S.M. BOYCE

WRAITHSTORM

THE WRAITHBLADE SAGA
BOOK THREE

Wraithmarked
CREATIVE

WRAITHSTORM: BOOK THREE OF THE WRAITHBLADE SERIES

Cover Illustration: Mansik YAM
Cover Design and Interior Layout: STK•Kreations
Art Direction: Bryce O'Connor

Trade paperback ISBN: 978-1-955252-52-2
Ebook ISBN: 978-1-955252-51-5

Worldwide Rights
1st Edition

Published by Wraithmarked Creative, LLC
www.wraithmarked.com

For Mom.

the hero from my storybooks,
my champion in the arena,
the silver lining in any storm cloud,
and a beautiful spark of the Divine.

"And once the storm is over, you won't remember how you made it through or how you managed to survive. You won't even be sure if it's really over. But one thing is certain. When you come out of it, you won't be the same person who walked in. That's what this storm's all about."

— Haruki Murakami

CHAPTER ONE

DEATH

In the soft amber glow of yet another sunrise, Death waited.

Deep in the Decay, He stood again amidst the bloodstained soil an old foe had salted to ruin so many centuries ago—the Wraith King. The Man with No Name.

A worthy rival, but one that had eventually succumbed to Him.

Same as all the others.

Even as the parched soil drank in the last of the lingering bloodstains, and though the corpses had already been burned to ash, the souls of the lingering dead lumbered toward Him.

Beaten and broken, the twisted things trudged closer, beckoned by the shadows in the rippling threads of his soot-black cloaks—the many, the varied, the wild. His cloaks fluttered about Him, rife with the ultimate power bestowed upon him by the Fates to stoke the fires of their creations.

On broken legs and shattered bones, the Fates' chosen spirits drew closer. Each dissolved into the eternal blackness He exuded, and they passed to His domain.

And each fallen soldier let out a breath of relief as they passed between worlds.

Visible as the dead were in the dawn and in the dusk, He wondered if the young man standing on the stone walls, staring out at him, could truly see. Most of the time, the living watched in somber silence, never knowing just how many dead walked past.

But sometimes, they saw glimpses.

Blood-drenched land fizzled with His magic for however long it took the fallen to find Him. Those chosen by the Fates brought with them a sliver of the in-between, if only for a time.

And they walked ever so slowly, for the one thing dead men have is time.

As the first ray of dawn hit the jet-black peaks of those dazzling, distant mountains, He studied the gates that carried His name. The morning's slow and steady creep inched toward Him, bringing with it the warmth and light of a day that would never reach Him.

But it was not the mountain that intrigued Him, nor the dawn.

In that citadel, not far away at all, was the man who had kept Him so *very* busy.

The man who bore His magic. The man He had observed, now, for quite some time. The man whose name He had already spoken twice before, and yet who had clawed his way back to the Land of the Living each time.

Connor Magnuson.

Another worthy foe, perhaps, but still a man—and one He would meet soon enough.

Just like all the others.

CHAPTER TWO

CONNOR

In the depths of Slaybourne, Connor crossed his arms over his broad chest. Intently, quietly, he watched the Soulsprite pop and fizzle in the darkness.

How strange it was to watch a god's heart beat.

From the moment he'd entered the once-silent vault, a soothing hum had echoed through the cavern like a distant song. It swam through the shadows, a light in the void beneath the citadel, and gave this dark place life.

He stood in the black-rock cavern, centered beneath the massive Saldian map with cities burned from its fibers, the Soulsprite's pedestal stood atop its platform, holding the greatest treasure on the continent. The glittering orb shone brilliantly gold, like it held a star at its center, and symbols made of light rotated incessantly across its edges. It hovered, brighter here in Slaybourne's darkness than when he'd first seen it in the Antiquity's chest.

How odd.

The goddess's sacrifice had fortified his home, and he owed the Antiquity a great debt for what she had done. Based on everything she had told him—and everything Dahlia had said—he suspected it was a debt he would have to repay soon.

Emerald flares of light twisted and spun off the orb's golden center, flickering this way and that like some enchanted fire that fed on the unseen, contained within a casing that could crack at any moment.

And in its depths, he heard whispers.

So quiet that they weren't even words—just voices, really—the whispers bubbled from the depths of the orb. A bone-deep chill raced down his arms, and a pang of dread stirred in his chest like a storm hitting the sea. The whispers continued, thick with the promise of secrets no mortal man should ever know.

If only he would come closer, perhaps he would understand.

He grimaced and tore his eyes away, his jaw tensing as the Soulsprite's magic nearly snared him. Whatever it truly was, whatever Death had done to create it, it still belonged to the Creator, and Connor had to be careful how he wielded it.

So very, *very* careful.

You heard them, the Wraith King observed. *The voices.*

It wasn't a question.

A rush of inky darkness rolled across the ground at Connor's feet, and the air shifted with the weight of eyes on his back. The light around him dimmed ever so slightly as the ghoul emerged from the depths of the in-between, but he noticed it all the same.

The Soulsprite's golden light flowed across the dead king's skeletal face like a reflection off water, rippling and unsteady, as he circled the pedestal. He watched it, and blips of light even stretched into the hollow sockets that had once been his eyes.

"What are they?" Connor asked. "Those whispers."

That is Death, the Wraith King explained. *And the Fates, I suppose.*

"Death," Connor muttered to himself.

To hear the voice of Death itself seemed insane. Surreal.

Impossible.

When he'd first taken the mantle of the Wraithblade, he never would've dreamed the world could be this big. That gods were real, and their magic trumped man's.

That everything—even spellgust itself—had belonged to Death from the beginning.

They were designed by Death, the Antiquity had told him when she had given him this awe-inspiring power from her own chest. *Formed in the forges of both worlds, and He infused them with my soul when He created me, long ago.*

"Think He's coming for it?" Connor asked with a nod to the Soulsprite. "Think he wants it back?"

At first, the Wraith King didn't answer. The old ghost hovered opposite him, staring into the gold and green lights of a magic that surpassed them both, and yet one which had given them power beyond reckoning.

I do not know, the ghoul eventually confessed.

"Comforting," Connor muttered.

Bah. The wraith dismissed Connor's quip with a flick of one bony wrist. *But look at us, acting like old fools staring at starlight when there is so much to do.*

"And he's back." With a sigh, Connor rubbed his jaw and shrugged. "It was nice to see you humble, if only for a second."

The dead king grumbled something unintelligible and shook his skeletal head. *You test my patience.*

"Don't I always?"

With a gruff cough, the Wraith King pivoted away from the Soulsprite and paced the length of the map hung on the far wall. *Focus, Magnuson, on the task at hand.*

Connor jogged down the steps that led to the pedestal and grabbed a handful of gold to refill the small bag he'd emptied in Tove's shop.

That woman was *expensive.*

"The task at hand, huh?" The gold clinked as he filled the coin purse to the brim. "Which one? There are so many. The Lightseers in the dungeons. The remaining Starlings on the way. The Deathdread we still haven't found. The dragons in Lunestone, locked away and feral."

So many bargains half-fulfilled, and so many favors still owed to others. In the nine days since he'd killed Teagan Starling, it was a miracle he'd gotten any sleep at all.

The surviving Lightseer elite are our greatest threat, the Wraith King said as he gestured past Connor, toward the door that led out to Slaybourne's walls. *You must do something with them soon. Even with those Bluntmar collars your necromancer made, they will recover soon. They are accustomed to torture. To prison. To Bluntmar blocking their powers. They are prepared for this, and you are not. Hell, some of them may even have hidden weapons on them, like the Starling woman did.*

"Quinn," he corrected with a terse glare toward the ghoul. "Use her name."

The Wraith King huffed indignantly but didn't reply.

"And it's something I've already considered," Connor continued, taking the ghost's silence as agreement. "That's why the undead are watching them. Four undead to every Lightseer. They won't try anything."

You underestimate a zealot's will to overcome.

Perhaps.

You must kill them, the ghoul demanded. *They see your mercy as weakness.*

"They, or you?" Connor's nose creased with disdain as he stared the dead king down. "Every time I think you've made progress, you say something absurd that proves me wrong."

This is no time for foolish nobility, the wraith chided. *I have held prisoners in this keep, whereas you have never contained soldiers like these. Unlike you, I know what I am doing.*

"Do you, now?" he asked dubiously. "Like you knew it was best to turn Nocturne feral? Or kill Quinn the moment we captured her?"

At first, the dead king didn't answer. He hovered midair, and those bleach-white bones clacked together as his hands curled into furious fists. An icy chill swam through the air, and once more, the brilliant light in the Soulsprite briefly dimmed.

These are dangerous warriors, the Wraith King explained in a grim voice. *Soldiers who do not share your ideals. Puppets for the Starlings who believe beyond a shadow of a doubt that you are the evil they were born to hunt, and which they will sacrifice all to destroy. These men and women you so kindly permitted to live think you aim to torture them. They believe you will leech information from them, and that you are merely letting them simmer. Stew. Wait. They do not see what you have done as mercy. They see it as a mistake, and they will decimate everything you've built here if you make even one error in judgment.*

Connor stood taller and met the old ghost's gaze. His shoulders ached with the weight of each word, and he considered the dead man's warning.

They cannot be allowed to live, the Wraith King said firmly. *They will be the death of you—and of me.*

"And if you're wrong?" Connor raised one eyebrow in challenge. "Some of them—the leaders, from what I've gathered—witnessed the real Teagan Starling out there. They heard what he was going to do to Quinn. To Zander. To me."

The man's threats had been vivid—and, frankly, hard to forget.

First, I'll gut this bastard, Teagan had said as he'd pointed Sovereign at Connor with a lazy shrug. *I'll break your legs and arms, Quinn, so that you can't do a damned thing but watch him die. I'll make it painful, far more than I had intended. Maybe I'll skin him alive, or maybe I'll take a finger at a time. What I do depends on how angry you make me.*

Connor's jaw tensed as he relived his duel with Teagan, and a muscle twitched in his eye. He took a deep and settling breath to bury the memory yet again.

With so much at stake, here and now, he had to focus.

"Those soldiers have influence." He gestured over his shoulder, in the vague direction of the distant dungeon. "The ones who witnessed Teagan's mask come off can convince the others to—"

To join you? The Wraith King laughed, so sharp and sudden it sounded almost like a bark. *You are the darkness they hunt, Magnuson. Hopeful kings die young. Don't be a fool.*

"I'm the darkness Quinn was hunting," he countered. "Murdoc, too. Nocturne, even."

Yet again, the ghoul went silent. He simply watched Connor with those hollow sockets in his skull, and the tense air crackled between them.

Truth be told, the dead man was right about one thing—it felt insane to keep a dungeon chock-full of elite warriors that wanted him dead. He knew the dangers of letting them live, but he wasn't about to kill that many people in cold blood. Even if he could live with himself after that—even if he could rationalize all that death away and find a way to sleep at night once he was done—the Finns would find out. They would look at him with horror. With fear. With the same terror as he'd seen on Kiera's face when he'd killed those slavers.

He could never live with himself if they thought he was a monster.

His new power as the Wraithblade tested his resolve at every turn. Too many others had succumbed to the allure of ultimate power. To a life of excess and greed.

He wouldn't be one of them.

Nocturne and Quinn had made a pact to kill him if he lost his way, and after Teagan had fallen on the battlefield, Connor had come dangerously close to the edge. Out there, among the carnage in his fully justified hatred of those who had dared attack his home, he'd almost lost himself in the bloodbath.

The insatiable bloodlust. The uncapped rage. The blistering hatred. It wasn't who he would let himself become.

With a furious growl, the Wraith King spread his decayed arms wide in frustration. *Magnuson, listen to me—*

"The answer is no," Connor said flatly. "At least for now. If they try anything or threaten the people here, then sure. Have your fun. But for now, they're off limits." His eyes narrowed at the ghoul, and he pointed one finger at the wraith's hollowed heart to drive his message home. "I mean it."

Magnuson, the wraith said with a frustrated sigh. *You are a damned fool.*

"So you keep telling me."

At least interrogate them. Take a few of the generals and force them to talk. You have three Hackamores. Use them!

"Two," Connor corrected. "One is Quinn's."

The ghoul let out a string of curses and threw his hands in the air, as if washing himself clean of their conversation.

"Blood and murder." Connor shook his head in annoyance. "It's all you ever do, and 'foolish idiot' that I am, I thought you were changing your legacy. I thought you said you were going to use this second chance of yours to redefine who you are. To be something better."

At that, the Wraith King went eerily still. With his back to Connor, the ghoul sighed, and he crossed his bony arms over his chest.

You have a point, the ghoul mumbled.

"I know." Connor turned his back to the ghost to hide a victorious grin. "You're welcome."

Through the corner of his eye, the wraith peered over one shoulder, and he could almost feel the piercing glare even as the dead king's vacant skull studied him without a shred of emotion. After a moment, however, the ghost's attention shifted to something on the floor, and Connor followed the dead king's gaze to find the man's former crown, resting on the floor by a pile of gold.

I told you I wanted the Deathdread, the ghost said.

"We'll find it," Connor assured him. "I promised you we'd go after it, and I'm a man of my word."

I know. The ghoul's tone was calm and, oddly enough, unflinchingly certain—as though it were an inevitability. As though it wasn't a matter of *if*, but *when* Aeron Zacharias's journal finally belonged to them.

Despite his better judgment, Connor stood a little taller at the Wraith King's unwavering faith in him. It was a nice change of pace.

He wasn't about to get used to it, but a man had to enjoy the little things when he could.

I still want to know how much Zacharias truly learned about what I am, the dead man confessed. *But the answers that matter most are not in that book. Aeron Zacharias is gone, and my legacy cannot depend on the notes he left behind. It is my own to create. In life, I pillaged and burned the world. In death, I will atone.*

"I won't lie to you." Connor scratched at the stubble on his jaw as he suppressed the impulse to whistle in surprise. "That's going to take a while."

The ghoul grumbled, annoyed as all hell, but the guttural growl turned into a frustrated sigh. *Perhaps it will. Perhaps not. I already know where I will start.*

"And that is?"

In life, I killed kings, the dead man explained. *To redeem myself, I will become a kingmaker.*

The ghost's head pivoted toward Connor, and a heavy silence settled between them. Only the soft whispers radiating from the Soulsprite filtered between them, and he fought the impulse to stare into its depths once more. His shoulders tensed with the unspoken implications of what it meant for the wraith to become even more involved in Slaybourne's growth, and he wasn't sure he liked the thought of the old ghost pulling strings.

You will wear this, Magnuson, the ghost said as he pointed a skeletal finger at the crown. *And far sooner than you think. You will step into the arena, and the world will try to break you for having the courage to be more than what they say you're allowed to be. Throughout time, there will be those who will flatten mountains to steal this and your freedom from you. Hell has already come for us, but it will only get worse.*

"Worse than hell?" Connor snorted in disbelief. "What could be worse than Teagan Starling?"

Only Death knows, the Wraith King answered, his voice tight with warning. *And before it—or, Fates forbid, He—comes for us both, I will do what I must to ensure you are ready.* The ghoul hesitated, and his shoulders straightened as his voice turned into a grisly growl.

He looked as if he wanted to say something else, something more, but the long-dead king went silent.

"I've *been* ready." Connor stared again at the Soulsprite, and his eyes glossed over with thought. He sifted through the Wraith King's words, sitting with each warning and weighing each threat. As his mind raced, he set one hand over his fist and absently cracked his knuckles. "The Starlings. The gods. The Fates. I've been buried by them all, hunted and burned within an inch of my life, but I always crawl out of the graves they dig for me."

Every time.

It was the only way of life he knew.

It's not your turn, his father had said.

In the depths of the star pool, back there in the Blood Bogs, he'd seen his father's face and heard the man's voice. It had been both kindness and cruelty, to be so close to the family he had failed to save, and yet unable to touch them.

Forever unable to right that old wrong, even as the bogs had teased him with the possibility of redemption.

Below the rippling jet-black surface, glittering as it had with impossible stars, his father had smiled so sadly. *You stay on that side for as long as you can, you hear me? There's still too much left for you to do. Don't throw it away now.*

Be patient, Ashlyn had added with a playful wag of her finger. *You'll get your turn to die, big brother.*

Every man did, eventually, but he wouldn't go willingly into the black.

Not yet, and if the Wraith King got his way, maybe not *ever.*

CHAPTER THREE

QUINN

As Quinn walked through the shadows beneath Slaybourne, she made no sound.

The distant drip of water echoed down the catacomb tunnel, almost in perfect sync to her steps. Beside her, Blaze growled softly, and his hum reverberated through the sconce-lit darkness ahead of them. Long shadows stretched across the floor as the firelight caught bumps and fissures in the walls' black rock.

She didn't know if she could ever call this place home. If it would ever feel truly safe, even with Connor manning it.

But after what the two of them had done to Teagan Starling, out there in the bloodstained dirt, Lunestone would never again be her home.

Around the bend in the tunnel ahead of her, two shadows stretched across the floor, longer than any others. Two men—or, at least, they had been men once. They stood at their posts to the dungeons, still as statues and just as silent.

Connor's undead.

Even as she rounded the corner, she stiffened at the mere sight of them. They guarded a pair of thick iron doors with massive black handles, and the glimmering threads of green light along the metal betrayed the enchantments carved into the entrance to an unending labyrinth of prison cells.

Beneath the undead soldiers' dark hoods, their eyes glowed green. The fabric of their tunics was half-rotted and littered with holes. An emerald light pulsed in their hollow ribcages like a heartbeat, and out of instinct, she reached for the hilt of her sword.

But *Aurora* was gone, and the sheath sat empty.

Her throat tightened painfully as she relived her father snapping it, and she barely suppressed the strangled little sob that tried so desperately to break free.

Focus, she chided herself.

That same prickling numbness seeped back into her chest and dulled all other sensation. Her face relaxed, though no relief followed. These were the only two things she felt anymore—either a deep, heart-wrenching sorrow, or nothing at all.

"Open it," she ordered when she reached the two undead ghouls.

Wordlessly, the two undead men obeyed, as Connor had commanded them to indulge her every demand. It was a sign of trust that the Wraith King had, apparently, not endorsed.

The soldiers unlocked the thick metal doors, and a flash of green light momentarily blinded her. A deep groan echoed through the air from somewhere beyond the corridor as gears turned in the myriad of interconnected locking systems hidden throughout the walls.

The Wraith King was, if nothing else, thorough. No prisoners would ever escape these cells on their own.

As the doors opened, the ceiling arched upward. A second story of cells opened up onto a wide cobblestone path cut through the prison, and each prisoner had his or her own cell. Farther down, the echoing snarl of caged vougels rumbled through the air.

A pedestal, drenched in shadow, sat in the center aisle, just far enough away that she couldn't make out what lay on its surface. Though she noticed the telltale flash of firelight off steel come from somewhere on the black stone, she chose to ignore it.

Four undead soldiers stood post in each Lightseer's prison, still as statues in every corner. A hundred additional skeletal warriors lined both sides of the center aisle, their hollow eyes staring dead ahead while they gripped their spears.

Immobile and armed to their bony teeth, like macabre gargoyles awaiting the order to spring to life.

Her eyes lingered on one as she passed him. A flash of firelight illuminated his stained yellow jawbone, visible through what stringy flesh remained of his face, and his skeletal hands reminded her of the Wraith King's.

A shudder raced down her spine, but she suppressed it. Nothing could kill these men. Even after the battle to defend Slaybourne, she had watched them reassemble, putting their own heads back on their shoulders and cobbling themselves back together in the aftermath.

The shudder came again, and this time, she couldn't fight it.

Instinctively, her fingernails dug into her palm, and she wished she'd had a Dazzledane vial with her. A sip would help steel her for what she was about to do, but she'd stubbornly refused to brew more after her father had confessed to using it as a means of control.

I allowed your addiction. His words echoed in her ear. She hated how crisp and clear his voice was, like he was there in the hall with her, baiting her even from beyond the grave. *It kept you in line.*

She swallowed hard.

As they entered the central aisle, each Lightseer's head shifted toward her. Fires raged in sconces between each jail cell, and the flickering orange flames illuminated the bloodstained faces of the warriors who had once fought beside her.

Teagan's elite. The ones who had survived, anyway.

"Good morning," she said flatly. Her emotionless voice echoed down the aisle, alerting any who couldn't already see her that they did, in fact, have company.

It worked. Some walked toward the bars to study her, while others watched silently from the shadows at the back of their cells. To her left, Blaze kept his head low, ears pinned to his head as he eyed each soldier, and he snarled.

Despite the threatening rumble, however, none of the undead moved. They waited, dutiful as ever, guarding the hall on Connor's command.

With a steadying breath, she gently felt for the Bloodbane dagger in its sheath on her waist, beside Aurora's empty scabbard—a reminder that even these undead men could be killed, if one had the right weapon.

That even Connor could be killed.

Her throat tightened at the thought.

In one of the cells to her right, Captain Edgars leaned his elbows on the iron beam that ran parallel to the floor to reinforce the vertical bars detaining him in a dark and ancient prison. The metal Bluntmar collar around his neck glinted in the firelight, but he relaxed against the iron as though he couldn't feel the sharp and icy pang of the metal on his skin. He held himself in much the same way as she had not long ago, when she was Connor's prisoner.

It felt like another life. A simpler time.

"Tell me this wasn't your idea," Edgars said as he pointed to a pedestal in the center aisle.

The one she had refused to acknowledge.

With a heavy sigh, she finally looked at the black stone table that had been dutifully set in full view of every Lightseer present. *Sovereign* rested on its sleek surface, cold and quiet without its master.

Teagan's Firesword.

The sight of it left her speechless, just as it had every time she visited, and the cold numbness ate deeper into her soul.

The Wraith King's idea, of course—to set the symbol of their fallen commander right in front of them, to break their will.

"It wasn't," she admitted.

Edgars wasn't satisfied. He slowly shook his head, and despite the two-dozen missions they'd completed together over the years, he studied her as though she were a stranger.

"Would you look at that?" a woman said from the cell closest to the door.

Quinn knew that voice. She shut her eyes briefly as she steeled herself against Major Halifax's grating tone.

This wouldn't go well.

With a casual sidelong glare over one shoulder, Quinn scanned the shadows in the Major's cell until she found a blonde covered with grime and dried blood. The thick scar across the soldier's cheek glowed briefly in the hazy firelight from the sconces, and the woman wrinkled her nose in disgust as she met Quinn's eye. "The Great Traitor has returned."

Despite the four undead soldiers in each corner of the major's cell, the Lightseer gave Quinn a mocking bow complete with sarcastic flourish. Behind them, the undead guards shut the only entrance into the dungeon. The resounding boom echoed down the central aisle, and for a moment, all was still.

No jeers. No curses. No clamor. Everyone simply watched her, and the Major likely spoke for the lot of them.

Quinn's eyes narrowed with barely masked annoyance at the insult, and Blaze snarled at the Lightseer's audacity.

"Traitor, am I?" Her steady voice filled the gaps between the crackle and pop of the firelight in the nearby sconces. She took slow and steady steps, closing the distance between them in moments as the Major met her by the bars.

"Aye." Orange and yellow light shimmered across the Bluntmar collar fastened around the major's neck.

At the sight of the enchanted circlet, Quinn's resolve faltered. Insults or no, it gutted her to see these powerful soldiers caged and collared. People she had fought with. The soldiers she had fought *for.*

They deserved better than this, but she couldn't free them. Not until they accepted what had really happened out there in the bloodstained desert.

"A sniveling, cowardly, heartless *whore,*" Halifax spat. The lines in her forehead deepened with hate.

To Quinn's surprise, she felt nothing. Though Blaze snarled at her side, she didn't bristle with indignation. Even her annoyance faded, and she watched the major like one would watch a child mid-tantrum.

"You've been conned," Quinn said quietly. Firmly. "He hollowed you out and molded you into whatever he wanted you to be. He did the same to me, Halifax. You never knew Teagan Starling, and you never fought for the light. You fought to make a rich man richer. Nothing more."

"You were his doll." The edge of the major's lip twitched and twisted into a wicked little sneer. "We indulged you to make him happy, but you never belonged. We all played along while you pretended you were a warrior, but we never wanted you there. Pretty thing like you? You just got in the way."

That ignited something amidst the numbness, and Quinn's eyes narrowed in warning.

The major met her gaze, already grinning in victory.

"You deserted us, Quinn," a man said from the shadows of the next cell over.

Captain Burns—part of Unit Zero, tasked with keeping the Master General safe.

He stood and met them both at the bars, glaring at Quinn with all the hate and ire she'd seen on her father's face the night he'd tried to kill her. "And for what? Power? Wealth? What did our enemy give you? What could he possibly have that the Master General didn't?"

"Honor." Her voice dripped with venom.

Burns grabbed the bars, his face flushing red with his hatred. "You vile, heartless, soulless little *fuck*!"

"Get ahold of yourself, Burns," a man snapped from above them. From this vantage, she couldn't see anyone standing by the bars, though he continued to speak from the depths of his cell. "Don't be an idiot. It's obvious she's being controlled. An opponent like that would have access to potions we'd never use on our prisoners. Bet you anything she has a Bridlecharge curse carved somewhere on her. Somewhere we can't see."

"We just have to find it," another man agreed from somewhere in the shadows.

"And break it," a third added from the row of cells behind her. "Why else would she fight alongside a necromancer? That raven-haired woman had the daggers of the Nethervale elite, not to mention the face of a Beaumont." He spat on the floor, as though the mere mention of the crime family's name left a sour taste in his mouth.

Quinn sighed and pinched the bridge of her nose. Every day had gone like this, and thus far, she'd gotten nowhere with them.

Insults and assumptions, and it always ended in an uproar.

As more voices joined in, each dissecting what possible spells she had succumbed to for her to debase herself to such a degree, Quinn took a settling breath. She'd known this would be difficult, but she hadn't anticipated the pain she'd feel at seeing them still lost in her father's delusions. He might've been gone, but his power over them remained.

At the thought of her father, a stabbing pain in her chest rooted her briefly in place. It left her breathless, as if someone had landed a blow in her gut, and Blaze growled softly at her side.

"I'm fine," she whispered.

He snorted, his large eyes narrowing as she dared lie to his face.

"...can't redeem her!" one snapped.

"Agreed," Major Halifax said. "She helped the Shade kill her father. The great Teagan Starling, tricked and cornered by his own blood as he tried to *save* her."

At that, something deep within Quinn snapped, and it snapped *hard.*

Too quick for any augmented soldier to see, much less one cut off from her magic like Halifax, Quinn reached through the bars and grabbed the major's collar. She pulled the woman forward, smacking the soldier's head against the bars, and the major growled with unrestrained hatred. Halifax reached through the jail cell, her fingers stretching wide as she tried to grab Quinn's hair.

Blaze nearly bit the woman's hand off, but Quinn was faster.

Still holding Halifax's shirt, and with the woman still pressed hard against the cold iron bars, Quinn grabbed the woman's wrist with her free hand and pulled. With an effortless tug, she yanked it out of Blaze's reach as his jaws shut with an audible *chomp.*

But she had no intention of saving the major from pain.

With a sharp twist, she rotated the major's arm and tested how far it could go. Quinn pushed the limb to its limit, letting Halifax linger on the edge of a broken bone.

Or several.

The Lightseer grimaced, but a second later, a pathetic little whimper limped through the mask of hatred and rage on her face. She winced and arched her head backward, teeth clenched as she tried to hold back a guttural scream.

Around them, the Lightseers shouted at her.

"Quinn!"

"...let her go..."

"...what the hell?"

But she snared Halifax in a hollow glare, leaning closer until their noses almost touched, and her voice dropped to a dangerous growl. "You will never call him 'great' again," she ordered, every word dripping with venom. "Not in my presence. Not if you like having limbs."

Halifax gritted her teeth, scowling even as her eyebrows pinched together with pain. In the cell next door, Captain Burns raced to the major's aid and reached for Quinn through the bars of his prison, but Quinn silenced him with a single glare. He slowed, arm still outstretched, and swallowed hard. He met her rage with a hateful glare of his own, daring her to do it.

Daring her to betray them, too.

"The Lightseers have never protected the people," she seethed. "You've been his dutiful, predictable little pawns all this time, and even now, you protect him. You didn't see the real Teagan Starling out there." Her grip on the woman tightened until the major let out a pained yelp. "But I *did*."

She waited, her words echoing through the dungeon as the last of the overlapping voices faded. With a sidelong glance, she pinned Halifax under one last paralyzing glare and finally released the woman. The major huffed and shuffled backward until her back hit the far wall. Wordlessly, eyes shaking with pain and with fear, she sucked in greedy breaths.

"He lied to you." Quinn pointed at the major to emphasize each word.

Halifax didn't respond.

"He lied to all of you!" Quinn's voice echoed as she gestured at the brainwashed fools around her who refused to wake up and see the truth, but the words hit too close to home.

This wasn't about them, not really, and she damn well knew it.

"He lied to *us*," she confessed, softer this time, not caring if all of them heard her.

Her eyes squeezed shut as she did her best to drown her grief and stuff it back in the box deep in her soul. Down there in the withered and hollow darkness, she wouldn't have to look at it.

She wouldn't have to *feel*.

"You deserve to know the truth." Her voice sounded far calmer than she felt. As she prepared to tell them what she hadn't been able to say before now—what she'd been too weak to share—she set her hands on her waist with a resigned sigh. "Out there in the desert, his mask came off. I saw who he truly is."

Her voice caught, and she cleared her throat.

"Who he *was*," she corrected, her voice shakier than she would've liked.

Beside her, Blaze growled softly, though he knew better than to give her a comforting nuzzle in front of so many witnesses. He would wait, still and observant, scanning the others in silence while she spoke. After all, he and Quinn were partners. They had to forever appear strong and united. Stoic. Unshakeable.

The caged Lightseers didn't reply. No one spoke, and even on the second floor of cells, hardly anyone breathed. They watched her, somber and still, as she relived the horrors of her father's final moments.

As she relived the painful truth she'd hunted for so long.

"Do you know what your 'great' leader told me?" She asked with a withering glare over her shoulder at Halifax. "Because I remember. I remember every *word*."

The major still cradled her arm, but her back remained firmly planted against the far wall.

"I'm not going to kill you," she said, quoting the words that had haunted her nightmares every night since the battle. "But part of you will absolutely die. I'll break your legs and arms. I'll make it painful."

Halifax swallowed hard, but even as her eyes shook, she seemed to brace herself against the words, like she didn't want to believe them.

"What father says that to his daughter?" Quinn asked in a cracked whisper. "He was not a wise and merciful man. Everything you knew about him was a *lie*."

Your eyes. His words echoed in her head, and she winced as he burrowed into her skull once more—dead, but still all too powerful. *Your eyes, Quinn, they always give you away. I will only kill the Wraithblade when your soul finally snaps, and then I'll drag you home.*

She pried herself away from the memory, lost in it as she was, and water burned at the edges of her eyes.

But she wouldn't cry here. Not in front of *them.*

"What did the Wraithblade do to you?" Burns asked in a stunned whisper. Horrified.

Interesting. Burns and Edgars had flown off toward Death's Door before she had revealed all of her father's lies. It would seem the few survivors of her confession out there on the battlefield had finally spread the word. Now, every Lightseer present knew the Wraith King's secret.

Good. With time, perhaps a few of them would lose their resolve. Perhaps a few would realize that Teagan had truly lied to them all. Maybe then she could let them out instead of watching her fellow warriors living like caged beasts for the rest of their lives.

For a moment, Quinn merely watched the Lightseer captain as he stared at her through the iron bars of his prison. Tears still burned in her eyes, trapped by her sheer stubborn grit, and she didn't know where to begin.

"We can scrub the Bridlecharge he put on you," Burns said before she could reply, and he glanced her over as he crossed his muscled arms. "Whatever he did to control you, it was a moment of weakness we can reverse."

The *nerve.*

"A Bridlecharge curse?" She scoffed, nose creasing with disdain at his audacity to suggest something so painfully *stupid.* "You think I don't have augmentations that protect me from a potion that could control my every movement? Do you really think my father didn't plan for that eventuality? Not one of you understands a Starling's resolve. Not really. You don't understand what my father did to me, all those years we trained in Lunestone, while you lot ate our banquets and lightly sparred each other in the training halls."

She took a menacing step toward Burns, whose jaw clenched under her furious gaze. "You. I've seen you fight. I've seen you spar. You broke a few bones and called yourself strong for going back out onto the mat. Do you know what my father did to me?"

The Lightseer captain swallowed hard, his resolve finally fading, but he didn't reply.

"I *burned.*" All of the pain and rage and agony of her father's training weighed on that one word, and a deathly quiet settled amongst the survivors. "I screamed and shattered in those rooms, behind those closed doors, in those sessions my father forbade you all to see. To make me strong, he broke and bled me while you all patrolled old roads that have been safe for decades. He pushed me to the edge and made me claw my way back on my own. He did to me what our enemies would do if I were captured, so don't you *dare* call me weak, you Fates-damned *fool.*"

The echoes of her voice faded into the steady drip of water somewhere deep in the dungeon, far beyond the occupied cells. Elite soldiers like these had spent decades under Teagan's thumb, and they needed a cold splash of reality to wake up from the dream her father had sold to them.

Just as she had awoken from the dream he'd sold to *her.*

"Out there, amidst the chaos and blood when he thought none of you could see him, Teagan Starling finally took off his mask." She stepped into the center of the aisle, back straight as she told them the truth they refused to hear. "I was only allowed to see through the lie because he intended to burn all memory of it out of me."

Her throat tightened, and she paused to keep her voice from breaking as she relived the horrors she was trying so desperately to forget.

"He didn't come to rescue me," she said flatly with a disgusted glare back at Major Halifax. "And he certainly didn't come to liberate anyone. He just wanted to drag me and Zander back to Lunestone to throw us in a cell. To starve us. To drown us within an inch of our lives. To shatter us. To drug us into obedience. To kill us and bring us back, over and over, until the fight in us died. Until we *obeyed.*"

She didn't care about her brother's life—not after everything he'd done—but it spoke volumes of Teagan Starling's moral boundaries to reveal what he would've done to his own son.

To their future leader.

In the dungeon around her, murmurs of disbelief filtered through the prisoners, and she caught snippets of their muttered conversations.

"...impossible..."

"...she's insane..."

"...no, she's a Fates-damned *liar.*"

The insults didn't matter. In fact, their reaction made sense. Lightseers protected the natural order, and only a necromancer would dare bring back the dead. Yet, when her father had admitted he would defy the fundamental belief every Lightseer lived by, not one of the soldiers had broken rank. Not one of them had even lowered his sword.

"Captain Oliver," she said, her voice loud and firm.

As the voices around her stopped, she shifted her attention to the only man still leaning his elbows against the metal crossbar running through the middle of his cell. The table bearing Teagan's sword had been placed right in front of his prison, and he stared at it with a blank expression on his face. No horror. No fear. No doubt. With blood still caked to his thick brown beard, he simply watched each flicker and flare of the firelight as it danced along the dormant steel.

Even as she said his name, he didn't look up.

"Tell them," she demanded, her voice dark and deep to mask the twitching muscles in her jaw as she relived a night she was trying to forget. "You heard everything. He confessed."

Captain Oliver had led Unit Zero. In every major battle for the last decade, he'd fought at Teagan's side. He'd been loyal. Devoted. A hardened soldier who feared no blood, and one who had faced Death time and time again for his Master General.

A man Teagan had been so willing to betray, just to protect the Wraith King's secret. Even if the Lightseer captain didn't want to admit it out loud, he must have known that.

Deep down.

Oliver's shoulders rose and fell with a weary sigh, but still, he refused to look up, and he didn't say a word.

"The lies." With slow and steady steps, she closed the gap between them. "The façade. All of it finally fell away, and you witnessed his casual cruelty. You saw the lazy shrug as he confessed to breaking Lightseer laws. You heard him admit to sustaining the lie that Lightseers had destroyed the simmering souls ages ago. You just don't want to believe what you witnessed. You just don't want to believe your life was based on a lie."

The captain swallowed hard, but he still wouldn't speak.

"And you didn't—" Her voice caught in her throat as she relived those final moments before her father had taken the first swing. "You saw everything. He stripped away the lies and attacked his own daughter. You swore to protect the Light, and you must've realized how he had used you. You knew he'd never let you leave that battlefield alive, knowing what you knew, what did you do?"

His eyes squeezed shut.

"Nothing," she hissed, her voice a pained whisper. "You stood there, unwilling to disobey a man that had betrayed us all, and you did absolutely *nothing*. Your Master General would have murdered you in cold blood for knowing too much, and you would have let him do it."

"You've lost your Fates-damned mind!" a soldier above the Lightseer captain's cell shouted. Overhead, he ran to the bars and pressed his face against them, glaring at her with the same unfettered hatred she'd seen on her father's face. "How can you speak of the Master General in such a way? You deserter. You—"

"Traitor," she finished for him, her voice calm despite the insult.

Though a sharp pain shot through the back of her eyes, her mind numbed as she mulled the word over. For the first time, she wondered if it was true. If she was every bit the traitor they believed her to be.

Perhaps.

That depended entirely on who the Lightseers were meant to protect—the greater good, or her father.

And she had chosen her side.

"Think of all I've done," she said, snaring the man above her in her gaze. "For the Lightseers. For my family. For all of you." She gestured across the dungeons, addressing all of them as her voice grew louder. "I've killed ninety-four necromancers in the field. I've raided over two hundred bandit enclaves across Saldia. Three dozen beasts in the Mountains of the Unwanted are only there because I captured them." She let the weight of her accomplishments sit on the air, far greater than most here could claim, but she didn't care about the accolades anymore.

The pomp. The prizes. The fame. It had all been a performance, and she was done with life as her father's doll.

"You lot think I'm the liar. The traitor," she snapped, her voice sharp and biting as she addressed every soldier here. "But all I've done is tell you the truth. All I've done is expose my father for who he truly is."

She wanted to continue, but her throat tightened to a stranglehold, choking the words into submission as she spoke of him in the present tense.

Her eyes shut, and she took a shallow breath as she tried to regain her composure. She fought to mask the pain, tried not to show it on her face, but a bit of her agony seeped through.

And they saw it.

She cleared her throat roughly. To regain her composure, she studied the caged Lightseers around her.

Most watched in silence. Some studied her face, brows twisted with confusion, while others wrinkled their noses in disgust.

Captain Oliver, however, had still not looked up from the floor.

"Remember," she ordered all of them. "Remember what I've sacrificed for *you.* I've led or joined half of you in missions you could never have completed yourselves. I've saved your lives in the Frost Forest, in the Enchanted Woods, on the road to Nethervale. Name it, and I've been there with at least one of you. I devoted *every* waking moment to the cause!" Her shout echoed through the dungeon, rife with her pain and regret.

But she wasn't alone. Not yet. They had yet to fully understand.

"With that in mind, think about why I'd be standing here. Think about why I would have defied my father and—" That stranglehold on her heart returned, and the words died in her throat. She let out a guttural little growl and stood taller, refusing to stop now.

Refusing to simply walk away and let them stew, as she had every day so far.

As the silence weighed on the prisoners who still believed they fought for the Light, she once again walked toward Captain Oliver. She grabbed the bars on either side of his head and stared at him until he reluctantly lifted his weary gaze to look her in the eye.

Good. At least he was man enough to face her.

"Think about what you stand for," she demanded, though only loud enough for him to hear. "You are the most senior man here. They look to you for guidance, and you know damn well what happened out there. You know who my father was. Tell them. Make them believe. They'll listen to you, at least. Fates know they won't listen to me."

"They listen to you," he corrected, and the creases in his forehead deepened as he said his first words since Connor had taken them all captive.

She swallowed hard in surprise, but she otherwise didn't move. In the bated silence, she waited for him to elaborate.

"You have more influence than you know." He groaned and rubbed his eyes as he leaned his forehead against the cold iron bars. "They just don't like what you're saying. None of us do."

He chewed the inside of his cheek, and he once again hung his head as his tired gaze returned to Teagan's lifeless sword.

"Make them see reason." She leaned in, until her body stood between him and her father's blade. "We don't have the luxury of time, Captain."

He didn't answer, and even though she blocked his view of the Firesword, he didn't move.

"Please," she added in the softest whisper. "I don't want you all down here forever. Think about what I've said—and which side you're on."

When he still wouldn't look her in the eye, she accepted defeat. This was everything she could do today, but as with every visit to her fallen brethren, it didn't feel like she'd done enough.

It never did.

With a sharp whistle for Blaze to join her, Quinn pushed off the iron bars and headed again for the lone exit. Her vougel trotted toward her and easily matched her stride.

But as she passed the last jail cell before the door, Major Halifax threaded her hands through the bars and watched her pass.

"For your crimes, I sentence you to death," the Lightseer whispered.

Quinn stopped midstride. The words were silent, barely more than a breath, but her ear twitched as the woman recited the Lightseer Code—the last words any criminal ever heard.

"Per my duty to the people," the major continued, "I will deliver your sentence myself, and—"

"A word of advice, Major," Quinn interrupted, not bothering to even look over her shoulder at the woman as she spoke. "Only threaten me if you think you can actually follow through."

Through the corner of her eye, Halifax pursed her lips together. A tense moment passed, but the woman wisely didn't finish her sentence.

"Good choice," Quinn said flatly.

With a snap of her fingers, the two undead soldiers nearest to the doors opened them for her, and she and Blaze walked out into the hall.

Before the doors slammed shut behind her, however, she stole one last glance at her father's Firesword. It glinted in the light of the sconces, cold and still and silent, and she impulsively grabbed the Starling crest that still hung around her neck.

The one she'd worn even as she had stabbed her own father in his back.

"As long as you wear this," her mother had told her once, *"you carry the fire of the Starling bloodline with you. Hold it tight and remember—you are one of us."*

She had worn the Starling crest every day of her life. Even now, with the shame of what she had done weighing on her soul, she couldn't bring herself to take it off—even though she could never again go home.

CHAPTER FOUR

CONNOR

On the outskirts of Slaybourne's ever-growing city, Connor paused to simply watch the ruins come to life.

What was once a few sleeping bags surrounding a dead campfire and some logs had become a proper little homestead. A dozen of Ethan's small cabins, thatched with dried grass from the enchanted meadows, lined a decayed old road that wandered up toward the lake. In the early morning sun, smoke billowed from one of the chimneys, and the toasted bite of rising yeast in an oven wafted through the air as someone baked their morning bread. A few of the homes even had windows going in where Ethan had left strategic holes in their wooden walls. Children giggled somewhere beyond the trees, and a woman's exasperated voice followed.

Beside the nearest home, a roughly hewn dining table served as Ethan's latest workstation. Wood curls covered half its surface, interspersed with the odd carving tool, and Connor ran his fingers along the inlaid design of a vast mountain range. He brushed a few of the loose shards aside to find a half-finished map of the valley, complete with the location for each house and the trail up to the lake.

And there, along the edge, was a single word—*home.*

Connor smiled. Slowly but surely, Slaybourne was waking up.

That carpenter needs to move faster, the Wraith King griped. *I want space for as many new subjects as possible if we're going to turn this into a proper kingdom. What good is a king if he only rules the deer?*

Connor grimaced, the peaceful moment shattered, and glared back at the ghoul. The dead man hovered behind him, his skeletal head half-covered with his frayed black hood.

The specter's skull pivoted toward him, and after a moment of irritated silence, the ghoul shrugged. *What? Why are you giving me that look?*

Instead of answering, Connor rubbed his eyes and continued his trek along the road they were slowly reclaiming.

He had work to do.

Murdoc's cabin was among the last before the road sloped upward toward the lake, and it was time to assemble his team. With more Starlings on the warpath and a few more bargains to fulfill, they had quite a bit to discuss.

Summon me when you finally do something interesting, the Wraith King muttered. Without waiting for a reply, the ghoul dissolved into a rush of black smoke, and Connor shook his head in annoyance.

That man was making progress, but he still couldn't prioritize worth a damn.

As he reached Murdoc's hut, a familiar shadow briefly blocked out the sun. With one hand shielding his eyes, he squinted upward as Nocturne spun through the sky, his silky black tail twirling. The dragon's wings clamped tight against his body, and his great head pivoted toward the earth. Mere seconds later, the regal creature dove into the forest to snare his next meal.

Nocturne was supposed to finish his hunt soon, but Connor knew better than to rush him. The dragon would join them after he'd eaten his fill of the forest, and then they could talk about their next flight out of Slaybourne. In the meantime, he and his team had plenty to tend to on their own.

He thumped his knuckle twice on Murdoc's door to see if the man was up—or if Connor would have to hoist his friend out of bed.

Again.

Arms crossed, he leaned against the frame as he waited for the former Blackguard to answer. Someone shuffled about inside, and a thud followed. After a bit of muffled cursing, a man's heavy footsteps neared.

The door opened to a bare-chested—and bare-legged—Murdoc. Connor's brow furrowed as he fought against seeing anything he didn't want to see, and he opted instead for glaring the man in the eye.

Murdoc, however, grinned broadly. "Morning, Captain. You're up early."

For a moment, Connor just watched his friend in silence. He wished he could've been surprised, but in the end, he wasn't.

"You're naked," he said flatly.

The former Blackguard awkwardly cleared his throat. "That I am, Captain."

There was a moment of silence, and Murdoc shuffled awkwardly by the entrance—though, notably, the man didn't reach for pants.

Connor let out a heavy sigh. "Care to explain why?"

"I—uh, that is—"

"What if I'd been Kiera? Or Fiona?" Connor raised one dubious eyebrow. "Pants, man. I can't believe I have to say this. Wear pants to open the door."

"Understood, Captain."

Connor's ear twitched briefly as someone shifted on the bed. Though the door blocked his view of the rough straw mattress, a woman's unmistakable whisper followed shortly after.

Though Connor's eyes narrowed in suspicion, he couldn't mask the mischievous grin that followed. "It seems I've interrupted something."

"Yes, well..." Murdoc retreated ever-so-slightly into his cabin as he attempted to shut the door. "I'll be out in just a minute."

At least he indulges his primal needs, the Wraith King huffed. *While you suppress natural urges with your stupid moral compass.*

Connor didn't take the bait. Even as Murdoc tried to retreat, Connor set one finger on the door. The subtle motion offered enough resistance that the former Blackguard couldn't close it, and Connor listened to the gait of the woman inside as she tip-toed out of sight. It took a moment before he recognized the almost inaudible shuffling of her bare feet on the floor.

"Did you have a good night, Sophia?" he asked.

Inside, the woman sighed in defeat.

Footsteps shuffled closer, and a frowning Sophia appeared beside Murdoc. Wrapped in a sheet, with her bare shoulders exposed to the morning, she lifted her chin ever so slightly in defiance.

Connor flashed her a roguish grin and leaned once more against the doorframe as he surveyed the necromancer who had finally succumbed to the inevitable.

"This isn't what it looks like." Though she stiffened with the obvious lie, her voice remained calm and certain.

"On the contrary, Captain." Murdoc kissed the top of her head. "This is exactly what it looks like."

Sophia smacked his arm, and though he winced, he couldn't hide his beaming smile.

"Get dressed, kids." Connor chuckled. "We've got a long day ahead of us."

"Don't we always?" Sophia asked curtly.

Instead of answering, Connor pushed off the doorframe and left the two of them to get dressed.

They knew where he would be.

In the brilliant morning, birds twittered. A few dove into the trees alongside the road as he ambled down the once-black street that had faded into the soil over the centuries. It was a familiar path, one he took several times a day, and it ended at the fallen pillar on top of a hill that overlooked the long stretch of the valley they'd reclaimed.

Alone and surrounded by a serene paradise, he sat on the ancient stone as he looked out over the massive plot of land they'd chosen for crops. His undead soldiers hacked away at the overgrown grasses, trimming the wild woodland to make it habitable.

Though everything moved so much faster with their help, not one of them had spoken a word—to him or anyone else.

"Can they talk?" he asked the ghoul.

Beside him, the Wraith King appeared in a puff of black smoke. The bony specter stared out over the fields as his resurrected army toiled at the dirt, and he shrugged. *I never cared to check.*

Connor shook his head. "Of course you didn't."

Maybe immortality had meant giving up much of what made them human, or perhaps they no longer cared enough to speak.

He might never know.

You need a general, Magnuson. Someone strong. As the grim voice echoed in

Connor's head, the Wraith King lifted one bony fist to emphasize his point. *Someone capable. Someone powerful. Someone you can trust with your life out there on the battlefield, when even our considerable strength falters. It will happen, from time to time, and you must possess at least one worthy fighter who raises their shield to protect you instead of themselves. Over time, you should find two or three great generals, but one will suffice for now. Who is that one?*

"Hmm." He paused to consider the suggestion, and as his mind raced, a few faces stuck out from the others.

Ahead, where the road curved back into the overgrown forest that had reclaimed Slaybourne in the Wraith King's absence, a silhouette crested the top of a small hill. They walked for a few moments with the sun behind them, nothing but shadow, but more details came into view with each step. Crimson hair, the color of fire. Loose curls, as wild as the ocean's waves. A curved build that belied her true strength. The confident stride of a warrior who could hold her own.

Quinn Starling, returning from yet another trip to the dungeons.

Moments later, her tiger-bird crested over the hill as well and padded after her, keeping her pace with ease. With his wings tucked tightly against his back, Blaze's fuzzy ears flicked every which way as he observed the buzzing forest around them.

Though Connor studied her approach for any tells of how her meeting with the Lightseers had gone, Quinn's eyes glossed over with thought. She stared at the undead soldiers tilling the fields, as if she hadn't noticed him or the wraith.

Right on time. Though he didn't always understand her, he could at least respect her punctuality.

No, the ghoul said firmly as he followed Connor's gaze. *She is the wrong choice. Pick someone else.*

"I'll decide my own damn general," Connor said tersely.

You're an obstinate idiot.

"So you keep telling me," he muttered, unfazed.

The Wraith King let out an exasperated sigh. *Think this through, Magnuson.*

"That's what I'm doing." He leaned back in his seat and shot the specter an irritated glare. "Thus, why I haven't even given you a name, yet."

I know that look. The ghoul pointed one bony finger in his face. *It's that mischievous glint you get when you're making poor choices.*

Connor shook his head and turned his back to the ghost, mostly to hide a smirk.

Damn. The old ghoul knew him too well.

"Poor choices, is it? When she's a natural-born soldier?" He raised one hand and ticked off her skills on his fingers. "Clever. Talented. Capable. Logical. Trustworthy. Influential. Widely respected. Adept with swordplay, and who knows what other weapons she's mastered?" He gestured toward her. "She's a Fates-damned Starling. Her father raised her to endure anything he threw at her. She witnessed her father's military trainings and watched him orchestrate and lead campaigns. She's led her own missions into enemy territory, only to come out unscathed. She holds her own in every fight, even the one against me."

You mean before she and that dragon made a pact to kill you?

"Only if I go dark." Connor shrugged to mask the pang of dread at the idea. "My point is this—she's efficient, brutal, and she's already proven she would face down her own family in the name of what I stand for. What else could you possibly want in a general?"

It's not her aptitude that concerns me. The Wraith King floated between him and the road, blocking Connor's view of Quinn as the Starling walked at a slow and steady pace. *For this to work, there are rules the two of you would have to obey.*

"I've never been fond of rules." Connor reclined, propping one leg on the pillar as he rested his elbow on his knee. "I thought you would've figured that out by now."

Oh, I have. The ghoul threw up his hands in frustration and turned his back, his robes hovering above the ground as the resurrected king paced along the grass. *But a general must sacrifice for his king. He must suffer and bleed. You must be willing to send your general to die for you, every time and at any moment. That is why you can never choose her as your general—because you're incapable of sending her to die.*

His eyes narrowed, Connor raised one eyebrow and dared the Wraith King to dig himself deeper into this hole.

If you were to take her as your general, then her body would be off limits. The Wraith King pointed at Quinn off in the distance, whose gaze darted toward them as the specter's attention shifted to her. *You think I didn't notice your intense urges for her back in Freymoor? You truly believe I haven't seen the way you watch her leave, or that I haven't felt the primal impulses that seem to get stronger the longer you're around her?*

Connor's knuckles cracked as his hand balled into a fist. He sat rigid on the pillar as the wraith walked the line between fair criticism and going too far.

You cannot lust for your general, the ghoul snapped. *You can never bed her. If you insist on choosing her to lead your armies, then we will have to find you another woman to ravage—and soon, you abstinent fool, before we both lose our Fates-damned minds.*

Connor groaned in frustration. "Do you ever think about anything other than sex and war?"

No! The wraith's harsh voice came out almost like a growl. *A man has needs, Magnuson!*

"No, a man has self-control," he corrected, though his attention shifted again to Quinn as she drew ever closer.

He had intended on saying something else, something poignant and biting, but a sharp and heavy pang hit him in the gut. He tensed, trying to rein in the primal urge snaking up his thighs before it could reach his chest. With seconds to spare, he squashed it before he had any visions of what he would do with her if he truly lost control.

With a grating cough, he cleared his throat and shook out one hand to distract himself.

Yet again, you've proven my point for me. The wraith grimaced in disdain. *My argument remains valid. Have whichever woman you want—or women, preferably, as I always had a harem—but if you truly decide to make Quinn Starling your general, she is off-limits. Understood?*

Connor didn't answer, but the wraith didn't seem to notice.

She has endured much, the Wraith King acknowledged. *She has earned her right to be here. Her duel with Teagan Starling, from what you claim, proved her merit, but I did not witness it. I will subject her to a test—not just of her ability or trust, but of her resolve to protect you at any cost, even to herself.*

"You and your damned tests," Connor muttered.

It is a test for the both of you. The ghoul looked at him over one bony shoulder. *You must trust me.*

To his surprise—and irritation—Connor found that he did.

"Alright." With a reluctant sigh, he scratched the back of his head. "What's the test?"

You have an irritating habit of telling this team of yours everything, the wraith grumbled. *I will alert you when the time comes.*

He wanted to demand more answers, but Quinn stepped within hearing range before he could say another word, and the opportunity passed him by.

"Go on, Blaze" she said as she nodded to the open fields. "Have some fun."

The tiger-bird growled happily and briefly rubbed his forehead against hers before charging into the nearest patch of meadow grass. With a happy little roar, he dove into the tall field. For a moment, there was silence—just the chirp of distant birds and the hum of a bee nearby—until the golden tip of a tiger's tail appeared above the meadow. It twitched merrily, moving at a steady pace away from them as he stalked something through the underbrush.

She laughed, watching her pet for a moment as he wandered and roamed, before ultimately closing the last stretch of land between her and Connor's perch.

"Have it your way, then." Connor lowered his voice to the barest whisper as he spoke to the Wraith King. "Where is this test going to happen?"

The catacombs.

"Cryptic, useless answers," he snapped. "You're worse than Dahlia."

The ghoul chuckled.

Connor, however, stood as he felt an oddly familiar pang of dread hit him square in the chest. His shoulders tensed, and his mind raced with the possibilities of what awaited him and Quinn both in the labyrinth of tunnels below the citadel. Those catacombs had nearly killed him once already, and he wasn't sure he wanted to know what other horrors the Wraith King had stored down there.

Sometimes, it seemed as though the grisly specter had even more deadly surprises up his frayed sleeve than all of the Starlings combined.

CHAPTER FIVE

CONNOR

As Connor and the wraith waited in the soft golden sunlight of another day in Slaybourne, Quinn Starling reached their spot at the top of a hill overlooking the bustling ruins.

"Good morning," Connor said with a nod.

"Morning, outlaw." Despite the jibe, she flashed him a rare and playful smile. With her hands on her hips, she stood beside him as they watched her pet stalk deeper into the glowing green grasses of the enchanted meadow.

"Any luck with our guests?" he asked.

The Lightseers—or, at least, the fifty-seven elite soldiers that had survived Teagan's onslaught.

Her smile faltered. "No."

He set one hand on her shoulder in reassurance, but he didn't say anything more. He didn't need to.

Shuffling steps along the road caught his attention. In unison, he and Quinn peered over their shoulders as Murdoc and Sophia hiked toward them. Though Sophia frowned in the dazzling sunbeams, as though it hurt her eyes to stand in light this bright, Murdoc stretched his arms over his head and sighed happily.

"Ain't it a gorgeous day?" he asked. "Bugs buzzing. Birds singing. Gorgeous."

"He's certainly chipper," Quinn said under her breath.

Connor laughed and nodded, but his attention drifted to the necromancer who still hadn't met his eye. "Is that a blush, Sophia?"

"No," she said with a withering glare.

"There's nothing wrong with it." He shrugged playfully, as if it didn't matter. "I'm glad you found someone to treat you right, that's all."

"That I can absolutely do, Captain." Murdoc grinned and set his arm around Sophia's shoulders.

A slow, knowing smile spread across Quinn's face as she watched them approach. "The great and fearsome Sophia Auclair has at long last settled down, has she?"

The necromancer scowled and crossed her arms. "I hate all of you."

Murdoc simply kissed her on the side of her head.

Whether out of genuine curiosity or a deep-rooted need to change the subject, Sophia gestured to the undead soldiers hard at work on the farmland beyond. "I know you like to think ahead, Connor, but this is ridiculous. There aren't even that many of us here, and the undead don't eat anything. Who are you trying to feed with this many fields? I don't even think we've found enough seeds to fill them, yet."

"I don't know," he admitted with a shrug. "Every time we leave Slaybourne, we seem to come back with someone new. Best to be prepared."

"You're expanding?" Quinn asked with a curious tilt to her head.

Yes, damn it all, the wraith said with an exasperated huff. *That's the Fates-damned point of having a kingdom! To be a KING.*

"The thought has occurred," Connor said flatly, ignoring the old ghoul's outburst. "The Lightseers clearly laid the groundwork for another siege, and more will probably follow. It would be ideal to find more specialists. Some carpenters to help Ethan, perhaps, and some more farmers who can take over when I'm not here." He paused and shot Quinn a sidelong glance. "And an augmentor, perhaps."

The Starling warrior raised one dubious eyebrow. "You want Tove to give up her life in Oakenglen to come here?"

Yes, damn it! the Wraith King snapped. *She has superior reagent knowledge even to Sophia and Quinn. Why in Saldia's name would we not drag her here? Fates be damned, do any of you even think these things through?*

Connor shot the ghoul a firm and furious glare over his shoulder, and the dead king groaned in frustration. The specter stalked off into the fields, hovering over the grass and grumbling half-incoherent obscenities to himself.

Strange. This was oddly out of character, even for him.

The thought hadn't occurred before, but perhaps the primal urges were corroding the Wraith King's self-restraint just as much as they tested his own.

"It makes sense." Murdoc's voice snapped Connor back into the moment. "It wouldn't hurt to have her expertise around here. With what she did in a few days, I imagine there's a lot she could do around here to help us rebuild."

"I wouldn't object to having her close by," Sophia admitted as she absently tapped the spellgust gem embedded in her chest.

"I agree," Connor said as he tried to ignore the lumbering ghost behind him.

"It's unlikely that she would come," Quinn confessed. "She doesn't get the respect and recognition she deserves, but she still has a good life there. I doubt she'll want to abandon it all to start over."

"Talk to her," Connor said. "See what you can find out."

"Alright," Quinn said with a weak shrug. "But don't get your hopes up."

You need spies, not carpenters, the ghoul chided, inserting himself into the conversation without warning. *An army. Powerful allies. A few spellcrafters to build you enchanted artifacts. These are the specialists that matter, Magnuson, and you are woefully behind on assembling talent.*

Connor scratched the back of his head, refusing to acknowledge the ghost's incessant interjections.

Truth be told, he didn't want strangers here. A host of Lightseers in the dungeons was bad enough, but letting people he didn't trust wander the streets, relatively unsupervised, set him on edge.

Law, order, and civilization had never exactly been his strong suits.

"All these people coming here…" Murdoc trailed off and rubbed his beard as he searched for the right words. "Seems risky, doesn't it?"

"It is," Connor said. "And though I see the benefit, I'm still not thrilled about the idea."

"It's necessary." Quinn crossed her arms as she met his eye. "Letting anyone new into the compound adds complications to Slaybourne's growth and food supply, sure, but the right additions can turn this from a smattering of huts into a proper city."

In Connor's periphery, the Wraith King gestured to the Starling warrior. *See? She understands, Magnuson. By the gods, man, you are infuriating.*

"I'm glad you're finally noticing," Connor said under his breath.

"That can't be our focus right now, though," Quinn continued with a nod toward the newly constructed cabins. "For the time being, I think we should focus on protecting the people who are already here. We have to prepare for what's coming next, and there won't be a lot of time to do it."

Connor scratched his cheek, mostly to hide the grin of pride at her command of the situation. The more he got to know her, the more confident he became about choosing her for the upper ranks of his growing military.

We can begin with proper clothes. The Wraith King crossed his bony arms and stared at Connor's shirt with disdain. *Those peasant threads need to be burned.*

Connor looked down at the scratchy shirt one of the newcomers had made for him. After the battle with Teagan, everyone's clothes had been too bloodstained to salvage, and he'd ended up in nothing more than an off-white shirt and tan slacks.

They itched like hell, but he'd endured worse. Itchy cotton hardly seemed like the death sentence the wraith believed it to be.

Warriors of Slaybourne must dress the part, the wraith continued. *In the catacombs, there is enchanted armor sealed in a spellgust vault. The vault will have protected the armor's enchantments, so its magic should be as strong as the day it was made.*

"Enchanted armor?" Connor tilted his head, intrigued.

"Do elaborate." Quinn shifted her weight to one hip and waited for Connor to share the conversation the two of them were having.

"He didn't tell us about *armor*?" Sophia scoffed. "Is there any reason we didn't get this *before* facing an entire army of Lightseers?"

"Agreed," Connor said as all eyes shifted toward the ghost.

In war, there must always be priorities, the ghost snapped, as though Sophia could hear him.

She couldn't, and unsurprisingly, her vexed glare didn't falter.

With our limited time, we had to choose wisely. The dead king shrugged, unapologetic. *This vault is sealed deep within the mountain, and it will not be easy to reach. Enchanted crypts like these require extensive fortifications and safeguards to make it nigh impenetrable, and after so many years away, even I'm not entirely certain what we'll find.*

At that, the old ghost pivoted his bony head ever so slightly. He now watched Connor, leaving something somber and unspoken hanging in the air.

Ah. The test.

There is more down there than armor, the ghoul continued. *Recipes. Weapons. Maps. It was my great trove, and it was where I kept my greatest treasures.*

"Looks like we'll have to make a detour into the mountain." Connor scratched at the stubble on his jaw as a cloud cast a brief shadow across them all. "I'm not sure what we'll find down there, or if the armor's enchantments have truly held after all this time."

Of course they have, the Wraith King muttered. *I saw to it myself.*

"I guess we'll see," Connor said with a sidelong glance at the ghoul. "In the meantime, there's a lot more to discuss."

"Like the prisoners," Sophia said, her dark gaze shifting to Quinn. "Learn anything useful this time?"

"Apparently, they think you're a Beaumont," Quinn said as she met the necromancer's gaze.

Sophia stiffened, but she didn't reply.

"How could they know that?" Connor asked, his eyes narrowing in disbelief.

"Wait. Are you..." Quinn's eyes darted between him and Sophia. "I thought they were making wild guesses. Are you actually a Beaumont?"

Sophia growled softly in frustration, but Connor didn't acknowledge it. These sort of secrets shouldn't stay buried, at least not between members of his team. With his eyes on the necromancer, he nodded silently toward Quinn.

Tell her, the gesture said.

"It's a long story," Sophia said with a begrudging shrug. "But the long and short of it is yes, and I have a Grimm on me from Gabor himself."

Quinn's head snapped back in surprise, and she whistled softly. "You must have done some serious damage for him to do that."

"You have no idea," Sophia said dryly.

"I can respect that."

The necromancer's head lifted in shock as a wry grin spread across Quinn's face. A silent second passed between them—whether it was rife with distrust or astonishment, Connor couldn't tell—and Sophia eventually smirked.

"How long have you had the Grimm?" Quinn asked.

"Years." Sophia admitted. "Long enough for the bounty to have gone up a few times."

"A few times?" Quinn laughed in her astonishment. "I absolutely *must* hear that story."

"It's a good one," Murdoc admitted.

Sophia nudged him in a silent demand to shut the hell up.

"Let's regroup," Connor chided. "We need an update on what else you learned down there, Quinn."

"Right." Quinn ran a hand through her long hair. "They don't know for certain if she is or isn't. As of now, it's just a guess, but these soldiers have surveyed or outright hunted enough of the Beaumonts to know one when they see one. They saw your Nethervale Elite blades, too, which certainly doesn't bode well. They know there's something amiss, and they're curious. That's a bad combination."

"It certainly is," Sophia said under her breath. She bit the tip of one slender nail as her eyes glossed over with thought.

"We're not letting the Lightseers out, right?" Murdoc asked. "Does it matter what they know?"

"We can't keep them in the dark forever," Quinn said, far more gently than Connor had expected.

Interesting. Apparently, she still had quite a soft spot for her former brothers-in-arms.

"What's the alternative?" Murdoc countered. "We can't let them up here. They'd kill us."

"Right now, they're staying put." Connor set one hand between the two of them to keep this from becoming a full-on debate. "They don't come up here until we know they're not a threat."

"They're Lightseer elite," Sophia said, irritated. "They'll always be a threat."

"Four undead and a collar on each one seems to be keeping them in line," Connor countered.

Sophia frowned, but she didn't reply.

"They're coming around," Quinn added, though she didn't sound confident. "Some will listen."

In unison, the Wraith King and the necromancer scoffed.

"I'm with my future wife on that one," Murdoc admitted. "I don't love that idea."

"We have to play it safe," Connor interjected. "There's too much at stake to trust them too early. We'll give them time, and once they've had a chance to reflect on what Teagan has done and what he said out there on the battlefield, maybe some will want to join us. Nocturne can help us figure out who's lying and who's telling the truth."

As he spoke, Quinn went suddenly still, and her hand flew to the Starling pendant hanging around her neck. She fiddled with it, flipping it this way and that between her fingertips, and her gaze drifted to the ground.

Likely at the mention of her father.

"They respect you, Quinn," Connor said, not sure how to respond to her sudden shift in demeanor. "The Lightseers will listen to you."

"We'll see," she said softly.

"Do you think any of the Unknown made it into those prisons?" Sophia asked. "It would make sense for Teagan to hide some of his secret assassins among his soldiers."

At her father's name, Quinn winced—subtly, almost imperceptibly, and only once—but Connor saw it all the same.

"Maybe," Connor admitted, giving the Starling warrior space to grieve. "An augmentation or potion would fade with their collar, but an enchanted item would hold, so it'll be hard to tell. Short of getting each to take a Hackamore, there's not much else we can do at the moment. Even with Nocturne's uncanny ability to detect truth and lies, those assassins seem crafty. I don't want to risk letting any of them out."

"What's next, then?" Quinn's hazel eyes darted toward him, and for a moment, he couldn't move.

Maybe it was the way her hair framed her eyes, or the faint scent of jasmine wafting from her, but a sharp and primal urge hit him square in the chest.

It *consumed* him. Ate away at him. In the crashing rush of whatever the hell this was, he knew he didn't dare move. If he so much as spoke, right in this moment, he would've grabbed her and wrapped her legs around his waist, witnesses be damned. He could already taste her, and the primal pulse of raw and carnal need demanded *more.*

And this time, he almost couldn't rein it in at all. It faded, ever so slightly, when he didn't indulge it right away, and that was enough for him to claw his way back from the edge.

Calmly, carefully, he closed his eyes and forced a settling breath.

A man has needs, Magnuson, the wraith said again, quietly this time. *Find a way to indulge yours before they consume you.*

Connor didn't reply.

Quinn's eyes narrowed, though he couldn't tell if it was with suspicion or concern. Irritating as the dead man was, the Wraith King was right about one thing—the urges were getting stronger, and he needed an outlet.

Soon.

He cleared his throat to break the tension in his shoulders, and he scanned the field around them while he tried to rein in the last of the primal urge's hold on him.

It faded the second he looked away from her, and he sighed with relief.

In the distance, children's laughter bubbled through the woods. It grew louder, and as he studied the edge of the trees, a small band of miniature soldiers with twigs for swords tumbled out of the forest. Fiona led the charge, giggling in their onslaught on some invisible enemy, and the others followed suit. They yelped and swung at the empty air, fully focused on their mission.

All, except for Isabella.

Though the rest bolted ahead of her, the Finn's middle child emerged several moments after the others, as if she were walking in a foggy daze. She sat with a resigned slump on a boulder poking from the meadow grasses and set her elbows on her knees as she watched her sister play. Unlike the others, she didn't smile—but from the sad tilt of her eyebrows, he could tell she was waging just as much war on an equally invisible enemy.

It struck him, then, that he didn't even know these other children's names, nor their mothers'. He hadn't spent much time in Slaybourne, and when he was here, he was always working. Farms. Fields. Cabins.

He barely had a moment to rest anymore.

And then he was always called away. Out there, beyond Death's Door, there was always some threat that needed his attention.

Isabella scratched at the thin silver scar on her face, and she hadn't been the same since she'd gotten it. Whatever horrors she endured out there in the Ancient Woods had broken her. Changed her. She had become painfully quiet, even more so than before.

In fact, here in the safety of Slaybourne, she seemed more afraid of the world than ever.

With a frustrated sigh, Connor rubbed his face. A smattering of houses out here in a lawless desert would never be a good enough life for her or any of these children. It suited him just fine, of course, but that wasn't enough. Not anymore.

It wasn't enough to hide them from the world. That wasn't a real life, and they deserved better.

"Alright," Connor clapped his hands together as he addressed his team. "Nocturne will join us later, and then we can discuss what we'll do the next time we leave the citadel. For now, there's a vault deep in the mountain that has a few things we need to get before we leave Slaybourne again."

"The armor?" Quinn asked.

"That, yes, but it apparently has more," Connor explained. "Recipes, weapons, and a few other key items, from the sound of it."

"Recipes?" Sophia perked up, and she smiled mischievously. "What kind?"

"No idea," Connor admitted. "This won't be easy. It's apparently hard to reach and heavily guarded."

"By what?" Murdoc asked.

Connor shrugged. "Haven't the foggiest."

"Fun," Quinn said dryly.

"Sounds like just the right amount of danger to make the day exciting."

Murdoc rubbed his hands together. "When do we leave?"

"You're sitting this one out, actually." Connor pointed at Murdoc and Sophia. "I need you two up here, keeping an eye on things and helping out where needed. There's still a lot to do."

"How thrilling," Sophia muttered.

"Quinn and I will head out soon," Connor continued, careful not to let his gaze linger on her for too long, lest the primal urge hit him again. "We'll bring back whatever we find down there."

Ever the soldier, the Starling beside him nodded and set her hand on the top of her empty sheath. He figured she'd been about to rest her hand on *Aurora's* hilt, more out of habit than anything else, and she closed her eyes as she remembered nothing was there. She swallowed hard as her fingers brushed the empty sheath.

From everything he knew of her abilities, her augmentations would be enough to protect her on their way down, even without a sword. But—just maybe, hidden deep in this mountain's depths—there was a weapon suitable enough for a warrior like her. Nothing could replace a Starling Firesword, but maybe they'd find something close.

"Let's go," Connor said with a nod behind him. "Lead the way, Wraith King."

Finally, the specter grumbled.

Quinn whistled once to her pet, who poked his head up over the meadow grass. She gestured toward him with the flat of her palm in some silent command, and he nodded. With that, she walked in perfect stride with Connor and cast him one more curious glance through the corner of her eye.

It was time to see if he was right to choose her as his general—because the day would come when she had to face her family once again, and this time, he trusted her completely.

Deep down in his bones, as much as he wanted to believe otherwise, he knew Zander was still out there. Waiting. Biding his time, maybe, or searching for the sort of magic that could tip the tides in his favor. Either way, the man would be back—and Connor would need a capable general if he were to have any hope of killing Zander Starling once and for all.

CHAPTER SIX

ZANDER

In the most lawless stretch of the Ancient Woods—farther south than even he had ever traveled—Zander crouched in the suffocating shadows on the darkest night thus far.

Crickets trilled nearby. Their gentle, steady song masked the quiet creep of padded feet across the dirt, but Zander heard the blightwolves' every step.

They were hunting, and yet again, he studied their every move.

He knelt at the edge of the tree line, looking out over a narrow clearing surrounded on every side by the woodland. The crunch of bones broke the night, and he shifted his weight as the blightwolves' prey munched happily on its kill, oblivious to the growing danger.

In the center of the field before him, surrounded by towering trees thicker than three men standing together, a horde of horned owls had gathered around a few half-eaten corpses on the ground. Whatever they had been—for they were nothing but skin and blood, now—the giant birds tore into them with gusto. Each owl towered over the carcasses, their bodies as large as his torso.

Sixty-three of them, gathered in two clusters. Twenty-two waited on the northern edge of the field, their beaks still bloody and their heads spinning routinely as they kept watch, while the rest stooped over their slaughter. Meat ripped off the dead beast's carcass. The crunch of bone came again, louder now as more limbs were broken off.

The stench of blood and rotting meat hung thick on the air, like mist off the ocean, strangling each breath he took. Despite all his time with the wolves—and how many of their kills he had witnessed—Zander's nose wrinkled with disgust at the birds' ravenous appetites.

They ate with a revolting gusto that reminded him of the blightwolves.

Though he didn't look forward to watching the wolves eat yet again, he looked forward to snaring some food of his own. He sniffed the air, hungry for something besides raw blood, and the distant char of a campfire meandered past. His mouth watered at the alluring aroma carried by the smoke—that of roasting meat, of rosemary, of blackened peppers and perhaps a potato.

The pang of hunger that followed nearly made him double over. It took effort to sit there, unmoving while the wolves took their positions, but he managed. He hadn't had a decent meal since they'd encountered those bandits in the farmhouse. Even now, so many weeks later, he could taste the steak and relive the sweet tang of honey-drenched blood on his tongue. He salivated at the mere thought, lost in it, and it was becoming harder to rein in his ravenous hunger. All he could think about, anymore, was *food.*

Unlike the wolves, he could never eat his fill.

His stomach growled, and though he salivated over the feast he would steal once this was done, he gritted his teeth and forced himself to focus on the meadow.

Not much longer to wait.

Even with a field this large, it wouldn't take the wolves more than a few more minutes to surround their prey. In all this time, he had begun to learn their every technique. The low crouch, the pounce approach, the belly crawl, the dive—he had named them all, watching for patterns in their approaches. He had studied their form. Their strengths and, more importantly, their weaknesses.

The observation alone had kept him sane in the weeks—or months, maybe, he had no idea—that he had wasted, trudging through the mud with monsters. Any number of horrors could've happened out there in the real world, and for all he knew, Lunestone had fallen to the Wraithblade by now.

But he had used his time with these beasts wisely, and the moronic Feral King had let him see so much more than should ever have been allowed.

In the pitch-black night, his vision sharpened, better even than the dragon blood Eyebright that had given his family superior vision to anyone else in Saldia. Though the Feral King had yet to reveal the powers Zander had acquired as the Feralblade, he had already discovered a few on his own.

Unmatched healing.

In a fraction of the time he should have needed, he was already fully healed. It had taken roughly two weeks before the last twinges of agony had faded, but none of his wounds from the duel with the Wraithblade affected him in any way. No pain. No limp. Nothing but scars.

Perfect vision.

In fact, he was so effortlessly attuned to the darkness that he wondered if he could see better than the blightwolves. In almost complete darkness, they had maneuvered through the thickest parts of the Ancient Woods. Even after the Ancient Woods' thick canopy had blocked out the last slivers of the waning moons, none of them had ever stumbled—including him.

An incredible sense of smell.

At the thought, his willpower snapped, and the distant trail of campfire smoke beckoned him again. He leaned into it, giving himself a moment to dig deeper into the scent, and he recognized the heady weight of deer meat. It had a complex undertone to it, and it took a moment more to recognize the sweeter, gamey hint of rabbit. A sprinkling of rosemary wafted past next, mixed with a new seasoning he'd never tasted before, and the bite of bay leaves followed.

No potion, no augmentation, and no enchantment had ever rivaled this sensation. This newfound ability elevated the world, opened him to new possibilities, and told him more about his environment than any other sense ever had.

His stomach roared again at the thought of roasted rabbit, far louder than before.

Beside him, the shadows moved. His eyes darted toward the darkness, and the vague outline of a blightwolf leaned toward him. On impulse, he set his hand on the hilt of his sword and watched its whisper-silent movements as its head pivoted toward him. It narrowed its eyes in warning and let out a quiet huff of irritated air.

Alistair—the same towering black blightwolf that had eyed him so intently after he'd killed their previous alpha. The one most likely to attack, if given the opportunity—and the one he had convinced the Feral King to let him ride through the woodlands, just to make the damn thing angrier.

Zander ignored the beast and returned his attention to the clearing.

What do you smell, human? The Feral King's now-familiar grim voice echoed through his mind, and Zander grimaced in revulsion as the abomination stepped into his head, unbidden.

Again.

If he didn't respond, the damn thing would poke and prod him, trying all the while to get a rise out of him, and he simply didn't have the patience to endure its attempt at insulting banter. For now, he chose to indulge its insipid questions.

"Food," he said under his breath, careful to keep his voice low enough that the owls couldn't hear. "Campfire."

Impressive, the thing admitted, as though Zander were a child that had completed a mildly interesting puzzle. *The enhanced sense of smell alone has driven all of my human hosts insane, and that's the simplest of the Feralblade's abilities. Yet, you endure. How very interesting.*

Zander peered over his shoulder, but only Alistair stood nearby. The blightwolf briefly looked his way before returning its attention fully to the owls in the meadow, awaiting the order to attack.

The ghoulish wolf wasn't standing anywhere nearby, but that didn't mean much. Since fusing with it, he hadn't had a moment's peace, nor a second alone, because the Feral King was *always* watching.

No matter. The stupid thing had revealed something important in that little interjection. The Feral King knew more about his newfound powers than it had let on. Once he'd had a good meal, he would be able to think clearly enough to extract the others out of the damn thing.

Through gaps in the darkened trees on the other side of the clearing, a white figure slipped briefly through the shadows. The lighter wolves had a harder time blending into the night, and as such, they had to move with more care than the others. It slowed the hunts, perhaps, but their added numbers compensated for the delay.

It wouldn't be long, now, before the Feral King gave the signal—and before these bone-chilling terrors of the Ancient Woods revealed even more of their secrets.

He'd already learned so much. Nocturnal. Isolated. Fast. The wolves traveled past several towns each night, faster even than vougels. Come dawn, they kept to the vast network of caves they had claimed along their hunting grounds. None of them had any young, despite the fact that spring was nearly over. In their drive to complete the Kurultai, the wolves were singularly focused on reaching the southern-most tip of the Ancient Woods as quickly as possible. He'd thought it would be a faster trip than this, but the timeless forest went deeper into the southern mountain ranges than Zander had ever realized.

It was almost as if this cursed woodland went on forever.

From the northern end of the field, a soft growl rumbled through the night. It was quiet, almost imperceptible, but three of the owls lifted their heads from their kill to listen. Their heads spun entirely around as they surveyed the forest for danger, and Zander tensed as their gazes passed his hiding place.

Their heads kept spinning, ignorant to the true danger that had already surrounded them.

On the opposite side of the field, a twig snapped. Ten more of the owls lifted their bloodstained heads, each looking at the southern end of the meadow, and Zander shook his head in disappointment.

With no real competitors in the forest, the wolves had gotten sloppy. Loose formations. Unclear direction. Uncoordinated attacks. A complete disregard for the element of surprise.

No subtlety. No grace. No precision at all.

Their raw power was *wasted* on the Feral King.

The last of the trailing shadows weaving through the trees stilled, and Zander took quick stock of the ninety-odd blightwolves circling the meadow.

They were capable, perhaps, but undisciplined, and he watched with irritation as they all settled into position. A large stretch of the field's northern edge, by the owl horde's lookouts, remained unguarded. At least a dozen birds would have time to escape, if not more. Three more inexcusable gaps in the assault line left obvious escape points along the edge of the forest opposite him, and a good ten more would escape there. Easily.

It almost hurt to see such potential absolutely *squandered.*

Besides, they would inevitably lose the element of surprise. The only signal the Feral King ever gave to attack was—

A piercing howl broke the night air, loud and sharp in his ear, and Zander winced at the sheer volume.

Damn it.

Though only he—and apparently the blightwolves—could hear the Feral King's call, the other wolves quickly joined suit. As expected, the howls shattered the night—and with it, the wolves' chance to preserve a few more precious seconds in their onslaught.

In a ruffle of feathers and wings snapping against the air, owls darted into the sky. It was a moment of panic, one where they realized they were now the prey, and they abandoned the half-eaten carcasses to their attackers. Despite their bulk, the feathery flutter of so many massive birds reverberated through the meadow like the deafening hum of an insect swarm. In seconds, half of them were out of reach, long before the wolves could even break the tree line.

The blightwolves didn't seem to care.

Growls and snarls dwarfed even the birds' overpowering escape. The lighter wolves jumped. The clomp of a dozen jaws snapping interspersed the chaos. Teeth gnashed at the air, catching clawed feet and digging deep into their meaty tails. Owls screeched in pain, their shrill screams drowned out by the chattering barks of ninety superior predators.

But it wasn't enough.

Seventeen owls on the northern end cleared the canopy. Ten more broke away to the east, and five more to the south.

Right in front of Zander, in the growing puddles of blood across the grass, a brown blightwolf snapped at a horned owl that had snaked its way out of the fray. The bird took off, clawing at the wolf's eye, and the blightwolf yelped in pain as a deep gash blinded it.

Zander scoffed in disgust. These things were supposed to be hell incarnate, and yet they couldn't even orchestrate a simple slaughter.

Still crouching by the forest's edge, he tugged the small dagger he'd used to kill Farkas free from his boot with an effortless twist of his hand. In one fluid motion, he stood and threw it at the bird that had blinded one of his wolves, more out of spite than anything else.

He certainly wasn't going to eat the damn thing.

The movement rattled the seven nearest blightwolves. They flinched sharply, as if they'd forgotten he was even there. All of them spun, growling at him as if he was about to attack them, but he didn't even look their way.

Instead, he watched his dagger as it flew toward where the owl would be any moment—and, one by one, each of the wolves followed his gaze.

As expected, his blade landed deep between the bird's eyes with a hollow *thunk*.

The owl's wings went limp, and its head lolled back. It plummeted to the dirt and hit the ground with a crunching thud, perfectly centered between the seven blightwolves that now stared at him in stunned silence.

Prior to the Feral King, it would've taken more than a dagger to down a horned owl, even with his superiorly enhanced senses. These damn birds had astonishingly thick skulls. In fact, thus far in his career, he'd only ever been able to crack one open with his Firesword.

Not now. Now, he exuded strength.

And he *liked* it.

As far as he could tell, this was yet another ability he'd acquired from the Feral King. His newfound speed and strength was far superior to anything the dragon blood augmentations had ever given him.

He had anticipated acquiring a few enhanced abilities upon becoming the Feralblade, but they were already exceeding expectations.

Across from him, Alistair pushed through the circle of seven blightwolves that had witnessed his kill. The great beast's eyes narrowed, and the towering black wolf lowered its head in silent challenge. He met its eye, waiting to see what it would do, but it was still a beast at heart. Even as it studied him warily, it couldn't mask the subtle flare of its nose as it sniffed at the dead bird before it.

Hungry, and begrudgingly impressed.

Zander walked to his kill and set his foot on the bird's beak. With an easy tug, he pulled his blade free and nodded to the carcass. "All yours."

Alistair hesitated, but Zander turned his back on the beast and wiped the owl's blood on his already bloodstained pant leg. It didn't matter what he did to these clothes. They were ruined, and he would burn them at the first opportunity.

The crunch of teeth snapping bone came shortly after, closer to him than the ravenous bloodbath happening in the center of the field, and Zander smiled in victory as he came ever closer to winning over the stupid things.

All beasts were the same—feed them, show them their inferiority, and they would always obey in the end.

He slipped the dagger back in its sheath on his ankle, and black smoke rolled across the grass beneath his feet. The air shifted, suddenly heavy with the eyes of something watching the back of his head, and he suppressed the shiver of dread that snaked down his spine each time the Feral King appeared.

"That attack was sloppy." Zander forced a bored tilt to his voice to mask his hatred for the sensation of being watched. He didn't bother turning around to look the abomination in the eye as he critiqued it.

Sloppy, was I? The wispy behemoth chuckled, the sounds quick and raspy.

Zander nodded. "You left too many gaps, and you squandered the element of surprise. No wonder so many escaped."

A nearby blightwolf growled at Zander's audacity, but he ignored it. He would own the lot of them soon enough. All he had to do was pass their little test, and they would belong to him.

The Kurultai—something which they had yet to explain in detail, but which he would master soon enough, same as every other challenge his father had ever given him. That's all these things were, after all.

Another challenge to conquer.

Behind him, the Feral King snickered, its wheezing laughter as harsh and grating as the final breaths of a dying man. *And I suppose your attack on the bandits was an example of well-coordinated military precision?*

"Of course," Zander lied. "I controlled every second of the encounter, including each man's death. Weren't you paying attention?"

In truth, he'd been too hungry to care about coordination. The bandits had all died, and he'd left no witnesses. That was all that mattered.

You still haven't told me why you let us have them, the abomination observed. *You funneled them right at us.*

A shadow appeared in his periphery, and Zander leaned against the nearest oak as feathers and bones flew into the air beyond the tree line. The blightwolves feasted, brutal and bloodstained, nipping and yipping at each other as all of them vied to see who could eat the most.

But from the darkness, stepped a true monster.

The Feral King's paw hit the dirt as the creature slipped out of the black smoke that appeared each time it materialized from thin air. Carved from the darkness itself, the wraithlike wolf lowered its head, watching him as thin slivers of blue moonlight snaked across the metallic spikes along its humped back. Its piercing yellow eyes glowed, leaving soft trails of light on the shadows around it as its head bobbed slowly back and forth.

And through it all, the thing studied him intently. Watching for what he would do next. Waiting for him to make a mistake. Always seconds away from pouncing, as though it were toying with its food.

Tell me, it finally demanded.

Zander raised one skeptical eyebrow at its nerve to demand anything of him, and it took a moment longer to suppress the surge of righteous indignation at its audacity. "I gave them to you lot because you were convenient. Those criminals had to die, and the wolves were hungry. Why would I care what you did to them?"

They are human, the Feral King explained. *Like you.*

"They were nothing like me." Zander shook his head at this beast's sheer stupidity. "I only protect those who obey me."

How curious.

"Don't gloat." Zander tilted his head in disdain. "You're hardly superior. You only protect these wolves because they obey you. The One Law, right? Respect yields obedience."

Well played. The Feral King chuckled again, and Zander grimaced at the sound.

As the blightwolves ravaged what little remained of the carcasses in the center of the field, he and the Feral King simply watched each other.

He knew its game. It wanted to lure him deeper into the woods, to play with his mind.

To break him.

Zander, however, had finesse, and he had far greater plans for this creature. Once he controlled the blightwolves, they would lead him back to Lunestone. Along the way, he would have to learn how to control the Feral King and keep it hidden, since he could never let a simmering soul be seen in the Lightseers' domain. There was no way to mask necromantic magic, and the Lightseers would leave in droves—if they didn't try to kill him outright—for being fused to something like this, even if they never learned the truth of what it was.

The abomination kept insisting the Kurultai would convince the wolves that Zander was a worthy alpha, but no contest would win the Feral King's loyalty. This thing exuded power, and with every passing day, it tried a little harder to poison his mind.

Thus far, it had failed.

To control it, his old methods wouldn't work. He had to treat this thing like a man—one whose loyalty could only be won through manipulation and strategy, rather than brute force. He had to dangle temptations in front of it and convince it only he could give it what it wanted most.

And this thing craved *fear.*

To the Feral King, fear was a delicacy, one the damn thing could almost taste on the air.

You are scheming, the abomination observed. *What plans are you crafting in that fragile human brain?*

Zander's nose creased in disdain, and he shook his head as he watched the forest beyond the clearing to break eye contact—and to hide a small smile of victory.

As annoying as this thing was, it dropped useful tidbits now and then. At least it couldn't read his thoughts. They had a limited connection, and he liked it that way.

"You'll see," he said.

I suppose we shall, it replied, unfazed by the unspoken implications in what he'd said. Any time he tried to play it, to goad it, to get it to react, it merely laughed.

Even though he never let on, that annoyed the ever-living *hell* out of him.

From the start, this thing was doomed to fail, and it just didn't realize that yet. He would be remembered as the Great Lightseer, and he could not be corrupted. This abomination would eventually bow to him, one way or another—or he would find a way to destroy it for good.

In the distance, almost impossible to detect, a howl cut through the air. Every blightwolf in the field lifted their heads, pausing mid-bite in their gory meals, to listen. It echoed, carried to them by the southern wind, and Zander pushed off his tree as he drank in the sound.

More were coming.

Loads more.

They would all assemble at the southern tip of the woods for the Kurultai, and each would challenge his strength. Each would ache to see him die. Each would unleash hell on him in their bid to dethrone their new rightful alpha, and he would kill any who challenged him.

Soon—if he played his cards right—each and every blightwolf in Saldia would belong to him. They would live and die by his command, and he already knew the first man he'd send them to kill.

Zander grinned in victory as the howl slowly faded. The Wraithblade's days were numbered.

CHAPTER SEVEN

CONNOR

In the depths of the catacombs beneath Slaybourne, only the crackle and pops of Connor's torch filled the silence. He led the way with Quinn only a step behind.

Together, they merely listened.

Now and then, the muted trickle of water somewhere in the darkness reverberated off the stone like endless ripples on a pond, too distant to pinpoint. It ebbed and flowed as the wraith led them deeper into the labyrinth. Throughout their descent, the steady drip occasionally disappeared for hours before inevitably returning.

They'd been walking for so long that Connor had lost track of time in the endless black that swallowed most of his torchlight. It ate away at the wooden handle, and the fire wouldn't survive much longer. The barest echo of his and Quinn's whisper-quiet footsteps followed them deeper into the unknown, and the soft orange glow from his flame illuminated only a few yards at a time. The darkness engulfed the light as though it were hungry, as though it were a living thing and its eons in the wraith's labyrinth had left it starved.

The distant rush of water faded into painful silence once again, leaving Connor with only the torch and their steady breath to fill the air.

Ahead of him, just out of reach and at the edge of the light, the wraith led the way. If the undead warlord hadn't already gone through hell and back for him, Connor would've thought the ghoul was leading them into a trap. The ends of that tattered old cloak shuddered, its frayed ribbons caught on the winds of the dead in an otherwise stagnant tunnel. The undead king's hood covered his exposed skull, and the slender bones on his hands appeared as bright white flashes in the shadows.

"Tell me where we're going," Connor demanded under his breath. It didn't matter how quietly he spoke, though, because his voice still carried down the chillingly quiet corridor in a haunting echo.

You will see soon enough, the wraith answered.

Nope.

He'd had enough of this.

Connor stopped dead in his tracks, and Quinn sidestepped him before she ran into his back. With the dying torch still in one hand, Connor squared his shoulders and glared the dead man down.

At this point, he didn't need to say anything to get his message across.

With an irritated groan, the ghoul pivoted midair. The dead man's skull glowed white beneath his hood as he studied Connor with the holes where his eyes used to be. He hovered off the ground, his legs long gone as he floated in the endless nothing beneath Slaybourne.

I told you this would be difficult to reach, the specter grumbled. *What exactly is your concern, Magnuson?*

"My concern is we've been walking for hours." Connor gestured with his torch to the empty tunnel around them, and the flame trembled as the sudden motion threatened to snuff it out.

Quinn ran a hand through her hair and leaned her back against the wall. Eyes closed, she rested the back of her head against the rock while she apparently waited for the two of them to finish bickering.

Connor closed the distance between him and the wraith, and he lowered his voice to the barest whisper. "Is part of your test figuring out how long a man can trudge through the darkness without going insane? Because the answer is however long we've been walking."

You irritate me.

"The feeling is mutual." With the heel of his free hand, he rubbed one tired eye.

Before the vault, you both must face a test. You will pass easily. The wraith dismissed any idea of failure with a flick of his bony wrist. *How she handles the challenges ahead, however, will tell us much of who she truly is.*

Connor shook his head in irritation. Quinn Starling had already dueled her own father to the death. As far as he was concerned, she didn't need to prove a damn thing.

We are almost there, the Wraith King promised. *Come.*

The ghoul gestured for them to follow, and Quinn kicked off the wall as their trek continued. Connor paused, even as Quinn passed him, and he watched her curved figure recede after the ghoul. His grip on the torch tightened, and his skin creaked over the leather wrap around its wooden base. He strained his ears, waiting to hear something alive over the roar of the flame and the muted drip of distant water.

He was about to join them—to follow—but something heavy thrummed through the air. He hesitated, leaning into it, trying to figure out what it was. It didn't make sense. It wasn't anything tangible, nothing to be heard or seen, but it was there nonetheless.

The tension weighed on his lungs, warning him of impending doom.

An ambush, perhaps, or a legendary beast the ghoul had trapped down here to butcher those who dared venture this far. Considering how many centuries had passed since the wraith had lived here, there had to be plenty of creatures lurking in these depths, perhaps even some who had ventured in long after the ghoul had faded from the mountain's memory.

Quinn paused and looked over one shoulder. She raised one eyebrow, evidently confused, and waited for him to join them.

Behind her, a flash of green light shot down the tunnel and blinded him. Connor grimaced, shielding his face with one arm as the torch crackled in his other hand, but the light faded as quickly as it had come.

He peered over his forearm as his vision cleared. At the end of the tunnel, just beyond the edge of the orange glow, more soft green light bent around a sharp corner. The black stone walls ended in an archway that led out to something obscured by pale light. Exaggerated shadows stretched along the walls as the humming energy beyond the archway illuminated every bump and imperfection in the stone.

The wraith had disappeared, leaving only a lingering trail of black smoke behind, but Quinn still stood between him and the archway. Fire crackled on her palms as she settled into a fighting stance, and her breathing slowed as she prepared to kill something.

They paused, and the tension in Connor's shoulders worsened as he waited for something to happen.

Nothing did.

"What the hell was that?" she finally whispered.

"No idea," he admitted as he cautiously led the way toward the light. "Let's find out."

As they neared, the light beyond the arch brightened just enough to hurt his eyes. He pushed through the pain, though, and didn't dare look away. He expected figures to appear, or statues, but no other shapes came into view. Only light waited beyond the tunnel, and Connor tightened his grip on the torch as he braced himself for whatever they might find.

Light in a long-dead tunnel suggested something magical lay beyond the archway, but he didn't trust anything in these tunnels—especially not something beautiful. Not with the wraith leading the way.

Bit by bit, the world beyond the archway came into focus. The tunnel ended in an open cavern that stretched farther than even Connor could see. The tunnel's footpath ended on a ledge overlooking thousands of natural stone pillars that rose from the cave floor like rocky lily pads in an inky black pond. Thick shadows stretched between the pillars, masking the cavern floor, and he couldn't even guess what a fall like that would do to a man's body.

Overhead, ribbons of spellgust snaked across the jet-black ceiling. The soft green light stretched across the pillars of stone like the first threads of an emerald sunrise breaking through a starlit sky.

As awe-inspiring as it was, sights like this were quickly becoming routine the longer he spent with the Wraith King.

Who, he noted, was nowhere to be seen.

"Wraith," he said, his voice tense with warning. "What do you—"

Good luck, Magnuson, the ghoul interrupted. *For your sake, I hope she's as good as you think.*

A rush of black smoke appeared across his feet, and he looked over his shoulder just as the wraith plunged his sword into the ledge overlooking the pit. The rock beneath Connor's feet rumbled, and his stomach lurched as he felt the inevitable happen seconds too late to do anything.

That fucking *bastard.*

The ghost dissolved into thin air, and Quinn charged through the black smoke he'd left in his wake. She reached for Connor as a deafening crack split through the stone, and the ground gave way.

He pushed off the rock, reaching for her open hand, and their fingertips brushed against each other as they missed by a breath.

His hand passed through air.

He fell, and Quinn reached uselessly for him with a look of utter horror on her face as he dropped into the sort of freefall that could kill even the strongest man.

One that could kill even *him.*

The torch fell out of his grip and plummeted along with the boulders that had once supported his weight. The crackling flames cast an orange glow across the edge of the cliff as the firelight fell ahead of him.

His stomach churned, and his survival instincts kicked in. He clawed at the rock wall as he plummeted down the cliff, kicking up dust and small stones. His heart skipped beats as he scrambled to find a handhold—a rock, a root, anything at all—to keep from plunging deeper into the never-ending darkness beneath him.

"Connor!" Quinn shouted, her voice already distant, as though she were leagues away.

The rumble of the rockslide echoed like an approaching stampede. Connor's shoulder scraped against the wall for several yards, and the burn of heating stone ripped a hole in his shirt. A jolt of pain shot up his neck from the steady scrape, and he gritted his teeth to ride it out as his boots scraped across the cliff. His fingertips slammed repeatedly against the stone as he struggled to find something—anything—to slow his deadly plunge. His left hand finally wrapped around a protruding rock, but the handhold snapped off in his palm from the sheer speed of his fall.

He shouted obscenities at the wraith, but the rockslide around him drowned out his voice. His pulse thudded in his ear as he scrambled to think of what to do—and how he planned to rip that wraith a new asshole once he figured a way out of this.

A puff of black smoke appeared alongside him as he fell, and the ghoul's bony face emerged from the fog. The holes where his eyes used to be studied the darkness below with cold indifference. *Given what awaits you down there, you face certain death. I have yet to see her act. Are you certain she was the right choice?*

"I'll kill you!" Connor shouted—or, rather, he'd meant to, but his stomach flipped from the free-fall. He risked a glance over his shoulder at the approaching ground.

As their ledge had been almost to the top of the enormous cavern, he had yet to pass the top of even the tallest pillar, but he was approaching fast. He had only a few minutes of freefall to come up with a plan.

Beneath him, a boulder protruded from the cliff not far below. If he could just reach it, this would be over.

As he fell, he twisted his body and shoved off the cliff with his left boot. The boulder below him neared at a dizzying speed.

He tensed, ready to grab it and have the wind knocked out of him. It would hurt, sure, but it was a far cry better than falling to his death.

When he hit it, he smashed clear through the rock. The boulder smacked him hard in the gut. Spots danced along the edges of his vision, and his world flashed white for a moment from the pain. Rock dust coated his face, and he inhaled pebbles. He coughed and sputtered, trying to clear his lungs as the last bursts of pain shot clear to his toes.

He fought to stay awake. He couldn't black out. Not now.

Hmm. The ghoul rubbed his bony jaw. *That was a poor choice.*

Connor roared with fury as he summoned the shadow blades into his hands and did the only thing he could think of. He dug the swords into the rock, hoping the resistance would slow his fall.

Instead of kicking up dust and debris, however, the perfect blades sliced clean through the stone. No resistance. No shattered rocks. Just perfect swords, having their way with the cliff as though it were made of freshly tilled soil.

They disappeared in a rush of black smoke as his backup plan failed.

You have yet to ask for help, the wraith said calmly. *From either me or the Starling woman. How curious.*

"Help me, then, you rat bastard!"

The ghoul chuckled. *No.*

A slender pillar of stone shot past him, and while the top soared above his head, its foundation continued on into the depths of the ravine. Far below, the orange light of his torch spun as it hit something in the darkness. With his heart in his throat, he peered after it, wondering how much time he had before he hit the ground.

Even with his enhanced strength, a fall like this would kill him.

He roared at the thought of everyone who wanted him dead, but most of all, he yelled with unfettered loathing for Henry. That man had brought only misery to Connor and his family. To his country. To this continent. If not for Henry, none of this would've happened. If not for that man, Saldia would still know peace.

If not for Henry, he would still have a father. A home. A purpose for something other than war.

Connor would not die here. Not like this. He had endured too much in his life to let Slaybourne's catacombs take him to the grave. After so long drifting through the Ancient Woods, survival was the only way of life he knew.

The shadow blades hadn't worked. His shield would probably fare no different. All he had left were his bare hands and his raw, stubborn grit.

Connor drove his fingertips into the rock, fully expecting this plan to fail. It was all he had left.

Shards of broken stone scraped against his skin. Blistering pain shot through his arms and clear up his skull. His biceps screamed in protest. The tendons in his hands threatened to snap. He gritted his teeth, but his furious war cry turned to one of agony as he braced himself for the worst.

Unrelenting and unwilling to give in, he pushed through the pain and dug his hands deeper into the cliff. The edges of his vision went dark as he funneled everything he had into this.

He simply refused to die.

The toes of his boots dug into the rock as he gave it everything he had. The leather corroded until his exposed toes dug into the stone and carved their way through the rock as well. His pulse thudded in his ear, as loud as the crack of shattering boulders as the rock broke beneath his might.

To his surprise, his plan worked—mostly. He slowed, though not enough to recover.

Far, far beneath his feet, the torch clattered onto the ground. From this distance, it was nothing more than an orange pinprick of light, but the flickering flame bounced along a metal spike protruding from the ground. The silver sheen glistened in the torchlight, thirsty for blood. A scattering of bones lay across the distant ground, and he would be next if he didn't figure out how the hell to get himself out of this.

That's a painful way to go, the wraith said. *I don't think you can rely on your so-called general to help you, Magnuson. You should probably find a way to stop your fall.*

Fates be damned. Sometimes, Connor hated this undead asshole.

"Connor!" Quinn shouted again—closer this time.

With his fingers still cutting through the rock, he peered through the cloud of rubble and dust to find her sliding down the cliff above. Focused on him, with her brows furrowed and jaw tensed to an almost painful degree, she skidded down the steep slope with her boots planted firmly on a flat slab of rock.

A strange sight, perhaps, but a welcome one nonetheless.

Her knees bent as she struggled to stay upright, but the unstable perch offered decent protection from the cliffside. She plummeted toward him at a breakneck pace, and bits of the flat slab broke off with each passing second. Before long, it would corrode completely, and she risked breaking every bone in her body from the sheer force of her own fall.

In her left hand, she carried a long shaft of black stone as though it were a spear. She let it skid across the cliff behind her, and its tip sharpened a bit more every time it smacked against the rock. Now that she was closer, she raised it and took aim. With a pained yell, she drove the makeshift spear into the rock by her head. Her bicep flexed through the long gashes in her sleeve, but she held it tight.

It didn't do much to slow her momentum, but it did give her even better control over each maneuver.

Her other hand reached toward him, palm flat and fingers splayed wide, and a sudden gale hit him from below. The wind tore past, stirring the cloud of dust into a violent tornado that swallowed them both.

It hit him, then how she could maintain that level of control despite her dizzying speed. She was using her Airdrift augmentation to slow their descent.

It seemed insane. Sure, she could control the air, but she damn well couldn't fly.

He studied her wobbly movements, certain he would have to reach out and grab her at any second to stop her from plummeting past him, but she remained upright even while approaching him. Each time she leaned too far to one side, her hand flew out in that direction, and the gale shifted. Though she rapidly closed the distance between them, her control over the air steadied her.

Mostly.

Together, they plummeted down the cliff in a violent spray of black dust that blocked out the vibrant green ribbons of spellgust overhead. The spear in her hand shortened, second by second, until it became at most a nub that was barely keeping her in control of the rocky slab she'd used as a stabilizer on the way down.

His hands ached, threatening to give out as he drove them deeper into the cliff, but he pushed through the pain. He looked over his shoulder at the quickly approaching ground, and this time, orange firelight glinted off metal.

The spike, pointing directly at him.

"Connor, I have a plan!" Quinn shouted.

"Is it a good one?" he yelled back over the thunder of clattering rocks.

She hesitated, squinting down at the ground below as they quickly approached it. "Yes?"

How comforting.

A low growl built in his throat as he struggled to come up with a plan of his own.

"Jump!" she shouted.

"Are you *insane*?"

"Do it!" She coughed as a thick plume of black dust hit her square in the face. "Grab my hand and jump as far away from the rock as you can!"

He shook his head, studying the ground as they approached, certain there had to be a better way to do this.

Absolutely *certain* there was another option aside from jumping to their Fates-damned *deaths.*

"Trust me!" she pleaded.

She leaned toward him, finally within arm's reach. The dwindling nub of black rock finally broke, and she wobbled on her precarious slab as it, too, slowly corroded to nothing.

They didn't have long to act, and he didn't have a better plan.

He was the man who saved his team. The one who stepped in seconds before the arrows hit. The one who held the shield over their heads instead of letting them get roasted alive. The one who took the blows for them so they could recover.

He saved others—but he wasn't the sort of man who trusted others to save *him.*

Here and now, though, it wasn't like he had much of a choice.

With a strangled growl of frustration, and with more spikes coming into view the closer they came to the ground, he roared in pain and pulled his knees to his chest. With a powerful kick, he slammed his feet against the stone and pushed off the cliff as hard as he possibly could. He grabbed Quinn's wrist with a second to spare, and together, they jumped into the spike-riddled abyss below.

To their deaths, most likely.

CHAPTER EIGHT

CONNOR

With one hand firmly holding Quinn's wrist, Connor fell toward the sharp spikes that lined the bottom of a pitch-black abyss.

And this plummet to what was most likely his death was all courtesy of the Wraith King.

That Fates-damned *bastard.*

Around him, the gale became a hurricane. He squinted as the wind stung his eyes, and everything around him blurred until he couldn't quite make sense of it. Somewhere nearby, Quinn grunted with effort, and the wind intensified. It lifted them, momentarily, and his stomach lurched as they abruptly changed direction.

But the air lifting them dispersed, and they once again fell.

The movement kicked the breath out of his lungs. The wind shifted violently, and as they tumbled, he lost track of which way was up. Something hard and warm slammed against his chest, and his grip on Quinn's arm tightened to ensure they didn't get separated in whatever chaos came next.

Another gust hit him hard in the back, sharp and cold as a breath of winter, and the rush cleared his head. He peered through one eye as the ground approached, thankful to spot an open stretch of dirt between three towering metal spikes. He instinctively tucked one shoulder as he prepared to roll.

This was going to hurt.

A lot.

One last gust of wind snapped against him as he fell, and it was enough to slow his freefall. He lurched backward even as he hit the ground. A jolt of white-hot pain shot up his shoulder, but years of training kicked in, and he tucked in his head as he rolled across the dirt. Whatever had landed against his chest pulled away, and the skittering tumble of something sliding across the soil broke through the howling wind.

Nausea burned in the back of his throat as he rolled, again and again. He held his head close to his chest, arms up to protect his skull and neck, and he let the momentum take him. Sticking out a leg now to slow himself down would only guarantee a broken femur.

Finally, blissfully, he slowed. He skidded the final few feet, and for a moment, he could only hear the ringing in his ears. After a while, the shrill scream faded, and his ragged breath mingled with the crackle of a lone torch nearby.

Connor opened his eyes to find the black ground illuminated by a soft orange glow, but his head spun, and he couldn't quite make out where it came from. Blood caked his fingers, but the ache had already begun to fade. He lay there, waiting for his vision to sharpen, and he cursed under his breath as he set his sweat-soaked forehead against the ground. A plume of rock dust stuck to the moisture on his face, but he didn't care. His chest rose and fell with greedy breaths as he did his best to settle his racing heart.

As his head finally cleared, a single name hit him like a lightning bolt to the chest.

Quinn.

He sat upright and pushed himself to his feet in a single motion, scanning the flickering shadows around him as his torch slowly died somewhere at the base of the cliff. At first, he saw only dancing darkness, the edges blurring and swaying at the whims of the firelight. His fingers curled and relaxed, again and again, as he anxiously searched for her body.

Fates above, she had better be alive. After everything they'd endured together, he wouldn't be able to live with himself if the ghoul's damn test had gotten her killed.

Someone coughed in a nearby shadow, and his head snapped toward it instantly. He jogged toward the sound, and sure enough, a lone figure came slowly into view. It walked toward him at an uneven pace, and seconds later,

Quinn Starling stumbled from the shadows.

As their eyes met, she smiled weakly. Chest heaving, she simply gave him a half-hearted salute and set her hands on her waist as she caught her breath.

Though she sighed with relief, the hazy alarm of a brush with death still thrummed through him. He stared at her—at the woman who had saved his life—and did the first thing that came to mind.

He grabbed her waist, pulled her close, and aggressively kissed her.

Rough. Raw. Hungry. The choice was a primal one, something he couldn't even control. Everything he'd experienced throughout the fall poured into that kiss.

Gratitude.

Relief.

Anger.

Bloodlust.

Need.

His grip on her waist kept her pinned against his chest, and he didn't even pause for air.

Magnuson! the Wraith King growled in his head. *You cannot bed your Fates-damned general! What the hell is wrong with you?*

That snapped Connor from his half-numb fog, and he broke off the kiss to glare around him for the wraith.

"What… how…" Quinn's dazed and dizzy voice trailed off into silence.

In his fury, however, Connor barely registered what she had said. His entire focus had shifted toward the Wraith King. The former warlord might've already been dead, but Connor was about to find a way to kill him again.

In a rush of black smoke and bone-white arms, the Wraith King emerged from a thick cloud of black smoke. Single-minded and focused entirely on the ghoul, Connor glared at the undead man who had once fought by his side. At the ghoul he had begun to consider his ally.

His *friend.*

The specter hovered nearby, just out of reach, as though he knew Connor wanted nothing more than to see if he could snap the dead man's bones.

"I warned you," Connor said in a dangerously low voice. "I warned you that I would find a way to end you if you ever—"

Your advanced training will not be gentle, the ghoul said. *Nor will I be kind.*

Even as Connor saw red, the words struck a familiar chord in the recesses of his mind. That sense of familiarity, of something close to nostalgia, was the only thing holding him back as he glared at the ghoul with unabashed loathing.

"Adapt or die," he finished for the Wraith King. "I know."

It was the warning the ghoul had given him back in the woods, before they'd ever found Slaybourne.

Precisely. The undead warlord crossed his bony arms and studied the cliff above them. *She certainly waited until the last minute, but I am pleasantly surprised by the outcome. I fully expected her to leave you to your own devices. Next time, though, minimize the theatrics and focus more on the task at hand, will you?*

"You infuriating ass," Connor spat.

Stop complaining, the specter replied. *We have work to do.*

Connor's biceps screamed in protest, but his body slowly recovered. Feeling seeped back into his fingers, and his breath eventually steadied. "You nearly killed us both."

You were fine. The Wraith King dismissed the accusation with a careless wave. *No Wraithblade worthy of my magic would let himself die on a metal spike.*

Connor scoffed as the nearest spike flashed in the firelight, easily twice his height. "A warning would've been nice."

The Fates have never been so kind as to give you the lesson before the test, Magnuson. Why should I?

Connor brushed dust off his tattered shirt and closed his eyes to stem the urge to reach out and wring the undead king's neck. The ghoul had warned him, in his own twisted way, of what awaited him here. As angry as he was, it didn't serve him to indulge his rage.

Down here, he had no idea what he would face next, and he had to be ready.

He listened to the darkness, ears straining to catch the next test before it hit him this time. Nothing slithered in the shadows, but he doubted the silence would last. If the wraith had hidden his citadel's enchantments in these tunnels, the catacombs must've been even more valuable than Connor had realized. With that much treasure to protect, plenty of living nightmares probably patrolled the darkness.

Behind him, a woman cleared her throat.

Quinn's voice snapped him from his foggy rage, and he looked over one shoulder to find her watching him with her fingertips resting against her lips. Her eyes narrowed slightly, and she tapped one finger against the mouth he'd ravaged seconds before.

We are close to the vault. Evidently oblivious to the tension in the air, the wraith pointed to the flickering fire lying on the stone floor not far away. *You will want your torch.*

Admittedly grateful for the distraction, Connor headed for the torch and grabbed it with an impatient huff. "You can pick things up too, you know."

Instead of answering, the dead king meandered through the cluster of metal spikes and towering pillars of stone. *This way.*

Quinn set her hands on her hips and watched the dead king float away. "What a jackass."

I heard that, the ghoul muttered.

"Good," Connor replied. "Because I second it."

Quinn's eyes snapped toward Connor, and she smirked.

As they walked after the wraith, the dying torch cast only a thin halo of light around him and Quinn as the murky darkness all but swallowed the fading flame. After their many hours in the catacombs so far, the fire wouldn't last much longer.

Then it would be Quinn's turn to light the way.

They passed a gap between two pillars, and two small orbs glinted just beyond the light. He paused, narrowing his eyes in suspicion as he lifted the torch. His shoulders tensed, and the knuckles on his free hand cracked as he balled it into a fist.

He prepared himself to find something staring back at him from the darkness.

The torch's light cast an orange glow on a fractured skull sitting atop a boulder. It stared at him with hollow eyes, and a centipede crawled out from between its teeth as his light disturbed its sleep.

Delightful.

As Connor took his next step, however, something skittered through the darkness just beyond the bones. Something small, about the size of his arm, and the firelight glinted off scales as the thing sifted its way through the shadows.

He paused, focusing more intently now on the darkness. The movement had reminded him of all those times he'd seen the michera darting through bushes in the Ancient Woods. The movement was singular. Distinct.

A slither.

"Connor?" Quinn asked from somewhere behind him. "What—"

"Quiet," he warned, his voice low and thick with warning.

The rushing whoosh of flame bursting to life followed, louder than the crackling fire of the fading torch in his hand, but he didn't dare look away from the nearby shadows. Their guest could attack at any second, and he had to be ready.

A shiver of dread snaked down his spine as he raised the torch to get a better view of whatever had joined them.

The orange circle of light bent and distorted as it hit the rocks and pillars piled on top of each other, down here in this cesspit the wraith had crafted in his life as Slaybourne's master. At its edge, something retreated into the darkness, always a second faster than the firelight—but too slow to remain completely hidden.

Something black.

Something scaly.

Something *fast.*

"Want to tell me what this thing is?" Connor asked the ghoul.

Michera, of course, the Wraith King said with a bored tilt to his voice. *One of my favorite creatures of the Ancient Woods, in fact.*

"Tell me you're joking."

I'm quite serious, the specter replied.

Connor groaned in a blend of disgust and irritation. He threw the torch on the ground, and it bounced once over the black stone as it rolled away. A plume of smoke churned over his arms as and summoned both blackfire blades, ready at any moment for something to charge out of the shadows.

He didn't have much patience left for this Fates-damned bastard.

"Get ready," he warned Quinn. "It's—"

In the inky black around them, two glowing green orbs appeared. They flickered and flashed with a fire of their own. It caught him off guard, and for a second, their light reminded him of vibrant spellgust gems. They hovered above the ground, and trails of green light traced behind them as they bobbed hypnotically from side to side.

As he fought to process what he was seeing, they blinked.

Before he could warn Quinn of the danger, the creature darted out of the shadows and into the light. As long as a sea serpent and just as ugly, the thing scurried frantically over the ground. Hundreds of clawed feet lined the full length of its body, and they clacked along the rock in a rhythmic motion like a wave rolling across the sea.

This wasn't like any michera he'd ever seen.

Whereas the michera of the Ancient Woods were usually blue with yellow tongues, this one was as black as the night. A single green line traced from the tip of its scaly snout, all the way down the length of its spine. It hissed at him, and to his horror, the damn thing had fangs.

Fangs.

The michera of the Ancient Woods were hard enough to kill with armored bodies and the bite power of a vougel. To add the threat of death by venom to the mix greatly reduced his and Quinn's odds of survival.

This just kept getting better.

It darted toward them and retreated in a dizzying display of inner chaos, as if it couldn't tell what it wanted more—to avoid the firelight, or to eat them alive. It bobbed and wove, never in one place for more than a second, and it snaked over the ground at a rapid, chaotic pace. The soft gray glow of his blackfire blades mingled with the amber firelight of his torch, and the surreal combination of light glinted along the beast's black scales.

Its hunger apparently won, and it finally launched itself at his face.

The second it came within reach, Connor sliced at its neck. His powerful blade cut clear through the thick defensive armor his silver swords had never been able to pierce back when he'd lived in the Ancient Woods.

A relief, really. A bit from this thing would've probably hurt like hell.

The creature's head plopped onto the ground with a meaty thud, and its black tongue flicked once across the rock beneath it. Its body landed with a wet thud. Bright green blood, more brilliant even than the spellgust overhead, oozed onto the floor in a rancid puddle.

Quinn's nose creased with disgust. "Why does it look like that?"

"They've been down here for centuries," Connor said as he recovered. "Trapped in the dark and surrounded by raw spellgust ore? It makes sense that they'd change."

"Still..." She trailed off as she nudged the beast's severed head with the tip of her boot. "Those eyes aren't right."

"We can worry about it later." He gestured toward the wraith. "For now, let's—"

An earsplitting buzz erupted from somewhere in the shadows, like a cluster of cicadas that all decided to sing at once. Both Quinn and Connor winced as the wall of sound hit their enhanced ears. His head snapped back and forth as he tried to place where it was coming from, and it took a moment to realize it came from everywhere.

They were surrounded.

Lewd little beasts, these michera, the wraith said with a dry laugh. *Left unattended and with no natural predators, all they do is mate.*

"Damn it," Connor growled under his breath.

The last flickers of the torch's orange flames cast long shadows across the nearby pillars, and he scanned the gaps between pillars for the first sign of attack. Even the subtlest movement through the void would be enough to pinpoint the stampede before it reached them, but he couldn't see anything.

Just darkness, even as the encroaching scream of clattering feet grew closer.

He spun, pressing his back against Quinn's as they slowly circled. "Michera. Loads of them. Be ready."

"They're solitary," she hissed under her breath. "How on earth—"

"Guess you were right," he interjected, his grip tightening on the hilts of his swords. "There's something off about these things."

"If we weren't about to die, I might've enjoyed that."

"What?"

"You admitting I'm right."

"Focus," he chided.

As quickly as it had come, the clamor stopped. In the eerie silence that followed, the torch finally sputtered out with a pathetic little fizzle. Some of the light faded, but the raging fires of Quinn's Burnbane augmentation now cast an even brighter glow across the ink-black stone under their feet.

Connor shifted his weight, prepared for the onslaught and already itching for the inevitable bloodbath.

From the shadows, glowing green eyes appeared. Just two, at first, but more followed. A dozen. Fifty. A hundred.

With each passing second, more of the beasts clambered toward them, climbing on pillars and slithering through the endless black beyond the rock.

"You might need your Volt," he warned.

Through the corner of his eye, Quinn shook out one hand until the fire hovering above her palm went dead. The amber light illuminating their circle dimmed, but since flames still raged in her other hand, it didn't go out completely. The clink of a metal chain followed.

"Ready?" he asked.

"As I'll ever be," she muttered.

"Have any good advice for me, wraith?" he asked, not bothering to look the ghoul's way as he sized up which of the michera might attack first.

This breed clusters around an alpha. Find it, and you might make them stop.

"Might?" He gritted his teeth to fight back another burst of rage for the Wraith King's insipid little pet projects. "What the hell do you mean by it '*might*' work?"

Just that, the ghoul answered. *It might fail. Pack culture changes over time. Only the Fates know what these things do down here in the dark.*

Fantastic.

"Want to let me in on the plan, outlaw?" Quinn asked under her breath.

"Look for an alpha," he answered. "I'm guessing it'll be the biggest, or the one leading the charge."

"That's helpful."

"It's all we've got," he countered. "We've kept them at bay this long, so maybe they don't like the light. Keep yours burning."

"I'll do my best," she replied.

A sudden hiss, like a rattlesnake quivering with warning, cut through the air. More hissing followed, and before long, the deafening sound was louder than the clattering claws had ever been.

There had to be hundreds of these damned things—maybe thousands.

This probably wouldn't end well.

Another of the beasts launched from the darkness toward them, and it was only a matter of time before the rest of the horde followed its lead.

The stalemate had ended, and the bloodbath had begun.

A blistering bolt of light shot through the air, followed by a deafening boom. The ground shook. The michera was gone, replaced by a blackened carcass that vaguely resembled a large millipede, and two dozen of the eyes in the shadows beyond had disappeared. Pebbles skittered down the pillars as they threatened to fall, and a large boulder broke free from one.

It fell toward Connor.

Quinn leaned into his back, and together they darted out of the way, never once breaking formation as they circled and kept their eyes on the threats beyond the firelight. The boulder hit the ground and rolled into the shadows, and the haunting wail of the michera followed. A crunching sound came shortly after, and the wails abruptly died.

That gave him an idea.

"New plan!" he shouted over his shoulder as the creatures hissed at them. "Don't use the Volt. We can't have the pillars crashing down on us."

Before she could respond, a dozen more darted out of the shadows behind him, and a torrent of fire met them. They screamed as Quinn roasted them alive.

Five more jumped off a nearby pillar, and Connor dropped one blade. In the rush of smoke that followed, he summoned his shield just as they reached him, fangs outstretched, and each hit the metal hard. They fell to the ground, writhing in agony, some of their fangs shattered from the impact.

He knelt and swung with his blackfire blade, cleaving each beast's head clean off in a single blow.

If these beasts were anything like the ones he had faced in the Ancient Woods, they were testing both him and Quinn. Assessing their strengths and sniffing out weaknesses before the big attack. He had to come up with a way to stop them before they realized how easily they could overwhelm even him and Quinn.

Hopefully these michera were just as stupid as their distant cousins in the Ancient Woods.

It was then that he spotted it.

The big one.

The alpha.

A towering michera clacked its way into the firelight, its hundreds of feet rhythmically tapping against the stone as it propelled its massive body forward. Hundreds of michera followed it into the light, waiting behind it as they clung to the sides of pillars to watch the spectacle from above.

"I think that might be the alpha," Quinn said dryly.

He peered over at her, only to find her staring over his shoulder at the beast quickly approaching them.

Something darted in his periphery, and they both snapped to attention at the same time. Three michera jumped off a nearby pillar, fangs extended, and he raised his shield. They landed with three heavy thuds, and he pivoted the shield to control their fall. They hit the ground hard, and he slammed the edge of his shield down on their necks. All three died in an instant, and the last threads of his plan formed.

"Hit the base of that pillar with your Volt." He nodded toward the towering pillar beside the hissing alpha michera.

"To take out the ones behind him?" Quinn asked.

"Exactly. I'll take the big guy while you aim. Between the deafening boom and their dead leader, that should be enough to make them stop."

"This won't work, Connor."

"That's the spirit." He took a settling breath to brace himself. "Ready?"

She let out a resigned sigh. "Yeah."

"Now!" he yelled.

He charged toward the alpha, and a cold blast of air shot across his back as he and Quinn separated. The alpha hissed, the sound deep and resonant enough to vibrate through the ground and up his legs, but he quickly closed the gap between them.

Connor had more important things to do, and this stupid creature was in his way.

It lunged, and he twisted his shoulder out of biting range only a second before its jaws clamped shut. He swung at its exposed neck, but its tail whipped toward his face before he could land the blow. He instead ducked and jumped over its thick body as its tail smacked against the stone. It left a little divot in its wake, the black rock cracked and shattered beneath its might, and he made a mental note not to let the thing hit him.

It was all the distraction Quinn had needed.

The air shattered, and another blast of light shot through the abyss, as white and blinding as staring into the sun. He squinted, unwilling to let his guard down even as sharp pain shot into the back of his skull. He kept his gaze focused on the alpha's silhouette as it retreated from the light.

A second thundering boom followed the Volt's attack, and the pillar he'd told her to hit shook violently. It groaned, almost like a tree on its way to the ground, and toppled across the makeshift arena. The michera in its path wailed as they finally realized the danger, and the panicked slithering of bodies scrambling to escape filled the air.

Too late. Most of those would die.

As the blinding brilliance finally faded, the alpha writhed on the ground in front of him, still blinded from the sudden light.

Connor made his move.

He raised his sword to cleave off its head, but the michera recovered. It hissed at him and lunged, its fangs perfectly aimed for his neck.

Enough of this.

Furious, raging, bloodthirsty and mad as hell, he'd had enough.

Focused as he was on the creature in front of him, Connor acted almost on instinct. He let his body lead and leaned into his raw muscle. He dismissed his blade and shield. With his bare hands, he caught the michera's open jaws, his fingers placed perfectly between the gaps in its hundreds of teeth. He stared into its open mouth, at the muscles flexing deep in its throat, and he did the first thing he could think of.

He ripped the damn thing apart.

It screamed in pain as he bent its jaw backward, farther than any jaw was meant to go, and something in it snapped. Joints popped, and the thing's eyes rolled backward in its head.

But he didn't stop.

His biceps flexed as he tore the top half of the michera's head clean off, and it took a moment for him to register that he was yelling. No, not yelling—roaring. His voice reverberated in his chest, raw and powerful, louder even than the michera clattering and screaming in the chaos of their own failed attack.

When he was done, he let the massive beast plop to the ground. Green blood oozed from all the parts he'd ripped off, and their alpha lay in a glowing green puddle of its own blood. The green ooze covered his hands, and his chest heaved as he glared across the gathered monsters that had tried to eat him and Quinn tonight.

They were still.

The surviving michera simply watched him, cowering and silent. He took one step toward the closest cluster of them, and they all shrank instantly backward.

Damn right.

They *should* be afraid.

He squared his shoulders and scanned the horde of michera one last time, searching for any among them that might attack anyway. Each of the beasts cowered under his glare. Most shrank into the shadows, and those trapped in place by the sheer number of other michera around them merely lowered their gazes.

"You." Connor pointed at the Wraith King, his voice dripping with fury as he spoke. "No more tests. No more surprises. Vault. NOW!"

To his utter annoyance, however, that damned ghoul only chuckled.

Careful, the specter warned as his laughter faded. *You're almost starting to sound like a real king.*

"Now!" Connor demanded, sick of the dead man's games.

Without answering, the hovering wraith set his skeletal palm on a small bump in the nearest stone pillar. In the darkness, right at the edge of the amber light from Quinn's Burnbane fires, a coat of arms had been carved into the stone—a shield with a roaring dragon etched on it, a crown above the beast, and two tattered flags billowing on either side. In a banner across the shield was a simple phrase, but one that hit home nonetheless.

Of blood and bone.

The Wraith King's coat of arms. No question.

Before he could order the wraith to explain himself, however, a door popped open in the rock. The gentle hiss of escaping air pierced the silence, and the michera flinched in unison.

That seemed to break the spell of terror he'd put on them.

All at once, in a deafening clamor, the michera retreated into the shadows. The thundering clack of thousands of claws against the stone echoed through the abyss, and Connor gritted his teeth to ride out the overwhelming wall of sound.

At least they weren't attacking again.

In the surreal quiet that followed, a soft green glow from deep below illuminated a curved stairwell. The cracked and weathered steps led further into Slaybourne, and Connor gave the wraith a single glare of warning. His expression conveyed all his anger, all his rage, all the Fates-damned *fury* he felt for this maddening ghoul who wouldn't stop testing his limits.

The warning was clear, and he let it weigh on the air between them.

Don't try me.

With fire still raging across both of her palms, Quinn walked up beside him and nodded down the stairwell. "If there's something else down there we have to kill, I'm going to grab my Bloodbane dagger and cut off another one of his fingers."

"I'd rather you didn't," Connor said flatly, though he understood the sentiment.

I am impressed, Magnuson, the undead warlord admitted, ignoring Quinn's threat. *You're mastering your power far more quickly than I anticipated. It won't be long, now, until you will finally have no equal.*

Connor scoffed, still too angry about the steep drop into the chasm to let a compliment soften his irritation. "Except for you, I assume?"

No. The ghoul shook his head slowly, almost sadly, and gestured for the two of them to follow him down the glowing green stairwell. *Not even me.*

The words burrowed into Connor's bones. They completely disarmed him, and he stared at the back of the ghoul's head in surprise. The tattered hood covered the Wraith King's cracked skull, and for all the undead man's power, Connor sometimes forgot that this titan of myth and legend was nothing more than a reanimated skeleton draped in a cloak.

Death had claimed the Wraith King, once, same as He had claimed Connor's father. Same as He had claimed Henry.

But for the first time, Connor let himself wonder if Death would even be able to claim *him.*

CHAPTER NINE

CONNOR

Unlike the curved staircase that led to the undead soldiers guarding the Soulsprite, this secret stairwell deep in a nondescript abyss below Slaybourne ended in something truly beautiful.

Doors—both of them perfectly aligned and carved from solid spellgust.

Connor paused before them as they glowed brilliantly green, with all the fire and shimmer of a star. A soft hum radiated from them, almost like a pulse, and he set his palm against their warm stone.

They had been built into the mountain, and not a trace of spellgust lingered anywhere else in the entranceway. The emerald light shivered along the dark rock like sunlight off a pond, casting thin rays of dazzling light in every direction.

"What is this place?" he asked the Wraith King. "A vault, sure, but what is it really?"

A tomb, the ghoul said softly.

With one eyebrow raised in concern, he looked over his shoulder at the hovering specter behind him.

Unaware of their conversation, Quinn set her hand against the glowing green stone and smiled. "I've never seen anything like this. With this much magic around it, whatever's inside must be perfectly preserved."

"Let's have a look, then."

Connor grabbed the indents in each door where a handle should have been, and at his touch, something hissed along the hinges. The resistance gave way, and the doors opened almost on their own.

Beware, the wraith warned. *Had the Starling woman tried to open them, she would have instantly died.*

He cast one irritated glare over his shoulder at the wraith. "Thanks for the warning."

You're welcome, the specter said with a lazy shrug.

Connor just shook his head in annoyance.

Ass.

The light only brightened as the doors swung aside. Connor squinted at first, until his eyes could adjust, and shapes slowly came into view amidst the emerald glow. Bottles, lots of them, stacked on shelves against the left wall. Weapons—everything from axes to spears and swords—lined the back wall. Soot-black armor lined the right wall, and display cases dotted the empty spaces along the floor.

In the center of the modest vault, a black book with a golden latch lay on a pedestal. Two dead men sat in the chairs on either side of it, leaning forward with their hands resting on the hilts of their swords. The tips of each blade dug into the spellgust floor, and small cracks radiated from where metal had pierced magic.

Connor summoned his blackfire blade, and fire erupted across Quinn's hands at almost the same time as they watched the men in tense silence.

The wraith had called it a tomb, but Connor hadn't been prepared for this. These men didn't look like the undead that had risen from Slaybourne's dirt.

These men had hair. Features. Skin. Their black uniforms hadn't corroded. The skin along their knuckles bleached white from the firm grip they held on their swords.

And yet neither man breathed. Even as the great spellgust doors swung slowly shut behind Connor's small band, neither so much as glanced his way.

"Who are they?" he finally asked.

At his voice, the dead men's heads pivoted upward, and they both looked directly at him. They had no whites to their eyes, and no irises—just an endless black, one that crept into the veins around each man's eye like thin, inky streams that leaked into their skin. The one on the left stared at Connor intently, as though he could peer into his soul with every bit as much skill as the Wraith King himself. The other, however, shifted his gaze to the ghoul floating at Connor's side.

"My king," both men said.

Beside him, Quinn flinched at the sound clawing its way out of their throats, and even Connor suppressed a shudder at the grating rasp with which these men spoke. Their voices reminded him of a demon whispering in the depths of a well, beckoning passersby to lean closer with lures of gold and treasures, only to drag them to their deaths far below.

It simply sounded *wrong*.

The two men knelt beside their upright swords, each leaning one elbow on his knee and bending his head until their hollow black eyes finally vanished from view.

These are my generals, Magnuson, the wraith explained. *They were the closest thing to friends I had in life, and you will treat them with respect.*

"How I treat them is based on how they act," he countered with a sidelong glare of warning.

The two men lifted their heads again, and this time both of them watched him intently.

"You seem to recognize him." Connor addressed them as he pointed to the Wraith King. "But I'm—"

"His heir," the one on the left said.

Connor's jaw tensed as the undead man's grating voice scratched on the air, but he roughly cleared his throat and forced himself to focus. "In a manner of speaking. I'm Connor. Connor Magnuson."

"I am General Gregori." The undead man gestured to his comrade. "And this is General Yao."

"Charmed," Quinn said dryly.

"And you are a Starling," Yao said, his unnatural eyes narrowing. "You do not belong in the great Slaybourne Citadel."

"On the contrary," Connor interjected. "She's your new acting general."

Through the corner of his eye, Quinn flinched in surprise and shifted her gaze toward him. When he didn't budge—or elaborate—she pursed her lips and patiently waited, apparently unsure whether or not this was a bluff.

She crossed her arms and waited, likely playing along until she found an opportunity to pull him aside.

Well played. With every test she passed, big and small, he was more and more certain she would be the perfect general.

This is your last chance to choose someone else, Magnuson, the wraith warned. *You kissed her out there, and I know what you actually wanted to do to her. What you would've done, had there not been pending danger.*

"No," he answered flatly. "I've made up my mind."

You're a damn fool. The ghost huffed indignantly. *And you're going to get yourself killed.*

Connor ignored the jibe, and he instead shifted his attention to Quinn. "Not sure why you're surprised. I need a general, and you're the obvious choice."

She shook her head. "Flattery won't get you anywhere, outlaw."

"Not flattery," he corrected. "Fact. I need someone who will watch my back when my guard is down. Someone who will fight at my side until the end. Someone who knows war even better than I do, who can point out flaws in my strategies and lead in my absence. That's you, Quinn."

Her jaw tensed, and though she stared at the dead men kneeling before them, she didn't reply.

"Say yes." Connor shifted his weight as he stared her down. "Admit you're the only logical choice."

"That's why you wanted the others to stay topside," she said, ignoring him. "This was a test."

"Several," he admitted. "None of them my idea, for the record."

"Noted." She chuckled, but her smile quickly faded. "I'm honored, Connor, but I won't let my ego blind me from the truth."

"And that is?"

"I'm not the right choice," she insisted.

Behind them, the Wraith King paced the length of the doors, his hands behind his back as he studied the Starling warrior before him. His head tilted to the side. The bones in his fingers clacked, slow and steady, as he curled them into a fist. The movements reminded Connor of a predator, prowling through the night, waiting for a chance to pounce.

"My father led the charges, not me," Quinn continued. "He commanded the Lightseers, not me. All I ever did was manage missions. Not an *army.*"

He leaned in and lowered his voice until only she and the wraith could hear him. "Your father raised you to need him. To rely on him. He trained you to doubt yourself, and I won't let you live like that anymore. I've seen you fight. I've seen you strategize. But more than anything, Quinn, I've seen you hold back. You're in my ranks, now, and you can't limit yourself anymore. I won't allow it, and I'll call you on your bullshit every time I see you do it. I want to see what you're really capable of. I want to know what you can truly do. Don't you?"

Her lips parted in surprise as she stared up at him, those hazel eyes as captivating as ever, and he forced himself to pull away even as another primal urge rocked him to the core. He blocked out the impulsive images of ripping off her shirt and did everything he could to focus on the moment.

In his head, the Wraith King's frustrated growl rumbled like thunder.

"I'm trusting you," he added. "With everything."

"I know," she finally said. "And I won't let you down."

"You two can stand," Connor told the undead generals. "One of you get her a sword."

The two men dutifully got to their feet, and each yanked his sword from the spellgust floor. They sheathed their weapons and stood with their hands behind their backs, awaiting orders.

Wait, the wraith interjected. *First, ask them where Lancet is.*

Connor's eye twitched with annoyance at the demand, but he ultimately indulged the dead king. "Where's Lancet?"

"Who's Lancet?" Quinn asked under her breath.

"No idea," Connor whispered back.

She sighed.

"He betrayed us," Yao answered.

"Lancet conspired with the queen to kill you," Gregori elaborated. "We took his sword and hung it here, for safe keeping, until you could appoint a worthier warrior."

The undead man pointed to the back wall, where a sword similar to theirs hung behind the large book still resting on its pedestal. A ribbon of green light flashed across the jet-black steel, and a single spellgust stone the size of an eyeball glimmered brilliantly in its hilt.

"As for Lancet, we had him drawn and quartered," Yao added. "Then we burned him. We knew you would succeed, Wraith King, and a traitor does not deserve immortality."

A low growl rumbled in Connor's head, and the wraith's hand curled into a tight fist. *That bastard. He helped her kill me. No wonder—now I know how she—*

His words overlapped, heavy with fury as each sentence fought the other for dominance, and the specter turned his back on them all as he processed what his men had told him.

Give her Lancet's sword, the ghoul said quietly. *A general must have a truly unique weapon.*

Given the specter's grief over the ancient betrayal, Connor resisted the impulse to gloat. Even as the Wraith King fumed over the traitor that had cut him down in life, he had finally admitted—in his own twisted fashion—that Quinn would be a worthy general.

Connor headed for the blade and nodded for Quinn to follow. She obliged him, and when they reached Lancet's sword, he lifted it off the wall. Hilt first, he offered it to her.

"*Aurora* might be gone," he said softly. "But you need a blade."

She swallowed hard even as her eyes roamed the magnificent steel before her. Her delicate fingers traced the sword's hilt, and she hesitated. It was brief—just a second's pause, one most people would've overlooked—but it showed her lingering doubts.

Not in him, but in herself.

When she finally took the sword, she angled it this way and that to inspect it.

"Flawless," she admitted.

Hmph. The Wraith King crossed his bony arms and resumed his pacing by the far door. *It's a blackfire blade. She will have to train to learn it. With time, perhaps she can begin to wield it even a fraction as well as—*

With a twist of her arm, blackfire erupted across the dark steel. She grinned, and the firelight reflected in her eyes as she studied her new weapon. The whoosh of blistering flames on the air cut through the vault, and she took a few practice swings to test its balance. The blade settled into her palm as though it had been forged for her, and she wielded it with ease.

Connor smirked victoriously and shot the wraith a sidelong glance. The ghoul merely grumbled in defeat.

"Yao." He gestured to the wall of armor. "I'll need your help removing these. Get four full sets."

"Yes, sir." The soldier bowed his head and immediately walked toward the wall of armor.

"Gregori," Connor added with a nod toward the rows of jars along opposite wall. "Are those reagents?"

"Almost entirely, sir." The other general nodded. "Enough to augment an army."

"Is there an inventory?"

"There is." Gregori tugged a thin brown journal from a narrow shelf built into the black book's pedestal. "This carries the vault's full inventory, at all times."

"Good. It's your job to keep that accurate, understood?"

"Yes, sir."

Connor lifted the black book into his hands, and his thumb brushed against the golden latch securing the pages. "This must be your collection of potion recipes."

It is, the ghoul answered. *The finest recipes ever recorded in Saldia. Use it well, Magnuson, and don't you dare lose it, or—*

"Or you'll find a way to smother me in my sleep, I know." Connor resisted the impulse to roll his eyes. "Come up with new threats, will you?"

The ghoul chuckled softly before he could stop himself.

"We'll have to come back with Sophia." Connor absently rubbed his jaw as he thought through the best way to handle this. "The book shouldn't leave this room, and she'll want access to the reagents anyway. The undead can carve a stairwell into the cliff to make the trip easier."

"And the michera?" Quinn asked dubiously.

"I think they've learned their lesson." His voice dropped an octave. "We'll post undead soldiers as guards, just in case."

"Fair enough."

One of my generals betrayed me, Magnuson, the wraith interjected.

Connor looked up as the ghoul spoke, his brows furrowed in concern. "That must be hard to accept."

It is, the ghost admitted. *And I never suspected it was something he would do. Let that be a lesson for you, then, that people can fail us in the most surprising ways.*

With that, the wraith disappeared into a rush of black smoke.

Connor stood by the pedestal, staring at where the wraith had been moments before, and sat with the dead king's warning. A numb ache crept up his neck, and for several moments, he could only stand there as the words echoed around in his skull.

"Are you alright?" Quinn asked softly.

Her voice snapped him from his daze, and he cracked his neck to relieve some of the tension. Her eyes narrowed—either in suspicion or concern, he couldn't tell—but she thankfully didn't say anything else.

"Gregori, help Yao with the armor," Connor ordered, unwilling to look her way.

"Yes, sir."

"Head topside. We'll meet you there."

The undead man saluted and joined his fellow general along the far wall. They hoisted glistening black armor onto their shoulders and yanked folded leather tunics from shelves built into the base of the wall. Connor would have to examine it in more detail later, but for now, he occupied himself by examining the wall of weapons behind him.

"Nice," he said under his breath as he spotted a dazzling black dagger as long as his forearm. He tugged it off the wall and slid it into his frayed boot.

He'd tell Gregori to mark the vault records later.

Quinn unbuckled the sheath on her waist and, with a heavy sigh, hung it on an empty hook. Instead, she replaced it with the jet-black sheath from her new blade.

Crouching with one elbow resting on his knee, Connor paused to marvel in the surreal sight of a Starling without the trademark blue and silver sheath of a Firesword. The black hilt stuck out at an odd angle, perhaps a little too big for her, and she crossed her arms as she studied the wall of weapons. Her eyes lingered on an axe, but she ultimately passed it over in favor of a throwing star.

"What will you name it?" he asked.

"The sword?"

He nodded.

She shrugged. "Too soon to say, honestly. Names come to you with time. I'm still getting to know it."

"That's fair."

After all, he still hadn't named his.

They returned to their survey of the weapons long after the generals had disappeared through the spellgust doors, and he figured they couldn't spend much longer down here. He could only imagine the chaos that might follow if two half-dead men emerged from the catacombs without him.

The earful he would get from Kiera alone wasn't worth it.

"Enough shopping." He clapped his hands together and nodded toward the exit. "Let's head out."

She followed without a word, her eyes glossing over in thought, and she didn't speak again until the spellgust doors had sealed behind them.

"What did you see in the star pool?" she finally asked.

He frowned in confusion. "Why?"

"Humor me."

"Alright." He wrapped one hand around his fist to crack his knuckles as he led them up the stairwell. He didn't really want to talk about this, but it seemed like she had something on her mind. "My family. They told me about the next life. They told me it wasn't my time to go."

"Hmm," she said softly.

It was still a bit strange, trusting a Starling like this, but he had to confess he didn't hate it.

Not as much as the wraith did, anyway.

"What did you see?" he asked.

"A memory. I think it's from when I was a baby." She scowled, like the thought hurt her. "I think it was my parents dying."

His head snapped back in surprise. "But how—"

"I don't know," she admitted.

They marched in silence for a bit longer, and the steady stomp of the generals' footsteps echoed down the stairwell.

"What do you think that pool showed us?" she eventually asked. "I mean, what was it, really?"

"Not sure," he admitted. "Murdoc saw the soldiers who died on the mission that got him kicked out of the Blackguards. Sophia saw everyone she's ever killed. We all saw something a little different, but it sounds like we all encountered the dead in one way or another."

"Perhaps," she said softly. "Whatever it was, it felt important."

"You'd best figure it out, then," he said with a casual glance at her. "It doesn't sound like something I can help you uncover, but it's clearly weighing on you."

"I know exactly who I need to ask." Her eyes drifted to the stairs ahead of her, and they glazed over once more.

"That sounded ominous."

Quinn Starling didn't answer, and he didn't press her to elaborate. Whatever she'd seen in that pool haunted her long after the rest of them had let it go, and that meant she had more to learn about herself—and, perhaps, Zander's belief that she wasn't a Starling at all.

CHAPTER TEN

CONNOR

Finally in the dazzling sunlight once more, Connor led his small band out of the catacombs and into the heart of Slaybourne.

Everyone had become accustomed to several thousand undead soldiers, so maybe two unnaturally grim generals wouldn't phase them all that much, either.

He snorted. Sure.

A man could dream.

His main focus upon their return had to be making sure the kids didn't get emotionally scarred just from looking at them.

At the prickling sensation of Yao's and Gregori's steady gazes on his back, he peered over one shoulder. The two men trudged through the tall grasses, perfectly in sync, and the sunlight gave their skin an almost gray tint to it. They said nothing, instead watching him with those all-black eyes while they each held two full sets of the Wraith King's magnificent armor. The ghoul, however, had not reappeared since the vault, and his absence had not gone unnoticed.

Lancet's betrayal had hit him hard, even after so many hundreds of years—and Connor couldn't blame the undead king for his grief. From what he'd gleaned of their partnership, it would be like Murdoc, murdering him in his sleep.

It was unthinkable.

Quinn walked in a steady cadence beside him, her eyes still unfocused, and thick tension bubbled between them as neither looked at the other for long. He'd lost his head back there in the catacombs, and that kiss had been uncalled for.

Mercifully, she hadn't mentioned it again.

"You're quiet," he said.

"Thinking," she answered without even a sidelong glance his way.

Hmm.

"About what?"

"What?" That seemed to break her from her daze, and she blinked rapidly as she finally looked his way.

"What are you thinking about?"

"Oh," she said absently. "Nothing."

"Sure," he muttered. "And I'm a northern princess, on my way to tea."

She laughed and, to his surprise, a soft snort escaped her as she shook her head. "You're an idiot."

"Guilty." He grinned. "Now, want to tell me what you're thinking about?"

Her smile faded, and her brow creased with focus as her gaze shifted again to the world in front of them. "The battle."

Ah.

Her father.

He cleared his throat, not sure what to say. "Murdoc can tell you that I'm not one for comforting speeches, but I know when to shut my mouth and listen. If you need to talk, just tell me."

She nodded, but she didn't reply.

As they trotted down a hill with the two undead generals in tow, he spotted Murdoc and Sophia sitting on a blanket in the grass. One of Kiera's picnic baskets sat between them, and the former blackguard munched happily on one of her famous sausage rolls.

"Hey!" Connor said. "You'd better have enough in there for me!"

"There aren't enough on this continent to satisfy you," Sophia countered as she bit into hers.

He tilted his head to hide his smile. "Rude."

The necromancer shrugged.

"I see you're keeping a close watch on the prisoners," Quinn said dryly as they reached the blanket.

"Oh, please." Murdoc waved away her critique with his free hand as he took another hearty bite of the last sausage roll. "It was an obvious ploy to keep us busy. Connor has enough soldiers to bury our prisoners in a bone pile."

"Now there's a charming image," Quinn muttered.

"Who are your new friends?" Sophia's nose creased with disgust as she peered around Connor's bulk. "And what the hell is wrong with their eyes?"

"Rude," Connor said again, more seriously this time. "These are the Wraith King's former generals. Show them some respect."

Through the corner of his eye, the two undead men briefly bowed their heads in greeting.

"General Yao, General Gregori," Connor said, gesturing to each man as he introduced them. "This is Sophia and Murdoc."

"And what is your rank among his Majesty's army?" Gregori's question slithered through the air, and the hair on the back of Connor's neck stood on end at the dead man's voice.

Though he and Quinn showed no reaction, Sophia and Murdoc winced.

"Please don't do that again," the former Blackguard said as he set his half-finished sausage roll in the basket.

"What?" Gregori asked, his brows pinching with annoyance.

"Speak," Sophia said flatly.

The generals growled in annoyance.

"Behave," Conner chided her.

She shrugged, but didn't say anything more.

He shifted his attention to his two new generals. "You can set the armor down by the blanket. Run recon on the ruins in the valley and tell me what you think is salvageable. Stay out of sight for now. I'll introduce you to the townspeople later."

"Yes, sir." With their hands still full, both men nodded instead of saluting and gently set the armor in four distinct piles by the blanket. In moments, they were off, walking in sync with each other as they obeyed his orders.

Sophia shuddered. "Tell me you found something more useful down there than two eerie dead men."

"Oh, *much* more useful." Connor flashed a mischievous grin as he sat on the blanket and rummaged through the basket for something to eat.

"It's empty," Murdoc said triumphantly. "Unless you like half-eaten leftovers."

Connor's stomach growled, but even he wasn't *that* hungry.

"Mostly, we found michera," Quinn added as she sat beside him. "Lots and lots of michera."

"Michera?" Murdoc's eyebrows shot up his forehead. "In the catacombs?"

As he set his palms on the grass behind him, Connor nodded. "There are hundreds of them, maybe a thousand, on the way to the central vault. Any expeditions need a full guard. We'll need to carve some stairs into the cliff to make it easier to access."

"How did you get to it, then?" Sophia asked.

"You don't want to know," Quinn said. "Be grateful you'll get stairs."

"I'll show you the route later, Sophia," Connor added. "The Wraith King's recipes are down there, and I don't want that book to leave the catacombs."

"He has a whole book?" Sophia's eyes lit up with excitement, and she sat up straight as a broad smile spread across her face.

Connor nodded. "That, and a wall filled with preserved reagents."

The necromancer's smile only widened. "Pinch me, because I must be dreaming."

Murdoc reached for her ass, and a second later she yelped. She smacked him, but he simply laughed.

"What's special about this armor?" Quinn pointed to the four carefully positioned piles of glittering black scales.

"Let's find out." Sophia stood and brushed her hands on her skirts as she studied the piles. She knelt beside one and lifted the chest plate to examine it more closely. The sunlight glinted off tiny black plates sewn together in a pattern that reminded him almost of dragon scales. In fact, as light glinted across the inky metal, they reminded him every bit of Nocturne's skin.

Fascinating.

"Look at this." Sophia pointed to a single green spellgust stone glimmering at the neckline, as vibrant as the day it was forged. She set it aside and lifted a gauntlet, brushing her thumb across the spellgust gem at its base.

"Wait," she said wistfully, still lost in thought as she sifted through each piece of armor. "Not just the chest plates. Every *piece* is enchanted."

"With what?" Connor asked.

"How the hell should I know?" The necromancer quirked one eyebrow in irritation. "You're the one with the connection to the undead king who made them."

But he didn't take the bait.

"You sound a little irritable," he said with a mischievous grin. "Did you not get enough sleep, Sophia?"

"Not nearly enough," Murdoc chuckled and reclined backward onto the grass. "As was the intention, of course."

"Idiot," she muttered under her breath.

They possess a unique Hygenmix enchantment, the wraith explained.

After hearing nothing from the Wraith King for so long, the dead king's grim voice seemed out of place at first. Connor scanned the meadow, but the ghoul had yet to make himself seen.

Blood will not stain it, nor will sweat, the ghost continued, still hidden from view. *A second Strongman enchantment makes it difficult to penetrate, though not impossible. The combination took decades to perfect, and this armor allowed us to campaign for months at a time without ever appearing exhausted, nor affected by the battles. Use it wisely.*

"That's fantastic," Connor admitted. "How many pieces of it do you have down there?"

Enough, the Wraith King answered simply.

"Sure, but—"

Magnuson, be silent, damn it, the specter grumbled. *I'm in no mood for conversation. I told you what you needed to know. We're done.*

Connor frowned and scanned the tall grasses again, knowing full well the undead king wouldn't be among them. Though they needed more information, he let out a slow sigh and simply nodded.

The Wraith King needed space to mourn.

A shadow flew overhead and circled them. Connor peered upward as the soft whistle of something falling cut through the calm morning, and a dazzling black blur shot toward them from the clouds.

Nocturne landed hard, and the ground shook beneath them. Some of the armor slid and clinked together as the delicately placed piles toppled.

"HELLO, MY FRIENDS," the dragon prince said. "THERE IS MUCH WE NEED TO DISCUSS."

Connor cleared his throat to break the tension. "Nocturne's right. Now that he's here, let's get down to business."

"What business?" Sophia asked as she claimed one of the piles of armor for herself.

"MY BRETHREN, OF COURSE," the dragon answered tersely. "THE ONES TEAGAN STARLING ENSLAVED."

Beside him, Quinn flinched briefly at her father's name, almost too subtly to even notice.

"WE KNOW WHERE THEY ARE," Nocturne continued, apparently oblivious to Quinn's discomfort. "HE IMPRISONED THEM ON A SMALL ISLAND BY LUNESTONE."

"It's a fortress," Sophia interjected. "Every necromancer that's ever tried to infiltrate it has never come back."

"It's not just the necromancers," Quinn said softly. "Not even I could infiltrate it. Father stopped me every time. It was like he knew where I was at any given moment."

The team paused, and an unnatural silence settled upon them as the southern wind rustled the meadow grass around the blanket.

The Starling warrior sat with one leg propped, her elbow resting on her knee, and she stared at the ground as she spoke.

"I've been thinking about this since we heard about his secret assassins," she admitted, her eyes glazing over. "He must have them positioned around the island, acting as invisible guards, and there must be some sort of enchantment that allows them to notify him if he needs to interject. Otherwise, they would've just killed me or captured me. He didn't want me to know they were there, so he came himself. It's the only thing I can think of that makes any damn sense."

"Is that kind of enchantment even possible?" Murdoc asked.

In unison, Quinn and Sophia nodded.

"Usually, it's blood magic," the necromancer added. "You can pair two items. If one breaks, the other will, too. It's rudimentary, and most recipes have a limited range, but it's effective enough as a warning sign."

"Without him there, we might be able to sneak in." Quinn's hand balled into a tight fist, but her voice was otherwise steady. "I need to gather information from his office first, though. We can't walk into that island blind."

"What would he have in his office?" Connor asked.

"Everything,"

She finally looked at him, and that infuriating primal urge to take her here and now slammed against his chest once again. He growled softly and forced himself to study the distant edge of the forest to quell the primal lust that was going to shatter his self-restraint at any moment.

To distract himself, he rubbed his palm with one thumb and tried to stay focused on the conversation. "Say we make it to the dragons, but they're feral. What do we do?"

Thunder rumbled in Nocturne's chest, and the prince of dragons lifted his mighty head toward the clouds as he sighed. "THEN WE GIVE MY FALLEN BROTHERS THE LAST KINDNESS, AND WE KILL THEM AS PAINLESSLY AS POSSIBLE."

The regal creature's words settled on their shoulders, heavy with implication and risk. No matter what information Quinn could find in her father's office, Connor could pretty much guarantee there would be something they didn't know going in. Something crucial. Something that would make the difference between success and failure.

"I MUST BELIEVE," Nocturne said quietly. "I MUST HAVE FAITH THAT SOME OF THEM HAVE PERSEVERED. I CANNOT LET MYSELF FALL INTO THE GRIEF OF LOSING THEM ALL."

"Then we will, too," Connor promised.

"He mentioned mind control and breeding," Quinn added.

Connor noticed she hadn't said her father's name, but he opted against commenting on that.

Nocturne growled with rage, and a plume of dark smoke shot through his nose. Sophia coughed as she waved it away. With an annoyed little huff, she hoisted her pile of armor into her hands and retreated to her spot beside Murdoc.

Take it easy, Connor said through his connection to the dragon. *Breathe.*

The prince of beasts closed his eyes and took several deep breaths. The torrent of smoke thinned until it dissolved completely, and the raging rumble in his chest faded into the gentle breeze around them.

"THERE MAY BE MORE DRAGONS THAN I ORIGINALLY LOST," Nocturne admitted. "THERE IS SO MUCH WE DO NOT KNOW."

"He also mentioned augmentations made from dragon's blood," Connor pointed out. "They're evidently much more powerful."

"DO NOT PUSH YOUR LUCK, WRAITHBLADE."

He chuckled. "It's something to think about. That's all."

"MMHMM," the dragon said dubiously.

A thought occurred to Connor, and he shifted his attention to the Starling warrior sitting beside him. "While you're in his office, look for anything you can find on the Deathdread. I promised the wraith I'd find it."

"It's in the Mountains of the Unwanted," Sophia said with an annoyed tilt to her voice.

"It can't hurt to confirm," he pointed out.

"Fine," she muttered. "But I'm right."

"I'll look," Quinn promised. "No guarantees, though."

"Noted," Connor said with a nod. "But it's not just for the wraith. Back in the Blood Bogs, the Antiquity mentioned another simmering soul. An active one."

"Fates be damned," Murdoc said, exasperated. "One's bad enough. Now there's another?"

I heard that, the ghoul muttered.

"She called him the newcomer," Connor continued, ignoring them both. "But she wouldn't tell me more."

"The newcomer?" Sophia frowned. "As in, newer than you?"

"Who knows?" he admitted with a shrug. "She's an eternal, ancient being. For all we know, 'new' is her way of describing anything that happened in the last century."

Sophia shrugged. "Fair point."

"Sounds like we need to pay Freymoor a visit," Quinn interjected.

"Seems so," he agreed. "She mentioned wanting me to find more Soul-sprites, too, so I'm sure there's quite a bit we need to discuss with her."

"Sounds like we're leaving Slaybourne," Murdoc leaned forward and set his elbows on his knees. "Again."

"Looks that way." Connor scratched the back of his neck and sighed. "Quinn, how long do we have until the rest of the Lightseers come for us? Who and what will they bring?"

"It's hard to say," she answered. "I doubt it'll be long. Give me a second to think through the scenarios."

Truth be told, it was a treat for her to give the information so willingly. Last time they'd had this conversation, the negotiations and bluffing had dragged on for ages.

"Alright." She leaned forward and clapped her hands together as the options came to her. "The biggest factor is whether or not Zander is still alive."

Murdoc let out an exasperated groan. "I'm telling you, he's dead."

"I'll believe it when I see his corpse," Quinn countered.

"He's probably been eaten, so that might be hard." The former Blackguard narrowed his eyes as he studied her face. "You'll never be satisfied, will you?"

She shrugged.

"Focus," Connor chided.

"We have a few months, I'd say," Quinn continued. "Without Zander in Lunestone, they'll squabble over who has the right to rule. I'm sure some of the Regents will try to take over, but Victoria and Gwen will keep them in line. My guess is Gwen will lead the charge, so we can probably mitigate this looming disaster with a simple conversation. If I can talk to her and get her to understand Father—" Her voice caught in her throat, and she cleared it roughly. "That he was lying to everyone, I might be able to get her to side with us. It would take some work, but we might be able to get the Lightseers to lay down arms. They might even become allies."

Sophia laughed, as though that were the most ludicrous thing she had ever heard. "That'll be a cold day in hell."

"It's possible," Quinn insisted, her voice firm.

"Wait," Connor interjected. "Why not send you back to take over? Your sisters are retired, and your brother is gone. That leaves you as the only heir. You can leave now and make your way out to the Ancient Woods. It'll be like you were never here."

"Too risky." She shook her head. "It's unlikely, but even one escaping survivor can unravel that whole story. I'd likely be forced to take a Hackamore anyway once I arrived home, as that's procedure when Lunestone recovers anyone lost in the field. If Zander does make it back, it will only further discredit me. Besides, I've lived a lie long enough. I'm done."

Frustrated, Connor scratched at the stubble in his beard. Those were all good points, and he needed a better plan.

"I need to infiltrate Lunestone, and I already have a way in." Quinn cracked her knuckles as she thought through her options. "While I'm in there, I'll speak to Gwen."

"I don't like it," Sophia interjected. "If she's anything like your brother, she will just ruin everything."

"She's nothing like Zander," Quinn snapped, her voice thick with warning as she defended her sister. "Gwen will listen."

"You're sure?" Connor interjected.

The Starling warrior's gaze shifted to him, and she nodded.

"You'd bet your life on it?"

She nodded again.

"My life?"

This time, Quinn hesitated. Her eyes never wavered, though, and she nodded a moment later.

Hmm.

Honestly, he didn't like this either. He wasn't a huge fan of the Starlings, present company excluded, and he didn't want to stake everything on a stranger.

But their options were limited.

"Alright," he finally acknowledged. "But talk to her after you've gone through the office and gotten everything useful out of that place. Understood?"

"Understood," she said, far more gently than he'd expected.

"It would be best for us to expose Teagan's lies." Nocturne's voice boomed around them, sudden and almost painfully loud. "Is there a way to reveal his deceit that would shift the tides of public opinion in your favor?"

Well, now *there* was an interesting idea.

"Looks like the Captain's weaving together another plan," Murdoc said with a roguish grin.

"Not sure it's a real plan yet." Connor tapped his thumb against his jaw as he slowly pieced it all together. "But the Lightseers' power stems from their position as the guardians of truth, right? They protect the people from the darkness. They're supposed to be these glorious warriors of light."

"I'm going to hate this," Sophia said dryly. "I can already tell."

"Think about it," he continued, ignoring the jibe. "The Lightseers are hunting me because of the Wraith King. I have a simmering soul when they claimed to have destroyed the simmering souls ages ago. My existence proves they've been lying to the people. What if we revealed what I am? What I *really* am?"

"Yep." Sophia sprawled out on the grasp with an irritated groan. "I hate it."

"Connor, it will make everyone despise you *more.*" Quinn shook her head, incredulous. "People fear the simmering souls because the magic undermines even the best augmented soldiers. The hosts are unstoppable."

"Exactly," he said with a smirk. "They expect a conqueror. A warlord. But when they realize I'll leave them alone, they'll understand they've been lied to all this time."

"They'll never believe that," she insisted. "They'll never change their minds."

"You did," he pointed out.

At that, Quinn went silent. She pursed her lips and sighed with irritation, but she didn't reply.

"I'm already everyone's enemy," he continued. "I'll always be someone's enemy. It's just a matter of time before the Lightseers rope the other kingdoms into an onslaught against Slaybourne. What do we have to lose?"

"Maybe *everything*?" Sophia said dryly.

"The Captain might be onto something," Murdoc said.

"Oh, don't *encourage* this," the necromancer snapped.

Connor shifted his attention to Quinn. "If Henry had told everyone he had a simmering soul, what would have happened?"

"He would've been overthrown," she answered. "He was already a warlord, but he'd destroyed people's will to fight. To have an ancient evil on the throne would've inspired them to keep fighting."

"Right, but I'm not forcing anyone to bow to me."

Quinn slowly shook her head. "I don't like it, Connor."

"Finally," Sophia muttered. "The Lightseer and I agree on something."

"This could easily backfire," Quinn continued. "It's assumed that the host will go darker and darker over time. If anything, it might only convince people to turn on you."

"THERE ARE TOO MANY UNKNOWNS," Nocturne begrudgingly agreed.

"Alright." Connor shrugged. "I'll think on it, and I want you all to think on it, too. Look for ways we can make it work."

"It won't," Sophia said with an irritated huff. "So why would we dwell on it?"

"Because the longer I hide the truth, the worse the fallout will be if the Lightseers ever get desperate," he said firmly. "If I tell everyone what I am, it at least gives me a *bit* of credibility."

A tense weight settled between them, and Sophia's dark gaze shifted to the ground.

"Why should anyone trust me if I'm living a lie?" He paused and, in the heavy silence, watched the Starling warrior through the corner of his eye. "You know what the fallout would be like."

She bit her lip and looked away, but ultimately nodded.

Even if nothing came of this for now, at least she understood.

"It sounds like we have a plan." Connor pushed himself to his feet and brushed the loose blades of grass off his hands. "We head to Freymoor and have a little chat. Quinn, you'll come with us to Freymoor in case there's any information you need before heading off to Lunestone. If the Antiquity needs us to go get her a Soulsprite, you'll head to Lunestone on your own. If not, we'll help."

"It would be better if you didn't." Quinn ripped apart a blade of grass as she grinned playfully. "Those tunnels probably aren't even wide enough for you."

He chuckled and shook his head. "For the sake of staying focused, I'll ignore that for now."

"How generous," she said, still smirking.

"Quinn will search—uh, search the office." He caught himself before he could say Teagan's name. "If you can do recon on the island, do it. If not, talk to Gwen and see if she can be swayed to our side. We'll meet up to discuss our plan to rescue the dragons."

"Simple," Murdoc muttered. "Yet insane."

"I have a safehouse in Arkcaster," Quinn added. "Fully stocked and isolated. I never shared the location with anyone, not even my family."

He raised one eyebrow, skeptical given the town's proximity to Lunestone. "Isolated enough to hide a dragon?"

Quinn nodded. "I'll sketch a map for you."

"Alright," he said, still doubtful. "Get that map to me, and we'll decide from there. Everyone else, get your things together. We need to head out soon, and there's a lot to be done before we leave."

Nocturne launched himself into the sky, and his leathery wings snapped against the air. The gusts from his wingbeats sent ripples across the meadow, like waves, and Quinn's hair danced around her face as he took off. Sophia gathered her armor while Murdoc scoped out the three remaining piles to choose his, but Connor's gaze fixed on Quinn.

His new general.

She stood and, as she brushed off her pants, caught his eye. Calmly, she tilted her head in silent curiosity as he watched her, and he leaned in. He gently grabbed her forearm, his massive hand nearly wrapping around her entire arm as his thumb rested against the bend of her elbow.

"Think about it," he told her, his voice low enough to go undetected even by Sophia. "If we can twist people against the Lightseers, I'm willing to step out into the public eye."

For a moment, Quinn simply looked off into the distance, in the vague direction of Death's Door, but she ultimately shook her head. "Sometimes, it's best to go unseen, Connor. Far too often, a soldier can do their best work in the darkness."

"And sometimes, that's just another way to hide," he countered.

It was an old proverb he'd learned from his father, all those years ago in Kirkwall. It was part of what had driven him, broken and battered, into the Ancient Woods to look for purpose and direction amongst Saldia's worst monsters.

Risks aren't as scary once we take them, he'd said. *And to live a life without a bit of danger, son, to never push your limits or test your boundaries? Well, that isn't much of a life at all.*

Live, he'd always said. *Live—and be man enough to fail.*

THE ANTIQUITY

In the darkness, the Antiquity slept.

It was a fitful sleep, the sort that left her more exhausted than before it had begun, and which, for all intents and purposes, seemed pointless in the end.

And yet, she endured. It was all she could do.

Her bogs were dying. Once, her homestead had stretched into the forests far beyond Freymoor, deep into the realms men had slowly begun to reclaim since her first Soulsprite had been stolen. Even with just two, her lands had driven off the worst mortals Saldia could produce.

With only one Soulsprite remaining, however, she could no longer stretch her vines deep into the homestead she had claimed so long ago.

For the first time in her existence, the Antiquity was weak.

Deep within the caves below the Blood Bogs, she curled around herself, conserving her energy for when her Champion returned. He would have questions—the mortals always did, it seemed—and she must conserve her energy for that moment.

But clinging to life took so much effort.

"Sister," a familiar voice said.

The word echoed, like a whisper through a deep and endless cave, beckoning her back to consciousness.

Back to the world of the living.

With the dwindling strength of a dying beast, she opened one eye. Not the eyes mortals saw, of course, but her third. The one situated in the middle of her forehead. The one that allowed her to truly See.

The one through which she spoke to her siblings—and to her Creator.

White light flooded her vision, its edges tinged with traces of green. The light fluttered and shook like shredded fabric, nothing solid for more than a second.

In this land between lands, she waited.

"Sister," the Morrow said again, louder this time.

"*Come to me*," the Antiquity replied.

Within the rippling lights the Fates themselves had designed, a silhouette appeared. Only a hint, at first. Nothing but shadow and a thin frame. It walked closer, and sleek curves appeared. Wide hips. Narrow shoulders. Billowing hair that floated in the figure's wake and shimmered in an ocean's current.

But still only a shadow.

It was all they could be, here in the void.

"The Soulsprites are no longer safe," the Morrow whispered to her. *"A floodgate has opened, and all will be found."*

A spark of fear shot through the Antiquity's hollow chest, and she impulsively pressed one of her vines against the cavity where her Soulsprites should be—and where only one remained.

"The Fates are certain?" she asked, though each word required such monumental effort. *"They have changed their minds before."*

Her sister sighed, soft and wistful. *"Not this time."*

Briefly, black threads of night cracked through the blinding white as the Antiquity nearly lost their connection. Tension rippled through her vines, clear to their ancient tips, and she grimaced as she forced her way back into the vision.

The connection had to hold. This was too important to leave half-spoken.

"You have the spare?" she asked.

The hazy silhouette of her sister nodded.

Good. She had plans for the last unclaimed Soulsprite in Saldia, and she couldn't risk losing it.

Not again.

The Morrow glanced over one shoulder, and her hair flung around her head as though she were submerged in water. *"You're sure about this one? This Champion of yours?"*

"Yes."

"You truly trust him to recover your power?"

Too weak to reply, the Antiquity simply nodded.

"Hmm." Her sister set her hands on her hips and sighed in defeat. *"I wish to meet him, but your health is more important. Send him to Kirkwall—and then to me."*

"But I sense more than one in Kirkwall."

"You are correct," her sister said flatly.

The Antiquity waited for her fellow goddess to continue, but only the quiet crackles of the light around them filled the void.

"Enough of these games," she snapped after the pause had stretched on too long. *"I must know what he will face on the island. He has already proven himself."*

"To you, perhaps, but I have seen what you have not," the Morrow countered. *"I have seen all the futures the Fates have woven for him, and there are many ways his story ends. I am not so confident in him, dear sister."*

How unfortunate.

The Antiquity leaned her head against the cold stone wall of her darkest cave, and again, her vision crackled as she nearly lost their connection. *"Where is my Soulsprite?"*

"Kirkwall Castle."

"And the second, whatever it may be?"

The Morrow took a second too long to reply, and the weight of that brief hesitation spoke volumes.

"The mountain," she admitted.

Ah.

The lost lands of a fallen brother. It made sense to hide dangerous magic in his grave—or what was left of it, at least.

"When will he leave?" her sister asked.

"Soon."

The Morrow clicked her tongue in disappointment. *"Your Champion must hurry."*

"I know."

Connor Magnuson had already caught Death's eye—and those who intrigued the Creator did not remain free men for long.

CHAPTER ELEVEN

CONNOR

With a tired sigh, Connor stood underneath the waterfall that gushed through an opening in the black rock above him. It fed into a small room that had been carved into the stone, from floor to ceiling, in an effort to contain the waterfall's heat. Though a thin trickle of steam escaped through the narrow archway leading into his new bedroom, the clever design contained most of the billowing mist.

The water, warmed from a natural spring somewhere in the bowels of the Black Keep Mountains, fed into a bed chamber the Wraith King had ordered carved into the mountain rock centuries ago. Though the room's furniture had long since rotted away, Ethan had been kind enough to have a bed brought up here, since the Wraith King absolutely refused to let him sleep in one of the carpenter's cabins.

Connor knew because he'd tried. For three nights in a row, the Wraith King hadn't let him sleep a wink, and he had caved to the dead king's demands for proper quarters.

After tearing down the cobwebs, he had to admit he rather liked his new accommodations. Windows along the northern wall gave him a stunning view of Slaybourne, and it had enough space to house ten beds side by side.

Not that he'd ever use all that room, of course, or admit any of this to the ghoul.

As the waterfall washed away the lingering bloodstains left behind by the michera, he sighed with relief. Ever-growing clouds of steam curled around him, obscuring the floor, and he breathed in the heavy air. It soothed him more than he'd thought it would, though it did remind him a little too much of the Blood Bogs.

"You ready to talk, yet?" he asked the wraith. "For a close ally to betray you like that, you must be—"

No, the ghoul interjected. *Especially not while you're as naked as the day you were born.*

Fair enough.

He shrugged, his last attempt made, and resolved to let the ghost speak if and when he was ready.

Connor leaned his head under the waterfall and closed his eyes as it drenched his hair. He leaned his hands against the wall and stood there, letting himself simply enjoy something for once.

He had to take these moments as they came, because they didn't come often.

The barest whisper of a footstep scuffed the floor outside his chambers, and his ear twitched briefly as he honed in on the source. Seconds later, someone knocked on his door.

And just like that, his moment was over.

With stealth like that, it had to be Quinn. She probably wanted to discuss their plan and make tweaks before the next day's bustle and chaos.

Time to get to work, then.

He stepped out of the waterfall and grabbed a folded towel off the floor. The scratchy cotton itched his face as he quickly dried himself off and threw on his loose cotton pants.

You have quality leather gear, now, the ghoul chided. *Why are you wearing that garbage?*

"Oh, *now* you want to talk?" Connor shot back.

The wraith grumbled in annoyance but didn't reply.

With every intention of getting back into the waterfall once their conversation ended, he didn't bother with a shirt. He opened the door to find Quinn leaning against the doorframe, arms crossed as she stared at the flickering sconces lining the long corridor that led to his new chambers.

"Oh good, you're awake. I—" Her head pivoted toward him, though her eyes immediately dropped to his bare chest, and she didn't finish her thought.

Her gaze lingered on his abdomen, and he raised one eyebrow in curiosity as the barest hint of pink flushed into her cheeks.

Quinn Starling, brutal warrior and killer of men, was *blushing.*

He couldn't resist the playful grin that spread across his face at the thought.

"You're up late." He stepped back into his chambers and gestured for her to join him. "Come on in. I assume you want to address things that shouldn't be discussed in the hallway."

Her blush deepened, but she roughly cleared her throat and followed him inside.

Connor shut the door behind her and grabbed the towel he'd thrown across his mattress. As the waterfall crashed against the black stone floor in the far corner, muffled by the alcove containing its steam, she leaned against the wall and scanned the room.

"It's still pretty empty," he admitted. "Not much to see."

Her gaze darted toward him and once more lingered on his chest. She quickly tilted her head toward the far wall and ran her fingers through her hair as she gave herself an excuse to look away.

To his immense frustration, something in her movements triggered another primal urge deep in his soul. Visions flashed across his mind, too fast to control or to stop, and he gritted his teeth as he fought them. He could taste her, just like he had down in the catacombs, and this time, it lingered. In a flash of dominating need, he imagined pinning her to the wall and using his knees to spread her legs wide.

This time, the primal urges he had denied for so long scraped away at the last threads of his willpower.

This time, they didn't fade.

"I've been thinking about what you said," Quinn admitted, still staring at the wall. "About revealing the Lightseers' lies."

Her voice didn't quell the urges like it had in the past. He forced himself to turn away from her, even as he tried to keep his tone even. "Ah. Come to your senses, then?"

She huffed in irritation. "Connor, be serious."

"I assumed you came to agree with me." He forced a laugh and ran the towel through his hair to dry off the lingering droplets of water.

"I understand what you're trying to do," she continued. "It's noble, and I respect that. Right now, however, there are too many unknowns."

"There are always unknowns."

"Not like these." She dismissed his argument with a flick of her wrist. "You asked me to consider it, and I have. I recommend we hold off. I *insist* we hold off, actually."

He tossed the towel back onto his mattress and crossed his arms over his bare chest. "Why?"

"To make this work, we need support," she answered. "Allies, and not just Freymoor. We need a majority of the other kingdoms Henry conquered to already be on your side. We need them to control the public narrative in places where we can't. If we leave the truth to the people, Connor, they'll listen to whatever the nearest sheriff tells them. Most people don't understand magic like we do. Most people don't understand nuance. Everything's good or evil to them. Light or darkness."

To distract himself from yet more visions, he scratched at the stubble on his jaw. "You're making some pretty serious assumptions about people you don't know, Quinn."

"I'm being realistic," she corrected, though she sighed in disappointment as she spoke. "I know because that's the way I used to be, back before I met you. I still catch myself doing it, sometimes, and I'm supposed to be the example people follow. The Lightseers have spent centuries—millennia, maybe—convincing people there are only two sides to this fight. Learning the truth will shake the foundation of what most people in Saldia believe. You can't shatter their understanding of the world and expect them to just go along with whatever you say."

His eyebrows shot up his head, and he nodded slowly as he sifted through her argument.

To his annoyance, he couldn't find fault with it.

"Trust me on this." Her voice softened, as though she understood more than he realized. "Someday, we will reveal it all, but we have to be strategic.

It has to be focused and intentional. Once we have allies, and once a solid plan is in place, I'll be there with you when you tell the world the truth."

He smiled and nodded once in gratitude.

"We're agreed?" she asked.

"Agreed." He scratched the back of his head and sighed. "That's why I wanted you as my general, Quinn. You see things I overlook."

She smiled.

"There's still a chance for you to recover your old life," he pointed out. "Once you're seen with me, it's over. You'll lose everything. Having a double agent in Lunestone might be the leverage we need to change public opinion."

Quinn shook her head. "I've been trying to think of a way to make it work, but yet again, there are too many—"

"Unknowns," he finished for her.

"Exactly." She rubbed her face and stifled a yawn as the twin moons crept across the midnight sky beyond the balcony. "Hackamores. Survivors. Zander possibly returning. Too many risks."

"Alright," he said with a shrug. "If you think Gwen will act as our double agent, perhaps it's not necessary for you to return."

"I think she will." Quinn leaned the back of her head against the wall behind her. "I hope she will, anyway. I won't give her key details until I'm sure, though, and I'll speak to her in a place with clear exits in case things go south."

"Fates be it doesn't come to that."

She shrugged. "With my family, who knows?"

He frowned.

Fair point.

Connor tried to carry the conversation, but his gaze drifted down her body, and the visions became more intense.

He had to make a choice, and he had to do it soon.

Magnuson, the ghoul said sharply.

He didn't reply to the ghost's sudden intrusion. He meant to, of course, but his focus narrowed instead on Quinn's waist.

Magnuson, don't you dare.

A pang of warning hummed in the back of his head. It was foggy and distant, but he figured the last threads of his willpower were doing their damnedest to hold on.

"Right." Quinn kicked off the wall and took a deep breath. She opened her mouth to say something else, but her gaze settled again on his chest.

"My eyes are up here," he said with a roguish grin.

Her gaze shifted up to his face, and she forced a thin, apologetic smile.

No king should sleep with his general! the Wraith King howled. *Find another woman, damn you! Any of them! Just pick one! Everyone must be replaceable, Magnuson!*

"That's why you're alone," Connor said under his breath.

There was a sharp hiss, like someone sucking in a breath through their teeth, but the ghost finally stopped talking.

A brief flicker of guilt cut through the primal urges rooting him in place, but it was something the Wraith King needed to hear. The more he tried to control people, the less control over them he would have.

"Quinn." His voice boomed in his chest, louder than he'd intended. He crossed to her slowly, doing everything in his power to restrain himself with each step. "I'm going to give you a choice."

Her brows pinched together in confusion as he neared. "Alright."

"This. Us." He gestured between them as he stood in front of her. "You choose what it is. If you want this to merely be a king and his general, I'll honor that."

"Or?" she prompted.

"Or it can be more," he said simply. "Your choice."

Quinn Starling watched him, calm and unwavering, and he would've given anything to know what thoughts were racing through her head.

"I want more," she finally answered.

"Good." He gently grabbed her chin. His thumb brushed over her lip, and he grinned with victory.

She was *his.*

QUINN

Quinn woke with a jolt of white-hot panic.

She shot upright in bed, breathing heavily, as her father's voice echoed in the back of her mind. It bounced around in her skull, distant and hazy, but she couldn't make out the words.

As she fought to make sense of them, her vision blurred. Her heart would not stop racing. She sucked in breath after breath, but it was never enough. Her lungs ached. Her eyes pinched shut, and she fought the surge of nausea burning the back of her throat as the lingering imprints of yet another nightmare danced on the edge of her memory.

It had all seemed so *real.*

Her father, reassembled from his ashes.

Her own Firesword, raised above her head as the Lightseer Code echoed in the night, sentencing her to death.

Snowfall in a forest as an arrow twanged.

"Get ahold of yourself," she chided softly, but her heart wouldn't stop thundering in her chest. "It was just a Fates-damned *dream.*"

With one hand, Quinn clutched the sheets to her chest, and she set her face in the other as sweat dripped down her bare back. Her breathing slowed, if only slightly, as the raging fear began to fade.

Someone shifted on the lumpy mattress beside her, and she impulsively lifted one hand to punch the silhouette in his throat—before she realized she wasn't in her bed at all.

Connor.

The memories came rushing back, and his presence chased away the last shreds of fear from the nightmare. He rolled toward her, still shirtless, and curled one arm underneath his pillow. She smiled, still unable to believe how they'd spent their evening.

The hunted, dominating his hunter until she'd begged for more. Her thighs still buzzed with numb pleasure as the memories seeped back, and she couldn't resist a playful smirk as she watched him sleep.

Not a bad night at all, really.

Quietly, she laid beside him and propped her head on one hand as she studied his face. Asleep, the creases of concern that always lined his brow were gone, and he seemed unfazed by the threats headed their way. Downright peaceful, even.

She rather envied that.

Eyes still closed, his free arm reached for her waist. She tensed, unprepared for whatever this was, but he didn't falter. His hand wrapped around her, and his strong grip pulled her close. In seconds, her chest pressed against his, and he burrowed his face in her hair. With his palm flat against her shoulder blades, he hummed with groggy contentment.

Perhaps she could've wriggled out of his grip. He was strong, sure, but so was she—and she had the advantage of being coherent enough to know what was happening.

But she didn't fight it.

Instead, Quinn nestled into the crook of his neck and closed her eyes. A fluttery sensation hummed through her, dizzy and warm. Strange as it was, she didn't entirely hate it, and she did her best to name it. Warmth. Ease. Safety, perhaps, or maybe it was just comfort.

Whatever it was, it was something she'd never felt before.

She closed her eyes and listened to the steady rhythm of his breath. Slowly, she relaxed, and she let herself sleep once again.

The word came to her, then, on the edge of sleep, and she smiled as she let new dreams take her.

Happy.

CHAPTER TWELVE

ZANDER

In the darkness, the blightwolves waited.

The full pack clustered around the weaker wolves, protecting them in the center, while Zander sat on Alistair's back at the edge. Each wolf scanned the forest around them, stiff with unspoken tension. Some growled, but most stood in a somber silence as they listened to the eerily still night.

Something wasn't right.

The Feral King had ordered them to remain here, but no one knew why. The ghoulish creature had long since faded into the wind, nothing but shadows and those lingering yellow eyes, and not even Zander knew where it had gone.

He needed to use this time wisely.

"Tell me," he said to Alistair, continuing a conversation they'd been having before the Feral King abruptly left. "It's only fitting."

The massive wolf growled with irritation, and those soft black ears darted briefly toward him as he spoke.

Truth be told, Zander expected the blightwolf to remain silent. Any time he asked about the Kurultai, the blightwolves had refused to answer. The less he knew, after all, the more likely he was to fail.

"The arena is a place of power," the blightwolf explained. "A place of heritage and home."

Zander's eyebrow shot up in surprise, and it took effort to restrain a small grunt of disbelief that he'd actually gotten a response. Perhaps it was because he'd fed the blightwolf, or maybe he'd earned the creature's respect somehow.

Either way, he wanted to keep it talking.

"How so?" he prompted.

"Only the alpha may enter," Alistair continued, his gaze still roaming the dark forest around them. "Any may challenge him, but only one may enter at a time. If he falls, the victor is the alpha, again and again, until no one dares enter to face him. Only the alpha may leave the ring."

Zander grimaced. How barbaric.

"We have no magic," Alistair added with a brief glance at him over one shoulder. "Therefore, you may not use yours. Your sword alone is permitted, since you are sadly lacking in claws. No fire. No lightning. Just your blade and your fists."

"And if I do use magic?"

"Then we will eat you." Alistair snarled in warning.

Zander scoffed at the very idea.

His pet blightwolf went silent, but he had gleaned more than enough from their short conversation. This Kurultai, in essence, was nothing more than a Lightseer Rite.

The Lightseer Master General had performed a Rite every five years for as long as the Lightseers had existed. It was mostly done in peacetime to showcase his power and remind the lower ranks of why none should dare refuse an order—especially one that came from him.

Teagan, of course, had chosen his opponents carefully and preferred not to kill them. Trusted captains and a few handpicked colonels, mostly, faced him over the week-long challenge to showcase his vast array of skills. Weaponry. Augmentations. Hand-to-hand combat, with both opponents wearing Bluntmar collars just to complicate things further. It was a spectacle with tourists funneling onto the island from every city across Saldia, as everyone came to witness the continent's most superior fighters—the Starlings.

Only three other humans have entered the Kurultai, said a haunting voice in his head. *None have walked out of it to claim the title of Alpha.*

Zander grimaced at the Feral King's blatant intrusion into his thoughts, but he did his best to rein in his disgust. He didn't want to give the ghoulish creature the satisfaction of knowing how much he hated that.

One blithering fool resorted to praying, the shadow-wolf added with a raspy bark of disbelief. *I laughed and laughed...*

"Charming," Zander muttered.

Soft growls rumbled through the blightwolves as Zander sat on Alistair's back. Despite the ever pressing need to reach the Kurultai arena, all ninety-three of his wolves waited in silence as the strange scent slithered through the towering oaks.

Musky. Sour. Heady and a little rank, like moss and mushrooms on a rotting log.

The southern wind stirred the scent again, carrying it closer, and this time a spark of warning popped in the back of Zander's head. It was sharp and sudden, like a cracking joint, and his body tensed at the unspoken warning that carried on the air.

Another pack had arrived.

Good, the Feral King said with a satisfied growl. *The western pack is here. We will finish the journey together.*

Despite the contented rumbling in his head, Zander didn't relax. His biceps flexed as he prepared for an onslaught, and he set one hand on the hilt of his sheathed Firesword.

"Let them come," Alistair growled, mostly to himself. The wolf snapped at the air, toward where the scent had originated, as if daring them to hurry. "Let the fools challenge us again."

"Let them try," another wolf snarled from nearby.

"They will die," a third added. "All who dare will bleed."

The Feral King didn't interject. Though Zander was still testing the limits of the ghoulish creature's connection to the blightwolves, he assumed they could hear the abomination speak. And yet, it didn't intervene or try to calm the gathered throng of snarling predators.

How curious.

In the distance, a shrill and piercing howl punctured the still night air. Others followed, echoing the first. Beneath him, Alistair tensed. The great black blightwolf threw its head back and unleashed a piercing howl of its own. The others in Zander's pack followed suit, and he braced his enhanced ears against the wall of sound that rattled even the trees.

Their cries faded, but the rumbling continued. The ground shook, stronger with every passing moment as the second pack neared.

Another large one, then. More wolves for his army.

The first one appeared through the dense trees, its metallic fur a chestnut brown unlike any he'd seen before, and it led the charge. Others followed it out of the dense shadows, more and more, an endless stream of white teeth and soft brown fur.

There had to be seventy of them, at least.

His grip tightened on *Valor's* hilt.

The wolf at the front towered over the others, easily a good head taller than the rest, and its cold black eyes settled instantly on Zander. It snarled in challenge, its ears pinning to its head, and it bared its stained teeth at him.

"You carry meat on your back, Alistair," it taunted. "Have you fallen so low as to become a pack mule?"

In answer, Alistair barked—once, and so sharply that it hurt even Zander's ears.

A warning to stop talking, or face dire consequences.

The challenger, however, didn't even flinch. Its snarl became a low growl, and its eyes never left Zander's.

"Perhaps the southern pack has lost its venom," it said. "How weak must you all be to let a human kill our alpha?"

The newcomers yipped and barked in agreement, pacing behind the wolf in front as it slowly inched steadily toward Alistair.

And, more importantly, toward Zander.

In mere seconds, the rumbling growls became an uproar. The wolves spoke over each other, grumbling and grousing, never in one place for more than a second as they all stirred with the anticipation of a possible fight.

"...to challenge us..."

"...blasphemy..."

"...treason!"

"The southern pack has spilled more blood than the rest of you combined!" Alistair barked. His heady growl punctuated the cacophony around them as he dared the newcomer to make the first move. The great black wolf shifted his weight, unable to be still for more than two seconds, and his ears darted about as he listened to each possible threat in the forest.

It took effort for Zander not to sigh impatiently. He'd had enough of this.

With an easy swing of his leg, he dismounted. As much as he would've preferred keeping the high ground, as Alistair dwarfed the challenger in terms of sheer size, he couldn't control the blightwolf yet. In an attack, one needed his mount to obey his every command, not pace and prance anxiously about.

Soon, Alistair would learn to trust him and submit. For now, Zander could only trust his own two feet.

With the movement, the newcomer's hungry black eyes trailed him.

You are not afraid, the Feral King said.

It wasn't a question.

Careful to keep the newcomer at the edge of his vision, Zander brief glanced over one shoulder at the towering shadow wolf that had trailed behind him throughout their short journey thus far tonight.

He did not, however, bother to reply.

How interesting, the ghoulish creature said.

The newcomer stalked slowly closer, inch by inch, and they wouldn't have long until it crossed the wide gap between packs.

Zander sniffed at the air, mainly to see if he could detect anything on the newcomers that would give him insights into where they'd been. At first, only the earthy bite of tilled soil stung his nose, but it carried with it the tangy undercurrent of stale blood.

Human blood.

"You've eaten." He took several steps forward, until he stood between the two packs. "How recently? How many?"

If they'd had a feast on their way here, they might have news of the outside world.

The pack of newcomers laughed, shrill and raspy, and many snarled at him in answer. Their yips became a roar of voices and snarls as they, too, spoke over each other in a rush.

"...he killed Farkas..."

"...impossible..."

"...no teeth, no claws..."

"Useless," the towering newcomer added, its voice louder than the others in its pack. It growled and lowered its head in warning as its gaze raked him over.

Looking for weaknesses, no doubt.

The western pack does not respect you, the Feral King growled in his head. *What will you do?*

At that, the southern pack behind him stilled. They waited in silence, and he could feel the full weight of their stares on his neck.

It was time to earn a bit of respect with the foremost blightwolf pack in Saldia, and he already knew how to stroke their egos. Man or mutt, flattery was the easiest way to make someone think Zander was on their side.

As the newcomer challenged him, he walked calmly toward it. The thing snarled, but he didn't hesitate. He didn't flinch. He barely registered the hulking beast's warning. It had no right to kill him, at least not before the arena. Thus far, he'd gleaned enough about blightwolf law to know the others wouldn't attack if this one did.

One paw out of place would start a civil war between the blightwolves, and the western pack was vastly outnumbered.

"You." Zander's voice dropped in warning, and he narrowed his eyes as he glared at the one that had insulted him.

The challenger snarled in answer, but the blightwolf's steady pace toward him didn't slow. They neared each other, neither backing down, neither so much as looking away as the challenge was made and met. Within seconds, he would be within reach of those gleaming white teeth.

"You've forgotten your place." His thumb tapped lightly against Valor's pommel as he prepared to draw it. "No house pet insults the southern pack, and for that matter, no one insults *me.*"

It snapped at his head. He leaned out of range at the last second, just as the beast's jaws closed with an audible *chomp*, and he landed a devastating left hook in its throat.

The creature wheezed and stumbled. Its shoulder hit a nearby oak, and the thick tree shook violently from the force. Something cracked in its trunk, but by some miracle, it didn't fall.

To his surprise, the southern pack yipped and howled in victory as his blow easily knocked his opponent aside. They celebrated the hit with all the gusto and reverie as they'd celebrated Farkas, back in the Decay, when the alpha had snared Zander in its jaws.

How times had changed.

When the chestnut-brown blightwolf had recovered, its menacing glare snapped again toward him. Its claws dug into the earth, and the muscles on its back tensed with hatred and hellfire, as if it would charge him at any second, consequences be damned.

Zander adjusted his stance and tilted his shoulders, preparing for an attack he was finally healed enough to deflect.

Instead, however, the blightwolf's gaze shifted over Zander's shoulder—toward the Feral King. Zander adjusted his head, keeping both the newcomer and the shadow-wolf in his realm of sight, and the Feral King nodded once.

Astonishing. Before attacking, this rabid creature had asked for *permission.*

In that moment, everything made sense. The Kurultai would earn him the respect of the blightwolves, but only the Feral King truly controlled them. Even back in the clearing when he and Farkas had dueled, the former alpha had honored the ghoulish wolf's command to fight to the death.

To command them, he would first have to earn the shadow-wolf's unflinching loyalty—and that was far easier said than done.

The Feral King didn't move. It didn't interject, and the challenger apparently took that as clearance to attack.

The blightwolf charged toward him, blisteringly fast, but Zander sidestepped it easily. As it passed, however, it snapped at his neck—and missed him by mere inches. If he had faltered even a little, the damn thing would've ripped out his throat.

This wasn't some idle challenge to test his boundaries. This was a fight to the death, in this makeshift arena surrounded by heathens and gnarled old trees.

Moonlight from a hole in the canopy glinted along the creature's metallic brown fur, and it growled with frustration as it skidded along the patchy grass. Dirt kicked into the air while the wolf tried to slow its own momentum, and Zander didn't have long before it recovered.

Around the small clearing in which he and the challenger dueled, the gathered blightwolves yipped and barked, each supporting their chosen champion.

And, surprisingly, the southern pack howled in victory as he stood there, patiently waiting for the next attack.

Framed by a cluster of towering pines, the Feral King merely watched the scene. Those piercing yellow eyes studied him, and he figured the infernal thing was giving him a test. These creatures lived and died by their one law, and he would never succeed in taming them until he played by their rules.

So be it.

Finally recovered from its long slide through the dirt, the attacking blightwolf launched off its hindquarters and once more raced toward him. He drew *Valor*, and though he was tempted to ignite its enchanted fires, Alistair's earlier warning suggested it was better to do this without magic.

For now, anyway.

The chestnut-brown wolf approached, and Zander held his ground. He didn't flinch, nor did he shift his weight anxiously as he timed his next move. Where once his heart would've raced as such a horrific creature charged him, he now felt nothing. No fear. No doubt. Just cold, calculating curiosity as to how he would kill it.

In the seconds before it reached him, Zander briefly scanned its stance. The thing ran heavy on its right paws, suggesting a weak left side, and that worked perfectly in his favor.

It entered his range of attack, and he shifted his weight easily. Its jaws opened, aiming again for his neck, but he swung *Valor* in a wide arc before it had the chance to bite. The blisteringly sharp steel sliced through its neck, through its spine, and clear out the other side.

Unfazed, Zander merely watched the blightwolf's head drop to the ground. Its body collapsed, and it slid the final yards toward the gathered throng of western wolves it had led here.

To him.

The yips and barks faded, and none of the roughly two hundred blightwolves moved. They stared down at the fallen challenger, and one by one, their gazes drifted upward toward him.

In shock, and with a hint of awe that hadn't been there before. It wasn't full-on respect—that, he would have to earn in the Kurultai—but it was a satisfying start.

Zander shot the Feral King a sidelong glare, and he was barely able to restrain his victorious smirk.

"Save your bloodlust for the arena," he chided the other blightwolves. "And to any of you western fools who would dare try again, no one will ever dethrone the southern pack. Not here, and not ever."

He turned his back on them and returned to Alistair. The black wolf towered over him, magnificent as ever, and the beast's ears perked with curiosity as he approached. He hoisted himself onto Alistair's back, and the blightwolf craned his neck to follow Zander's movements.

"More will come," Alistair said quietly. "More will challenge you."

"Let them." Zander shrugged as the silent company began its final trek through the southern-most edge of the Ancient Woods.

Once the blightwolves belonged to him, they would be far more useful on the battlefield than in Victoria's potions. When he finally returned to Lunestone, the monsters of the Ancient Woods would walk behind him in obedient, militant rows.

And *no one* would dare challenge him again.

CHAPTER THIRTEEN

CONNOR

The last cold gust of spring shot past Connor as he stood in a clearing not far from the cluster of cabins that had become their makeshift village. Death's Door loomed in the distance, a monolith towering over the trees, and he crossed his arms as he mentally mapped out their route one more time.

Just to be sure.

Freymoor. Arkcaster. Lunestone. Dragon Island.

Easy.

Behind him, the bustle and chatter of people gathering supplies drowned out the soft twitter of slaybirds in the trees. One fluttered past and landed on a perch, its body glowing as it gently sang in the breeze.

I don't see the need to leave. The Wraith King appeared beside him in a rush of black smoke and nodded approvingly. *With Slaybourne secured, this is a fortress.*

Connor stifled a surprised grunt. The ghost hadn't spoken to him since last night, and he'd wondered how long the silence would last. Now, apparently, the undead king was going to pretend nothing had happened at all.

Fine. Connor wouldn't press him if he didn't want to discuss it.

"We're leaving because we made promises to our allies," he reminded the ghoul.

Bah. The specter swatted away the comment like it was an annoying fly. *It's a waste of time, Magnuson.*

"It's not optional."

With an irritated groan, the ghost disappeared again into his dark void. *Alert me when something interesting happens, then.*

"Suit yourself," he muttered.

The metallic clunk of grinding gears lumbered somewhere behind him, and he smiled as he peered over one shoulder to find Ethan walking along the makeshift road with a full pack over one shoulder.

The carpenter clicked his tongue in disappointment. "Always heading off someplace. Can't you stay in one spot, Connor?"

"I try," he admitted with a shrug. "But then someone outside of Slaybourne starts a fire, and I've got to go put it out."

Ethan paused beside him and raised his eyebrows dubiously, much in the same way Connor's father had when he was about to get a lecture as a boy.

"It's not always on you to fix other people's problems, son," the man said.

Connor frowned, but he didn't reply.

"Are you sure about this?" Ethan asked with a gesture toward the gates. "We have a dungeon full of Lightseers and an undead army that answers only to you. Are the rest of us really safe?"

"I'm not worried." Connor smirked, and his gaze darted toward Kiera as she passed by with a basket full of bread loaves. "If the prisoners try anything, your wife will beat them into submission."

"Damn right, I will," she said with a dignified huff.

Ethan chuckled, and he waited until Kiera was out of earshot before he continued. "We've sealed their weapons away, of course, but those soldiers are more augmented than anything I've ever seen, Connor. What if they break free?"

"They won't." Connor set one hand on the man's shoulder to ease his worry. "You all are safe. I wouldn't leave if you weren't."

"And the undead soldiers?"

"I've already ordered them to obey your every word while I'm gone."

He'd taken care of it this morning. The thought of leaving his newfound family with so many threats in one place had unnerved him, too, and far more than Ethan seemed to realize.

"Slaybourne's in your hands until I get back," Connor added. "Take care of it."

"You know I will."

Connor nodded and pointed off toward the cliffs behind the cabins. "Start building homes out that way. The Wraith King's generals have already mapped out old foundations you can use, and the undead will make quick work of it."

The carpenter frowned. "Exactly how many people are we expecting?"

"I don't know," he confessed. "Maybe none. Maybe a lot. It all depends."

"On what?"

In answer, Connor merely shrugged. Only the Fates knew what would happen from here. Until the tide changed in his favor, all he could do was prepare.

"Best get to it, then," Ethan said with a resigned sigh. "Try not to be gone too long this time, you hear?"

"I'll do my best," he promised.

"Good man." With that, Ethan adjusted the pack on his shoulder and trudged toward the village. His enchanted leg whirred and clinked with every step, but he walked with ease.

"Connor!" a familiar voice shouted from somewhere nearby.

Wesley jogged over, the silver swords jostling on his back, and he paused to catch his breath as he reached them. The young man tugged on the criss-crossing sheaths on his back, beaming with pride. "I finally got them to fit!"

Connor nodded with approval. "Nicely done. They suit you."

The young man's smile broadened.

"It's going to be up to you to keep everyone safe, understood?" Connor adjusted the straps across Wesley's chest to tweak the one buckle he hadn't properly secured. "They'll look to you, Wesley. Be their strength."

The young man stood a little taller, and his smile settled into a determined line. "I won't let you down."

"Never doubted you." Connor patted Wesley on the shoulder, and the young man winced with pain from the sheer power of that subtle movement.

Oops.

"Sorry about that," Connor said.

"Nothing to be sorry about." Wesley rubbed his arm, but he smiled as the initial sting apparently faded.

Through the corner of his eye, Connor spotted Nocturne's hulking frame as the dragon lowered his head toward someone in the field. Fiona and Isabella stood side by side as Fiona offered the prince of dragons a flower. Nocturne sniffed it, his powerful breath stirring the grass around them, and Fiona giggled as her hair whipped about her face in the mini gale.

Isabella, however, simply held herself as she looked up at the regal creature. She hadn't spoken or smiled in days, and even then, it had been the bare minimum.

"Look after your sisters," Connor added as Isabella led Fiona away from the dragon and back to their mother. "Isabella isn't well."

"I know." Wesley's shoulders drooped slightly as he, too, watched the girls retreat back to the village proper. "I don't know what's wrong. Everyone else is recovering from—well, you know."

The slavers.

"Healing takes time." Connor shrugged. "She's strong, but she went through hell out there. Trauma like that can break people, Wesley, and she might not know how to ask for help. Be there for her. It's all you can do."

"Of course."

Over by Nocturne, Sophia and Murdoc clustered together with their backs to him as they spoke about something he couldn't hear from this distance. Quinn joined them, Blaze trailing behind her, and the vougel watched Nocturne with a wary glare.

"Go help your mother," Connor told Wesley. "I have a few more things to do before we leave."

"Yep!" The young man gave a lopsided salute and jogged off toward his family as the silver swords jostled on his back.

Over by the dragon, Quinn leaned toward her pet. She said something, and the tiger-bird's ears pinned flat against his head. He snarled once in irritation and took a step backward. His tail twitched furiously, and as Connor neared, he wondered what the hell she'd said to the creature to get that kind of reaction.

It couldn't have been good.

"...you're welcome to come along," Quinn said as Connor walked into earshot. "Hell, I *want* you to come. I'd love nothing more. I've missed having you out there with me, Blaze."

Her vougel's glare softened, and he nuzzled her hand as a gentle purr rumbled through the clearing.

"But you have to let Nocturne carry you," she added.

Blaze's ears pinned against his head again, and his gaze shifted up toward the dragon above him. At the same time, Nocturne yawned. The regal creature's wings stretched wide, and a flash of the fading sunlight glinted across his massive teeth. It was a mouth that could've swallowed Blaze whole, and the tiger-bird was apparently not fond of the idea.

The vougel snarled and shook his head. His claws extended from his paws and dug into the earth as his tail twitched more irately than before.

"Those are the choices!" Quinn said, exasperated. "We've been over this a dozen times already, Blaze. A dragon's just faster. It's nothing personal, buddy."

"Poor little kitty," Murdoc teased. "Doesn't want to be carried by the big bad dragon?"

Though Quinn shot him an irritated glare, Sophia snorted and lifted one hand to hide her smile.

The Starling warrior groaned. "Don't encourage—"

Blaze roared in annoyance, his full attention now focused on Murdoc, and the former Blackguard stiffened in surprise. He took a wary step back as Blaze lowered into a crouch, and Murdoc took off running.

Full of fury and vengeance, the vougel darted down the broken cobblestones after him.

"Quinn!" Murdoc shouted, his voice fading as he ran farther away. "Your tiger has no sense of humor!"

Blaze's soft snarl followed as they crested a hill and faded from sight.

Sophia and Quinn burst out laughing as they watched Murdoc flee. There was a distant yell, and seconds later, Murdoc returned at full speed, the winged tiger trailing just slightly behind.

The women laughed harder.

"Shouldn't you intervene?" Connor asked Quinn with a nod toward the yelping Blackguard being chased around the meadow.

"They're just burning off some energy." The Starling warrior dismissed his concern with a wave of her delicate hand. "Besides, Blaze would've tackled him by now if he wasn't enjoying this."

In the center of the meadow, Murdoc hollered incoherently.

Connor's gaze lingered on Quinn and trailed down her neck as he relived the highlights from last night. A mischievous grin tugged at the corner of his mouth, and she flashed him a playful smile as her eyes lingered on him.

"Well, well, well." Sophia set her hands on her hips as she looked between the two of them. "It's about damn time."

"What do you mean?" he asked, his tone steady despite the teasing tilt to her voice.

"Oh, don't play coy." The necromancer rolled her eyes and trekked off after the former Blackguard running circles in the field. "At least I won my bet with Murdoc."

Connor laughed. "Bet?"

Sophia nodded, and a wicked little grin spread across her face.

"What was the bet?" Quinn asked.

The necromancer didn't answer. As she stalked off into the field, Quinn simply shook her head. Her gaze drifted toward Death's Door, however, and her smile fell.

"Are you ready for this?" she asked.

"As I'll ever be," he admitted. "Are you ready to return to Lunestone?"

Instead of answering, she swallowed hard. Her eyes briefly glazed over, but she sighed and ultimately nodded.

For a moment, a surge of protectiveness corroded his better judgment. He considered leaving her here to ensure she was safe, but he knew better.

He couldn't protect a woman like Quinn from the world. Though he didn't want to send her into Lunestone, they had work to do.

As much as he hated to admit it, the Wraith King had been right. Falling for his general had consequences, but there was no going back now. Come dusk, Nocturne would take them back out into the Decay—and into a world that wanted to slit his throat.

CHAPTER FOURTEEN

TOVE

As she walked at a steady pace toward Oakenglen Castle, Tove could only stare up at the familiar spires with horror.

With every step, her hands trembled. She hadn't been back to the castle in years, and every time she returned, she could only remember the horrors that happened here when Henry massacred most of the original royal family—and her parents right along with them.

She held her hands in front of her in a last-ditch effort to steady them, but it ultimately made the tremor worse.

Two men from the king's guard walked on either side of her. The steady thuds of their boots on the cobblestone set a steady pace for her to follow as they led her through the main gates, their armor clanking as they marched in step with each other. When they had come for her, she had debated running. After all, Quinn had warned her that something terrible might happen, but she hadn't been prepared when these two had paid her a visit. They hadn't taken no for an answer, and she figured it would've served her better to come willingly than to come in chains.

If she made it out of this alive, she would expedite getting the last of her things out of Oakenglen. It seemed her welcome in the city would not last much longer.

On the other side of a glistening fountain in the center of the courtyard, the castle's main doors led into the sort of prisons people like her rarely escaped.

This was it.

They'd found out her secret—the one she'd kept, even from Quinn.

They knew who she was, and they'd ordered her here to wring information out of her.

She was a damn fool. She never should have stayed here. She should've fled, like the former prince and his mother did after Henry had taken over. She should've gone with them into the Westhelm Mountains, where she would've been safe.

Safe, perhaps, but purposeless. Without access to reagents and spellgust—of which, the finest existed in the Capital—she would've wasted away. No direction. No joy. No augmentations to make, and no potions to craft.

As she had told Prince Nicholas all those years ago, that just wasn't living.

Though her body shook with her fear, she did her best to stand up straight. If she was headed to her doom, she would at least go with some Fates-damned dignity.

To her surprise, however, the guards shifted to the right and led her toward the ornate stone archway into the palace rose gardens. Her eyes shifted between the castle doors and the garden, wondering if this was a trick or a mistake, but she didn't say anything.

Please, she begged the Fates. *Oh, please, let this be about something else.*

A winding stone path cut through hundreds of neatly trimmed roses, each of them in full bloom. Glowing green hummingbirds flitted past the pops of red and pink among the lush green bushes as the guards led her deeper into the garden.

Her heart thudded in her throat, and she hardly dared breathe.

Around a towering hedge stood a woman, her white hair pinned to her head in elaborate braids. Her golden gown spread across the stone, its ends gathered in bunches on the path, and she stared out at the lake with her hands clasped in front of her.

Celine Montgomery.

The Queen of Oakenglen didn't move, but her eyes darted briefly toward Tove. Tove froze under the glare, caught off guard by the chilling nothingness in the queen's expression. In her numb daze, Tove merely gaped at the regal woman before her, absolutely baffled as to what she should do.

It took a moment, but all her childhood years of growing up inside the palace walls finally kicked in.

"Your Majesty." Tove offered the deepest curtsey she could muster, and her long braid slid over her shoulder as she completely bowed her head. She held the pose, refusing to so much as blink until she was released.

"Leave." Celine Montgomery's sharp voice made Tove flinch, but she knew it wasn't directed at her. Sure enough, the two guards retreated, their armor clanking with each step as they made their way toward the exit.

Toward the only place, right now, where she wanted to go.

"Come," the queen ordered. "Stand beside me."

"Y-yes, Your Majesty."

Baffled, confused—and so far out of her comfort zone she thought she might faint—Tove lifted her head and stood beside the queen. She stared numbly off at the lake, mirroring the queen's stance, and she instinctively stood one step behind the monarch out of respect.

It was habit, forged from her days serving the Coldwells in their time at Oakenglen, and she didn't even think about it until after she'd already done it.

"You know your way around royalty," the queen observed.

Tove swallowed hard, but weakly nodded.

"How curious."

"I'm afraid there's no interesting story as to why," Tove lied, doing her best to recover from her stupid blunder. "I've researched etiquette in the hopes I would one day be able to meet you."

"Do not lie to me, my dear," the monarch warned. "Your pulse quickens when you do."

Tove shut her eyes briefly in terror, but once again nodded.

"I've been informed that you know Quinn Starling," the queen said calmly.

Shit.

Now Tove knew why she had been summoned, and this was almost worse.

"I do," she confessed.

After all, lying would do no good. Not in the company of someone so thoroughly augmented as a queen.

If she couldn't lie, then, Tove would have to be damn clever to keep from sharing anything meaningful—or giving the queen reason to force a Hackamore down her throat.

"How?" the queen asked.

"I merely augment her on occasion."

"Which augmentations?"

Tove debated calling upon the unspoken laws of privacy between an augmentor and their clients, but petulance wouldn't serve her here. "Hygenmix. Airdrift. Strongman. Eyebright. Hearhaven. I also—"

"Burnbane?" the queen interrupted.

"Yes," Tove admitted softly, and her head tilted toward the ground in shame of being caught.

"Interesting." The queen smiled—only a little, and with a wicked glint in her eye—as she studied Tove's face. "The Starling recipe?"

"Yes, Your Majesty," Tove admitted, and she did her best to retain her look of utter shame.

It was a carefully constructed lie, of course. Her recipe added nuance above the Starling concoction, but she refused to brag about her abilities to a member of the ruling royal family.

She did *not* want Celine Montgomery to think of her as useful.

"Hmm."

Through the corner of Tove's eye, the monarch's gaze lingered. Trapped under the powerful woman's glare, the thin hairs on her neck stood on end, and she ached for this to be over.

The queen pursed her lips. "Very well."

Tove resisted the urge to sigh with relief and kept her gaze fixated on the crack in the cobblestone at her feet.

"And what about enchanted items?" the queen continued. "What have you made for our dear Quinn Starling?"

Damn it.

She would have to lie.

Tove had only a second or two to spare before answering. Any longer, and it would be obvious she was stalling.

Inwardly, she focused her energy on her chest and took a soothing breath to quell her pulse. She forced her face to relax, and the creases in her brow faded. The fluttering flickers of panic eased, if only for a time, and she forced herself to think of other things.

Of all her books, waiting for her the moment she returned home.

Of her and Quinn, laughing as they sat at the table in her kitchen.

Of the dragon, towering above the canopy just outside of Oakenglen.

"Nothing special, Your Majesty. Most of what Quinn uses comes from Lunestone. If she came to me asking for something, it was only ever trinkets. I'm afraid none of my potions are suited for battle."

A *brazen* lie.

Time to see if she would get away with it.

For a moment, the queen didn't move. Tove forced herself to be still and passive, to appear as useless as possible, if only to make this conversation end.

In her periphery, a hand reached for her. She tensed, still refusing to let her heart race, and delicate fingers lifted her chin. Her eyes darted toward Celine Montgomery, and it took every effort to keep them from shaking under the powerful woman's gaze.

"You grew up in these walls." Without breaking eye contact, the queen nodded toward the castle behind them. "Your father served as the Master Augmentor for the previous royal family. He died with the old kings. The wrongful kings. The weak stewards who had tried to claim too much power."

Tove strangled the powerful urge to snap at the woman for repeating that Fates-damned *lie*. Henry was a tyrant. A warlord. He had stolen a powerful kingdom from its rightful rulers and slain any lingering heirs he found to cement his control.

He was little more than a thief.

Tove, for one, wished she had witnessed his murder. It would've brought a bit of much needed closure.

Though she wanted to scream at the indignity of it all, Tove managed to focus her full energy on keeping her face as expressionless as possible.

"Do you hate me?" the queen asked, her face as smooth as ice.

"No," Tove lied. Her voice sounded weak. Quiet. Almost like a whisper.

Almost like it wasn't there at all.

"Good." A dazzling smile broke across the queen's face, and for a moment, it seemed almost genuine. But her eyes didn't crease, not really, and that cold, piercing stare didn't falter.

"I spared you," the queen continued. "All those years ago. Do you remember?"

Tove stiffened. "I'm afraid I don't, Your Majesty."

"Henry wanted all of you dead, but you were just a girl. You couldn't possibly have known anything valuable. He took your parents, yes, but I ensured he spared you."

Locked there, under the woman who had married a murderer, Tove's throat tightened. Pricks of water threatened the corners of her eyes, but she refused to cry.

Not in front of *her*.

"Thank you, Your Majesty," she whispered.

She had tried to speak louder, but a whisper was all she could force out of her mouth. Anything more than that, and she would have screamed with her long-lost grief.

With her *hate*.

"I've heard good things about you, Tove Warren," the queen said with a self-satisfied nod. "Impress me, and one day I'll see to it you're moved to the Spell Market." The woman paused, her icy glare still pinning Tove in place. "Where you belong."

Tove's lip quivered, and this time, she didn't dare say a word. Instead, she forced herself to bow her head in respect and deference to the monarch who had forced her way onto a throne she didn't deserve.

"You may go." Celine Montgomery dismissed Tove with a wave of her delicate hand.

Bless the Fates.

With another deep curtsey, Tove retreated from the garden. She stared dead ahead, toward the two guardsmen waiting for her at the archway, and tears burned the corners of her eyes.

By the Fates, how she *hated* this place.

When Henry had come, he'd burned away the good memories of her childhood. The love. The joy. The safety. In their place, only bloodshed remained.

Bloodshed—and so much *pain.*

CELINE

With her back turned to Tove Warren, Celine listened carefully to the woman's fading footsteps. The pace had a fast and frantic cadence to it, almost like a racing heartbeat, and the faster retreat from the rose garden betrayed the young woman's relief to finally be leaving.

This augmentor knew so much more than she had let on, and that served Celine *beautifully.*

When Miss Warren's footsteps were the barest hint of a patter on the distant courtyard, someone else approached from the enclosed gazebo on the opposite side of the garden. His steady gait carried him quickly toward her.

On instinct, she reached for the silver dagger in her sleeve. Shaped like a feather and longer than her palm, the delicate knife rested in her fingertips, ready to fly.

She listened to the approaching man, tracking his pace among the roses. His steps were steady. Confident. Calm.

Familiar.

Ah, not a threat then, but Jensen Barrett—Oakenglen's General of Defense, and her reliable little pawn.

Celine took a steady breath and slid the silver feather back into her sleeve as he approached. "Good afternoon, Jensen."

"Good afternoon, Your Majesty." He paused a respectful distance behind her, and cloth rustled as he shifted in place. "The last stragglers have been captured."

Excellent. He'd finally rounded up the final rebels in the castle, and that meant the immediate threats were accounted for.

Now, she merely had to account for those outside of the walls.

"Tonight, we announce Henry's death and your position as reigning Queen."

Her heart panged at Henry's name, and for the first time since stepping out of the carriage, she paused to dwell again on what life should have been. Peace. Joy. Devotion.

Henry had made her *feel.*

And with him gone, her world had grown even icier than before she had met him.

Perhaps it would be easier to rule Oakenglen while the world thought he was simply ill, but it was a charade she could not sustain. Her new assistant had started the rumors of the king's ill health once she had returned, and now the people expected the heirless master of Oakenglen to die any day.

What they did not know, however, was who would rule in his place.

"Furthermore, the last..." Barrett paused, hunting for the right word. "...*complication* has been taken care of."

"Good," she said calmly.

The fools Henry had left to govern Oakenglen had fought her, at first, but none of the headstrong ones had lasted long. Those who didn't bow to her didn't live long enough to join General Davarius in his little rebellion.

Barrett's attention shifted again toward the edge of the rose garden and stared after the retreating Tove Warren. "Who was that girl? With everything at stake, I hardly thought you were the sort to take social visits."

"You should know me better than that by now, General." A wry smile tugged at the corner of Celine's lips. "Miss Warren is simply bait."

"For whom?"

"Quinn Starling."

There was silence, and she glanced over one shoulder to find the general watching her with one eyebrow raised in question.

"Keep an eye on her," she ordered, unfazed by his doubts. "I want as many soldiers as possible stationed outside of the augmentor's shop at all hours, hidden from view. If she knows we're watching, she will run."

"She won't get away," he promised.

"She had better not." Celine's icy tone dripped with warning.

He coughed and tilted his head away, likely to hide his tremor of fear, but she'd seen it all the same.

Celine smiled.

"And, uh—" He took a settling breath and returned his gaze forward. "What do we do if Quinn Starling takes the bait? Observe?"

"No," she said calmly. "You attack."

His head snapped back in surprise. "Attack a Starling?"

"It must be quick, and it must be devastating," she explained. "Bring them both to the castle. Separate them and collar them both. Store them in the lakefront prisons. I want Quinn to see Lunestone when I torture her."

"Your Majesty..." Jensen cleared his throat, hesitant to continue, but she already knew what he would say.

"You're reluctant to kidnap a Starling," she observed.

He sighed in defeat. "I am, Celine."

Her eye twitched at his informal tone, but she resisted the impulse to slice open his face in punishment. Once he was securely under her thumb, she would correct his overly familiar behavior.

For now, she would endure.

"Were Teagan Starling alive, he would have sent word by now," she explained. "Our spy network has not seen him in two weeks, when all reports indicated we would have gotten word at least six days ago." Celine paused and lifted her chin in victory. "He's dead, general, and Zander is missing."

Barrett went still, and his expression went briefly blank, as though he couldn't quite let himself believe it was possible.

As though he didn't dare let himself hope.

"If Zander is alive, he will return with a vengeance. That means we have a slim window in which to conquer Lunestone, and for an assault to succeed, I need Quinn Starling to tell me everything she knows."

"Quinn has been missing longer than Zander," Barrett countered. "What makes you think she's still alive?"

Instead of answering, Celine snared him with her cold gaze. "Do you know who visits Tove Warren's shop?"

He shook his head.

"Exactly." The Queen of Oakenglen stared again out over the lake, toward the distant silhouette of Lunestone on the horizon. "Almost no one goes into that woman's shop, and yet I heard she recently had company. She was cashing in favors for items she would never need herself."

"You think it was—"

"I do," Celine interjected. "I suspect Quinn is the one who led him to that woman's shop, though I don't know why she would have done it. Quinn Starling isn't dead, General, and she will be back. While you and I are gone, your best men must be ready for her. She will put up one hell of a fight."

"Yes, your Majesty."

"Good." Celine absently toyed with the blisteringly sharp tip of the knife hidden in her sleeve. She ran her fingertip over it again and again, relishing in the tantalizing risk of it slicing open her skin. "I expect her in the dungeons before my coronation. Is everything ready?"

"Nearly." He took a step closer, and his blurred silhouette appeared in her periphery. "But Your Majesty, you still haven't told me where we're going."

The silver dagger in her sleeve nicked her, and she rubbed her thumb against the bead of crimson that pooled on her fingertip. As ever, she felt nothing. No flash of pain. No jolt of surprise.

Just... *nothing.*

Blood smeared across her skin, and she stared at it, lost in thought.

"To tie up loose ends," she eventually admitted. "And to put General Davarius in his place."

CHAPTER FIFTEEN

CONNOR

With his back against a nearby tree, Connor shredded yet another blade of grass to bits as he stared absently down at his hands. His mind raced, and he couldn't sleep.

Sunbeams pierced the canopy, casting thin spotlights across patches of dirt and underbrush as the forest twittered around his makeshift camp. The rumble of a dragon's snore filled the air, so soft it almost faded completely into the breeze. Sophia and Quinn lay in their blankets nearby, both asleep, while Murdoc sat atop a towering boulder at the edge of the ring of bushes that offered them cover from any passersby.

This deep in the Ancient Woods, he didn't expect to run into anyone, but one of them still had to keep watch while the others slept.

You bore me, the Wraith King griped.

"Travel is boring," Connor replied, quiet enough to not wake those who were lucky enough to have fallen asleep. "You should be used to that by now."

Give me a campaign, the ghoul continued, as though Connor hadn't spoken. *A plot. A plan. Something to move toward, or someone to kill. Anything but this brutal nothing!*

Instead of taking the bait, Connor shut his eyes and leaned again against his tree trunk.

The rustle of leaves broke through the steady chirp and patter of the forest's inhabitants, and he paused to lean toward the sound. Seconds later, the rustle came again, right at the edge of his hearing.

Not paws scampering over the forest floor at all, but a footstep.

Someone was approaching.

Out *here.*

That made no sense—and it proved exceedingly dangerous.

He stood. The magic in his blood pulsed beneath his fingertips, aching to be freed, but he waited to summon his swords. He listened again, honing in on the distant footsteps as they became clearer.

Heading toward them, no less.

Connor whistled, soft and low. Murdoc's head pivoted toward him, and Connor pointed one finger off toward the sound. The former Blackguard frowned, and his eyes glossed over as he listened.

A second later, a twig cracked in the distance. Murdoc raised one eyebrow and nodded.

He'd heard it, too.

Connor held out one hand in a silent order for Murdoc to stand guard, and his friend gave him a salute.

Silent and focused, Connor darted into the forest. He wove between the trees, and his boots passed silently over the patchy grass as the sound guided him through the woodland. With each step, he adjusted his direction until the distant rustle became the painfully loud crack and snap of someone ripping plants up by their roots.

"Can you see anything?" he asked the Wraith King.

Not yet, the ghoul answered. *They're just beyond the edge of our connection.*

The soft rumble of a low conversation bubbled up through the clamor, and Connor pressed his back against a tree as he sought to make out the words. Two—no, three—men's voices punctuated the forest air, followed by a woman's soft whimper.

The barest whisper of a footstep brushed against the grass behind him, and he pivoted on his heel with one fist raised at whomever had caught him off guard.

Quinn stood by his tree and watched him with a curious smirk.

His shoulders relaxed at her familiar features, and he lowered his fist. "You should be at camp," he whispered. "Guarding the others."

"Murdoc is perfectly capable of watching a dragon sleep," she whispered back. Instead of heeding the order, she pressed one shoulder against the tree beside his and scanned the forest beyond. "Besides, it looks like we have company."

He sighed in defeat and opted against shoving her back toward camp. A man had to pick his battles, and this wasn't one he wanted to fight.

Mainly because he knew he wouldn't win it.

"Stay close," he told her.

She nodded.

He headed again toward the sound, and this time, Quinn trailed behind him. They walked in near-perfect sync, silent as ghosts, and the men's conversation quickly came into earshot.

"... get enough yarrow," one man snapped.

"Those reishi mushrooms are rank," another one added. "You trying to poison us, you old witch?"

The woman's whimper came again, but she didn't answer.

As the voices grew louder, Connor knelt behind a thick holly bush and peered through a hole in its leaves. Three men stood around a woman as she collected a clump of mushrooms from the forest floor. She set them in a basket on the grass beside her, and her wrinkled hands shook with each one she gathered.

The men circled her, swords on their waists as they glared down at her work. Green ink stained their arms in crude symbols and shaky lines, which meant that he and Quinn were up against augmented fighters.

Likely not a true threat, but he would be cautious all the same.

Not far away, three horses and a donkey clustered by a lichen-covered log. The animals ripped large chunks of grass out of the earth and chewed, their ears flicking every which way as they waited.

No reinforcements, then. The four of them were alone.

He slipped the cloth around his neck up and over his nose to hide most of his features. He tugged a second one out of his pocket, but with a quick glance at Quinn's fire-red hair, he wondered if it was worth the effort.

Starlings didn't exactly blend in.

She huffed at the offered scarf and, instead, tugged a thin vial out of a small leather pouch on her calf. She took a single sip, and almost instantly, the fiery threads of gold and orange in her hair darkened. It became auburn and, shortly after, turned fully brown. Before she had even corked the vial, her eyes had brightened to a stunning green, and she slipped it back in its place.

But her face—that was definitely still Quinn. Different hair, sure, and different eyes, but everything else remained the same.

"Take it," he demanded in an urgent whisper.

With an irritated groan, she snatched it from his fingers and tied it around her face. Her green eyes popped, brighter now in contrast against the black fabric hiding her features, and she shook her head in annoyance.

"Hurry up," the closest man demanded. "Haven't got all day, hag. This potion takes long enough to brew without you taking your sweet time."

"You've already taken everything," she said between tears. "Please, just leave me be."

"Gladly," he said with a mocking little bow. "Once you make this Rootrock, we'll be merrily on our way."

From his hidden vantage point, Connor's teeth clenched together as he resisted the urge to charge in and decapitate all three in one go.

"Spellgust poachers," he whispered.

Quinn's nose creased in disgust, and she drew her blackfire blade from its sheath.

Good. They were agreed on what to do next.

"I saw that!" one of the men shouted. He pointed down at the woman.

"Trying to kill us, are you?" another one snapped. "You think we're stupid enough to fall for that?"

She raised her hands over her head, trembling. "I—I don't—"

One of them shoved her hard, and she grunted with pain. As she shifted in her seat, a collection of wrinkled brown mushrooms fell out of her apron pocket. The little brown balls rolled toward the basket, almost the same brown as the reishis.

Clever woman.

Webcap mushrooms were fatal.

"What the hell are you playing at, you old bat?" One of the men took a menacing step closer to the frail woman and raised one hand to slap her.

Connor stifled a furious growl. He'd had enough of this.

Before the poacher could swing, Connor darted from the forest and grabbed the man's hand. The poacher flinched. He tried to pull away, but Connor's grip only tightened. Before anyone could speak, Connor bent the poacher's hand backward, and a sharp crack filled the air. The criminal screamed with pain, and Connor punched the man square in his nose to silence him.

The screaming stopped, and the poacher hit the ground with a thud. Blood rushed from his flattened nose, and his vacant eyes stared up at the canopy.

All that, before the other two could even draw their swords.

Both surviving poachers gaped at him, though one had enough wherewithal to at least draw this weapon. A second later, their eyes darted to his left. Quinn joined him, her sword already raised, and he summoned one of his own.

In unison, the blackfire along their dark steel roared to life, and they glared at the doomed men through the flames.

"The Shade!" one of them screamed. His scruffy black hair fell in his face as his dark eyes widened with fear. His sword shook so violently he barely kept hold of it.

Beside him, his blond friend inched slowly backward. The second man didn't speak. He didn't tremble. His eyes didn't shake with horror. Instead, his fiercely determined gaze darted between Connor and Quinn as he tried to assess the bigger threat.

After a moment more of deliberation, his eyes settled on Connor.

"It's the Shade!" the raven-haired poacher screamed again. Oddly, the man's own voice seemed to snap him from his terrified daze. His sword fell to the ground, striking a rock in the dirt with a resounding clang, and he bolted.

"All yours," Connor said to the ghoul.

Finally.

Dark smoke rolled across the field ahead of the poacher, and a skeletal hand darted from the shadows to grab the man's throat. With all the dramatic flair of an actor, the wraith's skeletal face emerged slowly from the inky haze as he lifted the criminal off his feet.

The man gasped for air. He smacked uselessly at the wraith's wrists, but the bony fingers only tightened. The poacher's legs kicked wildly at the Wraith King's billowing cloak, but he struck only air.

A thin stream of blood trickled from the man's eye as the specter choked the life out of him, and Connor grimaced at the Wraith King's bloodlust.

"Do it out of sight, "Connor ordered with a nod toward the trembling woman behind him.

The ghoul grumbled obscenities but dutifully shot through the trees. The gurgle of a man dying trailed after the tattered cloak, until the late spring day swallowed them both.

The lone survivor hadn't moved—whether from fear or stupidity, Connor couldn't tell—and the criminal didn't so much as glance toward his fallen friends. He simply watched Connor's face, as though looking for something.

When Connor had slaughtered the slavers, he had spared one of them to spread a dire warning of what would happen to the criminals traveling the southern road. Given how quickly rumors traveled through the pubs, there probably wasn't a soul in this forest who hadn't heard it by now.

"I warned you all," Connor said flatly.

After a moment's hesitation, the man nodded.

"And yet you're still here, stealing from an old woman. I know how you poachers work. You steal, and then you kill. She never had a chance on her own."

The poacher swallowed hard, and this time, he didn't respond.

Now, Connor had a choice. He could either show mercy one last time and use this cretin to reinforce his original warning, or he could enforce the edict he'd made that night he saved Kiera and the girls.

Back then, he hadn't wanted to let anyone out of that clearing alive. He had only done it because Keira was watching, but now he could easily let his bloodlust win.

With anyone you face, you must ask yourself one thing. Beck Arbor's voice rattled in Connor's head as a distant, hazy memory resurfaced. *Do you want them to fear you, or do you want them to respect you? Fear makes cowards listen. Sometimes, to survive, you must be brutal. You must be vicious. You must slit throats and draw a line in the soil that no sane mortal would cross.*

He had already drawn his line, and these damned fools had stepped right over it.

With an effortless swing, he cut the man's head clean off. The poacher's body collapsed in a heap, and the man's sword hit the ground with a dull thud. A small cloud of dust lingered over the corpse as it lay in the dirt, and he stared down for a moment at the criminal he had just killed.

It was easier to take a life when someone was actively trying to take his. This man, however, hadn't even drawn a weapon.

Killing him had felt oddly wrong.

The blackfire along Quinn's blade snuffed out with a hiss, and as she studied the corpses in the small clearing, she sheathed her new weapon. "That was excessive."

"Then you don't know spellgust poachers like I do." Connor dismissed his own blade with a flick of his wrist.

"Enlighten me."

"These were spellgust poachers." He nodded toward the decapitated corpse, but his eyes lingered on the body as he inwardly debated if he had, in fact, made the right choice. "They kill anyone with a potion and take it for themselves. They're vultures, and they never hunt alone. There's always a larger troupe out there, protecting the loot while smaller bands look for more. If we hadn't come, the woman would be dead."

Quinn's glamoured-green eyes roamed his face. "You've encountered their kind before?"

"Twice," he admitted. "Before I met the Finns. Nearly died both times."

He had no pity and no mercy for men like these. They'd heard of his warning to the slavers. They'd known the risk of stealing from the people in the Ancient Woods, and yet they hadn't stopped.

To let any of them live would have only meant letting them claim more victims.

A soft whimper punctuated the air, and Connor peered around Quinn to find the frail little woman curled in a ball against the base of a tree. She sobbed into her hands, her body trembling, and he froze at the thought of what this must've looked like to her.

Shit.

"Uh... huh." He scratched the back of his head, resisting the impulse to come closer and set a hand on her shoulder, since that hadn't worked at all when he'd tried to soothe the slavers' victims. "Madam, you're safe—"

The woman only cried harder.

"Mercy," she whispered, almost too quietly to hear. "Have mercy. Take everything. Please just spare me and Ned," she added with a weak gesture toward her donkey. "Please. I'm just a witch. I promise. Nothing special. I promise."

"Hey, now," Quinn said softly. Her tone and demeanor shifted in the blink of an eye. Every crease disappeared from her brow, and she gracefully knelt before the woman as a bird twittered in the canopy above. "None of that, love."

Slowly, deliberately, Quinn picked up each and every fallen reagent. She placed them, one by one, in the woman's basket. When the little pile of white flowers and mushrooms grew almost to the handle, she gently set the basket back at the woman's feet.

The frail little lady peered down at the collection through her fingers, and her sobbing slowed. Though her chest heaved with each terrified huff, the gasping breaths slowed to a calmer rhythm. She sluggishly lowered her hands and glanced between him and Quinn, again and again, as though she couldn't understand what she was seeing.

"That's better." Quinn tugged off her mask and smiled. "See? We're nothing scary."

Not to her, anyway, the wraith grumbled. *Honestly, it's a disgrace.*

Connor sighed impatiently.

"Ma'am," he interjected. "Are there more of those men back at your cottage?"

She shook her head. "Just those three, and I doubt I'll be seeing that last one again."

Quinn winked at her. "If you do, tell them we're in the woods waiting."

The woman laughed, and for the first time since they'd seen her, she relaxed. Her back slumped against the tree, and she breathed easy. "I'll do that, dear girl. I might just do that."

"Are you really…" the woman trailed off, her brows furrowing in awe as she stared up at Connor. "Are you really the Shade?"

Arms crossed, he simply nodded.

"The Shade," she whispered, as though it still hadn't fully registered. Her gaze drifted toward Quinn, and the woman scanned her face. "And you're… Mrs. Shade?"

"Uh—" A delicate blush burned along Quinn's cheeks. "I… I don't…"

"Come, now, Mrs. Shade." The black cloth across Connor's face hid his broad grin, and given the blush creeping down Quinn's neck, that probably worked in his favor. "Answer the woman."

Quinn flashed him an irritated glare.

He chuckled.

"I knew the Lightseers were wrong," the frail woman said quietly. A broad, brilliant smile inched across her face, and she clapped happily. "I knew it! I was right! Ha! Take that, you bloated zealots!"

With the soft pop of a cracking knuckle, Quinn curled one hand into a fist and cleared her throat.

"They told all sorts of lies," the woman continued, oblivious to Quinn's discomfort. "On their trip south, they spread rumors and made decrees. Oh, the Fates-damned *decrees.*" She threw her hands up in the air, as though she didn't even want to start on *those.* "Called you a tyrant, they did. Worse than King Henry. A thief. An assassin. A rapist, and a murderer. Said you'd set fire to us all and steal from every coffer you saw. Lies!"

Connor's jaw tensed as he sat with the weight of everything the Lightseers had said about him along the southern road. They would've only spread rumors like that to destroy his reputation and convince the locals not to help him.

Teagan Starling had been busy, and even from beyond the grave, the man was making Connor's life harder.

Damn it all to *hell.*

"But I never believed it," the woman continued. She lifted one thin finger and wagged it at the forest, as though the trees themselves had doubted her all along. "You've done too much good to be all those things the Lightseers claimed."

"Thank you," he said with a grateful nod.

"You still have friends along the southern road." The old witch leaned toward him, and her voice lowered to a mischievous whisper. "Look for us in the taverns, should you ever need our help."

With that, she clapped her wrinkled hands together and pushed herself to her feet, surprisingly spry for someone with so many years on her bones. She scooped up her basket and hummed to herself as she grabbed her donkey's harness. After one final smile over her shoulder, she wandered off into the sunny woodland.

Once she was out of earshot, Connor sighed and tugged off the cloth covering his features. Quinn stood and set one hand on his arm as they stared off into the trees, processing everything the woman had said.

"They've been busy," Quinn said.

"Yeah." Connor squared his shoulders and glared off in the direction of the southern road. "But so have we."

CHAPTER SIXTEEN

NYX

The rumbling roar of distant waterfalls echoed through the midday air. A warm breeze, thick with honey and the hint of approaching summer, rolled across the balcony of Mossvale Castle as Nyx Osana reclined on a silk couch that was never meant to be outdoors. Though lunch was still an hour away, she took a deep drink of the morbidly expensive wine she'd stolen from Otmund's cellars.

After all, the oaf wouldn't need it anymore. One of these days, she would find out who had murdered him. Once they'd told her everything of Otmund's final moments, she would torture them instead for robbing such a meaningful kill from her.

Otmund had much to atone for, and she had very much looked forward to skinning him alive.

Dressed in elaborate blue and green robes meant for Mossvale nobility, she enjoyed the gentle wind across her bare shoulders. Now and then, it suited her to discard the telltale black robes of the Nethervale elite in favor of something more comfortable.

Nothing else in Saldia soothed her skin quite like cool silk.

Another gust of wind carried hints of seaweed and the tide from the glittering sea at the far end of the gleaming city. The tension in her scarred back had almost vanished in these weeks of relaxation. Her necromancers were antsy, eager for something else to steal, but it took time to weave strings into a puppet state. Even now, some of her best had begun working on a crafted story to tell the locals as she slowly took over this paradise.

Otmund was a fool to ever leave this place.

Though she knew what had become of the Lord of Mossvale, she had yet to receive news on Teagan Starling's march through the Decay, and that intrigued her. A notice of victory should've begun floating through the kingdoms a week ago, but still—nothing.

Perhaps this Wraithblade had kept Teagan busy, and that meant this newcomer was a more formidable opponent than anyone had realized.

Even her.

With Teagan occupied, this could very well be the perfect time to steal the one thing she had always wanted from him, more than anything else. Something locked away deep in the Mountains of the Unwanted where few dared to tread.

Behind her, a hinge creaked as the door to her suite swung open. A glass bottle rattled on a tray. Leather shoes scuffed against the balcony tile, the person's pace slow and steady as they approached.

Too slow.

Too steady.

Unaugmented servants always tripped over themselves as they approached with her wine, but this person walked with intention.

Like they were *trying* to make noise.

With her back to the balcony doors, Nyx took the final sip of her wine and raised the empty chalice for the imposter to fill. Her ear twitched, her senses fully focused on her visitor as she lulled them into a false sense of security.

Yes, she thought. *Come closer, you little fool.*

Even she had to admit this was a clever ploy. To pose as a servant—to make noise when one had spent a lifetime training to perfect stealth—it would've caught nearly anyone off guard. It was unconventional. Crafty.

She almost envied the person's forethought.

Behind her, almost close enough to touch, the imposter paused. Glass rattled, as though they were about to pour, but everything about the position had been clearly timed. At this distance, she couldn't grab them, but they would be close enough to strike a death blow with the right weapon.

She cracked her neck, eager for a fight. It had been quite a while since she'd killed anyone.

The whistle of metal through the air shattered the late spring afternoon. Nyx shifted the goblet, and the shrill ring of metal striking metal followed as she caught the dagger easily.

A necromancer, then, using the poisoned blades she had commissioned for them upon induction into her ranks.

The *nerve.*

With an effortless twist, Nyx leaned forward and kicked the couch. Her boot slid underneath it, just as she'd intended, and the sofa flipped as it launched backward. It thudded against something hard. Boots and splintered wood slid against the stone. A woman grunted, the air knocked out of her.

It all happened within seconds.

The woman's second dagger sliced through the air. Unfazed, Nyx leaned to the left as it whizzed by her ear. Her cold gaze landed on her attacker as the chaise slammed against the balcony railing.

A woman she didn't recognize shoved aside the ripped silk and shattered wood of the now-decimated couch. Light brown hair. Brown eyes. Dressed in the black robes of the Nethervale elite.

A glamour. Had to be.

How clever—her assassin had even crafted an escape plan, should she fail.

The assailant set one hand on the balcony railing for balance. With the other, she grabbed one of the chair's broken legs and hurled it at Nyx's face.

A splintered spear, and likely nothing more than a distraction.

Again, Nyx sidestepped the attack as her would-be assassin raised both hands. The air chilled, and an unbidden shiver snaked down her spine as frost crept along the cutthroat's fingers. In unison, the rush of metal slicing through air sang from behind her.

Everything happened in the blink of an eye, each move almost too quick to register, but Nyx had been forged in the hellfire of Nethervale.

She *lived* for duels like these.

The thin hairs on her neck stood on end, warning of the approaching danger. Where others would have panicked, she took a deep breath to steady herself and time her next move.

Her assailant fired a dazzling blast of blue ice, aimed right for Nyx's chest. Again, clever—jumping would guarantee the two flying daggers would hit her in the head, while rolling would give her opponent time to call her enchanted blades back to her.

But she had more tricks up her sleeve than even the Nethervale elite knew.

Nyx jumped and twisted her body. One leg stretched out, horizontal to the floor, to balance her as she pressed her hands tightly against her chest. Her body spun, her blonde hair flying, and her eyes crossed briefly as one of the enchanted daggers sailed beneath her nose. The other dagger passed between her legs in the same moment that the blast of ice shot past her hip.

Her attacker gasped in surprise, and Nyx indulged a wicked little grin.

Before her foot hit the stone, she twisted both palms toward the sky. At the silent command, her two enchanted blades slipped from the small sheaths strapped to her wrists and hovered, ever so slightly, above the heels of her palms.

Her connection to the devastating power of the Nethervale daggers pulsed through her fingertips. Her augmentation linking her to her prized blades hummed as she delved into its magic, and for a moment, she debated giving this assassin a drawn-out death. The poison in her daggers would kill the woman instantly, and that almost seemed too kind.

In the end, however, self-preservation won.

With her fingers spread wide, she hurled the first dagger at her opponent. The second followed shortly after, and her boots hit the ground after that. She knelt as another blast of ice sailed over her head. Poised to strike, she kicked off the ground and raced toward her opponent, just in case her blades missed.

They didn't.

Both sank deep into the woman's eyes, and her head snapped back. Blood shot through her skull and splattered the stone behind her. She slumped, still leaning against the railing, and her body teetered as it threatened to fall over the side.

Nyx debated letting the corpse tumble and splatter against the ground far below. It would serve as a warning to anyone else who dared try such a foolhardy move.

With an irritated sigh, though, she grabbed the dead woman's collar and pulled. The corpse slid across the balcony, leaving a crimson trail in its wake, and Nyx waited in silence as the woman's last breath left her broken body.

With her death, the brown hair faded to strawberry blonde. Her skin darkened by a few shades. A single green tattoo of a thorn-covered bramble snaked up her forearm and into her sleeve.

Rooted in place, staring at the woman's body, Nyx seethed. It was Elaina—one of her favorites. One of the few she had entrusted with the task of shifting Mossvale into Nyx's control.

That *traitor*.

She spat on the necromancer's blood-drenched hair. With her eyes still locked on her dead soldier, she stretched her fingers wide and tugged on the invisible tether between her and her enchanted daggers. In her peripheral vision, two silver blurs shot toward her and only slowed as they approached her palms. Blood dripped onto her forearm as they slid back into their sheaths, and she relished the hot liquid rolling over her skin.

The hinge creaked again as the door to her suites swung open once more. This time, Reaver leaned against the doorframe, his arms crossed as he stared down at the fallen necromancer. Short white hair framed his ice-blue eyes, and the hilt of his sword protruded from the sheath on his back.

Another challenger—or simply an observer, waiting to see how the duel played out.

"Are you next?" Nyx asked her second in command.

Never one for words, he simply shook his head.

"Smart man."

He shrugged.

"Get potions and food," she ordered. "You and I are leaving."

Reaver didn't move. Instead, he raised one eyebrow in question.

"You don't need a reason," she snapped, refusing to let these fools think she'd gone soft. "You'll see when we get there."

He nodded again and bowed his head, setting one hand to his forehead in apology.

"Go," she demanded. "And take this traitor with you. Make sure the others see what will become of them, too, if they try anything this foolish."

With a heavy sigh, he pushed off the wall. Though he obeyed, he kept a safe distance from her—just far enough that he would have time to defend against an attack, should she decide he was a threat.

It was the distance he always put between them, no matter where they went.

"Orders?" he asked as he approached.

The word cracked like thunder. Any time he spoke, the air shifted around him. For a man of few words, his voice carried an impressive weight.

"Drain her." Nyx wrinkled her nose with disgust as she gestured toward the corpse at her feet. "Make sure her blood is only used for the cheap potions. I want her death wasted."

Reaver nodded.

Nyx stepped over the woman's body, and she intentionally stepped on the corpse's fingers to shatter them. With a satisfying crunch, she left Reaver to clean up her mess.

Her moment of respite was over. If one of the elite had dared tried to kill her, it meant the others thought she was going soft, too.

Useless idiots. All of them.

Time to remind them why so many Saldian peasants feared the dark—and why so many Lightseers feared *her*.

SOPHIA

Deep in the heart of the Blood Bogs, Sophia followed their small band through the darkened underground tunnels few knew existed. Sparse torches lit the damp space, far enough apart that their team frequently passed through stretches of pitch black with only the distant flicker of amber light to guide them.

How strange to be back in a land that tried to kill them—and this time, to be welcomed.

Withered brown vines lined the walls, their leaves wilting, and much of the forest where they'd landed had been equally shriveled to kindling. Without her second Soulsprite, it seemed as though the Antiquity was too weak to keep much of the land alive.

The thought struck Sophia as odd. Wrong, even, for a goddess to be dying.

Ahead, Quinn and Murdoc walked at a steady pace behind Duncan and Connor as the Freymoor General led them to safety deep underground. The two men in front spoke in hushed voices, discussing strategies and updates she would have normally killed someone to overhear.

But not tonight.

Not with everything at stake.

Right now, Sophia desperately needed a plan.

She trailed behind the others, distracted, and her thoughts raced through her limited options. Her eyes slipped out of focus, and no matter how many times she forced them to clear, they inevitably glazed over again as she followed her small band of allies through the cold stone corridors deep underground.

Whenever someone had hunted her in the past, her plan had always been to hide. That way, no one would figure out who she was, and no one would care enough about her to make an attempt on her life.

When she blended in with everyone else—when she didn't matter to anyone—she was safe. Before she'd met Connor, that had been her greatest chance of survival.

Her gaze darted toward Murdoc. The former Blackguard walked ahead of her, calm and confident, and he had a bit of wayward swagger in his step. As she studied the broad shoulders and muscled arms that had held her close on so many recent nights, a sharp pang hit her in the chest.

It wasn't dread, but it wasn't warmth, either.

It just... *was.*

Quinn's warning that the Lightseers had guessed she was a Beaumont unnerved her to no end. It was all she had been able to think about since they'd left Slaybourne.

If the Lightseers could guess she was a Beaumont after just one battle, others would, too. The more time she spent in public, the more likely it was that rumors would make it back to Gabor.

Her uncle understood the limits of forbidden magic better than most, and he was smart enough to piece the clues together. Once she was his captive, it would only take a Hackamore for her to bear her soul.

If she didn't hide in the shadows, her uncle would find her. He would give anything to the person who dragged her back to Hazeltide, to that terrifying cellar, deep below the manor, where all those bodies were rotting to bones.

To a place where she would never again see the sun, and where the world would simply forget she had ever existed.

Stupid.

The word rattled in her head, powerful and furious, and she wanted to slap herself for her own idiocy. Out of pride and spite, she had chosen a body that looked every bit like a Beaumont should. She could've chosen a blonde, for the Fates' sake, but *no.* She had to choose a woman who could've easily passed for Gabor's daughter. Her lifetime of wanting to belong to the family she had been born into could easily be what led them right to her.

She couldn't just steal another body this time and change her face. With the spellgust gem in her torso keeping her alive, this would be the one body that could sustain her.

Forever.

Her pride might very well get her killed, and now, she couldn't do a damn thing to stop it from happening.

The battle against the Lightseers had been brutal, and she'd been forced to use her skills from Nethervale to survive amongst the carnage. It was the sort of duel that had pushed her limits far beyond what Quinn had witnessed all those months ago, outside of Bradford. Back then, she had been able to play it safe to hide her true power. She had successfully played small to ensure she wasn't identified.

No more.

"We're splitting up."

Connor's voice snapped her from her daze. He paused at the head of their small band, and his eyes swept briefly over them. He towered over Duncan, ever the formidable force, and his broad shoulders blocked out the view of the tunnel ahead.

A dragon-tamer.

A Starling-killer.

A warrior unlike any the continent had seen for quite some time.

He and Murdoc were her last hope for survival.

"You three will meet Dahlia. She wants to talk to each of you before we settle in for the night."

A sconce ahead of them cast a golden outline around Quinn's fire-red hair as she set her hands on her hips. "Where are you going, then?"

"To speak with the Antiquity." He flashed the Starling warrior a mischievous grin, so quickly Sophia almost missed it—like a schoolboy showing off for a girl. "I'll catch up with you all soon."

It seemed as though Quinn wouldn't be sleeping alone tonight.

"Let's go." He clapped his hands together and nodded toward a fork in the path Sophia hadn't noticed, distracted as she had been with all of her wandering thoughts.

As he and Duncan took the path to the right, Quinn led them down the other route. Yet again, Sophia's eyes shifted toward the Scoundrel who had melted a few slivers of her icy black heart. The sensation of his kiss on her neck and his hands between her thighs sent a ribbon of warmth through her soul. With the memory of their last night in Slaybourne, the tension in her shoulders briefly eased.

To enjoy a lover's company, after all these years of torment, was... well, *strange*.

Perhaps it would have been wiser to stay in hiding, but now that she had tasted a richer life, she wanted more. Safety in the shadows wasn't good enough.

With Murdoc unaware of her gaze on the back of his head, a small smile tugged at her lips.

These two wouldn't let her uncle drag her into the darkness. Though her heart still skipped beats at the thought of Gabor glaring down at her again, she could finally let herself trust that these two wouldn't leave her there to die.

Trust.

It was still so new to her, and she clung to it with the desperation of a dying man hunting wreckage in a storm. Fragile, perhaps, but it was enough to stop her from disappearing again into the night.

For now, anyway. She could trust these men, but she didn't trust this strange feeling of *hope*—or the Fates, for that matter.

CHAPTER SEVENTEEN

CONNOR

The air smelled like death.

Connor's nose creased with barely restrained disgust as the lingering fumes of decay and rot mixed together with every step through the narrow stone corridor. The last time he'd walked down this path, Dahlia had led the way—this time, however, the Antiquity had asked to speak to him alone.

Once, brilliant green vines had covered these walls. Now, however, a gray twinge had overtaken them, like they'd been covered in grime and left to gather dust. The once-powerful pulses of light now shot through them with a dull cadence, weak and muted. Shriveled leaves covered the floor like a carpet, and even he couldn't step around all of them.

The goddess wasn't just weaker without her second Soulsprite. This was so much worse.

This is undesirable, the Wraith King said in a hushed tone, still out of sight for the time being. *Our ally cannot be dying.*

"Our ally can hear you," Connor reminded the dead man. "Let me do the talking."

The specter grumbled, but he ultimately didn't reply.

Good. One less thing for Connor to deal with.

As before, the corridor ended in a grand circular room. The rocky ceiling curved sharply upward, and the weakly pulsing vines covered every surface. Some slumped, revealing patches of mossy stone they had once covered, and their gray tendrils faded into a thick mist far above his head. The weak pulses of her heartbeat through the vines were barely bright enough to light the space.

"You're sick," he said to the empty room.

She didn't answer.

Instead, the vines slowly slithered back from the walls. It wasn't a powerful moment of movement, this time, but rather a trickle, like a stream slowly leaking from a dam. They assembled in the center of the stone floor, stirring the layers of dead leaves that covered everything.

They wove together, building the Antiquity from her feet. Legs formed. A torso. Arms. Shoulders. When her great, horned head finally appeared, her shoulders slumped. She studied him in silence, and no glowing white butterflies sprang to life this time.

"Very sick," Connor corrected. "You didn't tell me this would happen if I took the Soulsprite."

"Would you have changed your mind, had you known?" The Antiquity's voice was soft and soothing, far more powerful than her body. *"I wished to simplify our bargain. It is as I expected it to be."*

He frowned. That didn't make this any better.

"You have questions," she said with a weak flourish of her frail gray hand. *"And I have precious little energy. We must be quick. I will not withhold. Ask."*

Even the cadence of her voice had changed. No extended pauses. No longwinded riddles.

She was fading.

He gestured to her stooping posture. "How much time do you have left?"

"Years."

Connor raised one eyebrow, not buying it.

"I will not lie to you," she promised. *"Not with so much at stake."*

"Alright." He sighed and crossed his arms, still not happy with her answer. "Last time, you mentioned another simmering soul had found its host. Who is it? Are they a threat?"

"They are." Her great head tilted to the side, and her eyes fluttered briefly closed. *"Many centuries ago, the Feral King escaped his prison and found his way to the blightwolves. He has resided among them ever since."*

Despite his best judgment, Connor squinted at her in surprise. "You're actually going to give me answers? No riddles? No games?"

Though she slouched with all the exhaustion of a beaten soldier, she chuckled. *"Perhaps I was unkind in my tests, Champion, for you to believe I would continue to withhold such important information."*

"More than unkind," he muttered.

"The Feral King came from one of my brothers. The Hunt." She leaned backward against the wall, still towering over Connor despite her weakened state. *"He was the last of us to succumb, but Aeron Zacharias was experienced with the Soulsprites by the time he found the Hunt. He brought allies to that brutal fight, and the blightwolves ultimately ripped the Soulsprites from my brother's body."*

The blightwolves.

A chill crept through Connor's soul at the realization that Saldia's greatest horrors had allied with the darkness from the beginning.

In unison, he and the Wraith King sucked in a sharp breath. They had made a promise to the wolves, not long ago.

We're not unlike you, he'd told them. *We're creatures of death as well. Of murder. You have our respect, and as long as you give us the same, you will have our loyalty in this lawless world. It is a gift we rarely give.*

It was an oath made long before he'd known the depths of their treachery.

It was a mistake—one he needed to remedy.

"I see you have encountered them already," the Antiquity watched him with a curious tilt to her head.

"That's one way to put it," he admitted.

"Then you know the danger you face."

He nodded.

"With my brother's Soulsprites, Zacharias brought back the most fearsome of the blightwolves to ever exist. It was an abomination, one many thought could not be made by nature, and he called it the Feral King. I do not think he could control it."

"Fantastic," Connor said dryly.

"No one who wields the Feral King can live among men," she continued. *"I have watched its would-be masters from afar, in the centuries since it was found. Inevitably, they are called back to the forest—back to the land that once belonged to the Hunt."*

Connor raised one eyebrow in surprise. "If they were called back to the Hunt's domain, then there must be an element of the original god in all of the simmering souls."

"*There is.*" The Antiquity lifted her chin, watching something over his shoulder that he couldn't see, and he figured she was watching the Wraith King.

Who am I made from, then? the specter asked.

The goddess before them bristled at the ghoul's intrusion. The withered leaves clinging to the vines of her body shivered with a flutter of rage, and her great head tilted toward the air behind Connor.

"There's a better way to have worded that," Connor chided under his breath.

Perhaps, the wraith admitted.

"*You came from the Darkness,*" the Antiquity said after a moment. "*My brother who relished in war and blood. The one who adored the evil in men's hearts.*"

A heavy weight settled on the air, and for several moments, no one spoke.

"That's fitting," Connor said, mainly to break the spell of silence.

Ass, the wraith muttered.

"Last time I was here, you said there was a newcomer," Connor said to the goddess before him, doing his best to regain control of the conversation. "Another active host to a simmering soul."

They had much to discuss, and she had precious little energy to spare. Both he and the wraith had to stay focused.

"*Yes. The Feralblade. One who has ruled the blightwolves for the past twelve years.*"

Connor frowned. "I wouldn't exactly call him a newcomer, then."

The Antiquity shrugged. "*I suppose time does not mean for me what it means for you.*"

"Fair point," he admitted. "Do you know who this Feralblade is?"

"*Farkas.*" She reclined against the wall, her head drooping from exhaustion. "*A silver alpha who killed the last known human Feralblade to take the title for himself.*"

"You must be joking." Connor rubbed the back of his neck as he recalled the blightwolves teeth, inches from his face. "The alpha I met was actually a fellow blade?"

Impossible, the Wraith King said. *I would have seen the Feral King.*

"Unless he saw you first," the Antiquity corrected. *"Perhaps he did not want to be seen."*

Perhaps, the ghoul admitted with a frustrated sigh.

Connor paced the floor, his boots crunching softly over the leaves scattered across the stone. This was too insane to be real. Too wild.

The Wraith King had sensed something off about the silver blightwolf, and all this time, they hadn't realized they had already come face-to-face with the Feralblade himself.

"The remaining Soulsprites call to their old masters," the goddess continued. *"Mine have called to me. One beats within me, the only light keeping me alive. Another, I sense within Slaybourne—one I trust you will return with time."* She paused to watch him, and only a dull light pulsed within the curved vines that served as her eyes.

"I will," he promised.

She nodded weakly in breathless thanks. *"The third, I sense off the western coast. It is somewhere in the heart of a city called Kirkwall."*

Connor's jaw tightened. He stiffened, already knowing where this conversation was going, and a sickening wave of dread carved its way through him.

Home.

A place he never wanted to see again.

"To regain my full power, I need my own Soulsprites," the Antiquity explained. *"That is why, with time, we will find you one of your own to defend Slaybourne. You must return mine to me."*

"Understood," he said flatly.

"I do not know why it is there, of all places," she continued. *"I only pray no simmering soul has been crafted from it."*

"You can't tell the difference?" Connor asked.

The goddess shook her head.

He sighed and resumed his pacing, too irritated to stand still any longer. "So, when we find it, we might be in for a nasty surprise."

"It is a risk," she admitted. *"All I know for certain is the room in which it is hidden—a dark place with no sunlight, with only fire in the night and the day, surrounded by trinkets and gold."*

A treasury.

Great.

"Easy," he said dryly. "It's only the most fortified building on the island."

"Then you are familiar with Kirkwall?"

A knot formed in his throat. He coughed to clear it, and instead of answering, he simply nodded.

"Hmm." The sound came out like a gentle hum, but she thankfully didn't pursue the thought. *"Then you know the dragons used to own that island. It was stolen, centuries ago, by man."*

Connor frowned. "I've never heard that."

"How unfortunate. The era of the dragon was a captivating time." The Antiquity tilted her head and lost herself briefly in thought—or memory. *"One of my brothers claimed it as his homestead, and he gave his dragons a haven."*

"What happened to them?"

Her eyes pinched shut, and she gently shook her head. *"Not all gods were kind to each other. The Darkness craved the Flame's legendary homestead for himself, and the two of them brawled. Their battles shook the earth and ravaged the nearby islands. Even I do not know the full extent of the devastation, except that the Darkness acquired the Flame's Soulsprites. He desired to use them for himself."*

Delightful. Even the gods could be greedy bastards.

Frustrated, Connor rubbed his eye with the heel of his palm. "Do you know what he did with them? Those Soulsprites?"

"Squirreled them away," the Antiquity said weakly. *"I suspect Zacharias somehow acquired at least one of them, but I have no way of knowing. Either way, the Darkness failed. He never was able to conquer the Flame's homestead, nor its lingering magic."*

Connor narrowed his eyes in suspicion. "Then what are we going to find in that mountain?"

"I do not know," she confessed. *"The Soulsprites and simmering souls feel the same to me, on the rare occasions when I can sense them. Whatever waits in the mountain, it is no longer safe. The Fates' current has shifted, and the floodgates of chaos have opened. Before long, all of the gods' remaining magic will be claimed. We must not allow this one—whatever it is—to fall into the wrong hands."*

"Or claws," he added under his breath.

The weight of eyes on the back of Connor's head made the hair on his neck stand on end. He resisted the urge to turn around, to stare the Wraith King in the face, because he knew what the ghoul must've wanted so desperately to say.

The wraith wanted more—more blood, more magic, and more power. A simmering soul would deliver all of that in droves.

"Many bones lie within that mountain, my dear Champion," she warned. *"And many of its walls were built by the dead. Wherever this magic is hidden, it was never meant to be found. Those who brought it to the mountain died in their attempts to hide it. You will find no clues to its location, and you could easily spend your entire life wandering those tunnels, trying to find it."*

He squinted in disbelief. "Then why the hell are you sending me after it? It sounds plenty safe to me."

"Because there is one who can find it, and He is as fickle as the Fates."

At that little nugget of information, Connor stiffened. "Death? Death knows where it is?"

"Death knows many things," she answered. *"Including where all of His creations are, at any time. He forged the Soulsprites, and He knows where they linger."*

Frustrated, Connor pinched the bridge of his nose as he fought to understand the games these gods played with each other—and their creator. "Why would Death take me to something as important as a Soulsprite?"

Or a simmering soul, the wraith added. *Whichever this may be.*

Except for a sidelong glare at the empty space where Connor suspected the ghoul to be, he otherwise ignored the undead king.

At first, the Antiquity didn't answer. The vines comprising her face scrunched along her forehead, and the crinkle of withering leaves filled the silence.

Though the Wraith King scoffed impatiently, Connor didn't move. He didn't speak, nor did he try to hurry the conversation along. This was crucial information, and he wanted to ensure the goddess before him didn't dodge the question.

"You have not gone unnoticed," she eventually confessed. *"There are others like me who wish to see your true potential. Because of this—because of our interest in you—our Creator will test you. Death is wary, and He is wise."*

Now *that* sounded ominous.

"A map would be much easier," he said dryly.

"None exist, I'm afraid." The Antiquity shrugged, and her exhausted gaze settled on him once more. *"My Champion, if you encounter a simmering soul, you must not absorb it."*

Connor didn't answer. After all, he had no intention of fusing with yet more untested magic—especially if the new simmering soul was as irritating as the Wraith King.

The ghoul, however, disagreed.

Still hidden in the in-between, the old ghost scoffed in disgust. *Why should Magnuson not be given another simmering soul? He has proven himself to you through all of your ridiculous trials. Why would you degrade a king to become your errand boy?*

"Enough," Connor said firmly. "We owe her this much, that's why."

"It is not your worth I question," the goddess answered. *"It is the consequence of acquiring another simmering soul that concerns me."*

Now, that caught his attention.

"What's the consequence?" he prodded.

"To Death, each simmering soul is but another Soulsprite, and I have told you before how he reveres his greatest creations."

Ah. Right.

"To Him, how many you carry is irrelevant. It is how many you allow into your soul. It is not what you have, but what you do with them. Fuse with one, and you intrigue Him. Fuse with two, and you will meet Him. Fuse with three, and you will challenge Him." She lifted her hand and weakly gestured toward Connor. *"Trust me, my champion. Even you are not ready to challenge him. There is much you and I must do before that time comes."*

If it came at all.

"Promise me," she said softly. *"Swear to me that you will retrieve it."*

He sat with the weight of what she was asking him to do, but he ultimately nodded. After all she had sacrificed to protect his home, he owed her this much.

Probably more.

"Good." The Antiquity let out a quiet sigh and slumped further down the wall.

This must've taken more energy out of her than she truly had to give.

"We'll leave at sunset," he added. "For now, you should rest."

"Not yet." She waved away his concern with a weak flick of her wrist. *"There is more you must know."*

His brows furrowed in barely restrained surprise. Before today, it had been a chore to get her to tell him anything. Now, she had more answers than he had questions.

In a world where he had to bluff his way through most conversations, this was a rare treat.

"You must retrieve the magic in the mountain first. It is a dangerous journey through the dragons' labyrinth, and it will be even more treacherous now that such a powerful place has been left idle for so long. You will face dangerous creatures in those tunnels, and I cannot risk my Soulsprite being destroyed or lost to a lawless in-between."

He frowned. "What exactly do you think I'll find in there?"

"Horrors," she said softly. *"The homestead of a fallen god carries seeds of its dead master. In his absence, I'm certain creatures have made their way into his domain, drawn to it by its lingering enchantments. Homesteads are a bridge between the living and the dead. With no master to control it, it will have undoubtedly grown wild and untamed. The inhabitants will have strength and abilities they do not deserve."*

Connor's neck tensed with dread. He waited, immobile, for her to continue.

"While Quinn will survive its depths, you cannot bring Murdoc or Sophia with you," the goddess added.

He lifted his chin in a silent challenge. "I assume you have a good reason why."

"Murdoc will die," she explained.

Connor swallowed hard.

"His body repels magic. I witnessed as much myself, when my own bogs nearly suffocated him—and that was with me reining them in as best I could. Should he step foot in the labyrinth, it will bleed him dry."

With a frustrated sigh, Connor shook his head. Murdoc wasn't going to like that one bit. "And Sophia?"

"Undead as she is, her mere presence would tempt the creatures from the shadows. She would draw every demon in those tunnels to you, and you would be swarmed."

"Damn it," he muttered.

"A hidden door in the mountain will let you into the labyrinth," the goddess continued. *"Once inside, you must not lose your way. These tunnels were not made by man, and many have lost themselves in the endless hallways."*

Lost in thought—mainly with all the ways this could go terribly wrong—he scratched at the stubble along his jaw. "I'll figure something out."

"Be careful," she warned. *"Many strong men have died to hide this treasure from the world, and many of the dead no doubt hoard it for themselves. You are strong—stronger than any mortal I've ever known—but strength alone will never be enough to conquer the worst parts of your soul. Strength alone does not make a man worthy."*

The words resonated in Connor's core. He stood there, staring a goddess in the face with an undead king floating somewhere behind him, and the weight of what she had said grew heavier with each passing second.

"Tell me—" She grimaced, and though her hand briefly pressed against her chest, she continued. *"Tell me what you think of us. The remaining gods."*

"You're the only one I've met," he pointed out.

"And yet, I've told you so much about us. You are a smart man, and therefore you must have drawn several conclusions thus far." She lifted her head and studied his face. *"Surely, you've at least wondered what it would be like to join us."*

The Wraith King scoffed. *Obviously.*

Connor glared over his shoulder. Despite the empty air behind him, the ghoul huffed in annoyance at the silent command to stop talking.

The slow slither of vines sliding over wet rock ate into the silent air, and Connor frowned as he returned his attention to the goddess. Her head had already dispersed into the thousands of vines that composed her body, and her torso unraveled before his eyes. The glittering green Soulsprite keeping her alive peeked briefly through her unraveling chest, casting a bright glow across the leaves decaying on the floor, before it was swallowed by the snaking vines.

"My magic comes from the past." The Antiquity's weakening voice echoed through the air. *"But I have high hopes for your future, my champion. I see power you have not yet dreamed of. I see potential few could realize. And in you, I see a mortal who could become so much more."*

Another riddle, but this one made more sense than the others.

In unison, the vines along the wall stilled. A sudden silence overtook the space, and it hung heavy on the air. Try as she might, the Antiquity couldn't hide how quickly she was fading, and he suspected she had precious little time left.

Even with his mission to free the dragons, he had to help her.

But her final words weighed heaviest on him as he unwove the tendrils of her riddle. It seemed that he wasn't the only one who had contemplated immortality since meeting her.

This goddess had a plan for him. Whatever she had in store, it would require sacrifice—and, he suspected, quite a lot of blood.

CHAPTER EIGHTEEN

MURDOC

"You're upset, Sophia."

Murdoc watched his future wife as she sat on their borrowed bed in Freymoor. The door still sat ajar, and Dahlia's fading steps echoed down the hall as the fallen princess led Quinn Starling to another bedroom suite.

Probably.

He was a betting man, and he figured the odds were good that those two would rein in their hatred enough not to kill each other.

Sophia, however, simply stared at the floor, lost in thought. Even when he said her name, she seemed to barely register his voice.

With a heavy sigh, he closed the door to ensure they weren't overheard. The latch clicked, and he paused with his palm on the wooden entrance as he sifted through what he could possibly say to lift her spirits.

"My father used to tell me that we can't fight what is," he said softly. "That we can only accept it and make a choice from there."

"I'm not in the mood for this," she snapped.

The first words she had spoken since they landed. Despite the barbed irritation in her tone, he smiled with relief that he had at least gotten her to talk.

It was progress.

"I can see that," he admitted. "But let me finish."

She grumbled and rubbed her eyes in annoyance.

He crossed toward her, his boots hitting the wooden floorboards with pronounced thumps despite his best attempts to walk quietly. He kneeled on the mattress behind her and set his hands on her shoulders, just as he had done back in the forest outside Oakenglen while Connor was being augmented.

Under his touch, she relaxed. Only slightly, perhaps, but he felt it all the same.

"You're scared," he said quietly.

"I am *not*—"

"You are," he interrupted. "And you're perfectly justified in that fear."

She swallowed hard but didn't reply.

"You're scared," he repeated as he gently squeezed her shoulders. "But this time, you're not alone."

At first, she didn't move. She didn't speak, and she barely even breathed. He was certain she would push his hands away and make some snippy remark about needing sleep. He braced himself against the inevitable.

Instead, she reached for his hand and gently squeezed back.

Murdoc wrapped his burly arms around her and held her in silence. His nose pressed against her hair, and the sultry scent of vanilla and cinnamon swarmed his senses.

Nothing would happen to her. He would see to that himself. If anyone threatened her, he would kill—and die—for this woman.

QUINN

With Dahlia at her side, Quinn walked through the halls of Freymoor in silence.

Dahlia Donahue had yet to speak a single word to her. She watched the fallen princess through the corner of her eye, studying each of the woman's steps across the well-worn stone floor. Nobility didn't lead guests to their rooms, and Quinn could only guess that Dahlia had agreed to do so in order to make a point.

They were being watched—Quinn most of all.

The last time they'd spoken, their conversation had ended on painfully sour notes. Back then, Quinn had still been blind to her father's true cruelty.

She hadn't known who he really was.

She had defended him, in a way, and she now had much to atone for.

"Your room is there." Dahlia gestured vaguely at a door up ahead and, without a moment's pause, turned on her heel to head back down the corridor.

Quinn sighed. Now or never.

"Wait," she said.

The fallen princess glared at her over one shoulder, lips pursed in irritation, and her eyes narrowed with the silent demand that Quinn explain herself.

"Would you indulge me in a midnight stroll?"

"So that you can study the hallways and learn our corridors?" Dahlia scoffed. "I think not."

Quinn shook her head. "I just want to talk."

Dahlia's eyebrows furrowed in confusion, and she quickly glanced Quinn over, as though looking for the grift. "Very well. Follow me."

Without waiting for Quinn to join her, Dahlia set off down the corridor. It took only a moment for Quinn to match the noblewoman's pace, and for a time, they walked in silence.

There was so much to say, and yet the words simply wouldn't come.

Ahead, the corridor forked, and Dahlia wordlessly led the way to the right—away from the bedroom suites. In this endless warren of hallways, she could only imagine what treasures had been stowed for safekeeping from her and her family.

From Teagan Starling, who she now realized had tried on so many occasions to conquer this place for himself.

Together, they strode down a wide passage lined with flickering sconces. Windows dotted one wall, their glass glowing blue with the moonlight. A dimly lit meadow stretched out beyond the windowpanes, and the thick forests of the Blood Bogs towered above the grass. Wherever they were, it certainly wasn't in the city itself.

This place seemed familiar, but in this labyrinth of walkways and rooms, she couldn't say for certain.

"If I recall, you said you wanted to talk," Dahlia said flatly. "If not, I'm perfectly capable of walking the hallways in silence without you."

Like always, Dahlia was taunting her. This time, however, it didn't dig under her skin like it had before.

Instead of rising to the bait, Quinn chuckled. "That's fair."

The fallen princess frowned. "What exactly did you want to discuss?"

"I'm not sure if it will be much of a discussion," Quinn admitted. "It's more of an apology. The last time I was here—hell, all the times before—I was wrong about Freymoor. About my father. About you."

Dahlia flinched in surprise, and she paused midstride to study Quinn's face. Looking for the lie, no doubt.

Quinn let the woman have a few moments of silence to process what she had said. While she waited for the fallen princess to continue, she strode down the corridor in the direction Dahlia had led them. Within moments, the noblewoman matched her pace in a silent march.

Listening.

Alert.

And, most likely, *very* confused.

"You were right," Quinn continued. "You were right not to trust the Lightseers. The Starlings." She paused, and a heavy weight settled on her heart. "Or me."

A quiet breath escaped the noblewoman beside her as they walked in perfect stride with each other.

Quinn took a deep breath to steady herself. "Princess, I am truly sorry for everything I have done to you and your home."

Princess.

The word carried weight. Respect. Though Dahlia should have been Queen, she had never been granted a formal coronation, and Quinn settled for the next best thing in the hopes Dahlia would see it as the olive branch she had intended it to be.

In the past, Quinn had always used the fallen royal's insulting new title, given to the Donahue family by King Henry after he had conquered their home. Once, Dahlia Donahue had been a princess—but under Henry's rule, she and her family had been demoted to mere barons of the land they had once ruled. Every time someone addressed her as Lady Donahue instead of

Princess Dahlia, it was an insulting reminder that her kingdom had been dissolved, and that nothing but the castle and her people's pride remained. Quinn had done this intentionally for most of her life, rubbing salt in the wound because she had believed, for all those years, that traitors should be punished.

To call Dahlia a princess was a shift in tone that spoke volumes of her newfound respect for Freymoor and its people—and it was a change Dahlia seemed to notice.

The woman's eyebrows shot up her forehead, and her eyes widened with surprise. She stared dead ahead of them, as though this were all too baffling and bewildering to be real, and Quinn once more walked in silence to give the noblewoman time to process what she was hearing.

As the seconds passed, Dahlia's surprise became a chilling glare, and she clasped her hands in front of her as she lifted her chin in defiance. "I don't know what trick you're playing, Quinn Starling, but I'm not so easily fooled."

The icy words stung more than Quinn had imagined was possible, but truthfully, she hadn't expected to be forgiven.

"That's fair," she said softly. "You've spent your life looking for the lie. It must be hard for you to believe that someone who used to hate you might realize they were wrong for doing so, much less that they would apologize. But I was, Dahlia—and I am."

First, she had used the woman's proper title—and now, she had spoken Dahlia's name without a twinge of disgust in her voice.

Tonight was evidently a night of firsts.

Their silent march resumed, and as the minutes passed by without a word spoken between them, Quinn gave up hope that the conversation would continue. Instead, she enjoyed the soft blue moonlight filtering through the stone-lined corridor, and she studied the occasional portrait hung on the wall. Men and women draped in stunning blue robes with white fur lining stared out at her with cold, stern expressions.

"Thank you, Quinn," Dahlia eventually said. "That means more than you know."

The words pierced the air, and it was Quinn's turn to look at the woman in surprise. It was the first time the noblewoman had spoken her name without disdain dripping from every word.

Instead of responding—which risked shattering their fragile truce—she smiled.

"You've changed," Dahlia said, and a soft chuckle of disbelief followed.

"A lot has changed," Quinn admitted. "But yes, I've changed along with it."

"It suits you."

Quinn smiled in thanks but, ultimately, didn't reply.

"Whatever happened to spark this change in you..." Dahlia's voice trailed off, and she sighed. "It must have hurt deeply."

A knot formed in Quinn's throat, and she coughed once to clear it.

"I know what this feels like," the princess continued. "The void. The emptiness. That bitter, hollow ache."

Quinn let out a shaky breath. "I suspected as much."

"It gets better," Dahlia promised. "This time you're in—this is the descent. Every woman descends at least once in her life. She walks into the darkness, into the unknown, and she must strip herself of her old life before she can become something new. This is what the goddesses have done, and it is what we must also do to become better. To grow."

The knot in Quinn's throat tightened, and this time she didn't fight it. She let the pain sit there, splintering, as she listened.

"In that space between the old and new, there is nothing," Dahlia continued. "It's a frightening place, but it's not to be feared. It's the necessary quiet. It is our own winter, and it's a crucial time where thoughts incubate and seeds take root deep within us. Without this time, those seeds can never truly grow." The Princess of Freymoor took a deep and steadying breath before shifting her attention to the Starling woman walking beside her. "You are in your winter, Quinn, but I promise you will emerge from it stronger than you were before."

Impulsively, Quinn set her palm on the hilt of the sword strapped at her waist. In times like these, her Firesword *Aurora* had always soothed her. Instead of that familiar leather handle, however, the cold hilt of the unnamed weapon Connor had given her felt foreign in her grip.

Her jaw tensed, and she let out a slow breath to steady her pulse even as her thoughts raced.

"Thank you," she eventually said.

In Quinn's periphery, Dahlia lifted one hand. Her palm hovered in the air, as if uncertain whether she should set it on Quinn's arm, but ultimately Dahlia cleared her throat and clasped her hands together once more.

"I told you I saw everything in the mists," the princess said. "But I lied. I saw the apparitions that plagued you in the fog, but not whatever you saw in the Star Pool. Whatever vision you experienced, it snared you. Connor almost lost you to it."

"That it did," Quinn admitted.

"Moreover, he almost lost to you," Dahlia added. "I wonder which of you would win, if it came down to such a gruesome thing?"

"I don't want to find out."

"Nor do I," the princess confessed.

"What was it?" Quinn asked. "The Star Pool. It shows you the other side, doesn't it? Everyone else spoke to the dead, but not me. I still can't understand what I saw."

"Hmm." Dahlia pursed her lips in thought and sat with the question for several moments. "For starters, whatever you saw is personal. You don't have to divulge that to anyone, and in fact, it's best if you don't."

Oops. It was a bit late for that.

"But no, it's not a window into Death's domain," Dahlia continued. "It shows you that which you want most but believe you can never have. It dangles more than desire in front of you—it teases you with the impossible, all in an attempt to trick you into touching the water. The pool is a creature, same as you or me, though it comes from Death's lands. If you fall in, it eats you."

"Then those bones—"

"Its victims," Dahlia confirmed. "And its trophies."

Quinn wrinkled her nose in disgust.

"I know," the princess admitted with a grimace. "But it guards the bogs, and I have little choice but to let it exist."

Dahlia hesitated, and for a few seconds, she merely rubbed her hands absently together as she stared at the stone floor. "I mean no disrespect with what I'm about to say, Quinn, but you must understand that you would have failed the Star Pool's test if not for Connor. He did right by you."

"I know," Quin said softly.

That little fact only added to the mystery of the water's allure.

"What is it, then?" Dahlia asked. "What is it you want, but could never have?"

Quinn sat with the question as she pieced the clues together. Connor had seen the family he could never bring back. Murdoc had seen the brothers-in-arms who would never forgive him. Sophia had seen the family who had never accepted her, and whom she had murdered to survive.

But Quinn was a Starling, and her family had the wealth and power to acquire nearly anything they wanted. Even now, she owned several secret vaults across Saldia filled with gold, reagents, and weapons as a failsafe she had never intended to use.

The only thing that had ever eluded her was the truth—of what she truly was. Of why her father had claimed she was the child Death gave back. Of why her brother thought she was a bastard. Of why her body could sustain magic differently than any of Tove's other clients.

Quinn Starling was unique in some perverse way, but no one seemed to know *why*.

"You should get some rest," Dahlia said gently.

With a jolt, Quinn snapped out of her daze to find herself standing once again in front of the door to her suite. She groaned and rubbed her eyes, disappointed in herself for losing track of not just time, but of where Dahlia had been leading her.

It was strange, to already trust this woman who had once wished she would die.

Dahlia turned the knob, and the door swung gently open. Moonlight streamed through a window, and silk curtains shimmered in the pale blue glow.

The princess leaned one shoulder against the doorframe and studied Quinn's face. "You should know this is the first conversation we've had that didn't leave me wanting to kill you."

As she stepped over the threshold, Quinn laughed. "I feel the same."

"You should know you've done something few have done before," the princess added with a slight smile.

"And what's that?"

Dahlia Donahue watched her in the seconds that followed, but she ultimately bowed her head in a subtle sign of respect. "You proved me wrong."

With that, the Princess of Freymoor shut the bedroom door and left Quinn standing in the middle of a moonlit suite. Her boots sank into the plush carpet beneath her feet, and she crossed her arms as she sifted through everything she had learned on that fateful stroll.

Tonight, Quinn and Dahlia had begun to mend the chasm between them. It wasn't a true alliance—not yet—but it had the potential to become something more. For now, that was enough. Dahlia had also given her the clues she needed to unravel this mystery her father had set in motion.

And whatever she had seen in the Star Pool was the key to unlocking it *all.*

CHAPTER NINETEEN

CONNOR

In the early morning hours of an overcast day, Connor stood by the lone window in one of Dahlia's war rooms. Lost in thought as he was, he had barely slept, and Quinn helped him assemble everyone at first light.

Though they were squirreled away in the withered gray forests outside Freymoor, he was still surprised to see so many rooms above ground. They must've been deeper in the Blood Bogs than he had realized, and the shriveling leaves on each towering tree made him all the more aware of their limited timeline. If he didn't return the Antiquity's Soulsprite soon, the Oakenglen soldiers occupying Freymoor might get a little too adventurous and find bits of the bogs they were never meant to see.

Behind him, his team simmered on everything he had told them of his meeting with the Antiquity. The Wraith King hovered nearby, surveying the others with the air of a general inspecting his troops. Connor turned his back on the window as he gave the others time to process the news.

It was a lot to take in, and he wouldn't rush them.

He had already shared the highlights with Nocturne as he had waited for the others to arrive, and the dragon had gone off to hunt in the dying forests while he debated their options.

In the warmth of the war room, Dahlia and Quinn sat side by side, and not a single barbed insult had been thrown thus far. Sophia paced along the carpet, while Murdoc sat with his fingers woven together and his eyes glazed over in thought. Duncan wouldn't be able to join them for several hours, but Connor hadn't wanted to wait.

Of everything he and the goddess had discussed, he had only withheld one thing.

You didn't tell them about her plans for you, the Wraith King said haughtily.

Dahlia's ear twitched, and she raised one eyebrow as her gaze shifted to Connor. He growled softly under his breath and shot the undead man a sidelong glare, but the ghoul only chuckled.

"Ass," Connor muttered.

THIS DETOUR COMPLICATES OUR JOURNEY, Nocturne abruptly said through their connection.

I know, Connor replied. *It's not an easy decision.*

IT IS NOT, the dragon agreed. LET ME KNOW WHAT YOU ALL DECIDE. IF WE MUST TRAVEL FIRST TO KIRKWALL, I WILL UNDERSTAND.

Though Nocturne had agreed to a delay, there was a heaviness to the dragon's words. Much had been left unspoken, and the regal creature's grief had permeated every word.

Connor had to come up with a compromise—but he wasn't sure how.

"We expected this." Murdoc broke the silence first. "Or something like it, at least. That's why we came here first."

Connor nodded. "Exactly. The issue isn't where we're going, but rather how we can get all of this done in a limited time frame."

Sophia's gaze shifted to him, as though she could taste the lie. Of everyone in this room, only she had heard the full story of his time in Kirkwall—and why he had left.

He cleared his throat and scanned the others, not wanting to get into that right now.

"The Antiquity has precious little time," Dahlia said with a heavy sigh. "Rescuing the dragons from the Lightseers is critical, and I understand the risk they face. But without the Antiquity—" Dahlia swallowed hard. "If we lose her, then Freymoor loses everything."

Connor crossed his arms over his chest and let out a steadying breath. "I understand."

Quinn set her elbows on the table and shifted her attention toward him. "How long is the flight to Kirkwall?"

"If we travel at night, it's a two-day journey," Connor answered. "That's Nocturne's best guess, anyway."

"What if he leaves you three in Kirkwall?" Quinn gestured to Connor, Murdoc, and Sophia. "Then, he and I can scout the dragon island to see what we can uncover."

Connor shook his head. "I need Nocturne's help on the mountain."

"Right." Quinn tensed, and her brows furrowed in unspoken worry.

No one had any idea of what they would find in that mountain—or if they would even be able to get out.

"As much as I hate the idea of going back, Kirkwall is the best place to start." Connor sighed in resignation. "It has the fewest unknowns and the highest chance of success."

"Fewest unknowns?" Sophia scoffed. "All we know is there's a powerful artifact hidden in a mountain—that's probably full of the undead, by the way—and that the Soulsprite is in the castle."

"I said *fewest* unknowns," he replied. "Compare the two. In Kirkwall, we have clues and a place to start. The dragon island, however, is locked down, surrounded by the enemy, and from what little I know of it, nigh impossible to infiltrate."

"Trust me, I've tried," Quinn added.

With a groan of frustration, Sophia set her hands on her head and resumed her pacing.

"Hold on, Captain," Murdoc interjected. "Kirkwall's no moonlit stroll. I visited three summers ago, and the island was crawling with soldiers. The Oakenglen knights might not be occupying the city anymore, but the new king doesn't take kindly to any whiff of dissent. They're as murder-happy as ever."

Connor's jaw tensed, but he didn't reply.

"Not to mention, you're a tad recognizable," Murdoc added with a gesture toward Connor's broad shoulders. "Your wanted poster is in every pub across the continent."

"That's true," Dahlia conceded.

"Then we'll need glamours." Connor shrugged. "Easy enough. Even though you can't take one, no one has seen your face. Not even Zander. You should be safe to walk around."

"Ah." Murdoc cleared his throat awkwardly and sat back in his chair. "Provided the brotherhood doesn't spot me, then yes. I'll be fine."

"Brotherhood?" Dahlia asked.

"The Blackguards," Connor explained. He frowned as he studied his friend's face. "They have a presence there?"

"A massive one." The former Blackguard rubbed his eyes.

"Why were you there, then?" Sophia asked with narrowed eyes.

"If we're being honest, I was hoping one would run me through in a duel."

"Delightful," Connor muttered.

Murdoc shrugged. "It was a different time, before I met the woman that changed me."

Sophia huffed, but even as she turned her back on the man, Connor noticed the barest hint of a smile at the edge of her lips.

Don't be fools, the Wraith King snapped. *You're overcomplicating this. For the Fates' sake, Magnuson, you have a Fates-damned dragon. Wear that insipid mask of yours, storm the castle, and take the orb for yourself.*

"No," he and Dahlia said in unison.

The ghoul grumbled obscenities while everyone else watched them in silent confusion. Since Connor didn't want to plant the idea in anyone else's mind, he dismissed his team's unspoken questions with a quick gesture.

"Not important," he promised.

"We probably don't want to know," Murdoc said with a wry smile.

"You don't." Connor paused, and he used the momentary lull to redirect the conversation. "As for Kirkwall, we will have to lay low. We can't draw attention to ourselves, and that might be a challenge in such a well-lit kingdom."

Back when he was a boy smuggling goods through the roads with his father, the worst part of every night was passing under the street lamps. The tension. The fear. The palpable terror that choked him with every passing second, as he had wondered if this was how they would be found.

Damn it. Of all the cities in Saldia, the Antiquity's Soulsprite had to be in *Kirkwall.*

"Well-lit?" Murdoc frowned with confusion. "Captain, how long has it been since you were on the island?"

"A while," he admitted. "Why?"

"It's a ghost town at night," the former Blackguard answered. "Shadows, curfews, and military patrols. Whatever it was when you were there, it's a different place than you remember."

Though that worked in their favor, his stomach still churned as he thought of what horrors must've happened there after he had left.

"Once in Kirkwall, we scout the city," he continued, piecing the plan together bit by bit. "We find a way into the castle, and we find the Soulsprite. With an object that powerful, I'm sure it can't be hard to find. While we're scouting the castle, Nocturne will scour the mountain for the hidden door the Antiquity mentioned."

"Easy," Sophia said dryly.

Quinn leaned back in her chair and crossed her arms. "I have glamours. You all can use those instead of brewing new ones. It'll save us time."

"Save yours," Dahlia interjected. "You never know when you'll need one. I have plenty to share, and we rarely need them anymore."

"Thank you," Connor said.

"Of course."

"It's settled, then." He clapped his hands together once as he sifted through what lay ahead of them. "Our plan was to split up at this point, but I think that's unwise. It's better to divide and conquer. Sophia and Murdoc, you try to infiltrate the castle while Quinn, Nocturne, and I head into the mountain. It's all about timing and how quickly we can move. The biggest unknowns right now are what we will find and what obstacles might slow us down."

"I don't think I should go," Quinn said softly.

He frowned and met her eye. "Care to elaborate?"

"It's all about timing," she answered, echoing his words from moments before. "Infiltrating Lunestone is a deadly task in and of itself, and it's not something we should all do together. There's too much risk. Once inside, it's even worse. The hidden passages are narrow, and the more of us there are, the greater the risk is we're discovered."

Connor sat with that, but to his utter irritation, he couldn't fault her logic.

"With my father—" She hesitated, and her gaze drifted briefly to the table before her. With a rough cough, she cleared her throat and continued. "With my father gone and Zander missing, the Regents will convene regularly to run things in their stead. That means I can listen in. There are areas of the fortress that even my passages can't access, which might further complicate things. We need to know who is guarding the island, what their schedules are, how to deceive them, how to get in, and—most importantly—how to get out."

He sighed, knowing full well she was right, even though he hated to admit it. The last place he wanted to send her was back into the den of vipers that might kill her at the first opportunity.

To say Quinn and her family had a complicated dynamic was one hell of an understatement.

"One of us needs to go ahead and collect information," she finished. "I know the castle better than anyone here. I should go."

Connor scratched at the stubble on his chin as he hunted for a better alternative, but there wasn't one.

Damn it.

"Alright," he conceded. "Go, but Quinn, you *cannot* engage. You will be outnumbered, and you can't risk being overrun. You're only there to get information. Agreed?"

She nodded. Their eyes met, and he wondered if she could see through his logic to his genuine concern for her safety.

Even when she was perfectly capable of handling herself in a dangerous situation, a man wanted to keep his woman safe—and yet he was sending her into one of the most dangerous fortifications in Saldia.

It felt wrong.

This is why I said you couldn't bed your general, the ghoul snapped. *Your generals must be willing to die for you, and you cannot hesitate to send them into dangerous—*

"Stop talking," Connor interrupted. He shot a withering glare at the ghoul beside him, and the undead king merely shook his head in disdain.

Dahlia raised her hands to her mouth, but she wasn't able to hide the thin smile spreading across her face.

"There's only six days left of spring," Connor continued, mostly to redirect the conversation away from his sex life. "I want to be back here by the eighth day of summer. That should be enough time for us to do what needs to be done in Kirkwall."

"I'm not sure that timing works." Quinn adjusted in her seat and tapped one delicate finger against her cheek. "It's quite a trek to Lunestone from here."

"We can make a detour." Connor gestured over his shoulder to the forest beyond the war room. "It's not much of a flight from here. It might add a day to our trip, but we can make it work."

"Not likely," Sophia interjected. "Lunestone is on a walled island in the heart of Everdale Lake. We can't exactly fly overhead and land on a rampart."

"We don't have to," Quinn said. "The safehouse in Arkcaster that can serve as our meeting point. It's a little cottage deep in the woods outside the crossroads leading to Lunestone's main bridge. I keep it fully stocked and recharge the charms around the perimeter every few years to keep people away. It's the perfect spot."

"Wouldn't the Lightseers know about that?" Murdoc asked.

The Starling warrior shook her head. "This one is off record. Over the years, I've developed secret identities and vaults of resources that no one else knows of." She paused and swallowed hard. "Just in case."

A moment of silence followed as everyone shifted their attention away from Quinn, and only Connor watched the flash of grief cross her face.

"It was a smart move," he said.

Without looking up, she nodded in thanks.

Murdoc rubbed his hands together. "It sounds like we have a plan."

"It seems so," Connor said. "Quinn, if we haven't met you by the fifteenth day of summer, come back here."

"You'll make it back," she said.

"Damn right we will." He smirked. "Still, it's best to have a failsafe in place."

Quinn shrugged. "That's fair."

"If you're not at the safehouse by then, we'll come find you," he added. "Give us whatever you've got—maps, routes, intel. It'll help us if the worst happens."

"I will," she promised.

"One more thing," Dahlia interjected.

All eyes shifted toward the fallen princess, who gestured to the black armor he wore. "This is unlike anything I've seen before. I don't know how much of it you have in Slaybourne, but if you would like, I can have my craftsmen make more. I confess I would like some for my soldiers, if you don't mind me tweaking the recipe to my own devices."

For a moment, Connor debated whether or not that was a good idea. "I don't have an army to wear it."

"Yet," she corrected.

He raised one eyebrow in silent surprise, and for a moment, he didn't respond. While he was loathe to share ancient secrets, this would benefit them both. His allies were worth protecting.

"Alright," he eventually said.

The Wraith King bristled. *You are seriously going to give something that valuable to this little—*

"Choose your next words carefully," Dahlia interjected, and her sharp blue eyes darted toward the ghoul. "And may I remind you that you're no longer the King of Slaybourne. This is not your choice to make."

Connor grinned. Well played.

"I understand your hesitation," Connor told the wraith. "You're not used to having allies, but we can trust Dahlia. Even with something as precious as this."

Fine. With a few more muttered obscenities, the specter dismissed the entire situation with a flick of his bony wrist.

"This armor," Dahlia interjected. "What materials do you need?"

"It's quite a list," he admitted. "We can copy the design for you before we leave."

"This is quite the challenge, Captain," Murdoc said. "Finding long-lost ancient magic on a massive island? There's a forest covering half of it that not even the locals can tame. It's nigh impossible."

"That's never stopped us before," Connor reminded the man.

Murdoc sat with that for a second, and he eventually shrugged as something clicked for him. "That's true."

"We leave at nightfall," Connor announced. "Pack your things and get what sleep you can before we head out. It's going to be a long night."

Everyone stood, but he caught Quinn's eye as the others left. He subtly nodded to the empty space at the window beside him in a silent request for her to join him. Though she narrowed her eyes in playful suspicion, she ultimately indulged him.

"I know you want answers," he said quietly as she leaned against the windowpanes. "The nightmares are getting worse."

Her smile fell, and instead of answering, she glared out the window.

"The mission—and your safety—come first," he reminded her. "All your family has done is lie and manipulate you. Even without your father there, I doubt you'll get them to do anything else."

"Perhaps," she admitted.

"Be careful," he warned. "That's all I want."

"I know."

A heavy tension settled between them, however, and much was left unsaid. He had felt this before, back in his days of drifting along the southern road. Over his years of living off the forest, hunting for work when he could find it, he had accidentally charmed a farmer's daughter enough that she had asked him to stay. To build a home with her. A family. But she had deserved better than any life he could give her back then, and that night had ended with her bitter tears.

If he said anything else, he would only make things worse.

Instead, he squeezed Quinn's shoulder, knowing full well that she could handle herself. She wasn't fragile, and she didn't need him to protect her.

At the end of the day, a general had to make sacrifices for the greater good—even if it came at a great cost to themselves.

CHAPTER TWENTY

ISABELLA

At the edge of the darkness, where sunlight faded into the catacombs beneath Slaybourne, Isabella paused.

The steady drip of water echoed through the long, dark corridor that led toward the dungeons. The floor sloped downward at a steep angle, and she had no clue as to how deep into the mountains these paths went.

But she had a plan, and she was determined to see it through.

This wild idea had consumed her for ages, but now she felt the first flicker of doubt as to whether or not this was a good one. Her grip on the basket of freshly baked bread in her hands tightened, and her little heart raced with fear.

By the Fates, how she hated the dark.

Sconces placed along the walls raged with crackling fire, and their light cast a harsh orange glow across the uneven floor. That sparse light gave her the courage to walk onward.

Her mother hated this, of course. For Isabella to help Wesley in the twice-daily delivering of food to the prisoners meant she might be in harm's way, but she had incessantly tugged at her mother's skirts until the woman had finally given in.

It seemed so silly. With dozens of Connor's undead guards surrounding them, there was nothing to worry about. The soldiers all marched in unison, half of them carrying baskets instead of spears, and each stared straight ahead as they flanked her and Wesley.

Careful to go unnoticed, she tilted her head slowly to get a better view of the closest one. Torn muscle hung limply from the stained yellow bones in his forearm. The black fibers of a ripped tunic shook with each of his heavy steps, and a rusted metal chest plate rattled against his exposed ribs.

Isabella suppressed a shudder.

"Are you sure you want to be down here?" Wesley's voice echoed across the dank walls as they turned a corner. "You're only eleven. You shouldn't see this."

Irritated, she frowned. He had asked her this question seven times already, though he had phrased each attempt a little differently.

Her reply had always been the same.

In answer, she shot him another sidelong glare. No words. No sounds. Not even a groan of exasperation.

Just fierce, quiet annoyance.

For several weeks now, silence had been her answer to every question, no matter who asked it.

Her big brother sighed and shook his head. "Connor won't like this."

At the thought of their adopted brother's anger, a sharp pang hit her little chest. It wasn't fear, exactly, but it wasn't far off. She didn't know what to call this emotion. It had only come to her a few times in her life, and she didn't know how to describe it. She swallowed hard and straightened her back to brace herself for whatever might come, because she had to do this.

She had to see these Lightseers for herself.

"Fine," he said when it was clear she wasn't going to run back into the sunshine. "But there are rules. Stay close to me. Don't go near the bars. Stay near the undead soldiers at all times. Understood?"

She nodded.

He grumbled something under his breath, but their conversation died, and they continued in a stony silence.

After a while, more dark tunnels branched off of their main route. The soldiers led them straight, never veering from the primary path, and it didn't take long for her to feel utterly lost in the towering corridors. To pass the time—and to distract herself from the fluttering terror building in her chest—Isabella studied the divots on each wall in an attempt to build some sort of map in her head.

It didn't work.

The path curved again, and this time, she spotted a door down the hall. Eight undead soldiers flanked it, none of them moving an inch even as the clank of rusted metal and the thuds of heavy boots neared.

Seconds before they reached the door, one of the soldiers standing guard reached for the handle. Isabella flinched in surprise, but he didn't seem to notice. The undead man slid a heavy iron key into the lock, and an inhuman groan echoed through the air. Green light flashed across the door, and Isabella squinted as the mountain's magic hurt her eyes. Somewhere beyond the corridor, the harsh scrape of metal on metal clicked and clacked against the rocky walls. A steady hum built, ever louder with each passing second, until the guards finally opened the doors.

A rush of cold air hit her. It made her shiver, and even when the bright light finally faded, she kept her eyes closed longer than necessary. It wasn't until the march of soldiers' boots resumed that she took a settling breath and dared to look inside.

The ceiling towered overhead, almost too high to see, and a long cobblestone path cut through the stacked prison cells on either wall. Men and women in each jail turned to look at the door as it opened, and none of them spoke.

A pedestal with a shattered sword sat in the middle of the center aisle, but Isabella didn't know who the blade had belonged to or why it was there. She was more aware of the dozens of undead guards standing along the rows of metal bars, and she wondered just how many soldiers Connor really had.

A creature's roar, distant and somber, echoed in the otherwise dead-silent space.

Eyes wide with fear, Isabella swallowed hard and forced her feet forward. Her rigid body froze with the weight of all these Lightseers' gazes on her, and her body didn't want to obey.

Though she wanted to know what these people were like, her body wanted her to run.

"Remember the rules," Wesley said under his breath.

She gave him a curt nod, and his voice spurred enough of her stubborn resolve to get her through the prison door.

The undead soldiers around her dispersed, and each skeletal man passed dried meats and cheeses through the bars. Some Lightseers eagerly grabbed what they were offered, while others let it fall to the floor. Whatever choice the prisoners made, the undead army didn't falter or slow for even a moment.

As she and Wesley reached their first cell, her brother patted her on the shoulder and offered her a thin smile. That shook a bit of the terror from her bones, and she managed to walk steadily toward the first prisoner.

She had given their family hell to be allowed down here, but at least he wouldn't make her feel bad for being afraid now that she was seeing all of this for herself.

Breathlessly, she passed a thin loaf of bread through the bars of the first prisoner's cell, and she couldn't resist staring at the first male Lightseer she had ever seen up close. He watched her from the back of his jail with his arms crossed and his eyes narrowed. He leaned against the cold wall with dried blood still in his beard, and he didn't say a word.

For a second, she held the loaf above the other food he'd allowed to fall to the ground. She met his eye, and though another ribbon of fear snaked down her spine, she held his gaze.

Neither of them moved.

With a soft sigh, she let the bread drop onto the dried meats and hunk of cheese the undead guards had already brought this man. She felt the Lightseer's eyes on her back as she walked to the next cell, and she tried to ignore it as she trailed behind her brother.

The next few soldiers she passed all allowed the food to fall to the floor, and each of them watched her with strange, intense expressions she had never seen before. Wesley led her down the full length of cells with Isabella still in tow, and he doubled back to feed the others on the opposite side of the aisle.

With every new Lightseer she saw, she felt more and more confused. She didn't know what to make of them, these warriors who had attacked her home, and with each of them that she passed, she felt a growing tension deep in her core.

It wasn't fear, which surprised her. For so long, fear was all she had felt, and she didn't know what else this sensation could be.

The feeling fizzled within her as she puzzled over it. It took a few minutes of silently passing bread through cell bars to finally recognize it, as it had been years since she had felt this emotion, and she had never felt it this intensely.

It was anger.

No—it was *rage*.

"Keep up," Wesley chided.

Isabella ignored him. She had been taught to always respect adults, to listen to them, but lately she had begun to wonder if any of them knew what they were doing. The more adults she met, the more she had begun to wonder if they were every bit as lost and scared as she was.

They were just better at hiding it.

With a deep scowl, Isabella glared down at the floor, lost in her thoughts as she approached the last cell in this row. A woman's slender hands slipped through the metal bars, and this Lightseer rested her elbows on an iron beam.

Wesley stepped out of the woman's reach, but Isabella wasn't fast enough.

As Isabella reached for one of the last loaves of bread from her basket, strong hands grabbed her. An arm wound around her neck, and her back slammed against the bars. The basket fell. She saw stars. Her head spun. Her ears rang. The world went blurry, and for a second, she forgot where she was.

That had *hurt.*

Isabella lost her balance. Her feet slipped out from under her, and the Lightseer's grip tightened to keep her from wriggling free.

Voices overlapped each other as men and women alike shouted. The yelling deafened Isabella, and she struggled to breathe as the woman's arm pressed against her throat. Undead soldiers rushed toward the woman, seconds from ripping her to shreds. In response, the Lightseer dug her fingers into Isabella's jaw—as if she had every intention of taking Isabella with her.

The woman's nails drew blood. It burned, and Isabella winced. This hurt almost as much as when that horrible slaver had cut her face with that little kitchen knife she had used to mark their path through the woods.

But this time, Connor wouldn't be able to save her. This time, he was too far away to help.

"Order them to stop!" her captor shouted at Wesley. "Or this brat dies!"

Isabella bristled at the insult.

She didn't like this lady at *all.*

Wesley gritted his teeth but held up one hand in a silent order for the undead soldiers to stop. All of them paused midstride, some with their hands still outstretched toward the woman's arm, but not one of them moved after the order had been given to wait.

The loud din of soldiers yelling slowly faded as the Lightseers watched. Though Isabella tried to look at them, to figure out if they agreed with what this woman had done, spots shimmered along the edge of her vision. She couldn't see anything except for the small stretch of center aisle right in front of her.

Yet again, the soldier's grip on her throat tightened a little more. Trapped, Isabella clawed weakly at the woman's hands and gulped for air.

"Let her go," Wesley demanded, his voice a low growl.

"Release the child, Halifax." The voice came from a neighboring cell, and the man's tone was angry and firm. "That's an order!"

Isabella's heart skittered with fear at the furious edge to his words. It reminded her of all the times she and Fiona had pushed their father's patience too far.

"An order?" The woman behind her—Halifax, apparently, though Isabella thought it seemed like an odd name for a lady—laughed dryly. "Captain, all you've done since we were thrown down here is mope and lecture us. I don't give a damn about your orders."

"Stand down," the captain said again, unfazed. "We don't hurt the innocent. Release that child, or I will thrash you to death once we get out of here."

In a neighboring cell, someone gasped quietly with fear.

"What makes you think they'll let us out of here?" Halifax's grip on Isabella's neck only tightened, and Isabella coughed violently from the pressure on her throat. "I'm tired of rotting away in the darkness, and I won't die a coward like you. A hostage is the only way out of here. You know that, but you're not man enough to act on it. If you won't save us, I will."

Footsteps brushed against the floor, and somewhere out of sight, metal rattled.

"This is your last chance, Halifax," the man said. This time, his voice dripped with deadly warning, and his tone made Isabella's blood run cold with terror. He spoke with all the anger and rage Isabella felt—maybe more.

"Pathetic." Halifax's voice shook with fury. "Quinn got to you, didn't she? You're every bit the sniveling, cowardly, heartless traitor that she is!"

Isabella bristled. "Don't you dare talk about Miss Quinn that way!"

They were the first words she'd spoken in ages. She hadn't meant to say anything. She hadn't meant to get involved.

It just *happened.*

A surreal silence followed, and Wesley gaped at her in surprise. Her voice had sounded far more assertive than she felt, and in a strange way, that gave her a bit of confidence. Instead of scratching weakly at the woman's skin, Isabella's nails dug into the warrior's hands around her throat. She glared up at the Lightseer who had dared insult such a kind lady, ready to defend the person who had healed her face when no one else could.

Quinn had done right by them. Blaze, too.

"You don't get it, do you?" she asked the woman. Again, the words had come on their own, and this time she let them flow. "You don't understand why he put you down here."

Halifax's nose creased with disdain, and she glared down at Isabella through gaps in the metal bars. "Enlighten me, little girl."

"Because you did something bad!" she shouted, frustrated that this woman couldn't understand something so painfully simple. "You attacked our home! We never did anything to you, but you tried to hurt us! Aren't Lightseers supposed to protect people?"

Lightseers. After everything they had done to Connor, the word tasted foul in her mouth, like soap after a swear word.

These people weren't heroes. Now that she could see them up close, she realized they weren't any better than those slavers in the woods. Even though Connor had spared this woman's life, this soldier refused to see him for what he truly was—Isabella's hero.

At her furious words, the arm around her throat loosened its grip ever so slightly. Isabella wriggled again, and though she could at least breathe now, she still couldn't break free.

Tears burned at the corners of her eyes, and a knot formed in her throat. For weeks, she hadn't been able to speak. The anger had been brewing, deep down in her soul, but she hadn't been able to name the rage for what it was. She hadn't known how to express it or what to say.

Now, however, she couldn't stop the words from bubbling out of her.

"I used to pray you would come," she confessed. Unable to hold back her tears any longer, she started to cry, and her face flushed with her grief. "When I heard the blightwolves howl at night, I prayed you would come save us. I dreamed you would come and kill them all because I was so scared they would eat us. So scared that Papa wouldn't come back after—"

Her throat closed, and she sobbed. More hot tears poured down her cheek, and though she sniffled, her furious little scowl only deepened.

"But you never came!" she screamed. "All those stories I heard of how good you are were lies. The legends and songs I've heard lied about you, too. Year after year, I waited to be saved, and *none* of you came!"

Her tiny voice echoed, louder than it had ever been, and for once she didn't care who heard it. Everyone watched her, even the undead, and the horrifying weight of so many eyes rooted her to the floor.

With the endless flood of tears staining her face, she desperately wanted to close her mouth and make someone else the center of attention. Her body trembled with the kind of profound hatred she had never known before today, and she didn't want anyone to see her shake. It had been building up, day by day, since they had left Lindow. She just hadn't realized it until now.

Whatever had happened to her big sister had shattered their family. The day Kenzie disappeared was the first day she had seen her father cry, and it was the first time she had seen him afraid. Her father had always been her anchor. With him close by, nothing could hurt her.

But if he was frightened, then nothing could keep Isabella safe.

All this time, her hatred had been boiling below the surface. Festering. Sizzling. Waiting until she wasn't strong enough to hold it back any longer.

Now, it controlled her, and the anger burned as hot as her tears.

"I—I—" Behind her, Halifax stuttered. "You don't understand. We're trying to protect you. All those legends about the Lightseers are true."

"No, they're not," Isabella said flatly. "Heroes don't let mean, scary men kidnap a little girl and cut her face."

Isabella impulsively ran her finger over the long silver scar on her cheek—the one she could feel, but not see.

It lingered. It always would.

The woman behind her stuttered again. "We would have helped if we had known what was happening."

"I don't believe you." Isabella's voice broke, and she wasn't sure if anyone could understand her anymore.

She didn't care.

She looked at Wesley, only to find his brows pinched. He looked as devastated as she felt. None of them had talked about the slaver attack since Connor had brought them here, but the nightmares lingered. As she met his gaze, her brother closed his eyes and sniffled.

Back in the Ancient Woods as those horrible people had pushed her through the mud, her mother had refused to say where the slavers were taking them. Even now, Isabella still didn't know what the slavers were going to do to her and her family, so the truth had to be so much worse than she could imagine.

"Those people tried to kill us," she said flatly, too angry to cry anymore. "If we had relied on all of you to save us, we would be dead."

Behind her, Halifax gasped quietly. The arm around Isabella's neck released her, and the woman instead set her hand gently on Isabella's shoulder. With a little wriggling, she could've easily slipped out of the soldier's grip, but she didn't.

"Life isn't that simple, little one," the woman behind her said gently. "We can't save everyone."

"I don't think you tried." Isabella's head snapped around, and she glared up at the hardened soldier standing on the other side of the iron bars. The woman flinched, and after a tense moment, she looked briefly down at the ground.

No adult had ever looked at Isabella that way before.

With *shame.*

Halifax recovered, and the woman took a deep breath as she finally let go of Isabella altogether. "This man who's keeping you here—he's not the good guy, child. He's a killer."

Isabella took a step away from the warrior's prison. "And you're not?"

The Lightseer winced, as though that had hurt far more than Isabella realized, but it didn't matter. This woman deserved to feel this guilt, and Isabella had no intention of saving her from it.

"Connor is the only one who ever protected us," Isabella explained. "He's the only one who has ever cared about us. He saved us from the soldiers in the field, and he saved us again from the slavers. He killed them all."

The more she spoke, the more her words ran together, so fast that even Isabella couldn't always hear herself. She didn't really care. This wasn't about them. It was about her. She had to get this out or it would stew and rot and simmer once again into something worse than she was feeling now.

A tense silence settled on the air, but Isabella never looked away from the woman in the cell. She wanted to know if this soldier had seen the bloodshed. If she knew what Connor had done to save them.

Isabella wanted to watch this stranger realize that Connor had succeeded where the Lightseers had failed.

"This Connor fellow of yours is a criminal." Halifax's jaw tensed, and she glared down at the pile of bread and cheese between them. "He killed our Master General, child. He's dangerous. You don't know any better because you haven't seen him fight."

"I *have* seen him fight," Isabella corrected.

At that, the woman's head snapped up. Halifax furrowed her brows in suspicion, but it was the truth.

"I saw those bodies in the field," Isabella continued, her voice eerily calm after all that screaming. She didn't have much energy left, and as her white-hot rage slowly burned away, a cold numbness was filling the void her anger left behind. "Mama tried to cover my eyes, but I watched him slit throats. I watched men choke on their own blood. I listened as those horrible men begged for their lives. I watched them die, one by one. I saw the blightwolves eat what was left of them after he was done, and I thought—*good.* I'm glad they're dead. I'm glad they can't hurt me again. I watched Connor slice men in half, and I was *happy.* I always thought it was wrong, evil even, to be happy that someone else got hurt, but I don't care. It's the truth, and I don't know what to think anymore."

Isabella sniffled again, and her eyes glossed over as she remembered the screams. Even now, the hairs on her arms stood on end as she relived the horror.

Absently, she wiped her nose on her sleeve. She tried to clear her throat, like she had heard Connor do time and time again whenever he changed the subject, but it came out as a weak little whimper.

"I wanted to hurt them back," she confessed, ashamed of it even though she still spent her nights dreaming of new ways to make them feel the pain they had caused her. "But I couldn't. I'm too small. Nobody could hurt them except for Connor. He protects us in ways you all never did, and I will always love him for that. He's family. He's my brother, and you should *never* say nasty things about someone that good."

She glared up at the soldier who had pinned her to the cell bars. Halifax calmly held her gaze, and she couldn't tell what the woman was thinking.

Darn it. It was at times like these that Isabella wished she knew a swear word mean enough for these people. "Don't you dare say those things again, you—you—you *jerk!*"

Halifax didn't flinch, so that word clearly wasn't mean enough. The silence settled on them all again, and Isabella huffed in frustration.

Just like she had with the slavers, Isabella wanted these Lightseers to feel the same hurt they had caused to everyone who lived in Slaybourne. Maybe it was wrong, but she wanted them to hurt like she did.

But they were too big.

Too strong.

Though Isabella's bottom lip trembled with the threat of more tears, she did her best to stand up straight. She tried to mimic the way Quinn always arched her back when she and Connor were talking about something serious.

She waited for more words to come, but the silence stretched on longer than it should have. Her well of anger had gone dry, and now a familiar numbness was taking root in her chest.

This time, though, she tried to fight it. For the first time in ages, she had finally felt something besides fear, and she didn't want to let it slip away again.

All her life, Isabella had waited for someone to help her family. Fear had eaten away at her, bit by bit, year by year, and she was done being afraid.

Isabella Finn was done with waiting to be saved.

Furious, she bent down and picked up the loaf of bread she had meant to give the woman who had grabbed her. Refusing to even look the Lightseer in the eye, she set it between the bars and waited for the stupid lady to take it.

The bread left her palm. Without looking back to find out where it had gone, she left her mostly empty breadbasket on the ground and stormed off toward the exit.

Though she felt the weight of eyes on the back of her head, she refused to look at even one more of these so-called heroes. She had gotten what she'd come for, and they no longer seemed interesting.

With the anger finally gone, a deep and painful sadness soaked into her bones, and it made her little heart hurt.

"Listen closely, all of you!" Wesley's voice carried through the prison block, loud and clear, far more confident than hers had been. "Despite what some of you think, you really are down here to cool off. We don't want you to spend your lives down here any more than you do." He paused, and in the suspended silence that followed, she heard his boots scuff across the cobblestone toward her. "If it were up to me, though, I'd let you rot. You bastards deserve every second you spend down here in the dark."

Bastards.

Darn it. That would've been a far better insult. Isabella would have to remember that word for next time.

Silhouettes moved through the edges of her vision, but she didn't look up. With so many of Connor's soldiers nearby, she was safe—as long as she didn't go near the bars again.

Ahead of her, the doors to the hallway opened, and she stomped out into the cold stone tunnel that led up to the sunshine. The march of heavy boots mingled with the squeak of rusty hinges as the undead joined her in the corridor.

A hand rested on her shoulder, and she yelped in surprise. Though her heart skittered with a brief pang of shock, it was just Wesley. He smiled warmly, and though he was a good two feet taller than her, he did his best to wrap his arm around her shoulders.

They walked for a time in silence with the undead guards marching all around them, and her mind raced with everything she had said. It was more than she'd spoken in months, and her mother would feel a bit slighted after all the cold silences at the dinner table.

Oh well. Couldn't be changed now.

"Tell me something." Her brother's voice broke their silent march. "Do you want to learn how to fight?"

Hmm.

It seemed like a silly thing for a little girl to want, but deep down, she already knew the answer.

When she didn't reply, Wesley shrugged. "It's just an idea. Connor's stays don't last long, so I doubt we'll get much time one-on-one to practice with him. But who knows? Maybe he can get us started with our training. You know, give us some exercises to practice. We can run through them each afternoon."

"We can?" she asked quietly. "Together?"

He gently squeezed her shoulder and, with a broad grin, nodded. "Together."

A little smile twitched at the corner of her mouth, and a flush of warmth hummed through her chest. It chased away the sadness.

Her mother wouldn't want her to hold a sword, much less fight with one, but maybe that didn't matter. Maybe it was okay to disappoint people, just a little, even if she loved them.

Isabella bit her lip, hesitating at the thought of how this might upset the parents she adored, but she ultimately nodded.

"Good." Wesley took a deep breath and patted her back. "I'll get everything sorted. Leave it to me, Izzy."

Izzy.

He hadn't called her that in years. It brought back memories of running through glowing green grasses. Of giggling as he held a branch to his chest and acted out melodramatic deaths. Of a time when the world wasn't so scary, and when things made a little more sense.

Her smile widened.

When those horrible slavers had dragged her from her bed, she had felt helpless—and, by the Fates, she never wanted to feel that way again.

CHAPTER TWENTY-ONE

CONNOR

In the dead of night, somewhere deep in the forests that were too close to Lunestone for his comfort, Connor slid off Nocturne's back. His boots made no sound as he landed in the patchy grass, and he peered through gaps in the thick green canopy as a cloud covered Saldia's twin moons.

He didn't like this plan, but it was the best they had.

In his periphery, someone slid down after him. A moonbeam cast a brief blue glow across Quinn's face, and he took one more tense glance through the empty trees before returning his attention to her.

She stood behind him, those sharp hazel eyes already watching him. For a moment, only the wind made any sound as the midnight hour drenched the old oaks in darkness. He studied her tense expression, wishing there was another way to do this without sending her right into the viper's den.

We don't have time for this nonsense, the Wraith King chided. *She's fully capable of dismounting a dragon on her own. If this is the general you chose, that means—*

"Stop talking," Connor said under his breath.

The ghoul huffed in frustration, but the dead man thankfully remained silent.

"Be careful," he warned her again, mostly because he didn't know what else to say.

Her intense gaze softened. "You, too."

He nodded once in answer.

"This will work," she promised in a hushed tone. "You'll see."

Without pausing to think it through, he grabbed her bicep and kissed her roughly. It served where words failed, and for now, it would be enough.

"It had better," he said, his mouth barely an inch from hers. "Or I'll burn down the castle to get you out."

A thin smile tugged on her lips, but she didn't reply. With one final look back to Nocturne towering above them, she slipped into the shadows between the trees. In seconds, even the flash of her fiery red hair was swallowed by the darkness, and Quinn Starling was gone.

QUINN

As midnight bled into the early hours before dawn, Quinn knelt behind a bramble thicket and studied the cluster of trees before her. Six aspens huddled among a forest of oaks and firs, their trunks so close together they had practically fused into one giant tree. The aspens' golden leaves shivered in the night, a stark contrast to their bone-white bark even in the darkness.

The one and only hidden route into Lunestone, hidden on the coast and disguised as nothing more than another beautiful part of the forest. It wasn't meant to be used except in emergencies, and only her family knew where it was.

Or so she had always been told. Quinn didn't know what to believe anymore.

In the distance, the crash and rush of distant waves hit a nearby cliff. The familiar chorus of the massive lake's water over the rocks reminded her of home, of Lunestone, and of all the empty promises that awaited her if she ever returned.

No one could know she had come home, not even after she left.

With a settling breath, she waited and listened for the squeak of a hidden hinge, or for the telltale clink of Lightseer armor. A soft breeze stirred the leaves above her as the trees bloomed in the last days of spring, and a few of the thicker branches groaned as the ancient oaks around her gently swayed.

Aside from the forest, nothing moved.

She was alone.

Silently, she sprinted across the small clearing between the brambles and the cluster of trees. When she reached it, she pressed her shoulder against the rough bark and listened one last time for company.

Only the crash of distant waves and the subtle creak of shifting branches filled the otherwise still air.

With quick, fluid movements, she pressed her hands against the many knots covering the cluster of trees. The spring-loaded knob that opened the door was somewhere among these gnarled bumps, hidden with the same skill as the lines of the door itself so that no unsuspecting visitors to the woods could accidentally lean against it.

Her palms scraped against the bark as she hunted for it, and within seconds, one of them gave.

The thin layer of bark on the nearest tree popped open, and a hiss of stale air escaped. Her nose creased with disgust as a putrid rush of rotting meat rolled past, and she suppressed a burst of nausea at the intense stench.

But she didn't have time to hesitate. If anyone saw her enter, she would never leave.

Quinn braced herself against the odors of the tunnel and opened the door wide enough to slip inside. The hinges made the barest squeak, a sign that they had been neglected for far longer than she had realized, and it struck her as odd for her father to let such an important task go undone.

At the thought of Teagan Starling, her heart skipped a few beats. As the door latched behind her, she suppressed the thought of the man who had taught her, all those years ago, how to safely traverse the hundreds of traps littering this tunnel.

She gritted her teeth and shoved her grief deep into the darkest parts of her soul. This was the time for action, not memory.

Outside, the breeze and waves had kept her company. In here, however, there was nothing.

Just silence.

Painful, heavy silence, and a darkness so thick that even she couldn't see.

Her ears rang in the absence of any sound at all. With the door to the outside world once more sealed, the putrid stench of rotting bones engulfed her even stronger than before. It was worse than she had anticipated, and as the overbearing tang of death even settled on her tongue. Her eyes watered as the scent burrowed into her enhanced nose, and she swallowed in an attempt to quell the urge to vomit.

It worked—mostly. Acid burned against her back molars, and she braced herself for what lay ahead.

Every Master General throughout history had set his own traps in this secret tunnel, and her father had boasted privately of how he had made the cruelest ones of all.

It was time to move. She couldn't delay any longer.

Quinn stretched her fingers wide, and a flickering orange flame snapped to life on command. It hovered above her palm and cast an amber glow across a stone stairway that led into the depths of the lakeside cliffs.

On the very edge of the shadows, a skull stared up at her, suspended in the darkness. A spike protruded from one eye socket. The bony jaw was open, frozen in its final moment of surprise as the skeleton stared back at the exit it had almost reached in time.

Others apparently knew how to enter this secret passage, but few knew how to leave.

Death was not new to Quinn Starling, but she hadn't expected to see one so soon after entering. She hadn't even made it down the stairs yet, and this meant the Starling tunnel had been compromised. Others knew of its existence, and this complicated everything.

She had no idea what awaited her on the long, slow trek through this passage. For all she knew, living things had made their way down here, too.

With a deep breath—one she instantly regretted after the putrid air swirled through her lungs and burned her throat—she lifted her firelight to stare deeper into the darkness. She tensed as she mentally ran through the four dozen traps her father had set in the steep stairwell.

He had drilled her on each of them, after all, and allowed more than one to stab clean through her as punishment for anything less than perfection.

Quinn took the first step carefully, and her boot rested along the edge of the wall. Her firelight cast a dim glow over the thin outline of the secret trigger in the stone, and her gaze shifted to the narrow hole on the opposite wall. Something metallic glinted deep in the darkness, visible for only a second before the shadows swallowed it again.

But spikes were only one of the ways someone could die in this corridor, and it would take half a day or more to evade them all.

Quinn had a long night ahead of her.

Her boot hit the second step, though she twisted her foot at a slight angle to avoid the shallow button set into the lip of the stair. This time, she fought the urge to glance upward at the massive boulder, held in place by iron chains, that would've smashed in her skull if she had made even one mistake.

As she slowly made her way down the stairs, she noticed the corners of a leather pack poking out from under a rock the size of a man's head. The flattened bag lay on the step below the speared intruder. Only shattered glass remained of the potions he had carried.

She shook her head in disappointment. Those might've come in handy, if she had been able to decipher the contents.

What a waste.

On the tenth step, Quinn paused. Her foot hovered over the perfectly smooth stone, and her breath quickened with a flutter of instinctive fear. Her eyes darted toward the imperceptible slit in the stone wall to her left, but she couldn't even see the thin metal spike that had nearly pierced her heart on that first trip through the tunnel.

Her father had grabbed her shirt at the last second and yanked her backward. The spear had sliced a gouge across her stomach instead of instantly killing her, and in the blink of an eye, her father had saved her life.

I can't have you dying, little one, he had said. *I have big plans for you.*

At the time, she had felt so proud to think she was worthy of his plans. As a child, that had been her sign that she was important, no matter what Zander said, and that her father needed her.

Only now did she realize he had momentarily lowered his guard and shown her a glimpse behind the carefully maintained mask he always wore. That day, all those years ago, she had seen a glimpse of who he truly was.

He was dead, but his memory still haunted her. She would never truly be rid of him, nor would she ever truly escape the influence he'd had over her life. For better or worse, he had carved her into who she was today, and his mark would always linger.

As she pressed onward, the thought sent a shiver down her spine.

CHAPTER TWENTY-TWO

ZANDER

Zander felt the arena long before he saw it.

The buzz of magic older than time. The vibrations running underground. The raw power of natural enchantments that mankind had yet to harness.

The moment had come.

The Kurultai.

Even as the grumbles and growls of two hundred blightwolves permeated the air, he studied the circle of spellgust stones before him. They stabbed at the air like a titan's teeth, each glimmering green rock three times taller than him and ten times as wide. Beyond the spellgust pillars, the massive circle of ore encased a slab of black stone as wide and long as any mansion, its silky black sheen distorted and warped by the semi-transparent walls of priceless ore that surrounded it.

Zander stood at the entrance—the only way in, and the only way out. A throbbing green glow stretched and faded across the massive arena as the spellgust sizzled with a steady rhythm that reminded him of a heartbeat.

Deep in his core, something primal and unrefined wanted to claim this circle of spellgust stones for himself. To cage it. To kill all who dared walk across the polished black stone that served as this sacred structure's floor. To make it irrevocably *his*.

This place wasn't just a holy site. It was a mecca. A place of rebirth. Of charging. Of renewal.

Even open to the elements, this felt like a palace worthy of only the finest king—or, better yet, emperor.

Beside him, shadows pooled across the patchy grass where the Ancient Woods surrendered the soil to this monolith. Seconds later, the Feral King emerged from the darkness. Moonlight glinted off the metallic fur covering the ghoulish creature's mutated body as it, too, stared at the circle of jagged spellgust stones.

You feel it, the beast observed. *The magic that thrives here. The sense of home.*

How interesting. Apparently, even the Feral King had succumbed to the allure of this place. Even it was enraptured by its raw and primal beauty.

Silhouettes darted through Zander's periphery, and his gaze followed the movements. His wolves surrounded the holy site, and though they kept their distance, more and more filtered out of the woods with each passing minute. They crowded on the outskirts, none of them daring to tread closer.

The contenders.

Short cliffs towered over even the circle of spellgust, the topmost ledge of which offered the perfect view into the arena. More silhouettes stood on the edge, high above, their bodies backlit by the moon as they blocked out the twinkling starlight behind them.

The audience.

Spectators and contenders alike watched him. Two hundred wolves became a thousand, and the steadily growing snarls in the crowd of unholy beasts built to a rumble louder than any thunder. Thousands of massive paws, each the size of his face, shook the earth as they paced the uneven ground.

They think you are weak. The Feral King circled him, its eyes locked on the wolves watching from the high ground. *They think you are prey.*

"Then they're fools," he said calmly.

Unfazed.

Unafraid.

This is the birthplace of the Blightwolves, the beast continued, as though Zander hadn't spoken. *And it is therefore where each new alpha must prove himself worthy of the title.*

"I already know I'm worthy." Zander's gaze drifted toward the hulking monstrosity standing beside him.

Daring it to disagree.

Its lips twisted into a wicked sneer—though, on its mutated face, he couldn't quite tell if it was entertained or disgusted.

Either way, it didn't matter.

Perhaps, it eventually conceded. *But that still does not guarantee you will survive. Savagery. Ruthlessness. Power. Brawn. Bloodlust. Those are the traits an alpha must have to win the respect of every wolf here.*

"Easy," Zander lied.

Powerful as he was, this still would be the hardest thing he'd ever done. If he used magic, they would attack as a hoard—but that was only if they could see it. While he couldn't use flame, he still had his Strongman augmentation and his enhanced senses, not to mention the powers he had obtained from the Feral King thus far.

Even without access to his fire or his lightning, he'd been raised to rely on his fists and his sword to win any fight. No matter what entered the ring behind him, he could never show a shred of weakness. He would have to stand tall, even if he barely had the strength to keep his feet on the ground.

To walk out of here alive, the most horrifying creatures in Saldia had to learn to fear him.

No, they had to be *terrified* of him.

This would hurt. It would push him to the brink and possibly beyond, but he would walk out of that arena as the most powerful man in Saldia. This was the first of three rites he would have to perform to return home.

The Kurultai, to tame the wolves.

The formal challenge, to tame his father.

The Final Rite, to tame the Lightseers.

Not long ago, the thought of facing his father in a true, formal duel would have sent a cold pang of dread clear to his stomach. He would've vomited from the terror of facing the man who had broken nearly all of his bones, at some point in his life, and whom he had been raised to revere as a god.

But not now. Whether it was the Feral King or the Ancient Woods, something had carved the fear clean out of him.

"Our one law is the law of respect," a wolf said from behind him. It was a voice that had grown all too familiar in these weeks he'd spent wandering through the Ancient Woods.

Zander looked casually over one shoulder as Alistair stood behind him, the only wolf brave enough to approach the holy circle of spellgust stones. The black wolf studied him with that unwavering, steely gaze.

Equally unfazed.

Equally unafraid.

"Those who enter the arena do not fear you," Alistair continued. "Therefore, they do not respect you. As the challenger, you will walk in first. Many will follow you in, but only one living soul may leave."

A fight to the death—and every wolf here wanted him dead.

With one last glance across Alistair's face, he nodded back toward the arena. "Will I see you in there?"

"Most likely."

"Pity." Zander shrugged and began his short trek to the arena's one and only entrance. "I'd hate to have to kill my favorite."

When he took his first step into the arena, the snarls around the ring grew to yips and howls. The overwhelming wall of sound shook the very air as each wolf joined in. The ground quaked harder with the weight of their raw brawn as they nipped and slammed into each other. Through the semi-transparent green spellgust, he caught glimpses of a writhing mass of metallic fur and bone-white teeth.

Wild. Barbaric. Untamed without an alpha to rein them in.

All too soon, they would learn their place.

In the back of his head, a rough and heady growl reverberated through his skull as the Feral King lost itself in the combined packs' bloodlust. Just as it had when he'd faced Farkas, the ghoulish creature circled the edge of the ring, keeping to the outskirts as it scanned the area around them.

Already prepared for the first challenger to start the show.

When Zander reached the center of the ring, he turned to face the lone gap in the wall of towering spellgust stones. He unbuckled the scabbard around his waist and drew *Valor* from the sheath before tossing it aside. The stitched leather slid across the polished black stone beneath his feet and out of tripping range.

He needed to be light. Nimble. Unencumbered by anything.

The howling grew closer. Several wolves standing on the cliffs above the arena leapt off the edge and clambered down the rock toward him. The rumble beneath his feet grew louder as a few of the larger wolves among the pack raced toward the opening, each vying to enter first.

The sight would've terrified him, once.

Now, however, he felt nothing but anticipation for the inevitable bloodbath—and the hunger to win.

Within the throng of wolves and teeth, one broke free. It towered over the others, pushing its way through those at the front of the pack, and its cold blue eyes snared him. It darted toward the gap in the spellgust walls of the arena, and a sickly green glow shimmered over the white fur along its body.

Though Zander itched to summon *Valor's* enchanted fire, he resisted the impulse. One wrong move, and the match would end in the wolves' favor.

The first contender charged into the arena without a moment's pause. There was no hesitation. Not even a flicker of doubt. It barreled toward him like an arrow, closing the distance in seconds.

But he was ready.

It leapt into the air before him, claws extended and teeth bared, ready to rip out his throat. The second its feet left the ground, however, he rolled out of range. It was a quick motion, almost too fast to register, and its head pivoted toward him in that fleeting moment while it was suspended in the air. Seconds from landing, its muscles tensed, ready to pivot.

He struck first.

With his free hand, he tugged a dagger loose from his boot and hurled it at the soft spot behind its ear—the same weak point he'd used to kill Farkas.

It was dead before it hit the ground.

The blightwolf's corpse thudded against the polished black stone with a dagger's hilt protruding from its skull. A steady trickle of blood seeped from the wound, and Zander ripped his blade free with an easy tug. With a quick wipe across his already ruined shirt, he slipped it back in its sheath.

Briefly, the air stilled, and the wolves went silent. He glared at the opening, at the pulsating mass of blightwolves that paced by the entrance, waiting for their turn.

"Next," he said calmly.

The Feral King's raspy laughter filled his head like a morbid thunder, but he didn't have time to even glance toward the ghoulish creature as it circled the edge of the ring.

A second contender broke free of the others and charged into the arena. Its silver paws crossed the threshold, that metallic fur eerily similar to Farkas' own coat, though this one was much smaller than the former alpha. This new challenger raced toward him, faster than the first, and it closed the considerable gap between them in seconds.

With his dormant Firesword raised to the challenge, Zander waited. Any number of wolves might challenge him tonight, and he had to conserve his energy. Each blow had to be timed perfectly.

This blightwolf didn't jump at him, nor did it change course. Foolish and headstrong, perhaps, or saving up its energy for a last-second adjustment.

As his grip tightened on the hilt of his sword, he assumed it would be the latter and adjusted his stance for it.

Sure enough, at the last second, it darted left. He met the challenge with a swing at its throat, and it lifted its head with barely enough time to save its neck. His sword nicked its hide, and a trail of blood stained the wolf's silver fur. It contorted its body to avoid his second swing, and this time, *Valor* cut harmlessly through the air.

How annoying.

The wolf skidded across the sleek stone and recovered just as quickly as he did. Once more, it charged.

This time, he stood rooted in place with his weight shifted to the balls of his feet, ready to slip out of the way the moment it got too close. With his trap set, he lifted his chin to expose his neck.

Bait he knew the wolf would take.

It reached him and lunged. Those gleaming white teeth snapped closed, and he came within inches of its death grip.

But it still missed him, and now its own neck was exposed.

As it slid by, it clawed at him. Its deep nails carved into his shoulder in the same moment that he drove *Valor* clear into its throat. The beast's own momentum did the worst damage, carrying it across his Firesword, and the enchanted weapon ripped open the creature's neck with the ease of a fingernail cutting through the wax seal on a letter.

His shoulder ached, albeit briefly, and he glanced down at the bleeding claw marks as his failed attacker bled out onto the black stone arena. It would take several minutes for the thing to die, so he took a few moments to recover from this battle before he entered the next one.

Everything about tonight had to be carefully calculated, and he couldn't waste an ounce of energy.

Once he had recovered, he calmly walked toward the dying wolf as it drowned in its own blood. Without a shred of emotion, he drove his blade into the soft spot behind its ear.

Not for mercy or to give the thing a quick death, but for efficiency. Only one wolf could enter at a time, after all, and he had a long night ahead of him.

"Next," he said again.

Without a moment's pause, a blightwolf with fur the color of charcoal darted in. The wolf peered back over its shoulder, almost like it was gloating at someone in the gathered throng of contenders, and the movement exposed the weak spot behind its ear.

How utterly stupid.

Zander pulled his dagger from its sheath and hurled it at the wolf as it returned its attention to him, but it was too late.

His dagger hit, and the blightwolf collapsed onto the ground.

Next, the Feral King said this time, and the wolves beyond the arena's entrance perked up. Their ears pivoted toward a spot behind Zander, no doubt where the Feral King had circled in its pacing, and the next contender charged across the threshold.

Zander pulled a second dagger from his boot and launched it at the newcomer. Just as he had when taking out that horned owl, he didn't even pause to aim. This power, this magic, these enhancements he'd received as the Feralblade—he'd already begun relying on them.

With this much power now at his beck and call, he would've been a fool not to.

His second dagger burrowed right into the blightwolf's skull, and its eyes rolled back into its head as it collapsed onto the contender who'd entered right before it.

Death after death. Kill after kill. One by one, they drenched him in their blood. It rolled down his brow like beads of sweat, and the honey-sweet stench of death consumed him.

It was going to be a long night.

Next.

Another entered the arena. Brown, this time, or maybe black. He couldn't tell. In the rush of glinting fur and sharp teeth, the blightwolves started to blur together. They funneled in, one after the other, to their deaths.

They were wasting his army on this *drivel.*

On this useless ploy to prove wolves were somehow superior, when they weren't—and never would be. He growled with irritation as it quickly built to anger. To resentment.

This new contender barreled toward him, and he barely registered its path. His instinct already warned him where it would go, how it would dart to the left at the last moment, same as so many others had before it.

This bored him.

On cue, the blightwolf darted left, and *Valor* was perfectly positioned to spear it through the neck. His sword cut through the air, then skin.

The wolf yelped.

He drew his Firesword and landed one last devastating blow.

The wolf went still.

Next.

The rage grew. The impatience for these creatures who wouldn't stop challenging him. The resentment that he had yet to make it home. The disgust at what must have become of Lunestone and the continent with him occupied and that infernal peasant running amok with the Wraith King. The hatred for the Wraithblade, who had driven him here to a primordial hellscape filled with stupid beasts that needed to be murdered to learn respect.

Zander saw red, whether from the rage or the wolves' blood dripping down his face, and even his movements blurred together in the ceaseless onslaught. Without rest, his muscles ached, but he couldn't stop moving. He couldn't stop dodging, or one of them would rip out his throat. He couldn't hold back his strength or pull a single punch, since every wolf in the ring was fresh and strong, even as his energy wavered.

Though his back strained and his legs ached for even a second's moment to rest, he pushed through.

A Starling always persevered.

Another wolf entered.

This time, something deep within him snapped. It was subtle, more of a fracture than a break, but it popped all the same.

The wolf approached, and he was ready.

Hack.

Slash.

Blood.

Snap.

Next.

Zander settled into a macabre rhythm of swishing steel and whimpering wolves as he sliced them open, again and again.

Hack.

Slash.

Blood.

Snap.

Next.

With each blow, with each death, that fracturing *something* in his soul cracked a little more. It took his coherent thought along with it, and a deep rumbling replaced the steady cadence of his thoughts.

Instinct drove him, and in the heady daze of facing nonstop opponents, he leaned into its every command to survive.

He would win, he could feel it in his bones, and this powerful instinct would take him there.

Eventually, he lost count of how many fools had darted through the entrance. In the end, the number didn't matter. This was as much about survival as it was about pride, and he would kill the entire population if necessary.

A waste, but one he was willing to make.

With each new contender, all of them filing in one at a time from the pacing mob of candidates just beyond the entrance, more crimson smears coated his body. A few wolves snuck in a bite or two, just a hair faster than even his enhanced reflexes, but they died like all the others.

Corpses littered the arena. Dozens. Threads of silver-blue moonlight curved along their metallic fur as he added more and more bodies to the piles.

As he wasted more and more of his best soldiers, all on their insipid little game.

His chest rumbled as he grunted with each swing, growled with each death, his snarls blending with the feral beasts that charged him. The edges of his vision faded entirely, until all he could see was the next wolf to bolt through the entrance.

Deep in his soul, that fracturing *something* finally snapped.

It shifted.

It broke—and set him *free*.

A surge of raw and rabid power bubbled up from the depths of his soul, from the well of rage that lingered, untapped, in every man's core for those moments of dire need. It was primal perfection. For his entire life, he'd experienced the best of everything, but he'd never once felt this.

This—this was pure power, in its most distilled form. It was harnessed chaos. Bridled lightning. The magic of a god, blistering through veins finally capable of wielding its might.

And he would never be without it again.

A blightwolf lunged at his throat, those white teeth a stark contrast to the jet-black fur covering its head, and this time he did the unthinkable.

He threw his Firesword aside.

The flawless steel clanged hard against the arena's polished black stone. The sharp clatter pierced the ceaseless yips and barks of the blightwolves outside the ring.

As the contender closed the final gap between it and Zander, the other wolves went blissfully silent. They could tell something had changed, and they weren't sure if they liked it.

Zander met the beast with his bare hands, and he grabbed the hulking thing's jaws. His fingers slid between its teeth. He tightened his grip, and though a searing pain shot up his arms, he twisted its head with all his might.

The motion shifted the creature's trajectory, and it hit the ground hard. With his hands still on its jaws, however, Zander sank into his stance and tugged sharply backward. Its head snapped at an unholy angle, and it whimpered—just once, and reflexively, as though he'd surprised it. He released it, and the thing slid a few more feet before it finally came to a stop.

It lay there, motionless. Its chest heaved, and it watched him with drooping eyelids, as though it were struggling to stay awake. He stalked toward it, slow and steady, his body buzzing with both the arena's magic and his own primal power.

He was Death, come to collect on the thing's life, and yet this blightwolf watched him without a shred of fear. Its gaze remained fixed on him, unafraid even as he closed the final distance between them.

Even when faced with certain, painful death, it fought. Surrender was never a choice, nor one it would've made. It didn't beg, and it didn't cower. It faced death with courage and unyielding strength.

In so many ways, blightwolves were the perfect soldiers. Superior, in some ways, even to man.

Buried somewhere under the carnal need for blood, a hazy part of him wanted to say something. To speak. To lecture this thing in the final seconds of its life, perhaps, or use its death to make a point.

But the words didn't come, and he didn't care.

He grabbed its exposed ear with one hand and its jaw with the other. With a sharp twist, he snapped its neck the wrong direction, and its body finally went limp. Its head twisted backward at an unnatural angle, its snout aimed toward its tail.

And yet, he didn't stop.

He didn't let go.

Bruised and bloody, he roared with the effort of what his primal power drove him to do. The beast's massive head gave a little more, inching beneath him and giving under his immense strength, until a sickly ripping cut through the otherwise silent night.

With one final yank, he ripped the blightwolf's head clean off.

Blood rushed over his boots from the severed trophy as he lifted it into the air. The crimson goop seeped across the black rock like a fresh river carving through the dirt. A wet clump fell out of the severed head in his hands and splattered onto the ground as he lifted it higher, but he didn't care what it was.

All he cared about was the next contender, standing at the entrance with one paw hovering over the stone.

Alistair.

His favorite wolf watched not him, but the head in Zander's hands. Alistair's gaze lingered as it debated what it would do next.

Whether or not it would enter the ring.

He wanted to ask if these idiots were done dying.

He wanted to know if they'd had enough.

Instead of words, however, all he managed to let out was a strangled war cry. It reminded him of the front lines in the battle against Henry, all those years ago—of the charging men who had galloped on their warhorses toward trembling soldiers who had never seen true bloodlust in a man's eye before.

He carelessly tossed the blightwolf's head into a pile of corpses, and it landed with a meaty splat against another fallen brother. Its blood sprayed against one of the spellgust walls of this mighty arena, and the shard of ore glowed brighter.

Magic fed off death, after all, and he had given it a feast.

Alistair's paw still hovered on the threshold—uncommitted, but close. With one last glance around the bloodstained ring, however, the wolf retreated.

And this time, it lowered its head in surrender.

One by one, the other blightwolves followed suit. Through the semi-transparent spellgust surrounding him and clear up to the cliffs overhead, every blightwolf bowed to him.

Chest heaving, Zander simply stared at them all. He didn't feel much of anything. No pride. No horror at the bloodbath around him. No disgust at the wanton waste of life.

Any emotion or thought that might've arisen was buried deep beneath the buzzing roar of his primal power—and the thrill of a well-earned victory.

He had won.

Slowly, his vision sharpened. The black shadows in his periphery faded the longer he stood in the center of the bloodstained ring, chest still heaving, still on edge for one last fool to try him.

A silhouette slipped through the corner of his eye, and in his surprise, he stiffened. It circled the arena, its shoulder against the stone, and it took a moment for him to recognize the Feral King.

It sneered, and the green glow of the spellgust stones cast an eerie emerald light across its jagged teeth.

Well done, Starling, the beast said. *You have earned our respect. You are our alpha.*

But Zander was no fool.

Tonight had won him the blightwolves, but not the Feral King. He still had to test the creature's resolve. He still needed to poke it until it revealed a weakness.

Luckily, he'd had plenty of time during their trip south to map out the perfect plan.

CHAPTER TWENTY-THREE

CONNOR

After two nights of travel, Connor finally spotted the lights of Kirkwall on the horizon.

Damn it.

For close to an hour, they had flown over nothing but water and the occasional ship floating through the smattering of islands that surrounded Kirkwall. The vague silhouettes of a few smaller boats—and, oddly, a canoe—waited on the silent beaches below.

Behind him, Sophia leaned into Murdoc's chest, the two of them propped on one of the spikes along Nocturne's back as the dragon's powerful wings propelled them forward. Sophia dozed in the former Blackguard's arms, and the man set his chin on the top of the necromancer's head while he stared at the ocean water below them.

Neither of them had seen the island, yet, and Connor took the moment to center himself for whatever awaited them there.

They are memories, the Wraith King huffed. *Do not let them own you, Magnuson.*

It was the closest thing to comfort the ghoul had ever offered him, and for a time, he didn't reply. The dead man had a point, but that didn't mean Connor had to like it.

Ahead, a mountain towered over the northern end of the island. In the darkness, the dormant volcano was a mere shadow, nothing but a monolith backlit by the waning twin moons. A vast forest stretched across the island's middle, still as thick and wild as he remembered. On the island's southern tip, thin pinpricks of light marked the city itself.

Against all odds, Connor had come home.

I KNOW THAT MOUNTAIN. Nocturne's voice echoed through Connor's head, and the regal creature angled slightly toward the pillar of stone that dominated the landscape. IT IS THE FIREBREATH. FIREBREATH MOUNTAIN.

That's right, Connor admitted, confused. *How did you know?*

Nocturne hadn't been to Saldia before his trip through the Barrens, and he had certainly never made it this far north.

The great beast growled, and in the cool spring night, the sound hit the waves like thunder. BECAUSE DRAGONS NAMED IT, AND IT IS LEGENDARY. I HAVE HEARD THE TALES OF THE FLAME SINCE I WAS A HATCHLING.

Connor's head snapped backward in surprise, and he stared again at the towering volcano. *What—*

Without warning, Nocturne banked to the north, angling them toward the mountain with all the fire and speed of a falling star. Wind whistled past Connor's face, and he raised one arm to shield his eyes from the sudden gale.

Behind him, Sophia gasped. "—what the hell—"

"—hold on!" Murdoc's voice overlapped hers in the seconds before both voices faded into the wind.

Connor kept low against the dragon's back, and the regal creature's great horns blocked some of the airflow.

Focus, he chided through their connection. *I know this is important, but we need to go to the city first.*

As they quickly approached the mountain, Nocturne didn't answer. A cloud wandered past the moons, casting filtered beams of soft blue light across the black dragon's wings, and Connor cast a wary glance down at the city far below.

If they saw a dragon, even one backlit by the moons, any hope of infiltrating the castle would be gone. Everyone in Kirkwall would be on high alert, and there would be no sneaking through the night.

This could ruin everything.

Nocturne! he snapped. *Get ahold of yourself!*

LOOK, the dragon prince demanded. LOOK AT WHAT WE ONCE WERE.

With an irritated growl, Connor peered over the dragon's head at the rapidly approaching mountain. Even as they circled the rock, slowly curving upward toward the very top, there was nothing more to see than ash-gray rock rippled with shadow. The tall lip of the dormant volcano curved out at the very edges, and a deep red glow shimmered against the interior walls of stone.

In a lightning-quick shot, they crested the volcano, and they finally saw the source of the red light. Connor stared down at a bubbling lake of lava, deep within the mountain. The boiling red ocean popped and fizzled far below, heating the air until a murky haze blurred the edges of the ancient rock.

That snuffed out Connor's annoyance. Now, he could only watch the sleeping mountain with awe.

The closer they came to its steep slopes, the more detail appeared. First, a few caves emerged from the shadows along the mountainside. They bore into the stone, too deep for the moonlight to expose what lay within.

Next, symbols carved into the rock glowed with a faint golden light. The flash of moonlight on something metal made the markings clear enough to see, but not read. They circled the mountain again, and this time, he caught the brief flash of a dragon's silhouette, carved into the stone and lined with gold. The longer he stared, the more detail he saw—all of them depictions of a time before man found this island.

THIS IS A SACRED PLACE, Nocturne growled. ONE I THOUGHT I WOULD NEVER SEE.

Connor didn't answer. Words weren't enough, not now, and he instead patted his scaly friend's neck. He let the dragon circle again, and this time the regal beast growled wistfully to himself as he studied the remnants of a fallen world.

As the minutes ticked by, Connor shifted his attention to the city at the far end of the island. The night wore on, and they only had a few more hours before dawn. They would need to make their way down to the forest and sneak over the wall before the sun rose.

At least Dahlia's glamours would give him a modicum of anonymity. If anyone in Kirkwall recognized him, he was a dead man.

Nocturne once more banked around the mountain, and the distant outline of Kirkwall Castle came into view. It loomed over the trees, staring out at the domain no king had conquered, and lights glimmered from within its many windows. Of the city lights, the castle glowed brightest of all.

It didn't surprise him that the king had a god's magic, whether that be a Simmering Soul or a Soulsprite. If anything, he felt like an idiot for not figuring it out on his own. When Connor was a boy, the former king had hosted festivals to showcase the royal family's extensive collection of artifacts from across the continent and beyond. Those had been magical days where King Luc's treasures sat out on display, protected by enchanted glass and more guards than a ten-year-old could count.

The castle's vaults were legendary, and he had no idea how he could possibly steal an artifact without being detected.

With King Luc gone, however, it made sense for the newly appointed king to hoard the riches for himself.

Arlo Hunt—a man King Henry had appointed to power, and the man who had ordered the death of Connor's entire family.

There was only one person Connor hated more than Arlo Hunt, and that was Bryan Clark. Bryan had betrayed Connor's family and left them to die at Hunt's whim. As far as Connor was concerned, Bryan and Arlo carried the blame for the horror that drove him into the Ancient Woods.

Kirkwall was the link to both of those men. If he saw either of them here, he didn't know if he could be trusted to remember the mission.

What kind of man am I if I just move on? Wesley had asked him, all those weeks ago, when the Finns had narrowly escaped death. *What kind of man can forgive the people who did something that awful?*

Back then, it had been so easy for Connor to quote his father's wisdom. He'd told Wesley to let go of the past. To heal. He had known, even then, that avenging his family by killing those responsible would never set things right. Deep in his bones, in the depths of his core, Connor could still acknowledge that killing both Bryan and Hunt wouldn't solve a damn thing.

It still didn't soothe his fury.

If anything, being home only made the rage burn hotter.

Grief left a void that few things could fill. Revenge was an all-consuming bastard, but it chased away the pain.

And despite what he had told Wesley all those weeks ago, that broiling hatred was hard to ignore.

Come on, Nocturne, he said to his friend. *It's almost dawn.*

I KNOW. The great dragon's body inflated with a deep and mournful sigh. Without another word, the regal creature banked toward the south.

Toward Kirkwall Castle—and the long-lost home Connor had sworn to leave behind.

NOCTURNE

After several hours of crawling through the towering trees of a forest dragons had planted, Nocturne's humans were finally over the wall. Connor had infiltrated a city, and the people of Kirkwall had no idea of what chaos the man could bring.

Nocturne, meanwhile, had taken to the woods once more. Kirkwall was no place for a dragon to be seen, but the ancient redwoods offered him suitable cover.

In the last hour of darkness before the dawn, the Prince of Dragons finally had a moment to himself.

He stood at the base of Firebreath Mountain, on the edge of the tree line and still cloaked in shadow. He listened to the silence, and in the whisper and creak of an abandoned forest, he was alone. The wind rustling the late spring leaves mingled with the occasional croak of frogs, long and mournful.

Lonely, even, and tinged with a hint of grief.

With mother nature's song breathing life into a sleeping forest, he stared in silent awe at the dormant volcano's steep slopes. This mountain held the stories of his people, ancient tales that not even the sages of his homeland could remember.

These rocks, these caves, this forest. They were all a record of the age of the dragons—and of their fall.

As a hatchling, he had dreamed of seeing the Old Lands for himself.

It had seemed like an impossible dream, once, a mere story to tell the little ones, but now he stood at the foot of a fallen god's mountain.

With a weary sigh, he set his foot on the gray rock. His claws dug into the stone, and the mountain perfectly supported his weight. No crumbling pebbles. No risk of sliding.

Firm, like a good mountain should be.

He climbed the northern slope, hidden from the city by the mountain itself, and nothing but a shadow in the night to any onlooker in the forest. In minutes, he scaled half of the sleeping volcano's side. It was effortless, joyful even, and he closed his eyes to savor the air above an ocean.

A gust of salty wind rolled from the sea, carrying with it the tang of seaweed and the bite of a storm. He paused, scanning the dark horizon, looking for nothing in particular and enjoying it all the same. Waves crested in the distant sea. A smattering of small islands stretched out into the inky water, nothing but silhouettes in the distance.

And Nocturne let himself dream.

He could imagine a thousand dragons sailing on the ocean's air currents. He could see their smiles as the sky soothed their souls, while the sunlight glittered across the frothing waves like diamonds set ablaze by the sun. He imagined mothers nesting on the smaller islands, roaring at the hatchlings that buzzed through the trees, blowing smoke at each other, pretending they were flames.

This was a vibrant hive, once. Now, it was less than a memory.

His chest ached to see what had become of it in all its years of ruin.

A thin flash of moonlight cast a soft blue glow on the mountain, and Nocturne craned his long neck toward Saldia's twin moons. Only two thin slivers of pale light remained, and soon they would fade into a week of darkness.

The new moon. A time of renewal and introspection for the dragons, but a time that men ignored completely.

As he continued his climb, his darkest thoughts began to spill again from the deepest parts of his soul.

Perhaps this land of men could not be saved.

Perhaps this land of Saldia would become nothing more than ruin, much like this sacred mountain.

Time went on, in the end, and the world always forgot.

New civilizations razed and rebuilt the fallen ones. Old lessons were dismissed as legend, and history always repeated itself. How tired the Antiquity must've been, to watch old madness repeat itself with new players.

It made Nocturne think of Connor. Of the man's mission to protect Slaybourne, and of the cold reality Connor himself had yet to acknowledge. The Wraithblade wanted only to preserve his 'patch of dirt,' as the man called it, but Nocturne could taste a brewing storm that would thwart anything but war.

The headwinds signaled a shifting tide in the oceans of time, and the Fates would have their bloodshed.

A spark would ignite suffering, and this would end with unimaginable pain. In the end, there would be only rubble and ash.

The Fates kept Death very busy.

Connor Magnuson would never get the peace he so dearly wanted. His war would be a bloody one, and it might well last forever.

Perhaps the Wraithblade, like the gods, would grow tired.

Above him, a dark shadow in the mountain rock hinted at a cave, and he angled himself toward it on his rapid climb. As his head inched through the opening, he sniffed for signs of life. Though he caught the musky scent of a few spiderwebs at the back of the hollowed-out den, the other lingering trails were years old, or more. He couldn't even place what had lived here.

This beautiful hollow sat abandoned and forgotten, like everything else.

Big as he was, he had never found a Saldian cave to fit him just right. This one, however, was perfect—like it had been carved for him, all those centuries ago.

With a hearty stretch, he spread his wings wide, and the narrow claws at the tips of his wings gently brushed the roof of his little den. The muscles along his spine relaxed. A plume of smoke shot out his nose as he curled around himself, content. With his wings tucked tightly against his back, he nestled in for the night.

As he stared out over the ocean, at the line where the stars met the sea, his resolve faltered, and he let himself think once again of Storm.

Of his lost love.

Of the grief that had driven him toward Saldia in the first place.

With so many years lost in his search for her, he didn't know what could remain of his beautiful white dragon. He prayed to the long-dead god of his people that she had escaped and returned to their homeland. If the Fates had any kindness left in them, perhaps this entire quest of his had been a waste of time, and she had been waiting at home for him all these centuries.

If, of course, anything of home remained at all.

Perhaps, like this mountain, the dragonlands were nothing more than a ruin.

The thought drove the deepest stake into his heart, and he shut his eyes. Nocturne—Prince of the Dragons, King of the Nightlands, Protector of warriors and monks alike—once more buried his darkest fears into the depths of his soul, and in the shattered ruins of his people's legacy, he slept.

CHAPTER TWENTY-FOUR

CONNOR

Tense and on edge, Connor glanced at the soft pink ribbons of sunlight flirting with the horizon. The sun would rise any moment, and they needed to find an inn before that happened.

Ideally, they needed to find an innkeeper that didn't ask questions.

Connor, Sophia, and Murdoc sat crouched behind a stack of crates while the steady thud of soldiers' boots retreated down a side road. A towering warehouse to their left cast a long shadow across them, while the crates offered cover to their right.

From here, no one could see them—at least not until the city awoke. From what he recalled, the warehouse district came to life in the hours after dawn, and they didn't have much time before the first foremen unlocked the doors.

As they waited, a sleeve poking through a gap in the roughly hewn boards brushed against his arm, and the heady musk of freshly pressed leather coiled from within. The impulse to pry one open and find himself a change of clothes tempted him, but he quickly suppressed it.

He shook his head, frustrated with himself. He didn't steal, and it irritated him that he would even consider doing so. Sophia must've been rubbing off on him more than he had realized.

Slinking about in the dark, the Wraith King grumbled. *Again.*

"Quiet," Connor said under his breath.

Behind him, Murdoc chuckled. "The wife giving you trouble, Captain?"

Connor smirked, but he didn't reply.

Like a common thief, the ghoul continued, as though he hadn't heard either man speak. *This is no way for a king to behave, Magnuson.*

Instead of taking the bait, Connor peered around the wooden crates to gauge the distance between their hiding spot and the alley that would take them to the seedier part of town. A sector of the city, he noted, that hadn't been there when he was a boy.

Curious.

His mental link to Nocturne had limits, and he hadn't heard from the dragon since they'd gone over a thin stretch of unmonitored wall on the northern side, by the forest. To be safe, he had monitored the ramparts for close to an hour, costing them precious time.

But they hadn't been caught, and safe entry into the city was worth any delay. If they were caught, they would lose their one chance to recover the Antiquity's Soulsprite.

They had to lie low and, somehow, go unnoticed. In the meantime, Nocturne would hunt for a way into the mountain, and the regal dragon would reach through their connection once he had something to report.

"Now," he said with a nod over his shoulder to Sophia. "It's time."

He took one more wary glance at the brightening sky, but they needed disguises before he would let them go any further into a city that most likely had his wanted poster everywhere.

Sophia shrugged off her pack and set it gently on the cobblestone. She rifled through the bag and, seconds later, lifted two bottles filled with a dark green potion. The dull liquid sloshed inside the glass without a trace of glow to it, as most potions did, and Connor's nose wrinkled at the thought of drinking something the color of rotting meat.

The necromancer pursed her ruby red lips and quickly glanced him over. "Stop complaining."

Connor shrugged. "I didn't say anything."

She huffed indignantly and reached over Murdoc to offer Connor one of the bottles. With a reluctant groan, he took it. The cork left the glass with a soft pop, and oddly, the potion had no scent at all. Not sweet, not rancid. Just—nothing.

He paused once more as he raised the bottle to his mouth.

Between them, Murdoc frowned. The former Blackguard's gaze shifted between the two bottles. "Wish I could take one."

Sophia raised one delicate eyebrow as she, too, uncorked her potion. "Death by spellgust allergy isn't the way you want to go."

"I suppose not." The soldier grunted and tugged on the hood covering most of his face. "I've got this to hide my pretty face."

Right, because that's not suspicious, the Wraith King muttered.

"You're not missing anything, Murdoc," Connor said as he hesitated to take the first sip. "I can tell this is going to taste awful."

"Oh, just drink the damn thing!" Sophia hissed under her breath.

Without hesitation, the necromancer took a long sip of her potion. She grimaced as it poured into her mouth, and though her brows furrowed in a blend of determination and disgust, she drank a quarter of the bottle. She corked it and pressed the back of her hand to her lips as her eyes squeezed shut, and she roughly cleared her throat twice before anything happened.

A glimmer of green light snaked beneath her skin, following the course of her veins. Slowly, her body began to shift and shimmer. The edges of her features blurred, and her hair brightened to a soft golden tone within seconds. Her nose shortened, and freckles scattered across her cheeks.

When she eventually looked at them again, her black eyes had become green. She set one hand on her chest as the transformation finished, and the glimmering green light beneath her skin slowly faded.

The raven-haired beauty from the clearing outside Bradford was gone, replaced by a green-eyed blonde that could've passed for a governor's wife if not for the tattered hems on her blood-red dress.

Sophia didn't look anything like herself at all. Nothing even vaguely familiar remained, not even the shape of her eyebrows, and it was like looking at a complete stranger.

"A blonde, eh?" Murdoc grinned as he hungrily eyed her. "Good choice. Can you go for brunette next?"

The necromancer smacked him in the stomach. He lost his balance, and he caught himself before he fell to the cobblestone. Even as he gasped for air, he laughed.

"Idiot," she muttered. Her gaze shifted to Connor, and she gestured at him with a furious flourish of her slender wrist. "Why the hell haven't you taken yours?"

He grinned. "I was letting you test it for me."

As he and Murdoc chuckled like schoolboys, she groaned in exasperation. "I'm surrounded by idiots."

Honestly, Magnuson, the Wraith King chided. *I don't know why you're complaining. It tastes like honey.*

"I'm pretty sure you're lying," Connor muttered under his breath. "But we need to get moving."

Sophia lifted one finger in warning. "Remember—only a quarter of the bottle. Any more than that, and you'll waste it."

He didn't reply. Instead, he took a long swig of the putrid green potion, and the rancid rot of old cabbage hit his tongue. He gagged even as he forced himself to drink it. With a grimace, he swallowed a quarter of the bottle and shoved the cork back where it belonged.

Connor ran the back of his hand over his mouth and suppressed the urge to vomit. "Tastes like honey, does it?"

In his head, the Wraith King cackled.

The bitter taste faded in moments, and his body hummed with warmth. He looked down at his hands as the green lights of the potion's magic set to work, and his skin darkened a few shades. The hair on his arms lightened to the same golden hue as Sophia's, and he could only imagine what the rest of him looked like.

As the glow finally faded from his arms, Murdoc's face twisted into a strange expression Connor couldn't read.

"Now you two look like you could be related," the former Blackguard said. "I don't know how I feel about that."

"Because it's the same potion." Sophia reached for Connor's bottle, and he set it in her outstretched palm. "With our limited timeframe, did you really think Dahlia was going to brew two different versions? The same glamour will work differently on each person who drinks it. A single potion saves time."

"I still don't like it," Murdoc admitted.

"How long before it fades?" Connor asked.

"Two hours."

Damn. That didn't seem like long enough.

Connor shifted his attention back toward the main road and gestured for the others to follow. "We'd better get moving, then."

"Word of warning, Captain." Murdoc pointed at the alley they were about to take. "This tavern is where bad people go to hide in plain sight. Even the Blackguards don't go in there. If anyone picks a fight with us, we need to leave—not engage."

Coward, the ghoul muttered.

"He has a point," Connor said to the Wraith King. "We're here to observe. That means we can't bring attention to ourselves."

"I think you're going to do that by default," Sophia said as she scanned Connor's broad shoulders. "The glamour didn't change your figure, so you're still a behemoth."

"Thanks," Connor said dryly.

"What I mean is you'll draw attention," she said with an exasperated huff. "Even with a different face, you don't exactly blend in."

Behind her, Murdoc stretched and curled his fingers in an anxious rhythm. The man stared off over Connor's shoulder, toward the empty alley. Connor cast a confused look back at the shadows that awaited them, but the path ahead was still empty, and no guards had passed by since the first group.

"Are you alright?" he asked his friend.

Murdoc's head snapped toward him, and the former Blackguard roughly cleared his throat as he nodded. "Fine. Completely fine."

Sophia frowned. "You're a shit liar."

"It's—I just—down there…" Murdoc took a steadying breath and stared at the cobblestone beneath his feet. "There's a large Blackguard presence here. This is where I trained the new recruits. This is where I came to steal back my sword after they kicked me out."

Connor let out an aggravated sigh and pinched the bridge of his nose. "When were you going to tell us?"

"Hadn't planned on it, to be honest." The man swallowed hard, and as he tightened his hand into a fist, his knuckles cracked. "If they see me, we'll have trouble."

"Better hope they don't see you, then." Sophia swung her pack over her shoulder and nudged Connor's bicep in a silent request that they get moving.

Connor, however, studied the anxious lines on Murdoc's brow. His friend's body tensed with fear, and the man stared out at the road as though he had seen a ghost.

"It's different this time," Connor promised.

Murdoc's gaze shifted toward him, and for a moment, the worry lines in his forehead relaxed. Connor tilted his head in the same way his father used to, all those years ago, any time he had had figured out one of Connor's mischievous plans to torment anyone who teased his little sister.

I see what you're up to, the expression said. *And I'm here to help.*

A thin smile tugged on the edges of Murdoc's mouth, and the former Blackguard finally relaxed—only a little, mind, but enough. The soldier nodded in silent thanks, and in the first yellow ribbons of a new dawn, Connor led them through the city he had once called home.

A city that would behead him, if its people discovered who he truly was, to ensure he met the same grizzly end as his father.

MURDOC

Though Murdoc would never admit it to Connor, this hellhole of a tavern had always summed up Kirkwall to him. Belligerent drunks. Backdoor deals. Illicit goods hidden on the docks, represented here by crude tokens that passed more hands each night than any whore could handle.

For years, as he had plotted the recovery of his precious blade, this cesspit had been home.

The door creaked on neglected hinges as Connor shoved it open. The captain stepped from the early dawn light and faded into the tavern's pitch-black shadows. Sophia followed, the two of them with hair as gold as the morning sunlight, and Murdoc couldn't suppress the odd feeling that snaked through him when he saw the two of them like this.

It made him want to bend her over a table and claim her in front of anyone who had the balls to watch—but that primal urge didn't make a lick of sense.

With an awkward cough, he shoved the impulse aside.

As the tavern's dark shadows swallowed Sophia, Murdoc tugged again on the hood that cast most of his face in shadow. Hopefully, the tavern owner was asleep this early in the morning. While that old drunk would recognize Murdoc, the barmaid wouldn't. He had tried and failed for years to get between her skirts, but she never looked any man in the eye.

It had irked him back then, for a woman to reject his charm, but now he was damn grateful for it.

In a sudden rush, the feeling of eyes on the back of his head sent a shiver of dread down his spine. He paused on the threshold, fighting the urge to check the street behind him. It was empty. He knew it was empty. He'd checked twelve times already to confirm it was empty.

And yet, he couldn't resist the urge to check once more.

He knew instantly where to look. His eyes darted toward a lone figure standing at the edge of an alley across the street. The cloaked man stared at the inn, a hood hiding his features.

But it was the custom strips of silver cloth woven along the edge of the stranger's sleeves that truly caught Murdoc's eye. He'd had them once, too, when he was a second lieutenant within the Blackguards. It was an honor to wear one's rank in such a fashion, and he had always worn his with pride.

Evidently, Murdoc had already been found.

Numb, he did the only thing he could think to do—he followed his team into the tavern. Normally, he would scan every face for possible threats before he sat down, but this time he simply followed the two familiar silhouettes in his periphery as they chose a corner booth in the back of the open room. Even as he sat, he relived the figure standing in the first rays of dawn, watching him with all the silent intensity of a killer spotting his mark.

"Murdoc," Connor said firmly.

With a jolt, Murdoc snapped out of his daze. An ale had appeared before him. Connor watched him with a frown from across their small table, while Sophia sat to his left.

"By the Fates," Sophia muttered from beside him. "What the hell is wrong with you?"

Instead of answering, Murdoc took a long swig of his ale. It tasted like stale water, but he didn't care. It numbed him enough to clear his head, albeit only a little.

"You were spotted," Connor said.

It wasn't a question.

Murdoc rubbed his tongue along his back teeth and sighed into his beer. He set it down with an irritated thud and shook his head as he tried to find the right words.

"I don't know who it was," he eventually admitted.

A loud crack of wood hitting wood snapped through the air. Murdoc flinched, and he craned his head over his shoulder to look for the idiot who had kicked open the door.

Connor, however, didn't move. Through the corner of Murdoc's eye, the captain studied him with a fiercely stern expression, as though trying to read Murdoc's mind.

Hell, if anyone could learn how to do it, it was the captain. After everything he had witnessed since joining Connor's team, maybe that wasn't as impossible as he had once thought.

Instead of a contingent of Blackguards, however, eight burly men shuffled into the tavern. The last one slammed the door shut, and a bit of sawdust shook loose from the ceiling above him. They stumbled across the floorboards, already drunk, and collapsed into the first table they found. One man slumped over the bench and started to snore, which only made the group laugh harder.

Hunters—men who chased after any wanted poster with a reward attached. They did their best work at night, and when they made a catch, they always celebrated with enough booze to kill a whale.

Murdoc sighed with relief. These imbeciles made it harder to enjoy his time in a pub, but they were a far cry better than the alternative.

The rowdy bunch straddled the long benches on either side of the central table. One of them muttered about what he wanted to do to the barmaid when she finally got into work, and the rest of the men laughed.

How charming.

"Two of 'em," one man said as he slammed his fist on the table. He pointed at the bald man across from him with an aggressive glare. "I swear it on Mum's grave, Ed. Two necromancers, dead in the ocean thanks to me. Elites, even. I got their blades."

Sophia snorted in disdain and took a long swig of her ale.

"Protective?" Connor asked with a wry grin.

"Hardly." Sophia leaned back in her bench, though she kept her voice low. "These men don't look capable of killing a horse, much less elite soldiers. They're nothing but showboating liars."

As he took another sip of his ale, Connor watched the men as they clapped each other on the backs and laughed at each other's crude jokes. In his early days as a darts hustler, he would've marked these men as a threat to his safety and given them a wide berth. That many muscled men didn't take kindly to losing anything, much less their money.

"Did anyone see your face?" Connor asked.

After another long swig of his horrible ale, Murdoc leaned back in his seat and returned his attention to the warrior sitting across from him. Connor crossed his arms, those biceps bulging, and the booth barely seemed big enough to contain all that muscled bulk.

Sophia was right. Even with a glamour, the Wraithblade couldn't dream of fitting in or lying low.

"I don't know," he admitted. "I don't think so."

Connor raised one skeptical eyebrow. "Then why are you scared shitless?"

Murdoc shook his head. He wanted to put this sensation into words, but he simply couldn't.

"It's a feeling in my bones," he eventually admitted. "A knowing. I can't say how, and I can't say why, but they found me. I'm sure of it."

"Necromancers are well and fine," the man named Ed slurred, already two ales in even as Murdoc finished his first. "But I want that Shade man dead. I want him on a spike, I do."

Across the table, Connor went instantly rigid. Though the mug pressed against his lips, he didn't drink. His chest stilled, and he stared at the wall behind Murdoc's head.

Once again, Murdoc tilted his head to get a look at the goons who knew something they shouldn't. These men couldn't possibly have seen the Shade, much less hate him enough to want Connor dead. They were too far removed from the Ancient Woods.

"Gossip travels fast, I see," Sophia said under her breath as she, too, stole a glance at the men.

"Dead?!" Another man at the table shouted. "Have you gone mad, you old coot? He's the one who found the west dock rapist. Saved my daughters a sordid fate, that one."

"Weren't him," the first man insisted with a confident shake of his head. "He ain't no hero. Masked man running through the dark, taking girls from their beds. That's who he is."

"Right you are." The bald man—Ed—pointed at the first to emphasize his point. "How many wives disappear into the ocean, lads? How many daughters? It's the Shade. I swear it is."

"Incredible," Sophia whispered. Her lips twisted into a devious smile, and she raised her mug again to hide her grin.

"Incredible?" Connor snapped under his breath. "How could this possibly be good news?"

Sophia shrugged as though it were obvious. "It's the best possible cover. If the Shade is this mythical figure running throughout Saldia, his deeds can't possibly be traced back to you."

"I don't want that name used for evil deeds." Connor lowered his mug and snared her in a stern glare as he set his elbows on the table. "I don't want people to fear me when I'm trying to do right by them."

To Murdoc's surprise, Sophia didn't bristle. She didn't whip out a snappy response, nor did her delicate brows furrow in irritation. She simply watched their captain for a moment, and the silence weighed on all three of them.

"That's going to happen no matter what you do," she said softly.

Connor frowned, but after a tense moment, his eyes drifted toward the entrance. He seemed to be lost in a memory, and the conversation died.

As the burly men laughed louder, passing off outlandish stories and outright lies as their own heroic deeds, Murdoc and his friends didn't say a word. The watery thud of full mugs hitting each other punctuated the heavy silence that hung over Murdoc's table like a fog, and he stared down at his ale.

The captain was strong. Reliable. Someone Murdoc could trust. But sometimes, he forgot that Connor Magnuson lived with ghosts, same as the rest of them.

Though Murdoc couldn't place why, that figure in the alley had looked so familiar. Whoever it was, it was someone he knew—and someone who knew him. Blackguards were men of the night, and they wouldn't act until dark.

But when he saw the figure again, the stranger wouldn't be alone. Blackguards attacked as a unit, and they weren't the forgiving sort.

Whatever they wanted from him, they would eventually get it—and he couldn't lie low for much longer.

CHAPTER TWENTY-FIVE

QUINN

Quinn didn't have much time.

As the night wore on outside the windows in her suite at the heart of Lunestone, bottles clinked beneath her fingers. She stood in her bedroom, rifling through a wooden wardrobe she had converted into one of her potions cabinets. Her fingertips brushed over the corked bottles as she urgently restocked her bag, pausing here and there to inspect the scrawled symbols on each vial to ensure she only rescued the most important ones.

Her pulse raced. The longer she thought about it, the more ludicrous this mission seemed. Yet again, she cast a wary glance through the crack in her bedroom door to check on the main entrance into her suite. This late at night, no one would find her. The soldiers had all changed posts an hour ago, and the rest were asleep. She had timed this perfectly and with precise intention.

That didn't make this any less dangerous.

A thin layer of dust had settled on a few of the tables in her sitting room, as well as the nightstands beside her four-poster bed. It implied that the maids had fallen behind on their cleaning of her long-vacated room. The dust had even settled on patches of the floor, and it had taken careful maneuvering to avoid leaving footprints. At any moment, one could enter to remedy their mistake before any of the Starling family returned to witness their error.

Teagan's wrath had been legendary, after all, and few in Lunestone dared to disobey.

Her rapidly filling pack weighed on her shoulder, already stuffed to the brim with carefully wrapped and padded bottles, but she didn't know if there would be another opportunity like this to raid the coffers. She had to make the most of it before slipping through the secret passage that connected her bedroom to the litany of untracked corridors hidden within the castle walls. A small room built into the northern warren of passageways now served as her basecamp, and she could leave her things there while she continued to explore.

Being a Starling had many perks—including the right to choose her own rooms. This one had been selected with care, and her motivation for choosing it had been kept a secret.

The chatter she had overheard in the day she had spent in the castle corridors had revealed so much already. Teagan had missed his own targets for a triumphant return. The Lightseers had whispered about the massive rally of elite troops, as well as the eerie silence ever since. Rumors of her death, as well as Zander's had spread through the castle, and no one knew what would happen next.

All of Lunestone was scared. No Master General in history had ever disappeared like this. It set them all on edge, and she had encountered more stoic silence than whispers today.

She had, however, discovered that the Regents had been called. Lunestone's governing body—those who answered only to Teagan himself—would arrive in two days to discuss their options for Lunestone's future. That was a meeting she couldn't miss, and one of her passageways ended at the elegant war room that tradition demanded they use.

In the meantime, she would have to find her father's latest secretary and break into Teagan Starling's office.

The thought froze her in place. With one hand still outstretched toward the last Dazzledane potion in her stores, she swallowed hard. Throughout her life, her father's office had been a sacred place, somewhere she experienced either his pride or his fury.

Her neck ached from the tension in her shoulders, but she didn't dare think about him any longer. This wasn't the time or place for grief—nor anger.

With her last bottle pilfered, Quinn gently shut the wardrobe door and tightened the straps on her bag. She took a cursory glance behind her, ready to leave, until she noticed a familiar silhouette through the crack in her bedroom door.

Her heart skipped a beat, and she barely stifled a gasp of surprise as she thought—for a moment, anyway—that someone had somehow entered without her knowing.

But it was just furniture.

She let out a slow breath to settle her nerves and silently chided herself for being so on edge. Usually, her resolve carried her through far worse than this. None of her missions had ever forced her to sneak into her own home, however, nor to spy on the people she had once considered allies.

These were strange times.

Through the crack in her bedroom door, it was easy to see why she had been tricked. From this angle, the combination of a curtain loosely tucked into its holder and an old table with a dagger in it had the vague outline of something human.

Carefully, Quinn crept through the door and set her palms on the table. That familiar dagger cast a long shadow over the deep scars she had carved into the wood over her storied career. Tenderly, almost like a caress, she ran her finger over one of the seven crosses marking her failures.

How stupid she had been for all those years—to only notice failure in an ocean of achievement.

Numb, she stared down at the dagger. It was a sign to all who entered that she would eventually return. It was a promise to any who saw it that she wouldn't let the darkness take her. That she would live another day.

After all, it was hard to kill the child Death gave back.

She wondered if that was a lie, too. If her father had even woven tales about how she was born. If, perhaps, she wasn't nearly as special as he had always led her to believe.

At the thought, a flicker of her carefully controlled anger broke loose.

Though no flames erupted across her fingers, her palms burned hot as cast iron on a stove. The air above her hands sizzled, blistering enough to cast waves that blurred the table's surface. The heady char of burning pine drifted through the air.

She needed to rein this in. Of the soldiers in her units over the years, she had always been the one with superhuman restraint. It was her duty. Her obligation. Her debt to Lunestone and its Lightseers. That was what she had been taught, anyway—that the Starlings were superior, and that she was the gold standard for proper behavior.

More *lies.*

The dam had cracked, and her bitter rage poured through.

A black circle stretched out from her hands as she slowly scorched the pockmarked wood. In an instant, it shot across the table in every direction and burnt away every stab wound in the timber. The table corroded to ash, and the charred dagger fell.

Quinn caught it before the blade could clatter to the floor.

Only a pile of ash at her feet remained of the table that she had so religiously maintained over the years. To leave no mark of her presence, Quinn tugged on the air, calling upon her Airdrift augmentation to carry the soot outside. Her gale kicked open a window on the far wall, and the stained glass panes smacked hard against the exterior shutters.

That alone had kept them from breaking. In her anger, she was getting sloppy.

She briefly shut her eyes to rein in her lingering fury and, instead, focused her full attention on controlling the wind she had summoned. A dark gray haze spiraled on the funnel of air as she guided it outside, and she let the late spring breeze carried it all away.

Though she couldn't spare the time, Quinn watched the ashes disperse into the night sky. It reminded her of how, out there in the Decay, the wind had taken her father's ashes, too.

Nothing remained of the table but a soot stain on the floor, and Quinn slid a nearby carpet over the black mark to hide it. Her mother had always hated this table, and she had made many attempts over the years to have it destroyed. Quinn wondered, now, if her mother had realized how each cross on the wood had corroded a little more of Quinn's self-respect, but she might never know the true reason her mother had so desperately wanted it gone.

Anyone who entered would probably assume that the Starling matriarch had finally seen her opportunity to remove it. Coated in dust as these rooms were, however, Quinn doubted anyone would care enough to ask.

A fitting end, really, and one she wouldn't fight.

CHAPTER TWENTY-SIX

CONNOR

Connor hated the waiting.

The day had crawled by as they'd loitered around the rancid inn Murdoc had found for them. They couldn't move until dark, and there wasn't much else he could do but pace the full length of his tiny room.

The waiting. The debating. The constant check-ins with Nocturne—so many that the dragon had growled for Connor to leave him alone.

As with his time in Oakenglen, waiting in Tove's shop, the bustle outside the window had set him on edge. The shouts of merchants and rattle of old carts on the cobblestone. Of life passing them by. They risked exposure with each minute they were trapped in a room that smelled like piss and old beer.

It wasn't his favorite way to pass the time, but at least it was over. The sun had finally set, and their work could begin.

Connor now led his team along the cliff edge. Bathed in shadows, they darted unseen through the darkness, eyes and ears alert for any sign of soldiers or bounty hunters in the abandoned alleys along their route.

They had work to do.

A salty gust of sea air rolled off the ocean, and Connor paused as it hit him. The shuffle of Murdoc's boots behind him slowed, and he shut his eyes to savor the familiar scent of home.

It stirred something, deep in him, but he chose not to dredge up the past. He pushed aside the wistful pang in his chest and knelt by the waist-high stone wall built into the rock to keep drunks from falling into the sea.

"This is it," he said under his breath. "The western entrance to the secret tunnels is right over this wall."

He cast a wary glance across the row of homes lining the cliff edge, but this late at night, every window was dark. Another gust carried the tang of seaweed and salt over the rocky wall beside them, and he listened for any signs of life.

Old habits. Movements he had made almost a decade ago, as he and his father had stolen through the night to smuggle goods back to the family shop, now came back to him with ease.

He could so easily imagine his father in front of him, one knee pressed to the ground as they listened to the midnight air. If he and his team followed this road north, they would reach his father's shop in no time at all.

Connor hated being back here.

"Tunnels," Sophia said with an irritated scoff. "What a ridiculous myth."

"Not a myth," Connor corrected. "We used this cave system to get to the boats offshore. It's the only way we could smuggle goods into the city."

"I still can't see you as a smuggler," Murdoc admitted in a hushed voice. "The Shade, Champion of Justice, smuggling lace."

Connor couldn't hide the grin tugging at his mouth, so he turned his head to hide it. "Focus, Murdoc."

"Aye, Captain."

Connor waited for the Wraith King to interject himself, like the dead man always did, but the ghoul was unusually silent.

That suited him just fine. It gave them time to actually get things done.

Sophia peered over the edge of the wall, down at the moss-lined rocks that disguised the narrow footpath. "And you really think they go to the castle?"

"I do." Connor shifted his weight and set one knee against the cold grass on the edge of the narrow footpath they'd taken to get here. Lingering rainwater seeped into the fabric, leaving it damp, but he ignored the discomfort. "These tunnels are old—older than the castle, and some are even older than the city. Smugglers kept expanding them over the years, and I doubt they've been idle since I left. There are plenty of rumors of the tunnels hitting the castle's western side. The trick would be finding the passage."

"Easy," Sophia muttered dryly. "Look for the passage no one's been able to find and hope it's not bricked up."

Connor grinned. "A fun challenge, don't you think?"

Instead of responding, the necromancer shook her head in irritation.

With one last cursory glance around the darkened alley, he peered over the wall. He had done this so many times that he didn't even need to hunt for the footpath—he already knew where to look, and he spotted it instantly.

A trail, so thin it could be mistaken for a natural slope in the rock, meandered down the slope. It curved back into the cliff, and if he hadn't traveled down this route hundreds of times, he would've thought the path ended in the rock.

But he knew better. A short jump would lead to an entrance disguised by ivy, and he wondered if his father's pulley system had survived all these years.

Beside Connor, Sophia and Murdoc peered over the wall.

"That's a steep drop, Captain," Murdoc said.

Connor's jaw tensed as he followed Murdoc's gaze. Beyond the path, the rock angled out slightly, just enough to offer one or two chances to catch oneself before the steep drop into the rocks dotting the shoreline far below.

Connor's shoulders tensed on impulse, and he swallowed hard at the shredded memories of his back nearly breaking on his way down. He still didn't know how he had survived that fall.

He cleared his throat. The past was done, and it didn't matter anymore. He had to focus on the impossible challenge that waited for them in the darkness.

"It's a very steep drop," Connor admitted. "Don't slip."

"Good advice," Sophia said dryly. "Anything else we should know?"

"Avoid the cannibals."

"What?" Sophia and Murdoc said in unison.

"You heard me." Connor did his best to suppress the mischievous grin tugging on the corner of his mouth. By some miracle, he managed to keep his tone even as he shared the old folk story from his childhood. "The tunnels were carved by incestuous cannibals who needed a place to hide their victims.

It's alright though. They're long gone." He paused, mostly for dramatic effect. "*Probably* gone, anyway."

"How comforting," Murdoc said flatly.

"Let's get this over with," Sophia said under her breath. She set her hands on the edge of the wall and hoisted herself onto the flat rocks.

Connor shook his head. "It's a straight path. Head down. It'll look like it ends in the rock, but there's a short jump to the entrance. If you know what you're looking for, you can't miss it."

Reluctantly, Sophia slipped off the wall and crouched beside Connor once more. "Shouldn't you lead the way? You know it better than we do."

"We might not have time." Mostly out of habit, Connor scanned the road around them again to ensure they were alone. "It'll be up to you two to find a way into the castle once Nocturne uncovers that door."

"You mean *if* he uncovers the door," the necromancer corrected.

Connor cast a dubious glance over his shoulder at her. "Have a little faith, Sophia."

She shrugged.

"We'll go exploring," Murdoc nudged Sophia in the side. "It'll give us plenty of time alone, my love."

"The tunnels echo." Connor raised one eyebrow and cast a sidelong glare at his friend. "Behave yourselves."

"Fair point." Murdoc chuckled. "Sophia isn't exactly quiet when we do the deed."

Connor laughed, and even in the darkness, he could see the soft pink blush creep up Sophia's neck. She smacked Murdoc in the side, and the man grinned even as he winced from the blow.

"It's best to go into the tunnels at night," Connor suggested. "During the day, listen for more rumors on the Shade. I want to know what people are saying here."

"That's a waste of time," Sophia warned. "It doesn't matter what they say."

He shifted his intense gaze to the necromancer beside him, and he let the silence settle for a moment before he replied. "It matters to me."

"Honestly," she muttered. "Why can't you just drink to pass the time like a normal man? That's what Murdoc does."

"It's true," the former Blackguard admitted.

"I'm not a normal man," Connor said flatly.

"Also true," Murdoc said.

Sophia groaned softly—whether in disgust or irritation, Connor didn't know.

"This well-bred side of town is new to me, Captain." Murdoc pointed to the ivy weaving across the nearest home's white brick facade. "I don't know my way around. Do you know any side roads we can use to hide if we encounter patrols?"

With a heavy sigh, Connor nodded.

In fact, he knew all of them.

"This way." He gestured for them to follow and led his team through the long shadows toward the main road. He paused as they reached the cobblestone and peered around the edge of the building, but he couldn't hear anyone coming.

It was silent.

Eerily silent.

No dogs barked in the night. No babies cried. Only the distant sea spray crashing against the cliffs far below pierced the moonlit air.

It was almost as if the city held its breath at night and waited for some horror to pass it by.

When he was a boy, these streets had been lined with lamps. Pale yellow light had illuminated every inch of the street, and that light—coupled with the failed Prowlport Charm that bastard Bryan had concocted—was what had ultimately been their downfall.

Now, however, the road was dark. Along the entire street, a candle burned in only one window halfway between them and the intersection with the wider street that led up toward the castle. It reminded him of a lighthouse on a rocky shore, like a beacon that warned of danger if one got too close.

Strange.

Kirkwall Castle, meanwhile, glowed. Candlelight illuminated most windows in the massive stone structure, and fire raged along the walls protecting the wealthy from the common folk.

Much had changed in his time away.

This place wounds you. The ghoul's voice echoed grimly in his head, and Connor grimaced to hide his surprise at the sudden intrusion.

"I'm fine," Connor said under his breath.

I know you, Magnuson, the Wraith King said. *And that is a lie.*

The soft clink of metal pierced the air, hazy and distant, and Connor sank lower in his stance. He leaned his head to the side, searching for the source of the sound, and the subtle thud of leather boots on the stone followed.

Someone was coming.

He held his finger to his mouth and knelt. Behind him, Sophia and Murdoc followed suit and pressed themselves against the building that offered cover as the sound meandered closer.

One footstep became many, and the steady thuds grew louder. Seven men, based on the heavy footfalls, but it could be more.

Farther down the road, on a thinner foot trail not unlike the one under Connor's feet, a hazy amber glow illuminated a home's white brick walls. Seconds later, seven men ambled slowly onto the main street. Four carried lamps that cast the soft glow over the cobblestones around them. Each lantern had frosted glass panes that softened most of the flames. Clear glass circles on the front of each lamp cast long searchlights that swept across the road, over the windows, and into the side alleys.

One beam came within inches of Connor's feet, and he leaned carefully backward to ensure it didn't hit him.

None of these men wore helmets, and a few had streaks of gray in their hair. They didn't say a word as they strolled, and the tallest of them rested one hand on the thick pommel of his sword as he paused in the center of the street. The man glared toward Connor's narrow footpath, and as Connor peered cautiously around the corner of the building, part of him wished the Kirkwall soldiers would come this way.

It was a reckless wish, a stupid one, but he didn't care.

Given the streaks of gray in their hair, any of these men could've been here when his father was murdered. For all he knew, one of them swung the axe. His body tensed, and his biceps flexed while his mind wandered through a list of atrocities these soldiers might have committed. One of these men might even have heard his father's final words. Another might've been the one who put the severed head on a stake. Or perhaps these men were among those who barricaded his mother and sister in their family home to die in a fire set by the king.

Something hot burned deep in Connor's chest. Not hatred—he had felt that plenty of times before. This was new, and it was raw. Visceral.

Primal.

The tallest soldier turned his back on Connor's alley, and the urge to slit the man's throat hit him hard. It would be easy. He could reach them in less than a minute and kill them even faster.

In fact, it would be *effortless.*

"Captain," Murdoc hissed.

Connor flinched from the sudden sound, and he let out a shaky breath as the bloodlust slowly faded. He peered over his shoulder to find the former Blackguard eyeing him warily, his brows scrunched in confusion.

Let us kill them, the wraith suggested casually. *You look like you need to let off some steam.*

Instead of answering, Connor glared at the men. That familiar flicker in his chest burned again as one of them pointed to the lone candle in the distance. The tallest soldier gestured for the others to follow, and this time, they walked with purpose toward the light.

Now he understood the darkness. It seemed the king had imposed yet another oppressive law.

A pity, the ghoul muttered. *You missed a brilliant opportunity, Magnuson.*

"Stop talking," Connor said under his breath.

"What happened, Captain?" Murdoc asked. "You looked like you were going to kill them."

Connor's jaw tensed, but he didn't answer.

Once the soldiers were out of earshot, he darted into the darkened street and led his team down the road the men had just left. He sped along the path with ease, well versed in these winding old roads, and quietly pointed out each landmark as they passed it.

The old well, and the thicket behind it. Perfect cover.

The seamstress lines. The women always hung their newly washed blankets on the cables, and the soldiers never looked there. Perfect cover.

The carpenter's workhouse. He locked it every night, but he left the key under a rock in the small flowerbed beside the shack. Perfect cover.

Every landmark led them closer to the one he had sworn to never revisit, but his father's shop was a smuggler's haven. If they needed cover, they could hide in the secret bunkers for days.

As they turned the last corner, he abruptly stopped.

The last time he'd been here, the corner house and adjacent shop had been nothing but ash. A new home now stood where the cinders had been, and to his horror, it looked identical.

Same white brick siding. Same shop front, with the curved window to show the day's wares. Even the door was similar to the one from his childhood.

For a moment, he was sixteen again, broken and hobbling back home. This was the sight he had hoped for, all those years ago.

It was as if nothing had changed at all—as if he could knock on the door, and his father would answer, wondering where the hell he'd been for all these years.

Magnuson, the ghoul said roughly.

The undead king's voice snapped Connor out of his daze, and he blinked away the memories.

"What do you want now?" he hissed under his breath.

"Look," Sophia whispered, before the wraith could answer.

The necromancer pointed her pale finger down the road, toward a candle at the far end of the street. The pale flame flickered in the overwhelming darkness, and its light cast a soft yellow light glow across a man's broad chest. He held it in front of him, enough that most of his body was nothing more than a silhouette in the night.

But the cloth over the stranger's face looked strikingly familiar, as did the dark hood covering his head. The man lifted the candle, and the shifting light illuminated the twin swords resting in their sheaths on his back. For the briefest moment, dark eyes glared out over the road with all the fury and fire of a face on a wanted poster.

A specter in the night, wearing twin blades on his back.

A man with a cloth over his face.

A convict with a killer's glare.

The Shade—and a damn good imposter, at that.

CHAPTER TWENTY-SEVEN

CONNOR

As the cloaked man quietly surveyed the darkened street, Connor could barely think.

Someone hadn't just taken on the mantle of the Shade—they had done enough research to emulate him exactly.

That *bastard.*

"What the hell?" Murdoc whispered. "Captain, that looks like you."

Though Murdoc had barely spoken, the man's head snapped toward them. The light fluttered out, and the street was dark once more. Only a backlit silhouette remained of the man, almost the same color as the night, and he slipped silently into a thin path between two rows of homes.

Damn it. That route led to a stream and a thicket of old oaks, as well as a rumored entrance to the tunnels. If he didn't act now, he might never encounter this man again.

"You two, head down this road and keep an eye on the alley from this side," he ordered quietly. "I'll go around to the east end of that path to head him off."

"Connor, this is a waste of time!" Sophia whispered urgently. "We should—"

"It's not just a rumor anymore," he countered. "If someone is masquerading as me, that's a problem. Meet me back at the inn if you want, but I'm going after him."

"You can't just—"

He didn't wait for her to finish her thought. In seconds, he was out of earshot. He darted back down the road from where they'd come, pushing himself as fast as he could go, and he didn't stop until he reached the thin strip of old oak trees between two rows of houses. A thin stream trickled under a footbridge, and he jumped over the railing with ease. His boots hit the grass on the other end without a sound, and he bolted upstream on his way to catch the imposter.

At any moment, the man could disappear into the night. Every second was another chance he might lose the trail, and he refused to let the imposter slip through his fingers.

After a few minutes of running, the stream widened, and the strip of trees thickened until Connor couldn't see any of the surrounding homes anymore.

He knew this place.

During his days of fetching things from the town square, he had often wandered down this footpath and dreamed of adventures on the ocean. The thicket wasn't a thin strip of oaks, back then, but an untamed wilderness ripe for the conquering.

That was what children did, after all. They dreamed, and in those dreams, the impossible seemed close enough to touch.

Connor paused and knelt on the riverbank as he scanned the small footpath through the thicket for signs of the stranger. In the eerily silent morning hours before dawn, an owl hooted. Something screeched, far in the distance and out toward the sea, but he was otherwise alone.

No footsteps.

No breaths.

No sign of human life at all.

Pull yourself together, Magnuson, the Wraith King chided. *This is no time for—*

"Hush." Connor's voice was so rough and sudden that it sounded more like another bubbling sputter of the brook than an actual word.

Far upstream, something stumbled into view—just a silhouette, at first, but it took on shape as it eased through the shadows. Connor glared at the spot, and his enhanced eyes adjusted in the blanket of darkness beneath the oaks' thick canopy. Feet splashed through the water, closer with each second, and a man cursed under his breath. Another shushed him The swish of steel sliding against leather followed.

A blade drawn from its sheath.

In the silence, Connor approached them. He kept to the darkness, careful to remain unseen, and listened for more clues as he counted the silhouettes. Eight men, in total, lumbered through the water on the other side of the footbridge. Two hopped the railing and jumped into the shallow water on his side of the path. He took a few wary steps backward as both of them knelt a few feet in front of him. Their full focus remained on the bridge, and they didn't even glance his way.

Not one of them had seen him—not even the men within arm's reach.

You're getting better, the ghoul said approvingly. *Silent as a ghost.*

Connor didn't reply.

"Do you think this will work?" one of the closest men whispered to the other.

"Has to," the second man replied. "This damned Shade fellow is the only way we'll get in."

How curious.

It seemed as though these men were also hunting the imposter Shade.

"Dunno, mate," the first one whispered. "I don't like this one bit."

"You don't like anything."

"But how many times has he disappeared into these woods?" the first asked. "We never catch him. He's a ghost, I tell you. A ghost."

"He ain't a ghost, dumbass," the second man snapped. "He's a man, and a man can die."

Though Connor was fast, the imposter should've reached the bridge by now. He knelt and scanned the bridge again, wondering if he had lost the man's trail after all. He strained his hearing, searching for any sign of life on the path as those in the water went silent.

There.

He finally heard it.

Boots scuffed against the dirt path, but from the wrong side of the bridge. Connor frowned in confusion as the approaching footsteps padded along at a slow and steady pace. They came from the market side, instead of the road that led to his family's old house, and that didn't make a lick of sense.

Kirkwall soldiers were keeping a close eye on the city, and this wasn't the sort of place to take a leisurely midnight stroll.

Pale yellow light crept across the far end of the narrow footbridge, and the flame flickered with each of the approaching stranger's footsteps. The yellow glow brightened, until a familiar man clad in black stepped onto the bridge. He held an exposed candle in one hand, and a hood covered his face. The dark mask over his mouth obscured any recognizable features.

Another Shade.

Connor frowned, utterly baffled by whatever the hell was happening.

As he studied the newcomer, however, it became clear that this one couldn't have been the imposter he had seen on the street. This man was shorter, with a narrow chest and a head too big for his body.

To Connor's surprise, none of the men lying in wait moved. With one hand still holding the candle, the newcomer on the footbridge yanked back his hood and tugged off the scarf covering his face. A thick scar ran the length of the man's left jaw, and thick black brows hung heavily over pale green eyes.

"Nothing to the east," he reported with a frustrated grunt.

Interesting.

This was an ambush—and for some reason, the imposter Shade appeared to be the bait.

"This is a waste of time, boss," the man in front of Connor whispered.

"Keep quiet," the man on the bridge ordered. "Reggie hasn't returned yet. Maybe he got lucky."

Another clue.

Connor frowned as he pieced it together. It seemed these men had planted more than one imposter, but he still didn't know why—or what they were hoping to get out of this little ambush of theirs.

"It's been two weeks of nothing, boss," one of the men whispered from the other side of the bridge. "The Shade ain't gonna bite."

The short man standing on the bridge frowned. "He will."

Confused as all hell, Connor shook his head. He didn't know who any of these men were, much less what they wanted with the Shade. One of them had claimed the Shade could get them access to someplace restricted, which he assumed meant the castle. It was a stupid thing to believe, since Connor certainly couldn't take them over the walls. Hell, that was one of his goals in coming here, and something he needed to figure out for himself.

This didn't make any damn *sense*.

On the footpath, boots scuffed across the dirt. They thudded hard on the well-worn path toward the bridge, and a man huffed for air as he ran toward them.

"Get ready!" the newcomer whispered urgently. "I saw someone dart after me! He's here!"

On the bridge, the short man holding the candle sneered. He tossed his flickering light into the river just as the newcomer approached, and in the second before the fire hit the water, Connor caught a glimpse of the breathless man's face.

It was the man he had seen out in the street.

The imposter was part of this scheme after all.

The short man's candle landed in the stream with a hollow splash, and the flame snuffed out with a sharp hiss. The thicket plunged into darkness, as the two men on the bridge hopped over the railing. Boots hit the water with a splash, and all was silent once more.

Connor suppressed a disappointed sigh. As much as he hated to admit it to himself, part of him had hoped to find someone familiar under that mask.

Perhaps it was a lingering trace of the boy he used to be—the one who used to dream.

These had to be bounty hunters, and he figured they were after the coin purse that would go to whomever turned him in. It would take roughly five minutes, if that, to kill these men, but he had no reason to go through with it. This was nothing but a sloppy ambush orchestrated by amateurs.

He had wasted his time. Perhaps coming home to Kirkwall had put him more on edge than he had realized.

CONNOR.

Nocturne's voice echoed through his head, and he shut his eyes as he resisted the impulse to curse in surprise.

I HAVE FOUND IT, the dragon said. OUR WAY INTO THE MOUNTAIN.

Connor's heart skipped an excited beat, and he smiled. Finally, something concrete.

You're sure? he asked through their connection.

I AM CERTAIN, the dragon replied. I WILL MEET YOU AT THE NORTHERN WALL. WE CAN MAKE IT INTO THE PASSAGE BEFORE DAWN IF WE HURRY.

Excellent, he said. *I'll be there in—*

Despite the still air this far from the coast, the trees above him rustled. The quick huff of breaths followed, and a branch creaked softly enough that none of the men lying in wait seemed to notice. No one even looked up.

No one but Connor.

Across the footbridge, a silhouette dropped from the trees and landed on the bank without a sound. Another followed, and another, until ten men all dressed in clothes the color of the shadows now crept along the stream toward the bridge.

Well, now, the Wraith King said with a hint of amusement. *This is a pleasant surprise.*

Too focused on the evolving chaos before him, Connor ignored the ghoul. Slowly, steadily, he shuffled backward. With his eyes glued to the canopy, he didn't make a sound.

Four more silhouettes inched down the trees above him, each of them focused intently on the two men lying in wait by the footbridge. These silent soldiers moved with stealth few could rival.

The closest of them landed on the soft mud two feet in front of him, and Connor's fingers twitched as he fought the impulse to summon his blades.

What are you waiting for, Magnuson? The ghoul asked. *Surely you can use this as an excuse to let off steam, can't you? How delightful would it be to ambush an ambush who's waiting to ambush someone else?*

He wanted to tell the ghoul to shut his damn mouth, but he couldn't risk someone hearing him—something the Wraith King was likely using to his advantage right now.

With fluid, practiced movements, two figures in black crept behind each of the men lying in wait. In unison, one held a thick cloth over their victim's face, while the other stabbed him through the neck.

Connor's brows shot up his forehead.

Damn. That had been brutal, even by the Wraith King's standards.

I love it, the ghoul said gleefully. *This is a treat, Magnuson.*

In seconds, both of the men on Connor's side of the footbridge slumped over onto the grassy bank. The silent attackers slipped through the darkness toward the footbridge and knelt where their victims had once been waiting.

On the other side of the bridge, silhouettes dispersed into the darkness, and Connor caught only the occasional gasp or whisper-silent grunt as the gathered ambushers fell, one by one.

Almost as quickly as the attack had begun, it ended, and the thicket was silent once more.

Whatever Connor had stumbled upon went far deeper than anything he had expected to find in this place he had once called home.

A place he, apparently, had never truly understood.

The steady shuffle of boots over the dirt came once again, and another silhouette ambled casually toward the bridge. This man didn't wear a hood, and his wild brown hair stuck out at odd angles as he scanned the thicket. A black cloth covered his face, and even in the low light, the man's dark eyes caught Connor's attention.

This looked to be yet another Shade—but this one wore a darker cloak than the other two. He carried himself like a lord, with confidence and poise, and his inky black boots had a polished sheen to them.

Connor frowned, but after all the twists tonight had taken, he simply waited to see what would happen next.

I SENSE THAT YOU ARE NOT WELL. Nocturne's voice carried a twinge of concern. HAS SOMETHING HAPPENED?

There's… Connor fought to come up with the right words to describe the utter chaos before him. *There's a complication. I'm handling it. I'll meet you at the wall.*

Nocturne paused, and the ensuing silence carried the same weight as one of the dragon's questioning glares. DO NOT DAWDLE.

Connor resisted the impulse to reply. Even though he wanted to get into the mountain as quickly as possible, he couldn't exactly hurry someone else's ambush along because he was in a bit of a rush.

The third imposter Shade of the night strolled onto the footbridge. His boots thudded, slow and steady, against each wooden plank that carried him over the shallow stream.

A whistle cut through the air, and Connor heard the arrow before he saw it. The thing careened toward the man on the bridge, aimed at his heart.

The newcomer grabbed it, and the metal tip rested against the black cloth on his chest.

"You've been trying to get my attention for weeks." The stranger spoke to the darkness as he casually twirled the arrow between his fingers. "Congratulations, Mr. Jones. You have it."

"You always were a quick fellow," a familiar voice said from the bank on the opposite side of the bridge. Seconds later, the short man with the scar on his jaw hopped back over the bridge's railing and landed with a thud on the wooden planks—Mr. Jones, apparently. "Guess that's what makes you a good thief."

"Better than you," the newcomer said with a lazy shrug.

The short man scowled at the insult, and he cracked his knuckles as he paced along the far edge of the bridge. "You're a damned fool for coming tonight. You took my bait."

"Did I, now?" the Shade asked calmly.

"Aye." Jones lifted his chin in challenge as he continued to pace like a caged beast. "I figured out your game, and I told the king your little secret. There's more than one of you, and now the patrols know what to look for."

At that, the Shade went silent. The man glared at Jones over the scarf on his face, and he let the arrow in his hand fall to the ground with a hollow clatter.

He didn't, however, seem surprised. Either this man had known this all along, or he could bluff as well as Connor.

This gets more interesting with each passing moment, the ghoul said with a wry chuckle.

Connor nodded. It certainly did.

"I also found one of you." Jones laughed, but the sound came out more like a scratchy cough. "Turned him in to the crown. Got quite a pretty payday for it. Didn't think I'd be able to do that, did you? It's you I wanted though. You're the one that caught over half our crew. They've already hung for it, you bastard." Jones spat on the ground between them. "Figured watching your old man hang might make me feel a bit better."

At that, the Shade's hand tightened, and the man's eyebrows pinched with hatred. "So it was you."

"It was. He was just bait, though, to bring you here. I knew revenge would make you careless." Jones whistled sharply. "Get him, lads!"

Whatever Jones had been expecting, he was met with heavy silence.

In the seconds that followed, the short man's smile slowly fell. He glanced around the thicket in confusion, but only a gentle rustle in the trees answered him.

"You're right about one thing." The Shade's voice dripped with venom, and it took on a gravely tone not unlike Connor's. "There's more than one of us."

In unison, the dark silhouettes draped in black stormed the footbridge. They surrounded Jones in seconds, each of them with a mask over their face. Each wore the same black clothes. Each had wild hair, same as the man Jones had been hunting.

And each glared at Jones with all the hatred of a man more than willing to kill another.

Jones stuttered. His head pivoted frantically around as he gaped at the dozen or so men surrounding him. In his panic, he lost his one chance to dart through a gap between two of them, and the opportunity to live quickly passed.

One of the men shoved Jones hard in the back, and he stumbled forward. The Shade grabbed his shoulder, and Jones winced in pain as the man's grip rooted him in place.

"Here's the thing," the Shade said darkly. "When you threaten one of us, you threaten us all—and we don't take threats lightly."

In a dazzlingly quick thrust, the Shade drove a hidden blade deep into Jones's gut. The man doubled over, and the Shade just as quickly drew his sword. In one carefully aimed swing, he sliced Jones's head clean off. The severed head landed in the stream with a meaty splash, and the man's body slumped over the railing.

The circle of masked men stared at the corpse for a moment in silence as the Shade used Jones's shirt to wipe the blood off his weapons.

"I still think you should've made him suffer," one of the gathered men said. "After the hell he's caused us? After what's going to happen to Rockwell? He deserved it."

Rockwell.

The name struck a chord deep in Connor's soul. Liam Rockwell had been his father's best friend, but the surname wasn't altogether unique. Rockwell and Connor's father had been partners, and their smuggling ring impacted commerce on every inhabited island along Kirkwall's coast. Everyone involved with the smugglers—wives and children included—had died that night.

This couldn't be the same Rockwell. It wasn't possible, and yet Connor still couldn't kill the brief flicker of hope that the man had somehow survived all these years.

"Yes, Jones deserved to suffer," the Shade admitted as he sheathed his weapons. "But we're better than he was, and we're above his methods."

No one in the gathered throng spoke. In the silence that followed, Connor wasn't sure which of them agreed.

"Come on," the Shade said with a reluctant nod upstream. "We don't have long until dawn, and we need to dump the bodies before the city wakes up."

The men dispersed instantly, and most of them scaled the short railings on the footbridge as they returned to the corpses they'd left along the banks of the shallow stream. One, however, set his hand on the Shade's arm and rooted the man in place.

With a quick glance down at the hand on his bicep, the Shade lowered his voice to the barest whisper. "What are you doing, Wade?"

"You can't help, Owen," the second man—Wade, apparently—whispered back. "Like you said, it's almost dawn. You need to get back to the castle before someone notices you aren't there."

From his hiding place just out of sight, Connor's eyes narrowed, and he couldn't resist a victorious smile.

It seemed like he'd found his way into the castle after all.

"Don't be ridiculous." The Shade—a man named Owen, it seemed—yanked his arm out of Wade's grip. "I killed him. It's my duty to clean up my own messes."

"Put your stubborn pride aside," Wade snapped, though their voices remained the barest whispers. "I'll handle the jackass's corpse. You get back. Now. If you get caught, all of this goes under."

Excellent.

Connor had found the Shade movement's leader.

Owen growled in frustration, but ultimately nodded. "Don't be stupid, and don't—"

"And don't get caught." Wade finished with an impatient nod. "Now get the hell out of here."

With one last frustrated glare at the headless corpse slumped over the railing, Owen leapt over the railing and charged upstream.

Connor darted after him, careful to silently sidestep the men cleaning up corpses on the muddy banks, and he timed his route across the dirt footpath to ensure no one saw him chase after their leader.

As he raced through the trees after Owen, he noticed two silhouettes crouched behind the nearest house, watching from afar. He slowed, still hidden by the woods, and studied them. The Wraith King wouldn't let Owen go far, and Connor could risk a short detour to tie up any loose ends.

When he neared, however, he recognized Sophia's scowl in the darkness.

He slipped from the shadows. She and Murdoc flinched as he stepped out of the woods. With a silent gesture for them to follow, he darted back into the thicket after the leader of the imposter Shades.

Though his delay had cost him precious time, he caught sight of Owen's silhouette darting through two birch trees. The man jogged along the muddy bank and only slowed when he approached the towering boulder that marked the end of the thicket. The old stone had been there longer than anyone could remember, and the little stream trickled out from a narrow channel at its base.

In a well-practiced movement, Owen jumped onto the boulder. He landed with one foot on a crevice a few feet up the rock, and he used the leverage to propel himself even higher. Before he fell back down to the bank, he smacked a lump in the rock.

Owen landed lightly on the balls of his feet, just as something popped along the ground behind Connor. Connor slipped between the pitch-black trees in time to see an iron hatch pop up from underneath a carefully woven pile of ivy, and a thin beam of firelight spilled out through the gap.

As Owen grumbled incoherently to himself, he jumped over the stream and walked within a few feet of Connor. The man grabbed the edge of the latch and lifted it until the orange light illuminated his masked face.

And then, oddly, Owen paused.

His dark gaze scanned the trees Connor was using as cover, and the imposter Shade went still. His eyes narrowed, as if he could sense but not see the threat staring him right in the face.

Grab him, the Wraith King ordered.

But Connor obeyed no one, and the Wraith King least of all.

The stranger climbed down a ladder nailed to the stone. The latch closed behind him, and within moments, it was as if he'd never been there at all.

What a waste. The Wraith King materialized in a dramatic puff of black smoke, and the cloaked specter gestured toward the secret door with a frustrated flick of his bony wrist. *You had him within your grasp, Magnuson! Why let him go?*

"Because I'm not an idiot," Connor answered.

That has been debated, the ghoul snapped.

Connor didn't rise to the bait. "We found an entrance to the tunnels, and it's a far cry safer than the one on the cliff. We found the imposter Shades. And, more importantly, we found someone who can get us into the castle."

The undead king tilted his skeletal head. *I assume you have a point?*

"My point is simple," Connor said with a sidelong glare at the old ghost. "Whatever is in that mountain, we need to get it before we sneak into the castle, and that's not just because the Antiquity asked us to do it. If we steal something from the king, we won't have long to get the hell out of the city. Arlo Hunt doesn't take kindly to being robbed."

No self-respecting king would, the ghost said with a lazy shrug.

"That means we have to prioritize," Connor continued, as if the Wraith King hadn't spoken. "After everything we witnessed tonight, it's clear there's far more at play than any of us knows. Whoever these so-called Shades are, they're clearly organized, and there's a lot of them. Only an impatient idiot would capture their leader for interrogation until we have more information."

The wraith grumbled to himself but, to his credit, didn't argue.

The steady gait of two people raced toward him, and his ear twitched as he listened closely. It took a moment more before he recognized Sophia and Murdoc's footsteps.

When they reached him, Sophia set her arms on her waist and took a moment to catch her breath. "Don't ever race off like that again, damn it."

"Bless the Fates." Murdoc let out a long breath as his chest heaved. "I haven't run that hard in ages. Is that as fast as you can go?"

It wasn't, but Connor didn't answer. Instead, he nodded back toward the bridge. "Did you two catch everything that happened back there?"

"Most of it." Murdoc crossed his arms over his chest. "Seems like you have some stiff competition, Captain."

Connor shook his head. "This goes deep, and I bet there's much more that we don't know yet. Nocturne found a clue about the mountain, so I have to go. Until I'm back, I'd like you two to do a bit of scouting."

"Fun," Sophia said dryly.

"Trust me," Connor said as he stared down at the door he figured led to the tunnels beneath their feet. "Whoever this Owen guy is, he's our way into the castle."

"I don't know about that, Captain," Murdoc said with a shrug. "From what we've seen, he doesn't strike me as the generous type."

"Doesn't need to be." Connor looked his friend dead in the eye and shrugged. "Truth be told, I wasn't planning on giving the man a choice."

CHAPTER TWENTY-EIGHT

QUINN

With a shuddering breath and a silent prayer that this would work, Quinn Starling slipped into her father's office.

The sleeping woman draped over her shoulders and back snored softly. Quinn's eye twitched in irritation as another grating snort cut through the otherwise silent air. Her father's secretary grimaced in her drug-induced sleep, and the woman's head lolled again to the side.

The Dwelldoze potion would last another six hours, but Quinn only had another four until the guards on this side of the castle changed shifts. Despite traveling through the secret passages through Lunestone, there were too many open hallways she would have to traverse to return the secretary to her bed.

As the midnight hour wore on, Quinn waited for an alarm. For the thunder of soldiers' boots in the hallway, or the frenzied chatter from guards racing toward the room to catch the intruder. The secretary finally settled into her sleep, and Quinn listened intently to the eerie silence that followed.

No footsteps.

No voices.

Just that painfully empty *silence.*

This plan of hers was insane, but she had precious few options and even less time.

Teagan's need for a tidy office upon his return was ultimately his weakness. Though the enchanted knob would melt everything—and everyone—but him, few knew that he granted his secretary access to this room while he was away.

Quinn had used that to her advantage, but it had meant dragging his secretary through the castle just to use the woman's hand to open the door. Irritating, perhaps, but ultimately necessary.

What a sight they would've been if anyone had seen them—one of the lost Starlings, sneaking through the darkest hallways with her father's snoring secretary draped over her back.

Unwilling to believe his office had only the one enchantment on the doorknob, Quinn's heart slammed against her ribcage, and her racing pulse nearly drowned out the howl of wind hitting the windows. Across from the door, thick blue curtains had been pulled aside to reveal the glowing moonlight glinting off the lake. Mist rolled over the water in the warm spring night. Moonbeams crept across the carpet toward her, glinting across the silver fibers woven into the dark blue rug at her feet, and bookcases lined the room.

To her left, an empty armchair she had never seen him use. To her right, his desk—and the two chairs that always sat on the other side, awaiting whomever he had called into his office for a report.

She had spent so many hours of her life in this room, but never in the middle of the night. Despite her enhanced eyesight, the shadows seemed impossibly dark in here. Oppressive, almost, like a fog.

It sent a chill down her spine.

And yet, nothing had changed. His office was as it had been before she had left. It felt as though he would walk in at any moment and ask her what the hell she was thinking, coming in here without a summons.

Her throat tightened at the thought of him sitting there, watching her with yet another stern glare, and she swallowed hard to suppress the memory of the father whom she had betrayed.

Satisfied with the silent room and the lack of response from his guards, she pressed her heel against the door and gently closed it behind her. His secretary tossed again in her sleep, and Quinn gritted her teeth with annoyance. She set the dozing woman in the empty armchair to the left of the door and draped the girl's arm over the tall back to keep her in place.

With a deep breath to steady her nerves, Quinn adjusted the bag on her shoulder and stretched out her cramping arms. Even with her Strongman augmentation, carrying that woman through so many passages and hallways had left a lingering ache.

Her father spent most of his life in this office, and it held secrets beyond what most could imagine even existed. Everything she needed would be in this room, mostly because he wouldn't have trusted such sensitive information to be stored anywhere else.

Now, to begin her search for anything she could find on his assassins, the merlins, or the dragons he had imprisoned out there on the lone island between Lunestone and Oakenglen.

Quinn's heart thundered against her chest as she shifted her attention toward the desk. The moment she took her first step closer, however, her body froze. She willed it forward, trying to take the next step, but her feet wouldn't obey. She could only stare at the chair, angled away from the desk as it awaited his return, and it was all too easy to picture her father sitting there. She could almost hear his voice as the room stirred up memories of sunshine streaming through the windows during so many of their conversations.

For that brief moment, everything was as it was before she had discovered the truth about the horrible man who had raised her.

The grief hit her suddenly. Violently. The lump in her throat became a searing fire, and she fought the need to cry. She stood there, strangely still, unable to do anything but stare at the very thing that reminded her of her father more than anything else.

Even now, she couldn't believe how it had ended. She couldn't believe who he really was, or that he was really gone.

It seemed impossible—the legendary Teagan Starling, killed by his own daughter.

The shimmering blue glow of moonlight on the floor dragged her back, and she snapped out of her daze with a pained gasp. She shut her eyes to keep the tears at bay, and she didn't open them again until the surge of grief finally faded.

For now.

The quill he'd been using lay on the desk beside a small stack of papers, but the surface was otherwise empty. His chair sat to one side, waiting for him to return, and she fought the impulse to run her fingers along the fabric. Unlike her bedroom, which few would care to check, much less memorize, everything in Teagan's office had to remain exactly as it was before she had entered. Not many could sneak their way into this room, and even with her long disappearance from duty, she would inevitably be on the short list of suspects.

She knelt behind the desk, and her knee sank into the plush carpet as she ran her fingers along the full length of the desk drawers. She leaned in close, her nose nearly touching the wood as she studied it for any hint of a secret compartment.

Nothing. Not even the subtlest dent in the perfectly polished wood.

Damn. Any hidden compartments must've been built into the drawers themselves—drawers he had likely enchanted. No secretary would have access to these spaces.

With a cursory glance, Quinn scanned each drawer for signs of curses. A spellgust stone, perhaps, or dull green carvings that would glow if she set them off. Sure enough, on the underside of the desk itself, someone had carved the Starling crest right into the wood. Carefully, she ran her thumb across it to test how much life it had left, and it glowed brilliantly green at her touch.

Fresh. Damn.

Tendrils of emerald light snaked across the desk toward each of the drawers, betraying each one that he had enchanted in his absence. The thin flashes of light cast an eerie green glow through the moonlit night, and she cursed silently to herself as the light flickered across the window panes. Her hand snapped away from the carving, and the light mercifully faded.

If what she wanted was stored in that desk, she would lose precious days trying to figure out how to disable the curse.

Frustrated, she pushed herself to her feet and racked her brain in an attempt to figure out where else he might've hidden information no one else should see. Losing days to hunt down a recipe that could break open the desk drawers would take time she couldn't lose.

A thought struck her, sharp as lightning, and her head snapped up as she sat with its implications. Her father had been a smart man, someone who was used to being five steps ahead of everyone else. The possibility of someone breaking in would undoubtedly have crossed his mind, and anyone who did manage to find their way into his office would inevitably go to his desk to hunt for what they needed.

It was the obvious first step—a step he would've foreseen.

A step he would've *prepared* for.

Quinn took a wary step away from the desk and, once again, listened for any hint of alarms in the hallway beyond his office. Any hint of rushing soldiers, trying to be silent.

Nothing.

Not yet, anyway.

These enchantments on his desk could've easily been decoys to waste a thief's time, and she had an entire office to explore before dawn. A trap could spring at any moment, and she frankly couldn't risk staying in here for even a second longer than necessary.

With a cursory glance, she scanned the desk's surface for anything useful and rifled through the small stack of papers by the quill. Military orders, mostly, detailing his route through the Ancient Woods on his way to Slaybourne. He had called almost all of the Lightseer troops back to Lunestone, mostly in waves so as not to overwhelm the fortress's supplies and food stores, and there were clear orders for the next wave of soldiers to roll out the moment they received the order from him to come to Slaybourne.

Bless the Fates. Connor had come terrifyingly close to utter annihilation.

With this much information, memorizing the lines wouldn't be enough because she couldn't risk forgetting even the tiniest detail.

Quinn's jaw tensed, and she hesitated for only a moment before she folded the notes and slipped them into the otherwise empty bag on her shoulder. Her hunt tonight would inevitably turn up plenty more for her to steal, so she had left her potions and other belongings in the secret tunnels for safekeeping.

It took another few seconds to find suitable replacements for the papers, but she tugged a few identical sheets from the large pile on the bookshelf behind his chair. Since only his secretary had access, no one would know the difference until Quinn was long gone.

Finding such classified information laying out on his desk gave her hope. He'd gotten cocky, assuming that no one would ever infiltrate this room, and that meant she had a better chance of finding everything else without setting off further alarms.

A *chance*, perhaps, but not a guarantee.

It made sense to leave his orders for the lingering troops on his desk, so that his secretary could fetch them for any newly arriving officers who needed to see them. Quinn, however, needed access to records he wouldn't want even a trusted aide to stumble across whilst he was away.

Wherever they were, he had done a masterful job of hiding them.

They were somewhere in this room. With as much time as he spent here, drafting his plans for Saldia, they simply had to be.

There had to be a reason he'd chosen this room for his office. Of all the chambers in this wing, his office wasn't on the highest floor, nor was it conveniently located near the meeting rooms. It didn't have the best view of Oakenglen, or the lake, or even the dragon's island.

This office had to be special in some way, and Quinn only had until dawn to figure out why.

Perhaps one of them was a false door that led to a secret room, or a staircase that would take her to another part of the castle. Lunestone had dozens of secret passages, likely more than she knew of.

With few other options to explore, Quinn examined the nearest floor-to-ceiling bookshelf. It was one of dozens lining the walls, and she had a long night ahead of her if she ended up scanning each and every one.

Out of habit, she tugged on each one as she read its spine. Thick leather bindings, soft and worn with age, slid beneath her fingertips. Her touch sent small spirals of dust into the air, and she wrinkled her nose to stifle a sneeze.

Hmm.

Apparently his secretary wasn't much of a duster, and it seemed as though her father hadn't noticed.

That very much worked in Quinn's favor.

Of course, any one of these dull tomes could've been another decoy. A hollowed-out book had plenty of space to house secret information, but she didn't have the luxury of checking each one. Instead, she studied the dust on the shelves she passed in the hopes she would find a book that had been previously removed.

A thin layer of dust covered the entirety of this bookcase, however, and none of these books had been moved in quite some time.

Damn.

She quickly skimmed the titles anyway to be safe. Histories of the various kingdoms, mainly, with a few shelves of Starling biographies and journals on the lower shelves.

Nothing useful.

Time for a new approach.

This time, Quinn scanned each bookcase on her hunt for a shelf without dust. Only the eight bookcases on the far wall, opposite Teagan's desk, fit the criteria. Unlike the others, not a trace of dust covered any of these shelves.

These must've been the ones her father had actually used.

One after another, she thumbed through the titles. Military strategies. War-based augmentations. A twenty-three-book set of encyclopedias on regional reagents. An entire row had been dedicated to siege weapons, and though her heart panged happily at the prospect of finding information on the merlins, a half hour was wasted on those tomes before she realized they had been nothing more than inspiration. Wherever his actual notes on the merlins were, he hadn't kept them here.

Damn it.

With a frustrated growl, Quinn knelt and scanned the lower shelves. Perhaps he kept the useful books out of easy reach in an effort to con potential thieves.

Her thumb brushed over spine after spine, the various cloths and leathers scratching at her skin with each book she passed, and it took effort to ignore the nagging sensation that she was wasting her time.

Maybe she would never find what she was looking for—primarily because her father had never wanted her to find it.

On the very last shelf, tucked in the last bookcase on this wall, were forty-three notebooks. Each was only about an inch thick, and each had an identical beige cover. The spines were empty, with no titles or faded letters, and she braced herself to be disappointed yet again.

Quinn's heart sped up as she flipped open the first notebook, and her eyes trailed across the words in her father's handwriting. A date had been scrawled at the top—the fiftieth day of summer, over two decades ago—and she paused in awe.

These were his journals.

She stared at the perfect script, and her father's handwriting stirred up an ache in her that she hadn't expected. With a rough cough, she cleared her throat and tried to focus again on her task. The entry detailed Zander's training, how he was slow to learn the laws of the Lightseer Rite and the progression of power, but would figure it out soon enough.

Astonishing.

Quinn thumbed through the rest of the book, but the dates were all well over two decades old. She slipped it back on the shelf and skimmed the rest, looking for any out of place. Ultimately, she grabbed the last one in the row—only to find it empty.

An empty notebook, ready for notes her father would never have the chance to jot down.

She bit her lip as she fought a surge of tears. He would've probably detailed her torture in these books, if he'd won the battle for Slaybourne. She could imagine his quill tip scratching out perfectly clear lines, detailing her progress with all the dispassion she'd seen on his face out there in the Decay.

That eased her guilt, a little, and a flicker of rage replaced the grief.

One by one, she worked her way backward until she found a journal that wasn't empty. Two sheets of paper stuck out from the top right corner, and she flipped it open to the page he had inadvertently bookmarked.

In the center of the page was a sketch of a merlin.

A jolt of surprise shocked her to the core as she stared down at the drawing. The diagram had notes along the margins, each pointing to a unique area on the weapon and detailing something else of note.

With a broad smile and a sigh of relief, she scanned the pages that had bookmarked the sketch. Two reports—one on Zander's foray out into the

Decay, and the other on her failure to return from her own hunt for Connor.

Her smile faded, and she wordlessly folded the notes once again. She flipped forward a few pages, looking for more clues, but the last entry was nothing more than a short summary of the route he would take into the Decay.

The journal closed with a dull thud, and Quinn slid it in her pack. If nothing else, she at least had something useful on the merlins.

For good measure, she spent a few minutes skimming through the more recent journals, but nothing stood out to her besides a few disgruntled rantings about Wildefaire and the desire to replicate their Isletide solution out of spite. It was another source of revenue for the Starlings, and it would keep Whitney subservient to them moving forward.

She shook her head in disgust and returned the journal to its place on the shelf. She could spend a lifetime rifling through his notes, but nothing she found would be able to redeem him.

Moonlight glinted off something sleek on the floor behind a potted fern in the corner. She leaned toward the light to find a jet-black rock, roughly the size of a man's shoe, with the outline of a familiar dragon sketched into its flat surface. The coarse lines betrayed many attempts to make the wings curve properly, and the artist had forgotten to add one of its feet.

She grinned. She'd given him that for his birthday almost fifteen years ago. She couldn't believe he still had it.

Her chest tightened as she leaned forward to brush her hand along the surface. Her fingertips traced the uneven lines she had etched into the stone so long ago, and she wondered if, perhaps, she had been wrong.

If there was something about her father that could've been redeemed.

If there really was love, somewhere in him, that she had overlooked in her anger.

As her hand pressed against the rock, however, it slid backward. Well-oiled cogs clinked together somewhere in the wall behind the bookcase to her left, and the floor rumbled softly as something under her feet shifted.

The moment Quinn jumped to her feet, a narrow section of the wall behind the dragon stone popped open. It swung outward on perfectly silent hinges, and a cold breath of air shot past. She stifled a shiver as the draft toyed with her hair, and she stared ahead into the black void beyond her father's office.

It seemed as though her intuition had been right. Teagan Starling had most *definitely* chosen this room for a particular reason.

A spiral staircase curved upward in a tight curl of worn steps. A slight divot in the center of each stair hinted at just how many Master Generals must've taken this staircase to whatever secrets lay in wait above her.

Quinn stood at the threshold and craned her ear to listen for any hint of what waited in the darkness. The muffled howl of wind whistled from somewhere far above, but the staircase was otherwise silent.

There wasn't much time left for her to explore, and though she had no idea how long this little detour might take, she couldn't miss this opportunity. If her father had left his own journals within easy reach of his office, she could only imagine what secrets he'd chosen to hide away up there.

Silent as a ghost, Quinn took the stairs two at a time. Her eyes quickly adjusted to the sudden darkness. Her palm brushed across the wall as she raced upward, her senses always alert for threats or traps in the shadows.

The stairwell ended in a door built into a black stone archway, and to her surprise, it opened as she neared. She froze in place, stunned into silence by the sudden movement, and the darkness beyond the threshold was so black it could've easily been tar.

Her jaw tensed, but nothing else moved. Up here, even the wind had vanished. Only the faint ringing in her ear kept her company in the overbearing silence, and she took a deep breath before pressing onward.

Her boot hit the stone floor at the top of the steps with a dull tap, and she raised one hand as she prepared to hurl fire at anything stupid enough to attack her. She swallowed hard, and with the next step, she summoned flame into her open palm.

An orange haze spread across the vast room as she entered, illuminating hundreds of tomes stored in towering bookcases that loomed three stories above her. Walkways had been built at strategic intervals along the shelves, and the spiral staircases in each corner offered easy access to the upper stories. Neat rows of glass cases filled most of the space not occupied by books, and various swords or orbs rested on the blue pillows within. A desk sat in the middle of the room with its chair tucked neatly beneath it.

Her chest stilled in awe. The information stored in this room alone could've probably toppled empires and dethroned kings. Her imagination swirled with the possibility of what she might find in here, squirreled away from the rest of humanity, and she fought the fervent impulse to race up the closest staircase just to see what she might find.

Though Quinn wanted nothing more than to pore over everything in this room, she could almost feel the last threads of her available time slipping away.

She had to focus.

With her flickering flame held high, Quinn crossed to the desk. The light cast long shadows across the eerily silent room, and she fought the shudder down her spine at how heavy the air felt up here.

It felt almost like she was being watched by the darkness itself.

On the desk lay several books, each with gold lettering on their covers. She sifted through them with her free hand, trying to gauge their contents as quickly as possible.

LIGHTSEER RANKS.

Nope.

STARLING SPELLBOOK.

Quinn raised one eyebrow and, though she hadn't come for this, set the book aside.

UNKNOWN.

With a confused frown, Quinn opened the cover and skimmed the first few pages to find an endless score of names. Several surnames were familiar, though the first names weren't, and she didn't realize why until she saw the date in the top corner.

This book was over four centuries old.

As she thumbed through more pages, she came across mission assignments. Training regiments. Deaths. Replacements. Something about heirs.

How curious.

It hit her, then—what Duncan had said about his run-in with one of her father's assassins. When the assassin's glamour had faded, the man turned out to be a lord in the Freymoor court. A nobleman, dressed up in a brilliant glamour and sent to kill a Lightseer enemy. These familiar names in the ledger were all noble bloodlines that had been in Saldia for generations.

The Unknown was quite possibly the name of her father's assassins. To be safe, she set that tome on top of her family spellbook and continued her search.

The last book had worn lettering, much more faded than the rest, and she strained her eyes to read it despite the flickering firelight floating above her palm. Light glinted off the flecks of gold paint on its surface, and it took a few seconds to piece together what it said.

DRAGONS.

In the surge of relief that followed, Quinn felt almost weak. The night had worn on for what felt like forever, and she had so much left to do before dawn.

As best she could with one hand, she slid the three massive books into her bag. The stitching threatened to pop from the sheer volume of what she was trying to steal, but she managed to secure it well enough for her trip back through the castle.

There was no guarantee she had everything she needed—in fact, with a room this large, she could almost guarantee she had overlooked plenty—but what she had would have to do for now. She would review what she'd found thus far and, if necessary, return tomorrow night.

With one last look over her shoulder, she retreated down the pitch-black staircase that led down into her father's office. Her mind buzzed with all the things she and her father had left unsaid, but perhaps none of it mattered. No matter what she wanted to get off her chest, she would only be speaking to an empty room and the memory of a dead man who may never have loved her at all.

Teagan Starling was dead, and only time would tell if Quinn had made the right choice.

CHAPTER TWENTY-NINE

CONNOR

With a frustrated sigh, Connor crossed his arms and glared at the so-called door that Nocturne had found.

He and the dragon stood on a large cliff that protruded from Firebreath Mountain's northern slope. The Wraith King hovered beside them, the tattered ends of his cloak fluttering in the ocean breeze, and the three of them examined the steep slope halfway up the mountain. Instead of an iron entry, like Connor had expected, a flat stretch of rock towered over them all.

But that was it.

No hinges. No handles. Not even a crack along the edge to indicate it was something other than a flat stretch of stone.

A soft blue glow on the horizon slowly ate away the stars as dawn approached, and they didn't have time for games.

"Nocturne," Connor said flatly. "This is a rock."

Stupid beast, the Wraith King grumbled. *You wasted the opportunity to turn him feral, Magnuson.*

"Don't start with that again," Connor growled under his breath.

The ghoul shrugged.

"A PERFECTLY VERTICAL SLOPE THIS WIDE? ON A MOUNTAIN THIS LARGE? THAT IS IMPOSSIBLE FOR NATURE TO DESIGN ON ITS OWN," the dragon replied. "THIS WAS CARVED WITH INTENTION."

Connor rubbed his tired eyes. He hadn't slept since they landed, and he frankly didn't have the patience for this. "It's still just a rock."

"No." The dragon's voice boomed in the fading night. "It is a trick of the eye, and a fine one if it can fool even you."

"Alright." Connor craned his neck to look the dragon prince in the eye. "Show me, then."

"Soon," the dragon promised. "The sun will guide us."

"You're not making any sense," he said.

"Perhaps it is something you must see for yourself, then." The dragon huffed impatiently and glared down at him. "I have dreamed of seeing the famed Firebreath entrance since I was young, and I do not want this lifechanging experience ruined by your cynicism."

Connor shrugged.

Fine.

In silence, they stared up at the rock as the first threads of sunlight hit the sky. Connor waited, not altogether patiently, for something to happen.

At first, it was like any other dawn. The steady crash of waves hitting the shore hummed through the heavy air like a distant roar. Gulls cried on the ocean currents. Connor could almost hear the creak of ships in the harbor, or the light patter of his sister's feet on the stairs as their house woke up with the sun.

He roughly cleared his throat to bury the memory.

A flash of golden light blinded him, and he raised one hand to shield his eyes. The flash faded, and he squinted as he tried to make out what it was.

"It begins." Nocturne stood taller. He raised his wings and arched his long neck. The regal creature growled happily as more flashes of golden light erupted across the stone before them.

As the sunlight brightened, a strip of glittering gold appeared in the rock. It raced along the edges of the section of perfectly smooth stone, like the frame around a towering portrait. More ribbons of gold shot down from the others, until the outline of a gilded doorway appeared in the center of the cliff.

A doorway, yes, but one without a door.

"Remarkable," Nocturne said breathlessly.

I have no patience for this, the wraith growled.

Before Connor could say anything, Nocturne walked toward the newly formed doorframe. He reached his long neck forward, heading straight for the solid rock, and it looked as though he was about to ram right into the stone.

"Nocturne!" Connor shouted, baffled at the dragon's insane behavior. "Look out for—"

Instead of ramming headfirst into the mountainside, however, the prince of dragons stepped easily through. The regal beast craned his long neck and cast a mischievous glance back at Connor.

It took a moment for Connor to process what he was seeing. The illusion was so perfect that, at first, it truly looked as though Nocturne were standing in a bit of the cliff that shouldn't even exist. The dragon turned left, and this time he disappeared behind a slab of rock that had otherwise blended perfectly into the cliff.

Impressive, the Wraith King begrudgingly admitted.

It certainly was—but Connor wasn't about to admit that the old ghost was right. Instead, he looked at the Wraith King and smirked. "You can't stand to be outsmarted, can you?"

The ghoul scoffed.

Intrigued, Connor set his hand on the stretch of wall through which Nocturne had just passed, and his hand met air. It kept going, and he followed the wide tunnel until it forked. Both routes looked the same, though Nocturne's black tail curved around another bend in the left path.

A glimmer of golden light caught his eye, and he stepped backward to examine the circle of gold beneath his boot. A small carving of a sun, barely the size of his fingernail, glittered in the growing dawn. It lay on the floor at the edge of the left path. Behind him, on the path that veered to the right, a flame led the way into the darkness and an identical path to this one.

The sun will guide us.

Interesting.

Turn by turn, Connor followed the dragon through the maze. Nocturne's heavy footsteps shook loose pebbles from the ceiling far above them, and each of the looming walls reached beyond what the sunlight could pierce. A sun marked every change in direction Nocturne took. Out of habit, Connor tracked every twist and curve of the passageways anyway, just in case the symbols disappeared.

He didn't trust this mountain worth a damn, and he wouldn't rely on its generosity to lead him back out.

With each fork in the path, he eyed the routes the dragon didn't take. Sometimes, a flame marked the path. Other times, it was a bolt of lightning, or a gold coin.

Temptations, luring trespassers to fates Connor didn't want to consider.

With every step, the sunlight thinned. Bit by bit, it faded entirely, and Connor had only his enhanced eyesight to guide him through the darkness.

After roughly fifteen minutes, the Wraith King huffed impatiently. *Can't these scaly fools use proper doors?*

"Why would they?" Connor's words echoed through the towering labyrinth, and he impulsively lowered his voice. "Dragons don't have hands."

Instead of replying, the hovering ghost simply crossed his bony arms over his chest.

The steady thuds of Nocturne's heavy footsteps faded, and Connor rounded the last bend to find the dragon staring into a long tunnel. Empty stone sconces lined the hallway and faded into the endless shadows, long devoid of the torches that must've lit the way centuries ago.

An iron ring had been bolted to the edge of the passageway, and dozens of tattered cords were tied to it. Most had frayed and snapped with time, hanging limply as they trailed into the darkness, but two had survived. These two lingering cords were taut, their other ends secured by something deep in the mountain, and their bright white fibers led the way into the darkness.

Once inside, you must not lose your way. the Antiquity had warned. *These tunnels were not made by man, and many have lost themselves in the endless hallways.*

Judging by how many cords were still tied to the iron ring, he wondered just how many other people had walked into this endless void.

"MEN ADDED THAT RING." A plume of black smoke shot out of Nocturne's nose, and a soft growl rumbled in his throat. "THE NERVE OF THEM, TO TAINT SUCH A HOLY PLACE."

Connor patted his scaly friend's side. "I'm guessing none of them were the spiritual sort."

The dragon huffed again, and a second plume of smoke shot out of his nose.

As Connor studied the pitch-black corridor, he frowned. "Nocturne, this is as dark as the Slaybourne catacombs. If dragons love the sky, why would you live in a mountain?"

"Because this was never a home," the towering creature explained. "My ancestors lived in caves along the cliffs, or on the neighboring islands. The mountain itself is a place of worship and history, where kings were buried, and where legends were immortalized in its stone. In the center of this mountain is a holy site—a place of pilgrimage to be honored and preserved."

The dragon's eyes shut briefly, and Connor wondered what stories the regal creature had heard as a hatchling about this place. He spoke of it with awe and longing.

Fascinating.

A burst of wind shot down the tunnel, like a breath of air from the mountain itself, and it hit Connor square in the face. It carried the stench of rot, mixed with the sweet tang of honey. He gagged at the confusing blend of aromas, and the hair on his arms stood on end. His body hummed, as though it were picking up on an undercurrent in the air, and that gust of wind carried something with it.

Something more.

Something magical.

Something powerful.

Raw energy thrummed through the breath, and it lingered in Connor's bones even after the gust had faded.

"I guess this is it," he said.

"Be cautious," Nocturne warned. "The dragons of Firebreath Mountain built traps into their dens. This is a labyrinth few can escape, and we must be careful."

"Traps?" Connor asked warily. "When were you going to tell us about those?"

The regal creature tilted his head just enough to glare down at Connor. "Now is as good a time as any."

Fair enough.

"What kind of traps?" he asked.

"Secret paths," Nocturne explained. "Hidden doors. Tunnels that lead nowhere, and routes that end in a steep drop only a winged visitor could survive. This place is older than me, and my only guides are the stories. I cannot know for certain what my ancestors built into this mountain. Only they know for certain."

And they're long dead, the Wraith King added.

"Helpful," Connor said dryly.

"Follow the sun." The prince of dragons had a wistful air to his voice, the words light and twinged with awe. "The sun is the life-giver. It is our connection to the sky, to our true selves, and a marker of the divine. This is how my ancestors ensured future generations would make it safely through."

With a frown, Connor glared into the darkness before them—a darkness almost utterly devoid of light. "Suns, like the ones on the floor?"

"You were paying attention," Nocturne tilted his great scaly head and chuckled. "Yes, and there may be more. Whatever happens in there, the sun will steer you true. That is what the legends say."

Legends often lie, Wraith King muttered.

"Perhaps," Connor admitted.

From his experience, though, legends were always built on at least a kernel of truth.

Never one to walk into a battlefield unprepared, Connor slowly paced the entrance to the tunnel as he thought through all of the ways this could go wrong. After all, only Death could lead them to the Soulsprite locked away in this labyrinth, and that meant they had no true destination.

"Here's the plan." He squared his shoulders and returned his attention to his team. "The suns have to lead somewhere, and based on everything Nocturne has said thus far, I think they will take us to the holy site at the center of the mountain."

The dragon before him nodded, though the Wraith King impatiently gestured for him to continue.

Connor pointed at the sun near his boot. "That means we follow these and get to safety. From there, we figure out a way to summon Death. This is an in-between, and that means his magic is stronger here. Whatever we find at the end of this labyrinth, we should be able to do something that gets his attention."

This is a mistake, the ghoul said sternly.

"Maybe," Connor admitted with a shrug. "But it's what we've got to do."

The wraith growled in frustration but didn't reply.

"Stay alert," Connor added. "Even if the suns lead us through the dragons' traps, there's no telling what else is in there. I doubt the creatures from Death's domain will care what routes the dragons marked as safe."

"I SUPPOSE YOU ARE CORRECT," Nocturne admitted. "I DO NOT KNOW WHAT WE WILL ENCOUNTER IN THIS ABANDONED PLACE."

This will go well, the ghoul said dryly.

Connor ignored the old ghost. "Let's not waste any time, then."

He stepped into the darkness. With each careful step, he studied the shadows. His eyes strained as they adjusted, but the world came slowly into focus. With this little light, every trace of color practically glowed, and the two strings leading into the oppressive shadows ahead almost hummed with a faint white light.

Behind him, Nocturne walked with a slow and measured gait. He could feel the ghoul's eyes on the back of his head, and he didn't need to turn around to know the Wraith King was glaring at him.

Probably irritated with their slow pace through the darkness.

Without light, he slowly lost track of time. He didn't know how long they had been walking, and oddly enough, the endless tunnel reminded him somewhat of the catacombs beneath Slaybourne. The towering ceiling disappeared into the shadows he couldn't see, and Nocturne's hulking footsteps cast rippling echoes across the quiet rock.

In fact, Nocturne's steps were the only sound. No water dripped in the distance. No rocks clacked against the floor. Absolutely nothing in the tunnel moved at all, save for them.

Though Firebreath Mountain was a truly massive landmark, this tunnel seemed to go on far longer than it should have. The path never curved. It never sloped downward or led them to a stairwell that would take them higher. It simply continued straight ahead, endlessly, as though it were a portal to another world altogether.

Often, Connor was tempted to summon his blackfire blades to light their way through the void. He fought the impulse time and again, mostly because he didn't know what would be drawn to the flames.

He didn't want to attract attention. Not here. Not when any number of horrible things could live in this darkness.

And, through it all, they walked alongside those two taunt strings that were all that remained of the guides others had used to lead them through the darkness. There had simply been no other way to go. No turns to make. No emblems of a sun to guide their way down other corridors.

Nothing but a vacant tunnel that seemed to have no end.

One of the two strings ended at a wall up ahead. It had been tied off on a sharp rock that jutted from the mountainside like a makeshift sconce with no torch in it, and the loose end of the string dangled over the ground. Its frayed fibers hung limp, as though something had ripped the ball of yarn clean off, but no skeleton lay beside it.

The second string continued into the darkness beyond, and Connor frowned as he stared at that lonely, isolated tether that had ended in the middle of a corridor.

Odd.

His ears rang in the absence of ambient noise, and the shrill scream built to a steady buzz in his skull, loud and constant. Focused as he was on the darkness ahead, it took him a moment to notice that Nocturne's footsteps had faded. He frowned and looked over his shoulder, wondering why the regal creature had stopped.

But Nocturne and the Wraith King were gone. The mountain's tricks had eaten them, and only he remained.

CHAPTER THIRTY

CONNOR

Once again, Connor stood alone, lost in the depths of a place that wanted to eat him whole.

He stood in the tunnel, and in the oppressive silence, he heard only his breath and the sharp ringing in his ear. Slowly, the steady thud of his pulse echoed in his head, louder than Nocturne's steps had been, as the impossible silence weighed on his chest.

Nocturne! he said through their connection, not wanting to draw attention to himself by speaking. *Where the hell are you?*

But the dragon didn't respond, and the empty tunnel remained utterly still.

Answer me, damn it!

He waited several minutes for the dragon to reply, but that booming voice in his head never came. The Wraith King, too, remained uncharacteristically silent.

Yet another in-between had split him from his team. Much like his time in the Blood Bogs, he would have to face this mountain on his own until he could find the others.

If anything in this hellhole injured Nocturne or the Wraith King, Connor would find a way to cleanse every nook and cranny of this labyrinth.

He closed his eyes and took a steady breath to quell the dread stirring in his core. He and his team had tackled worse than this.

"Connor!"

He snapped his head toward the man's voice as it echoed toward him. Though no one moved through the darkness, footsteps raced toward him.

That voice was both unmistakable and utterly impossible.

Murdoc.

"Connor!" The man's voice echoed down the corridor, thick with terror, and the footsteps quickened. "Fates be damned, man, I need help!"

At his friend's panicked voice, Connor took an impulsive step forward. It was unconscious. Reflexive, even.

Somehow, through sheer force of will, he forced himself to stay put.

Murdoc knew not to follow. He and Sophia were in Kirkwall, and neither of them even knew the way past the door, much less how to get through the labyrinth. There was no possible way for Murdoc to be here.

And yet, that voice was so real.

"Connor!" the man screamed.

Close.

Too close.

"Help us!" a woman shouted, this time from right behind him.

Sophia.

He spun around and raised his fists, ready to knock out whatever creature was trying to trick him, but the air behind him was painfully empty.

Despite the voices, he was still completely alone.

His heart thrummed in his chest, painfully loud, and the echoes of his friends' voices faded to nothing. Footsteps darted over the floor toward him, louder every second, and he summoned his blackfire blades as he prepared to slice throats.

He was *not* in the mood for games.

"Connor," a woman said gently.

Quinn.

His head snapped around yet again, and this time, a pretty face stood a breath away from him. He flinched in surprise and took a wary step back before he registered her fire-red hair or the hazel eyes that so often snared him.

For a moment, he stood there, chest heaving as he stared at Quinn Starling in utter disbelief.

"You're not real," he said flatly.

She chuckled, and her smile lit up her face. She set one hand on her hip and raised her chin as she studied his features. "Is that so?"

He held his blackfire blade in front of him and nodded. This had to be just like the many tricks of the Blood Bogs.

Mirages. Illusions.

Lies.

"Where are Nocturne and the Wraith King?" he demanded.

Quinn frowned. "How the hell would I know? Connor, you're the one who summoned me here. Where are we? How did you make that portal?"

Confused, he took another wary step backward. "Portal?"

Her eyes narrowed, and she studied him for a moment in silence. "Connor, what's going on?"

At the genuine flicker of worry in her tone, his resolve faltered, and he lowered his sword. He studied her face, looking for every freckle that he had memorized in their nights together. The slope of her jawline. The angle of her eyebrows, especially when she was annoyed.

As far as he could tell, this was Quinn Starling—or a truly astonishing copy.

A heady perfume wafted by, as sweet and sultry as honey in summer. It hung on the air like mist off a waterfall, and his vision started to blur. His head felt light. Fuzzy. Unfocused.

A dull ache pounded at the back of his skull, and he grimaced as he fought the pain slowly spreading down his neck.

It is a trick, Nocturne had said about the door, in the moments before they'd entered the maze. *And a fine one at that, if it can fool even you.*

This mountain was apparently full of tricks, and even one of them could mean an early grave if he wasn't careful.

He couldn't let his guard down.

Not now. Not ever.

With a frustrated grunt, he rapidly blinked his eyes as he fought the daze.

"Stop it," he demanded.

But his words tasted strange, and his tongue felt too large for his mouth.

"Are you alright?" Quinn tilted her head in confusion, and she took a careful step forward. "Connor, what—"

With an effortless twist of his hand, he raised his sword to her chest.

The blackfire crackled over her skin, casting soft gray shadows across her plunging neckline, and she slowly raised both hands in wary surrender.

"Stay back," he warned.

For a moment, his head cleared, and he regained some of his control.

Thank the Fates.

"You're scaring me," she said softly.

In her mouth, he noticed the flash of light across something metallic. It was brief, and once upon a time, he wouldn't have noticed anything out of the ordinary at all. Her lips parted in surprise, just as they always did when she was piecing clues together. This time, he caught another glimmer of something long and slender swirling about in the back of her mouth.

He squinted, but her lips closed as soon as she saw him staring. In the painful seconds of silence that followed, he tried to figure out what the hell he had seen. Something deep in his soul warned him it was important, but he couldn't remember why. The voice felt small. Ancient. Distant.

"Connor, it's me." Quinn's voice snapped through his head, and he momentarily forgot what he had been thinking about.

Cautiously, she reached for his face. That heady scent of honey returned in a rush, and this time, it burned through his senses. His head swam. His pulse thumped like a drum in his ear.

Without warning, her hand pressed gently against his jaw. He tried to pull back, but his body wouldn't obey. She sidestepped the sword, and those haunting hazel eyes crept closer.

"Whatever's happening, let me help you," she promised, and her voice reminded him of a lullaby whose lyrics he had forgotten. All that remained was the melody, soft and soothing. "You and I can overcome anything."

As she spoke, she unwittingly gave him one last chance to figure out what was in her mouth, and why something deep within him kept warning him to look. Her lips parted, and he saw it, then, clear as day.

A slender tongue writhed in the deepest recesses of her mouth, far longer than it should have been. Scales covered the entire thing, and as she leaned forward to kiss him, that slender tongue darted forward.

Like *hell.*

He would sooner cut off his own arm than let this thing have its way with him.

This time, he pulled his head back just as that scaled tongue reached her lips. The blade of his blackfire sword pressed against her throat, and her skin sizzled in the enchanted fire's heat.

Quinn lifted her chin as far as it would go, and his blade followed the movement. As his head slowly cleared, he refused to give an inch.

This creature would pounce at the first sign of weakness.

It hit him, then—that warning, deep in his soul, from so long ago. His mother's lullabies swam through his memory, and he relived the tale of the sirens and selkies. One vile, one vibrant. One would kill, and one would show kindness.

But both could steal a man's heart.

"You're a siren, aren't you?" he asked.

Quinn's lips pinched together, and a quick flash of anger shot across her face. She recovered, but not fast enough.

That confirmed it.

"Selkies live in the waves," he continued, the threads of his mother's bedtime stories coming together as he relived a memory he had long since buried. "But sirens live in the darkness."

At first, Quinn merely watched him. Her eyes narrowed, and her nose creased with disdain. A slow, wicked smile spread across her face, and she tilted her head to one side.

"Until we feed on one of you lot," she finally said. Her voice was dark, deeper than Quinn's, and a blend of the two women's voices clashed with each other. "With enough of you fools dead, we can survive out there."

That heady scent of honey returned, and he shut his eyes as he fought it off. Whatever that poison was, it corroded his sense of reason, and he couldn't let it ambush him again.

"Come now, Connor." The siren chuckled, and with his eyes still shut as he fought off her perfume, her hands traced their way down to his legs. She pressed Quinn's body against his chest, and a pang of primal lust hit him square in the gut.

But this wasn't Quinn, and he wouldn't be fooled.

"That's enough!" he shouted.

In his empty hand, he summoned his second blackfire blade. He crossed them in front of her throat, and he glared down as the perfect copy of Quinn Starling stared up at him from between the blisteringly sharp blades.

His chest tightened at the sight of his woman, pinned in place by his swords. Deep down, part of him demanded that he step away, that this was insane, that he could never hurt her. It took immense effort to remind himself that this was nothing more than a perfect copy. Even then, there was a part of his soul that still didn't believe it.

"Could you do it?" the siren asked, still wearing Quinn's face. "Could you kill her?"

"No," he confessed. "But I can kill *you.*"

He twisted his blade, and the metal cut deep into the siren's throat. His heart twanged as the sword slit apart Quinn's neck, and it took every ounce of self-control he had left to remember that this wasn't really her.

Quinn was in Lunestone.

Quinn was alive, and this woman was a fake.

The river of red blood pouring from the gash in the siren's neck darkened until a sickly gray liquid poured over his blade. Disgusted, he took a step back as the creature's body browned. Quinn's pale skin rotted away before him, until it turned the color of ash and shriveled in on itself. Water poured over its body as the threads of her clothes burned away to ash, and the siren fell to its knees.

It croaked out garbled words he couldn't understand. With one last gasping breath, it keeled over. Its face landed on the stone with a nauseating squish, and the rest of its wrinkled gray body began to slowly melt into more of that putrid water.

At the very edge of what little he could see of the pitch-black tunnel, bare gray feet skittered back into the darkness.

More of them.

"You!" he shouted, letting the full force of his rage carry his voice down the tunnel. "Get back here. *Now!*"

The skittering footsteps paused, and warbling whispers followed. He arched his back, blackfire blade raging, and he glared into the shadows.

A king did not repeat himself—not when he gave an order.

On the edge of his vision, a few huddled silhouettes stepped forth. They stood a good two feet shorter than him, hunched over as they were. The cluster shoved one of their own forward, and it stumbled over its own feet as it tried to catch its balance.

When it stepped into the pale gray circle of light emanating from his blackfire blade, it peered up at him through stands in its greasy hair. Flecks of white floated through its otherwise jet-black eyes, and he resisted the impulse to grimace in disgust.

"You will find my two companions," he demanded in a dangerously low voice. "You will bring them here, alive and unharmed, or I will slaughter you all."

It gulped in horror, and squishy black eyes widened to reveal even more glowing bits of white floating within it.

"Go!" he barked.

The thing flinched and scampered off into the crowd of sirens behind it, and the lot of them raced into the darkness.

Good. After this little stunt of theirs, they shouldn't just be afraid of him.

They should be *terrified.*

CHAPTER THIRTY-ONE
THE WRAITH KING

Magnuson, the Wraith King snapped. *Tell me where the hell you are!*

But there was only silence, and he was alone.

He growled in frustration and tugged off his hood with one bony hand to scan the world around him for clues as to what the hell had happened. Seconds ago, Magnuson had led the way through the darkness. Now, the Wraith King hovered above a well-worn floor in a circular chamber lined with stone. It curved overhead, a roughly hewn dome carved from the mountain itself, and he spun in a circle as he tried to make sense of where he was.

These damned in-betweens.

How he *hated* them.

With no god pulling the strings in this place, however, the sudden isolation left him on edge. If ever he could be killed, it was in a place like this, where creatures from the lawless lands in Death's domain could roam free.

"Lachlann," a woman said from somewhere behind him.

A familiar voice. A soothing one.

He froze in place. The bones in his right hand clicked together as he curled his fingers into a fist. It took effort to kill the pang of longing that came with hearing her voice after so long.

From a woman he knew to be dead.

"Lachlann," she said again, just as she had all those centuries ago.

Lock-lenn.

Right.

That had been his name, once. He remembered it in a rush, and it seemed so obvious that he felt like a fool to have gone this long without saying it.

How strange, for a man to forget his own name.

It had annoyed him, back then, when she had called him by his first name. It was too familiar. Too intimate. It was a mark of disrespect that he should have seen for the warning sign it was.

Maeve, he replied.

Cautiously, he turned around. A woman now stood in the center of the otherwise empty room, her long blonde hair flowing over her shoulders and past her breasts. Her pink lips parted, and she smiled. The delicate skin around her piercing green eyes creased with genuine joy, as if she were truly happy to see him.

It was a lie, of course.

After all, she had hated him enough to slit his throat.

The golden silk of her nightgown touched the floor, and she took a timid step closer to him. Her bare feet padded across the stone, but she hesitated just out of reach.

"You must hate me." Her gaze drifted to the floor, and she took a fluttering breath. Her chest rose, and he caught himself staring at the plunging line of her cleavage.

I do, he admitted.

Maeve winced, as if the words were worse than his hand against her face, and she sighed. "I deserve that."

Yes, he confirmed.

Those piercing green eyes shifted toward him, and they snared him yet again. "Death has a way of soothing hot tempers. I was a fool."

You were, he agreed.

She laughed and shook her head. "As curt and cruel as ever, I see."

You killed me, Maeve, he reminded her. *And I am not the sort of man who forgives.*

"It would seem that you're not a man at all, my love."

She gestured to his flowing cloak, to the empty space where his feet should have been as he hovered over the floor. Her eyes roamed his body until they landed on his skull—and the long crack she had left in it.

Her smile fell.

"We have both tasted death." Her voice softened, and she closed the distance between them. Her palms pressed against his ribcage. She stared up at him with those doe eyes, perfect as ever, and those supple lips parted. "Can you forgive me, then, just this once?"

More out of impulse than intention, he set his hand on her neck, as he had done so many times in their years together. His thumb pressed against her throat, and he almost pressed down to block her airway.

From the second he touched her, however, the muscles on his hand began to regrow. Blood flowed over the tendons and fibers in his fingers, chasing up his arm as her touch repaired him, and skin followed. Legs grew from his broken femurs, and his feet touched the floor. He could feel the cold stone in his toes, every bit as icy as Death's breath on his neck.

In mere seconds, he was a man again—instead of some floating abomination of Saldian magic.

And, through it all, he never once let her go.

With his free hand, he studied the renewed skin of his long-dead body, and his brows knit with confusion—not at the magic itself, but at the sensation.

The feeling of being alive, once again.

The relief and rush of breath in his lungs.

The steady beat of a woman's pulse beneath his thumb, and the way it fluttered with anticipation as she stared up at him in awe.

Maeve leaned toward him, as she had so many times before, and her lips pressed against his jawline. A quick bolt of desire shot clear down his legs. Her tenderness brought back memories of the fun they'd had, with him between her thighs. Of the way her back arched when he drilled into her. Of the way she had moaned his name in ecstasy.

He wanted that back.

Her kisses trailed toward his mouth, and she hovered there, an inch from reigniting their renewed lust for each other.

"Do you still love me?" she asked quietly. "After everything I've done?"

He looked her in the eye, and his thumb brushed over her lip. His mind went blank, and he frankly didn't need to debate with himself to answer.

"I always loved you," he confessed, and it was so damn strange to feel his voice vibrate in his chest.

As if he were truly alive again.

Before she could kiss him, however, he grabbed her neck with both hands. He squeezed as hard as he could, harder than the night he had killed her, and her eyes went wide with shock. She gasped for breath, clawing at his hands just as she had back then, and she managed to choke out one last word.

"Please," she gasped.

That was it, then.

The confirmation that this wasn't truly Maeve.

"Whatever you are, I admire the deceit," he admitted. "Your attention to detail is astonishing. The hair. Those eyes. Her voice. It was perfect."

"Wh-what—"

He didn't let the imposter finish. "In fact, you got everything about her right except for one thing."

Those striking brown eyes stared up at him in panic as her face went pale. Her knees gave out, but he held fast to her throat. He towered over her as her full weight fell into his hands, and her knees hung limply over the ground in her final moments.

"Maeve never once said 'please,'" he explained. "And with her final breath, she called me a filthy bastard."

Before the girl could reply, her eyes rolled into the back of her head, and she went limp. Her hands fell to her side, and her head lolled backward as the last bit of life left her.

He dropped her to the floor, and her body hit with a wet smack. Her beautiful features melted away, and even her hair curled in on itself. Her skin turned green, and then a sickly gray, before it melted into a puddle of rancid water.

A strange creature lay where his dead wife had been, with gills along its neck and hollow holes for eyes. It gaped up at him with the same horrified expression as it had in its final moments, except now its withered gray body curled into a ball on the floor.

Dead.

Probably.

He didn't know what to expect in a hellhole like this.

As the hollow hole in his chest panged with a blend of strange sensations—loss, maybe, or grief, he couldn't tell—he stared down at his hands. They were nothing but bone once more, stained with time and the blood of all the people he had killed.

She will never forgive me, he said to the corpse of this disgusting creature that had, for a moment anyway, conned him. *And I will never forgive her.*

He turned his back on the creature and walked through the wall behind him, nothing more than a ghost in an abandoned cave. These walls could not hold him, not without a god to pull its strings, and he could be every bit as lawless as the monstrosities Death had allowed in here.

After all, there was much for him and Magnuson to do in the world of the living, and he wouldn't let either himself or that man die.

Not here.

Not *ever.*

CHAPTER THIRTY-TWO

NOCTURNE

In the painfully heavy silence, Nocturne listened.

He stood in a towering chamber lined with black stone. Its ceiling domed above him, taller than even he could see. A thin pinprick of light cast a narrow beam through a small hole high above him, and its edges barely pierced the darkness. Dust floated in the sunbeam, immobile and hovering in the ray of light, as though breathless to see what would happen next.

Nocturne stood in the center of the pale yellow circle cast by the withering sunlight, and he waited.

Whatever had drawn him here was undoubtedly already aware of his presence. He had no reason to hide, not in this sacred mountain that belonged to his people. This land had more tricks than he had anticipated, but he would endure.

One moment, Connor was leading the way through the endless darkness. The next, the man was gone, and Nocturne ventured into a towering room with no doors.

No way in. No way out.

But he was not alone.

Thick shadows drowned most of the chamber. Save for the few feet in front of him, he could see almost nothing—but his other senses sharpened, and they gleaned so much more than sight ever could.

Pebbles skittered across the floor. A footstep landed on the stone, soft and light, and claws scraped against the ground. He tilted his head toward the visitor, searching for more clues, but none came.

Not at first.

Once again, the chamber went silent, and he stood at its center like a gargoyle guarding what precious little light could be found in these long-abandoned catacombs.

A gentle breath rolled across the stone to his left, stirring the layers of dust on the floor. Though his eyes snapped toward the sound, the rest of him remained perfectly still.

Over the last few minutes, he had tracked his visitor's movements around the edge of the chamber. Its heavy footsteps. The hollow clack of its claws on the stone. The occasional breath. Movement in the shadows that never reached the edge of what he could see.

Above him, the spiral of dust motes still floated in their sunbeam, untouched by the visitor disturbing their air.

How curious.

FIGHT, his inner beast demanded.

The primal part of him. The feral creature against whom he fought for his sanity.

For control.

He ignored it. A dragon's feral nature could not be fed, and speaking to it only fueled its stronghold on the soul.

His visitor circled again, even more slowly than before, and Nocturne closed his eyes to listen to its path. He would not move first, not in this foreign terrain, not even with the impossible urgency of the task they faced.

And thus, he waited.

Abruptly, the footsteps stopped. Claws scuffled against the floor, and something screeched—fleetingly, quietly, and the sound died as quickly as it had come. The thud of something hitting the ground stirred the heavy silence, and the scrape of a body being dragged along the stone followed.

The rancid stench of rotting meat coiled through the air, and he growled in disgust. It burned his snout, sickly and vile, and it settled on his senses like the putrid stench of pond scum floating in a bog.

"ENOUGH OF YOUR GAMES," he finally demanded.

His voice carried across the stone walls, bouncing against the stone, again and again until his words overlapped themselves. A low growl built in his chest, and a flash of rage shot down his spine. Sparks skittered across his scales, and a low clicking rumbled from the back of his throat.

In answer, a gentle hum vibrated through the air, as sweet and light as the summer sky. Enchanting. Haunting.

Familiar.

Something scraped across the stone again, its body dragged by something larger, and the rancid rot spiraled through the air stronger than before. This time, a silhouette appeared on the edge of the light, as tall as he was.

A slender neck. Wings, spread wide.

A dragon.

His heart skipped a hopeful beat, but he forced himself to remain still. He watched the silhouette, waiting for answers.

Two blue eyes appeared among the shadows. They glowed from within, the color of a clear sky, and they watched him intently.

Beside the silhouette, a figure moved. It was subtle, small, but he saw it nonetheless. He tensed, ready for an attack, and a shadow shot toward him.

He bared his teeth, ready for war.

Instead, a creature's body landed on the floor with a splat. Water oozed from its gray skin, and greasy hair curled in on itself as the glitter of white scales faded from its arms. It slowly melted into a putrid puddle halfway between him and his visitor.

This gray blob before him didn't strike any chords, and he had no idea what it was. Even the patience of a dragon prince had its limits, and this visitor was quickly testing his.

"EXPLAIN," he commanded.

His visitor chuckled, and those blue eyes briefly narrowed. "WHEN DID YOU BECOME SO DEMANDING?."

That voice.

That *voice.*

After so many centuries without her, the sultry hum left him speechless. He stared into the shadows, lost in her eyes, unwilling to believe it was possible.

"You remember," she said.

"No sane dragon would forget you," he answered.

She laughed, and those blue eyes bobbed closer. A white dragon emerged from the shadows, and her scales glittered even in the weak spotlight from above. Lavender ribbons, glowing in the sunlight, snaked up her horns in two perfect spirals. In welcome, she spread her powerful wings, and the pale purple claws at the end of each wing scraped against the edges of the chamber.

With all the grace of a princess, she bowed before him. Her nose touched the floor in their ancient sign of respect, and she hummed again. Dust shot away from her as she commanded the forgotten chamber with all the presence and refinement of royalty.

Truth.

She—all of this—was real.

"Storm." He couldn't mask his astonishment, and he didn't want to try.

"Nocturne." She lifted her head and neared. With her, she carried the perfume of the sky, the softness of a cloud, and everything he missed about home.

The prince of dragons closed his eyes, and he savored the scent of her. It was one he feared he would never experience again.

He pressed his forehead against hers, and she hummed once more as she leaned into him. Their horns pressed together, and sparks ignited wherever they touched.

Home.

Yes.

Wherever she was, he was home.

"You came for me," she said. "I knew you would."

Nocturne sighed with relief, with joy, and with a hint of sadness. "I took so long, and we lost so many years. I was afraid I had failed you."

At that, she went silent, and the loving hum within her chest abruptly stopped.

"What is it?" he asked. "What's wrong?"

"You're mistaken, Nocturne," Storm replied. "It is I who failed you."

He snorted in his confusion, and a dark plume of smoke shot out of his nose at the ludicrous statement. "You're not making sense. You could never fail me."

"But I did. I failed them all." Storm sighed, and her regal neck curved as she studied the rotting gray corpse at their feet. "Look at that creature, Nocturne. Do you know what it is?"

He eyed her warily, on edge, but shook his head.

"It is a siren," she explained. "A soul-sucking creature, one who aimed to impersonate me to lure you to an early grave." Storm bared her blisteringly sharp teeth at the gray blob dissolving in a puddle on the floor. "Her deceit left its mark in Death's domain, and that is what called me here. That is how I found you."

At the unspoken implication, Nocturne froze. His blood ran cold, and he could only stare into her stunning blue eyes. "Death's domain?"

Her neck curled further in shame, and her gaze returned to him as she nodded.

"I couldn't hold on anymore," she whispered. "I protected the others as long as I could, but in the end, I succumbed."

Nocturne's world stopped, and a pang of horror rooted him in place. His mind went blank. Though she watched his face, waiting for him to say something, he could only stare at her in his paralyzing disbelief.

Truth.

His primal intuition kicked in, and it validated everything she had said.

"No," he said flatly.

The horror of what she was saying was too much.

Too painful.

Too raw, and he refused to accept it.

Her eyes pinched shut, so tightly that creases formed in the snow-white scales around her horns. She stifled a sob, and with the sound, her body shimmered. It was like watching a mirage flicker on the horizon, and in that flash of sorrow, he momentarily saw the cold stone floor behind her.

In seconds, she was back and solid again—but that had confirmed what he had refused to believe.

"I cannot stay long," she said softly. "I don't have the magic, any-

MORE, BUT I HAD TO SEE YOU. I HAD TO KNOW YOU WERE ALRIGHT."

His teeth clenched together, and he couldn't speak. He simply shook his head, unable to form words.

The pain was too great.

"YOU HAVE ALWAYS BEEN STRONGER THAN ME." She wiped her wing across her face and turned away, but he saw the tear she was trying to hide.

"NOT ALWAYS," he corrected.

Storm chuckled and, with a quick sniffle, she lifted her elegant head once more. She finally looked him in the eye again, all fire and grace, and his future queen composed herself as she had so many times before when they had faced hardship in the past.

Together.

"YOU MUST SUCCEED WHERE I FAILED," she said firmly. "THERE IS AN ISLAND IN A VAST LAKE, AND IN THE FORTRESS THERE, THE SURVIVORS ARE LOCKED DEEP IN THE GROUND. INNOCENT DRAGONS HAVE BEEN BRED LIKE CATTLE. HATCHLINGS HAVE BEEN BORN WHO HAVE NEVER TASTED THE SKY. TRUST NONE OF THE HUMANS YOU MEET, ESPECIALLY THOSE WITH FIRE-RED HAIR." Her eyes shook, and her nose flared with hatred. "THEY ARE MONSTERS. ALL OF THEM."

The Starlings.

He thought of Quinn, but ultimately, he said nothing.

Storm's body flickered again. A guttural growl of frustration hummed in her throat. Her eyes pinched shut, and she leaned toward him, as though resisting the pull of someone far greater.

Death was calling her back to Him, and even she would not be able to fight Him for long.

Sparks skittered over Nocturne's chest, and his body shook with his barely restrained fury. He had only just found her, and yet Death wanted to claim her yet again. His rage built, fueled by his grief, and through it all, he could say nothing.

He had no words for this.

For once in his long life, he was not prepared to quell the feral beast within him. His control began to slip, and the sparks grew stronger. Flashes of amber light rolled across the room, as it always did when he tapped into his primal power, but he had not summoned them.

And deep within him, the feral beast gnawed at the lingering threads of his willpower.

Soft scales pressed into his forehead, and Storm's soothing hum vibrated through his skull. He leaned into her, and with her touch, the frenzy within him quieted.

His world was once more still, and he could think.

"You are why I'm here," he growled. "You are who I came to save."

"I know," she said quietly. "But the other dragons need you more."

"I took too long." A white-hot flash of grief extinguished his rage. "A selfish man imprisoned me, and I lost my one chance to protect you."

"It is done," she replied. "It cannot be changed."

He growled again, low and deep, and words failed him.

"Save the others," she ordered. "Do not let loss distract you from what must be done."

"Of course," he replied.

It was all he could think to say.

Her body flickered once more, and his throat tightened. He couldn't lose her.

Not again.

Storm leaned back, just enough to look him in the eye, and the edges of her mouth lifted ever so slightly into a gentle smile. "There is more life for us to live, Nocturne. Death's domain is not the end of things. I will wait for you as long as it takes. This isn't forever. This is for now."

He growled again, louder this time, and he roughly pressed his forehead against hers. He relished in the soft brush of her scales against his, knowing it would be the last time. The sensation left a buzzing trail down his muzzle, and he savored it.

When she eventually faded into nothing, he wanted to remember her like this.

"Stay," he demanded, knowing full well that it was impossible.

Storm nuzzled harder against him. A soft plume of white smoke shot from her nose and rolled down his neck. "I WISH I COULD."

The words hit him like a spear to the heart, and his voice failed him.

"YOU GAVE ME STRENGTH THROUGH THE WORST OF MY TIME ON THAT ISLAND." Her voice purred through him, as soothing as sunlight on a summer breeze. "YOU ALWAYS HAVE BEEN MY PROTECTOR, BUT THERE'S NOTHING LEFT OF ME TO SAVE."

That gutted him.

"THE OTHERS STILL HAVE TIME," she continued. "THERE IS STILL HOPE FOR YOU TO SAVE THEM."

"I WILL," he promised. "AND I WILL TAKE THEM HOME."

She hummed happily. "THANK YOU."

"STORM." His voice carried through the chamber, and she leaned back as her dazzling blue eyes shifted toward him again. "I WILL NOT KEEP YOU WAITING FOR LONG. WE HAVE LOST SO MUCH TIME."

His queen chuckled, and the skin around her horns once again creased with her laughter. "SILLY THING. ALL I HAVE IS TIME."

Her body flickered again, until almost nothing of her was left at all, and she pressed her forehead against his one last time. His scales buzzed with the joy of her, and he closed his eyes to savor it before she faded away forever.

With a happy little growl, Storm nudged his jaw. It was light, more like a breath than a touch, and the buzzing brilliance of her scales on his faded completely.

Nocturne forced himself to open his eyes, and this time, she was gone. The isolated chamber was perfectly still and every bit as silent as it had been before.

He was alone, save for a rotting gray corpse and a solitary sunbeam.

Deep within, his feral beast raged. It railed against the cruelty the Fates had shown, to dangle his queen in front of him again, only to steal her away. It burned with hatred for the Wraith King, who had cost him his future with the dragoness he so loved. It seethed. It burned. It broke.

Nocturne held it at bay, just barely, with the thought of what she needed him to do.

As he remembered her last words to him, something within him shattered. An icy calm washed over him, and he went perfectly still. The savage creature within him finally quieted, and for the first time in so long, his inner world was still.

Storm had left him a challenge, and he would not fail her.

The metallic creak of old iron clicked through the chamber, and his glare darted toward the wall to his left. A loud pop echoed past him, and a hiss of air followed. Seconds later, a piece of the wall swung backward on hidden hinges, and seven tiny silhouettes bobbed in the darkness beyond.

Good. He had hatred to spare, and anything that came for him now would die a truly painful death.

In an instant, he stood and spread his wings wide. His claws dug deep into the stone at his feet, and he roared with all his might at the intruders. Sparks raced over his scales, and he summoned blistering lightning in his throat.

Death would claim more souls today, and Nocturne would help them to their graves.

The sharp yellow lightning brewing within him cast a brilliant glow across his visitors. They hunched their gray bodies as they gaped at him in horror through strings of their dark gray hair. White specks floated through the deep black eyes, and each of them looked identical to the corpse at his feet.

More sirens.

The *gall.*

Though he expected the silhouettes to attack, they instead bowed. The tips of their greasy hair brushed against the floor as they bobbed, stooping again and again, and their thin arms gestured down the hallway they had just revealed to him.

"I DO NOT TRUST YOUR KIND." He kicked the rotting corpse aside and lowered his head. The melting body squelched as it rolled across the stone, and as the lightning in his mouth grew, so did the sirens' horror.

The sirens all spoke at once, and despite their slurred panic, he caught the occasional word.

"—your commander—"

"—we concede—"

"—wait, please!"

He reined in his lightning and shifted his attention to the closest creature. "EXPLAIN!"

"You three are superior." The siren bowed, and it peered up at him with bulging black eyes. "We will not harm you. Your friend demanded that we take you to him."

TRUTH.

Nocturne snarled, fierce and low. The heady roar rumbled in his chest like brewing thunder. These things had tried to impersonate Storm, and in his hatred, he ached to obliterate them all.

But that was the feral beast within him, and he would not succumb.

"TAKE ME TO HIM," he commanded.

The sirens skittered out into the hallway, bowing all the way in their panic, and he followed. With each wary step he took, he surveyed the rocky walls around him for signs of a trap, but none came.

Whatever Connor had done to them had clearly terrified these creatures of Death's domain. The Wraithblade's power was growing, and so too was his influence.

Good.

When he met the fools who had contained his people all these years, Nocturne would ensure he had the full force of hell behind him. This wasn't just a rescue. It was revenge, and he would leave only scorched rubble in his wake.

CONNOR

While he waited for the sirens to bring back Nocturne and the Wraith King, Connor glared down at the rotting siren that had pretended to be Quinn Starling.

Admittedly, he took a bit too much satisfaction from watching it melt to a putrid slime. He still needed to find Nocturne and the Wraith King, and he couldn't stand here until this thing was nothing more than a puddle.

They had much to do, and hardly any time to do it.

He debated chasing after them. His command for them to return his friends had, after all, been something of a bluff. He had no idea where these things lived or how to find them if they failed to deliver. In his rage, he had commanded them to do something without being certain he could make them follow through.

But he had seen their terror. They knew the consequences if they didn't obey, and he was fully ready to rip this mountain apart to find them.

There you are, the Wraith King said.

Connor could barely hide the sigh of relief at hearing that old asshole's voice. He scanned the tunnel around him just as the ghoul materialized in a puff of black smoke. A skeletal face emerged from the mist as tendrils of inky night rolled over Connor's boots.

"Are you alright?" he asked the undead king.

Of course, the ghoul said with an indignant huff. *Don't go soft on me, Magnuson. There's work to be done.*

Connor squared his shoulders, and he eyed the ghoul in suspicion. For the siren to have emulated Quinn so perfectly, these creatures had to be skilled at deception, and that meant he had to be careful.

Before they continued, he had to ensure this was truly the Wraith King. Identifying a perfect copy was a difficult task, and the only clue Connor had so far was the siren's silver tongue.

"First thing's first," Connor said. "Open your mouth."

The ghoul's hollow eyes stared vacantly at him, and for a few seconds, there was only silence. Connor didn't waver, nor did he back down.

This wasn't a request.

I'm disappointed, the ghoul finally admitted. *You endured the Blood Bogs well enough, but this mountain has somehow damaged you. You're broken. How unfortunate.*

"I'm not—"

Perhaps you can be fixed. The undead king floated side to side, pacing as he examined Connor, and he shook his head in displeasure. *Broken by a little gray blob. Shameful.*

"Just open your damn mouth!" Connor demanded with an exasperated groan.

With an unrestrained growl of utter disgust, the Wraith King obliged. The undead king's teeth parted, each bone stained with the eons that he had been dead. Deep in his throat, there was only darkness—the sort of shadow that went on forever, as though it could snare any unsuspecting fools who wandered close and drag them to the sort of hell not even Death could fathom.

Connor's eyes pinched shut, and he grimaced as he peeled himself away from that horrific void. "Alright. You're you."

Idiot, the Wraith King muttered. *Why did you ask for such a stupid thing?*

"Its tongue was—no, forget I said anything." Connor dismissed the entire absurd situation with a flick of his hand. "We need to find Nocturne."

He turned his back on the Wraith King and scanned the tunnel around them. Any second now, he figured, they would be able to hear the steady echo of the great dragon's thundering steps.

But in the tunnel, there was only silence.

Did you... The Wraith King trailed off, and a strangely somber sigh followed. *What did you encounter while I was gone?*

"Sirens," Connor explained as he continued to look for Nocturne.

Ah, the ghoul said. *That explains it, then.*

Surprised, Connor looked over his shoulder at the hovering specter and raised one skeptical eyebrow. "Explains what, exactly?"

At first, the Wraith King didn't answer. The undead man stared off into the darkness, as though he saw something Connor couldn't see, and it seemed like he wasn't going to reply.

So be it.

Connor returned his attention to the tunnel, but the ghoul floated into his line of sight. The wraith's tattered cloak fluttered with the movement, and his bony hand stretched out at his side.

It hit him, then—what the specter had meant. If Connor had seen Quinn, he could easily guess who the Wraith King had encountered.

"You saw her, didn't you?" he asked. "Your queen?"

The wraith tilted his head away from Connor, and the undead king's shoulders slumped. *I did.*

Ah.

"It wasn't her," Connor reminded the wraith. "It was a fake."

A convincing one, the wraith replied.

"Yes." With his free hand, Connor rubbed the back of his neck. "But a fake nonetheless."

The Wraith King didn't reply. Instead, the ghoul pivoted toward the opposite end of the tunnel, and Connor followed the undead man's gaze.

At first, nothing moved. Connor's ear rang in the oppressive silence. Bit by bit, the dull thud of heavy footsteps overtook the shrill ringing, and a towering silhouette emerged from the darkness.

A long neck stretched forward, and two gleaming eyes appeared from within the shadows.

"Good. You are well." Nocturne spoke more slowly than usual, and a strange sense of longing hung from every word.

Connor let out a slow breath to steady the pressure building in his shoulder blades. Thanks to their connection, Nocturne was easier to test than the Wraith King. They could imitate the living, sure, but they couldn't emulate an augmentation.

What did you encounter while we were separated? Connor asked through their link.

The prince of dragons tilted his head toward Connor, as though he'd heard the question, but those dark eyes drifted to the Wraith King. Tension bubbled through the air, thicker with each passing second, and Nocturne's snout creased with a low snarl. Amber light flashed through his jet-black eyes. The growl echoed down the long tunnel, and he looked at the ghoul with all the bloodlust of a wolf about to attack.

Tell him to stop looking at me like that, the Wraith King demanded. *Otherwise, I'm happy to finish what I started all those years ago.*

Connor pointed one finger at the ghoul. "You. Stop talking."

The old ghost shrugged. *It's a fair warning, and the only one I'll give.*

Nocturne, Connor said, more firmly this time, as he returned his attention to the bristling dragon in front of him.

The regal creature's eyes cleared, and the amber glow faded. The thundering growl dissolved into the stagnant air, and the tension in his shoulders faded in a rush.

WHAT I SAW IS MINE TO CARRY, AND MINE ALONE, Nocturne replied. COME. WE MUST CONTINUE.

It was the real Nocturne, then, but something was still off. The regal creature brushed by him and led the way into the darkness. He passed the string that had been tied off on the rock in the middle of the tunnel. Instead, he followed the other string as that lone tether to the world outside led deeper into the mountain.

We had better find that damn Soulsprite, the Wraith King muttered.

"We'll find it," Connor promised as he followed the dragon. "The question is how the hell we get out."

CHAPTER THIRTY-THREE

NYX

Bathed in darkness, Nyx adjusted the black cloth covering her nose and mouth. Her eyes narrowed as she glared over the top of the fabric at the trembling silhouette of the young woman leading her and Reaver deeper into the mountain tunnels beneath Hazeltide. Aside from their guide's shuddering breaths and the swish of the girl's boots across the floor, the three of them walked in utter silence.

A soft green glow from thousands of tiny spellgust crystals in the walls offered their only light in one of the deepest tunnels that existed in the Mountains of the Unwanted. No one came down here unless they had to, and Nyx had played that to her advantage. Dressed in black, she and Reaver had gone mostly unnoticed in a city of whores and con artists.

While the Lightseers flaunted themselves, she and her soldiers moved unnoticed. Overlooked and underestimated, her necromancers always got away with so much more than Teagan ever suspected.

According to her spies, this sector of Hazeltide acted as a landfill, of sorts—a place where the king kept artifacts he feared.

That fat old king was too superstitious for his own good. He kept gold and spellgust gems in his treasury, only to leave the true power down here, guarded by fear and a handful of soldiers who could be bribed into taking an early dinner.

Though the cloth over her face hid her mouth, Nyx smiled.

How she loved to get away with mischief.

Up ahead, their guide cast a wary glance over one shoulder. The young girl's eyes lingered, wide with a blend of fear and awe.

Interesting.

Sometimes, Nyx wondered what she looked like to others. How she came across to them, and what they thought as they studied her. It was an annoying remnant of her younger self, to wonder how she was perceived. She had heard it all before, of course—cold, indifferent, terrifying enough to make a grown man piss himself—but sometimes she wished for the unfiltered perspective. To see herself from someone else's eyes and know, without a doubt, the truth of what they saw.

The magic was probably out there, somewhere, if she ever cared enough to hunt it down.

Behind her, Reaver stalked through the tunnel with all the dead-silent stealth she had come to expect from her best assassin. He studied the cave ahead, scanning for threats despite their guide's wide hips and narrow waist, but Nyx had caught his brief and hungry expression the first time he had seen her. He had likely catalogued her for the future, and she suspected Nethervale would soon have a new slave to train and feed.

She didn't care. He was worth the hassle. He always saw so much more than anyone realized, and that made him a valuable asset. The only one worthy of this mission—provided he didn't try to kill her before it was over.

Ahead, the tunnel curved sharply to the left. The girl disappeared around the bend, and Nyx flexed her fingers as she prepared to summon her blades. Any corner could be a trap. Any patch of darkness provided her enemies the opportunity to ambush her, and she never went into these things unprepared.

The blistering frost of her Crackmane augmentation shot through her veins. Her shoulders tensed, and she shifted her weight to the balls of her feet as she kept close to the wall and peered into the space beyond.

Their tunnel ended abruptly in a wrought iron door. A large circular lock with spokes sticking from its center, not unlike a ship's wheel, stretched almost from wall to wall. Along the frame, spellgust stones embedded in golden inlays glowed with enchantments. Their dazzling light overpowered the soft glow from the spellgust crystals in the walls, and she could only imagine the level of power required to contain the monsters in this mountain.

Runes etched into the door's surface glowed with a dull green fire, and though their soft light implied they had weakened over the years, Nyx knew better than to touch the iron herself. King Edward might've been a sex-crazed opium addict, but the scholars building his enchantments had made this kingdom powerful enough to survive every conqueror who had tried to claim it.

"Open it," Nyx ordered.

Beside her, Reaver crossed his arms as they both waited for their guide to obey.

With a shaky breath, the peasant girl tucked a lock of her frizzy blonde hair behind one ear and set her hands on a wheel in its center. At her touch, the lines of spellgust embedded in the door shone brighter, and she strained against the wheel as she tried uselessly to turn it. She grunted with effort, the latch unmoving under her grip, and Nyx raised one impatient eyebrow as she watched the girl flounder.

Pathetic.

They had picked this one intentionally. As a designated servant to one of King Edward's twin daughters, this peasant simultaneously had access to the castle's inner workings and was easily overlooked by the ruling class, making her the perfect guide to bring them down here. She had even been granted access to the forbidden vault, primarily to run errands for the princesses whenever they wanted a new toy from their father's piles of dark magic.

Surely, she could open the damn door on her own.

Though he rarely showed emotion, Reaver furrowed his brow and cast a sidelong glance toward Nyx in a silent request.

With an irritated sigh, she nodded.

He walked up behind the girl, his boots never making a sound even as he stood right behind her. The servant didn't even turn her head until he set his hands on hers.

The stupid girl panicked. She yelped in surprise and squirmed beneath him, trying to get away like a frightened kitten held by its scruff.

A futile effort, really, and a waste of precious time.

Reaver didn't budge, and therefore neither did she. His grip rooted her in place, her palms protecting his from the iron. He set his jaw against the side of her head, his mouth close to her ear, and the muscles in his back tensed.

A silent reminder of who was in control.

Though he didn't say a word, the girl whimpered and went still as a stone. His gloved hands never touched the metal as he turned the wheel for her, and though she whimpered again, it finally began to move. The shrill creak of scraping metal echoed down the tunnel, gaining traction in the otherwise silent space as the door finally opened.

When it began to spin more freely, Reaver released his grip and let her turn the rest on her own. He stood behind her, not giving her an inch as she worked, and her shoulders hunched in fear even as she spun the wheel faster.

Dramatic, perhaps, but effective. Nyx smirked.

After what felt like an ear-splitting eternity, given how accustomed Nyx was to stealth and speed, the door finally cracked open. The girl let go, and a line of pale green light stretched across the ground toward Nyx's boots. The Master of Nethervale tilted her head as the door slowly revealed what lay beyond, and though the sting of sudden light hurt her enhanced eyes, she scanned what little she could see of the room beyond.

Stairs, mostly, and a wide expanse of nothing—just darkness.

The Mountains of the Unwanted.

She had *finally* made it.

Reaver took a step back to give the peasant girl more room, and she scurried out from under him. With her back against the nearest wall, she hugged herself and stared at the floor. Her frizzy hair fell over her shoulders, hiding most of her ample chest, but it was too late. His gaze lingered on her for a second longer than strictly necessary, and Nyx figured he was cataloguing something about the girl to use against her later.

Nyx didn't care. What her most accomplished student did to let off steam didn't matter as long as he could focus when a mission required his attention.

Reaver drew the sword at his waist and pressed the tip of the blade against the door. A ripple of green light shot across the iron, the sword tip at its center, like a raindrop disturbing a puddle.

The door creaked again as he pushed it open the rest of the way. A long staircase led into the darkness, and only the green fire at the base of each step lit the otherwise pitch-black cavern beyond. Overhead, the tips of stalactites protruded from the oppressive shadows, hinting at a towering ceiling.

Their guide shivered with fear as she stared at the staircase. "The final door into the mountains is on the far end of this cavern. The stairs take you right to it. You don't need me to get through that one."

"Lucky you," Nyx said dryly.

"You know what's in there, right?" The girl's voice broke as she asked the question. Though she stood before two necromancers who had probably tortured more people than she had met, the girl's eyes slowly trailed toward the stairwell, and her raw terror seemed focused on the cavern beyond.

What a little idiot.

"Your mistress," Nyx said in a flat tone, unable to resist toying with Nethervale's new prey. "The princesses—they entertain visiting dignitaries with orgies. You must know that."

The girl's nose creased with disdain, but she nodded. "Hazeltide is a twisted place."

"It's tame," Nyx corrected. She drew the dagger at her waist and watched the girl with a sidelong glare. "Debauchery and drug dens, perhaps, but nothing real. Nothing of substance. You haven't seen much of life yet, child, but you will."

Their guide froze in place, and she stared at Nyx in breathless horror at what had been left unspoken.

Just as many terrors awaited her in the real world as could be found down here in the mountains. If Reaver ever got his hands on her, she would learn that the hard way.

Nyx passed the girl without a backward glance. "You remember the terms of our agreement?"

The girl didn't answer.

A flash of cold anger burned in Nyx's chest, and she shifted her piercing glare backward toward their guide.

The peasant girl flinched under her gaze. It took a second or two, but she finally nodded. "I open this door again in fifteen days, and you'll let my brother go."

Nyx narrowed her eyes in suspicion, still studying the young woman before her as she sniffed again for a possible trap. Nyx would never be able to open this door from the inside, but that didn't mean she would be trapped. Even if the girl never came back, the princesses would inevitably send a servant down here for something. Nyx would just need to be close by, waiting for some poor fool to open the door.

Their guide needed them far more than they needed her.

"I-I need you to promise." The girl took a timid step forward and picked at the skin around her nails as she trembled.

Ahead of Nyx, Reaver paused on the first step and cast an emotionless glance backward. Nyx crossed her arms and waited, intrigued by the girl's audacity. "Explain."

"My brother." The girl swallowed hard as her voice gave out on her. "How do I know you'll keep your word and release him?"

With most of her face still obscured by the cloth over her mouth, Nyx allowed herself a wicked little smile. "You're welcome to come back with me to Nethervale to see for yourself."

The girl went deathly still. Her chest didn't move. After a moment or two of silence, she took a retreating step backward into the darkness. Her lip quivered, and though she looked like she wanted to say something else, she wisely kept her mouth shut.

"Do what you're told," Nyx ordered. "When we leave Hazeltide safely, I will consider your brother's debt repaid."

The girl stared silently down at Nyx's feet and, after a moment, nodded.

Good. As long as this little pawn of hers remembered her place, Nyx would let her live.

Probably.

With his foot still resting on the first step, Reaver scanned her face and raised one eyebrow as he obediently waited for her next command. She brushed past him, leading the way down the stairwell as the emerald fires raged on either side of her.

She still hadn't told him what they had come here to retrieve. Fates willing, he wouldn't figure it out until it was too late for him to do a damn thing about it.

Saldia's greatest treasure had been squirreled away in these tunnels, stuffed into the darkness and forgotten by most. Teagan had left his most valuable possession unguarded, and she would find it in a place even the Lightseers feared.

The Great Necromancer's Tomb was finally within reach, and her patience had paid off. No one on this continent had any idea of the hell she was about to unleash—and the revenge she would take on this land that had tried so very hard to break her.

CHAPTER THIRTY-FOUR

CONNOR

What unnerved Connor most was the silence.

In the Blood Bogs, there had been the voices in the mist. The occasional tree would shiver, or something would rush by in his periphery.

Not here.

Deep in tunnels dragons had carved eons ago, there was only darkness—and that overbearing quiet. The longer they walked, the more Nocturne acclimated to the new environment, and the dragon's thumping steps became nothing more than light thuds across the floor.

Their one guide through the shadows was the solitary string leading from the entrance, still glowing ever so slightly in the endless black, as the taught string led deeper and deeper into the labyrinth.

Judging from where the last string had led them, he suspected this one would also end at something that wanted to kill them.

After the sirens, his small band had done its best to go unnoticed. Nocturne led the way into the void before them, his keen eyes seeing things even Connor missed, and the Wraith King trailed behind them.

None of them spoke as the hours passed. Thus far, they had only ever traveled straight—something that raised the hairs on Connor's neck. Even here in Firebreath Mountain, such a thing shouldn't have been possible.

And yet, their route only ever led them dead ahead.

"Look." Nocturne's voice echoed down the endless hall, and Connor's chest tightened on reflex at the sudden sound.

The dragon's head tilted toward the ground, at the entrance to the first passageway thus far to veer off from the main route. A familiar golden emblem marked the entrance to a new tunnel.

A sun.

The white string bent around the corner and led into this new passageway. It seemed as though the last person to wander through this maze had, perhaps, had an inkling of where he was going.

Connor took a steadying breath and glared at the white string that disappeared into the darkness before them. "Think this is it?"

His voice echoed through the labyrinth, and he hated the thought of something else in this cursed place hearing him.

Though Nocturne's dark scales practically faded into the shadows behind him, the great dragon nodded. "I DO."

With a cursory glance over his shoulder, Connor checked the Wraith King's ghoulish face for signs of disagreement. The specter crossed his bony arms and stared off down the new corridor, but he otherwise didn't indicate that he was even listening.

Hmm.

It seemed like he was still haunted by whatever his siren had said to him. He could only imagine what the Wraith King had seen, and he decided to give the undead king some space to process it all.

"Alright," Connor said with a nod down the hall. "Let's go."

Their small band took its first turn in their long journey into the mountain, and Connor cast one last glance over his shoulder back at the way they'd come. Part of him hated to stray from the path he knew could lead them out. A more rational side of him, however, figured it would be a pointless effort to try to take the same route out as they'd taken to get in. Given this mountain's magic, retracing their steps might well end with them walking forever in a corridor that never ended, and they would never truly make it out.

He'd hated his trip through the Blood Bogs, but in its somber vacancy, this desolate mountain was somehow so much worse.

Ahead, the corridor curved. A faint golden glow emanated from around the bend, and Connor's back straightened as he saw the first natural burst of light in this place.

Though he hoped to find the Soulsprite, he knew that would've been too easy.

This had to be another of the mountain's tricks.

When they turned the corner, the golden glow brightened. The solitary string through the darkness led to a stone platform placed in the center of the towering corridor, where a sculpture of a dragon's claw held a golden egg the size of Connor's head. The egg glittered and shone with a light of its own, casting thin rays of light across the walls.

And, on those walls, something twitched.

Connor summoned one of his enchanted blades, and its blackfire raged along the dark steel. The gray flames on his weapon cast their own pale light across the stone closest to him. Something oozed across the stone, as thick as pond slime, and it clung to the vertical walls like moss. The hulking gray mass pulsed and vibrated as the light hit it, and he grimaced in disgust.

Instead of the stale stench of rot or lichen, as one would expect when looking at something so fowl, a heady scent of nectar swirled through the air. It thickened each time the blob shifted in its perch on the wall.

Interesting.

That is truly disgusting, the Wraith King said with disdain.

"You're not wrong," Connor muttered.

He inspected the pulsing mass to find that it spread the full length of the wall, right up to the last beam of light from the statue of the golden egg.

Wary to keep his distance, Connor took a few steps closer to the pedestal as he hunted for more clues. "What the hell is this thing?"

"I HAVE NEVER SEEN SOMETHING LIKE THIS BEFORE," Nocturne admitted. "THERE HAS NEVER BEEN A LEGEND OR LORE OF THE DRAGONS CREATING SOMETHING SO FOUL."

This was probably something that had been born in Death's domain, then.

Delightful.

As Connor approached the pedestal, he noticed that the white string didn't, in fact, end at the statue. It instead curved around the back end of the egg's perch and ended in the wall, where a shriveled hand held tightly to a half-used ball of yarn. A half-decomposed body pressed against the wall, half-covered in thick layers of dark gray goop.

Connor frowned as he stared at the corpse. "Now we know what happened to the last person to wander into this place."

Fascinating. The Wraith King hovered forward, his bony hand scratching at his exposed jawbone as he inspected the corpse before them. *I have never seen anything like this before. It is almost as if the lichen is slowly eating the body.*

"Yeah," Connor said dryly. "Riveting stuff."

It almost looks as if this thing is still alive, the ghoul continued. *The face is almost perfectly preserved, as is most of its chest. Only its limbs are corroding.*

With a reluctant groan, Connor lifted his blackfire blade to see what the ghoul was talking about. Sure enough, gaps in the corpse's skin exposed large stretches of muscle and bone. Save for a few scratches on the man's neck and a large tear in his red shirt, however, the stranger's face and torso were in fact pristine. Brown hair. Strong jawline. Thick eyebrows, still scrunched tightly in concentration or fear.

That poor bastard. A burst of acid hit the back of Connor's teeth, and he cleared his throat to suppress the urge to gag at such a disgusting sight.

The corpse's bloodshot eyes snapped open.

In unison, Connor and the Wraith King leaned backward in surprise. The corpse reached for them, and though the thick layer of slime kept its elbow rooted against the wall, its fingers stretched wide. Those dark eyes, the whites riddled with red veins, stared unblinkingly at him.

"Fates be damned." Connor's heart raced at the sudden movement, and his breath quickened as he fought the urge to chop the corpse's head clean off.

It looked like a man, trapped and decomposing in this goopy prison, but the mountain had tricked him once already. He stole a quick glance down the full length of the slime-covered wall, in case this was a distraction to draw his eye from something far more sinister, but he and his team remained the only ones in the corridor.

For now.

Still on edge, Connor squared his shoulders and watched the corpse.

Despite the man's pitiful state, he shoved aside his pity for this poor bastard and reminded himself that this probably wasn't real.

The corpse opened its mouth, and a thick trail of slime drooped from between its cracked lips. Its eyes rolled briefly back, and a guttural squeal escaped its throat. The cadaver coughed, and more slime sprayed onto the floor where its feet should have been.

It spoke, but its voice was so quiet that even Connor's enhanced ears couldn't make out the words.

Connor kept his distance. He didn't trust this thing.

"Help," it said, barely loud enough to hear.

Leave him, the Wraith King ordered. *I am quite curious to see how this progresses.*

With a disgusted glare toward the old ghost, Connor relaxed somewhat in his stance. He returned his attention to the corpse and glanced it over. "What the hell happened to you?"

"This thing—" It gasped, the words apparently too painful for it to bear, and its eyes rolled back in its head once again. "This thing trapped me."

Instantly, Connor's gaze roved across the thick layer of goop clinging to the wall as he pieced together what the corpse had left unspoken.

This wasn't lichen, or slime. It was a *creature.*

Sure enough, a thin layer of its slime lay on the floor, trailing toward the golden egg's perch. In the darkness, the cluster of slime around the pedestal looked like nothing more than a puddle of water. As his blackfire blade illuminated its surface, however, the goop shrank backward from the light. Its edges shivered and moved away, and thin tendrils of slime stuck briefly to the stone floor like drool dripping from a mouth.

"The egg is bait," Connor said.

A low growl rumbled through the tunnel, and Nocturne snarled at the slime covering the opposite wall. "VILE THING. TO USE A CHILD'S TOMB AS A LURE FOR ITS PREY—WHAT A COWARDLY ACT."

"What—" Connor frowned, but as he studied the egg once again, he pieced it all together.

The egg wasn't a sculpture at all, but a monument to a dragon that had never been born.

"Look at what I've become." The corpse shut its eyes and sobbed, and a thick spray of slime shot out of its mouth. "Look at what it has taken from me. Don't let it take anything else. Kill me. Please, for the love of the Fates, kill me and make this end."

With a frustrated sigh, Connor rubbed the back of his head with his free hand. This could've easily been a trap, set by a talking corpse the slime was using as a puppet.

Or, worse still, this man was truly still alive, living forever in misery until the creature finally sucked him dry.

Either way, he didn't trust this thing, and he wasn't going to let it drag him under.

In a rush of black smoke, he summoned his second sword. The black-fire on both blades raged hotter, and the corpse before him braced itself. It grimaced, took one final breath, and nodded.

Magnuson, honestly, the ghoul chided. *Enough with your bleeding heart. This is worthy of study. Leave him.*

"No," Connor said.

That would be cruel, far worse than ending the man's pain, and he wouldn't let someone suffer.

He took aim, careful to ensure the blades would cut the man's head off without getting stuck in the slime, and he swung.

But the creature was faster.

A shrill scream echoed through the corridor, so loud that it choked his thoughts. All of them winced in pain, and a lightning-fast ripple spread across the creature's surface. Tendrils of slime shot across the corpse's torso, and the man screamed in horror. It dragged him deeper into its body and swallowed him whole. The ball of yarn still in the man's hand snapped, and the long string that had been his only lifeline to the world outside fell limp.

Barely a second later, the sludge muffled his terrified scream, and Connor's blades cut through nothing but air.

It was silent once more, as if the corpse had never been there to begin with. One more ripple spread through the slime, and then even it was still.

A chilling blast of ice-cold fury shot through Connor's body, and he glared at the creature before him. A sword wouldn't be enough to tackle this thing, but he refused to let it capture anyone else.

"Nocturne?" He caught the dragon's eye and nodded subtly toward the creature.

"WITH PLEASURE," the dragon growled.

The Wraith King sighed in frustration, but he was otherwise silent.

Good. Connor wasn't in the mood to argue, and the old ghost wouldn't get his way.

Connor backed away to give the regal dragon beside him extra room. A brilliant yellow light snapped to life, illuminating the slime's full body, and the egg's long shadow stretched across the goopy surface. A crackle of energy shot through the air, and the hair on Connor's arms stood on end.

"Leave nothing behind," Connor said.

Nocturne's deafening roar shook the tunnel, and a blistering crack of lightning hit the creature's ooze. It shrieked again, far louder than before, and ripples shot out from its center clear to its edges on the far ends of the tunnel. The shrill scream worsened with every second, but the dragon's blast of lightning never once weakened.

Arcs of lightning shot off the core blast, and each left smoldering streaks of black in the slime. The screech of a dying beast continued, and with each passing second, the burnt stretch of goop spread farther and farther along the creature's body.

An arc of lightning branched off the main bolt and hit the egg on its pedestal. The golden orb shattered, and fragments of eggshell fell to the stone floor. A thin plume of smoke coiled in the air above the now-empty claws that had held it, but nothing else remained of the unborn dragon's tomb.

The shriek ended, and so did the blast of lightning. In the sudden silence that followed, Connor's ears rang with the echo of the monster's scream. His eyes took several moments to adjust to the abrupt darkness, but when they did, the man's corpse now lay in a puddle of blackened scum. His body had been burnt to a crisp, but at least he wouldn't suffer anymore.

Nocturne lowered his great head toward the shattered egg, and his nose flared as he sniffed one of the golden fragments on the floor.

"Be at peace, little one," the dragon said softly.

In a rush of black smoke, Connor dismissed the swords in his hands and set his palm on his friend's scaly hide. In the heavy silence that followed, he gave the dragon a reassuring pat. "At least it didn't suffer in this dank hellhole."

"Yes," Nocturne said wistfully. "Our eggs lay dormant for decades before they hatch, sometimes even for centuries, but this child is long gone. When it is entombed in gold, an egg becomes little more than a shrine."

Connor pointed the tip of one of his blackfire blades at the shards on the floor. "Did we make a mistake by destroying it, then?"

"No," the dragon replied with a sad growl. "Monuments built to honor the dead are nothing but comfort for the living, and no one alive will notice this one is gone."

A bit grim, perhaps, but it was a fair point.

Connor took one last look at the devastation the dragon had left behind. "Come on, buddy. Let's keep moving."

"These abominations of nature have pillaged a holy site." A dark plume rolled over his feet, and another rumbling growl echoed through the tunnel as Nocturne's rage reignited. "These thieves. These monstrosities. These cowards. I have precious little patience left for any of them."

Connor didn't know what to say, so he opted for silence as their trio marched onward into the darkness.

Truth be told, he felt the same—and he wanted nothing more than to leave only charred corpses in this mountain when he left.

CHAPTER THIRTY-FIVE

CONNOR

Within Firebreath Mountain, the endless tunnels were no longer silent.

In the darkness just beyond Connor's vision, claws scuttled over the rocky walls. When the feet stilled, inhuman chittering filled the void. Whatever these things were, they came in a swarm. Dozens of them scampered over the walls, the ceiling, the floor—but always just out of sight, and forever out of reach.

"I don't like this," he said under his breath.

Nor do I, the ghoul confessed.

Instead of answering, Nocturne growled, and the rumble vibrated through the floor. At the dragon's voice, the walls shook—slightly, at first, but they quaked nonetheless. A thin ribbon of spellgust glowed within the rock, so pale that it barely existed at all.

When Nocturne's snarl quieted, the wall's green light faded as quickly as it had come.

Connor rubbed his eye with the heel of his palm, convinced it was a hallucination. Maybe this mountain was finally getting to him.

As with the first, this tunnel had gone on for ages. This time, however, dozens of side passages had veered off at steady intervals. He and his team had checked every threshold, always looking for a golden marker with a sun engraved on it, but they had yet to encounter even one.

In here, he had no sense of time. His stomach growled. His mouth was parched, and though he ached to take a swig from his canteen, he had to carefully ration what was left. His eyes stung with exhaustion, but he didn't dare sleep. Not here.

Perhaps only hours had passed. He couldn't tell. For all he knew, they had been in here for days.

The Antiquity had warned him that only Death could lead the way to the Soulsprite, but Connor was quickly beginning to suspect that the gods' creator wasn't home.

A metallic clack scuttled by overhead, like a bug knocking its pincers together, and Connor shifted his attention to the ceiling. Nothing moved in those vast shadows overhead, and he wondered what sort of hell they had stumbled into.

They had followed the suns, but those suns had led them astray.

The hairs on the back of Connor's neck stood on end, and the weight of something watching him settled between his shoulder blades. He took a cautious glance behind him.

As expected, it was dark, and he couldn't see a damn thing.

Nocturne, he said through his connection to the dragon. *It might be time for a show of force. Interested?*

INDEED. The dragon growled, his head low to the ground as his pace slowed.

Again, that faint ribbon of spellgust popped briefly to life at the regal creature's voice and faded just as quickly.

He ignored the spellgust so that he could focus on the task at hand. *One bolt of lightning, dead ahead. They'll either run away or swarm us.*

WHAT ARE OUR ODDS FOR EACH?

Connor frowned as he debated quietly with himself. *Probably fifty-fifty.*

THOSE ARE POOR ODDS.

Do you have a better idea?

A huff of irritated smoke shot through the dragon's nose, but Nocturne didn't reply.

Good. It wasn't like Connor wanted a fight—in fact, he was trying to stop one.

Magnuson. The ghoul's tone had a hint of warning to it. *Whatever you're plotting, stop. We don't want to antagonize these things.*

Connor disagreed, but as the scuttle of thousands of feet grew louder, he didn't dare reply. One word might ignite the firestorm, and he wanted the first attack to be on his terms.

Magnuson! The Wraith King snapped. *What the hell are you—*

Nocturne's earsplitting roar interrupted the old ghost's tirade, and Connor summoned both of his blackfire blades in the seconds before a blistering crack of lightning shot down the corridor.

In that flash of light, the corridor glowed with all the brilliance of midday. It was a snapshot in time, and Connor didn't like the view.

The long hallway was covered with beetles as large as his chest. Most of them, to his utter disgust, had clustered near him and his team, and all of them watched him intently. Flashes of yellow light glinted across their metallic bodies in the same way that sunlight slid across steel. Long pincers curved from their faces, and farther down the tunnel, a few had even taken flight.

Curse the Fates. Not only were he and his team vastly outnumbered, but these damn things had *wings*.

With the dragon's earth-shattering roar, the ribbon of spellgust returned. Brighter now than it had been before, it was joined by other ribbons of glowing green magic embedded in the walls. The spirals led the way down the hallway, toward the endless void, and it was no longer a figment of Connor's exhausted imagination.

It seemed as though this stretch of the mountain responded to Nocturne's magic, and they could use that to their advantage.

The bolt of lightning dissolved into a thousand thin veins of light. The darkness swallowed them all, and for a moment, there was an eerie silence. Only the crackle of his blackfire blades popped in the stillness, and he prepared himself for a brutal battle.

Idiot! the Wraith King seethed. *We were passing through them unseen!*

Bullshit.

In the lingering seconds before the first onslaught came, Connor didn't reply. Those little bastards had clustered overhead, and that meant they'd been queuing for an ambush. He was astonished that the ghoul had missed such an obvious cue, but right now, it didn't matter.

They do not seem deterred, the dragon said through their connection.

Evidently not, Connor replied. He shifted his weight onto the balls of his feet, ready to fight at the first sign of an attack. *Did you see where most of them are?*

Above us, the regal creature replied. But I cannot risk hitting you.

Don't worry about me. I'll get clear. You give them hell.

Nocturne growled in confirmation, and the dragon slowly spread his powerful wings wide. He bared his teeth, and everyone in the towering corridor prepared for war.

To Connor's left, the clack of little claws skittered across the stone. Just one of these bugs, isolated from the masses, darted past—and it was heading right for him.

At the edge of the gray light from his enchanted swords, two pincers came into view. They curved toward each other, each as long as his arm, and the pale light from his weapons glinted across the enormous bug's metallic back. In the darkness, he saw one beady eye—just watching him.

His grip tightened around the hilts of his blackfire blades, and he waited for his armored opponent to make the first move.

It screeched, and the shrill scream ripped through the overbearing silence. Those pincers spread wide to reveal three rows of teeth that gnashed on the air. Its wings shot out of the armor on its back, and it launched itself forward.

And it was *fast.*

"Son of a—" The bug's pincers snapped at his head, and Connor didn't have time to finish that thought.

He swung both of his blackfire blades before the thing could eat his face, and his swords sliced it into quarters. The beetle's pincers nipped his hair as they sailed past, and the bug's remnants smacked against the wall behind him.

That ignited the firestorm.

Around them, the buzzing drone of hundreds of insects filled the air. It settled into his bones, so loud that it threw him off balance, and he sank deeper into his stance to avoid keeling over.

There must've been so many more than he had realized.

In his head, the ghoul sighed in disappointment.

"Nocturne, now!" Connor shouted.

He launched himself forward as the dragon's lightning ripped through the air. It carved a path through the beetles above them and left a black mark along its brutal trail. The spellgust in the walls hummed to life, but the buzz of wings drowned out even the magic's purr.

An arc of lightning missed Connor by inches, and the hair on his arms stood on end as he dove out of the way. The blast singed the spot on the floor where he had been moments ago. Though Connor did his best to keep close to the dragon, the beetles swarmed. He hacked his way through the torrent, never pausing, and he could only catch glimpses of Nocturne's onslaught whenever he would cut down one of the beetles blocking his view. The dragon unleashed bolt after bolt, again and again, until the whole tunnel lit up with the dragon's power.

And with every blast, a hundred beetles burnt to a crisp.

The swarm around Connor only thickened. The bastards bit him, digging their teeth into his forearms, his torso, his legs, his neck—damn it all, how he hated these things.

"Are you going to help?" he shouted to the Wraith King.

I don't see why I should, the specter grumbled. *You ignored my warning, and look at the mess you've made.*

"You ass," Connor seethed. "You know they were about to attack!"

He cut open four more beetles with a single slice of his magnificent blades, and for a moment, he finally got a clear view of the hovering specter standing idly by the wall. Several beetles charged the ghost, and the wraith simply dissolved in a puff of black smoke. The beetles crashed into the wall and fell lifeless to the floor seconds before the ghost reappeared exactly where he had been.

One of the beetles bit him hard in the shoulder, drawing blood. He grimaced as a hot flash of pain shot down his spine, and he stabbed the little fucker in its mouth. The thing went limp and slid to the floor, but he sliced off its head for good measure.

He pointed one of his blackfire blades at the ghoul, who still hadn't so much as drawn his weapon. "If I die, you'll end up fused to Nocturne. I wonder how that will go for you?"

The ghost sighed in utter disgust, but that was enough to make him draw his weapon. *You owe me, Magnuson.*

He didn't, but Connor was too focused on the three new beetles launching at his face to reply.

As he cut the three bugs open, another brilliant arc of lightning ripped through the highest shadows in the tunnel. Hundreds of charred beetles fell to the floor like sickening rain, and he dodged one before it could land squarely on his head.

"What are these things?" he shouted over the din of buzzing wings.

I can't recall. The Wraith King cleaved three of them in half with his broadsword, and the ghoul's head pivoted as he scanned the walls for more. *They seem familiar, but my time in Death's domain is fuzzy. More like a dream than a memory.*

Connor hacked through another of the winged beetles. Its severed carcass dropped to the stone with a wet splat, and he resisted the urge to spit on it in his frustration. This was more like a nightmare than a dream, but he wasn't one to split hairs.

As the emerald light embedded in the walls fought Nocturne's blinding lightning for dominance in the darkness, Connor got an idea.

A crazy one.

The kind that didn't always have the best odds for survival—but they were trying to meet Death, and maybe this was the way to do it.

Only one way to find out.

CHAPTER THIRTY-SIX

CONNOR

As another one of those damned beetles dug its teeth into his back, Connor grimaced and ripped the thing off him. In the deafening buzz of hundreds of insects hurling through the air, he sifted through his insane plan one last time.

This would either be absolutely brilliant, or it would get them all killed.

He braced himself for a world of hurt, but he didn't have a better plan. This would have to work.

"Nocturne!" he shouted over the din. "Show these things who owns this mountain! Show them what your people do to those who desecrate a sacred place!"

The prince of dragons roared, and Nocturne's eyes glowed amber with his fury. The blasts of his lightning ripped holes in the walls. Boulders tumbled from the ceiling and crushed dozens of the bugs into dust.

Magnuson, the ghoul snapped. *What the hell are you doing? He will crush you. The tunnel will cave in at any moment. It cannot sustain this.*

Of course it could. This place was built for dragons, and Nocturne's ancestors had designed it as a haven for his kind.

If any mountain could take a beating, it was this one.

Ignoring the ghost, Connor raised his voice to ensure Nocturne heard him. "This is your land! Your kingdom! Take it back!"

The dragon's roar reached a crescendo, and the walls quaked. Another boulder ripped free of the ceiling above Connor, and he barely rolled out of the way before it flattened a beetle that had launched at his face.

In a puff of black smoke, the Wraith King disappeared seconds before a boulder could hit him. He reappeared in the center of the towering hallway and hacked through a beetle before the thing could sink its teeth into Connor's back.

Honestly, Magnuson, the ghost chided. *Sometimes, I swear you have a death wish.*

Connor grimaced and sliced through two more of the infuriating bugs. As much as he wanted to reply, he instead scanned the brilliant green glow rippling through the walls. These halls had enchantments buried in them, and Nocturne's lightning was the only thing they responded to.

Down the tunnel, Nocturne's tail smashed against the wall. The stone shook, and more boulders fell. Blackened beetles littered the floor, and yet more funneled toward them in an endless stream from every direction. The dragon's eyes burned gold, and to Connor's dismay, a flash of red shot through them.

Nocturne had been scarred by whatever had happened when they were separated. He had been silent and on edge, but now he looked like he was about to go feral.

They were so damn close, and Connor needed his scaly friend to hold on. The sooner this ended, the sooner he could talk the dragon down.

Nocturne! He reached out to the regal creature through their shared connection, primarily to ensure the dragon heard him over the deafening thunder in the corridor. *Give them HELL!*

"THIS MOUNTAIN IS MINE!" the dragon thundered. "ITS TREASURES BELONG TO THE DRAGONS ALONE, AND I WILL BURN ALL THOSE WHO TRY TO STEAL THEM!"

Nocturne's head arched backward, and the wildest bolt of lightning Connor had ever seen filled the hallway with brilliant white light. He grimaced and covered his eyes with his forearm to keep from going blind. The beetles shrieked in a deafening cacophony, but Nocturne's roar drowned out even their screams. A thunderous boom shook the floor, and Connor lost his balance. His shoulder hit the wall hard, and he grunted in pain as he fell to one knee.

Blinded, off balance, and with no idea if he was about to be crushed by a boulder. This couldn't get any worse.

The dragon's roar faded, and a smattering of falling pebbles filled the silence that followed. The shrill ring in his ear grated on his nerves. Nocturne's blinding blaze of white light faded, replaced by a steady green glow, but the world was otherwise still.

Fates be damned, the Wraith King said with a tinge of awe. *I knew that dragon was powerful, but he is far more impressive than I expected.*

Connor lowered his arm and cautiously peered over his bicep to survey the destruction. Spirals of smoke coiled up from piles of rubble on the floor. Scorch marks singed every wall, and black trails marred the glowing green spellgust as the mountain hummed with life.

Glowing green light raced along both walls at a breakneck speed, almost faster than his eye could follow. The magic collided up ahead at the end of the tunnel. Its emerald light meshed and bled together, like two bolts of lightning striking each other, until they took on the shape of a blazing green sun. Another flash of light followed, and the flickering sun split down the middle as two massive doors swung open.

Brilliant sunbeams rushed through the opening in the towering doorway, and Connor squinted as the brilliant sunbeams chased away the shadows. When his eyes finally adjusted, golden light filled the hallway around and ahead of them. A sharp line on the door's threshold marked the transition between the mountain's dark gray stone and the warm brown floor of whatever awaited them on the other side.

They had made it.

Connor laughed, relieved, and dismissed both of his blackfire blades in a rush of black smoke. "Nocturne, that was incredible!"

The dragon didn't reply.

Connor's smile fell, and he looked over his shoulder. An ocean of smoldering beetles lay along the stone like a carpet between him and Nocturne. The dragon stood in the center of the towering hallway, his head low to the ground, and the regal creature's eyes still glowed brilliantly orange. Pulses of red shot through the irises, and dark plumes of smoke wafted from his nose with every breath. He glared straight ahead, dazed and distant, like he was somewhere else entirely.

Nearby, the Wraith King overturned one of the beetles with his sword and nudged it aside as he floated over the charred corpses. He studied Nocturne with a dispassionate tilt of his head and chuckled.

Finally, the ghoul muttered. *If he goes feral on his own, you will have no choice but to break him.*

Connor cast a furious sidelong glare at the specter. "You know I'm not going to let that happen."

The Wraith King watched him with the holes where his eyes used to be, and though the skeletal ghost had long ago rotted away, his voice carried more menace than any facial expression ever could. *Looks like you won't have much input, Magnuson.*

Nocturne huffed again, and smoke as black as soot in a chimney shot into the air. Connor took a wary step forward, careful to walk around the hundreds of beetle corpses along the floor.

With the movement, Nocturne's glowing eyes snapped toward him, and the dragon growled in warning.

Easy, buddy, he said through their connection. *It's me. You know who I am. Stay with me.*

But the dragon didn't reply. Even as Connor tried to press against the regal creature's mind, Nocturne wouldn't let him in.

Damn it.

"Easy," Connor said gently as he approached. "Nocturne, it's me."

Red light flashed again through those glowing amber eyes. A guttural clicking vibrated in the dragon's throat with all the menace of a predator stalking its prey, and the regal creature before him briefly snarled in warning.

The feral beast within Nocturne watched Connor with hunger, and its body rumbled with hate.

With careful steps, Connor slowly closed the distance between them. He kept eye contact with the dragon, knowing full well that even one glance down at his feet might be the trigger for the beast to attack.

In Nocturne's eyes, red light seeped across the gold, claiming more space with every passing second.

Connor didn't have long.

Its jaws snapped at the air, and a thunderous rumble shook the ground below his feet.

"Hey!" he snapped, mostly to get its attention.

It glared down at him, daring him to walk closer, and he met the challenge.

"I'm not talking to you, you damn asshole," he said firmly. "I'm talking to Nocturne. He's my friend, and I won't let you take him."

Oddly, the dragon's eyes pinched briefly shut, and it shook its head. Another snort of black smoke rolled across the floor. As the hazy plume hit him, he raised his arm to cover his mouth and filter out some of the ash—but never once did he break eye contact. When the beast opened its eyes again, he was already watching it, studying its every movement for signs that his friend was still in there.

The red light paused, and that amber glow burned brighter.

"Good." He let out a slow breath at the first sign of hope that he could bring the dragon back from the brink. "Remember the dragonlands. Remember the promises you made to them. They need you, Nocturne. They're still there. I can feel it."

He didn't know it, but a man could hope.

"Think of our team," he continued, not pausing even as the dragon snorted and huffed in its internal rage. "Think of the home you've built back in Slaybourne. Think of Quinn, of Fiona, of the Finns who adore you. Think of them."

The dragon before him snarled, wincing once again, and it was all the confirmation he needed. This was working, and deep within this beast, Nocturne was fighting to regain control.

"That's it," Connor said as he closed the final gap between them.

If all else failed, he knew the one thing that could bring his scaly buddy back.

"Remember the sky, Nocturne," he said gently. "Think of the air currents rolling off the ocean. You can taste the salty breeze, can't you? Remember how your wings cut through the clouds? If you give in, you will lose it all."

Its eyes shut tightly, and the dragon pressed itself flat against the floor. The mountain rumbled from the regal creature's raw strength, and its jaw flattened a dozen beetle carcasses as it fell. It growled, teeth bared, but its raging war was internal. Connor was a mere spectator to the dueling dragons fighting for dominance, but he could at least give his friend a bit more strength.

As he reached the dragon's head, he set his hand out and pressed his palm flat against the air. With slow precision, he reached for his friend's nose.

Even one touch could be the final nudge that shoved the feral beast back in its cage.

Idiot. The Wraith King scoffed in irritation. *You're going to get your arm bitten off.*

"Will you shut your damn mouth?" Connor grumbled under his breath. Focused as he was on bringing Nocturne back, he didn't dare look away.

I'm here, Connor said through his connection with the dragon. *This is a battle you won't lose, and one you don't have to fight alone.*

The dragon's eyes snapped open, and now only the edges of the amber light glowed with red fire. It lay there, immobile, as he set his palm on its nose.

It let out a quivering breath, and a thick plume of smoke rolled over Connor. He suppressed the urge to cough, determined not to move an inch, and held his breath as the ash-riddled storm cloud passed.

As the air cleared, the last threads of red light finally faded from the irises.

THANK YOU, the dragon said through their connection.

Nocturne was back.

Connor let out a sigh of relief, and his shoulders finally relaxed. "Fates be damned, Nocturne. You had me worried there for a minute."

"THAT MAKES TWO OF US." The prince of dragons shut his eyes, and for several moments, he simply sucked in deep breaths of air. He relaxed into the stone beneath him, exhausted from the ordeal.

A pity, the ghoul muttered.

As Connor caught his breath, he set his hands on his knees and glared over his shoulder at the old ghost that was quickly trying his patience. "Ass."

The wraith shrugged.

"THAT DOOR." Nocturne lifted his head and squinted at the open doors before them. "THAT MUST BE IT—THE HAVEN FROM THE LEGENDS. THE SAFE SPACE WITHIN THE MOUNTAIN."

Perhaps.

Connor set his hand on the dragon's neck as he studied the world on the other side of the towering doorway. Specks of dust floated in the filtered sunbeams that filled a towering cavern, but from this distance, Connor couldn't glean many useful details.

In the ages since the dragons had left, he had no way of knowing if that part of the mountain was any safer than the tunnels they had seen thus far.

But he wasn't about to spoil Nocturne's sacred return to his ancestors, and he kept his mouth shut.

"Let's get going." Connor sidestepped the hundreds of carcasses littering the floor and made his way toward the doorway.

Death awaited them, somewhere in this mountain, and he wasn't feeling great about his odds of walking out of here in one piece. Whatever they found in this new chamber, it would take them to the gods' creator one way or another. Of that, at least, he was certain.

The tricky part would be finding their way back to the land of the living.

CHAPTER THIRTY-SEVEN

QUINN

In the half-lit shadows of yet another secret tunnel, Quinn waited.

The large book containing information about her father's assassins rested on her propped knee. With her back pressed against the stone, she flipped a page in the ledger, scanning the names for more she recognized.

In the excitement of her discoveries in her father's office, she had barely slept. For two days, she had spent most of her time flipping through the books to learn whatever she could, just in case she needed to return to her father's office to hunt for more.

But these records—they were meticulous. Her father had left behind a veritable treasure trove.

For starters, the dragons' island was more secured than she had ever realized. The traps laid throughout the surrounding area surpassed even those around Lunestone, and the enchanted alarms built into the stone itself made it almost impossible to access unseen. His assassins manned the walls, rather than traditional Lightseer guards, and their orders were to kill on sight. His journal detailed a brilliant array of shift changes, which he rotated at random and detailed in depth to ensure the patterns were never predictable. Judging by the date on the last entry, he had changed them yet again right before he'd left.

It was no wonder that her father had always intercepted her attempt to scale its walls. This place was little more than a giant death trap, and if she weren't his daughter, she would've been killed long before she got as close as she did.

The risk of capture was too high, even for her, and she wouldn't be able to survey the island fortress on her own. She would have to take this information back to Connor, and they would devise a better plan together.

Careful not to tune out the world around her entirely, Quinn paused her reading and leaned once again toward the small grate to her left. Light streamed through the thin bars, and she peeked once more through the slits to scan the meeting room beyond the narrow passage in which she sat. A shadow stretched across the carpet in front of the grate from whatever was hiding her little access window from those in the room.

A long table sat in the middle of the chamber, and tall windows on the left let in streams of brilliant sunlight. After all her time in the darkened passageways that ran between the walls of Lunestone, Quinn squinted at the blinding sunshine.

A woman's muffled whimper filtered through the closed door on the right. Muttered conversation followed, and Quinn only caught bits of their chatter.

"...already headed this way!"

"...any minute now..."

"...you missed the goblets!"

A woman in a long blue gown and a frilly white cap barged through the doors carrying a silver tray of wine goblets. One by one, she set them before the chairs. Her face flushed bright red as she hurried, and a few loose tendrils of frizzy hair fell from her tight bun.

"Honestly, a little warning would've been nice," she muttered to the empty room as she set the last goblet at the head of the table. "I would've liked more notice that so many were coming! Bless the Fates, do they think we're conjurers?"

The maid tucked her silver tray under one arm and grabbed her skirts as she hurried back out the door.

"...and get the apples!" someone shouted from the next room over, just before the doors swung shut yet again.

Quinn leaned her head back against the cold wall and sighed. From the chatter in the castle, it was clear that the Lightseer Regents would assemble in this room at any moment. When Teagan had failed to send word by the date he himself had set, the remaining officers in the fortress had summoned the rest of the governing council to decide what should be done.

Oddly enough, Quinn had never seen them all meet at once, nor did she know every name on the list. Their meetings only seemed to happen while she was away, and she only heard about it from the gossip fluttering about the castle after she had returned.

Perhaps, in her father's absence, they had gotten sloppy.

As the panicked chatter faded once again, Quinn thumbed through the book on her lap to find the most recent entries. Names filled each page in three columns, and a pattern began to emerge.

Each name represented one active assassin.

A black line through the name meant that person was dead.

Circled names were the assassins who had lived through their service, and a new name always followed theirs—their heir, set to replace them upon their leave.

No one left the Unknown without volunteering someone else to take their place. They even had a coded phrase to identify each other on missions. From several of the pages toward the front of the book, it was clear none of the assassins knew each other. They trained while wearing glamours, and it was forbidden to share their true identities with anyone in the Unknown.

Hence the name, apparently.

This baffled her. In all her years in Lunestone, she had never once seen even a hint of an assassin in these walls. Lords and ladies had come to visit, of course, but her father was a prominent member of Saldian elite. It only made sense for him to entertain important visitors.

Now, however, she suspected those meetings had been so much more.

Quinn flipped the page again, and this time a bold red line caught her eye. None of the ledgers had included anything other than the simple code of line, circle, heir—but this mark was thick. Rushed. Deep, like a scar on the page. It had clearly been made in anger.

She frowned and leaned closer, trying to make out the name beneath the mark.

Celine Jasper.

A chill snaked down Quinn's spine. Her body froze, and for a few seconds, she couldn't breathe.

When Celine had married, she became Celine Montgomery, Queen of Oakenglen.

In her silent shock, Quinn shook her head. It didn't seem possible. Celine had an air of authority, sure, but she walked with a light step and an even softer disposition. It had always struck Quinn as odd that such a demure woman would marry a bloodthirsty conqueror.

If this ledger was true, however, their partnership suddenly made far more sense. For that red mark to be drawn through her name, she must have defected. No heir was listed next to her name, despite her father having clearly retired.

As Quinn's mind raced with her newest discovery, the gentle scrape of muffled footsteps filtered through the meeting room's closed doors. She carefully shut the ledger and slipped it back into her bag just as the doors opened with a loud creak. Quinn rested her stomach on the cold floor and stared through the grate separating her from the chamber beyond. Her palms pressed against the dusty stone beneath her, and she tensed her core in case she needed to bolt.

One by one, the Regents filtered in. Several men and women filed through the doorway, each wearing a heavy cloak and a grim expression. No one spoke, and no one looked each other in the eye as they took their seats around the table. Some sighed wearily, while others set their elbows on the table and wove their fingers together in preparation for what lay ahead of them.

Furrowed brows. Deep frowns. From their expressions, it seemed as though they all had known the outcome of this meeting long before they had arrived.

When everyone had settled into their places, three seats remained empty—likely for Otmund, Zander, and her father.

Quinn's jaw tensed as she studied the faces she could see through the grate, but the room remained eerily silent. Whatever they had come to discuss, it seemed as though no one was in a hurry to start the conversation.

The muffled clack of heels stalking toward the closed doors pierced the silence. Confused, Quinn scanned the seats once again, but only three remained empty—those she knew belonged to men who would miss this meeting. She frowned in confusion and glared at the door as she waited to see who else would join the Regents.

With a dramatic flourish, both doors swung open, and a familiar redhead in a flowing green gown strode into the room with all the commanding presence of a queen.

Victoria Starling.

Another redhead entered behind her, and Gwen Starling paused by the entrance as the doors once more swung shut. Compared to the flowing gowns and prim suits everyone else wore, Gwen's black leather coat and riding pants looked painfully out of place.

As usual, however, her sister didn't seem to notice—or care.

How strange. Given that neither of the women had seats waiting for them, it was likely that neither were Regents themselves.

Gwen waited by the door with her arms crossed while Victoria strode confidently toward the head of the table. The eldest Starling child set her pale hand on the high back of their father's empty chair, and she cast a cold glance across those gathered at the table.

"Teagan Starling is dead," she said flatly.

In the painful silence that followed, everyone's full attention focused squarely on her. Victoria let the weight of what she'd said settle into everyone's bones. One by one, she looked each Regent in the eye.

"That's impossible," a man said.

Quinn's ear twitched, and she frowned as she tried to place the familiar voice. It took a few moments before she recognized him as Bernard Dupont, whose son had spent a good three years trying to romantically entangle her long enough to wear down her stubborn pride.

She rolled her eyes. *Of course* their family had connections to the Regents.

Victoria's gaze shifted toward the man, and she walked out of view. Quinn, however, didn't dare move. Even a scuffle could alert her sisters, both of whom had enhanced senses, to her location.

"Is my father sitting here, Lord Dupont?" Victoria asked.

Lord Dupont didn't answer, and Quinn could only assume the two were glaring daggers at each other.

"We have confirmation." Gwen's voice pierced the air, and for the first time since the two had entered, many of those sitting at the table shifted their attention to her.

"How could you possibly have confirmation?" a woman asked, though Quinn couldn't place the voice.

Though Gwen remained still at her post by the door, only her cold blue eyes shifted toward someone out of Quinn's line of sight. "One of the three survivors took a Hackamore. He told us everything he witnessed out there in the Decay."

An icy pang of dread stabbed through Quinn's chest, and her heart nearly stopped.

No.

It wasn't possible.

If any survivors had escaped the Decay, they would share information that could not yet be made public.

Fates be *damned.*

It took every ounce of Quinn's self-control to keep from pushing herself to her feet. She wanted nothing more than to find and warn Connor, but it wouldn't do any good. She still had over a week before they were supposed to meet at the safehouse.

"Colonel Freerock returned a few days ago," Gwen explained calmly. "He took a Hackamore and told us everything."

"How dare you!" Lord Dupont yelled, and the thundering smack of a man slamming his fist against the table followed shortly after. "Neither of you are Lightseers anymore. The two of you are here only as a *courtesy*, given that your father and brother are missing. You are not authorized to interrogate Lightseer soldiers, and you are certainly not entitled to the information you forcefully pulled out of a Lightseer officer!"

Gwen's glare slowly shifted toward the sound of his voice, and the steady clack of Victoria's heels punctuated the silence that followed.

"You are out of line," Dupont continued. "I demand that you both—"

"You do not make demands of me," Gwen said flatly.

"How dare you interrupt—"

"I interrupt those I do not respect," she interjected yet again. "You've never held a sword, Dupont. You've never fought with the troops. You're here on a technicality, and your word means nothing. I've killed men far more important than you will ever be, and if you give me another order, I will remind you of your true place."

An audible gulp came from Dupont's corner of the room, and Quinn smirked with pride at her sister's commanding presence.

"Now, to business," Victoria said. "I trust the rest of you are smart enough not to interject."

Many of those at the table sat back in their seats, their full attention once again on the eldest Starling sister.

"Lovely." As Victoria walked back into view, she studied the Regents before her with a wicked little smile. "The situation is more dire than we imagined. Our new foe in Slaybourne has access to an undead army that numbers in the thousands. We can only assume he will march northward to conquer whatever he can, just as all those with the Wraith King have before him."

Quinn's head snapped up, and she barely stifled a strangled growl of frustration. They knew about the Wraith King. Apparently, she had been the only Starling child without that knowledge.

"Undead?" One of the Regents balked at the idea. "Not even the Wraith King is capable of such a feat. If he were, Henry would've capitalized on it."

"That, or our new foe is even more clever than Henry," Victoria snapped. "Which do you think is worse?"

The Regent didn't answer.

"Freerock was unable to get close," Victoria continued. "However, it's clear that Father is dead. No one could take him prisoner, and the battle ended by dawn. Neither Zander nor Quinn were seen on the battlefield. If they're prisoners, they likely have little to no use now that Father is gone. It's assumed that both have been killed, if they weren't dead already. That leaves Lunestone without the leadership it needs to persevere."

Of those assembled, only Gwen winced at the statement of those who were presumed dead. Her gaze shifted toward the ground, and a flicker of grief broke through her stony mask of indifference.

With a pained grimace and a powerful flash of guilt, Quinn set her forehead against the cold stone beneath her. Her sister had always hidden her pain so well. For even this crack to show, she must've been in agony. Yet here Quinn was, mere feet away, and too much rode on her staying silent to ease that heartache.

Everyone else, however, leaned forward. Their eyes widened at the prospect of such power. Many stole sidelong glances at each other, and even more failed to hide the subtle grins at the corners of their mouths.

Disgusting, power hungry leeches. All of them.

"Lunestone needs a new Master General," Dupont said calmly. "With Otmund missing, the line of succession is clear."

"You will never lead the Lightseers," Gwen said flatly.

Dupont scoffed. "That isn't for you to decide."

"It's not a decision," Gwen countered. "It's a fact. No Lightseer would ever follow a Master General who wasn't a Starling. When you give your first order, Dupont, every soldier will merely laugh at you."

A strangled grunt of frustration came from Dupont's corner of the room, but the man didn't reply.

"The laws are clear," a woman said from somewhere out of view. "The Regents choose—"

"The laws were written by my ancestors," Victoria interrupted as she set her hand once more on Teagan's seat. "You lot will not squabble over the chair, nor will you plant someone you control in my father's place."

"The audacity," a man hissed under his breath.

"You have no control over this council!" someone else snapped.

That broke the tension, and everyone at the table yelled over each other. Some gestured toward Victoria, while others pointed to themselves. The din grew until Quinn couldn't keep track of the accusations and demands, and her nose creased in disdain.

These were the fools leading the Lightseers.

Disgusting.

Sunlight glinted off steel barely a second before Gwen slammed the flat of her sword against the solid oak table. The painfully loud tremor warbled through the room, louder than any one voice, and everyone present held their hands over their ears as they winced at the sound.

"Quiet!" she roared.

Though several of the Regents visible through the grate gritted their teeth in anger, no one else spoke.

"Sit," Victoria said firmly from the opposite end of the room. "And this time, behave yourselves."

Chairs scraped against the wooden floor as members returned to their seats. Several Regents tilted their heads toward each other, conspiring in barely audible whispers, and Victoria's cold glare swept across the worst offenders.

Though she said nothing, Quinn knew that expression all too well. They would be punished, eventually, when Victoria could hurt them the most.

"You are dismissed," Victoria said coldly.

The Regents stood, one by one, grumbling to themselves as they filed past Gwen and out into the hallway. She stood immobile by the door, glaring at anyone who dared meet her eye.

When the doors finally swung shut once again, Victoria set her palms on the table and let out a slow sigh.

"Does Mother know?" Gwen asked as she finally sheathed her sword.

"About our family?"

Gwen nodded.

"Not yet." Victoria stared at the table's surface as she spoke. "But soon. I sent her and Zander's children back to the manor in Everdale. None of them should be here when everyone finds out. I will fly out tomorrow to deliver the news myself before we announce anything to the public."

With a scratchy cough to clear her throat, Gwen leaned once more against the wall. "It will break her."

"I know." Victoria sighed, and to Quinn's surprise, rare threads of sadness dripped from those two simple words.

A gust rattled the windows behind them, and for a fleeting moment,

Victoria's brows twisted with grief. Lines formed in her forehead, and she bit her lip to keep whatever she was feeling at bay.

Victoria closed her eyes and swallowed hard. The lines in her forehead relaxed until they disappeared completely, and with one deep breath to steady herself, Victoria opened her eyes yet again.

Calm. Fierce. Commanding—as though she had never felt a thing in her life but a queen's irritation with the common folk.

"You can't lead the Lightseers." Gwen's voice punctuated the air, and she raised one eyebrow as she studied her sister's face. "You're already Queen of Dewcrest, Victoria. You can't be both."

"Obviously." Victoria sneered. "That's why you're going to do it."

Gwen frowned and crossed her arms, but she didn't reply.

"It's the obvious choice," Victoria continued. "As much as I hate to admit it, you're more capable than I am. They'll respect you. You'll pass the Rite, you'll earn their trust, and you'll take Father's place."

"How can you say that so casually?" Gwen's voice softened, and the furrowed lines in her brow relaxed. "Half our family is dead, Victoria, and you haven't shown an ounce of grief."

"Starlings don't cry." Victoria pushed off the table and slowly paced along the long rug by the windows. "Emotions make people weak. Don't go soft on me now, little sister. There isn't enough time."

Gwen's jaw tensed, and she looked away.

"Good," Victoria said with a curt nod. "Your new role comes with rules, of course. I know you well enough by now. For starters, you won't charge off into the Decay. Slaybourne is someone else's battle."

"Bullshit." Gwen's eyes narrowed at Victoria's audacity. "Our family is missing. That's an act of war, and we would be fools to leave that unanswered."

"No, you'd be a fool to charge into the unknown, little sister," Victoria snapped. "Whoever's out there killed better fighters than you."

Tension crackled in the air as the two women glared at each other, and for a few moments, neither spoke. Each was waiting for the other to snap first.

With slow and deliberate steps, Gwen closed the distance between them until she and Victoria were nearly nose to nose. "Father and Zander knew what they were getting into—but I won't let the man who killed my baby sister go unpunished."

"Don't be an imbecile." Victoria lifted her chin defiantly. "We're not touching Slaybourne. For now, you must wait."

"For what?" Gwen let out an exasperated grunt. "Father left behind key supply chains to make ground travel through the Ancient Woods much faster. It makes no sense for us to sit here on our laurels. Freerock even planted guiding markers through the Decay from Charborough to Slaybourne. Why the hell would we *wait*?"

"For him to march northward," Victoria explained, as though it were obvious. "If he leaves Slaybourne, he loses the advantage. We only strike if he walks into territory we control, and we fight on land we actually know."

Ever impatient, Gwen threw her hands up in the air and sat on the edge of the long meeting table.

Satisfied, Victoria set one hand on the tall back of the nearest chair and tapped her delicate finger against the ornate wood. "In the meantime, we need information. Quinn's augmentor is in Oakenglen, and I guarantee that she knows more than she lets on."

Quinn tensed, and her nails dug into the stone beneath her as she fought the fluttery panic in her chest.

If Victoria did anything to Tove, she would thrash her sister to hell and back.

"Ridiculous." Gwen shook her head. "Quinn doesn't divulge information to anyone, much less a gossip in the city's upper class."

"Don't be stupid." Victoria scoffed. "That augmentor is loyal. She has forged whole artifacts for Quinn over the years. That's no ordinary potion master, Gwen. That's a servant, and loyal servants won't willingly tell secrets."

Gwen's eyes narrowed in suspicion. "What are you suggesting we do?"

Instead of answering, Victoria snapped her fingers. The doors swung open yet again, and this time, three men walked in. Their leader strode ahead of the others with his helmet under one arm and his other resting on the pommel of the sword at his waist. His green tunic had Dewcrest's golden gryphon stitched into the fibers.

Dewcrest soldiers—likely those loyal only to Victoria.

"Find Tove Warren," their elegant queen ordered. "Monitor her first, and don't engage until you're certain she's alone. Wait for the summer festival to end before you detain her. Her guard will be down during the festivities, and neighbors will assume any commotion is simply a last bit of fun before the celebration ends."

"Victoria, this is insane," Gwen interjected. "You can't possibly—"

"Bring her to me," Victoria continued, as if her sister hadn't spoken. "But be careful. Dewcrest soldiers can't be seen kidnapping Oakenglen citizens."

The man wordlessly bowed his head to his queen. With a curt gesture for the other two to join him, he shoved open the doors and walked out into the hallway.

Quinn's nose flared with her fury, and her jaw clenched as she stifled the unbearable urge to wring Victoria's neck.

The Queen of Dewcrest had married young to join the royal family, and the rumors of how she toyed with the peasants in her kingdom made Quinn's skin crawl. According to whispers in the eastern pubs, many of those she interrogated in the castle's dungeons were never seen again.

And Tove was *not* a plaything.

As much as Quinn wanted to drop everything to save her friend, she had to be rational, and that meant she had to time this carefully. The First of Summer was two days away, and the festival wouldn't end until almost a full week later. If the soldiers were ordered to wait, that gave Quinn time to finish her work here in Lunestone. Entering and leaving the fortress was a deadly risk, and she couldn't take the chance that Victoria would post guards at either end of the secret passage beneath the lake, just in case one of the Starlings made their way home.

Victoria was nothing if not thorough, and like their father, the Queen of Dewcrest prepared for nearly every eventuality. Quinn had little else to recover here in Lunestone, and evidently her mother wasn't in the castle anymore. Everdale was on the mainland, enroute to Oakenglen, and Quinn likely wouldn't get another chance to speak to her mother if she didn't take this opportunity.

As much as she wanted to dash into Oakenglen to get Tove out of the city right away, Quinn had to finish her mission first.

It was the logical choice, yes, but she damn sure wasn't happy about it.

Apparently satisfied, Victoria clasped her hands in front of her waist, and her heels clacked against the floor as she made her way out of the meeting room.

Before she could, however, Gwen grabbed her arm. The firm grip rooted Victoria in place, and the regal woman went eerily still as she met her sister's glare.

"Quinn's augmentor isn't the enemy," Gwen's voice dripped with venom. "Whatever experiments you want to try out, you will not hurt that girl."

Instead of a burst of anger, as Quinn had expected, the edges of Victoria's mouth curled into a wicked smile. "But of course, little sister. Do you think I'm some sort of monster?"

Because Gwen was facing away from the metal grate by the floor, Quinn couldn't see her sister's face. The former Lightseer didn't reply, however, and the silence became her answer.

Victoria nodded subtly toward Gwen's hand on her arm, and Gwen released her. Victoria studied Gwen's face one last time before snapping her fingers yet again. The doors opened for her, and two servants who had been waiting in the hallway bowed as their queen strode elegantly down the hallway.

Now alone in the room, Gwen sighed and rubbed her eyes. She set her hand on the pommel of her Firesword and slipped through the doors seconds before they closed.

Quinn swallowed hard. Whatever Victoria had planned for Tove, it wasn't good. Despite everything else Quinn had to do before she could sneak into Oakenglen, she couldn't risk letting those men capture Tove.

But with Gwen so close by, Quinn had one more detour to make. It complicated everything, but as she mulled it over, she realized she had very little choice. If she couldn't convince her sister to become Connor's ally, the former commander of the Lightseer Elite would inevitably become his deadliest enemy.

CHAPTER THIRTY-EIGHT

QUINN

Finding a way to slip past the excessive charms guarding the corridor to Gwen's rooms had cost Quinn precious hours.

Hours she simply didn't have to spare.

Exhausted, eyes stinging, Quinn finally snuck through the main door into her sister's suite. Her bicep still ached from her run-in with a trap set into a picture frame—damn her sister's ingenuity, to hide a war hammer in the wall like that—and Quinn gently massaged the bruised muscle as she scanned the foyer for more traps.

The foyer opened onto a sitting room with a raging fire in the hearth. A dining table covered in daggers and axes sat beside the entrance, just far enough away so as not to provide good cover for anyone entering. A dark hallway, lit only by one lone sconce at the very end, led toward four more rooms. Each of the doors along the corridor sat firmly shut.

Empty—or so it seemed.

Roughly an hour ago, she had watched Gwen walk into this part of the castle, so she knew her sister had to be here. She craned her head, listening for any hint of life, but no one spoke. Nothing rustled, and no boots thudded against the floor. It was as if the suite were empty, but Quinn knew almost all of her sister's tricks.

The woman likely knew someone was here, and Quinn didn't want to end up on the sharp end of her sister's blade.

Just in case her sister wasn't alone, Quinn tugged her hood to ensure it stayed on her head. Her hair was tucked into the back of her shirt, and she wore a scarf over her mouth, like Connor did any time he donned his mantle as the Shade.

Her heart skipped a beat at the thought of him out there, fighting whatever hell Kirkwall had in store for him, but he could handle himself. Whatever he was enduring right now, she trusted him to survive.

Quinn took a cautious step forward, and the air instantly shifted. The weight of someone watching her sent a tingle down her spine, and she felt the impending threat long before she saw it. Driven mostly by instinct, she ducked and rolled into the center of the room as a knife embedded into the floor where she had been seconds before.

A backlit silhouette stood in the darkened hallway that had, moments prior, been empty. The only clue as to where the figure had come from was the first door on the left, which sat ever so slightly ajar.

"You're good." Gwen's voice was lower than normal, with a terrifying tinge of warning dripping from every word. "But unfortunately for you, I'm in a rather unforgiving mood."

The door behind her opened, and another silhouette joined her. A man's broad shoulders blocked out the light behind them, and for a horrifying second, it reminded her of Zander.

That was, of course, until a familiar man with dark brown hair stepped into the light from the raging fireplace. His dark eyes narrowed as he studied Quinn, and she let out a sigh of relief as she recognized Cade Vossen—her brother-in-law, and Gwen's devoted husband.

Gwen and Cade didn't keep secrets from each other, so there was no use hiding anything from him.

Before Quinn could say a word, Gwen drew another dagger from a hidden sheath on her leg and launched it in a single lightning-fast motion. Quinn rolled just as the blade embedded deep in the carpet behind her, and she jumped to her feet as she yanked off her mask and hood.

"It's me!" she shouted.

Cade's eyebrows shot up his forehead, and his mouth parted in shock.

Gwen, however, didn't move. Her expression didn't change, and the only indication she was anything more than a statue was the piercing glare that quickly roamed over Quinn's face.

Quinn cautiously raised her hands in surrender as she watched her sister's expression for any signs of what would happen next. This would either go brilliantly, or it would become a bloodbath.

With Gwen, there was no in-between.

The pop and fizzle of the fire behind her filled the heady air, and Quinn's brows slowly knit together in concern the longer her sister remained motionless. Even Cade's attention shifted to Gwen.

With any Starling family conflicts, it was best for others to never interject.

Gwen curled her fingers against her palm, and her callused knuckles cracked hard in the unbearable silence. Her frown deepened, and she slowly relaxed. Unblinking and focused entirely on Quinn, she took slow and steady steps toward her.

Quinn stood her ground, and her fingers twitched as she fought the urge to summon her Burnbane augmentation in self-defense.

Gwen set her hand on Quinn's shoulder, and after one more intense moment, she finally pulled Quinn into a tight hug. Quinn's bones popped from the painfully tight embrace, but she sighed with relief anyway.

That had been frighteningly close to going entirely wrong.

"I thought I'd lost you," Gwen whispered.

Quinn didn't reply, except to hug her sister back.

In the hallway, Cade smirked and leaned one shoulder against the wall. He crossed his arms and watched them for a moment before chuckling quietly to himself. "Aren't you dead, Quinn?"

She laughed—harshly, and just once—before shaking her head. "It's a long story, Cade."

"Lucky for you, we have all night to hear it." He quirked one eyebrow and tilted his head with all the ire of a disappointed father.

Gwen finally released her and took a deep, steadying breath. "He's right, Quinn. You need to tell me everything, starting with why the hell you're sneaking around your own home like a convict."

Quinn's smile fell, and she absently rubbed the back of her neck. Bless the Fates, she didn't even know where to start. She had so much to tell them—and so much to protect.

If Gwen refused to help, there was the risk she would share anything she learned tonight with Victoria and the Regents. Connor had plenty of enemies already, and he truly didn't need one more.

But Gwen would lead the Lightseers to hell and back to protect her family, and she deserved to know the truth. She had to know what really happened out there in Slaybourne—and who their father truly was.

Quinn had to at least *try* to shift Gwen's loyalty—if not for Connor, then to prevent having to face her own sister on the battlefield when this chaos inevitably came to a head.

QUINN

The next several hours were torture.

Quinn leaned against the wall, opposite the armchair where her sister sat, motionless, as she had revealed most of what happened since she had left home. Except for key logistical details and relevant information that would've compromised Slaybourne's security, Quinn had shared everything.

Their father's betrayal.

Zander's encounter with the blightwolves.

Connor's status as the Wraithblade.

Her own shifting loyalty to a man she had once hunted.

Nocturne's mission, and the dragons enslaved on the small island just beyond this very castle.

Everything.

Though Quinn still wanted more details about Gwen's knowledge of the Wraith King and the surviving simmering souls, she didn't bring it up. It hurt to think her sister had kept something so critical a secret from her, but Quinn wasn't exactly in a position to demand answers. She had kept the hidden passages to herself, after all. Evidently, all of the Starling children kept their own secrets, and Quinn left the matter alone.

Cade leaned against a bookshelf behind his wife, and the two of them remained eerily still throughout Quinn's confession. Even now, neither of them spoke. Though Gwen remained motionless, her gaze locked on the carpet at her feet, Cade rubbed his jaw and began to pace the far end of the room.

And yet, the minutes ticked on, one by one, in an endless, painful silence.

"Bless the Fates, Gwen," Quinn muttered with an exasperated groan. "Say *something*."

Her sister shook her head, slowly at first, and finally looked up from the floor. "Father is really dead?"

Quinn swallowed, and this time, it was her turn to stare down at the floor. She nodded.

"You helped kill him."

A jolt of pain shot down Quinn's neck from the tension in her jaw, but she nodded again. Though her arms remained crossed in front of her chest, she watched her sister through the corner of her eye and braced herself for a fight.

If they were going to duel, it would happen now.

"All those lies," Gwen whispered instead. She buried her face in her hands, and strands of her fire-red hair slid over her fingers.

"Impressive." At the far end of the room, Cade grinned. "I didn't think you had this much mischief in you, Quinn."

"Don't encourage her," Gwen chided.

"I knew something was off with him." Cade continued to pace the full length of the wall, and he set his hands on the back of his head. "I knew you weren't the only one he manipulated, Gwen. He's done it to all of you."

Quinn frowned. "What does that mean?"

Cade paused mid-step and caught her eye. "Teagan never wanted me to marry your sister. He wanted someone he could control, even though he knew some prissy lord from Oakenglen would make your sister miserable. The day of our contest, someone tried to kill me."

"He was furious." Gwen leaned forward and set her elbows on her knees. "I'd never seen him that angry in public. The moment Cade walked into the arena, I thought Father was about to strangle someone. His mask only slipped for a second, but I saw it. That was the first time—it was the moment I started to…"

Gwen trailed off, and Cade set his hand on her shoulder. He squeezed softly in a gentle show of support, and she tapped her fingers on his in gratitude.

"That was the first time I wondered," Gwen finished. "It was the moment I wondered if he wasn't everything he seemed to be."

"You knew?" Quinn asked, her voice cracking as she spoke.

Gwen shook her head. "I *suspected.*"

The crackle and pop of the raging fire filled the silence once again, and Quinn studied her sister's face. Gwen's eyes glossed over, and her eyebrows furrowed in thought. She was grieving the father she thought she'd known, just as Quinn had out there in the Decay, and this suddenly seemed so cruel.

If the roles were reversed, Quinn didn't know what she would believe—the sister she adored, or the legend of their father.

"What will you do?" Quinn asked softly.

For the first time since the confession had begun, Gwen stood. She walked silently toward the fireplace and leaned one arm against the mantle as she stared into the flame.

"I don't know," Gwen finally admitted.

"You risked a lot to come in here," Cade pointed out. "Why?"

"You both deserved to hear this from me," Quinn said. "It's going to get out sooner or later, and I wanted you both to know the truth. If you take over Lunestone, you would have the means to lead a charge against Slaybourne. I didn't—" Quinn's voice broke, and she roughly cleared her throat. "I didn't want us to fight on opposing sides."

Gwen looked over her shoulder. "Would you?"

"Would I what?"

"Fight me?" Gwen caught her eye, and her sister's intense gaze left her momentarily speechless at the unspoken implications of such a simple question.

Quinn raised her chin and, for a moment, thought it over. Her brow furrowed, and though her chest tightened at the very thought, she ultimately nodded.

By the bookcase, Cade let out an impressed whistle. "You're full of surprises. I've never seen this side of you, Quinn."

"I didn't know it was there," she confessed.

"What exactly do you want from me?" Gwen interjected. "Are you expecting me to join you and your Wraithblade in whatever chaos you're cooking up?"

"No," Quinn said flatly. "I'm *asking* you to spin the story among the Lightseers. I'm *asking* you to stop the onslaught and help us weave a new narrative—a true one, this time. Help me fix this, Gwen, before more people die. That's all I want."

"That's asking a lot of me," Gwen said flatly. "And all for a man I haven't even met."

"I know," Quinn admitted.

"I need to meet him." Gwen tightened her hand into a fist as she stared into the fire. "Whatever comes next, I need to know who he really is."

"Nonsense." Cade chuckled and kicked something on the carpet at his feet. "I'm already a fan."

"Can you be serious for two seconds?" Gwen's brows furrowed as she glared over her shoulder at her husband.

His head tilted to one side as he met her eye, and his mischievous grin softened ever so slightly. "I know you're grieving, Gwen, but you knew all along who your father really was. What hurts you most is admitting it out loud."

Quinn winced. No one but Cade could speak to Gwen like that and live to talk about it.

Instead of replying, his wife pushed off the mantle and stalked toward Quinn. Quinn frowned, momentarily, concerned, until her sister pulled her into a constricting hug. The embrace was tighter than before, and it lasted several moments longer than expected.

And, without another word, Gwen left them both in the sitting room. She disappeared into the hallway, and seconds later, a door slammed somewhere in the suite.

Cade let out a heavy sigh and ran both hands through his hair. He paced for a few more moments in silence, and Quinn rubbed her eyes in defeat.

Perhaps this had been a mistake.

Perhaps she had misread her relationship with her sister entirely.

Perhaps she had just ruined everything—and earned Connor a powerful new enemy.

"I've seen her kill so many people," Cade said quietly.

Quinn looked up to find the man standing in the middle of the room with his arms crossed, staring down the hallway where his wife had disappeared.

"I've watched her kill some of the best fighters on the continent," he continued calmly. "A unit of twenty assassins hit our manor two years ago. Twenty. I wouldn't have survived that on my own, but together, we managed.. I saw her spear a man in the neck with a candelabra, that night, and she took out four people with a single arrow. She's brutal. Always has been."

Quinn had never heard that story, but from what she knew of her sister, she believed it.

He shook his head, and his eyes glazed briefly over. "In all our years together, and with everything she's done in her time as a Lightseer, I've never seen her cry. Not once." His gaze cleared, and he shifted his attention toward Quinn. "Not until earlier today, when she told me you were dead."

In her shock, Quinn flinched and gaped at Cade in awe. She didn't know how to reply.

"Give her time," he added. "Meanwhile, you'd better get out of Lunestone. Victoria is sending this place into lockdown, and even the Starling entrance will be closed off." He quirked one eyebrow at the mention of a tunnel only the Starlings were supposed to know about. "Get out safely, and don't you dare die in that corridor, Quinn Starling. There's too much at stake."

"I'll be fine," she assured him.

"You don't understand." Cade took several steps closer, until he was only a few feet away. With his arms crossed over his broad chest, he frowned in a rare moment of solemn earnest. "If you die, it'll break her. I almost saw it happen today, and I never want her to go through that again. You hear me?"

Quinn met his eye and nodded.

"Good."

Without another word, Cade stalked off down the hallway after Gwen. He disappeared around the corner, just as she had moments earlier, and the suite was silent once more.

Left alone with the flickering fire, Quinn raised her hood and once again lifted the cloth over her mouth to hide her face. If Cade was right, she barely had any time at all to recover her things and slip out of Lunestone before her one and only exit closed for good.

She still wasn't sure what would come of her confession, but she knew one thing for certain—this little reunion of hers could have gone much, *much* worse.

CHAPTER THIRTY-NINE

CONNOR

As Connor and his small band stepped over the threshold and into the sunlight, the heady stench of sulfur wafted through the air. He pulled his scarf over his nose and mouth to filter out the smell and waited for his eyes to adjust to the sudden light.

Sunbeams streamed through thin slits in the interior walls far above them. The slender spotlights crisscrossed each other, their light playing against each beam, and they lit a vast chamber carved from the stone. It was easily ten times Nocturne's height—maybe more—and the sunshine glinting off the soft brown rock gave the room an amber glow.

To his left, a wide split in the stone revealed a pool of lava far below. Its churning red surface popped and bubbled, never still, and its overpowering heat scorched the air above it.

At the sight of the boiling goop, Connor took an unconscious step away from the steep drop to a certain death.

Along the walls, ancient paint flecked and peeled off the stone. Faded remnants of massive dragons had become barely more than sketches, loosely remembered by the curves in the rock and all but forgotten by time.

A place of dragons, now lying empty.

The only sign of life in the vacant cave came from the steady green glow at the far end of the cavern. A towering tree cast a long shadow across the floor toward them, and glowing green spellgust had crystallized its branches. Small white blossoms were sprinkled between the leaves, all of them perfectly preserved by the glittering crystals.

A metallic groan echoed through the chamber, so loud it nearly deafened Connor. It vibrated through the walls, across the floor, over everything, until the hair on his arms stood on end with the threat of another fight.

He braced himself and, ready for blood, spun around.

Instead of an onslaught, however, the doors closed slowly on their ancient hinges. His ears rang with the shrill scream of their work, and he grimaced as he watched their only exit close.

"That will keep the devils out." Nocturne's voice boomed over the squeaking hinges as the doors finally shut.

Or it's a trap, the Wraith King countered.

Connor didn't reply. Truth be told, he didn't know which of them was right.

Nocturne lifted his great head, and the sunlight skittered across his black scales. The dragon closed his eyes, and a sad growl rumbled through his chest. A thin stream of smoke spiraled from his nose with the sound, but he otherwise didn't speak.

Connor turned away, and he studied the crystallized tree in order to give his friend some space to process the empty void his people had left behind in this sacred mountain.

But this wasn't a shrine. Not anymore.

It was a tomb, and it had been reduced to a foggy memory.

As Connor cautiously approached the glistening tree, the hollow echoes of his footsteps bounced off the walls. He scanned every surface for signs of a trap or tripwire, but the expanse of brown rock remained empty except for the enchanted tree preserved beneath an alcove. The overhanging stone cast a shadow on the old oak, and in the darkness, the spellgust glowed brighter. The crystals clinging to the bark shimmered and shone, and a low hum pulsed from the spellgust that consumed its ancient trunk. Ripples of light danced across the wall behind it, like emerald ripples on a pond.

Its roots dug into the rock, wooden waves in a stony ocean, and it towered over the cavern with such ease that it almost looked as though it had grown from the mountain itself. The tree was a relic of another time, and even with the dragons gone, its ancient magic lingered.

Whatever the hell this thing was, it hummed with a powerful life of its own—and that set Connor on edge. Thus far, every living thing in this mountain had tried to kill them.

At a loss, Connor peered over one shoulder to find Nocturne staring up at the faded mural of a towering black dragon. As much as he wanted to give his scaly friend space to grieve, he had no idea how long they had been in this mountain's devious tunnels. As far as he knew, the sunlight through the slits overhead was yet another illusion, and they had been down here for years.

They needed to get the hell out of here.

"Nocturne," he said gently. "Do you know what this tree is?"

With a heavy sigh and the muffled thud of the dragon's feet on the stone, Nocturne joined him. "THERE IS NO MENTION OF SUCH A TREE IN ANY OF OUR LORE. WHATEVER THIS IS, IT CAME TO THE MOUNTAIN AFTER MY PEOPLE WERE GONE."

That's helpful, the ghoul muttered.

Instead of rising to the bait, Connor ignored the old ghost and studied the crystallized tree once more. It had been helpful—more so than the ghoul seemed to realize.

If the tree had come to the mountain after the dragons had left, there was a good chance it had something to do with the Soulsprite. After all, nothing else had infiltrated this center chamber, and the sunlit cavern appeared to have kept the dangerous things out.

This tree was likely supposed to be here, and they needed to figure out why.

He studied it for ages, examining every bump and line in its bark on his hunt for the Soulsprite. He lost track of how long he spent staring at it, wishing for a clue as to where the Soulsprite had gone. A carving in the bark, perhaps, or a notch in the flawless facets of the spellgust ore that had eaten this tree whole.

But he found nothing.

Despite its glistening beauty, it didn't seem to have the one thing they'd come here to get. It looked like they were going to have to ask Death after all—and he wasn't looking forward to it.

"How the hell are we going to summon Death?" Connor asked.

At first, no one answered, and his question echoed through the empty chamber. For a fleeting moment, he wondered if that would be enough. After all, it was insane for a man to walk into an abandoned in-between and announce himself.

Beside him, the Wraith King shrugged. *We could always kill the dragon.*

"Stop talking," Connor said firmly.

The old ghost grunted in annoyance and dismissed Connor's demand with a flick of his bony wrist. *I'm sure you could convince Death to return the stupid beast.*

"Enough," Connor said firmly. "The answer is no."

The ghoul huffed. *One of these days, you will listen to reason.*

Connor shook his head. "If that ever happens, it's proof I've lost my damn mind."

The specter chuckled.

"Whatever this is, it is beautiful," Nocturne said wistfully. The dragon prince watched the tree with a somber sorrow, and its green glow reflected in his black eyes.

"It is," Connor admitted.

The wraith let out an impatient groan. *It's nothing more than a dead tree and a hunk of glittering rock. We must focus. The Soulsprite is somewhere nearby, and you must acquire it. If possible, we must figure out how you will fuse to it before we leave. An in-between has the highest chance for success, and I question whether you would be able to do so once we leave.*

Connor cast a furious sidelong glare at the hovering ghoul. "That wasn't the plan."

It wasn't part of your plan, the ghost corrected. *But it was always part of mine.*

"You never learn." Connor's eyes pinched shut as he suppressed a surge of anger. "Don't even think about it."

I knew you would complain, despite it being the obvious course of action, the wraith snapped. *I know you well enough by now. You're a noble fool, and—*

"And you're greedy," Connor finished for him. "Greedy men always lose. It's never enough, and they inevitably do something stupid in their constant need for more. That's the difference between you and me. I know when I have enough."

The Wraith King straightened his back, and he rose a few inches as he stared down with cold dispassion. *If you don't seize the power you need, I will force you to do it.*

That bastard.

"Try it." Connor squared his shoulders and crossed his arms, his full attention focused on the Wraith King as the dead man challenged him. "See what happens to you."

The Wraith King watched him with the hollow sockets that used to be his eyes, and he went eerily still. A cold chill swept across the room, and the hair on Connor's arms stood on end. The air thickened, as heavy as an ocean weighing on his chest, but neither of them gave an inch.

A stalemate.

"I'm warning you," Connor said in a low voice as he closed the gap between them. "Do not try me."

The Wraith King said nothing, and for once, Connor wished he could see more than the time-stained patches on the ghoul's jaw. He needed an expression, a tick, a twitch in an eyebrow—anything at all to help him figure out what the ghoul was thinking.

"CONNOR."

Nocturne's voice broke his focus, and on impulse, he glanced toward the dragon prince. He hated being the first to break eye contact, but he'd made his point.

If the ghoul did anything stupid, Connor wouldn't simply take it. There would be a world of hurt, one way or another.

"CONNOR!" Nocturne said again, more urgently this time.

Connor spun on his heel, only to find the dragon staring at the far end of the room, toward the doors that kept the demons of this mountain at bay. The sunlight in the cavern had faded almost to nothing, and the sudden darkness set him on edge. The weight of something watching him settled on his chest like claws digging into his lungs, and he forced himself to take steady breaths. A deep, bone-chilling cold, like a trek through the dead of winter, seeped into his body, and his breath froze on the air as he once more became aware of his surroundings.

Damn it. Rookie move. He should never have let his guard down like that, regardless of the Wraith King's threats, and now something had joined them.

Beside Connor, the Wraith King shrunk backward, just out of sight.

Afraid.

Connor followed Nocturne's gaze, and his throat tightened with surprise as he saw a hovering specter at the far end of the cavern. It reminded him of the Wraith King, only larger. With no legs, the specter hovered in an eerily familiar way, and it watched him from the shadows of its soot-black hood covering its face—if there was truly anything beneath the hood at all. Its cloak—no, cloaks, somehow, more than one—fluttered in an endless flurry despite the still air.

And those cloaks beckoned Connor toward them.

Despite the chill in the air, despite the weight on his chest and the icy frost of winter in his lungs, Connor took a dazed step forward. His eyes slipped in and out of focus, and the pang of surprise faded into a numb sense of nothing.

Those cloaks.

They were all he could see, and they beckoned him toward Death's darkness.

A cold hand grabbed Connor's shoulder, and that snapped him from the daze. He found himself halfway between the tree and the towering specter by the doors, and he took a sudden breath as he once more became aware of the world around him. He looked over his shoulder to find the Wraith King behind him with one hand outstretched. Those bony fingers dug into Connor's shoulder, but that alone had pulled him back to the present.

Despite their argument moments earlier, Connor nodded in gratitude.

Nocturne stood by the tree, his black eyes glazed over. The prince of dragons didn't move and hardly breathed. Though he seemed trapped in the same daze as Connor, the regal creature thankfully hadn't stepped forward.

Perhaps because the specter's focus wasn't on the dragon, but on Connor.

"Impressive."

The word echoed through Connor's brain, much like the Antiquity's voice always did when the goddess spoke. He flinched at the booming voice in his mind. It rattled his skull, vibrating like a string on a fiddle, and Connor gritted his teeth as he fought the urge to hold his head.

He couldn't show a thread of weakness.

Not when he was finally staring Death in the face.

Death's head pivoted only slightly, and the rest of His body remained eerily still as He shifted His attention toward the Wraith King.

"Could it be that you have come to care for others after all?" Death asked.

The Wraith King didn't answer, and he never once released his grip on Connor's shoulder.

Death's attention returned to Connor, and the darkness beneath His hood pulled once again on Connor's soul.

Beckoning him forward.

Daring him to take another step closer.

"You tried to summon me, Connor Magnuson," Death said coldly.

A chill ran down Connor's spine. It seemed wrong, vile even, for such a powerful entity to so much as say his name.

Like he had been marked.

"But one does not summon Death," the specter continued. *"I appear when you are ready, and when your time has come. Yet again, you have my attention."*

Connor swallowed hard. He wanted to ask what Death had meant by 'yet again,' but he opted for silence instead.

Words seemed so Fates-damned difficult, standing here in front of the Creator, and stringing together a sentence felt near impossible.

With Nocturne still standing immobile by the tree, and with the Wraith King tensely waiting to see what would happen next, Connor knew this fight was his and his alone. As he finally faced the god he had gone through hell to summon, he wondered if he was truly ready for whatever came next.

After all, most people who met Death didn't survive the encounter.

CHAPTER FORTY

CONNOR

In the once-sunlit chamber within Firebreath Mountain, Connor stood before Death.

The Creator.

And, most curiously, the one thing the Wraith King seemed to fear.

The filtered sunbeams that had once lit the cavern no longer cast spotlights on the rocky floor, and a dark haze rolled through the massive chamber. As the light drained from the room, so too did the warmth. Connor's breath froze on the air, and a chill snaked down his arms as he fought the urge to shiver in the sudden cold.

It made no sense. Since fusing with the wraith, Connor hadn't once felt cold—until now.

His jaw tensed as the hair on his arms stood on end. Whatever Death wanted with him, he figured this wouldn't end well.

The Wraith King's bony hand on his shoulder kept him rooted in place, even as Death's pull beckoned him forward. The specter's cloaks billowed in the winds of the departed, and it took all of Connor's willpower not to look into their surging depths again.

If he did, he might walk into them—and next time, not even the Wraith King would be able to stop him from succumbing to the powerful call.

Death studied him from the shadows beneath that jet-black hood, and for several tense moments, no one moved. Connor hardly even breathed, mainly because of the pressure building on his chest, like someone was pressing hard against his lungs.

And still, he waited. Beck Arbor's lessons rooted him in place, and in this standoff, Connor knew better than to speak first.

"You have kept me busy," Death finally said.

Calm.

Cold.

Utterly indifferent.

The specter's voice boomed across the otherwise whisper-silent rock around them, and Connor nearly summoned his swords on impulse, just from the surprise.

Connor cleared his throat. "Is that a problem?"

"No."

Huh.

Alright then.

That wasn't the answer Connor had been expecting, but perhaps it worked in his favor. At least he hadn't acquired an immortal enemy.

Yet.

"My children sent you to me," Death continued.

It wasn't a question. Though Connor never liked to divulge key details to outsiders, this was probably not the best time to lie.

After all, it seemed downright stupid to try to bluff Death.

Connor nodded, still not entirely certain where this little conversation of theirs was headed. "That's right. The Antiquity."

"And the Morrow."

It took effort to keep his mouth shut this time, mainly because Connor didn't know who the hell that was. His eyebrow twitched—just once—but he otherwise managed not to betray any trace of his confusion.

Death glided forward, and though the rest of the specter's ghostly body remained perfectly still, the Creator quickly closed the gap between them. In unison, Connor and the Wraith King stepped aside. Even with their enhanced speed, they barely moved fast enough to get out of the immortal being's way, and Death continued past them as though Connor and the wraith weren't even there.

Those cloaks passed, far too close, and their call pulled hard on his chest.

It was sudden. Violent. Painful, and it nearly ripped the muscle from his bones. The enchanted robes sucked the air right out of Connor's lungs, and his head swam. He momentarily lost his balance, consumed as he was by the call of the dead, and only the Wraith King's grip on his shoulder kept him standing.

Death passed by in less than a second, and Connor sucked in a greedy breath as the weight of Death's cloaks finally lifted from his chest.

Fates be damned. He hated that sensation.

Worse, he hated the thought that his family had felt this, once, so long ago. It shredded him from within to think of his baby sister, charred beyond recognition, staring up at the towering cloaked figure before him now.

Connor's throat tightened, and he curled his hand into a fist to keep the memories at bay.

Death reached the tree almost instantly, as if he had been there all along, and a flash of light glinted across the glowing green crystal preserving the ancient oak. Though Nocturne still stood beside the tree, as vacant and unmoving as a stone carving, the dragon's gaze followed the ghostly specter. The regal creature remained dazed, watching everything before them as if it were someone else's dream.

As Death stood before the trunk, his bony fingers stretched toward its perfectly preserved canopy. One by one, the leaves within the crystal began to wilt, and the blight spread quickly across its branches. The vibrant green leaves browned and curled on themselves, rolling inward and rotting to ash in an instant.

Death's touch had power that exceeded anything Connor had ever seen, and he was once more grateful for the Wraith King's bony hand on his shoulder. If not for that damned ghoul's grip, Connor might well have suffered the same fate.

In a rush, the tree's spellgust casing shattered. A thundering crack rumbled through the cavern, and a flash of green light blinded Connor. He grimaced and raised his forearm to shield his face as fragments of the glowing green ore shot in every direction. A few chunks slammed against his skin, stinging him with all the fire of hornets protecting their nest. Each left a searing welt, and he gritted his teeth to ride out the pain.

When the patter of glass hitting stone finally faded, Connor cautiously peered over his forearm.

Gone.

Where the ancient oak had stood, only the withered husk of a rotting trunk remained. A thin tendril of black mist poked from its charred core, almost like a black sprout pushing through the soil. For a moment, it writhed in the rotting roots of the tree, flickering and fighting against the air until it erupted. Plumes of smoke and blackfire engulfed the entirety of the trunk, burning away whatever was left of the tree that had housed it moments prior. It danced and sputtered like a tar-black bonfire, and it cast a shadow across the cavern that was even darker than Death's.

Blackfire, Connor noted, that was eerily similar to the enchantments on his blades.

Within the flickering void, something glowed a soft green. It was faint, at first, like a dying pulse, but it grew stronger with each passing moment. It rose from the depths of the blackfire, and Connor braced himself for what would happen next.

The Soulsprite.

Thank the Fates, they'd finally found it.

When the glow finally broke through the thick tendril of shadow, however, it wasn't a familiar black orb at all—it was a simple green bottle, corked with a metal spike and carved from the same spellgust that had once encased the tree.

And this was a vial he had seen before.

Teagan Starling had brought two of them in his onslaught against Slaybourne, back when the former Master General had threatened to bottle the Wraith King for good.

Connor's gut churned, and he stared at the glimmering vial as a wave of dread washed through him. For a moment, he was numb, and the faint ringing in his ear was the only sound in the deadly silent temple.

Death hovered behind the bottle as the blackfire slowly died, and for a brief moment, a weak flash of gray firelight illuminated the exposed bone in

Death's jaw. The glimpse was gone as quickly as it had come, and through it all, the Creator merely watched him from beneath that dark hood.

The Antiquity had warned him he would meet Death, but this was more than a meeting.

This was a challenge, and Death had set his trap.

A distant laugh shattered Connor's numb haze, and the Wraith King's grip on his shoulder tightened. The laugh grew, louder and louder, echoing in Connor's head until he finally realized it was the wraith.

Cackling.

We weren't sent here to find a Soulsprite at all, the ghoul said in a gravelly voice. *Your goddess lied to you.*

Given that Death could hear the wraith speak, Connor shot a withering sidelong glare at the ghost behind him. He didn't want the Creator to get any ideas about his own intentions, even if the specter was a power-mad asshole who would've grabbed the powerful artifact for himself if he was still mortal enough to fuse with it.

Though the Wraith King was baiting him, Connor didn't reply. He didn't want to give the ghoul the satisfaction of knowing how those barbed words had crawled under his skin.

The Antiquity hadn't lied at all. They'd known it was a risk that they would find a simmering soul instead of a Soulsprite, but he hadn't wanted to consider the choice he knew the Wraith King was about to force him to make.

To Connor's surprise, Death didn't reply. The immortal being didn't even glance toward the ghoul, nor did he acknowledge the Wraith King had even spoken. With his hooded gaze still focused on Connor, the Creator stretched his bony hands above the green vial.

Death no doubt wanted to see if Connor, like the wraith, would succumb to greed.

The Wraith King released his hold, and Connor took a cautious step back as the wraith's gaunt form faded from his periphery. Without the spectral being at his side, Connor suddenly felt exposed. Though he was tempted to scan the cavern to keep an eye on that damned undead king, he knew better than to turn his back on Death.

"Don't do it," Connor warned the empty air, still uncertain of where the wraith had gone. "Don't you dare."

A dark chuckle answered him, but the Wraith King remained unseen.

That *bastard.*

Before he could say anything else, however, the edges of his vision went dark. Nocturne disappeared, and even the glowing green vial faded into the shadows that slowly engulfed him.

In a flash, Death stood before him, and the Creator raised one bony finger toward Connor's face. Close enough to touch, Death's mere presence sent a surge of frost into Connor's lungs, and his body went instantly rigid.

Even with his considerable strength, even with his enhanced senses and years of honed skill, Connor couldn't move.

Death had him pinned, and he had nowhere to go.

"You come to claim the Dragon King," Death said coldly. *"I desire to know your intent."*

The Dragon King.

At first, Connor didn't know how to respond. Visions of a powerful dragon, as dark and grim as the Wraith King, collided in the back of his mind. If the wraith could grant him so many unique powers, he couldn't fathom what a simmering soul crafted from a dragon could do.

He couldn't lie to himself—the very prospect tempted him.

To think of that much power, and of what it would mean to wield the strength and magic of a *dragon.*

As Death's finger hovered dangerously close, Connor swallowed hard and shoved the idea deep into the darkest parts of his soul. Greed had gotten the Wraith King killed, and Connor wouldn't fall into the same trap.

Tempting though it might be, Connor didn't need another voice in his head, and he certainly didn't want another soul fused to his—incredible powers or no.

And yet, the vial called to him.

It carried more than promise in the muted whispers rolling from its depths. Aeron Zacharias had figured out how to bottle the sort of raw power that could conquer whole continents—or liberate them.

Or, perhaps, destroy the poor fool who thought himself capable of mastering the sort of magic that could never be controlled.

CHAPTER FORTY-ONE

CONNOR

Surrounded by darkness, Connor stood face-to-face with Death Himself. A skeletal finger hovered just above Connor's forehead as the ghoulish specter watched him from the shadows beneath a jet-black hood.

Death had set a brutal trap, and Connor had no choice but to endure whatever happened next. Powerful magic rooted him in place, and even as that skeletal hand grew closer, Connor couldn't move.

Hell, he could hardly even breathe.

"You are not the first to reach this place," Death warned in that deep, echoing voice. *"Those who came before you met grizzly fates, Connor Magnuson. Fates you must see for yourself."*

Before Connor could reply, Death's finger pressed hard against his forehead. A burst of ice froze him solid, and he gritted his teeth as the pain crackled through every vein. He grimaced, brows furrowed in agony. His mind went blank. He tried to suck in air, but his lungs were full of ice. He held back his yell of raw pain until it had become truly unbearable, but even then, nothing came out but a strangled growl.

Fates be damned.

If this was what it felt like to die, Connor never wanted to experience it again.

Again, he thought of his little sister. Of his mother. Of his father. If they had felt even a fraction of this in their final moments, he would never forgive the Creator for causing them so much pain.

His body ached more with every passing second, but in his twisted rage, he managed to force open his eyes. The darkness still shrouded him, engulfing everything around him save for Death's grizzly form, and he once more saw the flash of the Creator's bone-white jaw.

"Curious," Death said dispassionately.

Connor tried to reply, but his mouth had frozen shut. Muffled grunts of agony and rage vibrated through his chest, but it was the closest he could come to telling Death exactly what he thought of the immortal asshole before him.

"This is a mere taste of their agony," Death explained. *"You must see the rest for yourself."*

A flash of light blinded Connor yet again, but this time he couldn't shield his eyes. Death dissolved into the searing glow, though the icy pressure from his finger on Connor's forehead remained.

The light receded, and another man now stood in the cavern. He raised the green vial, grinning broadly as it glittered in the sunlight and cast speckled spotlights across the dozen corpses strewn about him on the floor. He was the last man standing, and the Dragon King was finally his.

Though the edges of Connor's vision blurred and shimmered with all the murky haze of a dream, he could feel the man's greed. He felt the man's surge of excitement in his chest as if it were his own, and yet he still couldn't speak. He couldn't move, and he certainly couldn't warn the idiot of what the fool was about to unleash.

The stranger ripped the cork from its bottle, and he stood tall as a black mist shot forth. It hit him in the chest, and he sailed backward.

Screaming.

His greed and excitement instantly bled into panic. Into fear. The screams grew louder, and a blister of agony nearly ripped Connor's skin from his bones. He felt every ounce of the man's misery, of his death throes, and he was trapped in it.

Flickering plumes of burning air distorted the far side of the cavern, and the man inched closer to the steep drop to the lava below with each passing second. The man scrambled to his feet, his screams louder than before, and he hurled himself over the edge.

Connor felt a flash of intense heat. With that, the agony receded, and Death's somber form appeared in the memory. He raised the glowing green vial, and the tendril of smoke shot into it once again. The Creator corked the bottle, and as he set it on the ground, wooden roots encased it. A new tree grew from the very rock, protecting the simmering soul once more.

Another flash of blinding light burned holes through Connor's vision. He grimaced, still frozen in place, as a new vision replaced the last one. This time, a massive golden dragon towered over an ashen trunk as a familiar green vial hovered above the tree's charred remains.

The dragon roared, and the vial shattered from the sheer power of its voice. The black tendril shot forward again, though it landed square between the dragon's eyes. The dragon's powerful roar became a scream of horror, and a bolt of lightning shot clear through Connor's chest. It rooted him to the ground, fighting the ice in his lungs for dominance, and he barely stifled a miserable scream of agony.

He couldn't take much more of this.

No mortal body could.

The dragon thrashed, and flashes of gold burned in its eyes as it succumbed to the wild pain racking its body. The golden glow in its eyes bled into a fire-hot red, and the pain only worsened as it fell prey to its feral side.

It had all happened so fast. Even a dragon like this—one as formidable and commanding as Nocturne—couldn't resist the Dragon King's overwhelming power.

"Stop!" Connor demanded.

Or, rather, he tried to.

His voice came out as nothing more than a strangled gargle as the dragon speared itself on a rocky spike and went limp. Death appeared in the memory yet again, and he pulled a glowing green vial from the depths of his cloak. With a wave of his immortal hand, the Creator gathered the Dragon King from the contender's corpse.

And the visions only continued.

They bled into each other, one death after another, and Connor experienced every man's pain. Men melted. Many more threw themselves over the edge and into the lake of lava deep within the dormant volcano's core. Dragons went feral. Dozens of souls succumbed to the Dragon King's might through the centuries, and Death forced Connor to live them all.

And each time they died, the Creator was there to contain the Dragon King once again.

It was too much to bear.

Too cruel.

Too brutal, even for Death.

"Enough!" Connor yelled. In the dizzying haze of all these dying men, he couldn't tell if he'd actually spoken or not.

In the end, he didn't care. It didn't matter what Death heard as long as this agony stopped.

The icy claws gripping Connor's lungs released him, and he sucked in greedy gulps of air as he fell to his knees. He sputtered, his palms flat against the cold rock beneath him, and it took every ounce of his lingering strength to just keep himself from collapsing into a breathless heap.

If Connor had even a spare breath in his body right now, he would've told Death exactly what he thought of him—Creator or no. As it was, however, he struggled even to stay conscious. Tremors shot through his body, and his arms shook.

He kept himself upright, for the most part, out of sheer spite and stubborn grit.

"Fascinating," Death's grim voice was distant, almost watery, and it carried all the weight of the Fates themselves in each word.

"Fascinating?" Connor seethed. Though still on his hands and knees, he glared up at the hovering specter. Death stood behind the glittering green bottle on the opposite side of the room, exactly where he had been before, as if he'd never moved at all.

This couldn't go on.

Connor wouldn't entertain this immortal jackass for a moment longer.

"Fascinating?!" he repeated, louder this time as his fury gave his tortured body renewed strength. "Forcing me to experience death over and over, to feel every man's final moments—that was *fascinating*?"

"No." Death waved away the question with a bored flick of his bony wrist. *"You intrigue me."*

"And why is that?" Connor tried to stand, but he teetered at the last moment and fell to one knee.

"Because no one has broken out of the visions before they were done," Death explained. *"None but you."*

Not long ago, Connor might've taken that as a compliment. Now, however, it only made him angrier.

"You've let so many people die." He gestured toward the cliff to his left, beyond which lay the boiling lava that had claimed so many of the contenders who had come before him. "If the Dragon King is so powerful, why not simply destroy him? You're Death. You could do it."

"I could," Death agreed. *"But the Dragon King is not mine to destroy. You demigods live by different laws than mortals, and he is not yet ready to die. Nor, it seems, are you."*

The Creator gestured toward Connor, and the unspoken implications of that simple, careless statement weighed heavily on the air.

It spoke volumes of what Connor truly was, and of what the Wraith King had truly done to them that night they'd first met.

"You are tempted," Death said flatly. *"I sense the barely restrained threads of your greed. You know what you might become, should you survive. Is it worth risking everything you have to obtain what might well kill you?"*

Connor's gaze fell to the dazzling green bottle waiting for him between Death's outstretched hands. The emerald light shimmered, like sunlight off a pond, across the slender bones that served as the Creator's fingers.

But Connor didn't answer.

The Lightseers wanted him dead. The necromancers likely wanted to steal what he had. If the Wraith King could be believed, Celine Montgomery wouldn't tarry for long, and she would bring the might of an empire against him when the time came for them to face each other. His wanted poster hung in every town and city across Saldia, promising a considerable bounty for the lucky soul who caught him off guard and dragged him back to Lunestone in chains.

The world wanted him dead, and more power could be the difference between life and death.

So, yes, this new simmering soul was more than a temptation. Like it or not, it might be a necessity to his—and Slaybourne's—survival.

"I am watching, Connor Magnuson," Death's voice echoed through his very bones. *"Few ever manage to catch my eye, but the Fates have much in store for you."*

At that, Connor's gaze snapped back toward Death. The ghostly specter faded from the room, and as his body thinned to nothing but air, He took the darkness with him. The frost slowly melted from Connor's skin, and the icy puffs of his breath on the air dissolved as the sunlight returned.

Death was gone, but that glowing green bottle remained.

Beside the platform, Nocturne shook out his body. The dragon growled with frustration as his wings spread wide, and he shuddered as if ridding himself of the lingering grogginess after a long, deep sleep.

"WHAT—" The dragon bared his teeth, and his eyes flashed gold as he scanned the now empty cavern around them. "WHAT IN THE FATES' GOOD NAME—"

His gaze shifted toward Connor, and the dragon's breathing settled.

"He's gone. Everything's fine." Connor's voice was calmer than he felt, and he did his best to settle his own racing heart.

It might've been a lie, but it was one they both needed to hear.

Still resting on one knee, Connor finally pushed himself to his feet. His head briefly spun, but he managed to stay upright this time.

Fates be damned. That had been awful.

With Death finally gone—though Connor wasn't sure how much he trusted the Creator's sudden absence—he scanned the towering room in search of the Wraith King. The ghoul was still out of sight, hidden somewhere in this in-between, and Connor let out a breath of relief that the ass hadn't done anything stupid.

That had been close.

Too close.

Connor set his hands on his waist and studied his scaly friend's expression. "Are you alright? You went completely blank. Even when Death was by you, you didn't move."

"I—I can't..." Nocturne growled, and his giant head tilted toward the glimmering green bottle on the black pedestal where the tree had been. "It is fuzzy, like a memory or a dream. I heard enough."

The dragon caught his eye, and they shared a knowing glance before they both returned their attention to the spellgust bottle.

The Dragon King.

Connor forced himself to look away and sighed heavily as he rubbed his eyes. "We can't risk it, Nocturne. Back there—back when Death—" He sucked in a breath through his teeth, and the sudden rush of air was enough to quell the surge of tension that came with reliving the deaths of so many that had come before him. "Dozens of men and dragons have died trying to fuse with him. That thing stays in its bottle, understood? We have to take it back to the Antiquity."

A plume of black smoke shot from the dragon's nose, but Nocturne ultimately nodded.

Good.

You damned fool, the Wraith King seethed.

The specter's sudden voice boomed through Connor's head, and he grimaced as he settled into his stance and once again studied the room around him. A rush of black mist rolled over the pedestal, and the dark haze briefly shrouded the spellgust bottle. The vial's steady hum of glowing light flooded through the fog like candlelight in a twilight mist, and a skeletal face emerged above it.

Connor's heart skipped a beat at the thought of Death's return, but the sunlit air didn't darken. No frost rolled across his skin. This wasn't Death at all.

As the black smoke faded, the Wraith King appeared behind the vial, exactly where Death had hovered moments before. The ghoul drew his jet-black sword, and a flash of sunlight glinted across the dark steel as the ghost raised it above the pedestal.

After everything Connor had just gone through, this idiot was going to release the simmering soul.

The *nerve.*

"Don't," Connor demanded. He glared at the ghoul, knowing full well that the ghost could act before he reached the platform to stop this insanity. "We got what we came for. Neither Nocturne nor I want to fuse with that thing."

This is one of my fellow kings, the wraith explained. *He can hear you, even trapped as he is, and you would do well to show him the proper respect.*

"I'm only going to warn you once," Connor said fiercely, ignoring the wraith's remark. "If you break open that bottle, I will find a way to end you."

The ghoul chuckled. *You wouldn't dream of it. You and I are fused, Magnuson, like it or not—and you will never be rid of me.*

Deep in his bones, Connor knew it was true. This time, the ghoul had seen through his bluff, and there would be no going back.

In one fell swoop, the Wraith King sliced open the glowing green bottle. His steel cut through it effortlessly, and he cleaved the top clean off.

The shifting black tendril within the bottle rose from its prison, and in seconds, it shot toward the nearest living thing.

Toward Nocturne.

In the visions, Connor had watched dragon after dragon—some larger and more powerful even than Nocturne—succumb to the feral beasts deep within them. Every single one of them had died here in this cave, their eyes red as fire, and they lost themselves to their bloodlust until it destroyed them. Not one of them had even made it out of this mountain, much less survived.

If that inky black wisp hit Nocturne, the prince of dragons would die.

Nocturne flinched, but Connor had seen this before. Even as the dragon tried to dart out of the way, the wisp shifted direction. The simmering soul was going to hit *something*, and Nocturne was its closest target.

With only seconds until impact, Connor sprinted forward. He acted without thinking. It was the sort of split-second decision that could save—or end—lives, and he did the only thing he could think of.

He stepped in front of his friend a mere moment before the tendril made impact, and Connor braced himself for some of the worst pain of his life.

This was going to *hurt.*

Hell, it might even kill him.

After all Death had put him through already, Connor didn't know if he could take any more of the agony. His body had been through enough, and it was about to break.

But with Nocturne's life on the line, he didn't have a better option. Death had called him a demigod, but Nocturne was still a mortal.

Connor had the best chance of surviving this—even if that chance was a slim one.

With a bang as violent as a bolt of lightning, the black tendril of smoke hit his chest. It shot him backward, and in that suspended moment, he couldn't tell up from down. His head went blank, and the edges of his vision went dark as his body threatened to give out entirely.

He hadn't been this close to fracturing since he'd woken up on that battered shore below the cliffs of Kirkwall, broken and alone as the tide nearly washed him out to sea.

This island that he had once called home was cursed, and he refused to let it take any more of him.

Connor was just too damn stubborn to die.

CHAPTER FORTY-TWO

CONNOR

Pain.

That was the only thing Connor could think of—the agonizing *pain.*

Electric shocks snapped through his every muscle. The tendons in his neck tightened until he swore they would snap. His jaw fused shut as he held back a harrowing yell of utter and complete misery.

Even if he'd wanted to scream, he would never have been able to do it.

This was so much worse than when he fused with the Wraith King. Back in that field by those rotting ruins, the wraith had held a claw over Connor's heart. That grip on his very soul had tightened until his heart struggled to beat, and Connor had thought that was the end. That no pain could ever exceed what the Wraith King had done to him.

Connor couldn't have been more wrong.

The Dragon King carried all the power and chaos of a storm. It battered him, drowning him from within. His lungs filled with something else—something other—and he sputtered for breath as his muscles screamed for mercy. His head spun as violently as if a rogue tide had swept him out into the sea and done everything in its power to drag him below the waves.

The Dragon King had unleashed a hurricane in Connor's chest, and it wanted nothing more than to rip him apart from within.

Something hard slammed into his spine. His head snapped backward as his body was violently rammed against something—a rock, perhaps, or a tree. He remembered something about sunlight and red rocks on a cave wall, but that was it. Everything before this moment was reduced to a brutal blur of color and emotion. He couldn't recall who was there with him, or why it mattered, or what had led to this gut-wrenching agony.

All he could taste was blood and spite.

The pain ate away at everything—his mind, his vision, his hearing, and even his hope that it would ever stop. It was all consuming, and he swore his body would crumble to ash at any moment.

No mortal could survive this. He knew that much for certain, but he couldn't remember where he'd heard that.

It didn't matter.

An unnatural cold seeped into Connor's bones—the sort of chill he figured came in the moments before a man died.

Death.

That word triggered something deep within him, something buried beneath the frothing waves of his never-ending pain.

A figure in a long black cloak.

Skeletal fingers.

the shadows of a hood sewn by the Fates themselves.

The memory triggered a flash of clarity that broke through the unrelenting pain. That was enough to dredge up the memory of the Creator. Even as that flash of clarity began to fade back into the agony, Connor clung to it with all the primal panic of a man about to drown at sea.

Death wouldn't claim him.

Not yet.

The Dragon King roared in his mind, and Connor winced from the sheer might of the sound. It burrowed deep into his skull, like a worm tunneling through meat. Once, years ago, that would've made his heart sputter with barely restrained terror.

Now, however, it *infuriated* him.

To hell with this. Connor had a Fates-damned job to do, and no smoldering demi-god was going to keep him from it. The Dragon King thought it could break him, as it broke every host before, and it was dead wrong.

The Fates themselves had tried to break Connor on more than one occasion, and even they had failed.

Scream for me, mortal.

The voice in his head boomed like a crack of thunder in a black sky. It carried all the ferocity of nature's devastating strength, and the rumbling vibrations that followed nearly ripped the muscle from Connor's bones.

The jolts of lightning snapping through his body briefly faded, and the muscles in his throat loosened ever so slightly. It was the only part of him that no longer writhed in agony, and he figured the Dragon King merely wanted to give him a chance to obey the command.

To scream.

To surrender.

Though a pained, guttural yell threatened to break free any moment, Connor refused to give this demented Dragon King the satisfaction of watching him fracture. If he made even a sound, he would lose the last shred of his rapidly dwindling resolve. This would be over, and he would succumb like all the others.

Scream! The voice demanded yet again.

No.

He'd meant to say it, but he didn't dare open his mouth.

When he didn't obey, the agony built to a crescendo, and Connor's vision blurred at the edges. He couldn't possibly stay awake for much longer, but if he stopped fighting now, he would lose.

And that *pain.*

It somehow got *worse.*

Whatever this was—whatever the Dragon King was doing to him—it ripped chunks out of him. He could feel the tendons in his arms snapping. The bones in his legs splintered. He couldn't last much longer.

Enhanced magic or no, it seemed like even Connor might not win this one.

The thought seemed odd. Wrong, even, with all he had sacrificed to get this far, but the growing weight on his chest was slowly crushing him.

"Pain isn't so bad, son," his father had once said. *"Not once you're used to it."*

Despite the misery, Connor scoffed. It was quick, rough, and raw, but the little flicker of laughter was enough to clear his head again. A hazy old memory came back, and he pulled at the edges of it to distract himself. Those were words from his father, years ago, as the man had tended to the deep gash down Connor's leg.

And just like that, he was twelve again.

Summer sunlight streamed through the front window. His throat stung as he bit back tears, but the sharp jolts of pain shot up his side as his father applied pressure to the still-bleeding wound. Crimson ooze stained the white cloth around his leg, and he wondered if he would ever stop bleeding.

At twelve, everything seemed so dire, and so urgent. So immediate. So eternal. Surely, this was it. They would have to chop it off, and he would spend the rest of his life hobbling around on crutches. His life was ruined, and all because that idiot up the street had wanted to play with the leather ball his father had crafted for him.

"You're alright, son," his father had said. "I know this hurts, but you're stronger than you think."

He certainly didn't feel strong. Not right now.

"Listen closely," his father said firmly. "Pain always ends, just like everything else. Ride it out. The only way out of this is through it, my boy. Take a deep breath for me, Connor. Just breathe and let it pass."

Just breathe.

He forced a deep breath, and a weak flicker of relief fluttered briefly in his chest.

Let it pass.

Another excruciating jolt brought Connor back to the present. His back arched, and he clenched his teeth as tightly as they would go. With no other choice, Connor fought against the agony by preserving what precious energy he had left to rein in the last shreds of his self-control. Though he wanted nothing more than to claw out his own heart if that would stop the agony, he did his best to ignore it. To accept it. To let it be, because fighting it wasn't going to do a damn thing.

Break*!* the booming voice demanded.

It grated against his mind, grim and vile, and the word shot through him like another bolt of lightning. His arms curled underneath him, moving on their own and reminding him that his body was not his to control.

Not until the pain ended.

Sweat clung to his face as he pressed his forehead against something hard. Tension built in his skull, as if a boulder were slowly crushing his head, but he forced his eyes open. The world around him had been reduced to mere brown and yellow blurs, but he didn't care.

Any control at all was a victory.

DIE! the voice ordered.

"Never," he seethed.

A deafening roar echoed through his head, and he grimaced as the sound ripped through him. Every sound, every beat of his heart, every little sensation sent another blinding bolt of lightning through every one of his bones.

Fates be damned. He just wanted this to end.

"It always ends, just like everything else." His father's words came to him once again. *"The only way out of this is through it."*

Just breathe.

Let it pass.

YOU WILL REGRET THIS, the booming voice promised.

Yeah, Connor figured he probably would, but he didn't have the strength to reply.

In a violent rush, the pain faded. The pressure on Connor's head eased until it disappeared entirely.

He gasped, sucking in breath after greedy breath, and he collapsed onto the cold rock beneath him. Connor lay there, his body wracked with the lingering aftershocks of all that pain. He felt as if he had been struck by a lightning bolt, and small plumes of smoke coiled over his scorched skin. Spots fizzled across his vision, and he didn't bother looking around.

With a weak grunt, he rolled onto his back. He grimaced and laid there, savoring the cool stone on the back of his head, and he briefly closed his eyes as relief washed through him.

That pain was like nothing he had ever felt before. It was as if his insides had been ripped out, leaving him hollow and empty.

And so very, very tired.

The last of the pain lingered, and pressure built once again on his chest. A flash of alarm warned him to move, to stand, but he couldn't. He was barely able to raise his head, let alone get on his feet.

The prick of a sharp claw pressed into his ribs, and he realized the pressure wasn't the lingering pain after all.

Something was actually standing on his chest.

He glared upward, only to find two intense amber eyes staring at him. A massive head blocked out everything else in the room, and its snout hovered just above Connor's nose. Sparks of lightning skittered across the beast's black scales, a warning of an impending attack.

The Dragon King.

The massive creature before him bared its teeth, inches from his face, and Connor tried to roll to his left to avoid experiencing them for himself. The heavy pressure on his chest worsened, however, and rooted him in place.

Damn it.

The Dragon King roared in his face. It was blisteringly loud, and Connor grimaced as his ears rang. His chest vibrated with the sheer power of the furious scream, and he squeezed his eyes shut against the onslaught of sound.

Never in his life had he witnessed such power. If those dagger-like teeth weren't inches from his face, he might simply marvel at the Dragon King's majesty.

As it were, however, he needed to think fast.

A MAN, the Dragon King rumbled as that deafening roar mercifully faded.

The specter's grim voice shook Connor's skull from the inside out, and he tensed as he fought the panicked urge to claw out his own ears to stop the overbearing pressure building in his head. Each word sent a shockwave through his bones, and he gritted his teeth again to stifle yet another agonized yell.

This would end, just like his father had promised all those years ago. Pain always ended, eventually, and the only way out was through it.

He just had to breathe. Every breath was a victory, and not even the Dragon King would conquer him.

Not when he had so much to lose.

NO MAN HAS SURVIVED ME, AND YOU WILL NOT BE THE FIRST. The immortal dragon's golden eyes narrowed, and Connor glared right back up at them as the Dragon King continued. NOTHING BUT MEASLY LITTLE MONSTERS, YOU LOT. I WILL NEVER SERVE THE LIKES OF YOU, AND NO MAN WILL EVER WIELD MY POWER.

The pressure on Connor's chest worsened, and more tension built in his head. The muscles in his neck bulged as he fought for enough air to breathe, but he managed to choke out a few words.

"You're in for a nasty surprise," he warned the beast.

Deep in his mind, almost too distant to even hear, the Wraith King chuckled.

Above him, the Dragon King reared his head and growled. The burden on Connor's chest lifted once again, and he scooted backward across the rock as most of the strain faded to a dull ache.

At least he could move. That was another victory.

Though he managed to put some distance between him and the Dragon King, it wasn't enough. The beast towered above him, and the edges of the dragon's hide blurred and shimmered like a mirage. Connor's eyes slipped out of focus every time he tried to study the dragon's bulk, and it seemed almost as if the beast were slipping in and out of the waking world.

Those massive jaws opened, and blazing yellow light built in the back of the towering beast's throat. Familiar sparks skittered along the dragon's black scales, and Connor's heart skipped a beat at the thought of being roasted by a blast of lightning.

Fantastic. This beast who had just fused to his soul now wanted to roast him alive.

This day just kept getting better.

CHAPTER FORTY-THREE

CONNOR

The Dragon King loomed overhead. Lightning pooled in the beast's mouth, and the full force of its rage focused squarely on Connor's chest.

Back on the battlefield outside of Slaybourne, Nocturne's lightning had reduced several Lightseers to ash. Connor wasn't about to meet the same fate.

He rolled to the side, and a dizzying blast of lightning scorched the ground where he'd been moments before. A sharp pain shot through Connor's side as he forced his battered body to move, but he did his best to ignore it. His momentum kicked up dust, and pebbles skittered across the cavern floor as he slid to a stop safely out of reach.

The Dragon King's glowing eyes darted toward Connor, following his path with ease. A low warble followed, punctuated with the soft and curious clicks of a predator stalking its prey. It was the same sound he'd heard back when he and Nocturne first fought, and the idea of fighting an even larger dragon this time left a pit in his stomach.

His head cleared in a rush—just in time to hear the Wraith King sigh impatiently.

Stop running, the undead king demanded. *He can't hurt you.*

Maybe.

Given the circumstances, Connor didn't exactly want to test that theory.

CAN'T I? The Dragon King demanded.

The dragon pivoted. Connor sat up, sensing the attack before he saw it coming, but he couldn't move fast enough. The beast's tail nailed him in the gut, and he grunted as the air was kicked out of him.

Instead of throwing him against the far wall, however, the tail passed harmlessly through him.

Connor doubled over, and his vision briefly blurred. "I thought you said he couldn't hurt me?"

Stop whining, the ghoul chided.

Though he teetered, Connor forced himself to his feet. He muttered obscenities, exhausted beyond belief and fresh out of patience to deal with either of the simmering souls now fused to his body.

The thought of two dueling voices in his head for the rest of his life drained the final reserves of his energy.

A furious growl shook Connor's head, and he stumbled backward as the sound threatened to land him on his ass once again. He glared upward at the towering dragon-wraith above him, and the beast spread its great wings as it snarled.

If Death was to be believed, the dragon had never fused with any host. It had no idea what this partnership entailed, and it probably had no idea why he couldn't kill Connor. It would probably keep trying until one or both of them collapsed in furious exhaustion.

Delightful.

As the final shreds of pain faded, his senses and memory returned. A jolt of concern shot through him, and he quickly scanned the cavern to find Nocturne.

This new simmering soul couldn't kill Connor, apparently, but it could absolutely kill the prince of dragons.

At the far end of the cavern, beside the blackened husk of what had been the crystallized tree, Nocturne studied the Dragon King with bared teeth. The living dragon spread his wings wide and tensed, ready to lunge forward any moment, but it wouldn't do any good.

The worst was over.

"This is your doing." Connor nodded to the Wraith King and pointed up at the dragon. "Talk to him."

The ghoul sighed impatiently. *One day, you will recognize blessings for what they are.*

"Right." Connor scoffed. "Yet again, you've blessed my life. Now get the hell over there and fix this."

YOU SHOULD BE DEAD! the dragon growled. The words blurred together in the beast's frustration, and its mighty foot slammed hard against the ground. The mountain around them shook with the Dragon King's strength, but it was futile.

Their battle was over. Even if the Dragon King didn't yet realize the inevitable, Connor had won.

Connor needed to rest, and perhaps he could let the Dragon King throw a tantrum while he caught his breath.

Very well, the Wraith King muttered. *Yet again, I shall do your work for you. Be grateful, Magnuson.*

Too tired to take the bait, Connor waved away the taunt with a tired flick of his hand. "Eternally. Now, get your ass out there."

The ghoul grunted in annoyance but, true to his word, glided toward the dragon on the far side of the cave. The Dragon King's attention shifted toward the robed figure floating nearer, and the towering creature snarled yet again.

Calm down, the Wraith King ordered.

Connor shook his head. He wanted to warn the ghoul to take a more nuanced approach, but he figured he would be wasting his breath.

The Wraith King had never done nuance very well.

Smoke billowed from the Dragon King's nose as his full attention shifted to the swiftly approaching ghoul. AND WHO ARE YOU TO MAKE DEMANDS OF ME, YOU ROASTED PILE OF BONES?

With a heavy sigh, Connor rubbed the back of his neck and debated intervening. He wasn't sure what use he would be, though, until he'd had some time to recover. Besides, the wraith had brought this on them both. It seemed fitting for the ghoul to get a taste of the hell he had unleashed. Neither of these kings would treat the other with respect, but he doubted either would be able to kill the other.

It was fine. Connor could let them fight while he took a moment to himself.

Never insult me, you overgrown eel, the Wraith King warned.

Yep.

This would go *great.*

Now listen, you oaf. The Wraith King crossed his bony arms as he stared up at the dragon. *You've never had a host, while I've had many. We can be useful to each other.*

A plume of black smoke shot from the Dragon King's nose and rolled across the ground beneath the Wraith King. The dragon's raspy laughter filled the air, and a low growl followed—though Connor couldn't tell which of the simmering souls it had come from.

YOU ARE A MAN, EVEN IF ONLY THE REMNANTS OF ONE, the Dragon King said haughtily. YOU ARE OF NO USE TO ME.

Watch your tongue. The Wraith King drew his sword, and sunlight glinted over the black steel. *I am a king, same as you, and I demand respect.*

YOU ARE UNWORTHY OF IT.

The Wraith King's strangled growl echoed through Connor's head. *I will teach you respect, you damned lizard.*

I WILL ALLOW YOU TO TRY!

In unison, both simmering souls charged each other. The wraith's sword slammed against the dragon's teeth, and the beast's claw sliced through the ghoul's stomach. Both screamed in pain and rolled aside, only to charge one another yet again.

The sheer power of the dragon's might shook the cavernous chamber. The undead ghouls traded blows—the Wraith King's black sword sliced through the dragon's hide, and dizzying sparks shot across the Dragon King's black scales.

If demigods could bleed, it would've been a bloodbath.

Careful to keep one eye on the battle, Connor held his side and limped toward the far wall. The ground shook beneath him with each of the dragon king's heavy steps, and though he teetered now and again, he finally made it to safety. He sucked in air through his teeth as ribbons of agony shot through his core. When he finally reached the rock that could give him a bit of support, he leaned against it with an exhausted sigh.

Children. Both of them.

Through the corner of his eye, a shadow shot toward him. He flinched and raised his arms, ready for a fight, only to find Nocturne quickly closing the distance between them. His scaly friend watched the duel at the far end of the cavern even as he trotted closer.

Connor let out a sigh of relief, but a mind-splitting roar echoed in his head as the duel between two ghoulish kings continued.

Nocturne reached him just as another wail echoed through his skull. A plume of dark smoke shot out of the regal creature's nose as the prince of dragons studied the onslaught before them. "ARE YOU INJURED?"

Hell yes, he was injured.

Fusing with one ghoul had laid him out for an entire day, and the injuries he'd suffered afterward had taken weeks to heal. To fuse with a second left him barely able to stand. His body ached. A dull throb pulsed in his skull. His bones threatened to snap if he applied the wrong pressure to any one of them, and yet he had only won half the battle.

The Dragon King raged on, his sights now set on the Wraith King, but Connor figured his reprieve wouldn't last long.

"I'm fine," he lied.

Nocturne growled in annoyance, no doubt tasting the lie, but Connor didn't have time for pleasantries.

Like it or not, he had fused with two simmering souls. That meant if either one of them died, he would perish right along with them—and both of these ghoulish beasts were trying very, *very* hard to kill each other.

With a deafening roar, the Dragon King bit into the Wraith King and threw the undead man across the cavern. Connor's and Nocturne's heads pivoted in unison as they followed the Wraith King's trajectory and the subsequent curse-riddled landing against the far wall.

"YOU SAVED MY LIFE, CONNOR," Nocturne said. "THAT IS NOT SOMETHING I KNOW HOW TO REPAY."

"You don't owe me anything."

"ON THE CONTRARY. I OWE YOU A GREAT DEAL."

Too tired for a debate, Connor tried to shrug off the compliment, but a searing pain ripped down his spine with even that subtle movement. He grimaced as he rode out the wave of misery, and once it finally faded, he teetered. It was all he could do to simply stand, and his body screamed for rest.

Nocturne shook his great head, and the dragon's attention returned to the towering king on the far end of the cavern. "Power like that consumes the living. When the bottle broke, I did not understand what was happening, but after seeing your pain..."

Despite the raging war before them, Connor studied his scaly friend's face. The regal creature arched that long neck, standing tall as he watched the immortal war before them, and several minutes passed in silence.

Connor didn't interject. Silence wasn't something to be feared, and often it was the only way to process the past.

With each moment, a bit more of his pain faded, and he could think a little more clearly. Though his body still begged for rest, it became easier to stand. His breath came more steadily, and the lingering jolts of lightning slowly dissipated.

Thank the Fates.

That had been *awful.*

On the other end of the rumbling cavern, the Wraith King punched the Dragon King square in the nose. The beast stumbled backward and slammed against the wall, releasing several boulders and a plume of red dust from the mountain rock around them. Connor sighed impatiently.

"It was terrible," Nocturne confessed. "To see you in such pain and yet be unable to help at all."

The dragon's voice pierced the muffled yells coming from the two simmering souls across from them, and Connor jumped in surprise.

"Watching your pain reminded me of my time as the Wraith King's prisoner." Beside him, Nocturne lowered his head until they were eye to eye. "If a man could almost break me, I cannot imagine what a fellow dragon could do. Had the simmering soul hit me, I would have lost to my feral side. You saved my life, Connor, and that is a debt I will never forget."

"That's just what friends do." Carefully, he raised one hand and patted the dragon's hide. A twinge of pain pinched his shoulder blades, but it faded almost as quickly as it had come.

This was about as much recovery as he could expect without solid sleep and copious amounts of booze.

The dragon growled happily but didn't reply.

You vile, putrid pile of rotting meat! the Wraith King yelled.

The ghoul sliced at the Dragon King's face, and the dragon's head snapped back with a roar of agony.

This had to end now, or it might end badly.

"I guess that's as much rest as I'm going to get." Connor summoned his shield, and a rush of black fog rolled over his body as the enchanted metal settled against his arm. "As much fun as it is to watch the Wraith King get his ass handed to him, I should probably intervene."

The Dragon King smashed his wing hard against the ghoul's head, and the Wraith King slammed into the rocky floor. Dust shot out around him, temporarily covering the cloaked figure in a reddish haze.

Nocturne chuckled darkly. "PERHAPS GIVE THEM A FEW MORE MINUTES."

"Behave," Connor chided, though he couldn't hide a mischievous grin as he watched the ghoul sail across the cavern once again. "Any ideas? I need a way to make the Dragon King see reason."

"HMM." Nocturne tilted his head to one side as he studied the wraithlike dragon before them. "HIS EYES ARE NOT RED, WHICH MEANS HE IS NOT FERAL, AND YET HE HAS ATTACKED YOU BOTH. I WONDER IF HE WOULD ATTACK ME."

Connor shot a sidelong glare at the prince of dragons. "That's not something I'm willing to test."

"WE HAVE FEW OPTIONS."

Fair point, but Connor still didn't like it. "There's got to be a better way to—"

Nocturne snarled, and the regal creature's wings spread wide as he prepared for the inevitable intervention. "IN THE DRAGONLANDS, A KING MUST EARN HIS CROWN. YOU MUST EARN HIS RESPECT, CONNOR, AND THAT CANNOT BE DONE IN ONE DAY."

"Then how do we stop this?"

"I AM DESCENDED FROM ALL DRAGON KINGS BEFORE ME," the prince explained. "If he is truly a king at all, and not some self-proclaimed leader, then he is my ancestor. I will speak to him if you can stop the Wraith King's stupidity long enough to settle both their tempers."

Connor shook his head. "You might have the easier job."

With a furious scream, the Dragon King slammed his thick tail once again into the Wraith King's ribs. The skeletal specter shot backward, and for a moment, there was space between the two.

Now or never.

"Go!" Connor shouted.

Both he and Nocturne bolted toward the dueling wraiths. Nocturne charged ahead, still fresh and uninjured, while Connor pushed his screaming body to move. As his grip tightened on the shield in his hand, his muscles burned. His chest heaved. His throat closed more with every passing moment. It taxed the last drops of his resilience, but he managed to tune out the worst of the pain—though not all of it.

He had no choice but to persevere.

As the Wraith King snatched his jet-black broadsword off the ground, Connor grabbed the undead man's shoulder with his free hand and shoved the specter back toward the floor. The ghoul's hood had long-since fallen back and exposed the long crack on his skull, and now the wraith's head pivoted on his bony neck. It circled like an owl, until those hollow eyes stared directly into Connor's soul.

Once, long ago, that would have been utterly terrifying.

Now, however, Connor wanted to rip the damn ghost's head off in an effort to knock some sense into those hollowed-out bones.

"Enough!" he shouted into the Wraith King's face.

Never, the ghoul growled back. *Out of my way, Magnuson.*

But Connor didn't budge.

This—all of this—was the wraith's fault. They had too much to do and too much on the line to waste time drooling over more power, but now the Wraith King's greed might've cost them everything.

It made Connor think again about the oath he had taken all those months ago, on his way to Bradford.

There are ways for me to destroy you, he'd warned the undead king. *The old legends tell us that much.*

And now, after all this time, he wondered if he would finally have to deliver on that bloodstained promise.

CHAPTER FORTY-FOUR

CONNOR

Connor glared down at the Wraith King as the undead man held his jet-black broadsword in one skeletal palm. Connor's hand tightened on the ghoul's bony shoulder as they glared furiously at each other.

If he'd had a way to kill the wraith, he might've done it right here and now. This was worse than testing his patience—this was as bad as any sabotage.

Release me. The exposed bones of the Wraith King's hand clicked together as they balled into a tight fist, and anger rolled off the undead man in waves. *Stand aside, Magnuson, and do not stop me again. I will beat sense into this overgrown chicken if it kills me.*

"You *can't*!" Connor snapped. "That's the problem, damn it. Take consolation in the fact that you've held your own and stop this pointless duel. Neither of you can kill each other. You two could fight until Death comes back for you both, and you still wouldn't get anywhere."

The wraith let out a strangled yell of frustration. Instead of replying, his head pivoted back toward the two dragons circling at the far end of the cavern, and two low growls rumbled through the air—one in Connor's head, and one in Nocturne's chest.

"I AM NOCTURNE," the dragon said, though his voice was barely audible above the growling. "PRINCE OF THE DRAGONS, KING OF THE NIGHTLANDS..."

A loud snarl in Connor's head drowned out the rest of Nocturne's words.

"You started this," Connor added. "You brought him out into the open. What the hell did you think would happen?"

Instead of answering, the Wraith King shrugged Connor's hand off his shoulder. The ghoul rose, and he paced back and forth despite the empty air below his cloak where his feet should have been. He glared at Connor for a long moment in barely restrained fury, but he eventually nodded in agreement.

A silent concession—and one Connor did not trust.

Not with Nocturne's life on the line.

"Don't move." He raised one finger in warning as he met the specter's eye. "No matter what he says, you stay here."

Apparently too angry to speak, the wraith wordlessly dismissed Connor's concern with a careless wave of his bony hand.

"I mean it." Connor's brows furrowed with warning. "If you say even one word—"

I'm in no mood for a lecture, Magnuson! the wraith snapped. *Go talk some sense into him, and I will remain here—if only because I cannot stand that infuriating monster's face.*

Connor's eyes narrowed in distrust, and he glared at the Wraith King as he tried to figure out if the ghost was going to do something stupid.

Do not challenge me, little one, the Dragon King warned.

The snarling growls on the other end of the cavern built to a crescendo, and the two dragons snapped at each other. Heads low and wings spread wide, their claws dug into the rocky ground as sparks skittered across their scales.

The Dragon King was new to this, and he likely didn't realize Nocturne couldn't hear him speak.

With one last withering glare at the Wraith King's pacing form, Connor sprinted toward the dragons. His boots hit the hard ground at a rapid pace, and as the Dragon King's head lifted into the air, he pushed himself to go faster.

Judging by those bared teeth and the increasing fury rumbling through Connor's head, the undead dragon would strike at any time.

"Tell us your name!" Nocturne demanded. His voice shook the walls with all the fury of the Dragon King's footsteps, and the two regal creatures paused as they met, head-to-head. "No ancestor of mine would behave with such foolish rage!"

Connor winced, uncertain if that was the right approach, but he would have to go along with it.

"I AM DOOM," the Dragon King bellowed. He roared into Nocturne's face, though Connor suffered the full brunt of the wraithlike dragon's voice. "BUT YOU CANNOT BE WHAT YOU SEEM, FOR NO DESCENDANT OF MINE WOULD SERVE A MAN!"

Doom.

How fitting a name for a creature like this.

"He doesn't serve me!" Connor shouted as he finally reached the circling duo. "Nor do I want your obedience, Doom. All I want is for the two of us to have a civil conversation, damn it!"

"DOOM?" The amber light faded instantly from Nocturne's eyes, and he studied his ancestor with silent awe. "YOU ARE TRULY DOOM THE BATTLE-BORN? LORD OF THE SEVEN FIRES, SIRE OF WARRIORS AND KING OF THE BLOODY FANG?"

Doom's neck arched, but the raging growl in his throat finally faded. He narrowed his amber eyes in confusion, and his furious glare darted from Nocturne to Connor and back.

I HAD BEGUN TO THINK MY KIND HAD FORGOTTEN ME, the Dragon King confessed.

"He can't hear you," Connor explained, even as he lifted his shield to guard himself from more of Doom's rage. "Only I can."

On the other side of the cavern, the Wraith King grunted in disgust.

"Fine," Connor conceded. "I'm the only *living* thing that can hear you."

WHAT LUCK, Doom said dryly.

Caught off guard, Connor chuckled. He hadn't taken Doom for having a sense of humor, but he opted to keep his mouth shut.

No sense poking the beast.

Nocturne lowered his great head almost to the floor, and with his wings still spread wide, bowed to his ancestor. The Dragon King bristled, jaw raised in distrust, but he eventually tucked his wings against his back and bowed in return.

Connor's eyebrows shot upward in surprise, but he dismissed the shield in his hand as the tension in the air slowly faded.

Hopefully, the truce would last.

As Doom raised his head once more, his eyes faded instantly from amber to a soothing blue. He studied his descendant as Nocturne once more met the king's stern glare, and for a moment, neither dragon spoke.

TELL ME WHERE THE OTHERS ARE, Doom ordered.

"The other dragons?" Connor asked.

Doom's glare shifted toward Connor, and his eyes flashed briefly gold—though the glow faded almost instantly. With a frustrated growl, Doom nodded.

"There aren't any dragons in the mountain," Connor answered. "They've been gone for centuries."

The wraithlike dragon huffed impatiently, and a plume of black smoke rolled over the ground at his feet. Connor coughed as the haze shot past him, but he figured he would teach the Dragon King manners some other time.

For now, he was simply glad to be having a civil conversation.

"INCREDIBLE," Nocturne said softly.

"What is?" Connor asked.

"THAT SELF-CONTROL," Nocturne replied. "TO MOVE SO INSTANTLY BETWEEN RAGE AND SERENITY IS A LEVEL OF CONTROL ALL DRAGONS YEARN FOR, BUT WHICH NOT EVEN THE BEST OF US HAVE MASTERED. LEGEND SAYS DOOM IS THE ONLY ONE TO HAVE EVER ACHIEVED TRUE COMMAND OVER HIS FERAL SIDE."

IT IS TRUE, Doom acknowledged. AND IT IS POWER THAT WAS NEVER MEANT FOR MEN TO CONTROL.

The Dragon King's full attention shifted toward the only living man in the room, and Connor stiffened under the looming specter's glare. Those intense eyes flashed gold and then red before shifting back to that soothing blue.

He met the dragon's glare and stood his ground. "I don't want to control you."

Doom sneered. DO NOT LIE TO ME, MORTAL.

"I'm not lying," Connor said firmly. "Ask Nocturne."

"HE IS ONE OF THE GOOD MEN," Nocturne acknowledged. "HE HAS PROVEN HIMSELF TO ME."

But not to me, Doom countered. His head lowered until he and Connor were eye to eye, and another plume of smoke shot from the massive creature's nose. I know very little of this magic—of what I am, now, after that necromancer's meddling—but I know enough. You men clawed me back to this world to claim my power.

For a few seconds, there was blissful silence in Connor's mind as Doom merely watched him. Waiting for a tell, perhaps, or a sign of fear.

Connor met the dragon's eye with a fierce glare of his own, and he didn't give an inch.

When Connor didn't reply, Doom huffed in irritation. Have you nothing to say? No defense to be made?

"There's nothing to defend," Connor said curtly. "I'm not here to take anything from you."

The Dragon King laughed, and sparks skittered across his inky black scales with each huffing breath. You say that now, but I've seen this before. The honor. The nobility. It always burns away, once a man is tempted. Every man has his price.

"Not me," Connor said flatly.

You do. Doom snorted, loud and fierce, and the ground beneath Connor's feet shook. You only believe otherwise because no one has made a suitable offer.

Connor bit down *hard* to keep from saying something he would regret. This old dragon was an asshole from another time, and he wouldn't let the beast's prejudice get under his skin—even if he wanted nothing more than to throw down the gauntlet and teach Doom some Fates-damned manners.

That is why your kind hunted me, Doom continued, apparently oblivious to Connor's silent rage. They wished to claim my magic for themselves. My legendary Firebreath. My dragonscale armor. My unrivaled willpower and strength. My voice, which commands respect from men and dragon alike. They wished to steal what they could never possess, and you are similarly unworthy, Connor Magnuson. Perhaps you are indeed one of the good few, but you are still human. Not once have I seen a man worthy of the power

I ALONE CAN COMMAND.

Connor didn't reply. In fact, it took all of his self-control not to smirk in victory. It was rather refreshing for a simmering soul to tell him many—if not all—of the abilities he would acquire over their time together.

Provided he survived, of course.

YOU WILL FAIL, the Dragon King continued. SAME AS ALL THOSE WHO HAVE COME BEFORE YOU.

"I look forward to proving you wrong," Connor replied.

Doom growled and paced the full length of the towering cavern, trudging back and forth as smoke billowed from his nose.

"POWER IS OBTAINED NOT THROUGH BRAWN," Nocturne said calmly, still as a statue even as his ancestor paced the room. "BUT THROUGH WISDOM, PATIENCE, AND COMPASSION. YOU TOLD MY ANCESTORS THAT, LONG AGO, AND IT'S SOMETHING WE DRAGONS LIVE BY EVEN TODAY."

DO NOT LECTURE ME WITH MY OWN WORDS, Doom chided.

"He can't hear you," Connor reminded him.

Doom growled in irritation.

"OTHERWISE, WE ARE BUT BRUTAL BEASTS," Nocturne continued, oblivious to the growling chaos in Connor's head. "THE VERY BEASTS MEN TAKE US TO BE."

Doom paused and let out an exhausted sigh. For a blissful moment, the cavern was still. Quiet. At peace. The tension settled into a wary hope that it might finally be over, and Connor watched the shadowy dragon's face as he tried to make sense of this sudden silence.

A plume of smoke shot through the Dragon King's nose, and he tilted his great head toward the sunshine streaming through the makeshift windows above them. IT IS A COMFORT TO KNOW I HAVE NOT BEEN FORGOTTEN.

"I don't think you're the sort anyone can forget," Connor admitted.

The Dragon King shot him an irritated glare, but this time his eyes didn't flash with amber hatred. VERY WELL.

Connor crossed his arms and waited, uncertain of what Doom would do next.

Doom raised his massive head and studied Connor with one eye. SINCE

I CANNOT BE RID OF YOU, MORTAL, I HAVE NO CHOICE BUT TO TEST YOUR MERIT.

"How so?" he asked warily.

I WILL GUIDE YOU OUT OF THIS LABYRINTH, Doom answered. BECAUSE I WISH TO ENSURE MY DESCENDANT REACHES SAFETY.

"And then?"

THE TRIAL BEGINS. As he spoke, the Dragon King's head tilted with curiosity. BEYOND THESE WALLS, I WILL NOT HELP YOU. I WILL NOT SPEAK TO YOU. I WILL MERELY WATCH.

Connor raised one skeptical eyebrow. "What will that prove?"

YOUR MERIT. Doom growled, and the rumble echoed in Connor's chest. REGARDLESS OF YOUR TRICKS, YOU WILL EXPOSE BOTH YOUR WEAKNESSES AND YOUR STRENGTHS. YOU WILL REVEAL TO ME THAT WHICH YOU VALUE MOST. YOU WILL SHOW ME WHO YOU ARE, AND I WILL SEE WHERE DRAGON LIVES FALL IN YOUR PRIORITIES. WHEN I SEE THE MAN YOU TRULY ARE, I WILL JUDGE YOUR WORTH, AND WE WILL SEE IF YOU DESERVE MY DESCENDANT'S RESPECT.

"And if you think I'm unworthy?" Connor's eyes narrowed in challenge.

THEN I WILL FIND A WAY TO BURN YOUR SOUL FROM WITHIN YOU, the Dragon King replied calmly. AND WE WILL DIE TOGETHER.

A chill snaked through the air, and Connor didn't reply.

It was quite a claim, and one eerily similar to the promise he'd made the Wraith King, all those months ago when they had first set out toward Bradford. Back then, he'd meant every word of it—as did, it seemed, the colossal dragon standing above him.

"Suits me just fine," he said firmly.

The Dragon King's eyes narrowed in suspicion, but the hulking behemoth didn't otherwise move.

"I've proven myself plenty," Connor added. "I'm tired of the trials and tests. I won't jump through any of your hoops, and I don't give a damn what you see. As long as you stay out of sight, I don't care what you do."

Doom snarled at Connor's audacity, but Connor didn't flinch. Despite the dragon's sheer size, he took several steps closer and stared it dead in the eye.

"Just keep one thing in mind," he added, his voice dropping to a dangerous octave.

YES? The Dragon King asked impatiently.

"You're not the only one capable of ending this tense little truce of ours," Connor warned. "And if I have to destroy you, I'll make sure there's not enough of you left to come back from Death's domain."

He let the threat simmer on the air and turned his back on Doom for the first time since they had fused. The warning carried weight to it, and he hated the thought of leaving this life before he was ready.

But, if the dragon threatened his team or his mission, Connor had every intention of following through on it.

CHAPTER FORTY-FIVE

CAPTAIN OLIVER

Captain William Oliver couldn't peel his eyes away from Teagan Starling's sword.

Firelight glinted across the steel that had seen battle and bloodshed. This sword had taken lives—so many that the captain didn't dare try to count them all. After what he'd learned of Teagan's true nature, out there on the battlefield, he figured he would never know just how many lives his Master General had taken.

Oliver's friends had died out there in that cracked desert dirt. Men and women he'd spent his life defending. Deep down, he wanted to be angry. Furious. Vengeful.

But all he could do was stare at the soot-stained Firesword before him.

Death wasn't new to Oliver. He had seen death before, too often, but never had it come so close. Never had it been so personal. He could still hear the screams of the fallen, the clash of steel as men fought and died, all believing their Master General had led them to the Barren to protect Saldia.

Teagan had lied to them.

That bastard had lied to them *all.*

Oliver's hands curled into tight fists, and his knuckles cracked violently as he fought the urge to reach through the bars. It was too far for him to even touch the sword, much less grab it, but he longed to break the damn thing in half.

If only out of raw, unfiltered *spite.*

As fast as it had come, his fury fizzled out into that haunting numbness once again. He sighed a deep and heavy sigh, and he set his forehead on the cold iron bars. The bitter chill from the metal sank into his skin, and at least now he could *feel* something.

This had been his life for however long he'd been down here. Days, maybe, or weeks. Months. He couldn't tell, and he didn't care.

Seeing his true Master General had broken him, and in the fractured remnants of his ire, there simply wasn't much left to piece back together.

The sensation of eyes on the back of his head sent a chill down his spine, and he instinctively straightened. With a casual glance over his shoulder, Oliver once again studied the four undead soldiers manning each corner of his cell.

These statues hadn't moved in days, despite the glowing green magic powering their animated corpses. They simply stood in each corner, patiently and unblinking, as if waiting for something. At times, he had found himself staring at them and wondering what sort of magic could possibly have created them. This was something ancient, something other, and he hated to think of how such power could be abused.

Worse, he wondered what they told the Wraith King. There had been plenty of treasonous talk as the Lightseer survivors had grown accustomed to the grotesque ornaments in their jail cells.

"Eight days," Major Halifax's voice carried through the silent prison and echoed off the iron jail bars. "That's how long Quinn's been gone."

"Bullshit," a man in a nearby jail replied. "I can't tell night from day down here."

Halifax grunted impatiently. "They bring us food twice per day, idiot. I'm telling you, she's not in Slaybourne anymore. She and that assassin of hers left. There's no telling when they'll be back, and this is our chance to escape. We might not get another one."

"Think rationally, damn it." Captain Oliver slipped his hands through the jail bars and rested his elbow on the cold metal. "We have four soldiers on each of us. We have no weapons, and these Bluntmar collars cut off access to our augmentations."

He tapped on the metal ring around his throat for emphasis. It hummed with a short burst of life as he touched it, and he winced as a ribbon of pain shot down his spine.

Though he'd never wanted to believe it, he was getting too old for this.

"Don't kid yourself." Halifax gestured to the undead skeletons in her cell. "These soldiers haven't moved in days. I don't believe they're even active. It's a bluff."

"You can test it." Oliver shrugged, nearly out of patience for her incessant bloodlust. "Personally, I don't think you would stand a chance. Use this time to think and reflect, Major, not plot something stupid."

Across the aisle separating the two rows of jail cells, Halifax leaned against the iron bars and shot him a withering glare. "It's better than anything you're doing. You've moped in silence this entire time, when you should be crafting our way out of here. If you're just going to sulk, *someone* has to step up and act."

"You'd like that, I wager." He met the woman's infuriating gaze as he dared her to lie to him. "To lead the army, even if you end up leading them to their deaths."

She sucked in a sharp breath through her teeth and pushed off the bars with a furious flourish.

"She's right!" a man shouted from the row of cells above them. "How much longer are we going to rot down here?!"

"They killed our Master General!" someone else added.

Once again, Halifax stirred up a flurry of rage in the survivors. Their overlapping voices blurred together in a rush of anger and vengeance. Some slammed their hands on the iron doors. Others shouted above the fray, simply to be heard.

"—she's a liar—"

"—you all are insane—"

"—stab to the heart should be enough to—"

Yet again, Oliver tried in vain to tune them out. He figured Halifax was right, to a degree, and he should've been focused on keeping morale high and helping the others process everything they'd witnessed out there on the battlefield where they lost their brothers-in-arms.

But he couldn't. There just wasn't enough of him left for anyone else.

Through it all, those soldiers didn't so much as bat an eye. Whatever their purpose—whether bluff or reconnaissance—Oliver was certain they heard far more than anyone suspected.

"—lost your damn mind—"

"—what else can we do—"

"—rotting away in this Fates-forsaken hellhole—"

In the surging tide of conversation, something in Captain Oliver snapped. The last withered bit of his resolve fractured, and he couldn't hold back his white-hot rage any longer.

He slammed both palms against the iron bars, and they trembled under the blow even though the collar around his throat cut off access to his Strongman augmentation. The hollow ring of echoing metal sliced through the voices.

"Shut your Fates-damned mouths!" he shouted.

His voice reverberated off the walls, deafening even to him, and the raucous chatter faded to utter silence.

"Everything Quinn said is true." He spoke louder, and though he tried to keep his tone even, he couldn't hide the devastated quiver in each grief-stricken word. "Out there, he said things that never could've left that battlefield. Once it was done, he would've killed every member of Unit Zero. Every *one* of us."

Halifax snorted derisively. "You don't know that."

"Get your head out of your ass, Major," Oliver ordered. "Use your own damn brain for once and *think*."

"I think you've lost your damn mind." The grime-soaked blonde gripped the cell bars with both bloodstained hands, and she glared at him with unfiltered hatred. "I think you have a soft spot for that redheaded harlot because she saved your life once."

"She saved yours, too," he said coldly.

The major's nose creased with disdain. She paced the length of her cell, but she didn't look at him again.

"I dedicated myself to the light," Oliver continued, his voice loud enough for everyone to hear. "Not to Teagan Starling. It took watching the man unravel for me to realize that those two are not one and the same. Each of you should ask yourself where your loyalties truly lie."

A heavy lull settled once again on the prison. Many of the arms that had been poking through the bars now disappeared into the cells as soldier after soldier turned inward to answer that question for themselves.

"I know many of you are confused." He shook his head and leaned one forearm against the cold iron bars between him and Teagan's sword. "This isn't easy. This is forcing you to rethink things you thought were fact. This is forcing you to consider if, perhaps, you were wrong. If you dedicated your life to a lie."

His throat tightened, and he shut his eyes as he paused yet again at the thought. All this time, he hadn't been grieving Teagan Starling.

Not even remotely.

"But the Lightseers have laws," he continued. "And with the Master General gone, only a Starling has the chance to complete the Rite. Only a superior warrior can lead the Lightseers, and the Rite is the one way to prove their worth to the rest of us."

"You can't be serious," one man said from a nearby cell.

"I am." Oliver pushed off the bars and paced the length of his cell. "If she agrees to the challenge but can't compete with her father's power, then she dies. It's the law."

It was a trap, mostly for those like Halifax who clung to their idealism with the sort of zealous desperation only young soldiers had the energy to channel. For the old folk, like him, it carried so much more weight than a simple duel.

If Quinn couldn't complete the Rite, perhaps the Lightseers' time was done. Oliver certainly didn't have much fight left in him.

"Finally," Halifax snapped. "It's about time you came up with a decent idea to get us out of here."

"Let her prove herself," someone else echoed.

A murmur of agreement bubbled through the prison, but Oliver didn't reply. He hadn't been offering it as a choice, much less one for others to vote on. Among the few survivors of Unit Zero, he had the highest rank.

Only he had the seniority to lawfully impose it.

"Is it enough?" a woman asked from the cell above him. "I don't know if it would be enough to sway me."

"Then you hang up your sword," Oliver replied flatly. "That's the law. Elite soldier or no, you'll abide it just like everyone else."

His firm tone sucked the life out of the lingering murmurs, and for a time, only the shuffle of boots across the stone floor filled the air. The occasional frustrated groan filtered through the jail cells toward the entrance, but it was otherwise silent yet again.

"Maybe we let her think we can be swayed," Halifax added softly—just loud enough to hear.

To plant the seed in the others.

No one replied, and Oliver didn't bother to respond. Halifax was a lost cause, and he returned his attention to the sword lying on the pedestal in front of him. Firelight glinted across the storied steel that used to lead him into battle, and the fight in him faded.

Across the path between the two rows of jail cells, many of the Lightseers receded into the darkness beyond the bars. Silhouettes paced their little prisons, consumed with fresh ideas and a new perspective.

Some would follow his lead, but many would not.

With a weary sigh that ran bone-deep, Oliver rubbed his jaw. His eyes slipped out of focus as he stared dead ahead, as lost in thought as the rest of them.

He had fought with these good people for most of his life. He was a career soldier, one that had joined young and vowed to never leave. Lunestone was his home, and he loved these warriors like his own family. He had made brutal sacrifices, time and again, both on and off the battlefield to ensure their safety.

Including Quinn. She was as much one of them as anyone else here, and he adored her as if she were his own daughter. The young woman had saved his life once already, on a particularly deadly mission to the western mountains. That scorpion had nearly eaten him whole, and he wouldn't be here today if not for her.

Oliver gripped the iron bars tightly, and his knuckles cracked from the effort. Teagan was dead, and only the Fates knew where Zander had gone. That left Quinn as the natural heir to Lunestone anyway. More than one Starling had murdered their way to the top before, and each had justified their actions well enough to satisfy the law.

So be it.

Let her do the Rite. Let her prove herself in a fair fight. The Lightseer Master General wasn't a role that could go unfilled, and Quinn Starling had the only true claim.

He would be her first challenger, and he would not be gentle. If she proved herself, he would concede.

But there were fools among these survivors, fools who would never submit to anyone Teagan Starling hadn't endorsed. A Rite always ended with bloodstains on the floor, but hot-headed purists wouldn't follow the rules. Not against someone they believed to be an imposter unworthy of the stage.

When the Rite began, they would cheat. He would have to remind them of why the Lightseers lived by a code—and what happens to those who break it.

CONNOR

As Connor stepped into the last threads of daylight, the fading sunshine warmed his skin. He raised one arm to shield his eyes from the sun, but this pain was a welcome one after so long in the darkness.

For a time, he had wondered if they would ever make it out of Firebreath Mountain.

The sun shone down on the vast expanse of ocean as its surface glinted with all the fire and light of a gemstone. The sun danced on the waves, creating rippling patterns of light that filled the horizon with a soft shimmering glow. Waves crashed against the rocky shore below, and for that blissful moment, time stood still. For a few seconds, at least, Connor could set aside what they had seen in the darkness and let himself enjoy the sea's salty breeze.

No one in his small band spoke. Though the Wraith King floated past him and into the sunshine, Connor was too furious to even acknowledge the ghoul's existence. Except for the rare command from the Dragon King as he had guided them toward the exit, no one had said a word since leaving the abandoned shrine deep in the dragons' forgotten cavern.

Nocturne paused beside him, and together they studied the sheer cliff face before them. The prince of dragons sighed wistfully, but he turned his back on the home his ancestors had considered sacred.

Given everything they had endured in there, Connor doubted his scaly friend had much fondness left for the place.

A lingering ribbon of pain snaked through his chest, and he grimaced as he rode out the shockwave. He brushed his finger along his shirt, over the black mark the Wraith King had left behind, and the area burned at his touch.

He lifted his shirt and ran his hand over it again, only to find the black scar had gotten larger.

Much larger.

Green light bubbled beneath the surface, brighter than it had ever been before, and he sucked air through his teeth to stem a surge of cursing—most of which would've been directed at the Wraith King.

That *ass*.

I WILL BE WATCHING, CONNOR MAGNUSON.

The Dragon King's voice scraped against Connor's nerves, and he looked over one shoulder to meet Doom's eye one last time before the wraithlike dragon faded completely.

But there was nothing—only the rough black rock of the mountain as it swallowed the secret entrance to the tunnels. As they left, it was like they had never entered to begin with.

The surreal sensation made the hair on his arms stand on end.

A low growl echoed through Connor's mind, and Doom's voice rumbled through his chest yet again. LET US SEE WHAT SORT OF MAN YOU TRULY ARE.

"I have nothing to prove to you." Connor turned his back on the mountain. "Whatever you find out won't change a damn thing."

Doom snarled, and the weight of someone watching from afar sent a tremor of warning down Connor's spine.

If the Wraith King weren't enough of an audience, Connor now had to contend with an ancient dragon's judgment. He would be lucky to ever get a moment alone with Quinn again.

That damn ghoul. If he weren't already dead, Connor would kill him.

Even as that furious resentment built in his chest, however, he could only remember something his father used to say any time Connor made a mistake—especially when he broke something valuable.

"Can't change it now, son."

Connor closed his eyes and rubbed the back of his head as he let out a long, frustrated sigh.

"Take what you learned from this," his father would always add. *"Make me proud."*

He had learned much in those tunnels, but two discoveries stood out most of all—First off, Doom would stay out of his way for the time being, and that gave Connor room to master the powers that would come with being the Dragonblade.

Connor tilted his head until he could see the Wraith King. The ghoul paced along the rocky platform behind him with one bony hand holding the exposed bone of his jaw as he muttered incoherently to himself.

The second thing Connor had learned in those tunnels unnerved him most of all. It seemed he couldn't trust the Wraith King as much as he'd thought, and that left an immeasurable weakness in his armor.

The Dragon King had imbued him with incredible power, yes, but all Saldian magic came with a cost. With everything at stake, the Wraith King's greed might well have cost Connor and his team the valuable time—and allies—they needed to protect Slaybourne.

If Connor lost Slaybourne, he would never forgive those responsible, and he would spend the rest of his life hunting for the way to undo the Wraith King's tether to this world.

CHAPTER FORTY-SIX

CONNOR

In the pitch-black night of the Kirkwall oceanfront, Connor leaned his forearms against the wooden railing that separated the rickety promenade from the water. A gap in the railing led out to the main dock and the dozens of sailboats that took crews through the shallows and out to the large ships beyond the reef.

In the distance, the faded silhouettes of smaller islands blocked out patches of the stars.

Beside him, Sophia and Murdoc stood in silence. Both stared out at the sea, at anything but him, as they processed everything he'd told them.

He'd led them out here because the docks were always quiet at night when he was a boy. This was where his father and the man's lifelong friends had concocted their crazy idea to smuggle goods into Kirkwall, under the noses of two unjust kings. True to form, these docks were even darker now than they'd been back then.

A strangled city, shrouded in shadows. It pained him to think of what Kirkwall had become.

A twinge hit him between his lungs, and he grimaced as a lingering shockwave of pain shot through his torso. He set his palm on his chest as the sensation faded.

"I suppose it could've been worse," Murdoc said after a long stretch of silence. "You could've been melted."

Connor chuckled. "Fair enough."

"This is bad, Connor," Sophia finally said.

"I thought you'd have been the happiest to hear about this," he admitted.

Her thin eyebrows pinched together, and she glared up at him. "Two simmering souls? Are you insane?"

"I didn't have much choice." His eyes narrowed, and he peered over one shoulder in a vain attempt to find the Wraith King.

The ghoul had all but disappeared since they'd left the mountain, and he'd been eerily silent ever since.

Brooding, no doubt.

"And now there's a dragon looming over your shoulder, who could unleash chaos at any second!" she hissed.

Connor raised one hand in a silent request that she lower her voice even further, so as not to give the Dragon King any ideas.

"It's *insane*," she said again, her voice even more grating than before.

"What does Nocturne think about all this?" Murdoc asked.

Connor shook his head and stared out again at the lapping waves beyond the harbor. "He's not sure what to think about it. Nothing in there was what we were expecting, and something happened to him. He saw something in there but won't tell me what it was."

Connor had seen Quinn, and the Wraith King had seen his own lost love. It was easy enough to guess what Nocturne had witnessed, but it wasn't Connor's place to bring it up.

"For now, he's hunting," Connor continued. "Nocturne is out in the forest, searching for anything that can help us."

"He's wasting his time," Sophia said flatly.

"Maybe," Connor acknowledged. "But he said it's better than sitting idle."

The necromancer shrugged.

"You've been busy, Captain." Murdoc shifted his weight and pulled a stack of carefully folded papers out of his back pocket. "But so have we. No word on the Shade imposters, but we've been collecting their wanted posters—as well as yours, I might add."

Connor took the stack and rifled through page after page of his own intense glare. The drawings stared up at him from behind their masks, each more furious than the last as the artists got more creative with their interpretations of his face.

Fantastic.

He paused on the most sinister of them. These eyes were narrower than the others, and they glared with the soulless hatred of a man who had nothing left to lose.

Connor sighed. He wondered if his father would've even recognized him after all these years, or if he would've been just another stranger with menacing eyes.

He continued through the pile, and a few of the portraits had a thinner face. Others had larger eyes. Bit by bit, he pieced together the rough outlines of four other Shades, all of them distinctly different from his posters.

There had been far more, but the clues were there for anyone to find. These Shades were getting sloppy, and they were beginning to be found out. If he didn't move quickly, someone else might get to them before he had the chance.

At the bottom of the pile, a few pages had fused together thanks to a splotch of whiskey that had dried along their edges. Connor shot an annoyed sidelong glare at Murdoc, who simply shrugged.

"That wasn't me, Captain. I found it like that."

Connor peeled the pages apart, only to find the last two weren't masked vigilantes at all. One was a gnarled old stranger with a scar over his left eye, and the other stared up at him with a familiar sneer that had haunted him since he'd woken up at the bottom of the cliff.

Bryan Clark.

That son of a bitch.

The smug bastard stared up at him from the portrait, eight years older but undeniably the same man. Same jawline. Same nose, though it had a crooked tilt to it now. That same clean-combed hair, though a tad longer after all these years.

Wanted for murder, the poster said at the bottom. *Bounty guaranteed.*

Some men never changed.

With a flash of rage, Connor's grip on the posters in his hand tightened, and despite the crinkle of a dozen pages ripping at their edges, he couldn't take his eyes off the portrait that had been shoved haphazardly at the bottom.

Not only had this man had the audacity to come back here, but the damned fool had murdered even more people in the city.

"Captain?" Murdoc asked with an air of concern. "Are you alright?"

Though Connor's teeth gritted together, he forced a deep breath and nodded.

That settled him, and as the surge of hatred slowly faded, he could think a little more clearly.

Back in Slaybourne, Connor had confessed to Wesley that he would run Bryan through should they ever meet again. It wouldn't fix anything, but he couldn't bear the thought of letting a man like that live. Not after everything he'd done.

But bloodlust like this triggered something in Connor.

Something deep.

When he'd killed all those slavers, Kiera had watched him with horror. Those criminals hadn't deserved to live, and yet watching him murder them all had left Kiera trembling with fear.

Fear of *him*.

As much as he wanted to hunt Bryan down, Connor had to stay focused. The Antiquity's lost Soulsprite was somewhere in Kirkwall Castle, and he was the only one who could bring it back to her.

He had a debt to repay, and he wouldn't lose sight of that.

Even if it cost him his revenge.

WRAITH KING

This thing—this beast—was strange.

Watching from the in-between, the Wraith King hovered above the path as far away as possible from Magnuson and his little band of misfits. This time, however, he wasn't interested in anything they had to say.

He'd heard it all.

For now, he was far more interested in the hulking behemoth perched on an embankment on the other side of the harbor. The dragon's edges blurred and shifted as wisps of shadow and smoke radiated from its jet-black scales. Though it remained motionless, its spectral form rippled like a dark mist against the night sky. Its blue eyes gleamed with an otherworldly light as it intensely watched Magnuson and his team, and not once did it look away. Sinister and silent, the beast listened to the night. The air seemed to thicken around it, as if it were some ghostly apparition from Death's domain and not the lingering essence of raw power.

It was breathtaking, and the Wraith King desperately wanted to break it. To own it. To control its every movement.

The Dragon King was learning quickly. Doom, as it had called itself, had already tested the limits of its connection to Magnuson—and, by extension, the Wraith King. It had learned how far away it could travel, how much it could hear, and even how to slip through the land of the living and into the in-between Death used to hunt lost souls.

It didn't move. Rarely spoke. Instead, it listened. It watched the world around it with the hunger of a horned owl stalking deer.

And yet, it did nothing. No attacks. Barely a sound. It hovered on the edge of the waking world, nothing more than a shiver up men's spines. At times, even the Wraith King forgot it was there.

How curious.

This approach to studying a new host intrigued him. It seemed odd, foolish even, to let a host wander about with all that newfound power, doing as he pleased while the source of all that magic simply watched what he chose to do with it.

As much as he hated to admit it, this strategy made sense. In fact, he had adopted it for himself. Not to test Magnuson, of course, whom he knew would nag him like an old hen for that little stunt of his back in the mountain.

No, he had chosen to observe the Dragon King—and, more importantly, to hide his own abilities from it. A thing of that size and power had no business knowing the Wraith King's limitations, few as they were.

While it studied Magnuson, he would study it.

This creature was clever and observant, but he had faced similar opponents before and won. Like any beast, it could still be broken—either by Connor's hand, or his.

CHAPTER FORTY-SEVEN

ZANDER

In the dead of night, the southern wind raged through the trees. It carried a warning in its gale, something rank and raw, and Zander stiffened in the hurricane of battling aromas it brought to him.

It was almost as though the wind were speaking to him, with a voice only his most primal self could understand.

The wind carried more than a warning—it carried danger.

It carried death.

Warning or no, he pushed onward toward his manor on the outskirts of Briar Meadow. His stomach growled with hunger, louder than any blightwolf's snarl, and the back of his throat burned with the sort of gnawing hunger that left acid on the back of his tongue. If he didn't get food soon, his stomach might begin to eat itself.

Another wind hit him, and this time, a putrid stench hit his enhanced nose. He gagged on the disgusting scent. His cheeks flushed, and no matter how hard he tried to place what it was, his brain wouldn't cooperate. It was as though this smell—whatever it was—eroded even his self-control. It clawed its way up his nose and down his throat, leaving deep gouges in its wake, and he coughed to clear his lungs of it.

To regain some Fates-damned *composure.*

Alistair paused mid-stride, and his knees tightened around the wolf's back as they skidded to a stop. The blightwolf growled in rage and frustration, pacing and retracing his steps backward. Zander grimaced and held his breath, his eyes watering as his throat threatened to close on him, and he gasped for air.

Around them, the other blightwolves in his army did the same. The frontlines of his pack came to a dead halt, kicking up dirt and dried leaves as they fought to shake the stench off of them.

"The fires." Alistair growled and violently shook his head as he inched backward. "The humans are burning their putrid fires again."

The blightwolf fires.

That explained everything.

The aroma he had once thought of as soothing and even a bit floral now hit him like a hammer to the head.

He could barely *think.*

In pain, his throat closing by the second, Zander's vision blurred as he glared back at the route they needed to take to reach his manor. He wheezed, fighting for every breath, but they couldn't stop now. He needed to resupply, and the only Starling potions even remotely nearby were in that manor. Besides, every town along the southern road would be burning these fires, and it wasn't like he would fare any better somewhere else.

"Wait here," he ordered.

He slid off Alistair's back and stumbled. His shoulder slammed into a tree, and something in the towering oak's trunk snapped. The echoing crack of splitting wood raced up the tree and into its canopy, but Zander didn't care enough to find out what he'd done to it.

Eyes burning and about to vomit, Zander pushed his way through the woodland, toward the rank stench that now clawed at his lungs with every raspy breath. His hunger drove him onward, more than anything else. The need for meat, for substance. For potions to heal whatever the fires were doing to him.

Stop, the Feral King growled, furious. *Turn back, Starling.*

He didn't.

Zander pushed onward, until the oaks around him became nothing but black silhouettes. Very little made sense, anymore, as his lungs stopped working. He squinted through his swollen eyes, searching for the source of the fires and silently cursing himself for demanding the largest fire pots on the western tail of the southern road.

What in the wolves' name are you doing? The ghoulish blightwolf barked in his head, sharp and raging. *Do you want to die?*

No.

He wanted to bury this wretched fire pot in rubble.

In his head, the Feral King yelped in pain. It growled and snarled as it was as forced through the forest along with him, tangled in their connection to each other. He didn't even pause to breathe. He didn't dare, or else he might collapse from the weight of the blightwolf fires' poisons. Instead, he dragged the Feral King along with him as it became lost in its primal aches and abandoned any attempt to speak to him.

Good. At least now he could focus.

Beneath his feet, the ground sloped upward, and he squinted until he could spot the orange glow at the top of the hill. This close, the scent scorched his nose, and he took one final breath in an attempt to minimize the pain.

His shoulder hit a nearby tree before he'd realized he was falling, but he let the oak stabilize him as he raised one hand and took aim. The crackling majesty of his Voltaic augmentation sizzled through his veins, and he pointed one finger at the soft orange glow in the distance to guide the bolt that would break free any second.

A dazzling flash of light temporarily blinded him, and he winced. The familiar crack of thunder followed. As the lightning faded, it left imprints on his vision.

The orange glow was gone.

Instantly, he could breathe. He sucked in greedy breaths, his head already clearing, but the vile stench remained. He scanned the forest until he found a second orange glow, and he took aim once more.

With another crack of lightning, the last of the amber glows faded.

Zander collapsed against his tree and ran the back of his hand across his brow to wipe away the sweat. He sat there until his chest stopped heaving and his vision finally cleared.

When he opened his eyes again, the Feral King lay on the dirt across from him. It didn't move, save for its eyes, and they wandered his face with a curious hunger he'd never seen before.

You have done what no wolf could do, the ghoulish creature said, almost pensively, as though fascinated by a particularly curious bug.

"I'm full of surprises."

That you are.

After another deep breath, the dazed fog in Zander's head finally dissipated, and he pushed himself to his feet. The property would be lined with more fire pots, of course, but far enough away that knocking over one or two would give him and the wolves a clearcut path of entry.

All these years, he'd had no idea how effective the blightwolf fires truly were, and he'd hated discovering the truth for himself. Once he controlled the Lightseers, he would have to ensure those fires were never again lit.

He peered over his shoulder, back toward where he'd ordered the blightwolves to wait, and Alistair's dark head watched him through the trees, silent and obedient as ever. He would call for them if he needed them, but he doubted the need would arise. Several guards kept watch over all the Starling properties, and it was best for his new army to stay well out of sight.

Zander raised one palm in an unspoken command to stay put, and Alistair nodded.

With the fire in his lungs almost completely gone, Zander continued up the hill. He didn't bother checking his reflection in the steel of his sword, as he was fairly confident no one could recognize him under all the dirt and grime from his weeks in the Ancient Woods. He'd lived like a savage for ages, and he figured he looked like one, too.

It didn't matter. More than anything, this was a test of the Feral King's obedience, and one with low stakes. The manor would be vacant this time of year, and the non-military watchmen on the property would serve as his bait. He needed to see if the Feral King would obey an order to stay hidden, even in the presence of other humans.

And if the ghoulish beast failed, Zander could kill these witnesses with little consequence.

He crested the hill and gave a wide berth to the shattered brass pot that had once held the blightwolf fires. A lingering trail of smoke wafted from the dead embers, its last attempt to kill him. Rubble surrounded the shards of metal and clumps of singed herbs, and he spat on the ground to clear the last of it from his lungs.

Revolting stuff.

Ahead, a familiar cobblestone road led deeper into the woods, and he followed it toward the two stone towers that guarded the main gate into the manor grounds. His back straightened as he spotted the apple orchard through the gate's elaborate iron bars, and shadows passed through orange firelight in both towers' windows.

Fresh meat, the Feral King said with a wicked little laugh. *Tell me, will you eat these men raw? Or do you insist on burning more of your meals?*

"They're not for eating," Zander said quietly, still a good distance from the gate.

They're human, the ghoulish creature said, as though it were obvious. *That's all humans are good for.*

"On the contrary." Zander steeled himself against the carefully worded offer he was about to make, as all of his observation and plotting finally came to fruition. "They're your ticket out of these woods."

I rather like my woods.

"Of course." He shrugged, as though it were a given. "But you want more."

This time, the Feral King didn't reply, and Zander resisted a victorious smirk as he hooked the beast with the sort of bait it couldn't refuse.

"You've mastered this forest." He gestured to the trees around them with a careless flick of his hand. "You're bored. You think I haven't noticed? You try to strain every drop of fear from the beasts and beings who live out here, but it's all too easy. Too familiar, and too much work."

It is work worth doing.

"It's temporary." Zander clicked his tongue in disappointment, as though scolding a child who should've known better. "Out there in civilization, among my kind and in the cities I control, you'll find the sort of fear you can drink from for years. Generations, even."

Impossible.

"Not at all. I've done it my whole life."

At that, his mind went suddenly still. It was as though his thoughts had been racing before now, too fast for him to even register, and something had stopped all of them in their tracks.

For the first time since he'd fused with the Feral King, his mind felt calm.

Utterly still. Peaceful, even.

The Feral King was waiting with bated breath for him to continue.

Zander had learned so much from his time with this beast, but most of all, he'd learned threats would never work. He had to dangle treats in front of it and tempt it with the sort of bait it couldn't resist.

Simple, really.

"All you have to do is listen to me." They were closing in on the gate, and he didn't have much time left before the guards saw him.

And if I refuse?

"Then you will be bored for all of eternity, feeding off scraps." Zander glared at the thing through the corner of his eye as it trudged through the shadows beyond the road. "You'd hate to miss out on all that glorious fear, wouldn't you? Don't you at least want to know what it tastes like before you decide?"

It growled with annoyance, but didn't answer.

"Stay out of sight," he ordered. "Don't let anyone here see you."

A low, irritated grumble bubbled through him as he stepped into the circle of orange light that radiated from the guard towers. To his relief, however, the Feral King disappeared into a rush of black smoke, and a lingering puff of darkness rolled across his boot.

Zander allowed himself a thin smile of victory.

A door creaked, sharp and shrill in the night, and a man trotted down the staircase that led from the tower. He scowled at Zander and set one hand on the hilt of his sword, safe behind the iron gate. "You, there! What do you think you're—"

Without waiting for the dolt to finish speaking, Zander drew *Valor*. Flames erupted across the enchanted blade, and he pointed the Firesword at the guard in a silent command to let him through.

As two other men filed out of the tower and onto the main road to the house, the first guard staggered backward in surprise.

"Lord Starling," one of them said, his voice hushed with awe. "By the Fates, my Lord, what happened to you?"

"Do you need a healer, sir?" The third man spoke, this time, and he gaped at Zander while rifling through his pockets. After a moment, he pulled out a thick iron key from and unlatched the gate's main lock.

"Food," Zander ordered. "And wine."

"Of course, my Lord."

Zander's stomach growled again, and all three of the men paused to stare at him in silent horror.

"Now," he snapped.

His voice broke the three of them from their half-shocked dazes, and the gate opened shortly thereafter. He shoved his way through the gap before it had fully opened, exhausted and bored with their questions. Ahead, his manor dominated the top of a grassy knoll. In the darkness, the roof of the stables blended into the distant forest, barely visible. Yellow candlelight flickered in several of the manor windows, but he didn't care how much wax the guards wasted. He assumed they used rooms they weren't entitled to enter, and as such, he rarely left anything valuable here while he was away.

Footsteps tracked up the road after him, and he groaned in annoyance as the first man joined him.

"I'll announce you, sir," the guardsman offered.

Zander frowned, and he shifted his cold gaze toward the nameless peasant guarding his summer home. "To whom?"

"Your wife." The guard cleared his throat awkwardly, and his gaze shifted up toward the manor at the top of the hill.

He frowned with confusion. "My family shouldn't be here."

"Only your wife is here at the moment," the guard explained. "She's been traveling south on a goodwill mission to ease the locals' worries after your father's army passed along the southern road."

"My father? Military—" Zander's stomach roared again, and he grimaced in frustration. "No, not now. Prepare a report for me the moment I'm done eating."

"Of course, sir."

And yet, the man continued to walk beside him.

"Now," Zander barked.

"But your wife—"

"I don't need to be announced to my own wife." He nodded back to the guard towers. "Go."

Oddly enough, the man opened his mouth as though he were going to keep talking. To protest, perhaps, or insist, or slow them down as they quickly closed the distance toward the house.

Zander's eyes narrowed in silent warning, and the man's mouth quickly shut.

In that second or two before the guard slipped back down the road, a tantalizing aroma coiled through the air. It sizzled like butter on a hot steak and sang like honeysuckle on the vine, all at once, but Zander couldn't put his finger on what it was.

As soon as the man left, however, it was gone, and Zander was far too hungry to track down one trivial new scent in a world overflowing with better ones.

Hmm. The Feral King growled, thick and heavy in his head, but he ignored the beast in favor of finding food.

His wife wasn't supposed to be here, and it added considerable risk to his previously low-stakes plan. She was the mother of his children and a prominent figure in Oakenglen. He couldn't risk her life. She was too important.

Even as his steps slowed, though, he thought of his hand around her waist. The smell of lilies in her hair. Her skin beneath his palm, warm and soft. Her body was home, and he hadn't been inside of her since before this whole mess with the Wraith King had begun.

Oddly, it wasn't a carnal need. There was no lust. No visions of prying open her legs or hearing her moan his name. He imagined his nose against her neck, and with the memory of her scent came nostalgia. It was the same sense of peace and comfort he'd felt on the last holiday they'd taken to this very manor, years ago.

Perhaps this was for the best. A pleasant surprise in a string of plans gone awry, and the first kindness the Fates had shown him in quite some time. Besides, he controlled her. Even if she saw the Feral King, she wouldn't know what it was, and he would ensure she didn't tell a soul.

He needed this.

He needed *her*.

Zander grabbed both knobs on the dual front doors and swung them open in unison. Illuminated from the iron lamp posts on either side of the main entry, his shadow stretched into his house, across the foyer's white marble tile and over the mosaic star laid beneath the grand chandelier. The dual staircases met in the center of the ornate entrance, their dark mahogany railings a stark contrast to the bone-white marble that covered nearly every inch of the house's floors.

He paused, then, to savor the true depth of his victory. He had conquered the darkness and dragged it from the shadows of a fearsome forest. He had overcome the sort of challenges that could drive men mad, and instead, he had turned an abomination into a house pet.

Zander had *finally* come home.

The familiar fragrance of lilies spiraled through the air, sweet and subtle.

Eleanor. She was here after all.

Other scents blended with hers, almost too quickly to register. Roasted chicken and charred greens. Smoke. Burnt wood. Lemons and egg whites. The dull resin of polished wood. The distant, musky scent of men—that had to be a lingering scent from the guards.

But one of their scents stood out, stronger than the others.

Closer.

Upstairs, a woman spoke, her voice muffled by a door. A spring squeaked, and a boot hit the floor. She gasped,

Now, the guard's reservation made far more sense.

In his head, the Feral King growled with rage. With the snarl, a white-hot flicker of anger snapped in Zander's chest, almost too wild to control.

To be sure, he walked into the house until he stood below the crystal chandelier that had, during many a gala thrown in various fools' honor, welcomed dignitaries and monarchs alike from all over Saldia. He sniffed at the darkness yet again as he hunted down the man's scent.

It leaked down the stairs from a room at the end of the hall. He could almost see it, like a cloud of thin smoke rolling through his home.

Upstairs, the woman moaned. The slap of skin on skin followed, and the strange man's scent blended with Eleanor's. It thickened with the heady musk of salt and sex.

Zander's head cleared in a cold rush, and for several moments, he merely stared up the elaborate staircase. His fingers slowly curled into a tight fist as the slapping skin grew louder and more vigorous. Eleanor's moan of pleasure came again, followed by a happy little squeal.

That *whore.*

CHAPTER FORTY-EIGHT
ZANDER

Zander didn't know how he'd ended up at the closed door to the manor's master bedroom.

He'd walked, obviously, but he had no memory of it. It was as if he'd blacked out for a while there, numbed into a furious silence as he listened to the muffled moans of another man fucking his wife.

This cold fury—it was new. He'd endured hell, been burned and pushed to the edge of death, been cut open and left to bleed, been bitten and ripped open again and again.

But he'd never, not once, felt icy hatred this raw. It carved his chest hollow.

Your mate has betrayed you, the Feral King seethed.

Zander didn't answer.

He couldn't.

Briefly, he had the curious realization that the Feral King hadn't used this moment to bait him. It was as though they shared the same emotions. The same revulsion. The same rage.

"Frederick, what—*oh*!" Eleanor squealed with delight, the sound muffled by the door. "Yes! *Yes!* By the Fates, do that again!"

At that, Zander's curious thought flitted away, and the cold fury returned.

His hand grabbed the doorknob, the movement almost uncontrolled. Numb. The door swung open, and though the hinges gently creaked, neither of the two figures on the bed looked over at him.

His eyes adjusted instantly to the dark room. Behind him, the hallway sconces cast his lone shadow across the dark blue carpet toward the man with his pants around his ankles. The stranger's bare ass flexed as he grabbed the slender thighs spread before him. A delicate heel hung from the toes on the woman's left foot, and the other shoe peeked out from underneath a pile of silk sheets on the floor. His wife's long blonde hair stretched across the thick comforter as she hiked her skirts up higher, so that this man could go deeper.

She hadn't even taken off her dress. She'd simply lifted her skirts like a common harlot.

A sharp, fearsome growl rumbled in his head—or maybe his chest. He couldn't tell if he'd made the sound, or if it had come from the ghoulish wolf fused to his soul.

Instantly, Zander held one of his daggers in his hand. It was a throwing blade, one he kept strapped to his thigh for emergencies. It rested on his palm, ready to take another life, just as it had taken so many before.

He hadn't noticed himself draw the weapon, but that hardly mattered.

Sex. Salt. Sweat. The musky blend burned his nose, almost worse than the blightwolf fires, and it sickened him to think he'd ever been inside of her.

That he'd ever called her his own.

Zander threw the dagger, and it hit the man in the back of his neck, right at the base of his skull.

An instant kill. A kindness this bastard didn't deserve, perhaps, but Zander's efficiency won out in the end. He hadn't even recited the Lightseer Creed, as this was justice the Lightseers usually didn't have jurisdiction or clearance to deliver.

Besides, the true traitor in this room was his whore of a wife.

In a flash, the scents in the room changed. The rusty tang of blood permeated everything, staining the air and almost masking the salty musk of their pleasure. Eleanor paused, in those seconds before her lover toppled on top of her, and she screamed as he collapsed onto her chest. She wriggled out from underneath him, and he flopped sideways as blood trickled down his neck. In her panic, she had flipped him over, and tiny red streams leaked from one eye like tears. His body arched unnaturally as he lay there with a knife protruding from his neck.

Eleanor stared at her lover in dumb horror, her breast exposed from where he'd ripped open her bodice. Her legs still spread wide, her skirts hiked to her waist and her chest heaving as she tried to grapple with what had just happened.

Only then did her gaze shift to the door.

She screamed. It was the sort of blood-curdling terror that begged for mercy and help, all in one sound. With the front doors of their manor still wide open, he knew the guards would notice.

The question wasn't if they had heard it—it was whether or not they had the balls to try to stop him.

With her scream, however, came that tantalizing scent he had noticed earlier—the sizzling aroma of seasoned butter on steak, blended with the honey-sweet taste of honeysuckle in summer.

But he was too angry to care where it had come from.

Too furious to speak, he stalked toward her. She scrambled backward and fell off the bed. The comforter slid off the mattress and fell with her, breaking her fall even as she tangled herself in it.

Pathetic, the Feral King snarled.

Zander's nose creased in disgust. "I couldn't agree more."

As he spoke, Eleanor paused. She peered up at him from within the sheets, as though seeing him for the first time. Under the grime and blood of seven weeks' travel, he must've looked like a vagrant, come to rape and murder her.

But as her eyes widened with recognition, she didn't relax. She didn't breathe a sigh of relief, or ask him where he had been all this time.

Her look of horror deepened, and her trembling only grew more violent.

"Zander, please," she whispered. The mother of his children raised one shaky hand between them, as though that could quell his rage, and that decadent scent in the air grew stronger.

She was utterly terrified of him, and Zander finally understood where that indulgent aroma had come from. He finally understood what it was.

Fear.

Incredible, the Feral King said. *Her terror is sweeter than most. You must horrify her, Starling.*

Zander didn't reply.

"Please," Eleanor said again, and her trembling horror bled into uncontrollable sobs. "You leave for weeks, for seasons at a time, and I've been so alone. You're always in Lunestone. I barely know you anymore—"

"Shut your lying mouth," he snapped.

She flinched, and her eyes squeezed closed even as tears poured down her face.

"Tell me where the children are."

"Lunestone." Trapped in a pile of shivering blankets, Eleanor sobbed into her hands. "They're with your mother, Zander. They don't know anything about this. No one does. I swear, darling, I'll never do this again. I swear it. I *swear*—"

He scoffed in disgust. "Your promises are worthless."

"Tell me—" His wife sobbed, harder now, and she could barely form a coherent sentence. "Tell me what I can do to make this right."

"Make this right?" He tilted his head, astonished at her audacity, and he drew his Firesword as he slowly closed the distance between them. "Since his wedding, my father has had seventy-three mistresses—and those are the ones I know about. I'm sure there are more. With him as my role model, do you know how many times I've taken a mistress of my own?"

"T-the same?" Eleanor's voice squeaked out, barely audible.

"None," he seethed. "Yet here you are, putting his infidelity to shame. Fucking a man in my own bed—"

Zander couldn't even finish that sentence.

Utterly livid, with his blood burning through his veins, he drew his Firesword. Though he wanted to rip her to shreds, he yelled with frustration and instead sliced clean through the solid oak bedframe. It splintered and cracked under *Valor's* steel, and the violent rip of shredding cloth blended with Eleanor's fresh screams as his weapon came within inches of her face.

She sobbed harder.

What will you do? the Feral King asked. *Your mate does not respect you. She has disgraced you. What example does that set for the rest of the pack?*

As Zander debated how to answer, he glared down at the woman he had once paraded around with pride. A fair and stunning treasure. A beauty many men had courted, but one fit only for the best. A delicate flower, gorgeous as ever, with a stunning face and those beautiful brown eyes. Even as she watched him, terrified and silent, he could admire her flawless body—still perfect, even after giving him four children.

A gutting thought hit him, then, one he was ashamed of not considering sooner.

"Are the children even mine?" He scowled with revulsion at the whore kneeling before him. "And don't you dare lie to me, Eleanor. I'll know."

"They're yours," she answered, too horrified to speak in anything more than a quivering whisper. "I swear to the Fates, Zander, they're yours."

The ribbon of delightful terror snaking from her only thickened, and he caught her in the lie.

"You *whore,*" he seethed.

"They're yours," she repeated, but they were just words now, words that lacked any substance or meaning.

"Everything about you was a lie." He knelt in front of her, until he could feel her breath on his bloodstained jaw. "Even them."

"Don't hurt them," she begged. "Please, Zander, you're their father. The only father they know. They couldn't possibly—"

He tuned her out.

Though she sat there, blathering on, he ran through his options. If she disappeared into the Ancient Woods, people would notice. The guards would tell everyone he had been here, and her death would be traced to him. It was possible he would face consequences for punishing her outside the laws of the Lightseer Creed, and thus, he had to plan his next move carefully.

Or, perhaps, he could use this to his advantage.

He tilted his head and scanned the room for signs of the Feral King, but the dastardly creature remained out of sight—even in the heat of the moment, when Eleanor's fear enticed even Zander, the beast had stayed hidden.

It had obeyed him, even when tempted with what it craved most.

Perhaps it was time he gave it a reward, then, for its excellent behavior.

"Show yourself, Feral King," Even as Zander spoke to the ghoulish creature, his eyes never left Eleanor's. "And tell me what your kind do to unfaithful mates."

A rush of black smoke rolled across his boot, and his wife's gaze shifted over his shoulder. She screamed again, her voice so shrill it hurt his ears, and Zander clamped his hand over her mouth to stifle the sound.

Her voice vibrated against his palm, and her eyes darted between him and what could only have been the Feral King.

We eat them, the shadow wolf explained. *Together, as a pack.*

A humorless smile tugged briefly on Zander's mouth. "How fitting."

Humans are hollow. The creature snarled. *I told you before, Starling—all they're good for is their fear.*

"And you were right," he said, mostly to appease the ghost's ego.

To let it think *it* controlled *him.*

Zander grabbed a handful of her gorgeous blonde hair and dragged her toward the door. She screamed again, whimpering between the sobs, and she clutched at his wrists as she squirmed in his powerful grip.

But she wouldn't break free.

With a half-starved growl, he threw her into the hallway. She scooted backward across the carpet and looked up at him with those wide, trembling eyes. Her dress splayed about her, covered in white stains and the red-brown streaks of Frederick's blood.

"Zander, please," she whispered.

She didn't even have the courage to defend herself.

"I don't know how I didn't see it sooner," he admitted in a low, gravelly tone. "How weak you are. How *pathetic.*"

As he glared down at her, she sobbed into her hands. Her long curls fell over her shoulders, perfect and smooth as ever, but the nostalgic allure with which she had once snared him had now shattered. She wasn't home—not anymore, and not ever again.

She was dead to him.

He whistled, sharp and quick. Eleanor's head snapped up at the sound, and her brow furrowed with confusion while she searched his face for clues as to what he'd just done.

Beyond the house, a wolf howled. The deep and resonant wail echoed through the woodland, all too familiar after his weeks with the blightwolves.

Alistair was leading the charge.

In the seconds that followed, all was still and silent, as though the forest itself held its breath in fear.

The silence didn't last long, however, and a man screamed. Another yell of terror followed, and others shouted orders. The yips and growls of the blightwolves neared, close enough for Zander's enhanced sense to hear, and he looked down at the traitor he had once called his wife.

Through the corner of his eye, Zander watched as the Feral King lower its great head, ready to pounce. The devilish thing had danced for him tonight, perfect in its obedience and performance, and now he could reward it.

"You want to act like an animal?" he asked her, his voice deep and low as he looked her dead in the eye. "Then I'll treat you like one."

"Zander—" She choked on his name, like she couldn't bring herself to even say it. "Honey, what are you doing?"

Honey.

An endearing term. A last attempt to manipulate him into forgiveness she didn't deserve.

He knelt in front of her, until they were nose-to-nose, and he grabbed her jaw. It was a familiar movement, something he often did when he was inside her, and the simple motion had made her thighs tighten around him with pleasure more than once.

As he stared into her eyes, with men screaming on the manor grounds, he caught the barest glimpse of hope in her expression.

"I'm giving you a head start," he finally said, burning through her last shred of optimism. "Run, Eleanor."

Outside, the wolves' panting breaths grew louder, and the rumble of paws against the dirt quickly approached the front doors that still sat ajar.

His whore of a wife watched him in breathless horror. Though her lips parted, she couldn't speak. Her chest rose and fell, her bare shoulders exposed to the air, and he could imagine that bastard of a nobleman kissing her neck less than an hour ago.

That killed the last of his pity for her.

Awkwardly, still shaking like a leaf and struggling to get her balance, Eleanor tried to stand. Her bare foot caught on her skirts, and she fell with a loud thump. Zander stood as she attempted again, and this time, she scampered down the hallway—half standing, half stooping, with her palms against the wall for balance.

And in her retreat, she didn't look back.

Not *once.*

Zander watched, cold and quiet, as she bolted down the hallway. She gained speed with each passing second, and he quietly studied her trembling form until she disappeared around the corner that led to the back stairwell.

His chest tightened—not with grief, but with rage. It simmered in him, hot as hellfire, and he didn't move until the front doors slammed against the wall in the sitting room downstairs.

The Feral King growled, still rooted in place beside him, and Zander waited. It was a test, not just of his control over the thing, but also of its willpower. He had tempted it with what it wanted most, but he hadn't yet given permission to chase.

For a few moments, they simply stood there—the Feral King watching the hallway, and Zander watching the ghoulish creature restrain itself, even as the thundering blightwolves drew closer. Though a trail of black saliva dripped down the Feral King's jowls, and though its heady growl rumbled through Zander's head, the beast didn't move.

In the heat of the moment, the beast had obeyed. Even when tempted with a tantalizing prize, the shadow wolf waited for the command to attack.

It took immense effort to restrain his gloating smirk, but Zander somehow managed. Instead, he gestured at the corner where his wife had slipped out of sight. "She's all yours."

A wickedly dark chuckle rumbled through his head, grim and ghoulish, as the shadow wolf dissolved into a rush of black smoke.

I shall enjoy this, the Feral King said.

Zander shrugged. "I know."

Calmly, in no rush at all, he stepped into the open doorway that led into the bedroom he had once shared with Eleanor. He casually leaned against the doorframe and pivoted his head toward the stairs as the panting rasp of a dozen wolves became a deafening din.

They shot up the stairs and raced past him, snarling at each other as they funneled down the narrow hallway one at a time.

As he watched his perfect army run by, a terrified scream echoed through the air from outside. Once, not long ago, the sound would've made his heart race with panic.

Now, however, he simply sheathed his Firesword.

CHAPTER FORTY-NINE

QUINN

On the outskirts of Everdale, Quinn paused behind yet another hedge and listened to the night.

Boots crunched across the gravel path surrounding her family's manor, and she peered over the carefully manicured bush that framed the vast gardens to the south of the main house. Sure enough, a man walked along the path toward the guardhouse, his shift apparently over, and he hummed a gentle tune under his breath. His dark green tunic perfectly matched the thicket of trees surrounding the property, and if not for the moonlight on his bearded face, he might not have been visible at all.

Moisture from the wet earth beneath her knee seeped into her pant leg. Though the fabric clung to her skin, she didn't move. She waited, her focus entirely on the soldier, until he finally trotted down the gentle slope toward the small building at the main gates. A candle flickered in a window, and a silhouette passed in front of it as the man opened the door and greeted whoever was inside.

The door shut again, and the night was once more silent. Crickets chirped in the warming spring air, and the distant babble of the eastern brook filtered through the woodland.

At the top of the hill, framed by towering oaks older than some of the kingdoms in Saldia, stood Starling Manor. Her ancestral home all but glowed in the moonlight, its white paint as pristine as ever, and the solid spellgust pillars out front supported a balcony overlooking the manicured road leading up to the main doors. Gardens sprawled across the fields around the house, and a stable on the other side of the property sheltered her mother's prized Clydesdales.

The coast was clear.

With her overstuffed bag on her back, Quinn scaled the hedge and landed in the grass on the other side. She kept low, always scanning the fields around her for threats, and she once more checked the guard gate to ensure none of the guards had resumed their rounds. The door remained mercifully shut.

Out here in the gardens, she was exposed. Though hedge-lined pathways meandered through the roses and lilacs planted throughout the gardens, anyone on the higher floors would be able to see her stealing through the night. Even when she made it to the house, she would have a hell of a time getting in. Most of the doors had charms on the locks designed by Teagan himself, but she still had the key to one window in the attic. If she could scale the pillars and climb onto the balcony, she was halfway there.

A woman's quiet sob broke her focus.

Quinn dropped to her stomach, and her hands flattened across the damp grass as she listened for the source of the sound. Her ear twitched as she fought to make sense of where it had come from or who it could've been. This late at night, everyone in the manor should've been fast asleep.

As the crickets trilled in the warm spring night, the world remained otherwise still, and she began to doubt herself.

Maybe she had imagined it. After all, she hadn't gotten a good night's sleep since leaving Slaybourne.

Quinn lifted her head over the nearest hedge to get her bearings, and she heard it again.

Crying, coming from the rear of the house.

A flash of concern hit her hard in the chest, and she debated for only a moment before switching course. Carefully, she darted through the shadows and kept to the edges of the property as she curved around the manor.

The rear garden consisted primarily of a large brick courtyard designed around a bubbling fountain of a dragon. Instead of lightning, the giant marble beast spewed a steady stream of glittering water, and the spellgust basin beneath it hummed with life as the water splashed onto the pathway surrounding it. Brilliant red and orange roses circled the patio, each in full bloom.

A woman sat on the edge of the spellgust basin, perched on a small seat carved into the stone, and her pale blue nightgown practically glowed in the moonlight. Her blonde hair hung over her shoulders in loose curls, a light frizz to the edges, as she stared into the water below her.

Quinn's throat tightened as she watched her mother rest her hands on the edge of the basin so that she could lean over the water. Madeline Starling's shoulders trembled as she sobbed at the dragon's feet, her eyes pinched shut in her pain, and another breathless gasp escaped her as she surrendered to the tears.

Sobbing.

Broken.

Utterly *lost* in her grief.

The tears slowed, and her mother sniffled quietly. Unmoving, still staring into the water, she shook her head. "Oh, Quinn."

Quinn stiffened. Her mother had talent, of course, but Quinn had always been able to sneak past her unnoticed before.

"Quinn. Zander." Madeline sniffled again. "I've lost you both. I've lost you all. And for what? Why would the Fates do this to me?"

Quinn's heart fluttered as she realized her mother wasn't talking to her at all. Victoria had evidently delivered the news, and Madeline Starling thought half of her family was dead.

As much as Quinn wanted to race forward and comfort her mother, her body refused to move. She had rehearsed this in her head, again and again, but now she had no idea what to say. Nothing seemed suitable, and despite everything she needed to ask her mother, she now felt wholly unprepared.

It gutted her to witness her mother's pain, and she braced herself for the worst. She had to do this now, or she might well lose her nerve.

Now or never.

"I should've told you," her mother whispered.

Even as she had begun to stand, Quinn tensed and returned to her crouch behind the nearest rose bush. Confused, she listened intently.

Madeline's lips parted again, but instead of words, a strangled gasp followed. She sobbed again, this time into her hands. Tears leaked through her fingers and hit the water in the basin.

Quinn couldn't let this go on any longer.

Tenderly and carefully, so as not to scare her mother senseless, Quinn stood. She glanced warily up at the darkened windows above her, and though this wasn't where she had wanted to have this conversation, she had little choice in the matter.

"Mother," she whispered.

Madeline's head snapped up, and she pivoted toward the sound. Her eyes widened, and all of the color drained from her face. She gaped up at Quinn as though she were a ghost. In her stunned surprise, Madeline tilted in her seat, and she began to fall into the basin beside her.

Quinn lunged forward and grabbed her mother's shoulders in time to stop the fall. She knelt in front of the woman who had raised her, who had loved her all of these years, and her hands remained firmly planted on Madeline's arms to ensure she didn't fall again.

And as she met her mother's eye, she saw relief. It was all-consuming, and her mother joined her on the ground. Kneeling in front of each other, Madeline wrapped her arms tightly around Quinn's body and pulled her in close. It was a desperate embrace, a panicked one, as though Quinn might fade into thin air if she didn't hold tight.

Tears welled in Quinn's eyes, and her throat tightened painfully. She swallowed hard to clear it and, not knowing what else to do, held her mother just as tightly.

"My baby girl." Her mother sobbed again, and her voice broke. "I thought I'd lost you, Quinn. I thought you were gone."

Quinn didn't reply. Words didn't seem good enough. Not for something like this.

Madeline sniffled and leaned just far enough away to scan Quinn's face. "Victoria said you were dead."

"They think I am."

"Why? Why in the Fates' name would you do this to your family?"

For a moment, Quinn could only stare at her mother in stunned silence. The answer to that question was a painful one, a long one, nuanced and agonizing, and she had no idea where to begin.

"The less you know, Mother, the safer you will be," she finally admitted. "You're going to hear a lot of things, and most of them will be lies. You raised me to be true to myself, and that's what I'm doing. For now, just know I need to do this."

Her mother's tear-stained eyes shook as she studied Quinn's face, and her lip trembled. Eventually, however, she nodded.

Quinn wrapped her mother in another hug, and she shut her eyes as a ripple of gratitude fluttered through her heart. "Thank you."

"Darling, I need to tell you something." Madeline pulled away and set her hands on Quinn's arms as she took a steadying breath. "Something I should have told you a long time ago."

Quinn's heart skipped a beat, and she waited in silence for her mother to continue.

A gentle breeze wandered by, stirring the loose tendrils of her mother's hair. The roses around them bent and swayed, their petals shivering in the night. The gurgle of the fountain behind them blended with the chirp of the spring crickets, and for several minutes, nature's symphony filled the void.

"I don't know where to start," her mother finally confessed.

"I can go first," Quinn offered.

Her mother sniffled again. "Alright, darling."

"I had a vision," Quinn explained. "It was a memory, but it makes no sense. There was snow, and I was little. An infant. An arrow killed the person carrying me, and we fell to the ground."

Her mother went eerily still. Another tear fell from one eye, following the path the others had taken, and Madeline hardly took a breath as she watched Quinn in terrified silence.

"You know what that was." Quinn swallowed hard to quell the surge of fluttery panic in her chest. "You know what happened."

Madeline bit her lip, and for the first time since they had held each other close, she glanced down at the ground in shame. "I do."

Quinn's jaw tensed, and her brows furrowed as she fought the numb disbelief slowly eating into her bones.

Madeline shook her head and released Quinn. The woman shifted her weight and leaned backward against the spellgust basin until she could stare up at the stars. A curl clung to her neck, fused to it by her tears, and she closed her tired eyes. "I can't begin there. You'll think I'm a monster."

Quinn stiffened, but she didn't reply.

"Have you ever wondered, Quinn, why Gwen is nine years older than you? It's odd, isn't it, to have three children a year apart, only to wait almost a decade for the fourth?"

With a frown, Quinn watched her mother in confused silence, not certain of where this was heading—or if she would like it.

"Three powerful children weren't enough of a legacy for your father." Madeline's voice darkened, and she stared off at the roses with a vacant numbness Quinn had never before witnessed. "He wanted more. More power. More magic. More influence. He didn't just want to create life, Quinn. He wanted to create something *new*."

Breathless, Quinn shifted in her seat and propped her arm on one knee. Though she should've paid closer attention to their surroundings, she found herself enthralled by her mother's rare transparency.

All her life, her mother had been a beacon of light and positivity. No sadness. No grief. Just beauty and grace, from the day she was born.

Now, Quinn realized how foolish she had been to not see the mask her mother had worn for so long. This—this pain, this raw honesty—this was a side of her mother that had never been allowed to see sunlight.

"After Gwen was born, he started to experiment," Madeline continued. "Without me knowing, he gave her potions. She grew stronger. An unaugmented toddler should never be able to hold a sword, much less cleave a tree."

Quinn let out a soft string of curses.

Her mother nodded. "But the effects didn't last, and his attempts to create an augmentation failed. He told me all of this later, thinking I would be impressed, but it lit a fire in me that I didn't think I had. When I found out what he'd done, I did something I'd never done before."

"What?" Quinn whispered.

"I stood up to him," her mother answered quietly. "I told him no. I gave him the sort of hell I'd only ever seen warriors unleash on their enemies. I'd never been so furious in all my life, and I warned him that if he did it again, I would undermine him in front of his soldiers. In front of dignitaries. In front of anyone who would listen. His perfect little family would unravel, and I would burn it to the ground."

Despite the gravity of her mother's confession, Quinn smiled with pride.

"It made him furious," Madeline continued. "For me to defy him like that—he wanted to punish me. And by the Fates, Quinn, he succeeded."

Quinn's smile fell, and she listened on in horrified silence.

"With his children off-limits, he began to experiment on me." Her mother took a deep breath as she stared ahead, eyes glossy and vacant. "He fed me potions and did all he could to keep me pregnant. Child after child died from whatever he was forcing down my throat. Stillborns, all of them, and more of me died with each one I lost."

Madeline shut her eyes tightly and sobbed. Quinn slipped her bag off her shoulder and sat next to the woman who had comforted her through so many lows in her life. Now, her mother leaned her head on Quinn's shoulder, and it was her turn to grieve. The words bubbled away into sobs, and in the shivering spring night, Quinn let her mother have all the silence she needed.

"I couldn't birth a healthy baby," her mother whispered. "Not one. Eight stillborns in nine years, Quinn. They were born with scales on their beautiful little faces, or horns, or tails. Your father was disgusted by them, but not me. No matter what they looked like, no matter what he had done to them, I wanted them to live. I would've killed for them, Quinn. I failed them. I failed them all."

"You didn't," Quinn whispered. "Father failed *you*."

"I found out what was in the potions, then," her mother confessed. "Dragon blood, Quinn. It was some concoction based around dragon blood, meant to mutate his future child into something else. Something *other*."

At the unspoken implication, Quinn's heart panged hard against her ribcage. She froze, one arm still wrapped around her mother's shoulders, and her breath wouldn't come.

Other.

Nocturne had called her that, what felt like a lifetime ago, when they were alone out there in the Ancient Woods. He had looked into her soul, and he wasn't sure what he'd found there.

"By then, I refused to let him touch me," her mother continued. "I couldn't live with myself if I'd lost another baby, and I grew to hate him for what he was doing to them. To me. To Zander, who was already growing up in his image. Victoria was already under his thumb, but I did my best to protect Gwen. To give her a fighting chance. But he—he doesn't—" Her mother fought to find the words. "When I rejected him, I saw him change. I'd seen him look at criminals with that kind of hatred, but never at me. He forced himself on me, that night, and every night until I started showing."

Disgusted, horrified, and at a loss for words, Quinn shut her eyes as she processed what her mother had just said. She held her mother tightly as the woman stifled another sob. In that second, she felt like a child again—helpless, lost, and confused—and that simple motion was all she could think to do.

"I thought he adored you," Quinn whispered. "I thought you loved him."

"No," her mother replied. "He adored what I could do for him, and I pretended to forgive him so that I could keep my children. I love you all too much to lose you. You're all I have left."

A painful knot formed in Quinn's throat, and she bit her lip to choke back the tears. Right now, she had to be the strong one. Right now, she had to give her mother space to grieve.

Quinn had seen her true father out there in the Decay, but somehow, he had been so much worse than she had ever imagined.

"And then you came." Despite the horrific confession thus far, the hint of a smile brightened her mother's voice. "My little miracle, to survive all of that. The moment I started showing, I whisked you away to the north. The midwives of the northern forest have power even men fear, and I kept you there until you were born. If anyone could undo what your father had done, it was them."

Gently, her mother sat upright and once more leaned against the spellgust basin behind them. Even with tears glistening in her eyes, she smiled as she studied Quinn's face.

"These healers were some of the Freymoor Fallen," Madeline continued. "They escaped Freymoor when Henry overtook it, and they hid in the snows where he wouldn't dare tread. Rumors, of course, and ones even your father never heard. There are some secrets we women must keep for ourselves."

She set a hand on Quinn's cheek, and Quinn chuckled weakly.

"I made them a deal—I would burn any information Teagan had on them, and they would do everything in their power to keep you alive. No matter what it took. When you were born, you were beautiful. Perfect. You gave me hope because you took one glorious breath—before your little lungs stopped, and you turned blue."

Madeline winced, the pain as fresh now as it was back then, and her face contorted with her profound grief. "I couldn't lose you. I vowed to do anything—everything—to keep you alive. In the days before you had been born, someone left a baby on the healers' doorstep. It was a strange little thing with brilliant green eyes and green scales for skin. A pulsing light flooded through its body like blood. It was a Discovered, and from the moment it arrived, it was dying. Nothing the healers did could save it, and as both of you faded away together, the healers told me to leave. I refused."

Her mother leaned her head back on the edge of the spellgust basin and stared up at the stars. "They used dark magic, the sort necromancers know, but I didn't care. You were my last tether to this world. My last hope. If I lost you, I had no intention of going back to Lunestone. I would've walked off the cliffs and into the sea with your cold little body in my arms."

Quinn's eyes squeezed shut, and she swallowed hard to fight the tears that so badly wanted free.

"They worked quickly," her mother confessed. "They bathed you in potions and dunked you into enchanted waters like a weapon being forged from spellgust itself. They used my blood, and I gave them all they needed to make it work—my hair, my clothes, my coin. None of it mattered to me anymore. I gave it all."

"Thank you," Quinn whispered.

It wasn't nearly enough, but it was all she could think to say.

"I would do it again, my girl." Madeline shifted in her seat, and this time, she set her arm around Quinn's shoulders. "But this—what they did—can never be repeated. It was a fluke, nothing but luck and the Fates' blessing, and to this day I don't know how it worked. There's magic in the moment of death. That's all they would tell me—and they were right. The air gets thick, and for only a moment, new magic is possible. As that baby took its last breath, your lungs began to work again. I snatched you from that cauldron the second they let me by, and the two of us cried together."

Quinn's brows furrowed as she pieced it all together. "Then that memory—"

"I suspect it was the other child's," her mother confessed. "Freymoor's magic is rife with memory, and Death Himself seems to swim in it. Memories, especially the final ones, linger. That memory must have been that little boy's final moments before the cold took him. I think it was the last thing he saw."

Appalled, Quinn stared at the brick beneath her feet. Her breaths came in strangled bursts, and no amount of air could fill her lungs now. A numb tingle crept across her skin, and her lips parted with the horror of what she had just learned.

"Death didn't give you back, Quinn," her mother confessed. "I *stole* you back."

A painful cold seeped into Quinn's bones, as harsh as snow on bare skin. Her mind buzzed. None of this seemed possible. Her skin crawled, and none of this seemed real.

"Perhaps what I did next was spiteful," Madeline continued. "It took ages, but I burned all of his notes on those potions he forced me to drink. Every last one of them, so that he could never do to anyone else what he did to us. To you." She took a steadying breath. "I didn't want him to know that his horrible plan had worked, but more than that, I knew he wouldn't love you unless you looked like him. I wanted to spare you a life of isolation, Quinn. I wanted you to be more than another of his weapons, locked away in a vault until he found a use for you."

That snapped Quinn from her daze.

"What does that mean?" Quinn scanned her mother's face with breathless dread. "What are you saying?"

Madeline held her gaze, and those hazel eyes of hers were clear and steady. "His experiment worked, Quinn."

"What… I don't…" Quinn's voice trailed off as she stared at her mother in disbelief.

"I studied glamours long before I met your father," her mother said. "But I didn't master them until you were born."

Without another word, her mother tugged on the chain around Quinn's neck. The Starling crest that she had worn every day of her life slipped out of her jacket, and her mother reached around her neck to unlatch it.

When the pendant fell into her mother's hand, a sharp pain hit Quinn square in her chest. She gasped hard and fell forward as a current of power flooded through her bones. It bubbled and hissed through her veins, through every muscle, and it carried with it the very essence of life. Unimaginable strength swelled and tingled through her limbs. Her senses sharpened even more intently than before. The world around her brightened as her eyes adapted instantly to the night. Her field of vision deepened, and as she lifted her head to take a deep breath of warm spring air, she could see the bark on the trees at the far end of the property.

With power like this, Quinn could do *anything*.

But it wasn't just a physical sensation. She felt something else, something primal, something *raw* resonating deep within her. It was a feeling of connection, of belonging, of being an integral part of something much greater than herself.

It made no Fates-damned *sense*.

When the initial surge faded into a light tingle running across her skin, Quinn blinked away her daze. She scanned the world around her, drinking in new colors and ribbons of light in the sky that weren't there before.

Her mother still sat beside her, quiet and pensive, and the woman watched her with a curious expression. Quinn didn't know what was happening, but she knew she was no longer the same person she was only a moment ago.

"What's happening to me?" Quinn asked, her voice shaking.

With a sad smile, her mother took her hand and patted it gently. "This is your true power, Quinn. I hid this from you your whole life, but this is who you truly are."

Madeline gestured toward the basin full of water behind them. Still shaking and unsteady on her feet, Quinn stood and leaned both hands on the fountain's rim.

But even as she stared into its depths, she couldn't understand what she saw.

In the water's reflection, Quinn stared down at herself, but her fire-red hair had ribbons of lavender light running through it. Scales, each as pale and soft as purple silk, covered her forehead like a crown. More scales ran down her neck and into her cleavage. As she gaped down at the water, a flash of light snapped through her eyes, and they went briefly amber.

Just like Nocturne's, out there on the battlefield, when he had accessed his feral magic.

Quinn jumped backward, and her ass landed hard against the brick. In her shock, she shuffled backward, heart racing. When she backed herself against the row of roses surrounding the patio, she finally stilled.

But that numb disbelief remained.

"It's alright, darling," a woman said.

Her mother's soothing voice shattered Quinn's daze, and her head snapped toward the sound. Somehow, her mother had walked toward her without her noticing, and the woman now knelt beside her with the pendant in her open palm. Moonlight glinted off the metal as her mother lifted it toward her neck yet again, but Quinn grabbed her mother's wrist to stop her.

"Tell me what's happening," she demanded.

"Shh," her mother cooed. "This will help you, just like it did when you were little. I promise."

"Tell me what's *happening*," Quinn said again, her voice far more ferocious than she had intended. "What the hell did you just do to me?"

"Your power overwhelmed you when you were little." Madeline sighed, and her slender body slouched as she relived the memory. "That much raw power—it was so hard to control. It took ages, but I managed to modify a Bluntmar enchantment to limit the power you could access, but you kept outgrowing them. Every year, I had to make it a little stronger. Anytime I needed to fix the pendant, I stayed by your side and gave you a Dwelldoze to ensure you didn't wake up until I was done. I knew I had to keep it a secret, even from you."

Though Quinn's hand was still wrapped tightly around her mother's wrist, Madeline tugged gently on her grip in a silent request that she let go. Quinn obliged, but she scooted a little farther away—not from her mother, but from the pendant.

"You lied to me," Quinn whispered.

Her mother winced, and she stared down at the ground where Quinn had sat moments before. "I did."

"What am I?"

"I don't know," Madeline confessed. "Part dragon, perhaps, or something else entirely. If your father is truly dead, we may never know."

There wasn't a hint of sadness in her mother's voice, and if Teagan Starling was truly gone, it seemed that his wife would not grieve his loss.

Quinn's chest heaved with panic at everything she had just learned. As the buzzing numbness began to slowly fade, one word repeated endlessly in her head.

Other.

Other.

Other.

Not a human, not a Starling, but something else entirely.

Her gaze snapped up toward her mother, and though she wasn't proud of what she did next, Quinn jumped to her feet. She snatched her bag, mostly out of habit than coherent thought, and she slung it over one shoulder as she ran. She bolted into the night with no idea of where she could possibly go—she just knew she couldn't stay here.

She needed a moment to think.

Somehow, she needed to *understand.*

Quinn had gotten what she had come here for—but, as with all Saldian magic, it had come at a terrible cost.

MADELINE

As Madeline watched her daughter fade into the shadows at the edge of the property, she sat back on her heels. With her nightgown flowing over the ground around her, her body felt numb. A gentle breeze slid her frizzed hair off her shoulder and tried to carry it away into the sky as the sculpture behind her gargled and dripped onto the brick.

All she could do was watch her miracle child disappear yet again as that familiar grief built in her chest like a snowstorm.

Even a mother's strength had its limits, and Madeline had reached hers.

Alone in a manor that had once protected her entire family, Madeline sobbed into her hands. Quinn's crest slid from her fingers and clinked onto the brick below her, but she didn't care enough to look.

Quinn had always been her one great secret. In a world of lies and glamours, Quinn had given her purpose. That little girl had been Madeline's rebellion against the conman who had charmed a ring onto her finger. To keep her safe from him, to hide her true power from that horrible man—that had given Madeline strength.

In her darkest times, something her own mother had told her years and years ago had kept her going.

"A woman's greatest strength isn't in her body," her mother had said. *"It is her courage. It is her soul. It is her love. These powers are passed to the next generation, and to the next, and the next, so that they might live stronger lives than we ever dreamed possible for ourselves."*

"May you forgive me one day," Madeline said weakly, knowing her daughter was too far away to hear. "And may you forever know your strength, my darling little dragon."

CHAPTER FIFTY

QUINN

Quinn just needed a moment to breathe.

To *think*, and to make sense of everything she had just learned.

That word echoed again in her head, over and over, like a sick and twisted mantra someone else was screaming into her ear.

Other.

Her heart slammed against her ribcage, hard and violent.

Other.

Breath caught in her lungs, as sharp and cold as steel.

Other.

Her boots hit the dirt, one after another, faster with each passing second. She didn't know where she was going, only that she was trying to escape.

But not even she could run forever.

In the dark forest beyond her family estate, far beyond the edge of Everdale and even farther from the lake that held Lunestone in its waters, Quinn stopped and set her hands on her knees to catch her breath. Her chest heaved as she scanned the evergreens around her, all of them identical as they towered above the pine nettles from several years' worth of autumns.

Her overstuffed bag weighed on her shoulders, and she grimaced as she finally slid it off her back. It hit the ground beneath a thick pine with a thud, but she didn't care what broke. She knelt in front of it and rifled through it until she found the little vial with the clover on its label.

The last of her Dazzledane potion. The one thing that could soothe her tired bones, and this time, maybe she wouldn't limit herself to just one sip.

Maybe this time, she deserved a little more.

Quinn held it to her lips, but before she could drink it, her father's words hit her hard in the gut.

"I allowed your addiction," he had said out there in the Decay. *"It kept you in line. Child, you can't hide anything from me. I know it all."*

Her father had used her addiction to control her. It was yet another string he had pulled to keep her obedient, and there was no telling how far he would've let it go.

Though she didn't toss her cherished potion aside, she managed to cork the bottle without taking even a sip—and that, for now, was a victory.

The world around her came suddenly into focus, and a fuzzy sense of alarm burned somewhere in the back of her skull. She spun in a slow circle, trying to get her bearings, but every path from here looked the same—towering pines, patchy grass in the dirt, and the musky tang of moss wafting through the air.

The shrill ringing in her ear hit a crescendo, and she winced. She rubbed the skin behind it, where her scalp met her neck, and the shrill scream mercifully faded.

In the silence that followed, the crash of river rapids filled the air. The first blooms of summer poked through the dirt at her feet, and the soft tendrils of honeysuckle wafted by. The trees above her bent and swayed in a gentle northern breeze that carried the heady tang of jasmine through the forest. Moonbeams through gaps in the canopy glinted across dew gathered on the sparse patches of grass.

In the moonlight, the forest was at peace.

The quiet soothed her. As the woodland's perfume curled around her, she paused to take it all in.

Thunder rumbled, and her head snapped upward as a bolt of lightning shot across the sky. A dark cloud rolled above the trees, inching closer to the moons with each passing moment, and a shiver ran through the forest as the storm kicked up a gale.

Quinn's hair snapped against her skin like whips, but she didn't move. Lost as she was in her thoughts, she could only stare up at the rumbling darkness above her. It churned and rolled like a living thing, blacker than the night. Light cracked through its body with each lightning bolt as it burned itself from within, and the first smattering of rain drops pelted the forest caught in its wrath.

As the cold rain hit her face, Quinn closed her eyes to savor it. The wind filled her lungs, and the icy air cleared her head. She could think, finally, and the storm chased away some of her numb disbelief.

The Dazzledane potion slipped in her hand, and she tightened her grip around the vial to keep from spilling even a drop.

More rain pelted her face and neck as she stared down at the bottle, and this time she tilted her hands to study them. Where once her pale skin had been dotted with freckles, silky lavender scales now ran in a thin line over her wrists and across her forearms. She stared at them in disbelief as the storm worsened. A bolt of lightning lit the sky, and the crackling yellow light cast strange shadows across this part of her she'd never known she had.

Despite the tempest raging over the forest, kicking up leaves into the air as its power grew, Quinn felt oddly still. Silent. Dazed. Every fiber of her being had gone quiet. The warrior. The daughter. Even the general Connor wanted her to be.

In that moment, Quinn was nothing and no one. Everything she knew faded away, and she was one with the raging storm above her. It howled while she ached.

Death hadn't given her back to this world. Her mother had stolen from Him, and Quinn wondered if He would try to take her back sooner than she was ready to go. The Fates likely weren't fond of claimed souls slipping through their fingers.

As she closed her eyes, the rain fell harder. She leaned into it, savoring the icy chill each drop left behind on her skin, and the edge of her lips curled into a small smile. The rain brought fresh air with it, and the soothing aroma of water rolling off the leaves around her cleared her head.

In the raging thunder of a storm, everything finally made sense.

Through magic that could never be replicated, Quinn had been forged from the very fires her father had tried for so many years to conquer. She was a hybrid, and something neither man nor dragons could claim. Dragon blood ran in her veins, and it had forged her into something *other.*

There was that word again.

She waited to feel a twinge of shame or a pitter-patter of fear, but this time, she felt nothing. It wasn't a burden for her to bear, but rather a fact.

It simply was, and she wouldn't hide from it any longer.

A gust shot through the forest, and the trees bent in unison beneath its might. The gale hit Quinn square in the chest, but she leaned into it. Her boots skidded backward over the dirt as the wind kicked her hair around her face, and the chaotic clouds above her unleashed a torrent of rain. It fell in sheets, drenching her hair and clothes in an instant, but she didn't care.

This chaos, this power—it gave her *life.*

Lightning cracked across the sky, closer this time, and the sharp crackle of her Voltaic augmentation fizzled through her veins. The magic she had never been able to control connected with the sky, and in that, she felt somehow safe.

No sane woman would stand out here in a storm like this, but perhaps Quinn was no longer sensible.

Something teased the edge of her mind—something important but out of reach, like the tail of a fish she couldn't quite grab. It swam around her thoughts in circles. She grimaced as she fought to catch it, to reel it back toward her, but it refused to obey.

An earth-shattering boom rocked the ground beneath her feet, and Quinn opened her eyes in the second before a dazzling blast of lightning could hit. Her body acted on impulse, but instead of running, she reached for it.

And, to her astonishment, she caught it.

On contact, the vial of Dazzledane in her hand shattered. The potion instantly evaporated to nothing, and the singed cork flew to one side. The blinding light sizzled in her palm, and with a twist of her arm, she angled the bolt into the ground behind her. It scorched the earth and left a deep gouge in the soil. Sparks skittered across the dead leaves, igniting them with its dying breath, and tendrils of smoke coiled from the aftermath of their duel.

That cleared her head more than any potion ever could.

When people were afraid, she took the lead. She stood up for those who could not stand, and she fought for those with no voice. She was a killer, and though she fought for justice, she had made many mistakes in her life. She would make more—and she would heal from them when they came.

Quinn Starling was a warrior. It was who she had always been, and it was who she chose to be now.

A protector.

A soldier.

A general.

Thunder rumbled through the sky like a predator's growl, and Quinn raised one hand to greet it. Sparks danced through the clouds, and she called them to her. They bent and swayed, fighting her at first like the lightning always did, but she didn't relent.

Before, she had been afraid of this power.

Now, however, she *embraced* it.

A bolt of lightning tore through the clouds toward her, and she shifted her aim toward a nearby tree, just as she had seen her father and brother do so many times before. The arc of sizzling light obeyed, and it hit the old pine with a deafening *crack.* The force of nature's purest chaos scorched the bark in an instant, and dark lines spread out from its trunk as the bolt burned its way through the roots.

Sparks crackled over her body, dancing across the thin line of scales that ran up her arm, and she stared down at her hand in awe. A slow, broad smile broke across her face, and the last threads of her fear faded away.

Throughout her life, Zander had claimed to be one with the lightning. It was his reasoning for why she always failed to control it—she would never earn its respect.

But she was more than the lightning. Quinn Starling was the storm itself, and she would no longer be contained.

CHAPTER FIFTY-ONE

ZANDER

The dual windowpanes on either side of the bathroom sink opened onto the first day of summer. Three bluebirds darted past the open windows, and a sharp flash of light reflected off something in the pond on the eastern end of the manor, opposite the main road.

Zander buried his face in a plush black towel, still warm from its perch in a sunbeam, and he sighed into the cloth.

He'd been gone for nearly seven weeks, and he had missed most of the spring season. How strange, to think it was already summer. The summer festivals would be popping up all along the southern road as the peasants celebrated sunlight and the promise of renewal.

Summer was the fresh start everyone needed.

As the scent of his wife's blood still lingered on the air, he grunted in disgust.

The grime that had covered his body was gone, and so too was the overgrown beard. In the mirror set beside the clawfoot tub, he examined his handiwork once more to ensure he'd gotten it all. Shirtless and wearing only a fresh change of pants, he examined the scars littering his torso.

Teeth marks along his shoulder, courtesy of Farkas, now a shade or two lighter than the rest of his skin.

Two narrow gouges, from where the Wraithblade had stabbed him with his own Bloodbane dagger.

A sprawling black mark that began in the center of his chest and radiated outward, like a lake feeding into smaller rivers along its bank.

Zander ran his finger over the dark spot where the Feral King had fused with him, and the patch of black glowed briefly green.

Originally, he'd planned to spend several days recuperating in the manor. He'd thought civilization would be a pleasant escape from the constant yip and whine of his blightwolves, but now he missed the steady snarls that had accompanied him through the Ancient Woods.

How strange.

Besides, he didn't want to spend a minute more in this whorehouse than was necessary.

The sun inched farther across the sky, toward the horizon, and he estimated roughly an hour left until sunset. His wolves had retreated into the nearby forest to sleep, but many would already be waking as they prepared for their next movement through Saldia.

Time to make his final preparations.

Before he could move, however, a tendril of black smoke rolled across the floor toward him, and the air shifted. Something weighed on him, like eyes on the back of his neck, but this sensation hardly phased him anymore.

"Is there anything left of her?" he asked the Feral King.

Nothing, the shadow wolf confirmed. It circled the large bathroom, though its bulk barely fit even as it kept to the walls. *Nothing but bones.*

Zander nodded, satisfied. "All the leftovers are in the sitting room?"

Leftovers. The ghoulish creature chuckled. *As if they were never human to begin with.*

"Yes or no?" he prodded.

All remaining bones and bits are piled in the sitting room. Some of the pups from last year's litter fell asleep munching on them.

"How quaint," Zander said dryly.

While the Feral King paced the room, Zander dabbed at his face with the towel. In the mirror, he watched the creature on its route along the bathroom's walls. Never still. Always moving. Always twitching.

Always chasing *something*, even if it could only chase thoughts.

"You listened to me." He shifted his attention to his reflection and pretended to inspect his jawline for missed spots to shave. "Back there with the guards and with that whore. You stayed hidden."

In his periphery, it paused mid-stride. When it didn't speak, he glanced its way, and the thing watched him as a gentle breeze passed by the open windows. A sunbeam hit the mutated hump on its back, and the light cast a silky shimmer across the metallic blades of its fur.

I did, it finally said.

"And when we caught her—" Zander cleared his throat roughly and, instead of finishing that sentence, he returned his attention to his reflection. "You were every bit as enraged as I was."

The ghoulish creature growled softly. *To disrespect the alpha is to disrespect me.*

A small smile tugged at the edge of Zander's mouth, and he finally shifted his full attention to the Feral King.

"Back there, when she saw me..." His eyes slipped out of focus as he recalled the buttery aroma that had spiraled through the air. "I smelled her fear, didn't I?"

The great wolf nodded. *Tell me what else you can do, now that you are the Feralblade. Tell me what you've learned.*

A test, this time for him.

Alright. He could play this game, and he might even be able to trick it into revealing anything he had missed.

"I command the blightwolves," he began. "I have unmatched speed, superior strength, and a sense of smell that exceeds even the best potions in Saldia."

Good. The shadow wolf's mouth curled upward in a sinister smile. *What else?*

"I can see in almost total darkness. I heal on my own faster than any Rectivane could heal me."

What else?

Zander studied the wolf's face for signs of a bluff, but the ghoulish creature betrayed nothing.

In the end, he merely shrugged. "There's nothing else."

On the contrary. The Feral King resumed pacing, and its eyes never left Zander's. *You've already mastered my greatest gift. Something far more valuable than senses or speed.*

"What is it then?"

The shadow wolf bolted toward him, almost faster than the eye could see, and it skidded to a stop right in front of him. It snarled, its nose wrinkling with the threatening growl, and the beast barked sharply in his ear.

But Zander didn't move.

He stared up at it, towering over him, and waited for it to get to the damn point.

In his mind, the Feral King laughed. The deep-set creases in its face relaxed, and it shook its head as though it were obvious. *You have no fear, Zander Starling.*

How curious.

You want the Wraithblade, the ghoulish creature continued with a nod toward the windows. *That man is slowly taking control of the Ancient Woods, but that is our domain, not his. We must remind him of who truly owns this forest. We must remind him of his place.*

Zander smirked. "We will."

The Feral King's eyes narrowed, and for a moment, the beast didn't speak.

Then you have my respect, it finally said.

"And you have mine," Zander lied.

He tossed the towel into the tub, and the black fabric smeared a lingering red splotch along the white interior. Without servants to prepare his food or baths, he'd been slowed down considerably—but it was a small price to pay to not have to speak to any of the traitors who'd let his wife spread her legs for strangers.

A flicker of that same, white-hot rage flashed in his chest at the thought of her, and he spat on the floor to clear the taste of her name from his mouth.

He had more important matters to address, such as the Feral King's loyalty.

As Zander pulled on a fresh shirt and buckled his Firesword's sheath around his waist, he debated his options. This encounter had been fairly low-stakes. If the beast had failed, there would have been no consequences whatsoever.

It was possible the Feral King knew that, too. For all he knew, the thing might well be playing with him.

Lost in thought, he absently slid his various daggers and knives back into their hidden sheaths along his body.

He needed one more test. A big one. One with consequences, should the shadow-wolf fail. One where it would be tempted—both its impulsive urges and its desire to test his boundaries.

He needed to walk into a town, and he needed to speak to Lightseers. He needed to see exactly what the Feral King would do when faced with such decadent bait, but he also needed an escape route and a way to conceal his identity.

Luckily, he knew exactly where to go.

His pack leaned against the doorframe, already prepared with food, potions, weapons, and fresh clothes—the only possessions he kept in this place he so rarely visited. The rest of the things in this house belonged to his wife and the children.

None of whom, apparently, had truly been his to begin with.

At the thought, that flash of hatred in his chest became a bonfire. It took effort to rein in the rage, and he slung his pack over his shoulder as he tried to distract himself with the route they would take toward the southern road. Someone would find the manor soon enough, and he couldn't be anywhere nearby when they did.

No one could trace this massacre back to him.

He stepped over a guard's drool-drenched sword as he left the bathroom. Streaks of blood lined the hallway, interspersed with dark red puddles still seeping into what was once a royal blue carpet.

The rusty tang of iron and metal still hung on the air after all that death. Most of the men had died in the house, and all but a handful of rooms had been utterly ruined with claw marks on the walls and bloodstains across every surface.

It had truly been a bloodbath.

As he walked down the hallway, Zander stepped in one just to hear the *splurch* of a traitor's blood beneath his boot. Satisfied with the sound, he took a deep breath of the heady blood on the air. It filled his lungs like a perfume, and his stomach growled.

Oddly enough, all this blood made him rather hungry.

When he reached the bedroom he had once shared with Eleanor, he paused. His pack weighed on his shoulder as he studied the decimated room. The blankets strewn across the floor. The broken curtain rods, and the sunlight filtering through the window panes. The puddle of blood marking the spot where he'd killed her lover, and the trail of blood leading toward the door.

There was nothing left for him here.

Instantly, flame crackled across his hands. The fire raged, and in his numb hatred, he stared down at his palms. The red and orange flickers snapped at the air, ready to destroy and decimate at his command.

His magic, every bit as obedient as the blightwolves.

He unleashed a torrent of fire against the bed. The wood split and splintered under the enhanced flames, and its frame caved inward within seconds. The curtains were next, and then the bureau.

One by one, he burned her things. The trinkets. The trash.

The memories.

When there was nothing left in their bedroom to burn, he stood in the doorframe and watched the carnage. To ensure nothing remained—and that the bodies were assumed lost in the ash—Zander would have to burn every room on his way out the front doors.

A trifle, and one well worth the effort. By the time anyone noticed the thick plumes of smoke billowing into the air, he and his wolves would be long gone.

Eleanor had learned the hard way that he was truly the superior man, unrivaled. It was a lesson the Wraithblade would learn, as well—and in much the same way.

CHAPTER FIFTY-TWO

QUINN

A day had passed, but Quinn was finally ready.

In the tar-black sky, long after another sunset, Quinn stood on the balcony overlooking her family's estate. She waited with her back to the house while her mother stood before her, elbows resting on the stone railing as she stared off into nothing. The forests beyond the estate's towering walls were still, the rest of the world asleep.

Despite all she had learned last night, Quinn felt strangely calm.

The sunlit hours had been spent in the woods, thinking and remembering, and now her head was finally clear. In the filtered sunlight, she had spent her time thinking, grieving, and debating with herself about what would come next. What Gwen would say. What Connor would do. What Nocturne would think.

In the end, none of their reactions would change who she was. If they truly loved her, this wouldn't change a thing.

Finally dry after the rainstorm, she adjusted the pack on her shoulder. Mercifully, the trees had shielded the bag from most of the storm, and none of the books inside were damaged. A blessing, really, because she hadn't been able to think rationally enough to protect them.

With a quiet sigh, Quinn joined her mother at the balcony and rested her forearms on the cool stone railing. The guards had circled the property many times already, but Quinn had long ago memorized their shifting schedules. The estate had been designed to allow only Starlings to enter and exit unseen, and per her father's instruction, she had memorized every nook and cranny of her childhood home.

The Starlings kept to themselves, and the soldiers in charge of the estate's defense knew it better than most. Even now, as Quinn stood on the balcony, one of the men circled the house and whistled softly to himself. His attention remained on the walls, the gardens, and the forest—but not on the Starling matriarch as she stared up at the stars in the middle of the night.

Her mother didn't move, and for several minutes, neither woman spoke. They simply stared out into the darkness as the world slept on, oblivious to everything that had happened just hours before.

How surreal. Quinn's life had changed overnight, and she had gotten everything she had wished for—answers, power, and the truth her family had kept hidden from her for so long.

And yet, her heart felt heavy.

Quinn took one look at her mother, and she knew. Red eyes, swollen with tears, cheeks pink from the salt of hours spent crying, and a trembling lip that told more than words ever could.

As the guilt weighed heavy on her shoulders, Quinn's heart broke at her mother's pain. After everything she had done to protect her family, after all her suffering and sacrifice, Madeline Starling deserved so much better.

Exhausted, ashamed, and still a little confused, Quinn rubbed her face and racked her brain for something to say. Nothing felt suitable. Nothing was good enough, and when words failed her, she allowed the silence to continue. Together, they stared out past the walls and gardens, beyond the forests, into conquered lands.

Quinn had been taught to protect her family from danger, blood, and steel, but she had no idea how to shield them from sorrow or grief.

It left her helpless—and Fates be damned, how she hated this feeling.

Without warning, her mother wrapped her arms around Quinn's shoulders and pulled her into a tight hug. A delicate palm rested on the back of Quinn's head, cradling her with a gentle, tender touch.

Love.

Forgiveness.

Devotion.

That one gesture—a simple hand on the back of her head, stroking her hair now and then—said it all.

Quinn closed her eyes and leaned her forehead against her mother's shoulder, and she held the woman close. A gentle breeze wandered by, unbothered by anything but its rambling path through the sky, and Quinn smiled.

Right now, for just this moment, everything felt right with the world.

"I'm sorry," Quinn whispered. "I shouldn't have left like that. After everything you told me—after what Father did to you—"

Quinn's throat tightened, and she couldn't finish the thought. Instead, she held her mother tighter, as if that could somehow heal the pain.

Her mother kissed the side of her head. "You have nothing to apologize for, darling. I can't imagine how I would've reacted if I were in your shoes."

The guilt remained, and Quinn didn't answer.

Something had been eating at her, though, since the confession. Quinn braced herself as she began to piece together an explanation for even more of the things that had made her feel so very *other* for so long.

"I need to know… that is…" Faltering as she fought for the right words, Quinn took a deep breath to settle her racing heart and tried again. "Those glamours you made me—those never lasted very long, and they were weaker than the ones you made for Zander and Gwen."

"Because you were already wearing one," her mother confirmed. "It took ages to master the double-glamour, and even then it was flawed."

Quinn looked down at the ground. "And the Bluntmar collars left me so drained because I was unknowingly wearing one."

"A modified one." Her mother leaned back and lovingly set her hands on Quinn's shoulders. "Not a true disconnect from your magic, but a way to limit the surges of power you couldn't control."

"And the length of the chain?"

"Too tight to slip over your neck," Madeline confessed. "And charmed with a Strongman augmentation so that it wouldn't break. Just in case someone tried to steal it, or if you were in a battle where it risked snapping. I didn't want to leave it to chance."

Sluggishly and almost entirely unaware of the movement, Quinn nodded as the pieces of a lifelong puzzle fit slowly into place.

"Here." Her mother reached into a shallow pocket sewn into the side of her dress and pulled out two pendants with the Starling crest etched into their metal.

"I'm not wearing it again," Quinn said firmly.

Impulsively.

She closed her eyes and took another settling breath to recenter herself. "I'm not limiting my magic anymore. I'm not going to hide."

"You shouldn't show people who you are," her mother prodded. "Not yet. They aren't ready."

"They'll never be ready."

"Perhaps." Her mother shrugged and offered her the pendants anyway.

The two necklaces rested on Madeline's open palm, and their chains dangled through her slender fingers. Both Starling crests looked identical—a shield, dyed to a dazzling purple, and with a gilded phoenix in its center.

And, below the mythical beast, the family motto.

The wicked die at our feet.

Quinn winced and once more leaned against the railing, just to put distance between her and the cursed pendants in her mother's hand.

"My girl, I know it's a lot to ask, but you must trust me on this." Her mother leaned closer and brushed a loose lock of hair out of Quinn's face. "The people of Saldia see dragons as omens of death, darling. A beast only tyrants can conquer and control. I can't risk them thinking the same of you."

How fitting, given what Quinn's father had wanted from her.

"I can't lose you again." Her mother's voice quivered. "I've already lost Zander, and I don't think I can survive another of my babies dying before I do."

Guilt stabbed Quinn right in the heart, and she grimaced as she fought the surging tide of shame that came with it. Staying silent was probably the smartest choice, if only to keep her mother from hoping too hard for an unlikely outcome.

But she couldn't bear the grief in her mother's voice, and she ultimately succumbed.

"He might not be dead," she confessed.

Madeline gasped, and through the corner of Quinn's eye, she saw her mother stiffen. "What do you mean?"

"Blightwolves dragged him off," Quinn continued, still uncertain of whether or not this was a wise decision. "The biggest one sank its teeth into his arm and hauled him into the night, but I saw what he did. He let it happen. For whatever reason, he saw that as his chance to retreat, and he left me behind. We never found a body. Zander is strong, Mother. Even though he's been gone for so long, there's a possibility that he's very much alive."

"Bless the Fates." Her mother's body drooped with relief as tension flooded from her shoulders.

Though Quinn disagreed that it was a blessing, she kept silent.

"He's alive," Madeline said quietly, mostly to herself. "He has to be. He's too strong to let a blightwolf kill him."

"What would Zander say?" Quinn stared out again at the forest, even though she barely noticed it. Her mind raced at all the possible ways her brother might react after he learned the truth. "About me? About what I am?"

Beside her, Madeline went eerily still. Her body tensed again, and the relief faded from her face.

"Exactly," Quinn whispered, more out of disappointment than anything else. "You're not safe from him, Mother. You need to go into hiding."

"Nonsense." Her mother scoffed at the very idea. "I don't think your brother knows what you are, but I believe he has always suspected it. Your father likely shared tidbits, here and there, that Zander was able to piece together. That's why he's always been so cruel to you." Her mother shook her head in disappointment and sighed wearily. "I tried to get him to stop, and he did—for a time. But I eventually heard whispers of his cruelty whenever he thought no one was watching. So, no, it's not my safety I fear for, darling. It's yours."

Though she didn't agree, Quinn let the silence be her reply.

"You need these." Yet again, her mother offered her the two pendants in her hand. "Your pendant was due to be recharmed later this year, so I had a potion already prepared. I was waiting for the right opportunity to present itself, but... well..." The woman shrugged. "I suppose this is as good a time as any. They're both charmed with the same glamour, but only one of them will restrict your power. I painted a lightning bolt on the back of the one without the Bluntmar. Take both and use each as you see fit. You cannot let your magic get the best of you Quinn. You're older, now, and you have much better control—but I remember the rages you had in your youth, whenever your father pushed you too far, but you're stronger now. Think of the devastation you would cause if you let that consume you yet again."

With a reluctant grumble, Quinn took the necklaces. She flipped them over and, sure enough, one had a thick yellow bolt of lightning painted on the back. Each stroke of the yellow paint had been made with care and intention, and seeing it soothed her anger.

"Thank you," she said quietly.

"It's fitting, isn't it?" Her mother leaned again on the railing and wiped the tear stains from her cheeks. "Today is the first day of summer."

The summer celebrations had always brought Quinn such joy. The festivals. The lights. The sunshine, and the taste of strawberries fresh off the vine. The week-long festivals sometimes lasted all season because of the traveling performers, and she had always loved catching sight of their caravans passing along the roads.

It had always been a festival of sunlight and the promise of renewal. It was the fresh start everyone needed—including her.

"I've prepared a pack for you," her mother said. "Food, some potions, and the like."

Madeline's voice snapped Quinn from her thoughts, and she smiled with gratitude. "You haven't slept at all, have you?"

Her mother chuckled. "I couldn't have slept last night if I'd tried."

"That's fair. Thank you for the pack."

"Of course, darling. I included new glamours for you." Madeline studied Quinn's face and tilted her head with an air of curiosity. "You really are beautiful, my little dragon."

Little dragon.

Quinn went blank as she processed the simple words that somehow carried so much weight. She sat with them, mulling over them like a fine wine.

In the end, odd as it was to admit, the term felt right.

"I'm so grateful for you." Quinn wrapped her mother in another tight hug and once more rested her head on the woman's shoulder. "You gave me a real chance at life. You suffered to keep me safe. What you endured to protect me is more than anyone should ever have to give. Thank you, Mother. I don't know who I would be if not for you."

Madeline held her tightly, as if scared they might both fade away to dust if she let go, and a quivering sigh escaped her. "I gave it gladly."

The two of them held each other, standing there on that balcony under the starlit sky, as the evening stretched on. Quinn smiled, happy and at peace, as the two of them healed what had been broken by a lifetime of lies.

"Now, listen closely." Her mother cleared her throat and took a steadying breath. She pulled away and set both hands on Quinn's shoulders with all the poise and fire of a warrior queen. "You carry within you power unlike anything this continent has ever seen. As a Starling, you are of the fire. As a dragon, you are of the sky. Whatever you're up against, remember that, and face it with all the ferocity of the wildest storm."

Quinn stood taller, and her mother's voice gave her strength. "I will."

"Good." Madeline Starling lifted her elegant chin, and a gentle smirk tugged on the corner of her lips. "Give them hell, baby girl."

With a mischievous smile, Quinn simply nodded.

She was her mother's daughter, so it went without saying—but yes, that was most *definitely* the plan.

CHAPTER FIFTY-THREE

CONNOR

On the Kirkwall oceanfront, Connor waited.

He, Sophia, and Murdoc knelt behind a row of crates along the southern boardwalk. The cloth over their mouths hid their faces, but it was more precaution than necessity. Tonight was about gathering information, and he had no intention of letting anyone know he was here.

In the silence, a cool breeze rustled the moonlit docks. The wind carried the tang of rust and salt across the gentle waves, and the hollow groan of a lone ship's mast blended with the soothing midnight melody.

A calm, quiet night.

Perfect for a heist.

Up ahead, the lonely flicker of a single candle illuminated one window of an otherwise pitch-dark warehouse built along the cliff face. The loading bay doors had closed hours ago, and the merchants had packed up long before that. Only the caretaker remained, humming to himself as he had locked up the doors, and the man now sat at a worn wooden desk as his quill scratched away at a stack of parchment.

But Connor and his team weren't here for the caretaker.

In the patch of dark elm trees along the warehouse's eastern wall, eight silhouettes darted through the shadows. The cloaked men wore hoods, and the thick black cloth over their mouths hid most of their faces.

This warehouse had hosted more than one smuggler in Connor's day, and the familiar side entrance nearest to the cliff sat ajar—a clear sign that the building's illicit activity continued to this day. If these men wanted into that structure, they would have to walk right past the stack of crates Connor and his team had chosen for cover.

A strategic move, of course. Now, all they had to do was wait.

"Do you really think this is our mark?" Murdoc whispered from behind a nearby crate. "He's wearing a mask, just like all the rest of them."

"It's him," Connor confirmed. "His height, his build, his gait, his voice—I'm sure this is the one we want."

Owen.

The imposters' leader.

After two days of watching every figure who entered or left that secret hatch by his father's old shop, Connor had finally found their ticket into the castle.

Despite the Wraith King's griping—and, admittedly, Connor's own restlessness—they had not intervened since Connor had returned from the mountain. All this time, he and his team had simply watched from afar, studying the imposters and their routines. Their habits. Their weaknesses. Their numbers.

"How long until they *do* something?" Sophia whispered as she once again peered over the nearest crate. "For nameless thieves who sneak through the night, these people are surprisingly dull."

"I wouldn't go that far." Connor glanced at Sophia before returning his attention to the eight silhouettes up ahead. "They're using my image to break the law. I find that intriguing, to say the least."

"Petty theft, you mean." She scoffed. "They've done nothing but steal weapons from an armory vault on the west end and deliver Rectivanes to sick children. They're not even remotely interesting, Connor. Not by our standards, anyway."

"They did steal reagents from that potions shop yesterday," Murdoc said with a lazy shrug. "And that shop window showed everything they were doing. They didn't seem to care if they got caught. That was interesting, love."

"I hardly call that proper theft, since they paid for what they took." Sophia cast a sidelong glare at Connor. "Like someone else we know."

It was disgraceful, the Wraith King conceded, though he remained mercifully unseen as the stakeout dragged on. *It's clear that they've studied your exploits, Magnuson.*

Connor didn't rise to the bait—either from the necromancer or the ghoul.

"One of them stole that Bloody Beauty when the others weren't watching, Sophia." He raised one eyebrow in challenge. "The only one the shopkeeper had, too. He didn't pay. Not all of them are noble."

Sophia huffed, but didn't reply.

"We need leverage," he continued. "Their leader is our way into the castle, and I doubt he'll take us there willingly. If we're going to kidnap the man coordinating an illegal operation, we need to know how they'll retaliate. Even we can be outnumbered, Sophia, and we don't know how many of them there are."

"Sixty," she said flatly. "Give or take a dozen. That's my estimate based on what we've seen of their movements through that hatch. Easy for you to handle."

"And if you're wrong?"

Connor studied her face as her gaze shifted once more to him, and she frowned. The breeze toyed with one of her loose black curls, and she didn't reply.

He nodded. "Exactly. Without going down those tunnels ourselves—which is risky, given that they know the paths better than we do—we don't have enough information. We don't know who these men are, what they want, or what the risk is if we get on their bad side. You saw what they did to that group of criminals on the bridge. I don't know what they're capable of, yet, and we're not moving in on them until I do."

"Fine," she muttered under her breath.

Of course, their time monitoring the imposters had yielded useful information. The men always moved in groups of four to ten, depending on the mission, but they engaged with the townsfolk one at a time. For whatever reason, they clearly wanted to maintain the image of a lone vigilante stealing through the night.

Based on the green ink they occasionally caught on the men's arms and necks, they were heavily augmented—and that meant they had money. They stole through the night using old smuggler dens and more secret hatches to the underground tunnels than Connor thought could possibly exist, and they had a better understanding of the city than even the soldiers. On two occasions, the city's guardsmen had come within mere feet of the cloaked criminals, all without ever knowing they could've reached into the shadows and touched the very people they were hunting.

Most curious of all, however, was how many times Rockwell's name came up in their whispers. They met in back alleys and in the city's patches of forest, and their urgent tones were becoming more panicked with every passing day.

If they were going to save the man, they had to act soon—and that was Connor's leverage.

A cloud rolled past the waning crescent moons and further dimmed the already weak moonlight illuminating the docks. On cue, eight shadows darted from their cover among the thick cluster of elms.

It had begun.

Connor stiffened, his full focus on their rapid progress over the boardwalk's worn wooden planks. They ducked low to pass beneath the caretaker's window, each deft movement fluid and effortless, and their footsteps barely tapped across the ground. They neared, getting closer every second, and both of Connor's teammates tensed as they prepared for this to end in blood.

The goal, of course, would be to reason with this Owen fellow. Given what he wanted from the man, however, he didn't have high hopes that reason alone would work.

The men rounded the warehouse corner with tight precision that suggested military training and rigid discipline. Calculated steps. Practiced formations. Hand signals from the man in front, ordering each step and each pause.

These thieves weren't like the roving bands of mercenaries in the Ancient Woods. These men were professionals.

He remained still while they approached, but his thumb tapped against his thigh as he fought the urge to summon his swords. Sophia was right, after all. He could easily take all of these men at once and force them to answer his questions, but he didn't want to draw attention to himself.

Not yet, anyway.

Just as the silhouettes rounded the corner, the candlelight snuffed out, and the warehouse plunged into darkness. The muffled thump of heavy footsteps thudded through the closed door nearest to the window. Seconds later, the caretaker shoved open the door with his shoulder and slipped his hands into his pockets, whistling to the moon as he walked toward the city at a brisk pace.

How curious.

The man had left his post early, and as the man's tuneless whistling slowly faded, Connor realized why.

It was a signal. The warehouse was empty—and ready for whatever illicit dealings lay in store for them all tonight.

With their backs to the warehouse wall, the eight silhouettes paused yet again. Connor's enhanced senses picked up low whispers from the group, now that they were closer, and he tilted his head to listen in.

"… king's arms shipment," one man whispered. "It's in the second storage unit, halfway into the building. You all know what to do."

"This isn't possible," a familiar voice whispered back.

At the sound of Owen's voice, Connor scanned the men's faces until he spotted the man in the middle of the cluster.

Odd. It seemed as though the leader of this band wasn't even leading this mission.

Connor frowned in confusion, and for a moment, he wondered if he had been wrong. If this wasn't their leader at all.

Yet again, these Shades kept surprising—and confusing—him.

"There hasn't been any mention of this in the castle," Owen continued.

"Then they don't tell you as much as you think." Venom dripped from the first man's voice, but he kept his gaze trained on the door. "Come on."

The man in front pushed open the door. One by one, all eight silhouettes darted into the warehouse, and the old wooden walls muffled the fading patter of their light footsteps.

Curse the Fates, Magnuson, the Wraith King grumbled. *How long are you going to sit on your ass and watch other men do something useful?*

With an irritated sigh, Connor just shook his head. The ghoul wouldn't get a rise out of him tonight.

Wordlessly, he darted toward the door, and his team followed. He paused at the entrance to listen for any sign of lingering men keeping watch, but the footsteps faded further into the building.

Time to move.

He slipped into the shadows and quickly scanned the coiled ropes and riggings hung on every wall. Rolled up sails hung on the hooks far above them, and another open door on the far end of the room led deeper into the warehouse.

Connor knelt by the next door and scanned the second room just as the eight silhouettes clustered by a staircase on the opposite wall. Two rows of small sailboats offered a bit of cover between him and the thieves. As the minutes ticked on, all eight men scoured every shadow in the room beyond the row of sailboats—likely because they had swept this stretch of the warehouse already.

Hmm. The Wraith King muttered. *Well now, that's an interesting turn of events.*

"What happened?" Connor inched toward the stairwell as a few of the imposter Shades returned and huddled together at the foot of the stairs. He only paused when he reached the edge of the dingeys, and he signaled for his team to wait in the last few feet of shadow the boats could offer.

Sophia leaned closer and lowered her voice to the barest whisper. "Did you say something?" Sophia asked from behind him.

He cast a quick look over his shoulder and shook his head. "The ghoul."

She rolled her eyes but ultimately gestured for him to continue.

Oh, are you deigning to speak to me again? the ghoul asked with an exasperated grunt. *You've done nothing but brood and ignore me since we left the mountain.*

"I'm not in the mood," Connor growled under his breath. "What happened?"

There are no crates in this room, the ghoul answered. *As they've lazily trudged through each room, I've scanned every inch of this warehouse. There are no weapons anywhere in this building. Their informant was wrong.*

That was indeed an interesting turn of events, but Connor wasn't about to admit as much out loud.

Owen had been right after all.

One by one, the eight men returned to the stairwell. Each carried a long dagger in one hand, and even as they clustered together, their weapons remained drawn.

The last to jog down the steps sheathed his dagger with a frustrated growl. He tugged his hood and mask off his face with an irritated flourish. His shirt collar hid all but the tail ends of a spiraling tattoo of green ink that glowed across the base of his neck. Light brown stubble dotted his jaw, and he ran one hand through his wild hair as he scanned the nearest man's hooded face. "I *told* you. There's nothing here."

As Owen unmasked himself, Connor frowned. He knew that face, but he didn't know why.

Damn it all, he just wanted this mess to make *sense*.

"Who was your informant?" Another figure among the group sheathed his dagger and pulled off his hood and mask as well. His furious glare focused squarely on the tallest masked silhouette among them. Black hair. Dark eyes. Pointed jaw. Clean-shaven. A stranger, one Connor didn't recognize—and that only made the faint flicker of familiarity for Owen all the more unsettling.

"That isn't your concern, Wade." The taller figure sauntered up to the dark-haired stranger—Wade, apparently—and poked Wade hard in the chest. "Neither was this mission, for that matter."

Wade smacked the man's hand away, and his intense eyes only narrowed. "Give us answers, Darius. You've acted strange all week. You're a damned idiot if you thought I was going to let you lot take Owen on a mission alone."

Moonbeams filtered through the frosted windows along the wall. As the tension built in the air, the moonlight glinted over the steel in most men's hands.

"Enough." Owen stepped between the men and set a callused palm on each man's chest to split them apart. "This bickering stops *now*."

"And there's that hoity rich-boy tone again." Darius shoved Owen's hand off of him. "Demands. Orders. Commanding us like you're Rockwell's prodigy. Well, he ain't here to protect you any more, kid."

"Care to elaborate?" Owen's gravelly voice carried an unspoken warning that Darius would be wise to choose his next words carefully.

Darius chuckled darkly. "With pleasure."

In unison, all six of the still-masked men drove their blades deep into whichever unmasked man was closest.

Connor's head snapped back with surprise.

"What the *fuck* just happened?" Murdoc hissed.

What a delightful betrayal. The Wraith King laughed, deep and low, and Connor could practically feel the damn old ghost rubbing his skeletal hands together in wicked glee. *A fake mission to lure and isolate their target. The perfect moment to strike. I love it Magnuson.*

"I assume this is where we intervene?" Sophia whispered impatiently. "Heroes of the people and all that?"

As much as Connor wanted to stop this, he forced himself to stay put. He had no idea what these men had done to each other. He had no idea who these people were, nor did he know why they would turn on each other like this after everything he had witnessed on the bridge.

"When you threaten one of us, you threaten us all," Owen had said. *"And we don't take threats lightly."*

Connor didn't know Owen's motivations. Hell, the man had decapitated a rival and caught an arrow with his bare hands. This was not a scattered collection of novices. Whoever these men were, they had proven themselves to be dangerous professionals.

He couldn't allow any of these men to drive a knife in his back or hurt his team. Too much had been left unsaid, and any one of these men could be far more of a danger than Connor realized.

For now—and as much as he hated watching this—he had to wait.

With so many unknowns, he had no other choice.

CHAPTER FIFTY-FOUR

CONNOR

Connor hated this.

The waiting, while someone else suffered.

In an abandoned warehouse on the outskirts of town, far enough away that no one would hear even the loudest scream of agony, he and his team watched from the shadows as allies betrayed each other.

From this angle, the masked men's broad bodies surrounded their victims and blocked most of Connor's view. He could only catch glimpses of the two men's faces through a gap in the attackers.

The tendons in Owen's neck tightened until they nearly snapped, but he didn't scream. With a grunt of effort, he tugged one of the daggers out of his leg and hurled it at the far wall.

Wade, however, wasn't as lucky, and he stifled an agonized yell as the three men closest to him tugged out their daggers with a meaty squish.

Both victims were still standing, though only barely.

Metal clinked. Fabric swished against steel. Owen and Wade fell to their knees and blood seeped through their fingers as both tried and failed to put pressure on their wounds. One of the traitors pulled a tarp off a shelf along the wall to reveal two sets of heavy iron chains. Each link was as thick as Connor's wrist, and it took two men to carry each one.

Together, they dragged the chains over to their captives. In mere seconds, the attackers wrapped heavy iron around both Owen and Wade, and the two captives fell to their knees. The figures dispersed, one man holding each end of the chains. The emerald glow in Owen's augmentations faded, and he grimaced in pain as blood seeped from the deep gashes in his side.

"Bluntmar chains," Murdoc whispered. "Bet you anything."

Connor nodded. Given the way the bright green glow had faded from Owen's augmentations, there wasn't much else it could be.

"They're not very good fighters," Sophia muttered under her breath. "That was hardly a challenge."

"You saw him catch that arrow on the bridge," Connor whispered back. "I'd wager they're fine fighters. It's harder to stop a dagger when an ally stabs you in the back with it."

She pursed her lips, but didn't reply.

"You Fates-damned traitors!" Wade shouted.

Darius grabbed a fistful of Wade's hair and sneered into his face. "Took you long enough to figure it out."

"What the hell are you doing?" Owen sucked in breath after breath through his teeth, and his furious glare focused squarely on Darius. "Who put you up to this?"

"I volunteered, actually." Darius used Owen's cloak to wipe his blood-stained dagger clean. "Had to beat a few men at cards to earn my place here tonight."

"I knew it," Wade seethed. "I knew you lot were up to something—"

Darius kicked Wade hard in the teeth, and the dark-haired man slumped backward. Only the chains kept Wade upright, and the blow sent fresh blood trickling through the stab wounds littering his body.

"That's *enough*!" Owen roared. His voice echoed through the warehouse, and he pulled against his chains in an effort to break free. The two masked men holding his bonds yanked backward, dragging him farther away from Wade even as he fought to get closer.

Darius shifted his attention to Owen, and the two glared at each other as Darius towered over his captive. The silence settled on the air as tension brewed between the two men, fueled by a mutual hatred only they understood.

"You don't command me," Darius said, his voice low and dark. "You know how long I've wanted to slit your throat? How long I've fantasized about it? It's been a nightmare isolating you from the others. We had to accept killing this one just to get it done." Darius pointed his dagger at Wade. "It's a shame, too. A damn good fighter, wasted. His blood's on you, Owen, because your loyalists are poisoning the Shades."

Owen stifled an agonized groan as the bloodstain on his shirt spread through the fabric's fibers. "What the hell are you—"

"Don't play dumb," Darius interrupted. "I see your game. We all do. You want to overtake us. You want the Shades to be your errand boys. You've forgotten why we banded together in the first place."

"You rat *bastard*," Owen spat blood on the floor, but that didn't quell the raw hatred dripping from every word. "I've done nothing but help you. Coin. Weapons. Augmentations. Potions. I gave you everything you asked for and more."

"Aye." Darius grabbed Owen's hair and yanked the man's head back as far as it would go. "And you're a damn fool for doing it. That's why we kept you around as long as we did, but you're not useful anymore."

Darius drove his long dagger clear through Owen's arm. Owen's back arched with pain, and he barely stifled an agonized scream.

A wicked grin spread across Darius's face, and it only widened when he twisted his blade. Owen yelled this time, unable to hold it back anymore.

Connor's fingers twitched. He ached to draw his swords. To stop this. No matter what information he wanted to glean from Owen, sitting idly by as two men were tortured just wasn't right. Besides, it didn't seem as though Darius would let the two men live much longer.

He would have to act soon.

"Stop." Wade's head lolled forward. His body tilted forward, held up only by the chains, and a thin stream of blood leaked from his nose. His eyes slipped in and out of focus, but he managed to glare at Darius all the same. "This is madness. You're better than this."

"We thought *you* were better than this," Darius snapped. "All your talk all these years of wanting to make a difference. All the times you saved our hides. We thought you were one of us. A brother on the battlefield. And you're throwing it away for this spoiled rich boy?"

Wade coughed, and blood splattered the ground in front of him. "Owen's a better Shade than you'll ever be, and he'll be a better king than Victor could dream of becoming. So long as I'm alive, Victor will never get that throne."

"You've lost your damn mind," Darius seethed. "Victor Varon is our rightful king. Not this mutt, and not his tyrant father, for that matter. He and his family are a stain on this island. He ain't got a claim to that throne, and I ain't going to let you put him on it!"

Connor tensed as the last piece of this puzzle clicked into place. It seemed impossible. It seemed *insane*, even, and he didn't dare believe it.

"Wait," Sophia whispered. "Is he saying this man is—"

The faint hum of her words buzzed through Connor's head, but they faded into the shrill ringing in his ears. In his numb shock, he simply stared in utter disbelief at the man chained on the other side of the warehouse, every bit as trapped as Connor's mother and sister had been the night King Arlo had decreed they would be burned to death in their family home.

Owen had looked familiar because Connor had, in fact, seen the man before—well over a decade ago, when they were both boys. He had only seen Kirkwall's new crown prince in passing because Owen Hunt had rarely been allowed to leave the castle in those turbulent days of unrest and rampant poverty.

If not for Arlo Hunt's brutality, Connor's family would still be alive. There was only one man in Saldia that Connor hated more than Owen's father.

In a surreal twist of fate, here he was, with the crown prince's life hanging in the balance. For years, he had dreamed of causing King Arlo as much pain as the man had caused him—and now, he had the opportunity to do it.

"Why gloat?" Owen's voice snapped Connor out of his daze. The man's chest heaved as he struggled for air. "You could've killed us by now."

"You were never one of us, that's why." Darius's nose creased with disgust. "The smart ones among us remember that, even as you've bought and charmed the others. I've dreamed of this moment for a long time, kid. Don't spoil it for me."

Owen didn't bother masking his disgust.

"As for why I haven't killed you yet?" Darius drove his dagger into Owen's other arm, and Owen screamed with pain. "Victor ordered me to bring you in alive. Guess he needs you to fetch something for us from the castle before I can kill you."

Again, Connor's hand twitched as he fought the urge to draw his weapons and intervene. This time, however, an internal war raged between his thirst for revenge and his utterly infuriating conscience.

"I'm not helping you get a damn thing." Owen spat another clump of red blood onto the man's boots. "Get this over with, you Fates-damned coward."

"You'd like that." Darius tugged out his blade from Owen's arm and kicked the man squarely in the gut. Owen doubled over in pain as Darius continued to circle him. "Feeding your own arrogance and thinking you died a martyr. Not a chance, kid. You're going to die as nothing more than Victor's errand-boy. Seems fitting, don't you think?"

The masked men around him snickered.

"Nelson." Darius tilted his head toward the only other masked man not holding tight to one of their prisoners' chains. "Go get Victor."

"On it." With that, the man named Nelson jogged toward the shadows where Connor and his team had taken cover.

This was it.

Connor had to choose, and he had to do it quickly. He could either slip deeper into the shadows and let these men have the prince, or he could put his own vengeance aside and do what he knew was right.

Nelson jogged closer, and the internal war raged on. He didn't move, even as Sophia nudged him hard in the side.

Magnuson, the ghoul muttered in his head. *You cannot simply sit there like an imbecile. He will walk right into you lot on his way out. What the hell is wrong with you?*

In less than a minute, Nelson would be close enough to touch, but Connor still didn't reply. Returning to Kirkwall had been gruesome enough, but now he couldn't tell if the Fates were being kind or cruel.

His mind went blank, and he waited for a nugget of his father's wisdom. They usually came to him in times like these, to remind him of what it meant to be a force for good in this heartless, wicked world.

Nothing came.

Instead, he caught a glimpse of a memory. No words. No conversation. No haunting voices from his past. It was just a suspended moment in Slaybourne's forests, when sunlight had filtered through the pale green leaves of a warming spring day. Wesley sat on the ground, laughing through his tears as Connor's twin swords lay on the dirt beside him.

With an irritated growl, Connor snapped out of his foggy daze. The imposter Shade named Nelson had jogged close enough to touch, and the man's head snapped toward the sound of Connor's low growl.

Wordlessly, Connor stood. A thick plume of smoke rolled over his forearm as he summoned one blackfire blade, and he cleaved the man's head clean off.

In the second before the body hit the floor, an awestruck silence hung in the air. No one spoke. No one took a breath. The gathered imposters gaped at their fallen comrade, and even the two captives went eerily still.

Nelson's severed head hit the floorboards with a sickening splat. His body crumpled to the ground shortly thereafter, and the masked men took a collective step backward. Connor stepped over the dead man's corpse, and with a second rush of smoke, he summoned his second blade. Enchanted blackfire crackled over his dark steel, familiar and comforting.

"You call yourself Shades." Connor's voice was deeper and rougher than he'd intended it to be. Unfiltered hatred dripped from every word, and he surrendered to the rage. "I think it's high time you learn what happens to the fools who steal my name."

CHAPTER FIFTY-FIVE

CONNOR

Five men stood between Connor and Owen Hunt.

Their unlucky scout—Nelson, evidently—crumpled to the floor. Connor's mere presence had held the imposter Shades in a daze, suspended in their horror, but the meaty thud of Nelson's corpse hitting the floorboards snapped them from their stupor.

The metal chains holding Owen and Wade hostage clattered to the floor as all five men drew their weapons. Most held tight to the long daggers they had used to betray their fellow thieves, but Darius summoned a fierce burst of blistering fire into his palm.

Wounded as they were, both Owen and Wade slumped to the floor as their captors loosened their hold on the chains. The metal links wove around both men several times, heavy enough that even their struggling barely shifted the restraints.

Finally, the ghoul muttered. *A proper fight.*

"Stay out of this," Connor warned under his breath. "Owen and Wade can't be allowed to see you. Not yet."

The Wraith King mumbled obscenities, but the old ghost didn't reply.

"Don't push me," Connor added quietly. "After your stunt in the mountain, I have half a mind to uphold my original promise to end you."

The threat was met with eerie silence.

Doom, of course, was quiet as ever. The Dragon King hadn't spoken a word since they'd left the mountain, and sometimes Connor forgot the beast was even watching.

"Who the hell are you?" Darius shouted.

"He's the Shade, imbecile." Sophia's voice had an icy twinge to it. "The *real* one."

Both she and Murdoc stepped into Connor's periphery. All three of them still wore the cloths over their faces to mask their identity, and Connor could only imagine what this looked like to an outsider—eight people and a corpse, all masked and dressed almost identically, facing off in an empty warehouse on the outskirts of town.

Insanity, really, and almost too surreal to believe.

Murdoc drew the enchanted broadsword he had acquired in his time as a Blackguard. Sophia, meanwhile, closed her hand into a tight fist. On cue, the dazzling green augmentations inked into her skin began to glow.

"The Sh—what—" Darius stuttered. His chest heaved as his frantic gaze darted between the three of them. "Nelson was a good man! If you really are one of us, you would never have cut him down like—"

"A 'good man' doesn't laugh as he watches someone be tortured." Connor's deep baritone rumbled in his chest. "No, none of you are good men."

At that, he looked squarely at Owen. Kirkwall's prince stiffened, but he met Connor's glare with one of his own.

"Both of you watch the exits." Connor said under his breath to his team. "No one leaves this warehouse. If they run, no prisoners."

Through the corner of his eye, both of his teammates looked at each other. Sophia's head turned away from him, so he couldn't see her expression. He did, however, catch the flicker of concern on Murdoc's face. After a cursory glance back at him, both slipped silently into the darkness beyond the dingeys.

Tell me you're not going to show mercy, the ghoul said with a disgusted groan. *Surely these masked fools have earned your disdain.*

"They have," he confessed.

A wicked cackle bubbled through his head, but he ignored it.

It hit him, then—the revulsion. The unfiltered disgust for these cowards who would dare exploit his mantle as the Shade.

A fiery surge of anger snapped through his body with every breath. It beat within him like a second pulse from something else, something other, and it sent ripples of heat and hatred through his very core. His body burned from the sensation, and the air above his skin rippled from the sizzling heat rolling off of him.

Something hot pushed against his palms, and he instinctively tightened his grip on the blackfire blades in each hand. It pushed again, aching to be freed, and the crackling blackfire on his enchanted swords surged with the sensation.

This new rush of power left the charred hint of ash on the back of his tongue, and he knew exactly where it had come from. Thrilling as it was to get a taste of Doom's power, Connor had more urgent matters to attend.

Whatever this was, he would have to deal with it later.

Connor stalked slowly forward. Each intentional step landed firmly on the floorboards, one after the other, as he closed the gap between them.

Any sane man would have attacked by now, and yet they just stood there, immobile and about to piss their pants. Whatever they saw in his face, it rooted them all to the floor.

The five surviving traitors shrank under the weight of his mere presence. A few took wary steps backward. Others loosened their hold on their weapons, either because they were stunned or because they knew a dagger wouldn't save them from whatever he was about to do.

Connor looked each man in the eye, indifferent to their fear, and he silently dared them to run.

A floorboard creaked under Connor's foot, and that broke the silence. Darius launched a fireball at Connor's face, and Connor raised his blackfire blade with a lazy twist of his arm. The steel swallowed the flame, just as it had when he and Quinn first fought each other back in the Ancient Woods.

It didn't even slow him down.

All five of the traitors moved at the same time. Three charged him, but the two men farthest away turned tail and ran.

Though closest to Connor, Darius slowed just enough to let the other two masked men reach Connor first. One shot a blistering ball of ice at his chest. The other hurled a thin dagger laced with a thin purple liquid, aimed square for Connor's forehead.

Amateurs.

In a rush of black smoke that obscured his movements, Connor dismissed one blackfire blade and summoned his shield. The ice hit the enchanted shield's hot metal with a sizzling hiss, dissolving instantly to steam. Connor tilted his blade to block the clearly poisoned dagger, and a spark flashed through the air as steel hit steel.

With an effortless twist of his arm, his blade sliced through both men's necks. Death froze their stunned expressions on their faces, and both men crumpled to the floor.

Darius dropped his weapon and turned on one heel, but he wasn't fast enough. Connor grabbed the man's collar and, with a fluid tug, slammed the imposter Shade hard onto the floor.

It all happened within mere seconds. Owen and Wade barely had enough time to gasp in surprise before the fight was over.

The two men who had left their fellow traitors to die now bolted in a mad, panicked dash up the stairs. Each of them sprinted toward a door Connor couldn't see, but he didn't bother chasing them. He trusted Murdoc and Sophia to make quick work of the cowards who ran.

Unlike these backstabbing traitors, Connor's team would forever have his back.

"If I die, I'm taking you with me!" Darius yelled.

Instead of looking at Connor, however, the man turned the full intensity of his glare on Owen. He spread his fingers wide, and another torrent of blisteringly hot flame gathered in his palm.

He never got the chance to attack.

Connor drove his sword deep into the man's chest. Something gurgled in the back of Darius's throat, and his gaze wandered to Connor in the second or two before the light faded entirely from his eyes. The man went limp, and his blood snaked through long gouges in the floorboards left behind by all of the merchants and fishermen who had passed through this warehouse over the decades.

"He must've truly hated you, Owen." With one last cursory scan of the empty warehouse around them, Connor stepped over the bodies and dismissed his enchanted weapons in a rush of black smoke.

The Prince of Kirkwall didn't reply. He met Connor's gaze, broken and immobile, as blood dripped from the deep wounds covering his body. Each drop sent a ripple through the gathering crimson pool beneath him.

"Don't—don't touch him—" Only feet away from the prince, Wade's body shook as he struggled for air. Blood seeped from the wounds littering his torso. His cheek rested against the wood, and the man's eyes fluttered shut as the last of the color drained from his face.

Shit.

Wade was far closer to death than Connor had realized.

"Do what you want with me." Streaks of blood stained Owen's teeth, and his chest heaved with each labored breath. "But let him live. Please."

That killed the last of Connor's rage, and he let out an irritated sigh.

We don't need that one, the Wraith King interjected, still unseen. *Use him as leverage to get what we want out of this prince.*

"Find Sophia," Connor ordered.

You can't possibly expect him to know who that—

"I was talking to you," he interrupted.

The ghoul huffed in utter disgust, and the undead king grumbled the sort of obscenities that would make even whores blush.

Wordlessly, Connor knelt beside Wade. The man tilted his head, too weak to lift it, and he watched Connor from the corner of one bloodshot eye.

Owen struggled against the chains weighing him to the floor, and this time, he managed to loosen them ever so slightly. "Don't you dare!"

"Calm down," Connor snapped. "We're going to heal him."

While he waited for Sophia to return, Connor unwound the chains from around Wade's torso. More blood spurted from each wound with even the slightest movement. Despite Connor's best efforts to be gentle, Wade barely stifled his agonized screams.

When the metal chain finally clattered to the floor, both Wade and Connor sighed with relief that it was over.

A door creaked open from somewhere in the warehouse, and the barest patter of boots on the floorboards neared. Seconds later, Sophia appeared at the top of the stairs and leaned both hands on the railing as she stared down at the scene.

Behind her, almost one with the shadows, the Wraith King's skeletal face hovered in the darkness. He stared at Connor and, without a word, dissolved into the dark smoke coiling around him.

"Can you get him back on his feet?" Connor asked Sophia.

She let out an impatient huff of air, but she eventually nodded. She slipped off her pack as she trotted down the stairs and rifled through the contents on her way toward them.

"What—" Owen's gaze darted between Connor and Sophia. "What are you doing?"

"Quiet," she chided, still preoccupied with her bag.

"Where's Murdoc?" Connor asked.

"Dispatching the last one." Sophia knelt beside Wade's body, careful not to let his blood touch her sleeves. "If you ask me, he's milking it for a bit of a thrill."

"Who the hell *are* you people?!" Owen wriggled against the impossibly heavy chains still holding him in place.

Sophia groaned. "Deal with him, will you? I need to focus. You and your near-impossible demands on my magic—I mean, look at this one. He's lost so much blood."

"Don't lie, now." Connor clapped her on the shoulder. "You love the challenge. Besides, you make it look easy."

Though she didn't reply, she couldn't hide her proud little smirk.

"What about him?" Connor asked with a nod toward their royal captive. "Those injuries look bad. What does he need?"

"A normal Rectivane will work fine." Sophia fished out a bottle of bright green liquid and shoved it into his palm. "Based on the blood loss, his wounds aren't as dire. He might ache for a while, but this will do the trick."

"Wade!" Owen skidded his body over the floor as she tried to inch closer. "Wade, stay awake. You can't sleep. Not right now."

Connor pushed himself to his feet and shifted his full attention onto the chained prince. "I told you we would heal him, and I keep my word. Now, calm the hell down. You're only going to make this worse."

Owen's nose flared in barely restrained fury. The prince pressed his lips together, as if he were biting back a scathing retort. Whatever he'd been about to say, the man wisely kept his mouth shut.

Connor squatted in front of the prince and, with the potion in one hand, simply studied Owen for a moment. He had met with—and fought—some of the most influential and powerful people in Saldia. Having a prince in chains at his feet shouldn't have been so surreal, but he couldn't stifle that bizarre numbness that spread across his skin like ice.

Owen's father had killed Connor's, and yet Connor had just saved Owen's life.

Deep down, a hateful, bitter part of him resented that. It was the blood-thirsty part of him, and after all these years, it wanted *vengeance*.

CHAPTER FIFTY-SIX

CONNOR

It took effort not to reach out and snap Owen's neck.

Disgusted with his own bloodlust, Connor dug his fingernail into his thumb. The sharp burst of pain distracted him from his rage, and that was enough to quell his hatred.

Owen hadn't killed Connor's family. That blood was on King Arlo's hands.

Morally, Connor had no right to murder this man. That fact didn't quell his hatred, but it at least held the anger at bay.

Now that they were mere feet apart, Owen's eyes narrowed with recognition. His head tilted slightly, and the furious creases in his forehead relaxed. "I know you."

"You don't," Connor said flatly.

"I do." Owen tried to sit up, but he grimaced under the weight of the chains and his injuries. "Your wanted posters are everywhere."

Ah.

"Alright," Connor conceded. "Perhaps you do, then."

"You're really him," Owen couldn't mask the unfiltered awe in his voice. "The Shade. The real one."

"I already told you that," Sophia said with an exasperated grunt of disgust. "None of you idiots ever listen."

"Behave," Connor gently chided.

Bottles clinked as she set them out beside her, and she merely scoffed in reply.

"Look, Owen," Connor said firmly. ""I'm going to take that chain off of you. When I do, you're going to sit there and drink this potion. You won't do anything stupid. You won't move an inch. Understood?"

Owen hesitated, apparently debating his limited options, but ultimately nodded.

As he had with Wade, Connor lifted the heavy chains off Owen's torso. It took effort and a bit of careful maneuvering to avoid the worst of Owen's wounds, but he managed. With the weight gone, the prince managed to sit up and help shift the last metal links off of him. The chains hit the ground with a heavy thud, and Owen sucked in a deep breath of relief.

"Thank the Fates," Owen said under his breath. "That was awful."

"Bluntmar chains aren't exactly fun." Connor offered Owen the vial of green potion in his hand, and the prince took it.

"Is that what they used to curse those damn things?" Owen popped the cork from the glass bottle and tilted his head so that he could down the entire thing in one gulp.

Connor frowned. How trusting.

As the potion took hold, Owen's eyes fluttered shut. The prince swayed side to side as the magic worked through his body. The gaping wounds in his torso and arms slowly stitched themselves back together, and his breathing slowed with each passing second.

"That could've been a poison, or even a Hackamore," Connor pointed out. "You didn't even ask me to test it. For all you know, you might keel over or start spilling your darkest secrets at any moment."

"Oh." Owen's brows furrowed as he realized the risk he had unknowingly taken. "I'll keep that in mind for the future."

Connor shook his head. This man had a lot to learn about the world.

The muffled thud of a distant door closing echoed down over the boats behind Connor, and he peered over one shoulder just as Murdoc entered the room.

The former Blackguard gave him a quick salute on his way toward Sophia. "All clear, Captain."

Connor let out a quiet sigh of relief. "Good work."

"Who are they?" Owen set the empty bottle on the floor as he studied

Sophia and Murdoc. "I always thought the Shade worked alone."

"You thought wrong." Connor's voice had a harder edge to it than he'd intended, but it carried an unspoken warning in it all the same. "If anyone ever threatens them, they threaten me. And I don't take kindly to threats either, Owen."

The Prince of Kirkwall went eerily still. He met Connor's eye, and the color drained from his face.

"You all have been using my name," Connor said. "Tell me why."

As his wounds continued to heal, Owen propped one leg and rested his elbow on his knee. He sucked in a pained breath of air at the movement, and he pressed one palm against the still-healing injury on his left side. He sat in silence for a moment, and Connor let the quiet linger.

Owen would give him answers one way or another.

"Captain, is this the best place for an interrogation?" Murdoc pointed at the nearest corpse. "That caretaker could be back any moment."

Connor shook his head. "No one will be back until dawn."

Owen's eyes narrowed in suspicion. "How do you know that?"

Despite the new king on the throne, the smuggler dens hadn't changed. Smugglers had a habit of keeping to routines, and the family who owned this warehouse had a long history of flawlessly serving their clientele.

"I ask questions," Connor said flatly. "You answer them. That's how this is going to work, Owen."

As a matter of principle, he refused to address the man by his formal title.

Darius had been right about one thing, at least—the Hunts didn't deserve the throne they sat on. Owen clearly did, however, have a firm grasp on the secret passages through the city—passages Connor hadn't traversed in nearly a decade. If they left this warehouse, there was a risk these two would escape.

As much as he hated the idea of interrogating them here, of all places, Connor wasn't going to let these two imposters leave until he had the answers he was after.

"It was my idea." The Prince of Kirkwall sighed in defeat. "I saw your wanted posters on my last visit to Oakenglen, and I heard all the stories about what the Shade had done for people. The law told one version, of course, but

I learned a long time ago to listen to the stories in the pubs. They're closer to the truth. The Shade is a hero to them, but you've never been spotted this far west. My guess is you've been in Kirkwall long enough to realize that these good people need a hero, too."

Huh.

How interesting.

Now certain that Owen wouldn't try to do anything stupid after all, Connor sat on the floor across from the man and gestured to the empty potion bottle. "How are you feeling?"

"Better." The man winced and rubbed his shoulder. "But not great. Is Wade going to be okay?"

"She's the best at what she does," Connor promised. "Don't change the subject."

Owen frowned. "Apologies."

"How does a prince get mixed up in this sort of thing?" Connor gestured at the corpses. "Looks like your so-called heroes weren't too fond of you."

"I told you," Wade said weakly.

"Will you stop moving?" Sophia scoffed in unrestrained frustration. "I'm trying to heal you, damn it."

Wade ignored her, and he pushed himself upright with a pained grimace. His face contorted, and he gritted his teeth in agony as he pushed himself upright. Beside him, Sophia threw her hands in the air, too irritated to continue with a patient who wouldn't listen.

Connor caught her eye and raised his eyebrows in a silent question about how all that had gone.

"He's going to be fine." She dismissed his concern with a flick of her wrist. "He would heal faster if he just sat still, but I'm not going to coddle him."

At her side, Murdoc nudged her gently and smiled. She huffed, but the creases of irritation in her forehead smoothed as his touch relaxed her.

Wade leaned forward, and his chest heaved with every painful breath. With one hand on his side, palm flat against the fresh bandage wrapped around his torso, he glared at Owen. "I *told* you we shouldn't have taken this mission! I *told* you it was suspect that Victor wanted you on this squad. I *told* you he was up to something, and you refused to listen."

"I know." Owen rubbed his eyes. "And I'm sorry. This is my fault."

As he studied Owen's face, Connor scratched at the stubble on his jaw. From what he could remember of the Hunt family, they had never taken kindly to insults, nor had they ever taken the blame for their mistakes.

How interesting.

"I warned you time and again, for over a year." Apparently unsatisfied with the apology, Wade gestured to the corpses bleeding into the floorboards around them. "If you had just *listened*, we wouldn't be in this mess!"

Hmph. The Wraith King's grunt of disdain echoed through Connor's head. *I know what that feels like.*

"Not now," Connor muttered under his breath, not even certain if the ghoul was close enough to hear him.

"I didn't want to believe—" Owen let out a long, resigned sigh. "After everything I've done to be a part of the Shades, after everything I sacrificed to make us stronger, I just hoped…"

His voice trailed off, and for a time, only the clink of glass against glass filled the silent warehouse as Sophia returned her potions to her bag.

"We've been watching you all." Connor studied the prince's face as the man went rigid. "Your missions. Your targets. Your crimes."

Owen anxiously curled his fingers into a tight fist. "What did you learn?"

"That you're exceedingly boring," Sophia snapped.

Murdoc chuckled.

"Boring?" Owen's head snapped toward her, and he frowned. "That seems harsh."

Wade shifted in his seat, and he winced as he pressed his palm harder against the worst of his injuries. "No, I'm fine with boring. 'Boring' sounds a lot less painful."

"We found your access ladders to the cliffside tunnels," Connor said, regaining control of the conversation. "We know that one of your own is in prison, and you're desperate to break him out of there. We know you killed those thugs on the bridge, and we knew you had access to the castle. It's surprising what a man can learn with patience and a few days of surveillance."

"Damn," Owen muttered. "You're good."

Connor's eyes narrowed. "If you lie to me, I'll know."

The prince swallowed hard, but ultimately nodded.

"Let's begin." With the prince finally listening, Connor knew exactly where he wanted to start. "It's clear that one of your leaders is in prison. Tell me his name."

A muscle in Owen's jaw twitched as the prince clenched his mouth shut.

Connor cracked his knuckles. "This is going to be a long night if you don't start talking."

"You can threaten me all you want." Owen braced himself. "I won't betray one of my team."

With a quick glance at Murdoc and Sophia, Connor sighed. That had softened a bit of his anger.

"I know his name is Rockwell," Connor said firmly. "I need to know if his first name is Liam."

Owen's eyes widened briefly in surprise. Though the man cleared his throat to hide his shock, it was all the confirmation Connor needed.

Liam Rockwell was, in fact, alive.

To dangle his father's best friend in front of him, only to ship the man off to the gallows—the Fates could be so damn *cruel.*

"You live in the castle," Connor snapped. "If you truly care about this man, why the hell haven't you snuck him out on your own?"

"Don't you think I've tried?" Owen demanded. "That's all I've done since he was captured. He sacrificed himself to keep my identity safe, and I refuse to let him die for it!"

Yep.

That sounded *exactly* like something Rockwell would do.

"My father is using him as bait," Owen continued. "There are massive clusters of soldiers stationed strategically through the underground tunnels and the castle itself to ambush any of us who enter. He hates the Shades, and he's determined to destroy us after everything we've done to humiliate him. I know when I'm up against a losing fight, but I've done nothing but hunt for an answer since he was captured!"

Owen shut his eyes tightly and balled his hands into fists as he bit back whatever other scathing remarks he'd been about to say. His breathing slowed as he finally centered himself.

"But I guess this is where you dangle what I want over my head, isn't it?" Owen opened his eyes, and his furious glare landed squarely on Connor's face. "Your exploits are already legend. You can probably get him out of there, right? You have the upper hand, here, in more ways than one. This is when I realize I have no cards in my hand, and you wring me dry for everything I'm worth."

"You catch on quick," Connor bluffed.

Maybe the prince wasn't as bad at negotiations than Connor originally thought. If anything, this man had a sharp mind and only needed a bit of experience to hone his skill.

"What is it, then?" Owen clenched his teeth together as he braced himself. "Magic? Status? Coin?"

Sophia pursed her lips. "That's a good start, I suppose."

Connor cast a quick sidelong glare at her, and she rolled her eyes.

"Well?" Owen pressed. "Name your price."

Astonishing.

For a future king, the prince was an absolutely atrocious negotiator.

Yet again, the man's idealism corroded some of Connor's resolve. By the Fates, how he wanted to hate Owen Hunt, and yet it was becoming increasingly harder to do.

Damn it.

Tonight hadn't gone to plan at all. The more Connor learned about these imposters, the more chaos he seemed to uncover. He had stepped into a den of vipers, and now he had to charm his way out of it without setting off every snake hidden in the grass.

CHAPTER FIFTY-SEVEN

CONNOR

Connor sat on the warehouse floor on a stretch of wooden planks strategically out of range of the growing bloodstains oozing from the corpses around him. He met Owen Hunt's eye, and for a moment, he let the heavy silence between them simmer.

He didn't trust this man, but Owen was his only ticket into Kirkwall Castle.

Damn it.

With a frustrated sigh, Connor pointed one finger at Owen's chest. "If you want me to rescue your fellow Shade, then you're going to help me recover an artifact locked away in your family's treasury."

Owen scoffed in disgust. "Gold? That's all you want."

"No," Connor said firmly. "I have enough."

The prince scowled, apparently unconvinced. "What exactly is this artifact you want me to help you find?"

"A black orb." Connor hated giving away anything in a negotiation, but he couldn't risk wasting his time. If the prince didn't know where the orb was, Connor would have to find another way to track it down.

"Wait, the one with the runes on it?" Owen squinted in confusion. "It doesn't do anything. Why the hell would you want something like that?"

Connor chuckled. He couldn't help it.

This was too easy, and he almost felt bad for the man.

"A bit of advice for you," Connor replied. "If someone asks for something you think is useless, either bluff him into thinking it's priceless or ask yourself what he knows that you don't."

Owen's mouth shut with an audible click as he realized how much he had just given away. From a short way off, Murdoc laughed.

"But yes," Connor continued. "That's the one. If you get me that orb, then I'll save your man Rockwell."

A bluff, of course. The prince didn't need to know he would've done it for free.

"Is this who you really are?" Disappointment and a twinge of disgust dripped from every word Owen spoke. "A mercenary? You clearly know who Rockwell is. Would you really let him hang if I refused your deal?"

Connor almost lied.

He almost said yes, simply to keep the upper hand, but something in Owen's face disarmed him. The dejection in his tone, perhaps, or the way he stared up in disbelief that the Shade would truly do something so horrible.

As if Connor were his hero, and his hero had just stabbed him in the back.

With a half-strangled growl of frustration, Connor rubbed the spot on his forehead where a dull ache had begun to throb through his skull.

These damned Shades complicated *everything*.

"Look." The hard edge to Connor's voice faded, if only somewhat, and he met the prince's incredulous glare. "I'm going to save Rockwell with or without you. Consider the orb a favor to me, if that makes this easier to swallow."

A bit of the tension faded from Owen's shoulders, and the man sat a little taller. "Alright, then. It's a deal."

Connor laughed dryly. "There's a lot more you need to tell me before I trust you enough to follow you into your father's fortress, Owen Hunt."

The prince's eyes narrowed, but he gestured for Connor to continue.

"Tell me why a prince is stealing from his own father," Connor demanded. "A member of the ruling family shouldn't have to slink through the dark to do good deeds."

"I shouldn't, but I do." With a furious shake of his head, Owen glared at the floor. "Any time I try to give to the citizens, he stops me. To him, kindness is weakness, and mercy opens the door for betrayal. I defied him for a while, and he punished me for it by limiting my access outside the walls. Now I'm supervised any time I leave the castle."

"Sycophants, all of them." Wade didn't bother masking his overt disgust. "Greedy bastards, too."

Owen shrugged. "He thinks he can break me, and that only makes me despise him more. I've fought him for most of my life, but I truly started to hate him after the smuggling raids."

At the mention of King Arlo's hatred for smugglers, an excruciating jolt of grief shot clear through Connor's body.

Being back here—coming home to the island that nearly killed him—it was all too fresh. Too painful.

To distract himself from the memories, Connor cracked his knuckles and cleared his throat. "What about you, Wade?"

Wade frowned. "What do you want to know?"

"Your name, for starters." Connor gestured to the man's bloodstained tunic. "And why those sick bastards were willing to kill you to get to Owen."

For a moment, Wade chewed the inside of his cheek. He stared off at Darius's corpse, and it seemed as though he wasn't going to answer.

"Wade," Owen said firmly. "He deserves to know."

"Alright." Wade shifted in his seat and winced again as the movement jostled his injuries. "Alright, fine. I'm a Goldwyn."

Fates be damned.

Lord Goldwyn had ridden into town after Henry conquered the island, and the man had quickly claimed several estates that had previously belonged to loyalists of the former royal family.

A corpse-sniffer, his father had called them. Men who found their wealth in the smoldering wreckage left behind by war.

"You have got to be kidding me." Connor rubbed his temple at the staggering absurdity. Each new layer of this mystery unwrapped another utterly insane surprise, and he wasn't sure how much more of this he could take. "Another rich kid."

"This 'rich kid' killed an assassin," Wade snapped. "I'm not some coddled asshole."

"You are a regular asshole, though," Sophia said with a casual shrug.

Wade briefly glared at her over one shoulder, and she raised one eyebrow in a silent challenge to prove her wrong.

"Why are you here, then?" Connor gestured to the heir of the impossibly vast Goldwyn estate. "You must have almost as much wealth as the king."

"Almost." Wade shrugged. "Never used much of it, except to fund the Shades. Father gets fatter every year, drunk on wine and women. I don't think Mother has even seen him in six months, with as much time as she spends in Wildefaire, doing Fates-knows-what. That's not what I want out of life."

Connor's eyes narrowed in suspicion. "And what do you want?"

"Purpose," Wade said flatly. "Same as Owen. That's why we're here. We want to make a difference." The rich kid gave Connor a once-over and shrugged. "I figure you know what that feels like better than anyone."

Fair point.

With a resigned sigh, Connor slipped the mask off his face. He pushed himself to his feet and slowly paced the areas of nearby floor that weren't drenched in dead men's blood.

In unison, Owen and Wade leaned backward. They sat there, eyes wide, and stared up at his face in surprise.

"Finally," Sophia said dryly. She and Murdoc tugged their own masks off, and the two rich kids on the floor gaped at all three of them.

"The Shade," Owen said with a wistful little laugh. "I never thought I'd actually meet you."

"I should hope not." Connor gestured to the clothes the prince wore. "Most people don't take kindly to imposters."

"What were you all called before?" Murdoc asked. "That Darius fellow made it sound like the lot of you have been around for years before the Shade came along."

"There wasn't a name." Wade shrugged. "We just *were*. Rockwell helped us organize, but we just helped each other when someone wanted justice."

Rockwell.

There was that name again.

As he paced, Connor debated how much these two needed to know. If he asked about Rockwell, the truth of Connor's past would eventually come out—or, at least, be easily deduced. But if the man in that prison really was

Liam Rockwell, and not someone else with a similar name, Connor couldn't possibly leave the man to die.

Maybe, just this once, secrecy didn't matter.

With the Finns safe in Slaybourne and with no ties to any homeland, the risk of the public learning the Shade's true identity was minimal—but there was still risk, especially with a band of criminals so freely using his name and image.

Damn.

He wasn't sure what to do.

"How did you two even find these people?" Sophia nudged the nearest corpse with her boot.

Wade stared at the man she had kicked with a conflicted expression Connor couldn't quite read. "After I came of age, I developed a nasty habit of sneaking out at night. I'd studied combat since I was a kid, so I figured I would be fine without my normal guards. It was little things at first—potions for the sick, or food for the homeless—but one night I walked in on a murder. I didn't think. I just acted. The assassin was dead on the floor before I realized he was one of the king's enforcers."

Sophia dismissed the rich kid with a wave of her thin wrist. "You got lucky."

"Now, now, my love." Murdoc grinned and nudged her gently with his elbow. "Be nice."

"She's not wrong." Wade shrugged. "Turns out the woman I saved belonged to the underground, and she vouched for me. I joined young. Took a while for the others to warm up to me, but I was one of them within a year. Never looked back."

"And you?" Connor asked Owen.

"We've been friends our whole lives." Owen shrugged. "He vouched for me."

"Guess it wasn't enough," Wade said.

"It was to keep you close," Sophia said, as though it were obvious. "If you thought you were one of them, you would share secrets they could use against you."

Owen's shoulders drooped as he stared again at the corpses around them. "I realize that now."

"Is Victor Varon really here?" Connor asked.

"Yes," Wade answered. "The first members of the underground were Varon loyalists, and there's always been those among us who were only in it to get Victor back on the throne. He came back roughly a year ago when some of the men in the underground finally hunted him down."

"What will he do?" Connor asked. "When you come back, instead of the men he sent to kill you?"

"After an assassination attempt? Civil war." Owen nodded to Darius's corpse. "You heard what he said. Over the years, I've won a few of the others over. I wasn't trying to, but they listen to me. They've made me a better leader because I have to be. If I'm the one leading a mission, it's my job to protect the people who follow me."

What a noble idiot, the Wraith King grumbled.

Connor ignored the ghoul. This made Owen a true leader in the making, perhaps, but not an idiot.

And given the man's family name, Connor hated to admit that, even to himself.

"It's all so obvious now." Owen rubbed his forehead in frustration. "Victor wanted me to die on a mission so that the men who follow me wouldn't revolt. If my team knew what happened here tonight, there would be blood—and a lot of it."

As the silence stretched on, both Owen and Wade slowly shifted their attention to Connor. They waited, as though they expected him to say something, and he stopped pacing long enough to look each man in the eye.

"I'm not going to solve your problems for you," he said flatly.

"Huh," Murdoc said. "I really thought you were going to offer, Captain."

"So did I," Sophia confessed.

"This isn't my fight." Connor gestured between the two imposter Shades in front of him. "One thing you will do, however, is stop using my name."

"That's not how it works." Owen shrugged. "I mentioned the Shade folk story to Rockwell, and he loved it. He's the one who wove it into the fabric of who we are. If Victor has taken over enough to order a hit on my life, however, then my guess is even Rockwell couldn't put a stop to this now. Only the underground's leader makes those sort of changes, and as you can plainly see, I don't have that kind of influence."

Fates be damned.

Connor didn't have time for this.

An idea struck him, then, so sudden and so fiercely that he nearly staggered backward. A way to solve all of this and get what he needed from the castle in one fell swoop.

His breath quickened as his sifted through the many ways this might fail, but too much was on the line. With Rockwell sentenced to death and the Antiquity fading fast, Connor had to act soon.

Tonight, Victor Varon had declared war on Owen Hunt. These Shades were in the midst of a civil war, and all of Kirkwall would feel its effects. The turmoil within their ranks had driven a fissure between them all.

Connor could use that to his advantage in more ways than one. If he was clever, he might even be able to eliminate the need for bloodshed.

Unlikely, perhaps, given his luck—but possible all the same.

"I know that look, Captain." Murdoc pushed himself to his feet and brushed the dust off his hands. "That's the look that comes with mischief, and I'm in."

"Not mischief," Connor corrected. "This is going to be outright chaos."

The former Blackguard shrugged. "Even better."

"Chaos?" Owen frowned in confusion. "How is that going to help us rescue Rockwell? If anything, chaos would only make things worse."

"You'll see." Connor shifted the full weight of his glare onto the prince. "You're going to get us into the castle—just you, me, and my team. We will move quicker that way."

"And me?" Wade asked with a distrustful glint in his eye.

"You're collateral." Connor didn't bother masking the hard edge in his voice.

Owen scowled. "I would never—"

"You don't have a choice," Connor interrupted. "I'm following you into enemy territory, and I need assurance that you're not going to try anything stupid once we're inside. If my team and I make it out alive, nothing will happen to Wade."

"And after?" Owen stifled a grimace of pain and pressed his palm against his still-healing leg wound. "What about when you have what you want, and I've delivered you safely out of the castle?"

"If we wanted you dead, we wouldn't have healed you," Connor pointed out.

"True," the prince reluctantly admitted. "But you also clearly want something. How do we know you won't just kill us after you get it?"

"Guess you'll have to trust us," Connor said with a shrug.

Wade snorted derisively, and Owen didn't reply.

"Here's what will happen," Connor said firmly. "We get my artifact. We get Rockwell. Then, we get the hell out. No detours. No distractions. Understood?"

"Understood," Owen begrudgingly agreed. "I need a few days to get things together."

Connor's eyes narrowed in suspicion. "What things?"

"Coordination, mostly," Owen replied. "My men on the inside need to steal a master key, and that won't be easy. We need information on shift changes. These things take time."

Or the Prince of Kirkwall could just as easily coordinate a trap.

With a sidelong glance, he studied Wade. The prince's lifelong friend stiffened as he watched Owen, but neither of them so much as flinched. No twitch of the eye. No fidgeting.

Owen knew what was at stake.

"Fine," Connor conceded. "But we're taking Wade tonight."

The prince stiffened. "Like hell you are."

"It's not negotiable," Connor snapped. "Not with the risk my team and I are taking on. The deal's still good, and you'll get him back once this is over."

Owen gritted his teeth, but he was smart enough not to push his luck. "And the Shades? Unless you stop them, the other Shades will still use your name. Victor will still be after me. You seem to at least know Rockwell, but you'll be breaking him out of prison just to throw him in a snake pit. Once we escape, what will you do? Or do you not care what happens to this city?"

Connor didn't answer.

In a few days, the future of this island would shift, and much of his brewing plan depended on the outcome of their time in the castle. He had walked in on an uprising spearheaded by vigilantes who had abused his reputation and stolen his name. If he allowed it to continue, it could destroy his chance to establish Slaybourne as an independent kingdom among an empire that thrived on conquering its citizens.

After all, a group of criminals using his name without his consent undermined his authority and power. No leader would respect him unless he stopped this little rebellion dead in its tracks.

Whoever won this battle of the Shades would inevitably win Kirkwall as well. Whatever bittersweet memories he had of this place, his father had loved this island with all his soul. He'd fought for it. He'd sacrificed for it.

He'd *died* for it.

If Connor didn't intercede and stop this mess, there would be nothing left of his father's beloved island but bloodstains and rubble.

CHAPTER FIFTY-EIGHT

CELINE

In the warm summer night, Celine knelt in the shadows by a cluster of towering oaks. With her augmentations freshly enhanced, her feet made no sound. With a hood over her head to mask her snow-white hair, she had swapped her elaborate gowns for familiar riding gear that was eerily similar to the tunics she had worn in her days as Teagan Starling's secret assassin.

That felt like another life entirely—and yet, as she listened to the forest, it came back to her so easily.

The stealth.

The tension in her shoulders.

The twitch in her fingers as they itched to grab one of the two dozen daggers hidden on her body.

Around her, the Enchanted Woods trilled with life. Filtered moonbeams cast a soft glow through the silver leaves overhead, and crickets chirped in the distance. A stream gargled its way through the trees behind her. A lone frog croaked in the night, punctuated with the occasional cough from the sentries patrolling the compound's perimeter.

But the air was still, and the tantalizing aroma of spiced meat on a fire wafted through the woodland. This far into the Enchanted Woods, halfway between Dewcrest and Hazeltide, these fools had gotten complacent.

How sloppy.

Ahead, torchlight flickered in the deepest part of the woodland. It had been hell to find this place, and after pursuing more than one bad lead, she had finally found Hugh Davarius's camp.

Her nose creased with disdain. That bastard had already wasted so much of her precious time. The Wraithblade grew stronger every day, and so did the abomination fused to his soul. These petty squabbles had cost her dearly, and she would finally end the General of War's little rebellion.

Tonight.

Footsteps crunched lightly over grass. She crouched lower and tilted her head to pinpoint the sound. A boot brushed over a patch of dry dirt, and a man's low grumble punctuated the soothing woodland chorus.

He wandered closer, and Celine fought the temptation to close the distance between them. His silhouette neared, and she tugged a bright silver dagger from the sheath on her thigh.

For a time, she had been Teagan's favorite—mainly because she never made a sound, and her victims never saw her coming.

As he passed her stretch of shadows, Celine stood behind him and clasped one hand over his mouth. He barely had time to tense before she slid her dagger over his throat. A wet gurgle followed, muffled to near silence by her hand, and something wet splattered on the dried leaves beneath his feet.

Before the shock could wear off, Celine dragged him into the shadows. He thrashed under her grip, but her Strongman augmentation kept his head pinned to the dirt. She drove her dagger into his chest, and the man finally stilled.

Effortless—and, strangely, almost *fun.*

In the cold, withered void where her heart used to be, she felt a flicker of excitement. The thrill faded almost as quickly as it had come, but this reminded her of the old days. The mystery of what her target had done to anger the Starlings. The challenge of slipping undetected through the most secure fortresses in Saldia.

This time, however, she was killing on her own merit. She chose her own missions, and that liberation struck her as odd.

Delightful, even.

A makeshift wall surrounded the encampment, and she scaled it with ease. Her boots landed softly on the dirt, and she darted between the tents unseen. Torches crackled in their sconces as she passed, and shadows stretched along the ground toward her as soldiers patrolled the night.

With every step, she crept closer to her target—the largest tent, set squarely in the center of the camp. Davarius, after all, did not sleep in squalor.

This onslaught was weeks in the making. Coordinating. Testing. Interrogating. Curse the Fates, how she hated preparation. Usually, she slit throats and left the cleanup to others.

But Davarius needed to be an example of what happened to those who betrayed her.

Though she could have sent her new army in to clear out the camp, Davarius was an unmatched soldier. Few could kill him, and she couldn't risk him escaping tonight. He undoubtedly had something dire planned for her coronation, and he couldn't be allowed to see it through.

Only General Barrett knew she was here, and he would keep the other soldiers at a distance to ensure no one recognized her. On her orders, Barrett had this area surrounded, and his small band of elite soldiers stood by to capture any fools who tried to run. In one fell swoop, the last ribbons of dissent would finally be snuffed out.

Four guards stood watch at the entrance to the tent, and Celine paused just beyond the circle of orange light cast by the crackling torches that surrounded his makeshift chambers. Henry had used similar tents on his campaign through Saldia, and she knew them all too well. A foyer, of sorts, would lead to the main sleeping area, and this late at night, a privacy curtain would separate the two. Modified Prowlport charms enchanted the tent walls to ensure any discussions went unheard by eavesdroppers outside, and those enchantments would be his undoing.

Her mind buzzed with possible outcomes as she sheathed her dagger and summoned four of her custom blades—metallic feathers, carved by the best craftsmen Saldia had to offer, and not one of them with a hilt. The flawless steel daggers hovered out of the tailored pocket on her hip, and they floated a breath above her palm.

This little enchantment had been inspired by the necromancers, but it was one she had perfected for herself.

For a long while, she waited. To ensure no one witnessed what she was about to do, she had to time her next move precisely. Patrols tracked their way across the camp, nodding occasionally to the guards out front. Minute by minute, the routine became clear.

Another patrol passed, and her time had come.

With a flick of her wrist, she shot the first into the nearest guard's throat. The second and third soldiers fell before the fourth could even turn around, and her last dagger landed squarely in the center of his forehead.

The soldiers fell, and she slipped silently into the front entrance. A quick scan confirmed she was alone, and the privacy screen blocked her view of the makeshift bedroom beyond. Before the next patrol could walk by, Celine deftly hauled the dead soldiers into the front room, two at a time, and released the cord holding open the tent's front-most flap.

It was almost too easy.

Without so much as a breath to give away her position, Celine knelt and lifted the curtain. A circular table took up most of the space, and a few chairs sat against the tent wall to her left. Maps covered most of the surfaces, each pinned to the wood with a dagger, and trunks lined every wall in militant precision.

At the far end of the tent, Hugh Davarius slept fully dressed on a silk-mesh cot. His brown tunic nearly matched the table's dark wooden sheen, and the man even wore his boots. One arm rested over his eyes as he softly snored, and the faint outline of a broadsword lay beneath his cot.

Always ready for war, this one. Celine could respect that much.

As she crept closer, she braced herself for him to abruptly sit upright. To hurl a dagger at her head, perhaps, or to land a hard blow in her gut. They had fought in Henry's war together, after all, and they knew each other's habits better than most.

He adjusted in his sleep, and he let out a contented sigh as his arm fell off his head and slid off the cot. His fingers brushed the dirt-stained rug beneath him, just inches from the hilt of his sword, and Celine narrowed her eyes in suspicion.

If she had never met Henry, she would have married Davarius. He had courted her for so long, back when they were young, and he had asked many times for her hand. Though he hadn't known what she was, back then, she had nearly agreed. Of everyone in her life, Davarius seemed the most likely to outmatch her.

It was a trait she had always admired.

Her fingers stretched wide, and the subtle gesture summoned another of her feather-blades from the tailored pouch on her hip. It floated upward, obedient as ever, and she launched it at his throat.

In the second before the blade stabbed him through the neck, the general's eyes shot open. With a grunt of effort, he hurled himself off the cot. Just as he landed hard on the rug, her blade ripped through the cot where his head had been. He grabbed the sword from under his bed and jumped to his feet, brows furrowed and expression fierce.

Celine smiled. Good. At least she could have a little fun before she had to kill him.

With nothing to lose, Celine tugged off her hood. Her long white hair flowed over her shoulders, and she allowed herself one wicked little smile as she watched the color drain from his face.

This.

That look.

It was why she had opted against using a glamour.

Davarius frowned, trying and failing to mask the flicker of fear in his eyes as he recognized her. "Come for me already, have you?"

"Honestly, I felt like my hunt for you took too long. You're getting better at covering your tracks."

With a few steady steps, she placed herself between him and the exit. A tent like his would undoubtedly have Strongman charms on the canvas walls, and he would have a hell of a time running.

Not that his pride would allow it, of course.

"You sent that boy to his death," she taunted. "That little assassin of yours, the one that came for me in Wildefaire."

Davarius stilled, and a brief flicker of remorse broke through his stony exterior. Apparently, he had indeed cared for the young man she had tortured.

Interesting.

"He died with dignity," she assured him, though her tone remained flat and emotionless. "But he told me a great many things. *Damning* things. To think, if not for him, I might've made a truce with you."

Davarius tightened his grip and angled his blade toward her chest. "Don't lie to me, woman."

She shrugged. A lock of her hair, which he had so adored in their youth, fell into her face. "What use do I have in lying? I'm going to kill you regardless."

Instead of answering, he tugged a dagger from a sheath hidden in the small of his back and hurled it at her chest. She pivoted, and it landed with a dull *thunk* in the tent's center pole.

Celine smirked. "Good aim."

"Stand down, Celine," he warned, his voice a low growl. "Oakenglen is mine."

Henry's former General of War slowly circled, careful to keep the cot between them, and a pale glint of light flashed across a throwing axe resting on a nearby trunk. It took effort for Celine not to groan in disappointment as yet another man played perfectly into her hands.

But perhaps she could still have a little fun before he had to die.

She clicked her tongue in disappointment at his brazen ego. "Davarius, the world's players barely know you exist. The Starlings often forget your name. Even Otmund didn't consider you a threat. You belong to Oakenglen, but you will never rule it."

"And you will?" He laughed, harsh and hoarse, at her audacity. "With your carefully crafted image as our defenseless queen? You wanted the world to underestimate you, and I ensured no one would ever see you as more than a delicate flower. No one fears you, Celine."

"You do," she said coldly.

The general hesitated, and he watched her with all the hatred and ire of an enemy on the battlefield. She had seen that expression so many times before, and a jolt of surreal delight shot through her body as he focused his loathing on her.

"This won't end well for you," His tone was even. Cold. Matter-of-fact, as though the Fates themselves had revealed her future. "Perhaps if you had a claim to the throne, the people would listen—but Henry stole Oakenglen, and the citizens haven't forgotten the royal family that came before you. The Coldwells are still out there, woman. They want their kingdom back, and they will get it. If you're not killed at your coronation, you won't last a year."

Her eyes narrowed, but her wicked grin only grew. "That's quite a prediction, given that you know what I am."

"Assassins die all the time." Still at a safe distance, he gestured to her with the tip of his sword. "Even you can be killed, Celine."

A fair point—but one she had already considered.

The silence stretched between them like a taut wire, each of them sizing up the other. The tent's enchantments left the air painfully quiet, and only the rustle of fabric punctuated the silence as they circled each other.

"I've been weaving this plan since before Henry was coronated," Davarius said flatly. "It was only a matter of time before someone killed him, and I was ready the moment he died. This rebellion continues with or without me. You will never keep Oakenglen."

"I don't plan to," she admitted with a lazy shrug.

He frowned, caught off guard by her honesty, and she took the opportunity to do a quick scan for other weapons. Four sheaths dotted his thigh, and a bulge under his shirt suggested a larger knife hid within reach.

A respectable number to have nearby, at least whilst one slept.

Celine pretended to study the metallic feather hovering above her palm. "A few public trials. A hanging or two. Hard labor for some of your lower ranks, and strategic pardons here and there. Another month, and the last whispers of dissent will die as I make an example of your high-ranking officers."

With a lazy flick of her wrist, she launched her feathered dagger at his stomach. He dodged with a few seconds to spare and wisely used the opportunity to inch closer to the axe. Her dagger lodged into one of his trunks, and he fell to one knee with a feigned grunt of pain. With that one movement, he had perfectly positioned himself by the axe.

Another flicker of excitement snapped through her at the close call. By the Fates, Davarius was certainly a fun plaything.

"And me?" He made a show of setting one hand on the nearest trunk, and he angled his body to hide the axe behind him. "Will you parade my corpse through the street, Celine?"

"Maybe." She tilted her head, as though she were actually considering it. "Truthfully, I think you'll be more useful as a scapegoat for Henry's death. Our king, murdered by his most trusted ally in the dead of night. Maybe I'll add assassins. I'm not certain, yet, but I assure you it will be quite dramatic. You'll be remembered as every bit the villain you think I am."

Despite her taunts, the good general didn't reply.

In a lightning-fast movement, Davarius grabbed the throwing axe. With all his might—and a loud grunt of effort—he hurled it at her head.

Finally.

In the seconds before it embedded in her skull, Celine debated letting it hit. Perhaps that would be a decent way to go. Painless, really, and instant. She and Henry could be together once more, in the next life, and she would at least be done with this tedious world.

But her training refused to let her die.

With a well-practiced flourish, she caught the axe midair and spun on her heel to maintain its momentum. Her hand tightened around its handle as she took aim at her opponent's chest, and she launched it with every bit as much strength as he had shown moments before.

The sharp blade sliced through the air, and this time, it hit its mark.

Davarius stumbled backward into the trunks, and he hit the tent wall behind him. The tarp alone held him upright as he gasped for air and stared down at the axe protruding from his torso. His chest heaved for the air that wouldn't come, and blood bubbled from his mouth.

Hmm. The blade had missed his heart by an inch, and Celine frowned in disappointment. In her delight at having a worthy plaything perhaps she had gotten a bit sloppy herself.

He clawed at the tent walls, and she closed the gap between them to end this once and for all. Though he had tried to have her murdered, any more torture would waste precious minutes. Though she had enjoyed their tete-a-tete, their chat had already wasted more time than she truly had to spare.

She summoned another of her feather blades and, with her free hand, grabbed his collar. Her grip brought him closer, until they were nose-to-nose, and she met his eye.

"I had plans for you," she whispered to him. "What a waste."

To her surprise, he didn't fight. He didn't try to wriggle out of her grip, nor did he plead for mercy that would never come. Apparently accepting his fate, Davarius surprised her yet again.

He smiled.

She paused, her eyes roaming his face as she tried to make sense of what he was doing.

"B-beautiful," he sputtered, and more blood pooled against his teeth with each breath. Tenderly, almost lovingly, he ran his fingertips over her temple. His eyes slipped in and out of focus, but he gently tucked a lock of white hair behind her ear. "T-tell me something."

Celine raised an eyebrow, waiting for this to be over.

"H-how can you live like this?" He coughed, and blood splattered on her sleeve. "With no pain. No emotions. How can you not feel anything?"

For the first time since he'd awoken, Celine hesitated. The question caught her off guard, and she wasn't sure what to say.

Davarius gently held her jaw, and his head lolled as he fought to remain conscious. "I hated Henry, you know. F-for stealing you from me. I hated everything about him—until he showed me who you really were."

The *gall.*

Celine didn't reply. That numb void in her soul grew colder as a fresh wave of icy hate slithered through her veins. Without another wasted word, she held his gaze and drove one of her feather blades into his heart. The steel disappeared into his chest from the brute force of her blow. He grunted, eyes wide, and his brow furrowed as his last breath left him.

His body thudded to the floor, and Celine waited to feel a flicker of remorse. She had adored him, once, and part of her had wondered if killing him would make her feel again.

It didn't.

With a frustrated sigh, she watched rivers of blood snake away from his body. One angled under the cot and toward the door, but she couldn't dally.

The deed was done.

Celine lifted the hood over her bone-white hair and left the once-decorated war hero on the floor, marinating in a pool of his own blood. In minutes, Barrett would clear the camp and, on her orders, take credit for the man's death.

She, meanwhile, had a coronation to plan.

CHAPTER FIFTY-NINE

CONNOR

In the depths of Kirkwall Castle, deep in its labyrinth of dimly lit corridors and hidden passages, Connor paused behind Owen as the prince pressed one palm against a secret door.

Behind him, Sophia and Murdoc kept close and quiet. Even with the advantage of an insider leading them through this place, they understood the danger.

The winding path from the cliffside tunnels had been almost impossible to memorize. Their route had taken them through the castle's wine cellar, across exposed hallways, up a half-dozen ladders, and now to a six-foot portrait that masked a hidden entrance.

Without a word or a warning, Owen slid a wooden plank aside and peered through the gap it revealed. He stood there a moment in the silence, studying something beyond their secret door, but ultimately let out a sigh of relief.

"This way," he whispered.

He pressed against the door, and its hinges creaked as it swung quickly open.

At the shrill screech, Connor and his team collectively paused mid-step. Ahead of him, Owen winced and cast an apologetic glance over one shoulder.

Fates be damned, the Wraith King grumbled, still mercifully hidden in the in-between. *I've witnessed stampedes of howling blightwolves quieter than you four.*

Connor grunted in annoyance—both because of the ghoul's intrusion, and because the bastard was absolutely right.

"That happens every time," Owen whispered. "Father doesn't know about this one."

"Right," Murdoc muttered. "And I'm a pretty little fae princess."

Sophia snickered.

"Where are all the soldiers?" Connor asked, not bothering to mask the skepticism in his voice. "It's been eerily quiet this whole time."

"The ranks are spread thin," Owen whispered. "Most of his guards are out at night enforcing curfew. The rest are manning the ambush stations around the dungeon. Everywhere else in the castle is mostly unattended."

Connor frowned, not entirely convinced.

Suspicious as ever of Owen's intentions, Connor strained his enhanced senses to listen for approaching footsteps or the clink of metal armor. He waited for the inevitable ambush, but the trap didn't spring.

Yet.

It seemed unavoidable. At any moment, the prince would at least be tempted to lead Connor and his team into a horde of soldiers. He was, after all, leading an enemy into a castle brimming with a army that he could command. With one wayward gesture, Owen could get them caught—or worse.

If not for Wade being held as collateral, Connor wouldn't have dreamed of letting Owen Hunt lead him *anywhere.*

Nocturne, I need an update. Connor pressed on his connection to the dragon. *Is our collateral behaving?*

When he'd taken Wade to Nocturne in secret, with Murdoc and Sophia keeping watch on Owen, the Goldwyn heir's awe had lasted only moments. It was impressive, really, how quickly Wade had adapted, and he hadn't forgotten his role in Connor's plan—even if encountering a creature of legend had been somewhat of a surprise.

If tonight went sideways, neither Wade nor Owen would see the dawn.

An irritated growl rumbled through his connection to the regal creature. HE WILL NOT STOP GLARING AT ME. HE SIMPLY SITS THERE, ARMS CROSSED, LIKE A FURIOUS FLEDGLING WAITING FOR ITS PUNISHMENT TO END.

I—uh—alright. Connor frowned, not entirely certain he understood the reference, but he had a decent enough guess of what the dragon meant. *Has he tried to run?*

NOT YET. I SUSPECT THAT WILL HAPPEN ANY MOMENT.

If he does, scare the ever-loving shit out of him, Connor ordered. *A bit of growling will probably be enough.*

I AM A PRINCE, NOT A GOVERNESS! Nocturne growled. THIS IS DEMEANING.

Connor chuckled. *I owe you.*

UNDENIABLY, the dragon grumbled.

Connor nudged Sophia. "Got anything in that bag to solve a squeaky door hinge?"

The necromancer nodded and slipped her pack off her shoulder. "I'll catch up."

Connor signaled for Owen to move, and the Prince of Kirkwall slipped silently through the gap. The hinge squeaked again, much softer this time as Connor held the door in place, and the three men in their party snuck out into the castle.

Owen knelt at the corner where their passageway met the main corridor. Half-dead fires burned in the sconces along the opposite wall, and each flicker of the flames cast surreal shadows across the ornate red tapestries hung over the cold stone bricks to preserve what little heat the ancient castle could retain.

"There." the prince whispered.

Owen pointed at something just out of Connor's line of sight, and Connor leaned forward until he could see around the corner.

At the end of a lengthy hallway, two enormous oak doors took up the entirety of the wall. Sapphires and gold coated each door in a loose mosaic of waves on a turbulent sea, and four armored guards blocked the way forward.

Murdoc leaned around Connor, and the three men studied the vault entrance in a moment of stunned disbelief.

"That door costs more than I've ever made in my life," Murdoc hissed under his breath.

"I'm more concerned about the four soldiers you didn't tell us about," Connor glared at Owen through the corner of his eye.

The prince scoffed. "Did you think a king would leave his most valuable treasures unattended?"

A fair point, but Connor wasn't about to admit it.

Sophia knelt behind Murdoc and slung her bag over one shoulder, apparently done silencing the door. She caught his eye and nodded.

Good. They could continue.

In the hour or so before midnight, the muffled gusts of a howling ocean wind whistled through narrow holes in the old stones' mortar. The air was otherwise still, save for the odd sigh or grunt from the bored soldiers standing guard.

"What are we waiting for?" Sophia whispered.

"A sign from one of my men," Owen whispered back. "All four of those are loyal to my father, not to me."

Connor grimaced, but didn't reply.

The thud of footsteps on the carpet caught his attention, and he signaled for his team to slip back into the shadows. They pressed their backs against the wall, and Owen mimicked them moments before a soldier clad in white silk passed by. A black band lined the hem of his left sleeve, and he cast a knowing sidelong glance into their hallway.

He and the prince locked eyes, and Owen held up three fingers. With an almost unnoticeable gesture, the soldier coiled his fist and flashed two fingers in return.

The entire exchange lasted barely a second, and as the soldier continued down the hall toward the treasury doors, Connor narrowed his eyes in suspicion.

"Damn," Owen whispered. "He only bought us twenty minutes."

"Better than nothing," Murdoc whispered back.

Connor didn't reply. His body tensed, and it took focused effort not to draw his blackfire blades. Each corner of this place could end in devastating betrayal, and each passing second left him more on edge than the last. Everything about this heist set his nerves on fire, and he hated every minute of it.

The low murmur of men talking bubbled past, though they were too far away for Connor to hear. Their tones became more urgent, and the swish of cloth over metal followed. Footsteps raced toward them, thundering over the floor, and Connor shifted his weight onto the balls of his feet.

Ready to attack.

Four figures darted past their hiding place, swords drawn, and the man in front barked urgent orders as he led them down the hallway. The footsteps receded and, after a time, disappeared completely.

Not a trap, then, but a diversion. The prince hadn't lied after all.

Connor let out a slow breath to steady himself.

The clatter of a door handle rattling against wood broke the lingering silence that followed, and Owen peeked around the corner once again.

The prince gestured for Connor and his team to follow. "Now's our chance."

Owen darted out into the hallway. Before Connor followed, he cast a cursory glance around both lengths of the corridor to find that it was, indeed, empty—save for Owen's lone soldier clad in white.

The man grunted with effort as he pulled again on one of the towering door's handles, and Owen sprinted ahead to help him. The two yanked hard, and this time, the door slowly swung forward. A thin gap in the dazzling gemstone mosaic revealed some of the vault inside, and a silhouette walked past the opening.

Connor skidded to a stop, still staring after the shadow he had seen.

"There's someone inside," Sophia whispered from behind him. "We should—"

The door swung open, and the silhouette turned out to be another man dressed in green pushing from within. With one shoulder against the wood, he grimaced as he helped the other two open the obscenely heavy door.

Connor, Sophia, and Murdoc let out a collective sigh of relief.

Behind the newcomer, a towering chamber came sharply into focus. Iron sconces hung from the ceiling and cast a warm auburn glow over the dazzling array of gold trinkets and treasures lining every wall. Swords, axes, and even a few crossbows hung between ornate tapestries. Paintings framed in gold-plated wood filled the sparse gaps. Dozens of pedestals covered almost every inch of the floor, displaying a dazzling array of glowing artifacts resting on silk pillows. Daggers. Combs. A few jewel-encrusted boxes. It seemed endless, and the only gaps between the artifacts were the arched doorways that led to more rooms beyond what they could see.

Oddly, a jewel-encrusted chest rested on a circular marble platform in the center of the room. Light brown seal skins underneath the chest overlapped each other, and a white one covered in soft black spots hung over one end of the chest. A green spellgust stone the size of his fist glowed from the center of a large iron lock, as though taunting anyone who dared to open it.

"By the Fates," Sophia whispered. "I'm going to need more than twenty minutes."

"No," Connor said with a sidelong glance at her. "We're only here for the orb."

"But..." The necromancer pouted, and she blinked in awe at the treasures lying in wait for them. "Not even a few?"

"No," he said again, more firmly this time.

As the door fully opened, Connor spotted a familiar black sphere on the floor beside the soldier who had opened the vault from within.

The Soulsprite.

A thin ray of firelight stole through the gap in the doors, however, and the orange light glinted over the slick sheen of iron.

A decoy, perhaps—or evidence that Owen had duped them all.

The soldier dressed in all white pulled something from a satchel strapped to his thigh. Connor shifted his weight, ready to block any darts or daggers thrown his way, but the soldier opened his hand to reveal a dull gray key on his palm. A tiny green spellgust stone glittered in the base of the otherwise nondescript strip of wrought iron.

"Excellent as always," Owen said as he took the key. "You're sure it will work for Rockwell's cell?"

The man nodded.

"Good." The prince grabbed the key, and Connor made a mental note of which pocket he'd slipped it into. "Can you buy us any more time?"

"Thirty minutes is a stretch, sir, but I will try," the soldier in white said firmly. He cast a wary glance over Connor and his team and gestured for them to enter. "Better to assume the worst and find your way back sooner than that."

Owen clapped the man on the shoulder. "Thank you."

The prince led the way into the vault, and scoped up the decoy orb as he scanned the walls for something. As Owen darted by, the second soldier ignored him completely. The man's gaze instead lingered on Connor as he and his team followed the prince inside.

The man's unsettling glare reminded Connor of a wanted poster, not a trusted soldier.

Worse yet, there was a flash of something strange in the newcomer's expression, like the barest hint of recognition. It felt for a moment as if he had seen past the masks Connor and his team were wearing.

Connor's fingers twitched, and that odd blend of heat and hatred bubbled again in his palm. It pushed against his skin, aching to be freed. To burn something. To protect what was his.

Through sheer force of will, he quelled it.

"Now I need to remember..." Owen muttered to himself as he scanned the walls. "Was it in the southern corridor? Or the west? Damn it..."

"Are you insane?" Sophia grabbed the orb out of the prince's hands and gestured to the four archways in this room alone. "That's something you should've known before locking us in here!"

Connor wasn't worried. They would find it. He and Murdoc, however, were focused on another problem altogether.

Owen's two loyalists slipped into the hallway, and those heavy doors swung slowly shut. In the second before the doors closed, the stranger dressed in green caught Connor's eye once again. The doors shut with a hollow bang, and Connor listened to the ensuing silence.

Sure enough, one set of boots thudded against the carpet on their way down the hall. After roughly a minute of receding footsteps, the man's pace picked up—until he set off at a run.

One of Owen's men had left, and Connor figured he knew exactly which one had slipped away.

"Wraith," he whispered, careful to keep his voice low enough so that not even Sophia could hear. "Which of the men just left?"

The one in green, obviously. The ghoul huffed indignantly. *He kept glancing over his shoulder at the door, and even that oaf in white is suspicious. What a pitiful attempt at subterfuge.*

"Captain," Murdoc leaned close as he, too, glared at the now-closed door. "Did you see the way that second man—"

"Yes," Connor said under his breath.

Murdoc grunted in annoyance. "That's a problem, then."

"It is."

"Think he's loyal to the king?"

Of course not, the wraith huffed.

Hmm.

"No?" Connor quietly prodded the ghoul.

Don't be absurd, the Wraith King muttered. *Don't you know anything, Magnuson? Green is the color reserved for the highest officers in a king's guard in all of Henry's domains. It allowed him to easily find whoever was in charge, mostly so he could give them hell for every minor inconvenience he faced in his travels after the war. That man had the hunched shoulders and shifty eyes of a thief, not an officer. He's a fake, and those clothes are stolen.*

Well, now.

That had been far more useful than Connor had expected.

"Owen's conspiring, then." Connor shifted his attention to the prince as the man set his hands on his hips and stared up at the two archways at the opposite end of the main treasury room.

"It's one of these," Owen muttered to himself. "I'm sure of it."

Sophia groaned in utter disgust.

By the Fates, Magnuson, pay attention, the ghoul snapped. *The fool nearly sacrificed himself to save that Wade fellow. Your collateral ensures he will cooperate. No, I suspect this fake of ours belongs to someone else.*

"But who—"

It clicked for him, then.

There was only one other player in this game, at least that he knew of, who posed a threat to both him and Owen.

It seemed as though Victor Varon had been a busy man since his return to Kirkwall.

"Victor," Connor whispered to Murdoc.

The former Blackguard's eyebrows shot up his forehead. "That might be even worse."

Connor nodded.

Oblivious to their conversation, Owen gestured for Sophia to return the black iron orb to him. She studied him for a moment, but she ultimately indulged him.

"What exactly is that thing?" Sophia asked. "Surely you don't think that piece of junk is what we're here to find?"

"Of course not. It's a decoy." Owen flashed her a mischievous grin. "My father walks his vaults twice a day. He knows every artifact in this place, and he knows where each one goes. They never move unless he orders it. He would notice your orb is missing, but this fake will buy us time."

Clever.

"I'm impressed," Connor begrudgingly admitted.

"Careful, now." Owen chuckled. "That almost sounded like a compliment."

Fates forbid, the ghoul muttered. *The last thing you need is to adopt yet another wayward stray.*

Connor groaned in annoyance.

Owen gestured for them to follow. "This way."

The man darted off through the left rear archway, and Connor led his team after the prince. Weapons and vases blurred by, each set carefully on their pedestals, and glowing green spellgust gems hummed in nearly everything he passed.

The sheer cost to enchant objects that simply sat on pillows would've probably fed the people of Kirkwall for a year.

What a disgusting waste.

Nocturne, Connor once again pressed on his connection to the dragon.

WHAT IS IT NOW? the regal creature grumbled. IF YOU ASK FOR YET ANOTHER UPDATE, I WILL TORCH THIS ENTIRE FOREST.

Easy now. I need you to ask Wade how many of the Shades are loyal to Owen.

HE WILL NEVER ANSWER.

Try anyway.

There was a long pause as Connor followed Owen through the crisscrossing pathways and under another archway, leading to yet more rooms filled to the brim with ancient artifacts.

HALF, Nocturne eventually replied. HE WILL NOT TELL ME ANY MORE THAN THAT.

Connor suppressed a frustrated groan. He had wanted more specifics, but it would have to do.

Tell him to collect anyone who is loyal to Owen. He cannot breathe a word of this to any of Victor's men, nor to anyone who's neutral. Owen's men only. They need to meet on the northwest beach we used to enter the tunnels. Wade will know where that is. Tell him to stay hidden until I give the word.

The dragon snorted in confusion. YOU WANT TO RELEASE OUR COLLATERAL AGAINST A MAN YOU DO NOT TRUST?

Owen won't know that, Connor explained. *As far as the prince is concerned, you're moments away from eating Wade whole.*

Nocturne's curious growl echoed through his head. WHAT ARE YOU UP TO, CONNOR?

Hopefully nothing, he replied.

Connor wanted to be wrong. He wanted to walk out onto an empty beach. Best case, he would use the opportunity to draw a line in the sand and force the Shades to surrender his name. Worst case, he would walk out of the tunnel and into a warzone.

VERY WELL, MY FRIEND.

Up ahead, Owen skidded to a stop and pointed at a pedestal in the back corner. "There."

Connor's heart skipped a hopeful beat as he scanned the rows of blue silk pillows and glowing artifacts. True to his word, Owen had pointed to a lone orb in the very back corner, almost shrouded in shadow. Black as the night and coated in an ashy sheen, the inky spirals and ornate runes carved into the orb pulsed briefly—just once—with a faint green glow.

As though it felt his presence.

"Strange," Owen muttered. "It's never done that before."

"Yes, fine," Sophia said, not bothering to mask her impatience. "What enchantments does he have on these artifacts to safeguard against theft?"

"None," the prince answered.

Murdoc's jaw tensed, and he took a menacing step toward the man. "Do you think we're stupid?"

"I've checked this area a dozen times." Owen shrugged, as though he didn't understand it, either. "Over the years, I've stolen every enchanted dagger in this room. Everything you see on the walls is a fake. My father still doesn't know."

Murdoc cast Connor a sidelong glare. Neither of them liked this, but they didn't have the luxury of time.

"If we set something off, I'll kill you myself." With the decoy under one arm, Sophia slipped between the pedestals on her way to the Soulsprite. "Enough loitering. We have to move."

The necromancer rested the heavy iron fake in one palm, and she nervously stretched the fingers of her free hand as she eyed the Soulsprite before her. In one swift movement, she lifted the real one and rolled the decoy into its place.

All four of them paused, waiting for an alarm to sound or for the thunder of boots over the ornate blue carpet, but the silent night stretched on.

Sophia's shoulders relaxed, and the creases of worry in her brow slowly faded. She hugged the black orb to her chest and wove her way around the pedestals on her way to rejoin them. Murdoc slid his pack off his shoulder and tugged out the box made of vines that had protected the Antiquity's gifted Soulsprite on its way to Slaybourne. The two knelt, and Sophia set the Soulsprite on the cushion of leaves within it.

Safe.

Finally.

It seemed as though the King of Kirkwall had truly been oblivious to the raw power stored at the back of his treasured vault.

THIS WADE FELLOW UNDERSTANDS OUR URGENCY. Nocturne's voice snapped through Connor's head, catching him off guard. HE IS AWARE THAT I WILL WATCH HIM FROM THE SKY TO ENSURE HE BEHAVES.

Good. Try to stay out of sight. Connor took a settling breath with the hope he hadn't just made an egregious error. With so many unknowns, he had to protect his team to the best of his ability.

If things went wrong, he would let the Wraith King loose—even if it meant any survivors figured out what he truly was.

"Let's move," he ordered. "We've got a long night ahead of us."

Murdoc tied off the flap on his pack and slung the strap over his shoulder. "Ready, Captain."

"I'm trusting you," Owen said quietly.

Connor looked over his shoulder to find the prince standing in the middle of the aisle, both hands balled into anxious fists, as he stared at the three of them.

"You have what you want." The prince gestured to the pack on Murdoc's shoulder. "You have all the power, now. I'm trusting you to keep your word."

It was true.

If he wanted to, Connor could've left right now. He'd memorized the path they had taken through the warren of tunnels and secret passageways. He knew the way out, and he knew where the guards were stationed.

When Connor didn't reply, Owen's eye twitched. He shook his head, resigned, and pointed at the archway behind Connor. "We're nearly out of time. Come on."

How dull, the Wraith King muttered. *I was hoping for an ambush. I am quite bored, Magnuson.*

"Don't worry," Connor said under his breath. "If the ambushes are as bad as Owen claims, you'll get your share of blood."

The Wraith King's wicked laugh echoed through Connor's head, and he did his best to tune it out.

As the prince led the way through an almost endless array of interconnected aisles and archways, Connor watched the back of the man's head. Owen had thus far delivered on his end of their bargain. Though the prince could've called for soldiers at any moment, it became increasingly unlikely as the night wore on. He'd had plenty of opportunities already to spring a trap, and he hadn't taken one of them.

But they still had a long night ahead of them, and the prince would have plenty more chances.

CHAPTER SIXTY

CONNOR

The echoing crash of an underground waterfall masked every other sound in the giant underground cavern.

With Owen still leading their small band through the limestone labyrinth beneath Kirkwall Castle, Connor knelt with the others at the end of the narrow tunnel. This, supposedly, was one of the many hubs built into the cliff, and it allowed ample access to the three-dozen other pathways carved into the rock.

A tree's thick green foliage blocked his view of most of the cavern. A thin layer of dew coated its leaves as the waterfall's mist churned through the air. A waterfall fell from above in sheets that poured over the slick walls and gathered in a shallow lake as brilliantly blue as the sky. Rapids along the walls indicated possible exit points, but Connor had no idea if any were wide enough for a man.

Likely not.

Wide stones led the way through the shallow lake and a sparse collection of underground trees. Only the cluster of wooden barrels submerged beneath the calmer waters gave any hint of the cavern's time as a smuggling den, aside from the nondescript iron door at the far end of the cavern.

Twenty-six soldiers milled about in front of the door. Some sat on boulders, though most scanned the walls for signs of trouble. With broadswords in sheaths on their waists and spears resting against the wall by the door, these guards seemed prepared for an onslaught.

From a purely strategic standpoint, he didn't have a single advantage.

If he engaged, he risked revealing more than just his blades. For now, the Wraith King needed to stay a secret.

Besides, he didn't want to give the undead asshole the satisfaction of knowing he was needed.

"I take it that's the way in?" Connor asked as he pointed to the iron exit behind the soldiers.

"It's one way in," Owen answered rather cryptically.

"What's behind it?"

"A ladder that leads to a hatch in one of the prison cells."

"That's stupid," Sophia said. "Why would we want to enter into a cell?"

"For starters, I have a master key." Owen patted the pocket that still held the key the guard had given him. "Practically speaking, though, we don't. There will be roughly ten soldiers guarding it."

Murdoc frowned. "Then the plan is… what, exactly?"

"I found another way in." Owen pointed to a cluster of trees growing from a pile of boulders not far from the door. "There are some roughly hewn stairs behind those trees, hidden by an overgrown wall of ivy. I've cleared it out as much as I can, but I suspect the main door was added as a decoy in case the king ever found this cavern."

"Clever," Connor admitted.

"This is the closest I can get you," Owen said as he leaned one shoulder against the cold stone wall of their tunnel. "Anything closer than this, and they'll spot us instantly."

Damn.

"Great," Murdoc grumbled. "How the hell do we get past them?"

"That's yours to figure out," Owen muttered. "If I knew how to do that, I wouldn't have needed your help."

Fair enough.

To Owen's credit, the prince hadn't exaggerated about his father's military presence in the caves. They had narrowly slipped by three ambushes already, and an all-out brawl would've been inevitable if not for Owen's expert knowledge of every nook and cranny that the soldiers' hadn't yet found.

Owen had done his part, and he'd delivered on every promise he'd made thus far. The tunnels beneath Kirkwall Castle tunneled even deeper into the limestone than Connor could've imagined. It had taken an hour to weave their way back through the castle and underground passageways.

Without question, this mission would likely have failed without Owen's help—a fact Connor still hated.

Connor scanned the gathered throng of Kirkwall soldiers for any possible way to shift the tides in their favor. Limps, perhaps, or cover between here and there, but the soldiers kept a close watch on each other as well as the walls. Green ink along their forearms hinted at the weaponized augmentations each of them possessed, and he had no idea how varied their skills might be. All were within five feet of at least four other guards, and only a quarter of them rested or sat down at a time.

They were *good.*

From what Connor could assess of the terrain, there wasn't any possible way to make it across the lake, much less to the door, before all of them could grab their weapons. Even Sophia's enchanted darts would only take out a few at a time, and it wouldn't be a challenge for the soldiers to figure out where they'd come from.

My, my, the Wraith King grumbled. *If only there were a way for you to kill them all without betraying your position.*

With a resigned sigh, Connor rubbed his eyes. He hated giving the Wraith King what the old ghost wanted, but the mission was far more important than his pride.

"Owen, take the rear," Connor ordered.

The prince frowned with confusion, but Connor gestured behind Murdoc to emphasize the urgency.

Though Owen's eyes narrowed in suspicion, the prince obeyed. He pushed himself to his feet and darted silently to the rear of their small band and set one knee on the damp stone as he studied Connor's face.

"You will be tempted to watch," Connor explained. "Don't."

"This is ominous," the prince said. "What exactly are you going to do?"

"No matter what you hear," Connor continued, ignoring the man's question. "Do not look. Do not try to see what's happening. And for the love of the Fates, stay exactly where you are."

Murdoc patted the prince's shoulder. "Trust me, Owen. You don't want to see this."

"Alright," Owen said haltingly.

Connor rubbed the back of his neck, still not quite believing what he was about to do, but it had to be done.

"Have at them," he whispered to the Wraith King.

Truly? the ghost asked, unable to mask his astonishment.

"Yes. Be quick, and don't hold back."

A rough, wicked cackle bubbled through his mind. It drowned out his thoughts, and Connor grimaced with unfiltered disgust at the bloodlust brimming through the sound.

The laughter faded. For a suspended, eerie moment, nothing happened. The roar of water slamming into the underground lake muffled most of the scattered conversations among the soldiers, and not one of them suspected how they were about to die.

A twinge of guilt hit Connor deep in his gut, but it had to be done. Were he to simply walk out there, they would do the same to him.

A black cloud of smoke erupted in the center of the soldiers, and all of them flinched in unison. Several took wary steps backward, while others snatched their spears off the wall. The churning smoke hovered for a time, drawing them closer, and Connor shook his head.

The ghoul was milking it.

He should've known.

In a rush, a hand emerged from the smoke. It held a black sword forged from steel, and the ghoul's timeless weapon sliced effortlessly through the closest soldier's chest. The man slumped to the floor without even a whimper.

Dead in an instant.

That set a spark to the tension in the air, and chaos erupted.

The thick plume of smoke spread over the worn rock beneath their feet. It swallowed them, one by one, and agonized screams reverberated off the walls. The dark haze spat out bodies as it rolled toward its new victims. Swords clattered to the floor. Spears launched clear through the smoke, only to land harmlessly in the shimmering lake.

A bloodbath.

Maniacal laugher ricocheted through Connor's brain, and though he needed to keep an eye on the melee in case someone escaped, he chanced a quick look over his shoulder to see if Owen had behaved himself.

The Prince of Kirkwall stared at the floor, horrified. He pressed his fists hard against the rock beneath him, body tensed and muscles tight. He leaned forward and bit hard into his lip, as if he were barely able to restrain himself from pushing his way out of the tunnel to save the soldiers from whatever Connor had unleashed on them.

Murdoc shifted forward, his body strategically placed between Connor and the prince. The former Blackguard caught Connor's eye, and the subtle gesture conveyed an unspoken reassurance that he wouldn't let the prince see a damn thing.

Good.

As the black smoke swallowed the last of its victims, deafening screams filled the air. Even as swords clattered against the stone, the screams lingered. Bodies fell onto the rocky lakeshore with sickening plops, and ribbons of crimson snaked through the water from their corpses.

Vile.

If the wraith were close enough to hear him, Connor would've told the brutal warlord to end this now.

The last scream ended abruptly, and a wet gurgle followed. The black smoke dispersed in a rush, and a surreal calm settled onto the lush underground cavern.

Bodies littered the damp rocks. Some sank into the lake, sending swirling tendrils of blood through the current. Others slumped on nearby boulders. Most still had their heads, but there appeared to be two bodies missing.

"Where are the other—"

I got carried away, the ghoul explained. *There's nothing left of those two but some bones at the bottom of the lake.*

Connor grimaced in utter revulsion, but he opted not to reply.

"Let's move," he ordered.

He led their small band out into the cavern. A soothing chill snaked over his arms as the mist settled on his skin, and he deftly stepped between the stones that would keep him out of the water.

"Eyes front, Owen," he warned. "Focus on why we're here."

When the prince didn't reply, Connor paused and took one look over his shoulder. The man stood by the tree that had hidden them from sight, and he gaped at the carnage.

"Owen," Connor said firmly.

The prince blinked, snapped from his daze, and met Connor's eye. He tried to form words, but for several moments, he could only gasp incoherently.

"What did you *do*?" he finally asked.

Sophia and Murdoc shifted their attention to Connor, and all three waited for a reply.

But he didn't know what to say. In the face of such carnal devastation, nothing seemed suitable.

They had passed the closest cluster of guards on their way here, and it would easily have taken ten minutes for them to reach the cavern—if they could even figure out where the screams had come from in this endless warren of tunnels. The four of them probably had time to spare, but he still didn't want to test that theory.

"Not every choice is easy." Connor ran his tongue over his back molar as he fought another surge of guilt.

"But this..." Owen gestured to the corpses littering the rock. "This isn't... this is just..."

"It's brutal," Connor agreed. "Sometimes, a leader has to be."

Owen once again caught his eye, and the last of the color drained from his face.

But this was a lesson the prince would learn, one way or another. Better for him to face the real world's cold cruelty now, before all of Kirkwall bowed to him.

"You see all of this death? This blood?" Connor gestured to the corpses around them. "One day, you will face far worse. You won't just hear others die—you'll be the one giving the order for them to hang. It will fall to you to send men to their deaths, and you will watch as at least one person you love dies in front of you. If you're going to lead Kirkwall someday, you need to be ready for that moment."

"There must be a better way," Owen said breathlessly.

Idealistic as ever.

"Sometimes there is," Connor admitted. "But you still can't be afraid of bloodshed, Owen, because men can be brutal animals. We murder, we maim, and we destroy each other in the pursuit of more—more control, more power, more wealth. It's on people like the four of us to do better. To *be* better, and to protect those who can't hold a sword."

A memory flashed through the back of his mind, fast as an arrow flying by—the Slaybourne tapestry of the dragon's two halves. One lost in its feral bloodlust, and the other at peace in the sky.

Man was no less a monster, and he waged the same inner war.

No one spoke. All three of them simply listened, in a suspended, eerie silence. Everyone stood among the bleeding corpses, somber and still, and they needed something else. Something more.

Something that could make this right.

"We're here for Rockwell," he reminded them. "That man is willing to die for you, Owen. He's in that cell because he saved your skin. That's a man who would go to hell for the people he cares about and for those he swore to protect. We all owe a debt to people like that, and sometimes that's a debt you pay with blood—yours, or someone else's. So, listen closely," he added, raising one finger to emphasize his point. "If someone says they'll follow you to hell, it's on you to guarantee they make it back."

With that, he turned on his heel and sidestepped the blood cascading over the ground. That much noise would've inevitably caught someone's attention, and they likely had even less time to escape than they'd previously thought.

As they crossed the wide cavern, he felt Owen's stare on the back of his head. The unspoken question from all of them lingered like a taught cord that could snap at any moment.

But he'd meant what he said. Whatever happened, his team would make it out of here alive—even at a grave cost to himself.

CHAPTER SIXTY-ONE

CONNOR

Careful not to make a sound, Connor opened an iron hatch and peered through the thin gap.

Faint firelight spilled into the narrow tunnel leading up to the hatch, and his grip tightened on the metal ladder's top rung. Crates blocked most of his view of the dank storage room. Barrels of wine lined one wall, stacked one on top of the other, and a rat darted through the shadows along the floor.

No men walked by, however, and only that mattered. Rats wouldn't give away his position.

The heady musk of mold and wet soil stung Connor's nose, and he grimaced in disgust. Clumps of decaying straw gathered in the corners of the room, and the only light came from a lone sconce bolted to the wall just beyond the jail cell bars that kept inmates and soldiers alike from ransacking the stores.

Connor gently lifted the iron hatch, carefully watching its hinges to ensure it didn't make a sound, and it settled gently onto the stone floor. He hoisted himself out of the access tunnel and crouched behind a massive bag of grain to get a better view of the situation beyond the storage area.

The cell door sat ajar, its latch broken off altogether, and Connor's chest tightened. Maybe someone had gotten to the prison before them, or perhaps he and his team were about to walk into a trap.

But the aisle beyond the cell remained still, save for that one flickering sconce.

Before he gestured for his team to follow, he needed to track the position of every soldier and possible witness to what they were about to do.

Tendrils of smoke wafted from more sconces along a circular wall that angled downward into a dark pit. A wide stone aisle followed the wall, though no railing protected any fool who might fall off into the pit in the center of the dungeon. Prison cells lined the aisle's gentle slope, though the pitch-black darkness made it impossible to figure out which were empty. The open pit gave soldiers at the top an easy view at any fools racing up the aisle, which meant the dungeon's structure all but ensured no prisoners could escape.

Brilliant, the Wraith King muttered. *We must replicate this design in Slaybourne at once.*

Connor quietly groaned and opted not to reply.

The slope ended at a wide platform with the twelve jail cells that had the only windows, and the top plank of the gallows' wooden frame was visible through the windows' thin bars. Two figures sat slouched against the walls, and the chains rattled any time either of them fidgeted on the uncomfortable stone floor.

This stretch of wall had far more sconces, and the orange torchlight cast a warm glow across a few worn wooden tables and the long benches that offered the only seating at each one. Two mugs sat on the nearest table, alongside a neatly stacked deck of cards.

This had to be the soldiers' station, and yet he still hadn't seen even one of the guards.

A trap, clearly, and the only question was who wanted him to walk into it.

Connor inched around the grain and knelt behind a stack of crates to get a better view of this platform at the top of the sloped aisle. This gave him a view of every cell lining the walls of the soldier's station, and he finally spotted them.

The soldiers.

Seven guards surrounded a small drainage grate in the far corner of a distant cell. Four had their crossbows aimed at the grate, their shoulders tense as they waited, and the other three had their palms raised in front of them. The green ink along their exposed forearms glowed with Saldian magic, and flickers of light floated over one woman's hand as she scowled at the floor.

The ambush. Owen was right.

Connor gestured for his team to join him. Owen peered over the edge of the ladder as he scanned the environment for threats, but he ultimately hoisted himself out of the access tunnel. Sophia followed, and then Murdoc. The former Blackguard reached for the hatch to close it once more, but Connor shook his head.

The crates blocked all view of the hatch, and the soldiers hadn't surrounded this one—which meant they didn't know about it. If he and his team needed a quick escape, they couldn't waste a second on their way out.

Murdoc quietly saluted and knelt beside Sophia as all four of them clustered together to regroup.

"Don't speak when we're in there," Connor whispered to the prince, his voice muffled by the cloth over his mouth. Even without it, his voice was low enough to ensure the guards on the opposite end of the prison didn't hear him. "We can't risk any of the soldiers or prisoners recognizing your voice."

"Fair," Owen whispered back, his voice equally muffled by his mask.

As the prince spoke, one of the prisoners shifted their weight again, and the captive leaned forward into the torchlight. He had a mop of blond hair and a crooked nose, but Connor hadn't seen his face before.

The other stood, metal shackles clanking, and paced his small jail cell. This second man stepped into the torchlight at the edge of his cell, and his face struck a hollow chord in the back of Connor's mind.

Rockwell rubbed the dark bags beneath his eyes. The chains around his wrists clanked as he leaned his face into his hands with a heavy sigh. His graying hair, still flecked with bits of black even after all these years, stuck out at odd angles. The green ink on his exposed arms was dull and lifeless, which likely meant those cuffs had a Bluntmar on them.

Good. He was alive.

Owen nudged Connor and pointed at the man in the other occupied cell. "That's the Captain of the Guard. I bet he will ask us to free him and spy on us until he can get information back to my father."

Connor frowned and studied the blond man's face again, but the haggard figure hunched forward like any other criminal headed for the gallows. Dirt stained the underside of his nails, and greasy stains in his threadbare shirt suggested he hadn't bathed in ages.

"He certainly knows how to play the part, then," Connor admitted.

"He's good." Owen swallowed hard as he stared at the commander. "If anyone's going to recognize me, it's him."

Noted.

Murdoc and Sophia adjusted the cloths over their mouths as they both watched the seven soldiers gathered around the grate. Tension crackled through the air, as though the guards would flinch and fire off an early round at any moment.

"That's a sparse ambush," Sophia muttered.

"Agreed," Murdoc said. "I figured a dozen more would've been loitering around those tables, ready to catch any stragglers."

"Father doesn't think the Shades can actually reach the dungeon," Owen explained. "Those seven are mostly a contingency. His forces are spread too thin, and he's focusing his remaining manpower on the tunnels."

"They're on edge," Connor observed. "You're sure they don't know we're coming?"

"They probably heard the screams," Murdoc interjected. "Shrieks of terror have a way of drawing attention."

Sophia shrugged. "Depends on where you are."

Owen's brow furrowed, and his gaze darted between the three of them. "Seriously, who *are* you people?"

"Focus," Connor chided.

I will make quick work of them, the Wraith King said gleefully. *Now, to decide which dies first—*

"No," Connor whispered, as quietly as possible. "There would be witnesses."

Beside him, Owen stiffened. He kept his attention focused on the soldiers' ambush, and the only indication he'd heard anything was the subtle twitch of his ear.

The Wraith King groaned in disgust, but the old ghost thankfully didn't argue.

One of the unarmed soldiers unhooked a horn from his belt and held it tightly. He took a wary step backward, away from the metal grate, and the green ink along his arms burned even more brightly than before.

Terrified.

"We have to get those horns," Owen said. "They're deafening, and the entire castle will hear it. We can't risk any more soldiers charging in here until we're gone."

A good point.

"Alright, here's the plan. Sophia, tell us what you've got in that bag of yours that can give us some cover between here and there. Smoke, perhaps, or a bit of fog."

The necromancer smirked victoriously and rifled through the pack on her shoulder. "Take your pick. I could also melt them."

Yes, the ghoul replied. *I say we choose that method.*

Connor rubbed his eyes in frustration and, once again, opted not to respond.

"We need to divide and conquer." Murdoc pointed to the barred double doors on the far wall, beyond the soldier's station. "That beam is probably enchanted, but even that wouldn't be enough to keep reinforcements out. We need to move quickly and assume more soldiers will barge through at any second."

Connor grinned. "I take it you've infiltrated a few dungeons in your time?"

"A few," Murdoc admitted with a lazy shrug. "I'm something of a natural, you might say."

Owen sighed, but this time the prince didn't comment.

"I agree," Sophia added as she pulled three potion bottles from her bag. "As much as I'm sure you want to lead the charge, Connor, it's better for you and our guest here to find the prisoner while Murdoc and I handle these fools. Let us out ahead of you so that we can give you cover."

"Make sure you destroy that horn," Owen said.

"Yes, yes, fine." Sophia waved away his concern with a flick of her slender wrist. "We heard you."

"Sounds like a plan." Connor shifted his position behind the crates to allow room for the others to go through ahead of him. "After you, then."

Murdoc nodded and drew his sword. Sophia darted ahead, and it took effort for Connor to stay put. Letting his team walk into the line of fire before him felt wrong—cowardly, even—but those two knew how to hold their own.

Once the two of them had a head start, Connor followed. Owen darted behind him, and the four whisper-silent figures slunk through the shadows on their way to the torchlit platform.

As they reached the top of the sloping path toward the soldiers, Sophia tucked the three bottles under one arm and aimed her slender fingers at the horn in one soldier's hand. Frost crept over her skin as her augmentations glowed, and a blistering ball of ice launched from her fingertips. Before it could even hit, however, she threw all three of her potions at the open cell door, and a plume of white smoke erupted from the broken glass. The haze engulfed the soldiers in seconds. Something shattered in the fog, and the guards' frantic yelling followed.

This was Connor's chance.

He and Owen ran toward Rockwell's cell as blinding blasts of light shot out of the smoke. Silhouettes ran blindly through the haze, backlit by each bolt of white light, and several ran face-first into the cell's iron bars.

As much as he wanted to help them, Sophia and Murdoc were right. They had to divide and conquer, then get the hell out.

Both prisoners ran to the edge of their cells and grabbed the bars to watch the fray. The man with blond hair watched in horror, his knuckles white from his painfully tight grip, and his brow furrowed as he focused intently on the massacre happening four cells over.

Definitely a guard, then, and not a true prisoner. Yet again, Owen had told the truth.

Rockwell, however, never took his eyes off Connor. His mouth set in a grim line, and the deep creases of worry appeared among the wrinkles in his forehead. A flicker of fear snapped through his gray eyes.

Afraid of him, like everyone else.

As they reached Rockwell's cell, Connor quickly glanced at the melee happening at the end of the aisle. Murdoc stood at the edge of the haze as a dagger launched out of the smoke, and the former Blackguard sidestepped it with ease.

The Wraith King laughed, dark and deep. *Don't tell me you're jealous of all the fun they're having.*

In answer, Connor simply frowned.

"Get the hell out of here!" Rockwell took several steps backward to put plenty of space between him and freedom. "Both of you. That's an order!"

"Sorry, Liam," Connor said. "I don't take your orders."

He gestured for Owen to unlock the cell and cast another wary glance around the prison for any signs of backup hidden among the other cells.

In the cell next to Rockwell's, the disguised Captain of the Guard finally pried his eyes away from the chaos down the aisle. He shuffled closer and opened his mouth to speak. When he met Connor's gaze, however, the words seemed to die in his throat. There was a flash of recognition in his eyes, and the man froze.

Connor had never seen this man before, but that didn't mean much. Whether this soldier recognized him as the Shade or as the boy who had fled Kirkwall all those years ago, the fool was trapped.

"You're staying here," Connor warned in a hushed tone. "And you're not going to say a damn thing. You will sit there quietly, and if you use any of your augmentations, you'll die just like them."

Connor nodded down the aisle to prove his point.

The blond man's grip tightened on the bars, and he scowled. His flurry of panic was quickly replaced with barely restrained rage, and deep lines creased his forehead as his brows furrowed.

"Keep an eye on him," Connor whispered to the wraith. "If he tries anything, have at him."

The ghoul chuckled gleefully.

"I won't—I can't—" Rockwell sucked in a pained breath, and his stoic façade faded. "Boys, I can't risk you dying with me on those gallows, you hear? Get out of this hellhole. Save yourselves."

Something clicked, then, and Connor shifted his attention back to Rockwell. The man wasn't scared of him at all.

He was scared *for* him.

Owen growled in frustration as he fought to get the key into the lock.

The door rattled, and he leaned down to shove his shoulder against the enchanted metal in an effort to drive it deeper.

"We don't have time for this, damn it!" Rockwell snapped. "There are ambushes everywhere! I'm bait, boys. Fates be blessed that those bastards ran out of Hackamores, so they couldn't wring me for names, but they want as many of you as—"

"It's handled," Connor said flatly. "Now move. There's not much time until reinforcements arrive."

"It—you couldn't possibly have—" The man stumbled forward in a wild dash toward the jail bars. He grabbed the steel rods and pressed his face against the cold metal as he peered out at the chaotic haze by the door. The grunts and scuffle of the fight filled the air, along with the occasional sniffle from deeper down in the dungeons. Metal rattled, and the hollow echo of a rock plopping into water floated from the depths of the prison's darkness.

But no additional guards rushed through the doors.

"Bless the Fates." Rockwell rubbed his eyes, and his shoulders shook with either silent laughter or barely restrained tears. "This can't be real. They told me it's the gallows at dawn."

"It's real," Connor promised.

A latch clicked, and a sigh of relief followed. With an irritated huff, Owen set his foot on the iron bars and roughly yanked the enchanted key from the lock. Once freed, the door swung open, and Owen slipped the key in his pocket.

Rockwell stumbled through the jail cell, a slight limp to his left leg, and a thin smile tugged on the man's mouth. He set one hand on Owen's shoulder and squeezed. "Smart move, staying quiet. You become a better leader every day, kid."

Huh.

Apparently, Rockwell had recognized Owen without a word spoken between them. It suggested a familiarity that Connor hadn't expected. An affinity, almost. Perhaps Owen was Rockwell's prodigy after all, just as Victor's allies had feared.

Silently, Owen pointed toward the cluster of crates leading to the storage area and beckoned for Rockwell to follow.

Rockwell, however, ignored him.

"I know you," the man said, his eyes locked on Connor.

"Not now." Connor closed the jail cell door in an unspoken demand that they move.

"It can't be," Rockwell whispered.

"This isn't the time," Connor said curtly.

"This is the only time," Rockwell countered. His voice was every bit as firm and unwavering as it had been in Connor's youth, any time the man caught one of his friend's children causing mischief.

Connor, mostly. The others could never hope to compare to the hell he had raised as a boy.

With a cursory glance around the empty cells, Rockwell reached for Connor's mask. Connor snapped his head backward, out of reach, and grabbed the man's wrist.

"What the hell are you—"

"I need to know it's you, Connor."

Connor's jaw tensed, and he froze. To hear Rockwell say his name again, all these years later and after he'd been sure the man was dead—it disarmed him more than any potion ever could.

With a resigned groan, Connor lowered the cloth covering his mouth. It was a quick motion, only revealing enough for Rockwell to get the confirmation he needed, before Connor once again slid it over his nose.

Rockwell's entire body relaxed. The man stared up at him, stunned, and a lifetime of pain faded from the hard lines in his forehead. "Bless the Fates. It's really you."

Beside them, Owen's confused gaze darted between the two of them. He nudged Connor with his elbow in a silent request that they hurry the hell up.

"Look, I'll explain later," Connor promised. "For now, we have to leave."

"Soon. Buy me time." Rockwell patted him on the arm and darted in the opposite direction, toward a lone cell at the end of the footpath, set apart from the others by an angled curve in the downward slope. A silhouette in the cell's deepest shadows crawled forward, and a man's grunt of pain followed.

Connor grabbed Rockwell's sleeve, and the man came to an abrupt stop. "Have you lost your damn mind?"

His father's lifelong friend was the only reason they'd come to this Fates-damned hellhole, and the man seemed oddly reluctant to leave.

"I have to right an old wrong." Rockwell tried and failed to slap Connor's hand off his tunic, and that only made Connor's grip tighten. "You were only a boy. You wouldn't understand, but I have to do this."

"What could possibly—"

"See for yourself, then!"

Without another word, the man pointed at the cell at the far end of the path, right where the rough stone flooring curved and sloped downward to the next floor of cells. A silhouette shuffled forward from the back of the cell, but the dungeon's endless shadows obscured the figure's face.

Connor stifled a frustrated growl. "What the hell are you—"

"Take me with you!" The figure in the shadows stuck a filthy arm through the bars. Clusters of dirt under the man's nails stained them brown, and he desperately clawed at the air. "You can't leave me here to die! You're Shades, right? You have to help!"

Connor's blood ran cold.

He knew that voice.

His breath caught in his chest. The edges of his vision went black. He let go of Rockwell's shirt and gaped at the darkness. The whispers and rattling of a half-empty dungeon faded away into the shrill ringing in his ears, and he could only stare at the lone figure in half-mad horror.

In the years after escaping Kirkwall, that voice had plagued his nightmares.

"Better you than me, kid."

That voice had laughed at him as he relived his fall from the cliff. It had echoed, over and over, even after he shook off his terrors and finally woke up.

Bryan Clark.

That Fates-damned *bastard.*

A rush of smoke rolled over his arms, and the blackfire on one of his enchanted swords surged with a flash of heat. The weapon had come to him on impulse, as though it was a living thing that could read his mind, and he gripped it tightly.

Rockwell set his hand on Connor's shoulder, and the man's touch finally snapped him from his daze. Somewhere behind them, Owen's footsteps shuffled closer, and he grumbled incoherently to himself as they ignored his gestures for them to follow.

But Owen didn't understand. He couldn't possibly realize what was at stake, or why the two of them refused to move.

"Came in the day after I did." Rockwell's voice was eerily cold and devoid of any sympathy. It dripped with all the hatred and loathing Connor had felt for all these years. "That rancid coward is lucky I couldn't reach him. I've never wanted to snap a man's neck so badly, son, but I never thought I'd get to see you again. Maybe that's the Fates' way of telling me that I'm not the one to right this wrong."

"We have to go!" Owen's words took on a comically deep tone as he did his best to mask his voice.

"Give us the key," Connor ordered.

Owen's footsteps trotted closer, and the man appeared in Connor's periphery. "What's the matter with you? Reinforcements can't be far away. We need to get the hell out—"

"Do it." Rockwell opened his hand and gestured for Owen to hand it over.

The prince let out a strangled growl of frustration, but fished the key out of his pocket and slammed it in Rockwell's open palm. "It won't be long before the shift change, and we have to be out of the castle by then. Whatever this is, we can't waste time on it!"

"You know the way back." Connor's voice had a soulless, hollow echo to it. Vacant, almost.

It barely sounded like him at all.

"Are you insane? I just—" The prince scoffed and glared at Connor over the mask covering half his face. "You can't be serious. What if they catch you?"

"They won't," Connor said firmly.

"But—"

Connor's head snapped toward the prince. It was the first movement he'd made since the blackfire blades appeared, and something in his expression stopped Owen dead in his tracks. Above the mask that covered his mouth, the man's eyes widened with fear.

"We'll meet you there." Rockwell crossed his arms over his chest and leaned against an empty stretch of the prison wall.

To his credit, Owen simply nodded. He cast one wary glance back at Connor, but ultimately jogged back up the sloping path toward Murdoc and Sophia. The pair caught Connor's eye, and he tilted his head toward the prince in a silent request that they follow.

Sophia quirked one eyebrow, but Murdoc saluted and ushered Sophia ahead of him as they darted after their ticket out of here.

"Not sure what magic this is," Rockwell said with a gesture toward Connor's blade. "I don't much care, to be honest. All I want to know is if that'll hurt him as much as I think it will."

Connor nodded.

"Good." Rockwell pointed at the man who had betrayed Connor's family. "That son of a bitch is responsible for that whole night. He turned your father in, threw him in the line of fire to save his own selfish skin, and a few Hackamores later, your father was forced to out his lifelong friends. That man brought down the smuggling ring out of sheer cowardice, and all of Kirkwall suffered for it. Miriam—" Rockwell's voice caught as he said his late wife's name. "If not for this coward, my beautiful Miriam would still be here. Your father would still be alive. Everyone you know and love would still be around today if not for him."

That white-hot rage pushed against his palm yet again. Fueled by his hatred, the enchanted blackfire on his blade surged and engulfed the dark steel.

"He dies at dawn, son," Rockwell added under his breath. "Let's save the executioner some trouble."

Connor didn't reply. Seeing that coward after all these years rooted him to the floor. If he moved even one inch, he didn't know if he could contain the rage snapping through his body.

As cruel as the Fates could be, they sometimes delivered blessings. It was rare, of course, but the rewards were great.

If he ever met them, he would have to thank them for this.

CHAPTER SIXTY-TWO

CONNOR

Connor wasn't sure who had unlocked the cell door. Focused as he was on the trembling prisoner inside, he didn't register much at all until the latch clicked.

Before the cell could even open, Connor kicked it in. Iron screamed and twisted under his raw strength. He didn't care how much noise he made.

Something primal had overtaken him. Something raw. Something *hateful.* It corroded his self-control.

In this moment, nothing mattered but crushing Bryan Clark's throat with his bare hands.

Bryan scuttled backward in a futile attempt to put distance between them. The man's eyes widened with unrestrained terror, and his dirt-stained hand slipped on a wet clump of hay in his desperate bid for a few more seconds of life.

The sour bite of sweat coiled through the air in the cell like fumes off a bog. Connor entered, and his boots flattened the loose strands of hay strewn about the floor on his way toward the man who had destroyed his life.

"I'm innocent! I swear!" Bryan raised his hands over his head to shield himself from Connor's wrath. "I was in the wrong place at the wrong time. When I showed up in that alley, that woman was already dead. I couldn't—"

"You haven't changed." Connor's free hand tightened into a furious ball at the man's cowardice. "Still murdering. Still running. Too stupid to leave Kirkwall behind, and why? Are we easy marks for you?"

We.

It had come out so easily. After so long away from the island, he had tried to convince himself he didn't belong here anymore. Slaybourne was his home, now, but Kirkwall would always flow deep in his blood.

And he would always protect its people.

With a swift tug, Connor removed the mask covering his face. He had to know if this bastard even remembered what he had done to Connor's family, all those years ago.

Bryan's frantic eyes widened withgaze shifted between the two of them before a flash of recognition crossed his face. "You look familiar."

"I should," Connor said flatly. "After all, you looked me in the eye when you pushed me off that cliff."

Bryan went eerily still, and the blood drained from his face. He stared up at Connor in horror, and that look of raw terror was almost satisfying.

Almost.

It was what Connor had dreamed of in the dark, miserable southern woodland. In the pelting rain, when he had huddled in whatever cave he could find, shivering and praying no beast came looking for shelter, too. In the blistering sun, when he was working yet another farmer's homestead in the hopes of earning a bit of coin and enough food to ward off starvation. In those nights when he had almost wished death would come for him, to end the misery, he'd always imagined the same thing.

A fever-dream, of sorts, that had kept his hatred alive.

In those horrible moments when he hadn't thought he could keep going, he'd pictured Bryan in a tavern, chasing skirts and living his life a free man.

It had always been his fuel, and that rage would inevitably push him to at least survive until dawn. Back then, when he was broken and alone, it was often the only thing that had kept him going.

"What happened to you?" Bryan asked, breathless.

Connor's eyes narrowed. "I grew up."

"I'm so grateful you're alive." The criminal tried to smile, but the corner of his mouth simply twitched in the vain attempt. "I felt awful. That—pushing you—it was an accident. I never meant for you to get hurt, and I've carried that guilt with me ever since."

"Don't lie to me," Connor warned.

"You don't know what happened that night." The criminal on the floor set one palm in front of him, as though that could quell Connor's rage. "Your father, he tripped me on our way down that path. He was going to turn me in. I had to protect myself, and I panicked. I swear, that's all it was. I never meant to bump into you on that cliffside. You understand, don't you? Can you ever forgive me?"

A cold, deadly jolt crackled through Connor's veins. It corroded his self-restraint, and he momentarily lost control.

He grabbed Bryan by the neck and hoisted the man into the air. With a furious growl, he slammed Bryan against the wall, and a loud thud echoed through the quiet prison. Bryan gasped in pain and horror, his nails digging into Connor's hand as he gasped for breath. Every muscle in Connor's body tensed, and his bicep bulged as he held this putrid coward in place.

"I warned you not to lie." Though Connor felt the words rumbling in his chest, he didn't recognize his own voice. It was darker and deeper than ever before, heavy and hollow, and it sent a terrifying chill through the very air. Every bit of his body hummed with power and rage, as though he could summon the sky itself to do his bidding with a mere command.

The world around him went eerily still.

As his grip tightened on the hilt of his sword, something crackled over his skin. It blistered and snapped at the air, fierce and raging, as more of that strange heat shot up his arm. Still numb, still almost vacant in his raw fury, he slowly looked down at his weapon to figure out what the hell it was.

Blackfire.

Dark gray flames crackled over his sword, yes, but now also over his hand. It engulfed the weapon, hilt and all, as the crackling bonfire snapped over his skin. It didn't hover, either, like Quinn's fire in her palm—this rolled over his skin as though his fury alone could feed it. Though it bit at him like a whip hitting his skin, it didn't burn. It didn't ache.

If anything, it gave him strength.

Doom's low growl pulsed through his mind, deep and curious, but the Dragon King still didn't speak.

Even if he couldn't control it, it seemed as though Connor had adopted more of Doom's power than the ancient dragon had expected.

The blackfire went out with a violent hiss, and though Connor waited for it to return, it didn't. The seconds dragged on, and Bryan wriggled in his grasp, still wheezing for air.

The criminal's wheezing gasp hit Connor like a windstorm, and it blew away everything else. Doom. The Wraith King. Sophia. Murdoc. Quinn. Nothing and no one else mattered in this moment unless it could wring justice from this coward's sniveling whimpers.

"You don't deserve that breath." The haunting rumble in Connor's voice froze the air, and the full weight of his fury rested squarely on Bryan. "There is no punishment worthy of what you've done. No death is cruel enough. I couldn't possibly make you feel the pain you've caused this island, nor could I ever hurt you as much as you've hurt the ones you took from me. I can't carve the horror of eight years in the Ancient Woods into you. I can't burn you, break you, or bleed you enough to make you understand the grief and pain I've lived with for nearly a decade. I can't carve out of you what you stole from me—but that doesn't mean I won't try."

My rage stays on the battlefield, he'd once told Wesley. *Forgiveness isn't for them. It's for you.*

Back in the Ancient Woods, he had lied to himself and to Wesley. He had learned to fight not to protect himself from the horrors of the forest, but in the vain hope that he would one day see Bryan again. When he did, Connor wanted to know he could stab the man through the heart and watch him die.

He'd already had a taste of revenge, after all. He had avenged the Finns. He had murdered every slaver that had hurt them, and he had only allowed one to go free as a warning to the other criminals. If they were still alive, they would have only continued to destroy lives.

Those were dangerous people, and he had killed them all.

But that didn't erase what the Finns had endured. They would relive those days in their nightmares, and those were scars no potion could heal.

Sometimes you need the anger, he had said, what felt like ages ago in Slaybourne's peaceful forest. *It gets you through the hardest parts of life. Just don't let it burn away who you are.*

Connor gritted his teeth, furious at the words even as they echoed through his thoughts. The tip of his blackfire blade crackled on the air, a breath away from Bryan's skull. The pitiful bastard whimpered in the soft gray light radiating from the blades.

It's hard. The memory of his father's warning from long ago shot through his head like an arrow to the skull. Connor grimaced as the dead man's voice echoed, louder than his own thoughts. *Don't let anger burn away who you are, son. There's more to you than hate.*

His throat tightened, and though his heart still raced with his barely restrained fury, his breath slowed.

This was the life the Fates had given him—and the one they had given Bryan. Each man had made his choices, and perhaps the Fates were watching to see what he would do next.

This was a test—of his courage, perhaps, or his strength of will.

As much as he hated to admit the truth, it wasn't his place to decide Bryan's fate. Maybe his unfettered rage made him weak, but he didn't care.

Bryan was responsible for so much death. For loss. For grief. For the sort of wounds that never heal. He had tried to escape tonight, and with so few soldiers manning the castle's dungeons, there was a chance that he would succeed.

The man hadn't learned anything.

This coward hadn't changed.

Connor's palms burned hot with all the rage and magic of the Dragon King, and Bryan winced as heat radiated from the hand that held him to the wall. Connor waited for the fire to return, to engulf this bastard and burn him to ash, but it didn't. The criminal scratched at Connor's wrist, but Connor barely felt the nails digging into his skin.

He could barely feel anything at all.

His whole body had gone numb. The world around him—the dungeon, the dead guards on the floor outside this cell, the impending doom of reinforcements that would arrive any second—he didn't care about any of it.

He wanted *blood.*

Bryan must've seen something shift in his face, because the man stuttered incoherently until he was able to form words. "Y-you can't kill me."

Connor raised one eyebrow, astonished at the man's brazen comment. "Oh?"

"Y-you're the Shade," Bryan stuttered, either out of fear or because of the fingers digging into his throat. "I've heard about you. Y-you're supposed to be a hero. Heroes don't do this."

"You wouldn't know," Connor snapped, his voice dark and deep. "Don't preach to me about heroics, you fucking *coward*."

Bryan winced again, and his eyes squeezed shut as the trembling worsened. Connor's grip tightened to keep the man pinned in place, and Bryan gagged as the subtle movement cut off even more of his airway. The putrid stink of urine coiled from the criminal, and a slow trickle dripped from the man's leg onto the floor.

Connor's nose creased in disgust. "You're pathetic. That the people I loved died so you could save your worthless hide is *sickening*."

"Not much time left," Rockwell warned.

Rockwell's voice snapped Connor from his hyperfocused hatred, and he cast the briefest glance over his shoulder at the man who had helped shape his childhood. Rockwell had steered him true almost as much as his father, though the lessons he'd always taught were simpler. Straightforward. Fierce.

Rockwell was a man of fists, more than wisdom.

In this dank pit of despair deep below Kirkwall Castle, none of his father's life lessons floated from the depths of his mind. No caution against man's baser instincts. No golden moments toting forgiveness.

There was only silence, and the quiet splosh of urine hitting a growing puddle below Bryan's dangling feet.

Bryan gaped down at him, gasping for each breath, and his eyes were wide with panic. "A-are you going to k-kill me?"

Maybe.

He sure as hell *wanted* to.

Whatever Connor did next, he had spectators. He couldn't forget that. Rockwell. Doom. Death. Even the Wraith King had been eerily silent this whole time. Each had their own judgments about what had to be done, and each was waiting to see if he would do it.

No matter what he did, he risked losing *someone's* respect. There was no right choice, so he figured the only thing that mattered was the respect he had for *himself*.

The blackfire sword disappeared from his free hand, and the dark haze rolled over his forearm. It dispersed into the air between him and the man responsible for his family's deaths, and for a moment, everything was still.

Silent.

Breathless.

"A forgiving man wouldn't kill you," he admitted. "My father would've told me to let you go to the gallows. You die either way."

"T-thank you." Bryan let out a trembling sigh of relief. "Y-you're a merciful—"

"But because of you," Connor interrupted, "my father's not here to stop me."

In one fluid motion, he grabbed Bryan's jaw and forced the man's head backward into the wall. A sickening crack echoed through the prison, and Connor twisted the man's head sharply to the side. A second crack boomed through the still air, louder than the first. Bryan's grip on his wrist loosened, and the criminal's arms hung limply at his side.

Connor released his grip on the man's throat, and Bryan collapsed into a puddle of his own piss.

As the final flicker of life faded from Bryan's eyes, a shrill ringing buzzed in Connor's ear. It trilled like an insect, low and steady. The quiet hum tuned out the dungeon around him. Whatever he had been hoping to feel as he stared at the body never came.

He watched at the corpse for too long, spellbound and numb.

A hand grabbed his shoulder, and Connor flinched. After so many years of brawls and near-death experiences, he cocked his arm to punch whoever had touched him.

But it was just Rockwell, and Connor held back.

Rockwell stood behind him, one hand resting on his shoulder, and the man watched his face from beneath furrowed brows. Deep lines of worry creased Rockwell's forehead, and his grim frown only worsened the longer he studied Connor's face.

"It's done," Rockwell said firmly. "Let's go."

With one last glance at Bryan's corpse, Connor nodded. He lifted the cloth over his nose once again to hide his features and followed Rockwell out of the prison.

Doom hadn't spoken. Death hadn't interfered. The Wraith King stayed silent.

Something about tonight had felt like more than revenge. More than justice. Tonight, the tides of Saldia had shifted—but he wouldn't know if it was in his favor until it was too late to change course.

CHAPTER SIXTY-THREE

TOVE

Tove woke to a pang of icy dread.

She sat upright in bed and set one hand on her chest as her pulse raced. Her breath came in quick bursts as she tried desperately to figure out what had woken her this time, but the night was silent.

Still.

How strange, given the summer festivities happening throughout the kingdom. Even in the middle of the night, there was chatter, reverie, and light. It was part of what had kept her so on edge for these past few days. Every voice felt like a threat, and every footstep was an omen of approaching danger.

Muffled laughter filtered through her window, quiet and far enough away that it couldn't have been what woke her. Exhausted, anxious, and fed up after so many sleepless nights, she rubbed her eyes. Her long hair slid over her shoulders, and she pinched the bridge of her nose as she debated turning over and falling back asleep.

The low rumble of men's voices filtered through the glass panes from the north side of the courtyard outside her window, and she stiffened.

"It's a festival," she said under her breath, chiding herself. "Calm down, woman. You're safe. You're alright."

But a nagging sensation at the back of her mind didn't believe her, and she wouldn't be able to relax until she checked the window.

With a frustrated grumble, Tove slipped out of bed and knelt by the curtains, fully dressed and ready to run if the need called for it. She had taken to sleeping in her traveling clothes, just in case someone came for her in the dead of night, and all of her important possessions were stored in secret vaults set up under fake names. Everything was ready for her to disappear in an instant, should the need arise.

Cautiously—and, frankly, feeling like an utter lunatic for acting this way—she peered through the thinnest gap possible.

Below her window, three men rounded a corner and headed into the courtyard. They leaned toward each other, brows furrowed as they debated something intensely, and their path led them directly past her house. None of them climbed her front stairs, however, and not one of the men even glanced toward her shop. Within moments, they disappeared around another bend, and their conversation finally faded.

Exasperated as all hell, Tove set her forehead against the windowpane and sighed. Her eyes fluttered closed, and tired as she was, she nearly fell asleep right there, kneeling by the window.

Her heart panged—hard, and just once—and her head snapped up again. She cursed under her breath, frustrated and absolutely *done* with all of this stress and fear.

And yet, she couldn't make it stop. Her heart slammed against her rib-cage, wilder this time. It flared with all the panicked warning of a monster in the dark, despite the empty courtyard.

Maybe she needed to leave. Maybe this was more than she could handle. The waiting. The not knowing. The speculation about what she should do until Quinn returned, and the terror of wondering if her friend was ever coming back.

To make things worse, Tove had no way to let Quinn know where she had gone save for the few cryptic clues stashed around the house. To be safe, however, Tove had been forced to make them utterly cryptic and vague. Frankly, she wasn't sure if even Quinn could figure them out.

Tove was trapped in the very home that had brought her so much joy for all these years.

Through the window, something darted out of the dark alley on the other side of the courtyard. Tove stiffened once again, and she peered through the thin gap in her curtain to figure out what it was.

A stray dog, probably, or a few mischievous children out past curfew.

Infuriating, really, but the panic hummed through her all the same.

In the midnight darkness, the fountain's water was almost as black as the sky. It bubbled and splashed across the stone roses at the marbled feet of a dead king. Lamps surrounded the stone square, casting shadows across the fountain as water rippled through its basin, but the world was silent once more.

Until one of the lamps went out, and that shadow darted closer.

Tove pressed her shoulder against the wall, and a cold flicker of terror thrummed through her body. She waited for it to happen again, breathless as she watched, and her fingertips went cold as ice as the fear took hold.

She wanted this to be another close call.

Tired as she was, she still wanted to be wrong.

Another of the lamps went out, closer this time. The shadow darted through the darkness left by the extinguished light, and this time, the hazy outline of another silhouette joined the first.

A third light went out, even closer this time, and the pattern was clear. Whoever these people were—and whoever they worked for—they were heading toward her house with all the stealth and skill of professional assassins.

Tove went numb with the realization, and for a moment, she couldn't move. She could only sit there in a terrified daze, frozen in place by her fear, as these strangers darted toward her in the dark.

She could imagine them kicking in the door. Grabbing her. Shoving a gag in her mouth and binding her wrists. In the noise of the year's loudest celebration, her cries for help would never be heard.

It would've been genius if she weren't the one they were hunting.

The thought of them dragging her away snapped her from her daze, and she stood. Her body moved on its own, going through the motions she had practiced so many times since Quinn's last visit, and she barely registered any of it. The bag resting on a chair by the door was suddenly on her shoulder. Her boots appeared on her feet. She was suddenly downstairs, and every passing second, the shrill ringing in her ear got a little louder.

With a quick gate and shallow breaths, Tove darted through the empty front rooms of her shop. The shelves, the bookcases, the walls—everything was bare. The only evidence of her time here was the large throne where her clients sat for each augmentation.

She felt grief every time she walked through here, yes, but also gratitude. If these people really were coming here, Quinn's warning had saved her from losing her life's work—and maybe her life.

At the front door, she peeked as cautiously as she could through the window, careful to keep to the darkness as much as possible. Another light went out, and only one lamp remained between her and the approaching silhouettes.

They were *definitely* headed here.

Damn it. Hopefully none of them went around to the back door. They likely thought of her as a harmless augmentor who wasn't even good enough to be in the Spell Market, and she hoped they underestimated her. It would make this much easier.

She tugged a glass bottle from her bag and set it on a thin shelf that rested squarely on the bell above her door. The moment it rang—or if they reached for the bell to silence it—the potion would fall, and a nasty plume of smoke would choke them until they ran back out into the fresh air.

With that trap set, she ran back toward the stairs to set the others. With a delicate flourish, she summoned water from a metal pot in the corner. It snaked upward in a whirling spiral, and she stretched her fingers toward the floor between her and the door. The water obeyed, and it washed across the wooden planks.

Tove yanked a second bottle from her bag, and this time she poured it on the wet floor. Ice formed the second the Crackmane potion hit the water, and the sheet of icy death stretched quickly across the floorboards. It perfectly mirrored the wood, and her attackers wouldn't see it until they fell squarely on their asses.

But there wasn't any time to gloat.

Though there were more traps upstairs, she wouldn't get the chance to set them. Instead, she stepped over a thin trip wire running the full width of her hallway to the kitchen and uncorked one last bottle from her bag. With a twinge of guilt, she set the Duvolia potion on a thin shelf that was rigged to break if anyone so much as breathed on the tripwire.

Someone was going to die a horrible death tonight, and it would be her fault.

Her augmented ears twitched as the almost dead-silent whisper of footsteps on her front stairs.

They were here.

Tove darted to the back door and peeked through the curtain covering the narrow window in its center. The back road leading to the high street market was still, and a ginger cat trotted lazily across the cobblestone in the silent evening.

The handle on her front door turned. Locked and charmed as it was, it would slow them down—but not for long.

She set a trembling hand on her only way out of the house, still hoping against hope that they were underestimating her enough to leave this exit unmonitored, and she slipped out into the night.

The cool summer night sent a chill over her arms. She had purposefully not lit the lanterns on her house, but the neighbors' lights raged brightly. It offered just enough cover to look for any signs of danger, but she couldn't linger. The door closed behind her, and she rested her back briefly against the wood as she quickly scanned the dark street.

Boots shuffled across the stone beside her. With a stifled gasp, she spun toward it—but not quickly enough.

A man's callused hand grabbed her wrist, and another clamped down over her mouth. She yelled muffled curses as he pinned her arms behind her back. Though she wriggled, trying desperately to break free, his grip only tightened.

Inside her home, the front door creaked open. Glass shattered, and the sour stench of a skunk's cologne rolled from under the thin crack beneath the back door. Men coughed and sputtered, their cursing muffled by the door as she fought to break free from her attacker.

The man pulled her close, and the satchel on her back slammed hard against his chest. Her curses became panicked sobs as he cut off circulation to her wrists—likely with intention, to keep her from accessing her magic.

This bastard had her pinned.

Tove wasn't a fighter. She was the scholar, the mad alchemist who helped the warriors from afar with knowledge and wit. This was entirely outside of her comfort zone, and the frigid panic sent tremors through her body.

Without access to her magic or the potions in her bag, she had absolutely no chance of escape.

"This is going to happen," he growled into her ear. "If you keep fighting me, I'll make your life hell once we get where we're going. Your choice."

The sensation of his breath on her neck triggered more frantic wriggling, but his grip never wavered. She whimpered, horrified, but there was nothing more she could do.

The still night shifted around them, and a gale kicked through the sky. Her eyes darted around in her head, desperate to figure out if he was using some sort of Airdrift augmentation to do this, and she frantically debated her options.

Truth be told, she didn't have many.

A hard thwack shook the man's body, and he went strangely still. His grip on her mouth loosened, and this time, she managed to wriggle free. He stumbled to the side, and his shoulder slammed against the door. His face was covered in a hood, and a mask covered his mouth. He tugged both off, and if he weren't trying to kidnap her, she might've swooned over those dark eyes and that chiseled jaw.

Blood streamed down his neck and into his shirt. Dazed, he ran one hand across the back of his head and stared at the dark crimson smears left behind on his fingers.

"I'll kill you." He spoke calmly, as though it were a matter of fact and not a threat. His dark eyes shifted toward her, steady and cold, and he simply stared at her in the seconds that followed.

That broke her spell of terror, and Tove tried to run.

The gale picked up, blowing harder than before, and it pushed against her. She raised her arms to shield her face, even as the wind pushed her backward across the cobblestone toward her attacker. With one final gust, she fell hard onto the ground. Her elbow slammed against a stone, and she barely stifled the scream as an agonizing jolt shot up her arm.

He grunted in pain, and Tove peered backward to find him slumped on the ground just as the gale around her quieted. Tremors of agony shot through her arm, and she cradled her elbow as she stared, horrified, through the tousled strands of hair now in her face.

Where the man had been before, Tove now saw a new threat—another figure clothed in black riding gear, with a hood over their face and a mask over their mouth, standing over his eerily still body. The newcomer watched him for a moment, and when he didn't move, the stranger's focus shifted to Tove.

A savior, perhaps—or another assassin, come to steal her away to a different hellhole.

Too quickly for her to register, the stranger tugged a dagger from a sheath on their thigh and lodged it in the stone beneath the door. The rock split open like butter as the blade was driven into the stoop, and the dagger's hilt acted as a makeshift lock to keep the door from opening.

Inside, a man screamed in agony. Another pang of guilt hit Tove squarely in the chest at the thought of someone being frozen to death with the Duvolia she had left out, but that meant they had crossed through her other traps and were far closer to her than she had realized.

She needed to get the hell out of here.

With her elbow still smarting, she awkwardly pushed herself to her feet with her good arm. Stumbling, her head still fuzzy from the fall, she did her best to run—but after all of the panic and chaos of tonight, not to mention the pain, it was a challenge just to stay upright.

In seconds, the stranger reached her and grabbed her good wrist. The newcomer ran, dragging her along behind them even as she tried her best to wrench free.

No good. Whoever this was, they were damn strong.

Her captor darted down a back alley and past rows of buckets that had collected this week's rainfall. Tove's heart panged with hope, and as the pain in her elbow finally diminished, she reached for the nearest pool of water.

The enchanted ink along her neck hummed as she accessed her Taratatum augmentation, and the water spiraled up into the air at her command.

With the rush of magic through her blood, her head finally cleared—and her voice finally returned.

"Let me *go*!" she shouted.

Tove pulled hard on the stranger's grip just as she shot the spiral of water at their face. Just as she hoped, they let go, and fire erupted in their palms moments before Tove's attack could hit. Steam coiled past them both, obscuring the alley with a blisteringly loud hiss.

This was her chance.

She bolted, but yet again, the stranger grabbed her wrist. This time, however, they pulled back their hood to reveal familiar fire-red hair. The woman watched her with fierce hazel eyes, and Tove recognized her friend in the second before Quinn Starling pulled down the mask covering her mouth.

Oh, thank the Fates.

Tove let out a sigh of relief, and the terror coursing through her very veins dissolved in an instant. She set her hands on her waist as she looked up at the sky, doing her best to catch her breath after all that running and panic.

"Tove, what the hell?" Quinn snapped, her voice a furious whisper. "Didn't you recognize me?"

Tove's eye twitched with irritation, and she gestured to Quinn's jet-black riding gear. "How could I possibly recognize you? You were wearing a hood! You looked just like the man who attacked me, damn it!"

"But I was saving you!"

"I know that *now*!" Tove rubbed her elbow again, though the pain was finally gone. "And you hurt me, Quinn. I was so damn *scared*!"

Quinn's face relaxed, and creases of worry appeared in her forehead. She reached for the injury, perhaps to heal it, but Tove waved her hand away.

"I'm sorry," the Starling warrior said softly. "I didn't mean to. I needed you to stay close, and you kept trying to run away. I couldn't let him see my face or hear my voice. That's why I made you follow me."

"It's fine." Tove's heart finally settled, and she could breathe more easily now. "Really, I'm alright."

"We can't stay here." Quinn cast a wary glance around the alley and pulled her hood over her head yet again. "If anyone sees—"

Tove didn't let her friend finish, and she pulled Quinn into a tight hug. The Starling warrior hesitated, even as Tove buried her face into Quinn's neck. Moments later, though, she coiled her arms around Tove's shoulders and held her just as tightly.

"You were right." Tove couldn't hide the tremor in her voice. "I can't believe they actually came for me."

Quinn sighed. "I'm sorry I got you into this mess."

"What the hell is going on?" Tove released her friend and paced the narrow alley between two rows of white brick homes. "Why did they come? What happened with—"

"We can't talk here," Quinn interjected. She pulled the mask over her face yet again and gestured for Tove to follow. "I'll tell you everything once we're safe."

"Everything?" Tove raised one dubious eyebrow.

Quinn met her doubtful glare, and after a moment of silence, she nodded. "Everything."

Oh.

Wow.

Her friend never shared details, mainly to keep Tove safe. This entire mess must've been so much worse than she had suspected.

"Did you leave anything at the house?" Quinn asked with a brief glance behind them. "Anything important that's not in your bag?"

Tove shook her head. "It's all in storage. I've been slowly moving it out of the city."

"Smart. Come on. This way."

This time, Tove followed her friend through the dark alleyways. Somewhere beyond the rows of houses that offered her and Quinn cover, drunk revelers crooned to the bards gathered for the last day of the celebration. Lamplight in the distance marked their festivities, and laughter followed as the song ended.

How strange, to flee her beloved city during her favorite celebration of the year.

The thump of boots over the cobblestone nearby broke through her thoughts, and Quinn skidded to an abrupt stop. She craned her head, listening to the footsteps, and silently gestured for Tove to follow her down a different alley.

"What are we going to do?" Tove whispered through huffing breaths as she tried to keep up with her friend. "What's the plan?"

Before she answered, Quinn cast a wary glance at the dark windows above them. "Use glamours. Lay low. Get a few supplies, just enough to tide you over, and get to safety. We'll fetch your things later."

And, just like that, Tove Warren became every bit the outlaw as the man Quinn Starling had been hunting when all of this chaos first began.

So be it.

Quinn had always kept Tove safe, and through the years, they had dealt with mischief and danger as a team. Whatever happened next, Tove would do everything she could to help—because Quinn Starling was her friend, and she trusted this woman with her life.

CHAPTER SIXTY-FOUR

CONNOR

Blackfire.

That one word replayed in his mind, over and over, as he recalled the flame crackling over his skin. It had erupted across his hand, fed by his raw fury, and he hadn't been able to control it.

Not a good sign.

In the oppressively quiet limestone tunnels beneath Kirkwall Castle, even Connor's breath sounded painfully loud.

His small band took the labyrinth of passageways at a brisk pace. They needed to get to the northwest shore before dawn, and in a maze carved by hundreds of different smugglers over the centuries, that was quite an ask.

Layers of dust clung to the ancient walls, and their boots kicked up dirt and pebbles alike despite his team's augmented stealth. Up ahead, Sophia sneezed, and a plume of dust lit by the flickering flames of her Firestarter dagger floated past.

The damp air weighed on Connor's chest, heavier with each breath, but no one spoke. Though he hadn't felt truly cold since fusing with the Wraith King, the chilled air sent an unpleasant ripple of numbness down his arms.

They needed to get the hell out of this place—and fast.

All the while, he kept a close eye on the two new additions to their small band. Per his orders, Sophia and Murdoc led the way while he and Rockwell stayed to the rear. That left Owen smack in between them, where Connor could keep an eye on the island's crown prince.

A man he still didn't fully trust.

Rockwell once again peered over his shoulder at the pitch-dark corridor behind them. Even the distant torches of the lengths of tunnel occupied by the king's guard had long since faded, none of them had wanted to risk their voices traveling down the passageway.

Now, however, the man's gaze lingered, and his pace finally slowed as he let out a relieved breath. "It's clear. We're far enough away that no one could possibly hear us, even if they're down the tunnel."

Without a moment's hesitation, Owen yanked off his mask and grabbed Rockwell's shoulder. Connor instinctively tensed, his fingers itching to summon his swords, but Owen pulled Rockwell into a tight hug. Rockwell sighed happily and warmly patted the young man on his back.

"Thought I was a dead man," Rockwell admitted.

"Never." Owen pulled away, though he kept one reassuring hand on the man's shoulder. "I never would have let it happen."

Interesting.

Though Connor relaxed his stance, he kept a wary watch on the Prince of Kirkwall. Ahead of them, Sophia sighed impatiently as she and Murdoc begrudgingly stopped their hurried pace to watch the reunion.

"Owen, you're not safe." Rockwell set both hands on Owen's shoulders and looked the prince dead in the eye. "Those thugs didn't catch me on their own. They were after you, and they had help. Victor told them enough to find you. That smug asshole Jones told me everything. The damn fool couldn't keep his mouth shut and gloated right up until he turned me in."

"Don't worry," Murdoc said as he leaned against the tunnel wall. "Jones is dead."

"Our prince here saw to that." Sophia set one hand on her hip and tilted her head as she let the unspoken implications settle on their royal guest.

"How much of that did you all see?" Owen asked.

"All of it," Sophia answered.

"Oh," the prince said quietly. "You lot are full of surprises."

Murdoc crossed his arms over his chest as he got comfortable against the cold limestone. "You have no idea."

"Jones isn't who matters," Rockwell continued, his tone more urgent this time. "Victor wants you dead, Owen, and he wanted me out of the way so that he could do it."

"We know," Connor said flatly.

Rockwell frowned with confusion as his gaze shifted between the four of them. "You can't possibly mean—"

"He already tried to kill me and Wade," Owen patted the man lightly on his arm. "If not for these three, he would've succeeded."

"That son of a bitch." Rockwell's jaw tensed, and his eye twitched with hatred. "I'll kill him. I swear to the Fates, he's dead."

"It's not that simple, Liam." Owen rubbed his face and paced a small stretch of the tunnel. "He's swayed half of the Shades. They'll do anything he says."

"Maybe," Connor said flatly.

He debated sharing a bit of his brewing plan—and, more importantly, what he suspected would happen once they reached the oceanfront—but he desperately wanted to be wrong. Nocturne still hadn't flown within range to contact him, and he had precious little information at the moment.

Ultimately, he left it at that.

The prince, thankfully, didn't pry. An eerie quiet settled amongst them, and only the crackle of Sophia's lone light source snapped through the still air.

Rockwell cleared his throat to dispel the tension. "We should keep walking. Owen, let me have a chat with our friend here."

"Right, of course." Owen briefly scanned Connor's face, as though searching for something in his expression, but the man ultimately followed after Sophia and Murdoc once again.

Rockwell, however, resumed at a slower pace. Connor cast a sidelong glance at his family's lifelong friend, and he matched the man's gait.

It was strange, really, this silence. To find someone from his past, someone he'd thought was long dead, would have once ignited hope within him. It would've renewed his vigor and helped him focus. It would've sparked a well of questions that would've poured out of him like water through a hole in a bucket, but now he couldn't think of a single thing to say.

After so long, words hardly felt good enough.

"You've made quite a name for yourself, Connor," Rockwell said after a while. "Ancient Woods, huh? Never would've imagined you'd go there."

"No one would have," he confessed. "That's why I went."

A dry laugh escaped his father's friend, and another strange moment of silence weighed between them.

"I thought you were dead, son," Rockwell admitted.

Son.

The word gutted him, and his throat tightened. It reminded him of home. Of his father. Of the family he'd once had here, and of everything he had lost.

"Yeah." Connor roughly cleared his throat. "I thought the same about you."

"In a way, I did." Rockwell hooked one thumb on the edge of his pants and stared into the darkness far beyond Sophia's torchlight.

The man's voice echoed with a hollow emptiness Connor had never heard before, and it once again left Connor at a loss for words.

"Seeing all my friends..." Rockwell shook his head, slowly at first, and his eyes glazed over. "Seeing them all up there, on spikes and in the gallows, it broke me. Seeing our houses burned to ash with our wives and children inside. I lost everything that night. The hatred was the only thing that kept me going."

Connor swallowed hard, and he resisted the wave of memories that tried to overtake him. The charred ash on his tongue. The heady smoke that choked him. The searing agony in his back that splintered his resolve with every step, daring him to just give up and die like all the rest.

He knew that feeling all too well.

"Your head wasn't up there," Rockwell continued, more quietly than before. "It gave me hope. I thought that maybe, by some miracle of the Fates, that you had escaped. I believed it, too, right up until Bryan ended up in that cell. He told me everything. He thought those bars would keep him safe from me."

Connor took a ragged breath, but given the aching lump in his throat, he didn't dare speak.

"What you did back there..." Rockwell squared his shoulders as he glared down at his feet. "With Bryan..."

Ah.

The man likely wanted an explanation. He wanted to know what the hell Connor's magic even was, or how in the Fates' good name he'd gotten ahold of something that powerful.

They were questions Connor wasn't ready to answer.

"That anger," Rockwell eventually whispered. "Even I was scared of you, for a second there, but I don't blame you one bit. He deserved what he got."

Maybe.

Even though it was done, Connor still wasn't sure.

"You think I did the right thing, then?" he asked. "Killing him like that?"

"It's what I would've done," the man confessed. "But that doesn't make it right."

Fair point.

"Doesn't matter." Rockwell waved away the question and took a deep breath. His expression shifted, and he once again looked up. Though Connor had never once seen this man cry, Rockwell's eyes watered. He smiled, big and broad, even as his eyebrows knit with grief. "I missed you, kid. Truly."

"I've missed you, too," Connor admitted quietly.

It was the truth, and yet it hurt his heart to say it out loud.

Finding Rockwell after all these years had brought him joy he thought he'd never feel again, but it also reminded him of everything they had both lost.

Rockwell sniffled—once, and almost violently, as if that was enough to quell it all—before abruptly laughing. "Can't really call you a kid anymore, though, can I? Look at you, son. Fully grown. Hardly recognized you at all."

"Yeah," Connor admitted as his attention shifted to the crown prince walking ahead of them, just out of earshot. "I suppose a lot has changed in my time away."

"Hmm." Rockwell's gaze shifted between Connor and the back of Owen's head. "I know what you're thinking."

Connor raised one dubious eyebrow and glared at the man. "Do you?"

"Don't give me that look," Rockwell warned. "And yes, I do. He's not like his father. Not one bit."

"You'd really vouch for him? Of all people?"

"With my life," Rockwell said with a resolute nod.

Connor still didn't like it. He shoved one hand in his pocket and curled it into a tight fist as he studied the walls they walked by. Anything at all, really, was better than acknowledging that Rockwell might be right.

"He's got a good heart," Rockwell's voice softened as he continued. He shrugged, as though it didn't make sense to him, either. "His mother's influence, I think. The queen is a gentle woman. I don't know how a bastard like Arlo convinced a sweet lady like that to marry him."

Money, probably, but Connor kept his mouth shut.

"I wanted Victor back on the throne until I met him." Rockwell pointed to the back of Owen's head as the prince walked dutifully ahead of them to give them space to talk. "After that, I didn't know what to think. I went back and forth on it for years, convincing myself I'd keep Owen safe when we overtook the castle, but meeting Victor for myself convinced me that man can never sit on that throne. He's a coward."

Connor frowned. "Should be easy to run him out of town, then, shouldn't it? What's the problem?"

"Aye, cowards aren't a threat until they assemble a little army of sycophants." Rockwell's nose creased with disdain. "That's when they get dangerous, Connor. That's when they stoke fires, and that's when good men die."

Damn.

"Well said," Connor admitted.

"He tried to kill me and Owen both." Rockwell's voice dropped to a dangerous, gravelly tone. "And now, he's tried to kill Wade, too? I'll kill him, Connor. I'll kill him with my bare hands if I have to."

As Connor's thoughts raced, he rubbed the back of his head. His hair scratched against his callused palm while he debated the best course of action, but he couldn't deny the inevitable.

He would have to intercede.

"I'll do it," he eventually said.

"What? No. Not what I meant." Rockwell waved away Connor's offer with a quick gesture. "A man has to settle his own debts, son. This one's mine."

"It's not." Connor set both hands in his pockets as he watched his father's lifelong friend through the corner of his eye. "For starters, you're family. No one threatens my family and lives to brag about it."

A proud smile broke over Rockwell's face, and he nodded in silent thanks.

"Second, there's the group itself," Connor continued. "I am the Shade, and you all, though well-meaning, have taken my name. Owen said the others won't give it up easily, especially Victor. That means I have to give them a choice—stop using it, or obey me. There's no other way."

Rockwell's smile fell, and his eyes briefly roamed Connor's face. "Aye. Fair play."

Yes, it was. Connor didn't need the man's endorsement to know as much, but he appreciated it all the same.

"Those stories..." Rockwell shook his head as he tried to find the right words. "What I've heard from the Ancient Woods is astonishing. Saving two lovers on the southern road from blightwolves. Killing fifty slavers and freeing their captives. Is all that true?"

"It was closer to seventy slavers, actually," Connor admitted. "But, yes."

"Seventy?" Rockwell let out a low, astonished whistle. "By yourself?"

More or less.

You're going to lie, aren't you? the Wraith King asked with an irritated groan.

Obviously. That should've been a given. Neither Rockwell nor Owen needed to know the truth, yet—if ever.

In answer to Rockwell's question, Connor nodded. In the back of his mind, the ghoul muttered frustrated obscenities.

Connor smirked, taking perhaps a little too much glee from the wraith's annoyance.

"Astonishing." Rockwell grinned proudly and shook his head in awe. "I wish your father could see you now. He would be so proud."

Connor's throat tightened again at the thought of his father's head on a spike. It relaxed, however, as he recalled his family's faces, what already felt like a lifetime ago, floating beneath the water in that pool of stars. The Blood Bogs had many secrets, and to this day, he still didn't know if what he'd seen was real.

He wanted to believe it was.

"I wouldn't be who I am without him," Connor eventually admitted.

"That's true." Rockwell nodded a few times, though he added a casual little shrug at the end. "But you should take a little credit, too. You made the choices that brought you here. Don't forget that, son. You've done good deeds, so don't stop. This power you've attained—and don't worry, I won't pry—it can be devastating in the wrong hands. I mean, look at Victor. That boy lost himself in his greed, and that can happen to anyone. Even you."

Hmm.

Connor sighed as he thought it over. Somewhere in the ether nearby, watching from the in-between, the Dragon King was likely studying his every move. He suspected Doom noticed more than Connor realized, and Rockwell's warning hit home.

One man could only attain so much power before he lost himself in it. He'd felt it himself, out there in the Decay, as he'd witnessed the carnage his undead army had wrought on the Lightseer Elite. For a moment, he had actually enjoyed it.

He couldn't lose himself like that again.

ANSWER ME! Nocturne's voice roared in his head, all-consuming and sudden, and those two simple words rattled like dice in his skull.

Connor winced as the dragon's powerful voice rumbled down his spine. He stumbled, and his shoulder hit the wall. Though he recovered his balance with his next steps, Rockwell's forehead creased with concern, and the man watched him with wary suspicion.

"Are you alright?" Rockwell asked.

"Yeah. Fine." Connor forced a half-hearted smile and focused his attention on the tunnel ahead of him.

FOR THE LOVE OF THE OLD GODS, CONNOR! Nocturne shouted. CAN YOU HEAR ME YET?

I'm here, he told the dragon. *Quit your screaming, damn it.*

FINALLY! Nocturne growled in frustration. THAT MUST MEAN YOU ARE CLOSE TO THE BEACH. WADE AND WHAT SHADES HE COULD MUSTER ARE LYING IN WAIT AROUND THE OCEANFRONT EXIT TO THE TUNNELS, BUT ANOTHER CLUSTER OF MEN ARRIVED LONG BEFORE THEM. THIRTY-SEVEN,

BY MY COUNT, TO WADE'S TWENTY-FIVE. THE LARGER BAND HAS CIRCLED A MAN WEARING A LUDICROUS DARK ORANGE TUNIC.

Dark orange and black—the Varon royal colors. It seemed as though Victor had spies in the castle after all, and the coward probably thought he was safe when surrounded by so many of his newly acquired soldiers.

Though Connor had prepared for this, he had desperately wanted to be wrong. This added a complication he truly didn't want to deal with right now.

Stay in the clouds, he warned the dragon. *I take it you're circling overhead?*

I AM.

Good, Connor replied. *Don't let them see you. There's no telling what they'll do if they think they can wrangle a dragon like you into submission.*

LET THEM TRY, the regal creature seethed.

Hey, now, he chided. *No need for that quite yet. I have a plan.*

THESE MEN LIE IN WAIT TO AMBUSH YOU ALL, the dragon said with a furious snarl. SURELY YOU WON'T BARGAIN WITH THESE COWARDS?

No, Connor admitted. *But if we can avoid more bloodshed, I want to try.*

A low, rumbling growl echoed through his mind, and he couldn't be sure which of the dragons in his head made it.

The low whistle of wind through the rocks wandered down the passage, and a thin sliver of blue moonlight stretched across the tunnel's floor up ahead.

"There," Owen pointed to the shadow-drenched silhouette of a circular door at the far end of the tunnel. "We're almost to the beach."

"Wait," Connor ordered.

His team stopped midstride, and each head pivoted toward him as they paused silently for him to elaborate. For a moment, however, Connor simply stared at the door as he pieced together the last threads of his ever-evolving plan.

"Victor's out there," he finally explained. "And he's not alone."

"Damn it." Rockwell smacked his palm hard against the uneven limestone wall and paced the full width of the tunnel. "How could he have known?"

"Spies." Connor gestured down the tunnel, in the vague direction of the castle.

"What?" Owen stiffened, and his nose creased briefly with either disgust or disdain. "How in the Fates' name could you know that?"

"Basic observation," Sophia said dryly. "And a bit of common sense."

"Exactly." Connor glanced briefly toward the necromancer as she leaned against the wall. Behind her, Murdoc chewed the inside of his cheek and stared at the floor, thinking.

Owen stuttered. "What—"

"Whomever brought you that decoy orb betrayed you," Connor said flatly, hardly in the mood for games and guessing. "It was almost painfully obvious, Owen. He works for Victor."

"But—" A muscle in the prince's jaw twitched violently, and the man swallowed hard as he quietly pieced it all together. His eyes flashed with recognition, and within seconds, he glared down the tunnel. "That bastard."

"There are probably more traitors," Connor warned. "He's surrounded by men, and he's wearing his family's colors. It's clear he has plans for you. When we go out there, be ready for a fight."

"He'll get one." Rockwell's voice scratched against his throat, and he glared at that door with all the rage of a caged beast eyeing the only way out.

"No, Liam." Connor stepped between the man and the exit and gave a definitive shake of his head. "I told you, I'll handle this."

"You had your fight," Rockwell spat. "This is mine."

"Don't let that rage take you over," Connor said firmly, echoing a bit of advice the man had told him nearly a decade ago.

Rockwell grimaced with disgust and kicked a rock across the tunnel floor. "Don't chide me with my own advice."

In Connor's head, the Wraith King chuckled. *All that time in prison made him hungry. How delightful.*

"I mean it," Connor warned Rockwell, ignoring the ghoul's intrusion. "Look at yourself, damn it. You're malnourished. You're sleep-deprived. You're in a weakened state, and you're letting your Fates-damned pride get the better of you. Snap out of it!"

A sharp huff of air shot through Rockwell's nose, and he hooked one thumb over the waistline of his pants. With a furious, stifled growl, he shook his head and shut his mouth.

Thank the Fates.

A silent surrender.

"Listen closely." Connor's gaze swept across each person in the tunnel. "Whatever happens out there, you need to trust me."

Murdoc gave a mock salute. "As always, Captain."

"You're up to something." Sophia's eyes narrowed with suspicion, and she studied his face more intently than ever before. "What exactly are you going to do?"

"You'll see," he assured her.

"Mmhmm." The necromancer pursed her lips, but that curious glint in her eye didn't fade.

"He's going to gloat," Owen said flatly. He watched Connor through the corner of his eye. The man kept his back to the wall, as though he had begun to wonder if anyone in this tunnel had a dagger reserved just for him.

"He might," Connor admitted.

"You all can still leave," Owen pointed out. "You said it yourself. This isn't your war. We aren't your Shades."

"On the contrary." Connor's voice dropped an octave, and he took several threatening steps toward the prince. "After tonight, the Shades will either disband—or you all will belong to me."

A heavy silence settled between them, and to his credit, Owen didn't bat an eye. The Prince of Kirkwall glared at him, focused and intense, and his mouth set into a grim line as he silently dared Connor to say that again.

But Connor wouldn't repeat himself. He had made his point, and the prince could make his own choices from here. Either way, Connor would hold the man to the same standard as everyone else out there on that beach.

"Stay behind me," he ordered. "You and Rockwell take up the rear. Sophia, Murdoc, and I will handle this."

"Fates damn it, *no!*" Rockwell snapped. "I won't let you shield me like I'm some maiden at the faire!"

"Enough!" Connor shouted.

His voice carried down the tunnel, far louder than he'd intended, and everyone around him went eerily still. They watched him intently, as though the mere sound of his command had rooted them firmly to the ground and sewn their mouths shut.

It wasn't what he had intended to do. Hell, he didn't know how he'd done it in the first place, but it worked in his favor.

"I'm not *asking*," he said firmly. "I'm telling you what's going to happen, and you need to fall in line."

A rush of black smoke rolled over his forearm as he summoned his shield, and the warm metal hummed against the tunnel's cool air. The familiar weight settled into his palm, and he met Rockwell's eye as he silently warned the man to back down.

Though his family's lifelong friend stiffened under his gaze, Rockwell eventually nodded.

Good.

That was it, then. The last thread of his plan fell into place, and his pulse settled as he finally figured out exactly what he needed to do.

He didn't want to kill anyone else tonight—but if Victor did something stupid, he would not hold back.

After everything these would-be Shades had put him through thus far, he'd had enough. These men had delayed him for too long, and he had more urgent matters on his mind. They had stolen his name. They had overtaken his home. And if he didn't step in, they would ignite a bloody civil war that would split this island in two.

Kirkwall had seen enough blood. It didn't need to lose more good people to a rich man's unfettered greed.

Victor Varon had come to claim Owen Hunt's throne. Tonight, out there on that dark stretch of sand, Connor would decide which man would one day have it.

CHAPTER SIXTY-FIVE

CONNOR

Waves crashed against the distant beach, their thunder muffled by a thick wooden door.

Still standing in the limestone tunnels that carved through Kirkwall's cliffs, Connor waited. He set his hand on the weathered oak and, as much as he wanted to charge through and end this once and for all, he forced himself to listen to the beach outside.

At first, only the ocean's chorus rustled through the night, and he held up one hand in a silent order for the four people gathered behind him to wait a bit longer.

He needed to know where Victor's men were, and how close they could get before the door even opened.

In the lull between each wave that hit the shore, he heard it—a distant murmur. The man's voice was faint. Loud enough to register, but not close enough to make out the words.

Good. That gave him room to work.

Marvelous, the Wraith King said with a wicked chuckle. *It has been so long since I've had a chance to rip through so many.*

"You just took on twenty," Connor whispered, quietly enough that those behind him couldn't hear. "That's enough for now. Stand down."

The ghoul scoffed. *This is an opportunity to show them your might. These are not strays for you to adopt, Magnuson. Make them fear you. You're the Fates-damned King of Slaybourne, not some aimless assassin stumbling through the dark.*

"No," Connor said firmly. "After your stunt in the mountain, I'm not in the mood for your bloodlust. We do this my way."

The wraith huffed in utter revulsion, but mercifully said nothing else.

With one last warning glance over his shoulder at Owen and Rockwell, he pulled his mask up over his nose to hide his face. Sophia and Murdoc followed suit, though the two Kirkwall locals didn't bother.

Victor already knew who they were. He had, after all, tried to assassinate them both.

Ready for the onslaught, Connor gently pushed open the door. It swung out into the sand on silent hinges, and a salty gust rolled off the ocean as he took his first breath of fresh air. It carried the bite of seaweed floating on the tide and a taste of freedom, all in one.

This had always been the smell of home, and his chest ached at the memories it stirred within him.

The whisper of steel on the air cut through the night. With an effortless twist of his hand, Connor raised his shield. Masked as it was by the shadows, the dagger appeared in the second before it clanged against the enchanted metal, and his shield absorbed the blow with a resonant twang.

He peered over his shield, his body still blocking the narrow crack in the door, as two more daggers whistled toward him. He took a few measured steps closer as the blades collided with his enchanted metal and thudded harmlessly into the sand at his feet.

Though green ink glowed across his opponents' muscled arms, he doubted they would pose much of a threat. The lot of them would last maybe ten minutes against him—or less if they tried to taunt him.

But he wasn't interested in a massacre. If he played his cards right, he would leave Kirkwall with something far more valuable than blood.

With a quick scan of the beach, he spotted a dark thicket a short way off. The trees gathered on a grassy knoll that rose above the sand, and dune grass rippled in the occasional gusts off the ocean. The cluster of scraggly trees matched the vague description Nocturne had given him, and his attention lingered as a silhouette crouched beside one of the weathered bushes.

Owen's men, lying in wait.

Good. Now, to find Nocturne.

Connor glanced quickly upward just as the vague shadow of something large passed between two clouds. It shot past the twin moons like a trick of the eye, barely lit by the waning moonlight, and its edges blended in with the stars far above it.

Everyone was here.

Across from Connor, standing almost in the waterline, more silhouettes clustered around a tall figure at their center. Moonlight glinted off steel in the gathered throng, and the taught warning of tightening bowstrings creaked in time with the sea's thunderous song. Four of the men at the front of the line cocked their arms to throw the next round of daggers.

Fine.

If they wanted a show of force, he'd give them one.

Four daggers launched toward him this time, and he tracked each one through the air. One would reach him a second faster than the others, and that gave him a solid shot at taking out two of his opponents.

Doom had bragged of his unrivaled strength and speed. Time to see how much of that Connor could use for himself.

The first dagger reached him, and Connor snatched it out of the air. He spun to keep its momentum and hurled it back at the man who'd thrown it. The second it left his palm, he grabbed the next one mid-flight and raised his shield to block the last two daggers. They clanged harmlessly against the enchanted metal in his hand. He peered again over the edge of the shield for only a moment—just long enough to aim—and he launched the second dagger with a perfectly timed twist of his arm.

The two blades meant for his skull landed hilt-deep in his victims. One in a man's forehead, and the second in another man's eye.

Connor frowned. He hadn't meant to take out someone's eye, but it had worked all the same.

His two marks slumped to the ground, dead before they'd even seen the threat, and he stood. Though he kept his shield in front of him, he lowered it enough that these fools could see his face—or, at least, the part of it not covered by his mask.

Under his furious glare, the gathered crowd went eerily still.

Sloppy, the Wraith King chided. *You didn't even hit your target.*

Connor stifled an irritated groan and did his best to mask his annoyance as he searched the crowd for Victor.

It took only a second to spot him. The man waited in the middle of the others, taller than most, and his dark orange tunic stood out in an ocean of black silhouettes. Once his eyes adjusted to the dark island night, Victor's angled features came into sharp focus. The former Prince of Kirkwall watched him with a twisted smirk of satisfaction, as though this were a performance he had waited years to see. The clouds shifted, and Saldia's twin moons peeked briefly through the stars. A sliver of the waning moonlight accentuated Victor's sharp cheekbones and illuminated the cruel glimmer in his eyes.

He'd just lost two men, and he didn't remotely care.

"Impressive." Victor gestured at those gathered around him, and they slowly stepped aside to let him through. "That shield. That speed. Those eyes. It would seem that the rumors are true. You're the actual Shade."

"I am." Connor's voice rumbled in his throat like a stifled growl.

"You killed Darius, then?" Victor reached the edge of his men, though he silently gestured for two to remain in front of him.

Human shields, most likely. The fools obeyed, and it took effort for Connor not to grimace in disgust.

"I did," Connor replied. "And I'm in no mood for games, Victor."

Victor's eyebrows shot up his forehead, and he grinned in surprise. "I'm impressed. I didn't expect you to know who I am. Has my reputation preceded me?"

"You don't have a reputation," Connor replied. "You're a coward who hides behind other men, and you want a throne that's not yours."

"It has *always* been mine," Victor snapped. His demeanor shifted in an instant, and he scowled with unfettered disdain. "That petulant brat who led you through the tunnels has no right to this island."

Behind Connor, Owen bristled. Connor shot a warning glare over one shoulder, and the Prince of Kirkwall clenched his teeth with barely restrained rage.

Holding back, no doubt.

"An odd claim to make," Connor said flatly. "Given that you have no right to use my name, and yet you're using it anyway."

"Hmm." Victor's expression softened, as though he'd already forgotten his burst of anger from moments ago, and he flashed a haughty grin as he met Connor's eye. "Well said, peasant."

He's unbearable, the Wraith King growled. *If you don't kill him, I will, if only to keep him from talking.*

"Stop it," Connor said under his breath.

"It must be irritating for you, I'm sure," Victor said with a lazy flick of his wrist. "Unfortunately, your legend is quite useful to us. It's suitable cover. Both the king and the castle's soldiers fear you more than I ever anticipated. The idea of you coming here has stirred them into a frenzy, and that's important to my plans for this island. I must continue to use it."

Connor hated to admit it to himself—and he would never have said it out loud—but the Wraith King was right.

Victor Varon was utterly insufferable.

The imbecile had shared one little nugget of useful information, however. The King of Kirkwall feared the Shade, and that could work out well for him in the future.

For now, he had an entitled asshole to deal with.

"I know Owen's with you." Victor set the tips of his fingers against each other and nodded toward the door. "Give him to me."

In a rush of black fog, Connor summoned one of his swords. Everyone in the cluster before him—including Victor—flinched at the sudden movement, and many of them gaped at the blackfire crackling over his enchanted steel.

The magical flames cast a dim gray glow over the white sand beneath his boots, but he otherwise didn't move. He simply watched the color drain from Victor's face as the former nobleman stared wide-eyed at the weapon in his hand.

"You don't make demands of me." Connor's voice punctuated the silence, and his tone carried an icy warning.

"Look—" Victor's voice quivered briefly. He cleared his throat and tugged firmly on the ends of his tunic to steady himself. "This can end peacefully. I don't want you, after all. Give me Owen and give me what you stole from the castle. Whatever he has on you—however he made you help him—I don't care. You can leave my island peacefully, and we can part as unlikely friends. It's a generous offer. If you don't take it, tonight will not end well for you."

The *gall.*

"You've heard what I've done," Connor said flatly.

Victor ran his tongue over his front teeth, as though debating how to answer, but nodded.

"The slavers," Connor continued.

Again, Victor nodded.

"You know what I can do," Connor added, more to drive home the point than anything else.

"Yes," the former prince said. "All of Saldia does."

"Then you're a Fates-damned idiot." Connor's tone didn't waver, and he never once broke eye contact. "Because no sane man would dare to threaten me."

Finally, the Wraith King muttered. *You and I can agree on something.*

A smile tugged at the edge of Connor's mouth, but he managed to hold it at bay.

Victor bristled. "It seems as though you don't realize the danger you're in. The only reason you're alive is because I want this to end amicably. I have augmented soldiers. You're alone."

"Am I?"

At the unspoken invitation to join him, Sophia and Murdoc stepped out of the tunnel. They flanked him, and Murdoc drew his sword with the careless confidence of a man who'd survived far worse odds. Sophia, meanwhile, set one hand on her hip and twisted her other palm toward the sky. A sleek, silver dagger hovered over her palm, sharper than any steel, and her red lips curled into a sinister smile.

"Fine," Victor said with an irritated huff. "There's three of you and a disgraced prince. Those are still poor odds."

"I'm sick of his drivel." Sophia wrinkled her nose in disgust. "Can't we just kill him and be done with this?"

Connor met Victor's eye and nodded. "Soon."

Victor stiffened and took several steps backward as his soldiers flanked around him yet again. "Don't do anything stupid, now. My terms are fair, and you know it. What you stole and why you took it doesn't matter to me. It belongs to my family, and I want it back. I assume you want to sell it for a fair bit of coin, and I don't want an heirloom lost to the Saldian black markets. I'll give you double whatever you want to ask for it. This is a good offer, peasant. Don't be a fool."

Murdoc shook his head, laughing. "I almost feel bad, Captain. This is going to be too easy."

"You turned Rockwell in," Connor's eyes narrowed with hatred, and this time, he didn't keep the fury at bay.

At the surge of anger, that overwhelming heat pushed on his palms once again. The air sizzled, like the haze over a bonfire, as Doom's blackfire threatened to erupt yet again.

This time, Connor reached for it.

He embraced it.

As he always did with his blades, he beckoned it closer. He wanted it to come. He wanted to learn more about it, to study it, to master it—but it refused.

The heat merely pressed against his palms once again, and Connor frowned in disappointment.

"You think I turned Rockwell in?" Victor scoffed. "Don't be ludicrous. Why would I—"

"Yes, Victor." Rockwell stepped around Sophia and crossed his arms over his broad chest. "Why *did* you try to have me killed, hmm?"

With a sidelong glance at Connor, Owen followed Rockwell from the tunnel and stood beside the man that had sacrificed himself to keep Owen Hunt alive. Connor watched the prince like a wolf stalking prey, but he didn't intercede.

Though he hadn't given them the signal, the timing still worked in his favor.

Many of the men gathered around Victor relaxed the moment they saw Rockwell. Their swords lowered, and several of those armed with bows pointed their arrow tips toward the ground as they smiled with relief.

"Rockwell, you're—" Victor stiffened, and his mouth twitched once before he managed to force an almost convincing smile. "Thank the Fates you're—"

"Cut the horseshit," Rockwell ordered. "Your friend Jones wouldn't shut his damn mouth. You set me up, you conniving traitor!"

Those who had moments before smiled with relief now turned their rage—and, some, their weapons—on Victor. Two of the men with bows aimed their arrows at Victor's heart, and the soldiers beside them flinched in surprise.

Men shouted. Steel swished over cloth. A few muffled gasps of surprise turned into a roar of shouting, and in moments, the gathered crowd of would-be Shades turned their weapons on each other. Everyone in the crowd trained their deadly steel on one of their brothers-in-arms, and some even turned their back on Connor's team. The distance between each man grew as they tried to retain the upper hand on those they had, moments before, fought beside.

Good. At least Rockwell still had loyalists within Victor's ranks. This was why Victor had worked so hard to make Rockwell's capture look like an accident.

"Shut your damn mouths!" Connor roared.

His voice carried over the ocean, out to the sea and the foggy horizon, and even the stars went momentarily still. The panicked shouts died in an instant, swallowed by the sheer power of his words, and everyone abruptly looked at him. Even Murdoc and Sophia eyed him warily, as confused as the others, as the water washed gently over the sandy shore. A moonbeam filtered through the rolling clouds above the chaotic scene, and the light glinted off steel that had, not long ago, been trained on him.

"Look at yourselves." He gestured to the lot of them with a disgusted tilt of his sword. "Look how easy it was to turn you against each other. A bit of truth, and you crumbled. You've forgotten what you even stand for. You've forgotten who you truly serve. The people of Kirkwall need you, and you've failed them all. Maybe you started with good intentions, but those are long gone. Now, you serve a rich man's greed."

Several men in the cluster swallowed hard. Others looked down at the sand, and still more glanced among themselves, as though looking for others who agreed that this was utter lunacy.

Only a few glared resolutely at him, angry as ever, apparently convinced beyond reason that anything he said would be a lie.

"This isn't about greed." On the other side of the throng, with his back to the ocean, Victor raised one finger at Connor to emphasize his point. "This is about justice. This is—"

"No," Connor growled. The word rumbled in his chest, as loud as any thunder, and his grip tightened on the hilt of his sword. "You don't get to speak. Not to me. You sent your men to kill Owen and Wade. You set Rockwell up to take the fall. You pulled the strings of this brotherhood to make them dance for you, and half of them want so badly to believe your lies that they'll ignore your utter ineptitude."

"I—how dare—" Victor blinked rapidly, apparently stunned by the sheer number of insults, and his face burned red with anger. "You're talking to a king, peasant. You will treat me with respect."

Connor laughed.

He couldn't help it.

Even with everything he had seen over the past few days, Connor hadn't been entirely sure of which man deserved to rule this island. Common sense told him Owen was the only suitable choice, but resentment was often a more powerful force than reason. He could no longer ignore the facts, and he'd seen enough to know what choice he had to make.

He'd wanted so badly to hate Owen Hunt, but his feelings about the man didn't matter. Not anymore.

Rockwell had lost as much as he did in the smuggler raids—if not more. If that man could learn how to forgive, then so could Connor.

"That's the future King of Kirkwall." Though Connor met Victor's eye, he pointed the tip of his blade at Owen. "That's what a leader looks like."

In his periphery, Connor noticed Owen flinch with surprise. The prince glanced briefly toward him, as though caught off guard by the statement, but he cleared his throat to regain his composure. The entire episode had lasted barely three seconds, and the man recovered before anyone else could detect his unease.

Quick to adapt and good with a bluff. Owen really was the best choice.

Damn it.

"Wade, get out here," Connor ordered with a sidelong glance at the dark trees on the outskirts of this small stretch of beach. "And bring the others."

At his friend's name, Owen stood a little taller. He followed Connor's gaze toward the thicket as silhouettes strode from the shadows. Wade walked first into the moonlight, his furious glare trained on Victor, and he tugged the cloth off his face with an angry flourish.

Owen let out a small sigh of relief. The prince caught Connor's eye, and he pretended to stroke his jaw to shield his smile from Victor.

He'd been played, sure, but he didn't seem too upset about it.

"This is what's going to happen." Connor's voice carried over the beach and out into the sea, but no one beyond this splintered group of vigilantes would hear him this far north of the city. "Tonight, you're all going to make a choice."

Rockwell raised one curious eyebrow, but he otherwise remained stoic and still.

"Anyone who calls himself a Shade obeys me," Connor continued. "He takes his orders from me and me alone. Any leaders I appoint will also take their orders from me. This is not negotiable."

Connor paused, and in the silence that followed, he made a point of looking Owen dead in the eye. The prince went still under his glare, and after a tense moment of silence, Owen nodded.

Good.

"There is a creed," Connor continued. "Laws you must follow. You will not torture your captives or your marks. You serve the people of Kirkwall, and it is your duty to keep them safe. Many of you are assholes, and I won't try to change you—but you will not let that get in the way. If you wear my name and my mask, you do right by others. There is no middle ground."

Victor slowly shook his head, as though he were more disappointed than anything else. "It didn't have to go like this. I could've been your ally, peasant. Now, you've only made an enemy of me."

"Then you are not a smart man," Connor said flatly.

The former prince narrowed his eyes in warning, but Victor clearly didn't understand his position.

"This is my offer," Connor continued, raising his voice enough that everyone present could hear. "One—you join me and honor my law. Two—you stand aside and hang up your mask forever. Or, three—you die."

Victor shook his head in disgust. "And if they make the wiser choice to stay with me?"

"I already gave that option." Connor's eyes narrowed. "It's option three."

An icy chill snaked through the air, and several of the men on Victor's frontline took wary steps backward.

"Choose," Connor demanded of the men present.

For a breathless, suspended moment, no one moved. No one spoke. No weapons were sheathed, but no new ones were drawn. It was a stalemate, the sort of silence that follows either chaos or clarity, as each man debated his options.

To Connor's surprise, Wade took the first step.

The man walked past Connor and stood at Owen's side. Wade scanned the breathless figures around them and crossed his arms over his chest as he waited for the others to make their own choice.

That simple movement broke the spell, and the rest of Owen's band followed suit. One by one, those who had previously gathered behind Wade joined him at Owen's side, and the Prince of Kirkwall nodded in thanks to every man who passed.

Another soldier broke away from the group around Victor—the first to abandon him—and the man didn't look back as he crossed the long stretch of beach to stand at Owen's side.

Good. At least some of them had common sense.

More followed suit. One by one, at first, but groups of two and three began to splinter away. Most stood by Owen, but some walked past him entirely. These men stood off to the side, between the two groups, apparently done with all of it.

Most of the Shades, however, abandoned Victor to stand with the current Prince of Kirkwall. Owen stood taller with each passing second, emboldened by the show of faith in him. With his loyalists firmly on his side, Owen shifted his attention to Victor and raised his chin in silent challenge.

Victor, of course, fumed more with each man he lost. When each man had made his choice, only fifteen still stood at the former prince's side.

Nocturne, Connor asked with a cursory glance at the clouds. *Not sure how much patience I have left for these people. Care to join us?*

WITH PLEASURE.

Overhead, the clouds parted. Their edges swirled against the stars, stirred by something unseen in the void above the ocean, and a sharp whistle cut through the night. Those around Victor shifted uneasily, each of them trying to place the sound as it grew louder. A few looked upward as a silhouette passed in front of the twin moons, and even the Wraith King chuckled with wicked glee.

A touch of theatre, the ghoul said, unable to mask a hint of pride in his voice. *You've improved, Magnuson. I'm impressed.*

The towering silhouette landed in the shallows with a deafening crash. Water shot in every direction as moonlight glinted off the creature's teeth, and it spread its wings wide in the seconds before pale moonbeams shimmered across its jet-black scales.

Nocturne—with perfect timing, as always.

The prince of dragons roared, and his voice shook the earth. Waves sloshed over the regal creature's legs, and a blistering yellow light built in the depths of his open jaw. The lightning in Nocturne's throat cast surreal shadows across his teeth, and the overall effect made it seem as though they had lengthened on command. Sparks skittered over his hide, and his leathery wings beat once against the air. A gale swept over those unlucky enough to be gathered beneath him, and four of the men collapsed to the ground in raw fear.

Connor glanced in the distant direction of Kirkwall Castle, half-wondering if anyone had heard Nocturne's introduction, but the locals wouldn't know what it was. If anything, someone would claim to have spotted a sea monster in the waves offshore. He'd heard those tales every summer when he was a boy, and those were the sort of legends a drunk could revive any time he had one too many.

"Fates be—" Rockwell managed to stifle the rest of the curse by slapping his hand over his mouth, but he still took a terrified step backward.

Owen's eyes went wide, and though he stiffened, he somehow managed to stay rooted in place. He gave almost nothing away, and to his credit, only the faintest hint of fear flashed across his face as he saw Nocturne for the first time.

After all, Connor hadn't exactly told Owen who was keeping an eye on Wade. It didn't seem like the sort of thing a potential enemy needed to know.

"You have a *dragon*?" Rockwell hissed under his breath. "How in the Fates' bloody name do you have a *dragon*?"

Connor caught the man's eye and, instead of answering, shook his head once in reply.

This wasn't the time.

Those clustered around Victor scattered. Nearly all of them stumbled toward those who had opted to quit altogether, though four tried to join Owen's ranks. Wade clocked one in the jaw, and the man fell hard on the sand at Wade's feet.

"You're a traitor," Wade spat. "You didn't make your choice until you had the piss scared out of you, and you're not welcome."

The man on the ground rubbed his jaw, but he slowly lowered his gaze in silent surrender. He pushed himself to his feet, stumbling the first few steps, and ultimately ambled toward the cluster of those who had opted to leave.

"Alright! Alright, you win!" Victor's voice trembled with fear. Alone on the beach and frozen beneath Nocturne's furious glare, the former prince dropped to his knees. He bowed before Nocturne with his palms on the sand, his body shaking.

"You surrender?" Owen asked.

The prince of dragons snarled. His lip curled as he lowered his jaws toward the sniveling man at his feet, and he only stopped when his teeth hovered a breath above Victor's neck.

"I surrender!" Victor whimpered and pressed his cheek into the dunes in a vain attempt to put some distance between him and the dragon.

Beside Connor, Owen let out a slow breath of relief. His shoulders finally relaxed, and he clapped Wade on the back in silent gratitude for the man's show of force.

Connor's attention shifted to those who had opted to leave the Shades altogether, and he toyed with what they could do to ensure none of Owen's secrets made it to the king. "Sophia, what potions do you have for—"

"None of that, now," Rockwell interjected. The man set one hand on Connor's shoulder and shook his head. "You've done enough, son. We have procedures in place for those who want to quit. Trust me. They won't remember this clearly enough to betray anything useful."

Curious, Connor tilted his head and studied the man's face. "That sounded ominous."

"Huh. It did, didn't it?" Rockwell laughed. "Not to worry. It's quite dull. Potions mostly."

Sophia huffed indignantly, but she ultimately didn't comment.

"Don't worry, darling," Murdoc whispered, almost too quietly to hear. "I'm sure yours are better."

Though the necromancer didn't reply, she couldn't resist the smile tugging on her ruby red lips.

"Now, go on," Rockwell gestured toward the distant city.

Connor shook his head. "There's work to do."

"Aye, and we'll do it." Rockwell raised his eyebrows in challenge. "You know what your father did after a successful night of smuggling?"

"No," he admitted. "You two always left me at home and came back by dawn."

"Blind drunk," Rockwell added. "Your father knew how to celebrate his wins, Connor. It's time you do the same."

Connor frowned, but the man had a point. "And Victor?"

"Leave him to me." Rockwell's eyes narrowed as he glared at the sniveling traitor still cowering at Nocturne's feet.

Hmm.

Connor debated it, but he ultimately waved away the idea. "I know how you get when you're angry, Liam. My laws apply to you, too, even with our history. No torture."

"I won't," the man lied.

"I mean it," Connor said firmly. "I'll kill him myself. You're too close to this."

Rockwell snorted derisively. "Damn right I am. The bastard tried to murder me."

"And us," Owen added with a quick gesture toward Wade.

"Burn him," Wade agreed. "I want to watch."

"You won't be here for every deliberation about justice," Rockwell added with a stern glare. "Trust me, Connor. Trust *us*."

From the water's edge, Nocturne snarled down at the sniveling coward as Connor mulled it over. He couldn't be here for every judgment, and Rockwell had a point.

Murdoc nudged Connor in the arm. "Face it, Captain. You just want to kill him yourself."

"Damn right," Connor admitted.

No one tried to kill his family and lived to talk about it.

"This one's mine." Rockwell smacked Connor lightly on the arm, as if that settled things. "Now, go on. But son, before you leave, you owe me an explanation for the dragon."

Connor nodded.

"Now go," Rockwell shooed them away with a few lazy flicks of his hands. "Wade and I will clean up this bastard's mess. You all rest. You've earned it."

"Hey, now," Wade said with a tired groan. "I want to rest, too."

Owen laughed.

"Tough," Rockwell frowned at Wade and gestured toward the cluster of loyalists slowly circling those who had chosen to quit. "They need their memories fogged, kid, and Connor's lot have spent the night running through the castle. Those four get to rest. You and I, however, have work to do."

Wade raised his palms in half-hearted surrender. "Fine, old man. You win."

"None of that 'old man' nonsense," Rockwell chided. "Come on. Help me get a Bluntmar on that bastard pissing himself beneath the dragon."

"Don't be ridiculous," Owen said. "I'll help. I can't leave this all to you after that show of support."

"Maybe," Rockwell admitted. "But you know where the entrance to the pub's safehouse is. These three don't."

"Ah," Owen said. "Noted."

Murdoc grinned and rubbed his hands together. "Well, if you're buying..."

"You all saved me from certain death," Rockwell said. "Of course I'm buying. I owe you a hell of a lot more than a drink."

"Nothing owed." It was something Connor had often heard his father say on those nights when the man had been the only thing between his friends and a jail cell. "That's just what family does."

With his back to Connor, Rockwell paused. He stretched his fingers wide and curled them into a tight fist, again and again, before roughly clearing his throat.

"Aye." He didn't turn around, but he couldn't mask the twinge of pain in his voice. "So we do."

With that, Rockwell walked toward Victor and never once looked back. Shoulders squared and head held high, he carried himself like a lord surveying his estate.

A pity, the Wraith King grumbled. *I wanted to torch that coward myself.*

"Yeah," Connor admitted as he gestured for the others to join him on the long trek back to the city. "But he isn't our coward to burn."

In a way, Rockwell had been right. This wasn't his fight. Not really. This was something for the Shades to settle, and he trusted them to handle it.

CHAPTER SIXTY-SIX

MURDOC

Murdoc listened intently to the calm city night—mostly because he didn't trust the quiet.

Owen led the way as their small band navigated side streets and cobblestone he had long ago memorized. Not far off, light spilled through a tavern's open door in a row of otherwise dark shops and storefronts. The signs hanging over each door swayed in another cold gust from the ocean, and the various symbols carved along each wooden panel suggested a few of these shops had changed hands since he was last here.

The tavern, though, hadn't changed a bit. Silhouettes stumbled past the open doorway, casting long shadows across the midnight cobblestones as they slurred their way through a drinking song about the sea.

Murdoc's' makeshift band had only taken a day of rest, but even that had helped. Murdoc's eyes stung with exhaustion, but he was used to odd hours by now. Sleep was a luxury for people like him, and he would sleep once they were back in Slaybourne.

After all, they had much to do before then, and almost no time in which to do it. Par for the course with Connor's plans, but Murdoc couldn't begrudge the Wraithblade's ambition.

Given Connor's history with this island, Murdoc hadn't shared much of his own experiences with Kirkwall's seedy underbelly. The Blackguard presence here was stronger than he remembered, and tonight, his team had already passed two faces he recognized.

Unfortunately, their gazes had lingered on him as well. He had returned to a Blackguard stronghold, and they were fully aware he was here.

Yet again, he reached into his pocket and ran his finger over the folded note he'd stored there. It had appeared a few days ago, same as orders always did when the Blackguards had given him missions, and the unspoken message was clear.

We will always find you.

The note itself had a fairly dire warning of its own, written in a vaguely familiar handwriting he couldn't quite place.

He itched to read it again, more out of habit than anything else, but this was something he wanted to deal with on his own. He wouldn't bother Connor with it, and Sophia had enough on her mind already.

Ahead of him, Owen glanced quickly over one shoulder before leading the team down a dark, narrow alley beside the pub. The drinking song faded, muffled by the stone walls and foggy windows, and Murdoc's boots crunched along a gravel path littered with weeds and wilted spring daisies. Connor's towering bulk blocked most of Murdoc's view of what lay ahead, and the subtle swish of Sophia's skirts across her boots were the only indication she was still following closely behind.

Stealthy as ever.

His footsteps were the only ones to be heard, and he shifted his weight to the balls of his feet as he did his best to follow suit. He still sometimes wished he could get an augmentation of his own, but this was the lot he'd been given in this life, and he wouldn't complain.

No point, after all. Wouldn't change a damn thing.

Owen disappeared into the shadows behind the pub, and it took Murdoc's eyes a minute to adjust. Trees towered above them on a steep hill behind the building, and their evergreen canopy blocked most of the buildings lining the top of the hill. Only the occasional beam of candlelight gave any indication that there were buildings up there at all.

"This way," Owen whispered.

The prince reached for the door handle on a lopsided shed leaning against the tavern's back wall, hidden from the street and propped up on one side by a pile of chopped wood.

"That?" Murdoc snorted derisively and pointed to the ancient shed. "It's practically rotted away. If you touch that, it'll dissolve to dust."

Owen shrugged, but he couldn't hide a proud smile. "It's one of my better glamours, I admit."

"That's glamoured?" Connor asked.

The prince nodded. "Let's go. No time to waste."

Behind them, Sophia sighed impatiently, but otherwise said nothing.

The hinges squeaked—softly, and just for a second—as Owen opened the shed's slanted door. More wood piled against the edges of the narrow structure, and a cloth tarp on the back wall of the shed blocked any hint of this so-called secret passage.

"You must be joking," Sophia muttered.

"Come on, now." Connor cast a sidelong glance at the two of them, but he didn't bother to hide his own mischievous smile. "I know you both need a drink. It's been a long couple of days."

Murdoc groaned and rubbed his tired eyes. "To put it mildly."

The prince reached into the shed and pulled aside the tarp to reveal a wooden door built flush into the tavern's stone wall.

Clever.

"I—uh—need a bit of fresh air." Murdoc feigned a half-hearted cough to hide the lie. "I'll meet you all inside."

Sophia frowned. "Since when do you put 'fresh air' before whiskey?"

Beside her, Connor crossed his arms and raised one doubtful eyebrow.

Damn.

Neither of them had bought it.

"I'll be fine," he said with a lazy flick of his wrist. "I just need a minute to myself."

"Don't take too long," Owen warned. "This area of town isn't the sort of place you want to wander alone."

"I'll keep that in mind." Murdoc lifted one hand to his forehead in a mock salute. "Now, you all get drunk. Or, rather, try to," he added with a playful grin at Connor.

"Alright," Connor said as he held open the ramshackle door. "Let's go, everyone. This isn't the place for debates."

Owen darted inside, and Sophia followed with a resigned shrug, apparently too tired to argue.

Connor, however, paused a moment longer. He watched Murdoc with an intense stare that would've set any man on edge, and Murdoc fought the urge to fidget under his friend's knowing glare.

"Be safe," Connor warned.

"Aye, Captain." Murdoc gestured toward the tavern. "Go have yourself a well-earned barrel of whiskey."

Connor chuckled dryly and ducked as he walked into the shed. The door closed without a sound, and the dark alley behind the pub went eerily silent.

Good. Murdoc had to do this alone.

For roughly the tenth time today, Murdoc tugged the yellowed note from his pocket. He unfolded it as he tread a familiar path through the southeast slums. Though he had already memorized the time and place of this meeting with his former brothers-in-arms, he studied the handwriting again each time he passed a streetlamp.

He still couldn't make out who had written it, and that could only mean the Blackguards had been *heavily* recruiting since he'd been banished.

Obviously, Connor would've told him not to go, but the man didn't understand what was at stake. It wasn't just the stolen sword in the sheath on his hip, and it wasn't the fact that he had returned to a Blackguard stronghold after they had stripped him of his rank and life's purpose.

As long as Murdoc carried this sword, he thought of himself as a Blackguard. Even with the disgraced mark on his chest, the sword kept him rooted to the only way of life he had ever known, at least before he had stumbled into Connor's strange world.

Tonight, he would finally put his past behind him. So long as he didn't provoke them—and so long as they got what they wanted—they wouldn't attack him.

Probably.

His team would've rallied behind him, giving him much needed support in a standoff that would most certainly leave him outnumbered. He knew that. This wasn't a matter of his safety, but of theirs. Blackguards would recognize a Beaumont if they got too close, and that meant Sophia wasn't safe. Connor was a wanted man fused to ancient magic, and he knew how their kind thought.

These were men accustomed to taking on powerful foes and winning. If they caught wind of Connor, they would kill him. With the sort of power that man wielded, he was the kind of enemy the Blackguards would do anything to take down—even if it meant destroying themselves.

Quicker than he had expected, he ended up at the southern cliffside. A salty wind blew in off the sea, and black silhouettes on the horizon were the only indication of the smaller islands just offshore. An overgrown footpath carved through a cluster of trees along the sheer cliff, and his feet led him down the familiar route.

How strange, to be back here after so long—and to head into these woods for a different reason altogether.

The canopy blocked what little moonlight the crescent moons provided, and long stretches of tar-black shadow offered plenty of opportunities for his former brothers-in-arms to hide.

The creak of tightening bows caught his ear, and he casually glanced up to find two men in the branches above him. They glared down at him as he passed below, their arrows aimed on his chest, and he gave them a lazy salute.

He'd been through hell since he'd left the brotherhood. They didn't scare him anymore.

They.

Not *we*, but *they.*

The thought struck him as odd, and he paused for a moment to savor the sudden rush of clarity. He had come so far since his time in the Ancient Woods. Back then, he had been nothing more than a lost man with a death wish.

Now, he understood the true meaning of brotherhood. He finally knew what loyalty really felt like.

A series of tripwires up ahead marked the only clues of the traps lying in wait in this darkness, and he easily stepped over each one. It was effortless, as familiar as the air he breathed, and he tried to catch glimpses of what lay in wait as he passed each one. He saw nothing but the oppressive shadow.

Too bad. He had always loved seeing the new contraptions for himself.

The path curved around a thick dogwood tree, and he heard the cluster of men on the other side before he saw them. He fought the impulse to draw his stolen sword and squared his shoulders as he rounded the bend.

Four men stood in a small clearing, and the blue moonlight cast a surreal spotlight on their faces. Three sat on a towering boulder at the far end of the clearing, their crossbows already pointed at his heart.

Johnson. Miller. Fischer.

He'd lost count of how many missions the four of them had gone on through the years. Now, however, the three senior officers glowered at him with the same ferocity as he'd felt on so many of their campaigns.

The fourth man stood in the center of the clearing with his hands on his waist. Silver hair had finally overtaken his once jet-black locks, and the aging Commander's eyes narrowed as Murdoc closed the gap between them.

Commander Wells.

Damn it.

Murdoc had assumed that Wells would've been in the north this time of year. Any of the other three commanders would've been a better audience than the man who had banished him to begin with.

Just his luck.

"Gentlemen." Murdoc forced his shoulders to relax as he surveyed the four of them, knowing full well the woodland was teeming with more of the brotherhood. He could only imagine how many of them had volunteered for this, if only to see their disgraced second lieutenant get his due.

"You got nerve, boy." While Commander Wells kept his glare firmly on Murdoc, the man spat on the ground to emphasize his point.

Once, Murdoc would've said something stupid. Something antagonizing. Something just cocky enough to get under their skin.

This time, however, he kept quiet and focused on his breathing. His heartbeat settled, and his shoulders never slumped.

He wasn't going to back down from this.

"Walking back into the fray like that," Wells continued. "Strutting into our lands with a stolen sword on your waist and new company we ain't seen before. Can't tell if you're brave or stupid, kid."

Wells kicked a rock on the ground. It skittered over the patches of grass and hit Murdoc's boot.

An insult, and one Murdoc chose to ignore.

"That girl of yours is pretty." Wells gestured back toward the path behind Murdoc. "Looks dangerous. Both of them do. Ain't seen either in the last day or so, though. Did you figure out that we were looking into them?"

"I did," he said flatly.

"Who are they?" Wells asked.

"These aren't questions I'll answer," Murdoc said firmly. "Nor am I going to take this bait. Get to the point, Wells. Is it the sword you want? Or me?"

Wells spit again on the ground, and his eyes narrowed with barely restrained disgust. "Both."

"See, now, that's a problem." Murdoc shrugged lazily, as though this were a mere negotiation. "Pretty as you think I am, you can't have me."

"Cut the shit, Murdoc," Wells growled. "You came here for a fight, and you're getting it."

"I didn't, actually."

"Horse shit."

"No. It's the truth," Murdoc corrected.

He reached for the strap holding the sheath to his waist. The three officers on the boulder tensed, and their arrow tips recentered on his heart. In the shadows around the clearing, more bowstrings tightened. A few men muttered obscenities under their breath, and he managed to catch one voice among the sudden cacophony.

"I dare you, fucker," one man muttered.

Murdoc waited for that to sting. To think of the people he had once considered to be family, now eager to stab him through the heart.

But he didn't. Oddly, he felt nothing at all.

Not even fear.

"Easy, now." Cautiously, Murdoc raised his hands to show he meant no harm. "I'm just going for the buckle."

"Lying to my face." Wells shook his head, disgusted. "You ain't never giving up that sword on your own."

"You're not often wrong, Wells," Murdoc lied as met the man's furious glare. "But this time, you are. If I try to attack, sure. Kill me. But there's only one reason I would've come out here, alone, into a clearing where I knew I'd be outnumbered."

Once again, he reached for the buckle holding the sheath to his waist. The metal clicked as he unfastened it, and he let the blade slide off his thigh. It hit the ground with a thud, and he once more raised his hands in surrender. With a gentle twist of his foot, he hooked his boot under the weapon and kicked it over to the commander.

The enchanted blade kicked up a small cloud of dust as it slid the last few feet toward the officer. Even when it tapped his boot, Wells didn't budge.

"What are you playing at, Baynard?" one of the men on the boulder asked.

Fischer.

The blond man glared down the length of his crossbow, and Murdoc caught the man's eye. "Nothing to play at. Not this time."

The officer scoffed. "You're just giving it up?"

Murdoc nodded.

"Bullshit," Wells snapped. "No Blackguard gives up his weapon without a fight."

"I'm no Blackguard." Murdoc scowled at the commander this time. With a quick tug, he pulled up enough of his shirt to expose the large slash inked through the Blackguard shield on his chest. "You lot made sure of that."

The clearing was silent, and something shifted in the commander's expression. Recognition, perhaps, or understanding. Maybe even a hint of respect.

Either way, it didn't matter.

"You got what you wanted." With his hands still raised in surrender, Murdoc nodded toward the path behind him. "I just want to leave."

Wells barked out a hoarse laugh. "You stole from us, Baynard, and I don't like the look of those people you brought here. You ain't leaving until I say so."

"Wrong," Murdoc corrected, his voice cold and even. "I stole that sword back from you because it was mine, and because I became a scapegoat for your own shit judgment. You know as well as I do that there wasn't a thing I could've done different out there in Norbury, but you needed someone to blame. I owe you *nothing*."

Behind Wells, Fisher's trigger finger tightened, a breath away from firing. Unfazed, Murdoc met the man's eye.

"My aim has improved since our last target practice," he warned the officer. "Has yours?"

Fisher ran his tongue along his teeth, and in the heavy silence that followed, he loosened his hold on the trigger.

"My company is none of your concern," he warned Wells. "And neither am I. You sniff around my business again—or if you leave me more cryptic notes, or threaten my friends—then you're going to walk into a world of hurt. I'm in deeper than any of you know, and that death's going to be a painful one for the fool who follows after me. I'll see you dying, and I won't lift a finger to help."

Wells sneered. "Is that a—"

"It's a fair warning," Murdoc finished for him. "Are you smart enough to heed it?"

A lull settled into the woodland, and for a time, only the crash of waves against the rocks at the base of the cliff filled the air.

"Now," Murdoc said firmly. "I'm going to walk out of here. The moment I leave this forest, you will never so much as look at me again."

He cast one lingering glance around the clearing, making sure to stare each man in the eye before he turned his back on them.

"Still ain't sure," Wells said flatly.

Murdoc looked over his shoulder at his former commander. "Of what?"

"Whether you're brave or stupid."

"Bit of both," Murdoc confessed with an apathetic shrug.

Without waiting for a reply, Murdoc returned to the overcast shadows of the lone trail that led back to the city. He could feel the soldiers' eyes on the back of his head as he left the Blackguards behind him.

The sensation of being watched slowly faded, and Murdoc kept his eyes trained ahead of him. He didn't want to give any of them a reason to shoot, and he didn't once look back.

As Murdoc returned to the city's cobblestone streets, he sighed and slipped his hands in his pockets. A few carts rumbled past, their wheels rattling over the rough stones, and a horse's soft nicker floated by.

After this much time, his team would have questions that he didn't know how to answer. He wasn't in the mood for a lecture, nor did he want to explain himself.

The past was buried, at least, and he could take solace in that.

As he turned down an alley to take the back route toward the tavern, a silhouette stepped into his periphery. He flinched and raised both fists, ready to land a blow on the idiot who thought he could mug him.

Connor stood there, smirking, and raised one eyebrow in silent challenge.

"Damn it, you're quiet." Murdoc let out a relieved sigh and rubbed the back of his neck as he pieced together what must've happened. "You followed me, didn't you?"

"Sure did."

"What did you hear?"

"All of it," Connor admitted.

Murdoc gestured behind them, in the vague direction of the Blackguard's woodland. "Let's hear it then. The lecture."

"What lecture?" Connor stepped around him and led the way down the alley, back toward the pub.

Grateful and exhausted, Murdoc chuckled and matched his friend's gait as they trudged through the dark alley between two red-brick shops.

"Guess you'll need a new weapon," Connor said.

"Looks that way."

The Wraithblade grinned. "Good thing we've got an armory, then."

"Lucky bastards, aren't we?" Murdoc laughed. "Now buy me some booze. I'm parched."

As Connor led the way back to the tavern, neither man spoke. Nothing needed to be said, and the silence served as all the confirmation Murdoc needed.

'Lucky bastard' was an understatement. After getting rid of that sword, he felt *free*.

CHAPTER SIXTY-SEVEN

SOPHIA

In a hidden back room of a local tavern, Sophia and Owen waited in a tense silence. They sat at a long wooden table, each on opposite benches, and both of them nursed their mugs of ale. Two cups marked the places where Connor and Murdoc were supposed to be sitting, and she once more debated going after them.

If Connor hadn't asked her to keep an eye on the prince, she would have darted out the door this instant. Murdoc had clearly been up to something, and Connor added to the chaos just as often as he curbed it.

Those two knew more about raising hell than any necromancer could dream of mastering.

Sophia stared at the floor, her eyes tracing the grain of the wood panels as if they held some clue as to what was to come. Owen shifted uneasily in his chair, his eyes scanning the room as if he could somehow catch a glimpse of the future within the pockmarked tavern walls.

Distant drinking songs, muffled by a closed door and the long hallway outside, filtered into their silent space. Firelight flickered in the sconces on the walls, casting black shadows across the warm room, and thin tendrils of smoke coiled up toward the thin vents above.

A loud huff of air shot through Owen's nose, and he took a long drink from his mug. The Prince of Kirkwall watched her over the rim, and after another sip, he cradled it between his hands. "You look tense."

Sophia shrugged. "As do you."

"Fair enough." He grinned and pushed his empty cup to the end of the table. With a heavy groan, he propped one leg on the bench and leaned his back against the wall. The prince shut his eyes and relaxed into the wooden planks behind him.

Still lost in her thoughts, Sophia stared into the half-empty mug in her hand. Ripples darted across the surface each time she fidgeted in her seat.

"What's bothering you?" Owen asked.

Sophia quirked an eyebrow as his voice snapped her out of her daze, but his eyes were still closed. He hadn't moved an inch, but she had heard the question all the same.

And, curse the Fates, she had a list.

The Lightseers had recognized her out there in the Decay. With all of their traipsing through Kirkwall, she had run out of glamours. Her new life was supposed to be spent in hiding in rural areas far from Nethervale interests, not bumbling about taverns and major cities with an easily recognized outlaw.

Worst of all, she had a dark little inkling that the Grimm on her life would be fulfilled—and soon.

"Nothing," she said flatly.

Owen chuckled. "I always assumed necromancers were at least half-decent liars."

Her eye twitched in irritation, but she didn't reply.

A man's slurred voice drifted through the wall, and faint echoes of laughter followed. The twang of a lute blended with the occasional thud of a fist slamming onto a table, and she wondered how many people out there had connections to the Beaumonts.

Any one of them could've recognized her already.

A chorus of drunken jeers erupted from somewhere in the back, followed by a raucous rendition of a bawdy song. The sound of footsteps, heavy boots scraping against the wooden floorboards, grew louder before fading away again.

On the other side of that wall, lives were being lived in the hours leading up to the town's curfew. Songs were being sung. Old men were telling exaggerated war stories. Friends were toasting each other's successes. All of that life, happening while two fugitives had a beer just feet away. A good many of those people would return to homes and families that actually wanted them.

Sophia wondered what that must've been like.

"I figure you're on the run," Owen said quietly. "There's plenty of people after Connor, but my guess is you're running from something else."

"This doesn't concern you." She didn't bother masking the dripping venom in each word.

Sophia didn't take well to people prying into her life—especially those with connections to royalty.

"You're right. It doesn't." Owen adjusted in his seat, but his eyes remained shut. "I've seen you fight, woman, and you're terrifying."

A little grin tugged on the edges of her mouth, and she took a sip of her ale to hide it. "Flatterer."

Owen chuckled. "I know it's not my business, but sometimes I can't help myself. You looked miserable."

"It's fine," she lied.

"Whatever's on your mind, Sophia, remember you're not alone. I haven't known you all long, but Connor is clearly a good man. He does what's right, and he protects his team."

She pursed her lips, but the man had a point. With Connor on her side, she stood a chance—even against the most feared crime lord in Saldia.

"And as far as I'm concerned, you're a Shade." The prince peeked through one eye. "That means I—and the others—have your back. From what I've seen so far, you're one of the people Connor cares about the most. I pity anyone who comes after you because there's no telling what will be left once Connor's through with them."

Once again, a lull settled between them. She sat with everything he'd said, and she had to admit it made her feel the tiniest bit better.

Footsteps thudded on the floorboards beyond the door, but this time, they didn't fade. They neared, louder with each second.

Sophia tensed. Her mug hit the table with the barest tap, and her now-empty fingertips twitched. On demand, her enchanted daggers slid from the sheaths hidden on her wrists, and she angled her body toward the door.

If anyone other than Connor or Murdoc entered, a poisoned dagger would lodge in their neck.

Owen heard it too, and he set one hand on his sword as the footsteps reached the only entrance to the room.

The door slowly opened, and a familiar rogue with long brown curls stuck his head through the gap.

Murdoc.

"It's us," he said with a mischievous grin. "Rein in the murder, please."

In unison, Sophia and Owen relaxed. Sophia's blades sank back into their leather holsters, and Owen sheathed his sword with a soft clink.

The door creaked open, and Connor dominated the hallway behind Murdoc. The former Blackguard ducked into the room with an air of relief—and no sword.

Sophia raised one eyebrow as she waited for either man to say something. "Is it handled?"

With a tired groan, Murdoc slid onto the bench next to her and planted a wet kiss on her cheek. "It is."

Irritated by the slime on her cheek, she wiped the worst of it on her sleeve and shot him an irritated glare. Unfazed as ever, he simply planted another on her lips.

Connor hadn't entered. He still stood in the hallway, one hand on the doorframe, and gestured for Owen to join him. "A word?"

"Of course." The prince jumped to his feet, but he paused at the exit to flash a reassuring smile back at Sophia.

With that, both men disappeared into the hallway, though Sophia could only hear one pair of boots on the hardwood. Connor's stealth was improving.

"What was that about?" Murdoc glanced between her and the door.

"Jealous?" Sophia grinned and watched him over the rim of her mug.

"I'm not sure." Murdoc made a show of setting one hand on his heart as he feigned deep thought. "Is it—curious? Nosy, maybe?"

"Loud?" she offered flatly.

"Aroused." Murdoc nodded once, as though that settled it. "Definitely aroused."

Sophia laughed and shook her head at his ludicrous banter. "You're an idiot."

"Your idiot," Murdoc corrected.

"That's right." This time, she didn't try to hide her broad smile. "My idiot."

CHAPTER SIXTY-EIGHT

CONNOR

On the edge of the Kirkwall cliffs, with Saldia's twin moons half-asleep in the sky, Connor leaned against the wind-worn fence that kept drunks from falling to their deaths. He stared down at the rocky shore, far below—at the stretch of beach where he nearly died.

This was where Bryan had shoved him off the cliff.

The night had a somber weight to it. Over the centuries, smugglers had used this same dirt path to pass unseen through the night. He stood where many men had stood before him, and where many would stand when he was gone.

With Owen next to him, neither man spoke. The starlit sky cast a silver glow over the sea, but the stars on the horizon burned brightest. Waves rippled and crashed in the calm ocean breeze, and the wind carried their salty tang over the island's cliffs.

In his youth, Connor hadn't thought of this place as peaceful—but it had a surreal serenity to it now that he had paused to simply listen.

The two of them stood there for what seemed like hours, lost in thought and the beauty of the island night.

"I overheard what you told that man," the prince suddenly said. "Back in the dungeon when you went rogue. That man. Bryan. He killed your family. He's the reason Rockwell lost everything."

A sharp breath of air shot through Connor's nose. His fingers coiled into a fist, so tight that his knuckles cracked, but he eventually nodded.

"I'm sorry that happened to you," Owen said quietly.

"Thank you."

In the somber silence that followed, the two of them stared out at the sea. The distant islands faded in and out of the shadows as a midnight ocean roared over the rocks below. A lone star shot through the sky, far off across the waves, and faded to nothing in the pitch-black horizon.

"I was lost, out there in the Ancient Woods," Connor admitted.

His voice broke the peaceful silence, and Owen tilted his head closer as he listened. Calm. Collected. Focused and present, waiting to help carry this burden if Connor felt inclined to share.

A natural-born leader.

Connor roughly cleared his throat. "I would've preferred a world where my family was still here. I miss them. Coming here—coming home—this hurt worse than most of the fights I've been in."

Owen sighed, soft and somber, but he let the silence linger.

"Can't be changed," Connor said with a shrug. "I suppose this is the path the Fates gave me, same as you. All either of us can do is our best."

Through the corner of Connor's eye, the prince wove his fingers together as he watched the midnight sea. "I suppose you're right. At least you got your revenge."

At that, Connor looked down at his hands.

He chose not to reply.

"Will you ever tell me what you did in the cavern?" Owen asked without looking over. "All of those soldiers, dead without so much as seeing you."

"No," Connor said flatly. "Not today."

"Someday, then?"

Hmm.

Do it, the Wraith King said. *Tell him now, Magnuson. It's foolish for you to continue to keep what you are secret.*

Connor frowned at the intrusion, but he ultimately shrugged as he returned his attention to Owen. "Maybe."

The Wraith King sighed in disappointment. *You cannot hide forever, Magnuson.*

With an irritated glare around the empty path, Connor stifled the urge to tell the undead king to shut his damn mouth.

"A 'maybe' is better than a 'no,'" Owen said.

Connor studied the prince's face, even though he wasn't entirely sure what he was looking for. Fear, perhaps, or a hint of disgust. "Are you scared of it?"

"No," the prince said flatly.

Bullshit.

Connor let the silence linger as he watched Owen's face more intently for any tells of a lie. A twitch of the eye, perhaps, or a bit more fidgeting than normal. But the prince stared out at the sea, calm and still, and leaned a little more into the wooden barrier keeping them both from plunging to their deaths.

Interesting.

"Careful, now," Connor said with a wry grin. "It almost sounds like you trust me."

Owen chuckled.

Connor shrugged. "That, or you've lost your damn mind."

"Maybe it's a little bit of both."

A gust of wind shot over the ocean. The sharp blast hit him square in the face, carrying the heady aroma of seaweed on the tide, and a happy shiver snaked down his spine. The midnight hours sauntered by, and once again, a peaceful tranquility settled between them. Far below, the sea roared across the base of the sheer cliff as wave after wave smashed against the shore. Wind whistled through the rocks, filling the air with the ocean's salty song, and he closed his eyes to savor its chorus.

"Is this pointless?" Owen eventually asked. "The Shades. Our fight. Our attempts to make Kirkwall better."

"It depends," Connor admitted. "What makes you think it's pointless?"

"Because it never ends." The prince pushed off the railing and set his hands on the back of his head. "Because no matter how much good I do, I'm only one man. It's never *enough*."

Huh.

How interesting.

Connor lightly tapped his knuckle on the railing as debated what to say.

"Small steps make big progress. Even drops in a bucket add up over time."

Owen frowned. Instead of replying, he just glared out at the ocean.

"Do you want to quit?" Connor asked.

"No, of course not. I just—"

"Say you did quit," Connor interjected. "Would you regret it on your deathbed? Would you look back and wish you'd kept going?"

Owen sighed and shut his eyes. "Yes."

"There's your answer, then." Connor gestured out at the raging waves beyond the island. "Be like the sea. The tide never stops, even though it sometimes slows. Whatever happens, don't stop."

At that, Owen smiled. His shoulders relaxed, and the Prince of Kirkwall set his hands on his waist. "I suppose you're right."

With a mischievous grin, Connor shrugged. "I *am* right."

Owen laughed, and the last of the man's tension faded away. He leaned against the railing once more as another gust of wind carried the sharp bite of pine bark across the path.

"It seems daunting at times," Connor added. "There are times when it feels like you're doing this on your own. Even with a brilliant team and all the stubborn grit in the world, the fight sometimes feels impossible to win."

"Is it?"

"I don't think so," Connor answered. "Not as long as there are good people out there like you."

It was something he never thought he would say, and yet it rang painfully true.

"And you," the prince added.

Hmm.

Words failed him, and Connor mulled over how best to reply. This entire exchange seemed so strange, so surreal, that he almost couldn't believe the future King of Kirkwall was standing next to him, asking for advice.

In the end, he opted for silence.

"I was going to return that bastard to the throne." Owen spat on the ground, as if the words were rotting on his tongue. "I didn't want to believe he would do something like this. That he would try to kill me."

"It's a lesson worth learning." Connor shifted his weight against the railing so that he could study the prince's face as they spoke. "If you're not vigilant, you'll miss the snakes in the grass. Look at everyone you meet and ask yourself what drives them. What makes them who they are? What do they fear? What do they want? Given your position, a good number of them will want you dead, Owen, and many more will try to manipulate you for power or profit. You can't let your idealism blind you anymore."

Instead of answering, the prince scowled out at the sea. After several moments of silence, it became clear he wasn't going to respond.

Yet again, that surreal sensation nestled deep in Connor's gut. He'd often glared out over the ocean, just like that, when his father had given him one too many lectures. With his mind racing and his anger burning in his veins, he had often started to tune his father out. Looking back, there was no telling the wisdom he'd missed, simply because he had been too lost in his own thoughts.

What he would give to go back and change that.

"Tell me something, Owen," Connor said firmly, loud enough to break through those buzzing thoughts in the prince's head. "What makes a good leader?"

The prince frowned. "I don't know anymore. I guess it isn't something I've thought much about, since I didn't want the throne."

"Didn't? Or don't?"

Owen rubbed the back of his neck for a second or two before answering. "My family doesn't deserve it, Connor."

"Maybe not," Connor said calmly. "But it's yours. Victor isn't a threat anymore, and that means you have to learn to live with your place in this world. That's the path the Fates set for you. Ask yourself who you need to be to deserve it, when all is said and done, and work toward becoming that man."

Owen sighed. "You sound like Rockwell."

"Then he's not wrong."

"I know." The prince rubbed his eyes. "I just—I mean—Look, it's not that simple. From the day we set foot on this island, one I'd never even seen before my father was declared king of its people, I've felt like a fraud."

"Was Victor any better?"

With a heavy sigh, Owen shook his head. "I suppose not, but maybe I'm still not the best option. Maybe I'll never deserve that crown."

"Few kings do," Connor admitted. "And no king does until he proves himself to his people. Wear the mask. Be the Shade. Let the city see the difference between you and your father. Let him hate you for it. One day, you're going to take off that mask, and your people will judge you for who you are—not for who your father is."

A thin smile tugged on the prince's mouth, but Owen didn't look up from his hands.

"You changed Rockwell's mind," Connor pointed out. "All those years ago, when you two met, did you know your father had ordered his wife to be burned to death in their home?"

The color drained from Owen's face, and the prince gaped up at Connor in horror.

"I'll take that as a no." Connor shook his head. "That's Rockwell for you. Didn't want you to carry that guilt, I suppose."

"My father is a monster." The prince's nose creased with unrestrained disgust. "I can't stand him. Every time we speak, I want to punch him in the face. He's such a *coward*. He hides in that palace and hoards the city's wealth. He couldn't dream of spending all that money in one lifetime, and yet he lets a fifth of our city starve."

For a moment, Connor didn't know how to reply. He wasn't used to men like the prince, not really. For someone in power to actually want to protect those he was responsible for—well, it was a refreshing surprise.

Something about Owen's earnest desire to help extinguished the last tendrils of resentment deep within the spiteful part of Connor's soul.

Despite warning the prince not to carry the weight of his father's legacy, Connor had often done the same. His father had been such an integral part of his life that Connor had all but given him full credit for who he had become.

As the ocean's song thundered below them, Connor wove his fingers together and watched the starlit sky. "Our fathers influence who we become, but only we can choose who we are, Owen. I'd say you chose well."

The prince smiled. "That almost sounded like a compliment."

"It won't happen again," Connor assured him with a playful grin.

As the minutes ticked by, Owen's smile slowly fell. "Wade—he was going to die for me. He didn't even hesitate."

Connor nodded. "That's a true ally. Find more people like him."

"You don't understand. I don't want people to die for me."

"No good man does," Connor explained. "But it will probably happen anyway. It's on you to protect them as best you can. Remember what I said. If a man follows you to hell—"

"—it's on me to ensure he makes it back." Owen pinched the bridge of his nose and let out a long, slow sigh. "I know."

Connor clapped the prince on the back. "I'm trusting you with the Shades, Owen. Prove me right."

Owen sat with that, for a moment, before nodding. "I will. Thank you."

"It won't be easy," Connor warned. "When I leave, you need to better organize. Learn how to lead and weed out those who won't listen. Rockwell will teach you what you need to know. Take risks. Make mistakes. Learn from it all. Keep your men focused, and don't let them lose sight of what drove you all to join."

"You have my word."

"Good." Connor pushed off the railing and brushed a wayward leaf off his shoulder. "It won't be long before the city wakes up. Let's head back."

In the tranquil night, their boots passed silently over the dirt path. Owen walked beside him as the ocean's roar slowly faded into the night. Out here, away from the blinding lights of Oakenglen, the stars burned brightly overhead as clouds rolled past the twin moons.

Arlo Hunt hadn't drained the magic from this island.

Not yet, and not ever.

"I owe you more than my life." Owen's voice broke the early morning stillness as they found the narrow alley that would lead back to the tavern.

Connor smirked. "That's true."

Owen didn't laugh. Instead, the man stuck his hands in his pockets and looked Connor dead in the eye. "If you ever need anything, the Shades and

I are always here for you. Just ask."

Connor's smile fell, and he scanned the shadows around them as the offer stirred up thoughts of the chaos to come. Even with Teagan gone, the promise of death and slit throats simmered on the horizon like a bloody dawn. He had a dungeon full of Lightseers and a horde of other enemies that he had yet to even meet.

As much as he wanted to believe otherwise, he would one day take Owen up on that offer—and that day would likely come sooner than either of them could imagine.

CHAPTER SIXTY-NINE

DOOM

The two waning crescent moons hung low in a tar-black sky, like a haunting pair of eyes floating among the stars.

Somber.

Silent.

Still.

As Doom flew above the thundering waves beyond Kirkwall, he scanned the mainland's distant cliffs. Somewhere beyond that rocky shore, a goddess waited—one he had never met, but only heard of in the awestruck legends that had wandered out to his domain. The Daughter of Death. The Keeper of Memory. She had so many names, and he had always desired to meet her.

Perhaps this new human of his would prove useful after all.

At peace and finally reunited with his beloved sky, Doom waited to relive its melody. For the tug of the current on his long-dead wings. For the ache and shimmer of the blackfire in his chest to rage against the cool air. All those centuries ago, the wind had always whispered across his scales, soft and soothing, as it carried him toward the stars. It was the sensation of life, of freedom, and of joy.

Yet he felt nothing. Only the icy surge of magic through his ancient bones kept him company in the night.

Aeron Zacharias had tempted him back to the land of the living, mainly with pretty words of the destruction they would rain upon this mortal world. The necromancer had charmed him with the promise of a servant's obedience, all to convince him that men would pay for what they had done to Firebreath Mountain.

Lies dripped from every word the conniving mortal had spoken, so Doom had used the fool to bring him back—but his second chance at life had not gone to plan.

Immortality had a cost, and it was one he had not been prepared to pay.

Ahead, along the rapidly approaching cliffs, a flock of seagulls dove in front of the jagged stone. More of them shot from hidden nests among the sheer rock, their flight jarring and sudden, and his feral nature flashed hot with the urge to chase this fresh new prey. It had erupted in this new world of sensations and sights, and it was starved for blood. Any deaths would do to sate its ravenous hunger, but he had long since grown accustomed to its savagery. It had never spoken to him, and he would never let it free.

If he did, it would swallow each living thing whole and still be hungry.

Below, between Doom and the raging sea, his descendent carried three humans like some belabored pack mule. One had even tied herself to his spine, as though this mighty warrior were but a ship's mast in a raging storm, and the sight set Doom's blackfire raging. His feral side pushed again for liberation, harder this time, and he once again restrained the urge to light them all on fire. Nocturne's hide would protect him from the worst of the blast, of course, and the scars would remind the young prince of a dragon's place in this world—far above the men.

His people were not to be conquered.

Three figures perched on Nocturne's back, each staring at a different part of the horizon, and that infernal Wraith King hovered beside them. He and Doom flew through the in-between, separate from the land of the living in this white-washed landscape between worlds.

This was the world in which he had lived since fusing with Connor Magnuson, and Doom had learned so much.

The self-proclaimed warlord, for all his boasting, obeyed this mortal man. The Wraith King griped and moped, of course, as rabid and irrational as any man Doom had known before, but Doom had witnessed something far more interesting. In fact, he was beginning to understand why these way-laid misfits had banded with Magnuson in their journeys through this life.

Murdoc, the disgraced soldier who had finally found purpose.

Sophia, the destructive necromancer who secretly yearned for a home.

And Nocturne, who saw Magnuson as an equal. A friend, even, with whom he had struck a bargain—though the two had yet to discuss it in detail.

...being foolish, the Wraith King's voice faded in and out of the wind as the undead man hovered by Magnuson's side.

Doom angled downward, and he leveled out after mere moments of descent. This position gave him the advantage—far enough away to blend into the sky, but close enough to listen.

"Stop talking," Magnuson ordered, careful to keep his voice low.

Why are we returning this? the Wraith King pressed, as though the man hadn't spoken. *You heard Death. You know what you could be—what you could do—if you kept this for yourself. She doesn't have the power to stop you. You're letting that damned nobility get in the way yet again.*

Magnuson growled in annoyance, but he didn't reply.

One more, the ghoul pressed. *One more, and you're a god. You would sacrifice such power?*

Doom's eyes narrowed, and a low snarl rumbled in his skull as he waited for the human's answer.

"I'm keeping my word," Connor said. "This isn't open for discussion, and I won't listen to this anymore. You try anything, and I'll finally make good on my promise."

The wraith scoffed. *You wouldn't dare.*

"Try me." Magnuson's voice dropped an octave, and the unspoken threat thundered in his chest. "You set Doom free. I warned you what would happen if you threatened me or my team. You're an ass, and I'll tolerate that—to a point. What you did in the mountain went too far, and you're lucky I haven't already tried to end you."

Floating through the air at Magnuson's side, the ghoul went eerily still. His bony hands curled into tight fists, and he lifted his chin in defiance at the man's audacity.

And yet, the Wraith King did nothing.

Astonishing.

This nobility—this honor—it could not be real. This had to be an air to win Doom's favor, and a dragon of his caliber could not be so easily fooled.

Strangely, however, Magnuson seemed to forget at times that he was being watched. It was what Doom had wanted, of course, but thus far the man had been tolerable. Enjoyable, even.

To admit something so absurd set Doom's blackfire raging yet again.

As Aeron Zacharias had hinted, all those centuries ago, Doom's powers had seeped into the man who served as his tether to this world.

Doom's blackfire raged through the man's blood at each pulse of anger. It had erupted, hot and fierce, when his resolve had faltered. Even now, Doom could feel it trying to break free, and yet Magnuson betrayed nothing of the ache he must've felt in his very bones.

Doom's tenacity, too, had slowly begun to strengthen the man's resolve. Though pangs of hunger and lust hit on occasion, Magnuson had yet to succumb to them. Sometimes, it seemed as though he hardly felt them at all.

Even Doom's overbearing power had seeped into Magnuson's voice. Out there on the beach, his mere presence had been so powerful that it made those unruly fools go still after a single command. They had obeyed, albeit begrudgingly, just as the dragons had submitted to Doom in ages past.

However, no impenetrable black scales had grown into that feeble flesh, and it seemed likely that none ever would. Not all of his powers had transferred, then, and Doom could take solace in that.

To Doom's astonishment, the man had not abused even one of them.

Not yet, anyway.

This Connor Magnuson—the first man to survive fusing with a king of legend—carried himself with the confidence only a true warrior could embody. He had blood on his hands, but every good king did. It was the way of law and the fate of a leader, to carry those burdens for his people.

But this man carried an inferno within him.

That fight. That fire. A blend of wisdom and courage, of honor and mercy, that burned within every great king. These were traits Doom's own son had displayed, time and again, as the hatchling had grown into a dragon worthy of being remembered in myth and lore. Back in his time, when breath could fill his lungs and the sky's currents sent happy chills across his hide, Doom's son

Pyre had displayed all the subtle makings of a great leader—but it had been Doom who had pushed him to accept that power and become a true king.

To see his child thrive, after all, was a father's duty.

How strange, to think a human might not be so different from Doom's own son. It seemed like an impossible thought, treason to even consider. In his day, Doom would have roasted the fool stupid enough to suggest such a thing in his presence.

Yet he was all these centuries later, considering it for himself.

It was not yet the time to act. Magnuson had a Soulsprite, one that belonged to a living goddess, and the inklings of its true power had already been mentioned in passing by that infernal ghoul. To resist the allure of having it so near, when it had already called to him once, astonished Doom to no end. In the treasure chamber, it had hummed with life and longing, as if begging Magnuson to take it.

But the man had refused temptation.

Clearly, Magnuson knew what would happen if he kept it for himself. He would soon be forced to choose between what was right and what was easy. That would tell Doom more than any observation ever could.

Should the man succeed, Doom would strike a bargain. This human seemed prone to them, after all, and Doom only wanted one thing—to know the price at which Connor Magnuson's honor could finally be bought.

CHAPTER SEVENTY

CONNOR

The steady clack of Dahlia's heels on the worn, weathered stone echoed down the tunnel.

As she led Connor deeper into the tunnels below the Blood Bogs, her hands trembled. She wrung them in an anxious pattern, her knuckles bleached white with tension, and goosebumps covered her exposed arms.

Dahlia Donahue was afraid, and that meant something had happened while he was away.

"Are you going to tell me what's wrong?" he asked. "Or are you going to make me pry it out of you?"

The fallen princess flinched, sharp and sudden, and her foot caught on a raised stone in the floor. She stumbled, but Connor grabbed her arm to keep her upright.

They stood there for a moment, his hand on her arm as her chest heaved with surprise, but she looked up at him with foggy eyes. Whatever she was thinking about, it had dragged her far away from him and the tunnel through which they walked.

She gently patted his hand in a silent request for him to let her go. He indulged her, though he kept a wary eye on her face, and she took a shaky breath to steady her nerves. The fallen princess raised her chin and relaxed her shoulders, but no amount of decorum or composure could hide the shake in her hands.

"She's worse," Dahlia said softly.

Connor frowned. The Antiquity was fading faster than anyone had expected.

"Let's go." He adjusted the bag on his shoulder—the one that carried her Soulsprite—and gestured for Dahlia to lead the way.

Decaying vines littered the walls, more and more of them the longer they walked, and the blanket of dead leaves on the floor thickened. The sickening stench of rotting wood and swamp bile choked the air, heavier with every step. It weighed on his lungs, filling them and refusing to leave. Desperate for air, he lifted the cloth around his neck to cover his nose. It filtered some of the stench, but not enough to quell the nausea biting at the back of his throat.

Dahlia was right. This was far worse than he had expected.

Unfazed by the stench, Dahlia paused at an archway that led into a familiar circular chamber deep below the bogs. Muted light filtered through the vines, almost too dull to see, and the fluttering pulse of a dying goddess rippled through what little greenery was left.

Dahlia's gaze wandered the withered vines along the walls, some of them black with decay, and she swallowed hard. "Goddess?"

The woman wrung her hands again, her shoulders tight with worry, and she scanned the walls. Her body tensed more with each moment, as though she were afraid the Antiquity might not answer.

"I am here," a weak voice replied.

One by one, the surviving vines slithered back from the walls. The room shifted slowly, like a trickle of water through a long-dead stream, and the vines ambled toward the center of the towering chamber. They curled over each other along the floor, stirring up the decay along the stone, and a plume of rotting dust rolled over the ground like a sickly fog.

Connor grimaced, and he braced himself for the worst.

Though long stretches of the living vines were brown with rot, they wove tightly together as the Antiquity rebuilt herself from what was left of her magic. Frayed ends and withered leaves snapped off, slowing her growth, but her body formed all the same. Long legs. A torso. Arms. A neck. The elegant curve of her horns emerged last from the flowing vines, and her body flashed briefly green as the dying goddess stared down at them.

No time to waste, then.

The bag slipped off his shoulder, and he knelt to open it. Buckles clacked and leather slid across skin as he gently pulled the long woven box from his pack and stood. Its vines clustered tightly together, and the stunning green shine on each one reminded him of how the goddess had once appeared.

Strong.

Vibrant.

Alive.

An irritated groan rumbled through his mind, but the Wraith King otherwise remained silent. At least the undead king knew better than to interfere.

He opened the lid to reveal a dull black orb nestled on a cushion of leaves. The Soulsprite hummed in her presence, stronger than it had for him back in the Kirkwall vaults, and a flash of light snaked through the ancient runes carved along its surface.

"You found it." Breathless relief flowed through every word the Antiquity spoke, and she raised one hand toward the dull black orb. At the gesture, the Soulsprite hummed again, louder this time, and the flash of green light lasted a little longer than before.

"Take it," he insisted.

The goddess did not reply.

Instead, her fingers spread wide, and vines slithered over the box to lift the Soulsprite into the air. It hovered, suspended on the tips of what was left of her power, and the orb rolled gently as the slithering mass of roots and decay carried it closer to their master.

The dull light throbbing through the room quickened like a racing pulse. One by one, the vines in the Antiquity's torso snapped open to reveal the hollowed hole in her chest. A lone orb, pulsing with dull green light, rested on a cluster of rotting brambles and black soot in the pit of her stomach.

With a sigh of relief as loud as a torrent of rain through a woodland, the Antiquity closed her eyes. She leaned toward the newfound Soulsprite as it neared, and the orb settled gently in the hollow cavity. The thick vines closed tightly, as though afraid someone else might remove what she had only just recovered.

And, for a moment, the world was dreadfully still.

A low hum built in the air like an approaching storm, soft and gentle on the horizon, but it grew to a crescendo. Connor grimaced as his ears rang from the shrill melody that came from everywhere and nowhere at once. It buzzed in his head, and he set his palms on his ears to quell its earth-shattering screech. Beside him, Dahlia did the same, and they teetered as the floor trembled under their feet.

It stopped as suddenly as it had come, but Connor didn't trust the silence.

A burst of magic shot through the very stone around them. Green light rippled through the rock, through the vines, through every dead thing on the ground, and the decayed leaves hovered above the dazzling energy. The air itself crackled with magic, with power, with life, and the sweet nectar of fresh peaches ripening in the summer sun swam through Connor's senses.

All around him, decayed leaves regrew. The grays and browns in their withered stems brightened into a vibrant green yet again. Any long-dead leaves faded to dust, as if they had never existed at all, as the goddess of the Blood Bogs reclaimed her power.

The Antiquity's once-dying pulse shimmered in the light of the Soulsprite now nestled in her chest, and the thick horns on her head lengthened. White butterflies sprang to life along her arms, fluttering through her hands, as she was once more made whole.

Beside him, Dahlia's brows knit with relief. Her eyes watered, and she set her fingertips on her mouth as she watched the goddess come to life. Her lip quivered, and she wrapped one arm around her torso as she let the emotion take her.

"Thank the Fates," she whispered softly. "Connor—thank you. With all my heart, thank you."

As a tear rolled down her cheek, the fallen princess smiled up at him. She beamed, refreshed and happy, and all of the tension melted from her face.

He shrugged, uncomfortable with the sudden attention. "It's what allies do."

"I suppose it is," she said, standing taller. "And it's only fitting for us to return the favor."

His eyes narrowed in suspicion, and he briefly scanned her face. "What do you mean?"

"We will join you in Arkcaster." Dahlia gestured back down the tunnel, in the vague direction of Freymoor Castle. "You dropped everything to save the Antiquity, and we will do the same. My army and I will meet you in the forests, and we will help you free the dragons."

"Don't be ridiculous." He waved away the idea with a flick of his wrist. "You need to be here with your people. With the Antiquity. I'm not going to let you risk your life for us."

Dahlia tilted her head and frowned, as if incredulous at the very idea that he could stop her. "I'm not giving you a choice. This is what allies do for each other, isn't it? You helped us. Now let us help you."

Connor frowned. He didn't like this one bit. Though he could use the manpower and backup, he had never coordinated an onslaught this large—especially not one against such an impregnable fortress. He had always preferred having his team with him, rather than a larger unit, since he knew every face and who he could trust.

Strangers, even those among his allies, only added to the risk.

"You can give me the map to your rendezvous point," Dahlia prodded. "Or, if you're difficult, we can simply track you. Either way, we will meet you there."

He groaned. "You're insufferable, you know that?"

Dahlia smirked in victory. Though the skin around her eyes crinkled with delight, she didn't reply.

"Fine," he conceded. "Yes, I'll give you the map before we leave."

"Wonderful." Her eyes returned to the towering goddess above them as more and more life seeped into the immortal being's fingers. The green light pulsing through every vein beat brighter with each second that passed.

A sigh of relief rushed by like a gale through the canopy. It quivered like a leaf on a warm summer wind, and it carried with it the promise of budding new life.

"Such sacrifice." The Antiquity's voice echoed through the room and seeped into his mind, and he tilted his head in surprise at the sheer power of her voice.

With her so weak for so long, he had almost forgotten her sheer majesty and presence.

"Death showed me everything," she continued. *"In that mountain, my fears came true, and you have now returned with yet another simmering soul. You knew what you could claim, should you keep my Soulsprite for yourself. You knew what you would become if you fused with it, instead of giving it to me. And yet, you kept your word."*

"I do that a lot, actually," Connor muttered. "And yet everyone always seems so surprised when it happens."

"Not surprised," the goddess corrected. *"Validated. I knew you were worthy of my sacrifice, Connor Magnuson. But now, I know you are ready for so much more."*

He frowned, curious as to where this was going—and not entirely sure he would like whatever happened next.

"Ready for what, exactly?" he asked.

"To face Death," she replied.

"I did that already," he said. "Not really interested in trying it again."

The goddess chuckled, and another flurry of white butterflies appeared around her great horns. *"You met him, yes, but you did not face him."*

Connor raised one eyebrow in surprise, but he wasn't quite sure how to respond to that.

"I have heard whispers," she continued. *"Whispers of the future. Whispers of what your new magic can truly do."*

Ah.

Great.

The nonsensical riddles were back. Though he didn't like seeing the goddess so weak, he rather preferred how straightforward she had been with only one Soulsprite.

"You are a demigod," she explained. *"The magic of the simmering souls has made you distinctly 'other.' You are not of the gods, but neither are you of men. You exist in an in-between of your own, of neither and watched by both. You are my Champion among men, yes—but so too are you my Champion among the gods. I have chosen you as the first to replace my fallen brothers. I have chosen you to join me and the Morrow in our immortal lives."*

Though Connor's mouth parted in his dazed shock, no words would come.

Unfazed by his silence, the Antiquity raised one hand and studied the butterflies made of white light as they fluttered along her fingers. They left a thin trail of glittering diamonds in their wake, and the dazzling pinpricks of blinding magic faded into the air above her palm.

"You must find two more Soulsprites," she continued. *"One to replace the one I gave you, and the other to fuse with your soul. You will be immortal, Connor. Once you face Death, you will be a god."*

"You planned this," he said quietly as the pieces began to click into place. "You knew from the start what would happen."

"Some," she admitted. *"Not all."*

He narrowed his eyes at her audacity. "You played me."

"Connor!" Dahlia chided, her voice so furious and low that it came out almost like a hiss.

"I tested you." The goddess's glowing eyes narrowed as she corrected him with a firm tone. *"Through the eons, only ten will be worthy of that which you will have. You will never taste the land of the dead. You will never age. You will never weaken. You will join us as an immortal protector of this realm, and we will restore balance to this long-dead hellscape that men have pillaged. It is our duty to the mortals to protect these lands, and the world will once more know peace when enough of us are reborn."*

"I've been around long enough to know magic has a price," Connor said flatly, ignoring Dahlia's fury. "Especially magic like that."

"It does," the Antiquity conceded. *"And you are wise to be wary. If you are conquered, someday in the ages to come, then you will cease to be. Mortals move to other lands, and there, they can reunite. You will never be allowed such a blessing. You will never cross over to Death's domain. When those you love die, they will be forever lost to you."*

That sent a chill through his heart.

He would never see his father. His family. Quinn. Murdoc and Sophia. The Finns. Even Nocturne. They would all die, someday, and he would never follow them to whatever awaited them all in the Beyond.

It seemed futile, really, for him and his team to have sacrificed so much to protect Slaybourne—only to live in it forever alone, surrounded by remnants of the friends he would never again see.

Irrelevant. The Wraith King's voice pierced his daze, and the ghoulish words dragged him back to the chamber below the Blood Bogs. *You will always have me, Magnuson.*

"That's not the reassurance you think it is," Connor muttered.

"This is the path you have taken," the Antiquity said. *"There is no turning back. There is no surrendering your power. To take that final Soulsprite—or simmering soul—is to fully commit. When the moment comes, my Champion, whatever choice you make will push you into the kind of life you cannot yet imagine. You cannot be afraid of its power."*

"I'm not," he said firmly.

"Perhaps." The goddess tilted her head, as though she didn't quite believe him, and a soft hum fluttered through the chamber. *"But other people are. People you adore."*

Kiera's face, twisted with horror, flashed through his mind. Her unfiltered terror as he had cut through the slavers still haunted him, all this time later. Try as he might, he would never forget the way she had held the girls tight, as though he was the most fearsome monster in the darkness.

Back in the cavern beneath Kirkwall, he had unleashed the Wraith King's true devastation. Thus far, he had held the undead king's bloodlust at bay—but in so doing, he had held himself back as well.

Out of reason, yes, but also out of fear for what he might become if he truly tested his limits.

"You are correct," the Antiquity said, more gently this time. *"All magic does, indeed, have a price, and that is usually a price paid with someone's blood. This will be the most expensive sacrifice you have ever made, my Champion, but with it will come all the power you need to protect your homeland. Your people will know peace, even though you will lead them from a lonely throne. Can you do this?"*

Obviously, the Wraith King grumbled.

The Antiquity ignored the ghoul and, instead, lowered her great head toward Connor. The white butterflies fluttered with renewed vigor, and every vine that composed her horns thrummed as her steady pulse fed light through her body. Her body glimmered with magic, with life, and he could almost sense a smile on her otherwise empty face.

"The world is vast, my Champion," she said. *"It's humbling, isn't it, to see how many more lives are at stake than your own. Many will rely on you, in the years to come—so many more than you can imagine. It is your sole duty to protect them with all that you are."*

It was an echo of something she had said not long ago, but it rang truer this time. Louder. More resonant. He met her eye, his mind still buzzing with everything they had discussed, and he didn't reply.

"I have found your Soulsprites," she said calmly. *"They wait for you in South Haven, with the Morrow. Should you choose this path after all, go to her. She will find you. For now, I must rest—and rebuild my bogs."*

With that. The vines in the Antiquity's face unwove themselves, and her great horns vanished. The roots slithered over themselves as she faded into the air, and a happy hum filtered through the chamber. The chittering buzz of insects in spring echoed down the tunnels, and with that, she was gone.

But in her wake, she had left Connor a tantalizing offer. To join the gods seemed so absurd, so impossible, that he could hardly fathom the idea. But it would give him the last shred of power he needed to secure Slaybourne once and for all—and, perhaps, destroy his last thread of humanity in the process.

Saldian magic always came with a catch. The more powerful it was, the greater the cost, and he had a feeling there was far more at stake than perhaps even the Antiquity had realized.

CHAPTER SEVENTY-ONE

QUINN

Six days.

Six days of grueling travel and pushing through the night to make it to her safehouse without being spotted. Six days of wearing nonstop glamours, and of taking an entirely new brew each time the old one faded—just so no one would recognize them, even in a glamoured form.

But they had made it to her safehouse in record time, and in these woods, they were finally safe.

With an exhausted groan, Quinn collapsed into an overstuffed armchair by the door. She leaned backward, letting the aged leather all but absorb her, and she finally closed her weary eyes.

Without her Dazzledane to help her push through, this had nearly broken her—but each time she had unconsciously reached for the vial, only to find it gone, she had relived that moment in the storm. The rumbling sky. The churning clouds. The lightning, fast and fierce, coursing through her blood.

With the raw power in her veins, she could survive this.

She could survive *anything*.

The gentle creak of the log cabin's wood shifting in the soft breeze outside registered in the back of Quinn's mind, and she forced her tired eyes to open. She had already done a routine check of the property to ensure her charms were still active, but no visitors had found the house while she had been away.

Even so, she couldn't get complacent.

Across from her, at the other end of the small sitting room that served as most of the small house's main floor, Tove Warren dove headfirst into a sofa by the stone fireplace. Her bare feet stuck out over the armrest, and the augmentor let out a slow sigh of relief.

Another familiar creak echoed through the house from the rooftop, but this house had always groaned in the wind. More out of habit than need, Quinn leaned toward the window and peered cautiously through a thin gap in the curtain covering the glass panes.

Pale blue moonlight filtered through gaps in the towering canopy, and the forest's leaves shivered in the night's gentle breeze. The muffled croak of a distant frog mixed with the hoot of a midnight owl. The breeze faded, and then the world was momentarily still.

She had always found this place strangely soothing. Perhaps it was the rustic nature of a cabin stowed away in the woods, or perhaps it was the fact that she could disappear here for days or weeks at a time, knowing full well no one would find her. A thick layer of bark coated the cabin's exterior walls, and the overall effect made the structure fade into the surrounding trees. Unless one got close—which her charms and traps prevented—nothing at all looked out of place among the old oaks and willows in this stretch of the forest.

Even Blaze's modest stable blended in with the trees. No one would catch a glimpse of the horses they'd bought to carry Tove's things from her secret vault in Everdale.

Tove's packs now lay in heaps by the door—books and reagents, mostly, with a few high-value items tucked delicately in secret pockets along each bag. Tove had apparently sold most of what she owned, and another twang of guilt hit Quinn squarely in the gut.

Her friend deserved better than life as an outlaw.

"Are you going to tell me now?" Tove asked.

The augmentor's voice snapped through Quinn's head, sudden and jarring, and she flinched as the question broke the tranquil silence.

When her heart settled, she stood and stretched the aching muscles in her back. "Which part?"

"Everything." Tove sat upright and brushed a frizzy lock of hair out of her face. "Like you promised, back in Oakenglen."

For a moment, Quinn didn't answer. She had been simmering on this for their entire journey, wondering if she had promised too much. If Tove wanted nothing to do with this mess, the augmentor would need plausible deniability and a safehouse of her own until everything quieted down.

Hell, maybe she needed to find a way to get Tove out of Saldia altogether. Maybe this continent was no longer safe.

"Stop *thinking*, damn it." Tove groaned and pushed herself to her feet. "Stop debating. Stop deliberating. Stop sifting through that sharp mind of yours, Quinn, and just tell me what the hell is going on!"

Quinn chuckled and rubbed her eyes. "It will put you in danger."

"In case you hadn't noticed, I *am* in danger." Tove gestured to the safehouse around them. "I don't think this could possibly be any worse."

"It can," Quinn said flatly. "And it is."

A heavy silence weighed between them, and Tove's frustrated scowl slowly faded. The augmentor sat once again on the sofa and set her head in her hands. For a moment, they simply listened to the gentle creaks and moans of the cabin, and Quinn gave her friend the silence she needed to make her final choice.

"Tell me," Tove finally demanded. "Tell me all of it."

"I'm not sure where to start." Quinn stood. After a moment of quiet deliberation, she paced the room and tapped her fingertip against her lips.

"Tell me about that outlaw," Tove suggested. "Tell me about where that gorgeous dragon came from—the one I augmented. Tell me what happened when you went out into the Decay. Tell me what you found out there, and where you've been. There's plenty for you to tell me, and any of it will do as a decent start."

Quinn sighed.

One secret weighed heaviest on her. Out of everything Tove deserved to know, one reveal carried the greatest risk, and it would either bond them further or rip them apart.

Quinn had yet to tell anyone what she really was. Though she trusted Tove more than almost anyone on this continent, Quinn still felt a wave of dread at the thought of sharing this part of her.

It didn't matter. She had made a promise, and she braced herself for the worst.

"You've always commented on how augmentations last longer on me," she began. "You always thought there was something unique about us. About the Starlings."

Tove went eerily still, and she watched Quinn with an awestruck, wide-eyed expression. "You figured it out, didn't you?"

Quinn bit her lip, but ultimately nodded.

"Tell me, please." Tove leaned forward, breathless and waiting. "I *must* know what's so unique about your family. It has baffled me for years."

"It's not all Starlings," Quinn corrected. "It's just me. My father—" Her throat tightened, and she coughed roughly to clear it. "My father experimented on me before I was even born. He did awful things to my mother to transform me. To change me. To forge me into a weapon unlike any Saldia had ever seen."

Tove's brows furrowed, and she quickly scanned Quinn's face. "You're not making sense."

Carefully, Quinn reached for the clasp on her Starling family pendant. Since learning the truth, Quinn had only worn the necklace with the little lightning bolt painted on the back of it, as she never wanted to limit her power again. The original one—the one with the Bluntmar—would remain in her pack.

When her fingertips pulled on the little hook, she paused to brace herself for whatever came next. She wasn't ready to do this, but she never would be, so she took off the pendant anyway.

Tove gasped, and she covered her mouth with both hands as her eyes went wide with shock. Her gaze roamed over Quinn's body—her face, her neck, her arms, her hair. The color drained from Tove's face, and the augmentor blinked rapidly as her forehead creased with either worry or baffled concentration.

Quinn swallowed hard as the stunned silence stretched on.

"Say something," she finally demanded.

Tove's hands lowered, and the woman smiled broadly. "You look *incredible*."

Quinn laughed, and she ran her fingers over the silky soft scales on her neck. They still felt so strange, so foreign, and it was surreal to think they had always been there—just masked by a brilliant glamourist's magic.

Tove's smile fell, and she blinked rapidly, as if she had only now pieced something together. "Your father did this to you?"

With a somber glance at the floor, Quinn nodded.

"He *experimented* on you?" Tove's voice cracked with astonished disbelief. "On his own daughter?"

Quinn crossed her arms and resumed her pacing, mostly to keep from looking Tove in the eye. "Yes."

"Then the legend—the child Death gave back—"

"It was a lie." Quinn's mouth twitched as she suppressed a flicker of white-hot rage. "I'm no miracle. I'm an experiment. He wanted to create something new—something powerful that he could manipulate and control—but his concoctions killed all of the attempts before me. Death didn't give me back, Tove. My mother *stole* me back because she couldn't take losing another one of her babies. Whatever I am, it can't be replicated. The magic she used that night was a fluke, and the midwives who helped her do it disappeared. I'm lucky to be alive at all."

Tove's eyebrows tilted upward, and she abruptly stood. With a few quick steps, she crossed the distance between them and pulled Quinn into a tight hug. "I can't imagine what you're going through right now. You must be reeling."

Though she returned the hug, Quinn felt numb. Vacant, almost, or void of any feeling at all. There weren't words that could explain the sensation, so she opted not to say anything at all.

Tove leaned backward, and yet again, her friend's gaze wandered across the ribbons of lavender scales that now covered narrow stretches of her skin. Silently, the augmentor tilted her head this way and that as she studied the ribbons of iridescent scales with an intense frown. She lifted Quinn's arms and examined them, studying the shimmers from every angle, and her examination ended with a full circle around Quinn as the Starling warrior waited in awkward silence for Tove to say something.

The longer this went on, the more she felt like a sideshow oddity.

"Stop it," she finally demanded.

Snapped from her daze, Tove blinked rapidly, and a red blush crept up her neck. "Oh my, I'm sorry. It's just that this is all so *fascinating*. What are these scales? Do you know?"

"Dragon scales."

"Dr—dra—" Tove stuttered, unable to form a single word, and she gaped up at Quinn in disbelief. "You're part *dragon*?!"

Quinn winced at her friend's sudden shout, but ultimately nodded.

"Dragon!" Tove threw her arms up in the air and laughed like a child in a sweets shop. "Dragon blood! All this time, *that's* what I've been missing! Your reactions to the potion ink, your connection to the brews I made for you, the way even enchanted items worked better when you use them—it was dragon blood!"

"Focus." Quinn chided.

"This is incredible!" Tove plowed ahead as though Quinn hadn't spoken. "How does it feel? Where did the glamour come from? Have you always known, or is this a recent discovery? Are there any additional charms on the pendant, or is it just the one glamour? Oh, it was your mother, wasn't it? No wonder she became such a legendary glamourist—good gracious, your mother is brilliant. Do you think I can ask her a few questions about—"

"Bless the Fates, woman," Quinn interjected. "Calm *down*."

Tove did not, in fact, calm down.

"They glimmer!" The augmentor brushed her finger along the scales on Quinn's arm, and a soft purple sheen raced over them like moonlight over steel. "Look at that! They did it again. What do you suppose causes this reaction?"

"Stop that." Quinn smacked her friend's hand away.

Tove yelped, and she rested the offending hand against her chest. That seemed to break her fixation, and she finally looked Quinn in the eye once again. "Oh, goodness. I overdid it again, didn't I?"

Quinn took a settling breath, and with a flick of her hand, she waved away Tove's concern. "It's fine."

But it wasn't fine.

Not really.

A revelation like this could change their entire dynamic, and Quinn wondered if Tove would ever look at her as more than an oddity for her to study.

Tonight, she very well could've lost her only true friend in the world.

The deep creases Tove's forehead softened, and the fascinated glint in her eye faded entirely. The augmentor's smile fell, and it seemed as though she saw something in Quinn's expression that Quinn hadn't meant to give away.

"I'm sorry," Tove said softly. "Truly, I am. I got caught up in the moment. But Quinn, you're wrong. You *are* a miracle. It must be isolating to think you're the only one of your kind that will ever be."

Quinn looked at the floor, but she didn't reply.

Tove tilted her head to one side, and she frowned. "Wait, do you think I'm going to see you differently?"

With a frustrated sigh, Quinn nodded.

"Then you're an idiot."

At that, Quinn's head snapped back, and she looked up to find Tove with a wide, playful grin on her face.

"Thanks," she said dryly.

"You know what I mean." Tove rolled her eyes. "Nothing's different. Not between us, anyway."

Quinn smiled, and the tension in her shoulders finally faded. "Thank you."

"Now, enough squishy emotional chatter." Tove clapped her hands together and took a settling breath. "You probably need at least one augmentation revived, right? Or new potions? We went through quite a few glamours to get here."

With a confused tilt to her head, Quinn did a quick glance-over of the easily distractable augmentor in front of her. "Don't you want to know about the rest? Or, hell, sleep? You're every bit as exhausted as I am. I can see it in your face."

Tove shook her head. "We can talk about that later. For now, I need to *do* something. I can't just stand there and talk. Now, give me a potion you need completed. Anything. I don't care what it is. I just need to do something with my hands."

Quinn chuckled, and she rubbed the exhaustion from her eyes. If Tove wasn't going to sleep tonight, it meant she probably wouldn't, either.

"Alright," she conceded. "I wouldn't mind a—uh—well, a Rushmar augmentation."

After all, she didn't want to get pregnant, and Connor was almost as utterly insatiable as she was.

In the silence that followed, Quinn cleared her throat awkwardly and became suddenly very interested in a small crack in the wooden plank of a nearby wall.

Through the corner of her eye, a mischievous little grin spread across Tove's face. "You *didn't.*"

Quinn smiled.

"You *did*!" Tove giggled and clapped her hands happily. "Tell me everything!"

"I thought you needed to keep yourself busy?" Quinn nodded to the bags by the door.

"Demanding as ever, I see." Tove leaned her weight on one hip and crossed her arms over her chest. "First, admit that I was right about everything. I knew you couldn't resist."

Quinn smirked. "Everything."

"Damn right." With a playful shrug, Tove knelt beside one of her bags and rifled through the pack. "Let's see, we'll need my spellbook, of course. Now, where are those clovers? I need the fresh ones for this."

And just like that, Tove's focus shifted entirely to her work. Creases in her brow. Eyes narrowed with concentration. Biting her lip anytime she wasn't mumbling incoherently to herself.

Quinn had seen that expression plenty of times before. Even if she said something, Tove wouldn't hear her until the potion was made.

Despite her exhaustion, Quinn pressed her back against the wall and peered once again through the window. The silent night swayed in the gentle wind, but otherwise, the forest was just as it had been before. No footsteps. No huffing breaths. Just a silent woodland, peaceful and asleep as the midnight hour wore on.

Good. She could use some fresh air.

Quinn gently opened the door to the rustle of hands through a knapsack behind her. The quiet mutterings of the brilliant augmentor faded as the door silently closed.

Finally alone, Quinn pressed her back against the closed door and listened to the night. Her enhanced senses drank in the world around her, no longer encumbered by the Bluntmar around her neck, and the forest came alive.

The soothing chill across her arms.

The fluttering rustle of leaves in the canopy.

The soft chirp of crickets, blended with the distant crash of water on a rocky shore.

Her cabin had been chosen more for its location than its luxuries. The thick forests around Arkcaster refused to be tamed, and it gave her easy access to both Lunestone and the well-trod crossroads that led to every corner of the continent. Close to a cliff and in the farthest reaches of the woodland, this spot had always offered her and Blaze an effortless way to leap into the night and blend into the sky.

Lightning cracked through her veins, sharp and fierce, and she grinned at the violent rush. A low growl rumbled in her throat, and she abruptly tensed.

How...

...odd.

It made her blood boil.

It made her want to *run*. To nowhere in particular, and more to feel the earth slam against her feet with each step.

And it demanded she listen.

So, she did.

She charged into the night, silent as a ghost, and the oaks whizzed past her in a blur of shadow and branches. The water's peaceful lullaby neared as she ran toward the cliff to get a better view of the sky.

The forest thinned, and a gust hit her as she reached the cliff. A wet tang clung to the air, like the sweet scent of grass after a rain, and the wind whipped her hair around her face. The lights of Arkcaster stretched out below her in the one area along the coast where the trees had been conquered, and Lunestone towered over the lake beyond Arkcaster's shores.

The city had always served as the main passage into Lunestone, and from here, she had a clear view of the long bridge out to the island she had once called home.

Her heart raced, happy and fluttering from the jog, and her chest heaved with each breath. The stars glittered overhead in a vast and never-ending sky, and the glittering lights winked at her from afar.

Tempting her closer.

Another surge of lightning crackled within her veins. This time, sparks skittered over her hands and up her arms. She studied the arcs of yellow light, fascinated by their patterns over her soft scales, and she ached to know more.

Maybe she would, someday.

Or maybe she would forever be *other*.

It didn't matter. Not really. Whatever came next, she had the strength to face it—and she had a ragged team of misfits who had become like family.

Her father had tried to break her. To control her. To make her dance. Little had he known that his cruelty had made her strong enough to burn everything he'd built.

CHAPTER SEVENTY-TWO
ZANDER

This was it.

The ultimate test.

With his shoulders squared and his back arched, Zander took one final swig of the glamour that would stain his features enough to hide his identity from the townsfolk who would become his unsuspecting bait. To be sure it had worked, he drew his sword and checked his reflection in the steel—black hair, brown eyes, black stubble to obscure the skin around his mouth.

Good.

The moment someone recognized his sword, of course, the ruse would end. On his way through the woods, he tugged a leather strap free from his boot and wrapped it around the dazzling spellgust gem that powered *Valor.*

It wouldn't hold in a fight, but he ideally wouldn't get caught in one.

To his left, the Feral King walked beside him. The wraith-wolf's shadowy feet pressed against the ground, despite leaving no indent in the soil, and the creature sniffed at the air. A child's squeal of delight filtered through the trees, shrill and distant, and the clang of a blacksmith's hammer echoed after it.

He checked his reflection once more in his blade. The last of the red hair gave way to the rich black tone, and he sheathed his weapon.

It was time.

Look at you, the Feral King scoffed in disgust. *Why have you donned this—what did you call it? Glamour? To hide what you are from these peasants is the ultimate insult. They must know you. Fear you. Tremble before you!*

"They will," Zander assured him. "But today isn't about fear. It's about answers. I can't go out there as me, or they'll slow me down. Everyone out here wants something." He shook his head in annoyance, and that, at least, wasn't a lie. "I need to access the Lightseer encampment without the common folk begging for scraps along the way."

The shadow-wolf growled in annoyance, but didn't reply—and that suited Zander just fine.

A town? the Feral King scoffed. *If we're meant to terrorize a town, we should have brought the pack. Why did you demand they wait in the forest?*

"Because we're not here for terror," Zander explained. "We're here for something more valuable."

The ghoulish beast snarled. *Nothing is more valuable.*

"On the contrary." He knelt behind a blackberry bush and gently pried apart the thick brambles as he peered out onto one of the towns along the southern road.

Guthram.

The mining town sat nestled between the mountains and the forest, and even from here, Zander spotted the entrance to one of the town's hundreds of mining tunnels. The cliff towered over this cluster of thatched roof cottages, and lanterns along the mine shaft's walls cast a pale-yellow glow into its depths. Outside, two little girls chased each other through a patch of glowing green grass, and tendrils of emerald light shivered into the air as they disturbed the meadow.

His heart skipped beats at the sight of humans. He had been in the woods for so long that he hadn't given real thought to civilization in weeks. There had been plotting and planning to get here, sure, but to actually be around humans again seemed odd.

He wasn't even going to kill them. After so long in a forest rife with bandits and degenerates, that almost seemed odder.

The Feral King growled in frustration. *And what could be more valuable—*

"Information," Zander interrupted curtly. "Now, it's time for you to disappear. I'll let you know when you can show yourself."

He expected a grumble. A protest. A snarl, even, or an outright challenge. Instead, he was met with silence, and he peered over one shoulder to find the towering shadow-wolf staring down at him with narrowed eyes.

Skeptical.

And thus, the test. Not of man, and not of beast—but of his control over the most powerful darkness on the continent.

Of course, he had come equipped, and he knew just the bait to set out for it—both to test its self-restraint and incentivize it to obey.

Today, he would finally find out if he could control the Feral King. If the beast failed, he couldn't return to civilization until he found a way to destroy it, and time was against him.

This *had* to work.

"You don't want bland horror," Zander said flatly, daring the ghoulish creature to disagree. "You're bored of repetitive terror. You crave something more."

The Feral King tilted its head, watching him more intently now.

"You want obedient fear." He stood and took a step closer, letting a devious little smile break across his face as he neared. "You want the kind of dread that rolls around a man like a fog, the sort that makes his heart thunder in his chest even as you circle him. You want the sort of fear that makes powerful men jump to appease you. To please you. To give you everything you desire, all while suspecting that you'll rip out their throats if they fail you in the slightest." He paused, inches away from the Feral King now and more certain than ever that he was right. "That's what you want, and only I can give it to you."

What makes you so certain?

"You've had centuries out in these forests." Zander nodded disdainfully to the trees behind the creature. "IF you could do it on your own, you would've accomplished it by now."

A short, low growl echoed through Zander's head at the insult, but the ghoulish creature didn't disagree.

"Listen," he added, staring the towering beast dead in the eye as he spoke. "Restrain yourself. Rein in the bloodlust and be patient." His voice lowered to a gravelly tone to drive home his point. "Do what I tell you, and you'll have all the obedient terror you can stomach."

A low chuckle rumbled through his mind, and the wolf's eyes crinkled with an expression Zander couldn't quite read. As they glared at each other, the shadows comprising the wolf slowly thinned, until the beast faded away into nothing.

We shall see, Starling. The ghoulish creature's voice echoed, dull and hollow, as it left him alone in the woods.

The wolf's ominous words lingered, and for a moment, he wondered if it was now testing him. Perhaps this encounter carried weight for both of them, or perhaps it still thought it was in control of this little partnership.

Let it believe so. That would make this so much easier.

With a settling breath, Zander stepped around the blackberry bush and into the sunlight.

He'd chosen this side road intentionally, as it gave him quick access to the main town without anyone noticing.

Anyone important, at least.

The two little girls giggled and ran around the meadow right until he passed them, when they both stopped mid-stride and watched him warily. The littlest one bolted over to her sister and hid behind her, though they were both too young to do much in the way of protecting one another. Wisps of brown hair floated about their faces in the southern breeze, but he didn't care about them.

At that moment, a devastating pang of hunger hit him.

The urge to kill them both hit hard and fast, and he barely suppressed it in time. He could imagine bloodstains on their white aprons, across the grass, over his hands. It was visceral. Vivid.

Beautiful.

No, he couldn't indulge this. He had to overcome.

To distract himself, he scanned the cluster of cottages for the blacksmith. Though the hammer still clanged against metal, somewhere among the wooden walls and the bedsheets hung on a line to dry, no one appeared.

Good.

He walked along the road toward the main street, and already he could spot the bustle of people hustling about the town square. Everything about this town seemed so *beige*—the buildings, the roofs, even the clothes people wore.

Bland, but then again, that was why he'd chosen Guthram for his experiment. This far to the southwest, on the route toward South Haven, Lightseer contingents would exist in smaller numbers simply because no one cared about these towns.

If he had to kill everyone here, it would be easy, and he could escape into the forest unscathed.

In his head, the Feral King snarled with the same rumbling tension as he'd felt when they'd attacked the bandits in the farmhouse. Any second now, the beast would appear. He would charge the girls, and he would relish in the chase as they tried desperately to escape.

Perhaps this was it.

Perhaps the test had already come, and he would now witness the shadowwolf's true colors.

His heart thundered in a frantic cadence—not from the vivid thought of killing the children, oddly enough, but from the idea that the Feral King might fail.

"Discipline," Zander chided the ghoulish creature in a low whisper. "You only need a little to get what you really want."

The low rumble continued, and though Zander watched the meadow through the corner of his eye—just in case—he shifted his attention away from the girls and turned his back on them.

Now, to see if the wolf would do the same. If it would reveal itself as something he could control, or something he would have to eradicate.

The seconds ticked by, agonizingly slow, as the rumble vibrated in his chest. It hummed through his body, desperate with need and with *hunger*, but he fought the urges that shook through him with each of the Feral King's rasping breaths.

As savage as it might've been, he wouldn't succumb to simple impulse.

He finally neared the end of this short road, and the bustle of the crowd grew louder. The scent of sweat and meat tempted him, sparking his ravenous appetite, but he again did his best to suppress the urge to find the nearest hunk of steak and eat it raw.

Finally, blissfully, the hungry snarl became a frustrated growl, and the pang of bloodlust slowly faded.

This obedient fear you speak of had better taste amazing, the Feral King warned.

A victorious smirk tugged at the edge of his mouth, but he managed to restrain it. "It will."

With one final, guttural moan, the Feral King surrendered, and the primal urge to kill everything he saw faded.

It *faded.*

Completely.

He had *won.*

It took everything in Zander to not yell with victory. With satisfaction. With the absolute thrill of conquering something powerful and bending it entirely to his will. He wanted to fuck the nearest woman he found and eat the finest meal in celebration, but he settled for a few deep and excited breaths.

The celebration could wait. For now, he had work to do.

It was finally time to go home.

Glamoured from head to toe, Zander slipped into the current of people. The scent of each person he passed assaulted his enhanced senses, but differently than it had before his time as the Feralblade. Once, the smells had blended together, stiff and obscure, but now he could detect each one. The daisies in one woman's basket. The dirt behind a young boy's ear. The heady bite of tobacco in a man's cigar, or the sweet tang of the corked whiskey in his hand.

The scents blended into a stunning cacophony of sensations, and he relished the story each one told him. Their scents gave away their life story, and no one here had the slightest clue how many of their secrets they had betrayed to him without even a passing glance.

Even in the throng, the Feral King's bloodlust flared only sparingly. It came in hits and bursts, each easier to control than the last, and it took everything in Zander's power to keep from beaming with pride.

He had truly tamed a monster.

Before long, he reached the Guthram office. Blue and silver banners hung the full length of the three-story building, and the large silver horse emblem on each reminded all who passed of those who truly controlled the city.

His boots passed silently over the wooden steps leading up to the door, and he paused briefly to listen for footsteps on the other side. Scents mingled together as they slipped under the door and out into the sunlight—whiskey, charred steak, and the sharp musk of sex.

These fools had gotten sloppy.

With a creak, the door swung open, and he stepped into the main hall. Four Lightseers mingled around a desk, each holding a clear glass filled with an amber liquid, and the sweet scent of rye lay heavy on the air. The one farthest from him stank the most of sex, and a strange pang hit Zander at the musky aroma.

Not of disgust or bloodlust, oddly enough, but of *envy.*

Of hatred for what his whore of a wife had stolen from him.

A white-hot flash of anger ripped through him as he shut the door. The soldiers stood, each frowning as they glanced him over, and the nearest one crossed his thick arms over his broad chest.

"You look a right mess," the soldier said. "Care to explain what the hell you're doing?"

At first, Zander didn't speak. Instead, he listened. He craned his ear and scanned what he could hear from the rest of the building. The shuffling feet of two dozen people above. The clatter of dishes. The rush of water, somewhere in the back of the building. The racing hearts of the dozen-or-so rabbits that would become dinner.

More importantly than that, however, was what the Feral King would do next. Zander listened intently to the cues of his body, waiting for another pang of bloodlust. Waiting for the ghoulish creature to lose control, now that they were in the presence of the people he most needed on his side. He waited for the beast to betray him, now that it had the power to undermine everything Zander had done thus far.

The four Lightseers glanced among themselves, each looking to the other for a hint of what the hell was going on. The biggest one among them—an older man with graying hair and a thinning beard—took a few threatening steps closer.

Zander's eyes darted toward the Lightseer as the man set his hand on the hilt of his sword.

"Explain yourself," the man warned.

But Zander wasn't listening. Not really. He suspected, deep down, that the Feral King would appear. That he would ruin everything.

Any moment, the glamour would fade. He had timed his sips perfectly, wanting to ensure that it would last only long enough to run his test, but the seconds dragged on. His fingers itched, and he pressed his hand against the bottle stored in his pocket.

Any moment now, he would need to take another sip to prolong the glamour's magic.

I warn you, Starling. The Feral King's grim voice flooded his thoughts, drowning out everything that didn't belong to the ghoulish creature. *Should you fail to deliver what you promised me, no pain you have felt in your life will compare to what I will do to you.*

Zander smiled.

Though a growl rumbled through the back of his mind, nothing happened, and he finally let himself relax.

"Explain myself," he muttered, chuckling, entertained by the idea that he, of all people, would ever explain himself to them.

In one fluid motion, he drew his sword. The movement was too fast for any of the Lightseers to react, and he had his blade in hand before any of them had even wrapped their hands around their weapons.

"Hey, now," one in the back warned.

Another summoned ice into his hand, and glowing white lights swam across the last man's palms.

Drunk and drenched in a whore's aftermath, but still ready for battle.

Excellent. Perhaps they hadn't gone soft after all.

Instead of attacking, however, he tugged off the leather strap that hid *Valor's* spellgust gem. Almost in unison, the glamour began to fade, and the jet-black hairs on his arm lightened until they were red once more.

The soldiers' gazes fell to *Valor* and snapped back to his face, again and again, and they all blinked in utter shock.

"Zander Starling," the man closest to him said in awe. "Never thought I'd see the day, sir. We—we all thought—"

"That I was dead?" Zander finished for him.

Reluctantly, the man nodded. Around him, the soldiers quickly sheathed their swords out of respect.

Zander laughed and sheathed his Firesword as he surveyed the first Lightseers he'd seen since he left for the Decay. "You should know the Starlings are hard to kill."

A hush settled across them, and each man looked at another as they shared knowing sidelong glances. He frowned, watching each man's face as he tried to understand what was being left unsaid between them.

"Tell me," he finally demanded.

"It's—" The eldest of the soldiers roughly cleared his throat. "It's your father. He's..."

Though the man trailed off, Zander waited. Normally, he would've snapped at the man to spit it out. He would've barked orders or doled out punishments until they all stopped wasting his time.

But, for the first time in his life, he merely waited—and his intense glare only narrowed with warning.

"He's dead," the soldier finally said.

Zander's head snapped back in surprise, and he scanned the man's face for signs of a tell. A twitch of the brow, or fidgeting of the hands.

Nothing.

It was the truth.

"Dead," he repeated, mostly to soothe the startling disbelief that had shocked his system.

The great Teagan Starling.

Dead.

Zander waited to feel grief. Anger. Rage. The lust for revenge. He waited, in that tense and heavy silence, to feel something. Anything at all.

But he felt nothing.

"We all grieve our Master General," the soldier closest to him continued. "But we can't begin to imagine what you must feel, sir."

No, he suspected they couldn't.

"There's no time to waste," he said quietly, doing his best to force a hint of sadness into his voice. "I haven't been idle."

"Of course, sir." The commanding officer snapped to attention, and the other three followed suit. "What are your orders?"

"Send word that I'm coming home," Zander ordered. He turned his back on the men to hide a wicked smile. "And I'm bringing quite a surprise with me."

CHAPTER SEVENTY-THREE

CONNOR

In the chilled air of a midnight forest, no one spoke.

Connor held his fist up at his side in a silent order to hold. Though they sat on Nocturne's back, massive boulders and thick vines along the edge of the clearing offered plenty of places to hide. A low growl rumbled in Nocturne's throat as they surveyed the darkness.

Waiting.

Arkcaster was different than he had expected. The untamed forest tangled over the hillsides and valleys, unforgiving and covered in thorns as big as his arm. They'd heard the whinny of the black unicorns that made their home in these forests, but thus far hadn't seen one.

A stroke of luck, really, given how bloodthirsty those damn things were.

Yet again, the faint thud of footsteps caught his attention, coming from somewhere to the east. Focused as he was on the sound, he closed his eyes to listen. A gust of wind snaked through the trees like a whisper in the dark, the only sound in the otherwise silent world.

Yet again, the world had gone still.

Unconvinced, he opened his eyes and scanned the shadows for any sign of an ambush. Nothing stirred in the darkness between the trees, save the occasional flicker of an owl's wings as it swooped from branch to branch.

Fine. Whoever was there, they either hadn't seen them or weren't planning on making themselves known any time soon.

With a quick gesture toward the ground, he gave the silent command to his team to dismount. One by one, they slid off of Nocturne's back, and the dragon kept his head low as his unwavering glare surveyed the edges of the clearing.

Though he had followed Quinn's map to the letter, they hadn't seen a cottage. No hint of a roof as they'd flown over, and no smoke billowing into the air from a fire. By every indication, this forest was devoid of any human life.

But he knew her well enough by now, and he had expected nothing less.

Through the corner of his eye, a figure stumbled across the grass with a rope hanging loosely from her waist. Sophia muttered a few curses as she fought with it, and Murdoc set a steadying hand on her arm to help her balance.

There, the Wraith King said. *The boulder.*

The ghoul's voice punctuated the night, loud and commanding, and Connor's gaze swept the clearing yet again as he followed the wraith's clue.

Sure enough, a large boulder rested on the edge of the clearing, half-submerged in the forest's canopy. A backlit silhouette stood on it, watching them from afar. Green augmentations hummed along the figure's skin, and her hair danced around her head in the night's gentle wind.

Though she didn't move, he heard the footsteps yet again. The soft crunch of boots on fresh grass, slightly louder than before, headed straight for them. Moments later, a second figure walked around the boulder with a green glow buzzing through the ink in her skin. The hem of her skirts brushed across the grass at her feet, and she rested one hand on her waist as she studied them as well.

Connor frowned, and his fingers twitched as he fought the impulse to draw his sword. He cast a sidelong glare at Nocturne, and a plume of smoke shot through the dragon's nose as he nodded in silent agreement.

Quinn hadn't told them anything about bringing along company—and these two were heavily augmented.

Beside him, Murdoc reached for the sword that was no longer at his side and frowned as he glared at the newcomers. The warning crackle of splintering ice cut through the air as Sophia, too, shifted her full attention toward the boulder.

His team, ready for anything and unafraid of blood. He couldn't have asked for more.

The silhouette jumped off the boulder, and a familiar voice hummed with curiosity as the two figures walked toward them. Clouds still rolled across the twin moons, obscuring their already fading light, and Connor's company were still far enough away that he couldn't make out the details on their faces.

An enchanting perfume coiled through the air—the soothing aroma of jasmine, blended with the sweet bite of honeysuckle. It reminded him of all the nights he had inhaled that scent, tangled in the blankets as long legs wrapped around his waist.

Quinn.

He relaxed in the seconds before she walked into view. A familiar brunette walked beside her, and the augmented rose inked into her neck glowed green in the night.

Tove Warren.

At the sight of them, his team let out a collective sigh of relief.

"Don't *do* that," Sophia snapped.

Quinn chuckled. "I thought you enjoyed a fair bit of theatre?"

"Of course," the necromancer said as she shook the ice from her slender hands. "But only when I'm the one orchestrating it."

The Starling warrior shifted her attention to Connor, and her smile melted away the last bit of tension from his shoulders—only to be replaced with the image of his sword against the siren's throat.

That creature had looked exactly like her. Sounded like her. Everything had seemed so real, and the thought that he had killed something that so perfectly emulated her sent a cold rush of self-hatred clear through his core.

He shook away the thought.

"You made it," he said.

Her gaze flicked to the ground, and her smile fell. It hit him, then—a flash of warning, like the change in the air before someone tried to throw a punch. His eyes narrowed as he scanned her face, and the longer he looked, the more certain he became.

Something about her had changed—and maybe not for the better.

"We've been busy," Tove interjected. "Though I'm sure the four of you haven't been bored, either."

Murdoc grinned and snuck a quick glance at Connor. "I suppose you could say that."

"Come on." Tove gestured for Murdoc and Sophia to follow her as she led the way through the darkness. "I'll take you to the cabin. Quinn has something to tell those two while the rest of us get some food."

Connor's eyes narrowed, and he shifted his attention to the Starling warrior standing in front of him. Quinn frowned at her friend, but she ultimately met Connor's eye and nodded.

"She's right," Quinn said quietly, barely loud enough for him to hear. "In fact, it's something I need to show you—and we can't do it here."

"Captain?" Murdoc's tone conveyed concern for the strange tension in the air, and the unspoken question lingered. The former Blackguard stood beside Sophia, and both of them watched Connor's face with wary alarm.

Whatever the hell was going on, they wouldn't leave if he needed backup.

But this was Quinn, and she wouldn't hurt him.

After a moment of deliberation, he nodded and gestured for them to follow Tove. "I'll meet you there."

"Alright then," Murdoc said with a shrug. "I won't say no to food."

"And whiskey, I'm sure." Sophia feigned a half-hearted smirk and followed after the augmentor leading them into the darkness. As she reached the edge of the shadows, however, she cast one wary glance back at Connor. She frowned, and the silent warning was clear.

Be careful.

A low growl rolled through the field like thunder, and Nocturne took a wary step closer. Though the dragon lowered his head to Connor's side, the regal creature didn't speak—nor, thankfully, did either of the undead kings fused to Connor's soul.

"Alright," he said with a wary nod toward the forest. "Lead the way, Quinn Starling."

CHAPTER SEVENTY-FOUR

QUINN

Standing a short way from the cliff's edge and shrouded in enough woodland shadow to hide even Nocturne, Quinn's heart fluttered with nerves at what she was about to share. She stood with her back to Connor and Nocturne with her hands on her hips, and she braced herself for what she was about to say.

But this—her nerves—all of this was so *stupid.*

If anyone would accept her, it was Connor. Even if the rest of the world saw her as an abomination of nature, he wouldn't toss her aside. Not after everything they had endured together.

Eyes shut and pulse still racing, she took a settling breath before she faced the outlaw she had once hunted. Nocturne sat behind him, the regal creature's long neck arched as he watched her intently, and his eyes narrowed with recognition.

"You are different," Nocturne said, as quietly as a dragon could muster. "You have changed."

"What the hell are you talking about?" Connor glanced up at the prince of dragons behind him.

"He's right." Quinn took a deep breath. "There's something you need to see."

Quickly, before she could hesitate or change her mind, she unclasped the pendant around her neck, just as she had when she told Tove this very secret. Instantly, lavender scales pushed through the enchantments that had disguised her arms, but she had already memorized every one of them. The pendant fell into her palm, and her shoulders tensed as she met Connor's eye.

His eyes widened with surprise, and his mouth dropped open as he stared at her, dumbfounded. Nocturne studied her, equally confounded, and no one spoke. A dark plume of smoke rolled through the forest, and the wraith's grim figure emerged from the shadow as he, too, gawked at her.

The silence stretched on, and she cleared her throat in an attempt to snap them from their collective stunned daze.

Connor was the first to regain his composure. His jaw clamped shut even as his eyes continued to roam her face. "What happened? Are you—"

Before he could finish, a thick wave of black smoke rolled through the forest behind them. It consumed them all, shrouding everything in a thick layer of tar-black fog. Wary and already on edge, Quinn tucked the glamoured pendant in her pocket and lifted the scarf around her neck to protect her nose and mouth. Tremors of warning shot through her arms, and the panic left a tingling weakness in its wake that made her fingers twitch with dread.

She squinted through the darkness to pinpoint the oncoming threat.

A figure loomed in the murky haze, larger even than Nocturne, and she drew her sword as she prepared for war. Blackfire raged across the dark steel, and she was ready for blood.

The beast's head drew closer, astonishingly fast.

Toward *her*.

"Don't you *dare*—" Connor's voice faded into the smoke, and in seconds, disappeared completely.

A black snout broke first through the fog, and blue eyes glowed in the wispy haze. They stared down at her with all the intense fire of a blistering blue flame. They carried power. *Authority*. That simple glare had weight to it, and something painfully heavy pressed against her back.

She grimaced as the force drove her to the ground, and her knees hit the wet grass as she succumbed. Her sword fell, and its blackfire fizzled out with a sharp hiss the moment it left her palm. She glared up at her attacker's face, confused as all hell, but the weight of its glare forced her to kneel before it.

No, not *it*.

Him.

She frowned as the thought hit her, but it wasn't a guess. It was a knowing, and she felt it in her very soul.

The last of the smoke cleared, and a towering black dragon loomed over her. His snout hovered barely an inch from her face. A gap in the canopy above them perfectly framed his face, and pale moonlight glinted over the majestic creature's hide. The edges of his body faded and blurred like a mirage, as though he were dissolving into the very stars above.

Her initial panic faded in a rush. As she studied his face, she instead felt oddly calm.

Snared as she was by the strange dragon that had appeared from nothing at all, she didn't see Connor until he elbowed the stunning creature hard in the jaw. The dragon snarled, baring his teeth at the intrusion, and the two of them glared at each other with unfettered hatred.

Unfazed as ever, Connor angled his body and put himself between her and the towering dragon. A surge of dark smoke rolled over his arm as he summoned one blackfire blade and pointed it up at the wraithlike dragon above them.

It hit her, then.

That smoke.

This new dragon had appeared just as the wraith always did—in a rush of black fog, like a grim predator emerging from the darkness of another world.

"You're a simmering soul," Quinn whispered as she stared up at the dragon, almost too numb to register what she was even saying.

Connor looked at her over his shoulder, and his body relaxed as he let out a heavy sigh. "It looks like we've both been busy."

Her brows pinched together in vacant horror. "You took another simmering soul?"

Instead of answering, he dismissed the blackfire blade with a puff of dark smoke and offered her his hand. She took it, and as he pulled her to her feet, he grabbed her sword off the ground.

"I did," he said as he offered her the blade.

His ear twitched, and his brows furrowed with anger as his intense glare once again shifted toward the fierce dragon looming overhead.

"What?" Quinn glanced between the two of them. "What did he say?"

"Nothing," Connor lied.

Her eyes narrowed, and her lips pursed tightly together.

Connor caught her eye, and he grunted in annoyance. "Glare at me all you want, Quinn. I won't repeat what he called you."

She frowned, and this time her furious attention shifted to the dragon looming above her. The moment she met his eye, however, her fury dissipated into awe.

None of this made any *sense*. She couldn't stay angry with this dragon, even when he was apparently insulting her.

"What the hell is wrong with me?" she muttered. "Who is this?"

"Besides a gloating asshole?" Connor asked.

A plume of smoke shot through the regal dragon's nose, and those intense blue eyes shifted toward him.

"This is Doom," Nocturne answered through the fading shreds of tar-black fog. "An ancient king. A legend, and my ancestor. He commands the respect of all dragons." Nocturne paused, and his dark eyes roamed her body as he raised his chin defiantly. "Which, I suspect, is why you knelt before him."

"What?" Connor asked. "What are you..."

The Wraithblade paused as he pieced the impossible thought together, and his full attention shifted slowly to her. He raised one dubious eyebrow as he silently asked if that was true.

If she was, in fact, part dragon.

Though her back ached from the tension in her body, she nodded.

"Part *dragon*?" Connor asked incredulously. "How is that even possible?"

"My father," she answered flatly.

"Ah." Connor scratched at the back of his head, and for a moment, no one spoke. He paced a small stretch of grass between the trees, and his eyes glazed over with thought. "That actually explains a lot."

Quinn laughed.

She couldn't help it.

Of all the possible reactions he could've had, that wasn't one she had expected. It was refreshing, really, to find a man who wanted nothing more from her than what she already wanted to give.

"That's it?" she asked once she had composed herself. "I tell you I'm an impossible hybrid between humans and a dragon, and that's all you have to say?"

He shrugged. "You're still you. That hasn't changed."

That disarmed her, and she tilted her head to hide a smile.

Nocturne stalked closer, the ground shaking with his every step, and he lowered his head as the wraithlike dragon had done moments before. His snout brushed against her forehead, and a hot rush of air rolled over her face. It smelled of sulfur and burnt wood, and she coughed to clear her lungs.

The prince of dragons shifted, and this time he pressed his nose against her ear. Another hot breath shot over her neck, and she shivered impulsively as the air tickled her exposed skin.

"Stop that." Quinn leaned back as his scales again pressed against her ear. "Nocturne, what are you—"

"YOU CARRY STORM WITHIN YOU." His voice ached with sadness, with grief, and a third huff of his roasted breath hit Quinn squarely in the face. "I KNOW THOSE SCALES. I SEE HER LIFEFIRE BURNING WITHIN YOU. IT IS COMFORTING TO KNOW SHE LIVES ON." His eyes pinched closed, and his wounded growl rumbled deep in her chest. "I TAKE SOLACE THAT PARTS OF HER LINGER."

That *pain.*

That *sadness.*

His words echoed with the hollow pang of ultimate loss.

Nocturne set his forehead against hers, and his deep growl rumbled through every fiber of her being. Quinn didn't press for answers. Though she had no idea what he was saying, she set her palm on the soft scales along his jaw. She let him rest there, aching, and gave him space to grieve.

His pain wasn't hers to understand. She could only listen and be here for her friend when he needed her.

Through the corner of her eye, Connor once again shifted his attention toward Doom. The two of them watched each other in silence. Now and then, Connor simply shook his head, as if he were settling a debate each time.

They were speaking—or, rather, Doom was speaking to him. Whatever it was, Connor apparently didn't like what the ancient king of dragons had to say.

"How?" Nocturne asked, his voice rumbling through his skull and into her chest. "How could this go unseen for so long? I sense your dragon nature now, but I could not before. You simply felt strange. Other."

"The glamour," she explained. "Mother charmed my Starling Crest with a Bluntmar to contain the power surges."

"A crime." Nocturne snarled, and he bared his teeth at the very idea. "There is no telling the damage that may have caused to your developing abilities."

Quinn frowned. "She did what she could."

"You have much to learn." Nocturne's head slipped away from her, and he turned his back as he receded into the cover of the forest. "Dragons learn their natural talents within their first thirty years, and yours have been dormant because of that blasted charm. Your horns will grow soon, if they grow at all."

"What?" she and Connor asked in unison.

"Horns," Nocturne repeated flatly, as though they simply hadn't heard him the first time. "Though, because of your unique nature, there is no telling what will or won't develop. Watch for intuitive warnings and, most importantly, pangs of savage hunger. We must remain vigilant—especially when it comes to your feral nature."

Quinn raised one doubtful eyebrow. "I don't have a feral nature."

The prince of dragons paused, and his regal neck arched as he looked back at her. "All dragons have a feral nature."

That struck her as odd. Wrong, even as she felt the twang of fear deep in her gut. The sensation left her on edge, and her fingertips tingled with a buzzing numbness.

Nocturne once again turned his back on her. He led the way into the woods without another glance over his shoulder, and seconds later, he disappeared entirely into the shadows beneath the trees. His footsteps receded into the distant lap of the lake's gentle waves and eventually faded altogether. In the silence that followed, only a few broken branches on the ground indicated that he had ever been there at all.

The weight of eyes on the back of her head sent a ripple of warning down Quinn's spine, and she glanced upward to find Doom already watching her. Those fierce blue eyes never wavered, and she met his glare with one of her own.

The dragon dissolved into a thick black fog, and the Wraith King soon followed. Black smoke rolled over the grass, past Quinn and Connor's boots, until the wind carried it off into the sky. For the first time since their visit to Freymoor, Quinn and Connor were alone.

Or rather, as alone as one could be with two simmering souls nearby.

Wordlessly, Connor set his palm on the back of her neck and pulled her close. He pressed his forehead against hers, and they stood there for a moment in the peaceful silent night. She drank in the scent of him—of oak and leather, and a hint of sweat—and she smiled.

They were safe, if only for now.

"Part dragon, huh?" he asked, his voice low and rough.

She grinned. "Two simmering souls, huh?"

"Guess so." After a pause filled with the rush of wind and waves, he laughed. "We're quite a pair, aren't we?"

"Wildly insane," she agreed. "But I like it."

"I don't mind it, myself." He grinned, mischievous as ever, and playfully nipped the skin on her neck. "Now that we have a minute to ourselves, how about you and I find a way to burn off some of this tension?"

Quinn grabbed his collar and clicked her tongue in mock disdain. "There's still work to do, and I have much more to tell you all."

He set his hand on the back of her head, and that devious grin of his only widened. "Don't worry, Quinn. The world will still be on fire when I'm done with you."

She looked away, but she couldn't hide her smile. "You're an idiot."

"You like it."

"Maybe." Quinn let out a slow breath of relief and finally relaxed into his chest. "Never change, outlaw."

"Hadn't planned on it," he confessed.

In the back of her mind, Quinn's training screamed at her to stop. To focus. To meet with the others and share what they had all learned. After all, Connor had no idea of the bloodshed that lay in wait for them all.

Worse yet, if Nocturne was right, she could have the untamed chaos of a feral dragon brewing within her, biding its time before it took her over completely.

The world was, indeed, on fire—but perhaps Connor was right. It would always burn, to some degree, and maybe she could let herself live a little before they faced certain death yet again.

Just this once.

CHAPTER SEVENTY-FIVE

CONNOR

In the early hours of the morning, Connor watched the distant island where Teagan Starling had secretly enslaved dragons.

His legs dangled off the edge of the steep cliff that gave him a perfect view of the world below: Lunestone, with its torches raging along every battlement; the forests shrouding much of the smaller dragon island from view of the mainland; the vast lake, almost an ocean in and of itself, that led toward the distant glimmer of Oakenglen on the horizon.

A gust of wind sailed off the lake and hit him square in the face. He squinted through the surge, focused as he was on the islands below, and he inwardly debated how the hell they were going to do this.

Freeing dragons from a secret island base teeming with assassins wasn't exactly a surefire way to see another sunrise.

Quinn had told them everything she'd found, and they likewise shared what had happened in Kirkwall. While his team had shared what they'd learned, there had been so many silences—so many moments where everyone secretly wondered if this was even possible, or if this was how they would die.

Dahlia would arrive in another few days with a small army in tow, and after everything Quinn had discovered, Connor was grateful for the backup. He wasn't about to admit it, of course, but he figured Dahlia would somehow know anyway.

Whether from sheer exhaustion or the impossibility of what lay ahead of them, a dull throb built in the back of Connor's skull. He rubbed the palm of his hand against his eye and, with a frustrated groan tried yet again to pick apart the flaws in each new plan that surfaced.

With Nocturne keeping watch for the next few hours, his team had all gone to bed. He needed to sleep, too, but he couldn't stop his mind from racing. In the morning, the rest of them would look to him for a plan, and he somehow needed to come up with one.

A thick plume of smoke rolled over the cliff beside him, and he suppressed an irritated sigh. He had sent the Wraith King off to patrol the surrounding forest, mostly to keep the ghoul occupied, but it seemed as though the undead king had grown bored of his task—and Connor was hardly in the mood for a lecture.

"Don't," he warned the billowing shadows in his periphery. "I don't want to hear it."

IS THAT SO? Doom's voice vibrated through Connor's skull.

Caught off guard, Connor leaned back and stared up at the undead dragon towering over him. Doom's piercing blue eyes watched him from afar as wisps of black smoke rolled from the dragon's hide. His broad wings were tucked tightly against his back, and Doom sat there with all the poise and composure of a king surveying his army.

"I wasn't expecting you to speak to me," Connor admitted. "I thought you were the Wraith King."

YES, HE IS INSUFFERABLE, ISN'T HE? Doom snorted, and a plume of ash shot from his nose.

Connor chose not to reply.

Any moment now, Doom would make more demands. Threats. Orders. Though the dragon's presence surprised him, he didn't expect this would end well. Though Connor wasn't the diplomatic type, he figured antagonizing an immortal dragon king was a fairly stupid choice, and he opted to let Doom speak first.

After all, he still had no idea what the dragon really wanted.

The quiet night rolled past them, carried by gusts off the lake, and the warm summer air carried a floral perfume Connor couldn't quite place. Clouds rolled across the waning moons, and their pale light spilled over the lake's glassy surface. Along the lakeshore, a line of glowing green algae dotted the shallows in an emerald green ribbon of light.

And through it all, only the wind's whisper through the trees filled the silence.

How strange, really, to think that such a tranquil place had become home to bloodthirsty bastards like Teagan Starling. Lunestone's fortress loomed over the water, a torchlit beacon in the night that dared any fool to cross its bridge and try to claim it for himself.

THE GHOUL IS OCCUPIED. Doom's voice crashed through the peaceful night, and Connor winced as the deafening roar filled his head. HE CANNOT HEAR US, AND WE CAN THUS SPEAK FRANKLY WITH EACH OTHER.

"Alright," Connor said hesitantly, more curious with each passing second as to what Doom was about to say.

This decorum and composure seemed out of character for the unruly king who had tried to roast him alive when they'd met. If Connor didn't know better, it might have even come across as respect.

Careful to feign disinterest, Connor propped one knee and scanned the horizon. "What's on your mind?"

YOU, Doom said.

When the dragon didn't continue, Connor frowned. "Care to elaborate?"

HMM. Another plume of smoke shot through Doom's nose, and he lifted his chin with a regal huff. YOU AND THAT PRINCE—OWEN, WAS IT? WHEN YOU LAST SPOKE, YOU TREATED HIM WITH RESPECT. YOU GAVE HIM ADVICE. YOU CHANGED HIM.

"I did." Connor tilted his head to look up at the dragon beside him. "Why is that relevant?"

YOU WANTED TO HATE HIM, the dragon explained. YOU DESPISED HIM, WHEN FIRST YOU MET, FOR WHAT HIS FATHER DID TO YOUR FAMILY. TO YOU.

Connor swallowed hard, and his hand tightened into a fist as he focused his attention again on the horizon.

AND YET, THE MORE YOU LEARNED OF HIS INTENTIONS, THE MORE YOU HAD TO BEGRUDGINGLY ACCEPT THAT YOUR INTERESTS WERE ALIGNED. THAT, AS MUCH AS YOU WANTED TO HATE HIM, YOU COULDN'T. BY THE END, I DETECTED A HINT OF RESPECT.

Huh.

"You were watching more closely than I realized," Connor admitted.

Yes. Doom growled, low and deep, but his body remained relaxed. You impressed me, Magnuson. I was not expecting a human to have such self-awareness as to admit when he is wrong.

"Thanks," Connor said dryly.

Inwardly, however, he reeled at the compliment. Whatever the dragon had come to discuss, Connor sure as hell hadn't been expecting *that.*

It resonated, Doom continued. For that is what I have come to believe about you. I despise that you are a human, but I cannot deny my respect for who you are.

A bit bewildered by whatever was happening, Connor let the silence linger. He ran his thumb over the tip of his finger, lost in his thoughts, and he didn't quite know how to reply.

The wraith-like dragon curled his regal neck and shifted the full weight of his piercing blue eyes to Connor. You surprised me. I was expecting to witness devastation. Cruelty. Control. You need refinement, but you have potential to be a king worthy of leading even the dragons.

Connor quirked one eyebrow at the backhanded compliment, but he ultimately resisted the urge to poke the bear.

Apparently, he wasn't the only one who needed a bit of refinement.

I do not expect you to trust me, Doom continued. Nor would I, if I were in your position. I have left you to fend for yourself, to learn your new abilities on your own, and I have been silent.

"It's fine," Connor said. "I understand why you did it."

Do you? A dubious chuckle rolled through Connor's head, and it sounded strangely similar to the one his father had made any time Connor had tried to lie as a boy.

"You don't know me. You needed to figure out who I am and what I wanted from you."

In part, the dragon replied with an impressed snort. *But it is more than that. A wise leader listens before he acts. He observes before he commands. He thinks, he plans, and he is—above all else—intentional.*

Hmm.

The sentiment echoed something Beck Arbor had told him all those years ago, back when he was just an orphan lost in the Ancient Woods, chopping wood for the grumpy old man who'd taught him how to fight.

True leaders—the ones history remembers—they don't choose to lead, Sir Beck had told him once. *I already know where you fit into the world, Connor. Do you?*

Doom's inquisitive growl echoed in Connor's head, and the deafening sound snapped Connor out of his memory. He returned to the windswept cliff and the towering dragon looming above him.

There is something I do not understand, Doom said.

"And what's that?" Connor asked.

You have incredible power that most men would abuse, and yet you are hesitant to use it.

With a halfhearted chuckle, Connor returned his attention to the Lightseer fortress below them. "I bust open heads just fine, thank you."

Not your fists, the dragon corrected. *And not your blades, for that matter. Your true power is so much more. As you found in the cavern below Kirkwall Castle, you do not need to strike every blow on your own.*

Connor's smile fell, and he ran his tongue over his teeth as he grappled with the gravity of what the dragon had left unspoken.

He is a murderous ghoul who happily kills at your command, Doom continued. *He is a demon who can slip between worlds and rip your foes to ribbons and bone.*

"And?"

The dragon snorted impatiently at Connor's tone. *And you appeared ashamed to have used the Wraith King's power.*

"Not ashamed," Connor corrected.

What, then?

"Reluctant."

Hmm.

Connor picked at a lone blade of grass poking from the cliff's rock and ripped it from its roots. He slowly shredded it as he debated how much the dragon needed to know, but he didn't want to lose this opportunity to win over an immortal ghoul that would be fused to him forever.

"People fear me," he explained. "Even the ones I'm trying to protect. Even my own family. The ones I love have only witnessed a fraction of what I can do, and I'll still remember the horror on their faces for the rest of my life."

Or the rest of eternity, perhaps, if the Antiquity got her way.

And that holds you back? Doom asked.

"It keeps me grounded," he said with a sidelong glance at the dragon's face. "It reminds me of why I'm doing this. It keeps me from losing control."

Maybe.

"No, definitely," he corrected.

You're mistaken, Doom said flatly.

Connor snorted, doubtful. "How so?"

I razed cities, the dragon answered. *I burned kingdoms whole. My blackfire melted bone and metal. I toppled empires and scorched the kings who would invade my lands. I was a force of nature, of bloody vengeance, and my people cheered me for it.*

Unsure of what to say, Connor absently stared at the shredded blade of grass in his palm and remained silent.

It is not your power or its devastation that breeds fear, Doom explained. *It is the way in which you wield it. You know the raw depth of your abilities—most of them, at least—and you have earned my respect. I will never obey you, Magnuson, but I will at a minimum consider your requests of me.*

"It's progress." Connor chucked the grass over the edge of the cliff, and the wind carried the remnants out over the water far below.

Embrace your devastation, Doom said firmly. *Embrace what you can do. You have incredible power at your fingertips. Wield it well, and do not fear it. The time has come to use it—or others will steal it from you.*

Huh.

That was actually damn good advice.

"Thank you," he said.

And, to his surprise, he actually meant it this time.

I will help you free my people, Doom said as his blue eyes shifted toward the small island beside Lunestone. *And I will teach you what you need to know to wield your new magic.*

Wait.

No, this couldn't be real.

Connor's eyebrows shot up his forehead, and he braced himself for the trap to spring. "You're going to help us?"

Doom's gaze shifted toward him, and the dragon ultimately nodded. *But you were right, back there in Freymoor, when you told the Antiquity that all great magic has a price.*

And there it was.

The catch.

This wasn't making amends between two kings. This was a bargain, same as all the others. It annoyed him that, for a moment there, it had almost seemed as though the rift between them had finally healed.

"Out with it, then," Connor demanded. "Tell me what you want."

It concerns that woman of yours.

"Quinn? What does she have to do with this?"

She is an abomination. Doom's voice was cold, dispassionate even, as though he weren't insulting the woman Connor had chosen for life.

"Not this again, damn it all." Connor pushed to his feet and raised one finger in warning. "I told you not to call her that."

It is not an insult, Doom replied calmly. *That is just what she is. Nocturne sees his lost love in her, and that means she has been bred from the blood of fallen dragons. She was hobbled together from the ghosts of my people, stolen from their very veins. She should not exist.*

"And you should?" Connor gestured to the hulking behemoth on the cliff's edge, as dark as the night around them and barely visible while backlit by the stars. "You're cobbled together from a stolen simmering soul. Don't preach to me, you royal ass. You're no better."

Doom's head snapped back, as though Connor had backhanded him in the face, and neither of them spoke.

Connor fumed. He paced along the cliff's edge, furious that this overgrown lizard had once again insulted Quinn after it had clearly taken so much out of her to tell him the truth.

The *gall.*

She is new, Doom said after a while. *She has a feral nature, Magnuson. I can almost taste it on her, like a lie she's trying to hide from us all. It has been repressed for so long that it will become untamable now that it's free. Her power radiates from her, raw and wild, and it will only grow. There will come a time when even you cannot stop her. You cannot claim to protect this land or its people if you do not stop this madness before it begins.*

At that, Connor went still, and his blood ran cold.

It was all suddenly so obvious—what Doom wanted him to do.

"No." Connor's voice reverberated in his chest like a growl, low and deep. His body tensed as he met the dragon's eye, and his glare narrowed with unfettered hatred.

He would not kill Quinn Starling.

It will be painful, Doom said calmly. *But it must be done. If you are reluctant to access the depths of your own magic, you cannot begin to fathom what she will destroy when she turns feral. Nothing and no one will be safe. Not even you.*

"No," he repeated. This time, the word was even less recognizable as anything other than an enraged snarl in his throat.

Doom's blue eyes briefly scanned his face. *You are becoming emotional. This is unbecoming of a king.*

"Shut your damn mouth," Connor ordered.

His voice snapped through the air like a whip to the face, and Doom's eyes narrowed in contempt. The dragon's nose creased with disdain, and the two kings stared each other down in breathless challenge.

For my help in this onslaught, that is my price, Doom said firmly. *What is your answer?*

"Fuck no," Connor spat. "How's that for an answer?"

Doom bristled. His jaw raised into the air, until Connor could barely see his eye over those sleek black scales, and charred black smoke churned from the regal creature's nose. *Then I will not help you.*

"You're all talk." Connor gave the dragon a once-over. "Look at you, lording your power over me as if you could strongarm me into submission. If you call that respect, I don't want it. My mission isn't to save humans, or even to hunt information. I'm saving dragons. Your people, Doom. Yours, not mine. You're going to let them die? For what? Your own damn pride?"

It is not pride. Thunder rumbled in Doom's chest as dark clouds gathered on the distant horizon. *It is reason. You do not understand what she will become.*

"Neither do you, apparently," Connor snapped.

Doom snarled, low and fierce, and he lowered his head until he and Connor were eye to eye. *Put your lust aside, you mortal fool. Think about what is best for your people as well—not just for yourself.*

"Right now, you're holding your own people as leverage against me. You're last on the list of living beings who can preach to me, damn it."

An abomination like her cannot be allowed to live! Doom roared.

"She's the last bit of Storm that Nocturne has left." Connor pointed back toward the forest, in the vague direction of the cottage. "Even if you hate Quinn, are you really going to take that from him?"

He has been with men too long. Doom snorted, indignant at the very idea. *You all have made him soft. Emotional. He sees his lost love and not the abomination that was created with her corpse.*

Connor grimaced. "You hate humans. Fine. You think dragons are superior. I don't care. But if you lay one claw on Quinn, I will end you. One way or another, I'm sure Death will take you back."

Then you will lose my power.

"I've managed just fine without it."

You disgust me! Doom growled, deep and low, and spread his great wings wide. A flash of amber light shot through his eyes as he accessed the depths of his own feral power. His head raised such that Connor couldn't make out a thing beyond the Dragon King's massive body, except for the ribbons of black smoke rolling from his scales. *It is as I thought. You cannot handle my power. You do not possess the courage to become a king. You are weak!*

At the devastating echo of that all-consuming voice in his head, any other man would have cowered. He would have knelt. He would have obeyed. The words shook every bone in Connor's body, and it took effort to even breathe.

But his rage outweighed even the weight on his chest.

Cold fury sent surreal chills down his arms. He felt nothing in that warm summer night, save the flicker of something devastating deep in his soul. His boot flattened the sparse wildflowers poking through cracks in the rock at his feet as he took one ominous step closer to the Dragon King of legend.

His glare, his posture, his presence—it all carried an unspoken warning.

"Some king you are." Connor's gravelly voice dropped an octave. "You dangle your people's lives like bartering chips, and you lecture me on what it takes to lead. For as much as you preach about how men will sell their morals, you seem all too willing to sacrifice your own. You still haven't figured out my price, Doom, but it looks like we discovered yours."

The amber light in Doom's blue eyes faded in a rush, and the wraithlike dragon went still. He watched Connor in stunned silence, but the Dragon King did not reply.

"I don't know what you are," Connor admitted with a disgusted huff. "But you're no leader."

With that, he turned his back on the immortal dragon who, for a moment there, had seemed to come to his senses. Furious and fuming, Connor didn't even know where he was going. He didn't care. He knew Doom would be tethered to him for life, forever the infuriating hypocrite who would judge any move Connor made, but none of that mattered. Right now, Connor needed to put as much distance between them as possible.

For Doom's sake, really, as much as his own.

Wait, the dragon said.

Connor shook his head, and he didn't even look back at the dragon on the cliff's edge. He wouldn't take orders from this colossal jackass.

It is a request, Doom explained. *Not an order.*

With a frustrated sigh, Connor paused midstride and set his hands on the back of his head. "What is it now?"

No one has ever defied me, the undead dragon said.

"Get used to it."

To his surprise, Doom laughed. The raspy chuckle echoed through his mind, and Connor frowned in confusion.

I will help you.

"Maybe I don't want your help," he said coldly.

Perhaps, Doom acknowledged. *But you need it anyway.*

Skeptical, Connor scanned the dragon's face for any hint of a lie. Honestly, though, he still hadn't mastered dragon tells quite yet, and he had almost nothing to go on.

"I'm not killing her."

I know.

Connor's eyes narrowed in suspicion. "And you won't either."

Doom watched him, and the silence lasted a moment too long. *I will not harm her.*

But there was something there, between the words, that the Dragon King had left unsaid. The tense threat lingered between them, heavy and unsettling, and Connor could almost hear the tail end of that sentence.

Two words lingered between them, unspoken but there all the same—*"for now."*

Quinn would live, and Doom would share his power.

For now.

CHAPTER SEVENTY-SIX

CONNOR

It was time.

As daylight poured through the open windows in the isolated cabin, Connor stood with his back to the fireplace. As he waited for Nocturne to join them, he took a moment to scan his team's faces. His small band of misfits had grown, and even after all this time, he still found it surreal to think that such a diverse group of powerful warriors would all look to him for answers.

The Fates were certainly full of surprises.

The Wraith King and Dragon King were somewhere out of sight, and Connor preferred that for the moment. Quinn and Tove stood to his right, and though Tove flipped through the pages of one of her books, Quinn scanned the gathered throng along with him.

Sophia and Murdoc lounged on the long couch across from him. Sophia absently tapped one finger on her lips as she skimmed the assassin's log Quinn had stolen from Teagan's office. Murdoc, meanwhile, draped his arm around Sophia's shoulders, and he leaned his mouth toward her ear. Connor tuned out the man's whispers, though, since he figured he didn't want to know whatever raunchy nonsense was about to take place.

Dahlia and her small army had arrived overnight. She and Duncan stood by the door, whispering among themselves. He caught snippets of their debate about tents and supplies, but he would ask Quinn to help them shelter their fifty-odd troops they had brought from Freymoor.

A blessing, really, and an act of loyalty he wouldn't forget.

Outside, a hollow thud shook the ground. The floorboards vibrated beneath Connor's boots, and he studied the nearest window as he waited for the visitor to make himself known. A shadow passed through the sunlight, black as the midnight sky, and a low growl rolled through the air.

Everyone inside the cabin went silent, their full attention on the window, as the shadow reached the house. Its massive head lowered, and bits came into view one at a time—black scales, sharp teeth, and then a single black eye, peering through the curtains.

"I HOPE I DID NOT KEEP YOU WAITING LONG," Nocturne's voice boomed through the cabin and shook the very walls.

Good. They were all here, and he could begin.

With her eyes locked on Nocturne's face, Tove leaned toward Quinn and lowered her voice to a whisper. "You don't need me for this, right? While you all discuss the next steps, I'll be outside. I want to sketch Nocturne so that I can—"

"Focus," Quinn chided.

"But—"

"Later." The Starling warrior's eyes narrowed, and she raised one eyebrow in an unspoken warning to sit still.

Tove pouted. The augmentor crossed her arms and leaned against the wall, her eyes trained on the dragon just outside the open window.

With a settling breath, Connor braced himself for the debate that lay ahead. Even with Doom's help, what they were about to do seemed nigh impossible.

"Listen closely." Connor's jaw tensed as his piercing eyes swept across the small band of warriors gathered around him. "Things don't look good. The island fortress where the dragons are located is crawling with Unknown assassins. Every one of them is wearing glamours, and we have no idea how many more were added after Teagan went missing. We can't scout the island because of their numbers, and anyone who comes too close will get an arrow through the eye."

Tove grimaced. "I really didn't need that image in my head."

"It's the truth." He cast a sidelong glance at the augmentor to ensure she realized what they were up against. "The Lightseers and Starlings both rely on the money generated by that one fortress. Those spellgust gemstones aren't made by humans, like we all thought, but by their enslaved dragons. Though the Isletide solution being crafted on the island will cover some of that lost income, the dragons are the foundation of Starling wealth. Lunestone has a lot to lose if those dragons disappear, and that means that island is even more secured than we know."

In the brief lull that followed, everyone in the room looked at Quinn. To her credit, she didn't falter, nor did she fidget under the weight of so much attention. Instead, she kept her eyes trained on Connor and nodded for him to go on.

"It gets worse," he continued. "Celine Montgomery has returned to Oakenglen, and she is secretly an Unknown assassin. She's brutal and not to be underestimated."

"It explains a lot," Tove said under her breath.

Connor frowned. "How so?"

"Oh." Tove stiffened as the room's attention shifted to her, and a soft pink blush crept up her neck. "It's just—her presence. Something isn't right about her. She summoned me while you were away, Quinn, and just standing near her made me want to run for cover. She's terrifying."

"She summoned you?" Quinn's brow knit in confusion. "Why?"

Tove's lips parted, but the augmentor didn't speak. Instead, she tugged on the ends of her braid and stared at the floor.

"Tove, what aren't you telling me?" Quinn asked. "Why would Celine Montgomery summon you to the castle? What did she want?"

"It's—ugh." Tove pinched the bridge of her nose and sighed in defeat. "My parents were potion masters for the last kings of Oakenglen. The Coldwells. They were murdered in the onslaught when Henry took the crown, but I was too young. Henry sent me to live with a family friend who had done a better job of hiding their loyalties to the Coldwell crown, but I suspect those in the castle have kept an eye on me ever since."

The room went still, and Quinn blinked rapidly in stunned surprise. "That seems like something I should've known a while ago, Tove."

"No, it's—it's not like that," Tove said. "It's because I didn't want you to think less of me. That and, well, I never wanted to discuss the way my parents—" The augmentor cleared her throat and swallowed hard as she once more toyed with the ends of her braid. "I didn't want to dwell in a past I couldn't change. I want to live in the now."

Connor scratched at the stubble on his jaw, but he couldn't deny her logic. Not when he had demons of his own.

Quinn's glare softened, and after a tense moment of silence, she gently set her palm on her friend's shoulder.

"Celine is a threat," Connor said, mostly to shift the attention off of Tove. "We don't know the number of Unknown she controls, if any. We need to use the utmost caution if we have any altercation with her at all."

"Noted," Dahlia said dryly.

Fair point. The fallen princess didn't need to be reminded of the Montgomery's brutality.

"Tove can't return to her shop," Quinn added. "Of us, only Murdoc can show his face in public—though Sophia is also safe until Zander returns."

"If he returns," Dahlia corrected.

Quinn sighed, and though she stared at the ground, she slowly shook her head. "When. I can feel it."

Dahlia pursed her lips, but she didn't press the matter.

"We have one goal," Connor interjected, regaining control of the conversation. "Free the dragons on that island."

"They deserve their freedom," Nocturne's voice shook the walls, and he growled happily.

You and your damned bargains, the Wraith King grumbled from somewhere in the in-between. *They slow you down, Magnuson.*

Connor opted not to reply.

"My fear," Nocturne continued, "Is that there are no dragons on that island to save."

The air thickened with unspoken dread, and Connor met his scaly friend's eye. "There have to be, don't you think? For the Starlings to continue making the spellgust gemstones?"

"DRAGONS, YES," Nocturne answered. "BUT IF THEY HAVE GONE FERAL IN THEIR CENTURIES AWAY FROM THE SKY, THERE WILL BE NOTHING LEFT OF THEM TO SAVE."

"Do you think that's likely?" Quinn asked.

A thin plume of smoke shot through Nocturne's nose, and he nodded. "I FEAR IT IS INEVITABLE. MAY THE FALLEN BE AT PEACE."

Connor let out a slow breath to steel himself against the thought. It was one of the great risks of this mission—that they would attack an impregnable fortress, possibly losing some of their own in the process, only to find no one there to save.

He hated not knowing what they would face in there. With anything built by Teagan Starling, he had to assume the worst.

"It doesn't matter," he said firmly. "We're going. If they're feral, it's our duty to put them out of their misery."

A pained growl rumbled through the floorboards, but Nocturne ultimately nodded.

With a flick of his hand, Connor gestured in the vague direction of Lunestone. "We have one shot at this. The military force on that island is fierce, even without the Unknown. There won't be a return trip, so anything we have to do needs to be done before we leave."

Sophia shut the ledger of Unknown assassins and tapped her fingernail on the cover. "Judging from this book, Connor, we're doomed to fail."

"Come on, now," he chided. "Everyone in this room is clever. We can think of something."

"Any ideas, Captain?" Murdoc asked.

"Some," he admitted. "But I need to make sure I understand all of the risks before we act."

"Where do I start?" Sophia let out a wry laugh and lifted the book in her lap for emphasis. "We can't do this quietly. Freeing a band of dragons from an island fortress is going to draw attention, even if we succeed brilliantly."

"Celine will be watching," Tove added with a shudder. "Even if the weather is foggy, she will at least notice the dragons flying south over the city."

"No one knows dragons even exist," Quinn chimed in. "To the common folk, dragons are creatures of doom and destruction. Anyone who sees one will assume those responsible are evil."

"DELIGHTFUL." The prince of dragons standing outside the open window grumbled obscenities at the very idea.

Quinn shrugged. "They don't know better, Nocturne. Maybe we can change their minds with time, but that's the reality we have to face right now."

The dragon huffed indignantly, but he ultimately didn't reply.

"The Lightseers will respond," Duncan interjected. "If we attack an island that belongs to their fortress, even those who don't know about Teagan's dragons will fly over to assist those in the fortress. We will be quickly outnumbered, even beyond the original forces."

A good point.

"And what about the dragons themselves?" Sophia asked. "If they've been down there for centuries, chained in a dungeon, the muscles in their wings will have atrophied. They can't possibly fly."

Damn it.

Connor hadn't even considered that.

"THE SKY CALLS TO ALL DRAGONS," Nocturne replied. "THE YOUNG, THE OLD, THE BROKEN. WHEN THEY SEE THE STARS, THEY WILL FLY."

Sophia shook her head. "That's not how atrophied muscles work. They might want to fly, but they will be too weak. They won't get off the ground, and you may not be able to carry them all."

"He can't carry any of them," Connor corrected. "We won't have much attack power without Nocturne and Doom unleashing hell on that island."

At the mention of the Dragon King's name, the room yet again went still. Everyone stiffened, even Sophia, and their eyes slowly drifted toward him as they each asked the same silent question.

Like Connor, no one here was certain they could truly rely on Doom for help.

He raised one palm to reassure them that he, too, had considered the risk. "Let's take on one bit of chaos at a time."

Dahlia and Duncan frowned, neither of them apparently satisfied with the consolation, but no one protested.

"Here's what concerns me," Murdoc interjected. "Like Sophia mentioned, this can't be done quietly. There's a lot at stake. Namely, the reputation of everyone in this room. Captain, if anything goes wrong—if a survivor recognizes you and tells others what happened—you'll be more vilified than ever. This might be the tipping point that sets the entire continent against you."

Connor nodded. "It's a risk."

"Same with Quinn," Murdoc added. "Quinn, you're going up against the Lightseers again. It was hard enough out there in the Decay, but now you're in their land. You know the terrain, but so do they. It's a risk that they will recognize you, too. If they do, you lose everything."

"I know," the Starling warrior said softly. "But it's better to stand for what's right, even if it means a harder life. If this costs me my place in Saldia, so be it. I won't live a lie anymore."

With everyone watching, Connor resisted the urge to set his hand on her shoulder. Instead, he took a step closer in solidarity. Her gaze shifted to him, and a thin smile of silent gratitude tugged on her lips.

Connor gestured to everyone in the room. "This is deadly. When we go out there, anyone here could die. Everything we do needs to be strategic."

Sophia crossed her legs and snorted derisively. "That's hard to do when we have no idea what's down there."

"You're not wrong," Quinn admitted.

"We need scouts," Connor agreed. "Luckily, we have two wraiths who can pass through walls undetected."

On the couch, both Murdoc and Sophia sat a little taller. A mischievous smile spread over Sophia's ruby red lips, and even Quinn chuckled deviously.

"Brilliant," the Starling warrior muttered.

In Connor's head, the Wraith King groaned in unrestrained irritation. *One day, Magnuson, you will finally grasp the profound sacrifices I make for your ungrateful hide.*

"Consider it redemption for your stint back in the mountain," Connor replied under his breath.

Bah, the wraith said dismissively. *You will be better for what I've done.*

Doom growled, low and fierce, and the conversation from the in-between died.

"The two of them have already agreed to scout," Connor explained. "The rest of us will wait with Nocturne in a holding pattern over the fortress. We won't have long before we're spotted, even overhead, but it will be enough. Doom and the wraith, meanwhile, will wait to attack until they can give us a clear view of what lies in wait, and that gives us a momentary advantage. Once we have a clear path to the dragons, those two will launch the first attack. Nocturne, you'll unleash your lightning while Doom breaks through the fortress from below. It will cause enough chaos that no one will know what we're doing until it's too late to stop us. It's not an elegant solution, but it will be an effective one."

Nocturne snorted, and a plume of dark smoke rolled through the air around his face. Connor took that as silent agreement—and, perhaps, a bit of bloodlust.

At the thought of unleashing bloodthirsty murderers on hundreds of unsuspecting people on that island, a twinge of guilt hit Connor hard in the gut.

But it had to be done. The people on that island would kill him and his team on sight, and there was no other way.

"And once we get to the dragons?" Dahlia asked. "What do we do if they can't fly?"

"Or if they're feral?" Quinn added softly.

Connor roughly cleared his throat at the memory of Nocturne deep under Slaybourne. One dragon had nearly been the death of him, and he could hardly fathom what more might do if they got loose—but he and Nocturne had already gone over this in detail.

"If we find a feral dragon, it'll be gruesome," he admitted. "One thing on our side, however, is that Teagan probably isn't letting dragons wander free through his fortress. Anyone who has gone feral will likely be chained, just like the sane ones, and those locks have got to be heavily enchanted. They won't attack us, but you still won't get close enough to a feral dragon to put them down humanely. It's not going to be pleasant."

"A FERAL DRAGON'S GOOD DEATH LIES IN HELLFIRE," Nocturne said firmly. "WE WILL GIVE THEM THAT INFERNO AS THEY LEAVE THIS LIFE."

"Brutal," Murdoc said under his breath.

"It is." Connor ran his fingers along his jawline as he stitched together another hole in his plan. "I don't, however, know what to do for those who can't fly."

"Dazzledane." With her arms crossed over her chest, Quinn leaned against the fireplace behind her and propped one leg on the brick facade. "That's what got me through the worst times. It worked more intensely on me than on others. I never understood why, but maybe it has something to do with the dragon blood."

"Part dragon," Dahlia said quietly. "I'm still having a hard time absorbing that."

"You and me both," Quinn admitted.

"That became an addiction," Connor reminded her. He scanned her face, not bothering to mask his concern, and gently shook his head. "Giving dragons that potion seems unwise."

"There aren't many options," she said with a shrug. "I built that addiction over fifteen years, and I took it despite the risk because it *worked.* It made me stronger. Cleared my head. Gave me energy. Sometimes, that potion was the only reason I could pull through something dire. It will work for them, too. Even if it's temporary, it'll be enough to get them airborne."

"Unlikely," Sophia said with a halfhearted gesture toward Nocturne. "Potions are brewed for humans, not dragons. We have no idea what reagents we would need, nor do we know how the ingredients would need to be adjusted for their unique bodies."

"We concentrate them," Tove said.

Though she stared at the floor, lost in thought, a slow smile spread across the augmentor's face. Every head in the room turned toward her, and the others waited for her to elaborate.

"Think about it." She paced the length of the wall as she pieced together how this might work. "The Starling recipe is already superior to any recipe I've encountered, and the result is a far more intense effect. What are augmentations but concentrated forms of a potion? It's distilled and, for that reason, far more potent. The effects last longer, especially when inked into the blood, and dragons are obviously more susceptible to the effects of magic."

Tove gestured toward Quinn, who frowned.

"Thanks," the Starling muttered.

"It will take time," Tove continued, oblivious. "But I can do it if Sophia helps me."

Connor caught the necromancer's eye and raised one eyebrow in a silent request that she do it.

"Yes, fine." Sophia waved away the thought with a flick of her slender wrist. "It will be a curious experiment, if nothing else."

Connor smirked. "That's the spirit."

"What about the babies?" Murdoc asked. "He was breeding them, right?"

Outside the window and in Connor's head, the two dragons snarled.

"I think so." Though Quinn briefly glanced at the prince of dragons by the open window, she shrugged. "That's what I gleaned from his ledgers, anyway."

"And he kept *meticulous* notes." For emphasis, Sophia tapped the ledger in her lap.

"Right, so they've never flown," Murdoc said. "How would we get them airborne?"

"A DRAGON IS BORN WITH INTUITIVE FLIGHT," Nocturne replied. "IT IS CLUMSY AND UNSTEADY, BUT IT IS THERE. IF WE GET THEM INTO THE AIR, THEY WILL DO THE REST. THOSE WHO TRULY CANNOT SUSTAIN FLIGHT WILL LIKELY BE SMALL ENOUGH TO RIDE ON THE ELDERS' BACKS."

"It's a long trip," Dahlia pointed out. "The Dazzledanes will wear off long before you reach Slaybourne."

"We will have to make extra," Tove said with a shrug. "Dragons can't exactly sip from a bottle, but I doubt the glass will hurt them even if they eat it."

"CORRECT," Nocturne said.

Connor frowned, not sure if he wanted to know how the regal creature had figured that one out.

"That will work, then," Tove continued. "Dazzledanes will get them into the air. If they're coasting on the air currents, that should get them to Slaybourne. It means flying during the day, when they can be spotted, but it's like Murdoc said—we can't do this quietly. They'll be spotted nonetheless."

"We should still keep to the less populated areas of the Ancient Woods," Connor interjected. "The fewer people who see the dragons headed south, the better. Let the rumors confuse everyone as to where they really went."

"A good idea," Dahlia said. "I'll send some false information to Wildefaire to pass through their chain of gossips. That will further confuse the general public."

"Excellent," Connor said with a grateful nod.

"And if they dive? If they hunt?" Duncan shook his head at this insane idea. "You cannot risk even one of them breaking off from the core flock."

"THEY WON'T," Nocturne said with a firm growl. "I WILL ENSURE IT."

"They don't know you're their prince," the Freymoor general pointed out. "They won't know to obey you."

"THEY WILL LEARN." Nocturne snarled again. "AND I WILL NOT LET THEM FORGET."

In Connor's head, Doom chuckled approvingly.

"It's risky," Duncan insisted.

"You're right," Connor conceded. "It's not perfect, but it's the closest thing to a plan that we've got."

Duncan opened his mouth to protest, but he wordlessly shook his head as his eyes shifted out of focus. The man thought through the options before them and, ultimately, shrugged. "I suppose you're right."

"I appreciate the vote of confidence," Connor said dryly.

The Freymoor general snickered and rubbed his eyes, evidently too tired after their long trek to indulge any banter.

"There's still the matter of the Lightseers." Dahlia's cold voice pierced the air, and her eyes narrowed with a brief flash of hatred. "From what I read in that ledger of the island, there is some kind of alert in times of danger. Whether from that or the onslaught, the Lightseers will respond."

"That's true," Connor said as he studied the princess's face. "And I have a feeling you already came up with a solution."

Dahlia smirked. "Duncan and I have discussed it, and we believe we've found a solution."

"We will give you cover," Duncan explained. "The island isn't far from a lone stretch of the mainland cliffs, and I've already ordered some of my soldiers to scout that area. We should find at least three acceptable vantage points that give us a clear view of the Lightseers who fly toward the island."

"And?" Sophia pressed. "Will you be throwing menacing glares at them, or something useful."

Murdoc chuckled and gently nudged the necromancer beside him. "Be nice, darling."

"Something useful," Duncan answered, though he didn't bother to mask his disdain. "A new enchanted weapon of ours has been in development for years. It's time to deploy it in the field."

"That sounds ominous," Connor admitted.

"It's *effective*," Dahlia corrected. "The black ice arrows haven't failed a single test in over a year. When fired in the dark, they're undetectable. Upon impact, they instantly freeze the target. Those who are hit will not even know they've died. If it's dark enough, those behind the target won't even see the arrow land—but if anyone *does* witness the attack, they won't have enough time to react before an arrow hits them, too."

Damn.

Connor didn't know whether he was impressed or outright disturbed by a weapon with that sort of impact.

While the rest of the room went eerily silent, Murdoc stared at the princess as though she had grown fangs. "That's terrifying."

In answer, Dahlia simply smirked.

The Wraith King's wicked cackle echoed through Connor's mind. *You must acquire that recipe, Magnuson. I wish to have that in the Slaybourne arsenal as well.*

"Focus," Connor chided the ghoul.

"It's a good idea," Sophia admitted. "While they're on the mainland, the four of us can infiltrate on Nocturne's back."

Ah. Right.

Connor braced himself to deliver the edict he had, to some extent, been dreading—mostly because neither Murdoc nor Sophia was going to like it.

"Not four," Connor corrected. "Two."

Sophia's eyes narrowed, and her lip twitched with a barely restrained reply—one that likely involved a fair number of scathing insults.

"You can't be serious." Murdoc planted his boots firmly on the floor, and any hint of his usual lighthearted grin faded from his expression. "We couldn't give you backup in the mountain, and now you're not letting us give you backup on this, either?"

"You will die in there," Sophia said coldly. "Those assassins, those soldiers—all of them want you dead. They will focus on you, and even you can be overrun."

She has a point, Magnuson, the ghoul interjected.

"This is happening, Connor, whether you like it or not." Sophia raised her chin in defiance, as though that settled things. "You can't stop us."

"I can," he said firmly. "And it's for the same reason you couldn't join me in the mountain. That was an in-between, and this fortress probably has enough spellgust in it to cook you both alive. Murdoc, you could barely breathe in the Blood Bogs. Imagine what you would endure on that island."

"I've endured worse," the former Blackguard said darkly.

"Maybe," Connor admitted. "But dragons likely aren't being kept far from the spellgust. If you go in there, your throat might close before you can get a word out to warn me. I won't risk it."

The man's nose flared with anger, but he muttered obscenities as he conceded to reason. He sank back in his seat with one fist resting on his leg and refused to look Connor in the eye.

"And me?" Disdain dripped from every word Sophia spoke. "You need me, Connor."

"I do," he acknowledged. "But it's the same. The magic keeping you alive is new, and we don't know what will happen if you get that close to so much spellgust."

"Cook you from within, probably," Tove said flippantly. "And it will hurt the whole time you're dying."

"Thank you for that disturbingly vivid image, Tove." Connor didn't bother to mask the wry disgust in his voice as he glanced at her over one shoulder.

Tove shrugged.

Sophia sneered at the augmentor. Her dark eyes drifted to the floor, and she pursed her lips in thought. After another few moments of silence, she reclined against the sofa and crossed her arms in defeat.

Good. It was settled.

"We have to time the onslaught," Duncan added. "For the black ice arrows to properly work, we need utter darkness. I say we wait for the new moons."

"THEY HAVE WAITED LONG ENOUGH," Nocturne growled.

Connor grimaced as he considered the idea. "I agree with Nocturne. I don't like it. With every second that passes, we risk another one of them going feral. If we wait for the new moons, that means delaying by almost a full week."

"It's a trifle compared to how long those dragons have been in the dark," Duncan pointed out. "In the meantime, it will give us time to prepare."

Connor sucked in a sharp breath through his teeth, still not a fan, but he couldn't deny the logic. Duncan had a point. If they rushed this, the loss could be even worse—both for the enslaved dragons and for his team.

"Alright," he conceded. "Nocturne, I think this is our best option."

The prince of dragons growled, and though the walls yet again shook with the power of his voice, Nocturne didn't press the matter.

"Should we get your sister to help?" Tove asked Quinn.

The Starling warrior sighed and shook her head. "We need her to maintain deniability. She knows I'm planning something, but she can't be involved with this. When she hears that something is happening on the island, she will stay away. For now, that's the best scenario."

"It might still be best to have her on board," Connor said. "There's no telling how useful she could be, especially if she delays the Lightseers or stops them altogether."

"I know," Quinn admitted. "But we have to look at the long-term risk of that plan. If she's responsible for stopping a unit from assisting what ultimately becomes a full-on attack of part of Lunestone, she will become a suspect. That severely limits her ability to influence other matters in the future."

Connor frowned, but she had a point.

"This is your choice," he eventually said. "Whatever you decide, I'll support it."

Quinn nodded. "Trust me."

He did, and she knew it.

Murdoc leaned back in his seat and got comfortable. "Alright, then. That still leaves the small matter of what to do with Oakenglen. The city isn't exactly close to Lunestone, but it's close enough to see a bunch of dragons flying toward them."

"Right." Connor scratched the back of his head as he sifted through the possible ways that could go wrong.

There were *many*.

An idea came to him, then, as bright and fierce as the sun rising over a mountain's peak. It would solve two problems at once, and he didn't even try to mask the mischievous grin as he paused to consider possible holes with this new plan.

"I know that face." Murdoc laughed and slapped his thigh. "Out with it, Captain. I want to know what sort of hell you're going to raise."

Connor's grin widened. "We can't hide dragons over Lunestone, but we can control what happens after they're spotted. If we time things right, we make Oakenglen think Lunestone is attacking."

The room erupted, and in the stunned muttering that followed, everyone spoke over each other.

"—death wish—"

"—what could we possibly—"

"—would never work—"

Murdoc, meanwhile, just laughed. "I love it."

"Then you're as crazy as he is," Sophia muttered.

"Connor, that could never work," Quinn stepped closer and scanned his face, as though she were trying to see if he had officially lost his mind. "How could we possibly make them think it's Lunestone attacking?"

"We bluff," he said with a shrug. "I'm sure Dahlia's soldiers can secure a few Lightseer uniforms. We wear them as we fly over. Hide our faces. Nocturne unleashes a bit of lightning, and Doom rains hell on another part of the city. We keep to the walls and castle to minimize casualties. We wait for them to fire every ballista along the ramparts, and we let them think they've chased us off. We fly east and split up. The weaker dragons take the air currents to the south, while Nocturne and Doom loop north. When we're over an isolated stretch of land, we loop back south and go unseen. The detour will take minutes—short enough that the weaker dragons can't cause any trouble. If they're just coasting on the currents, we will catch up instantly."

A lull settled over the room, and everyone gaped at him as flashes of doubt or understanding crossed every person's face, one at a time. Slowly, mouths began to close and eyes began to gloss over in silent debate.

But this would work.

"I LIKE IT," Nocturne eventually said.

The dragon's voice pierced the silence, and those gathered in the cabin slowly nodded in agreement.

"I'll be damned," Quinn muttered. "That's actually brilliant."

Connor laughed. "You're surprised?"

The Starling warrior chuckled, and though she looked at him with a playful smile on her face, she didn't reply.

"This keeps my name out of the rumors," Connor added. "At least for the most part. Lunestone and Oakenglen have had a tense alliance since Henry forced them into submission, and I'm sure there are those among the Lightseer ranks who want every last Montgomery burned alive."

"There are many," Quinn admitted.

Connor slowly paced a small stretch of the floor in front of him. "Exactly. The motivation is there. There hasn't been any mention of me in the area, right Tove?"

"None," the augmentor confirmed.

"Perfect." He paused mid-stride and took a moment to look every member of his team in the eye, silently waiting for any other points of contention he might've missed.

When no one spoke, he tightened one fist until his knuckles cracked.

"It's settled, then," he said firmly. "We have our plan, and we have five days to prepare. Let's not waste a second of it."

His voice broke the silent spell on the air, and everyone in the room headed for the door. Each person glanced briefly at him as they walked outside, and Quinn held his gaze a second longer than the rest.

A pit formed in his stomach as her unspoken concern lingered. In the past, more than one of his best strategies had unraveled in the heat of the moment.

In matters of life and death, things rarely went to plan. More people were relying on him than ever before, and no matter what happened out there on that lake, it was his duty to ensure that his team made it out alive.

At *any* cost.

CHAPTER SEVENTY-SEVEN

CELINE

The first threads of dawn cast a golden shimmer across the lake that separated Oakenglen from Lunestone. Each castle dominated its respective horizon. Cliffs surrounded each fortress, and waves crashed against the rocks beneath both strongholds of Saldian power. A cool breeze rolled over the dawn-stained water, rippling the ribbons of pink and orange light, and it carried the first taste of summer on its breath.

Two domains, long at war with each other.

From her balcony in Oakenglen's northern wall, with her palms resting on the cold stone railing, Celine stared off at the distant shimmer of Lunestone. Its towering silhouette loomed over the watery horizon, nothing more than a mirage hiding in the last shreds of shadow. How often she had stood here, in her days with Henry, and watched the island's lights flicker in the distance.

She had escaped that life, only to be dragged back into the fray by incompetent men too drunk off their own egos to recognize their own greed.

Without a sound, a man stepped into her periphery. Her heart skipped a beat, as it always did when her father surprised her, but she otherwise gave no indication that she saw him at all.

Charles Jasper, retired Unknown. The man who had elected her to take his spot as Teagan Starling's favorite.

Her father stood beside her with his shoulders squared and his hands resting behind his back. His long silver beard ended in a well-groomed point over his chest, and the carefully tailored mustache above his mouth curled at both ends.

Together, they stared out at the lake with nothing but the wind to fill the void between them.

"You found Davarius before me." Her father's voice punctuated the calm morning, and Celine's eye twitched once in annoyance.

So few people appreciated the beauty in silence.

"I did," she replied.

"Well done," he said flatly.

Celine didn't respond. This was how their conversations always went—curt, straightforward, and civil. He had yet to even look her in the eye.

It was his way, and she had long ago stopped trying to change him.

Yet again, the conversation died. They stood on the balcony as Celine's loose hair danced on the chill wind. A hawk screeched somewhere over the water, and a shadowy blur dove from the clouds. It snared something at the surface of the lake, and the predator sailed off into the sky with a dark shape wriggling in its claws.

"That peasant has Henry's wraith," Charles said flatly.

It wasn't a question.

Her father leaned his elbows against the railing beside her, and she frowned in confusion as he relaxed against the stone. It was as if she had witnessed the stiff, unyielding assassin fade into an old man that couldn't help but think out loud.

"That shouldn't be possible," he continued. "Necromancers cannot transfer their abominations after death. Whatever they created ceases to be."

Celine didn't answer.

"Teagan Starling didn't want it for himself." Charles stroked his silver beard as he pieced it all together. "I knew that much. But his hatred for it—that surprised me. It was something more. Something that scared him. Something, I think, that could even *destroy* him."

How curious.

Silent and alert, Celine waited for her father to connect the final clues.

"It could only—" A frustrated huff of air shot through her father's nose as he grappled with the only possible explanation. "No, it can't be."

"It is," she said calmly.

The simmering souls, every bit as powerful as the day Aeron made them. The Lightseers had never destroyed Aeron's dark magic, and to this day, Celine suspected it was because those greedy bastards had secretly wanted that power for themselves.

They just couldn't figure out how to get away with wielding it.

"How many?" her father asked calmly.

Too calmly for someone who had just unearthed one of Saldia's most damning secrets.

For the first time since he had joined her, Celine caught his eye. The man who had taught her everything she knew about murder was already watching her. Waiting for an answer.

Eager to see what she knew.

"Four," she answered.

He nodded gently, mostly to himself, as though that confirmed something he had already suspected. "Fascinating."

"Is it?" Celine closed her eyes as another breeze rolled off the lake, carrying with it the subtle hint of jasmine. It soothed her bones and quelled the raging current of thoughts through her mind, if only for a moment.

"You knew." Charles pushed off the railing. "You knew what Henry's wraith was all along, and you kept it from me to protect him."

She nodded.

Nothing to hide anymore.

Her father rapped his knuckle against the stone, but he ultimately chuckled. "You continue to impress me, Celine."

At that, she allowed herself a small smile.

She didn't care if he saw it.

"What next?" her father asked.

"We kill it." Her attention returned to the waves on the vast lake before her. "We destroy them all."

"Is that possible?"

Celine's fingers twitched on impulse, and for a moment, she could recall the weight of the Bloodbane dagger in her palm. The power to kill anything, perhaps even Death Himself, resting in that one little blade.

It was power she had been foolish to relinquish.

"Yes," she eventually confessed.

"Good." Her father rested his palms on the railing beside her, and they stared out over the water once more. "Your return, at last, makes sense—but we will need more than the Oakenglen army to succeed."

Celine raised one dubious eyebrow. "Oh?"

He nodded. "I've heard whispers of what this peasant can truly do. He's a fierce opponent, my dear, and you cannot underestimate him."

Hmm.

"Zander's return..." Her father trailed off as he fought to find the right word. "It complicates things for us. The Lightseers cannot be bought, not with him in power. But we may be able to secure loyalty from the other Unknown before his grasp on them tightens. He cannot see this as the moment of weakness it is, and though it will be brief, it is one we can exploit."

"Perhaps," she conceded. "I leave that in your capable hands, Father."

For a while, he simply watched her face. She let him stare, studying whatever it was he thought he could decipher, and instead focused her attention on the small island just off Lunestone.

In all her time spent in this castle, staring out over the lake's rippling current, she had always wondered what Teagan Starling kept there.

"You can still leave," her father said calmly.

Celine blinked herself out of her daze and frowned in confusion. "Why would I?"

"Why wouldn't you?" he countered. "Let the peasants burn what's left of this continent. Your mother is gone. Your brothers are dead. Only you and I are left, and there's nothing rooting us here. You never cared for power. You never cared for glamour. You're here for the army, and even it will come to bore you."

Her father's cold eyes snared her as he dared her to disagree.

She didn't, and she wouldn't give him the fight he was looking for.

"Without purpose, what use is there in living?" she asked calmly. "I've found mine, Father. Leave me to it."

He pursed his lips in disappointment, but ultimately shrugged weakly in defeat. "So be it, child."

Celine's eyes narrowed in challenge. "You know something I don't."

"Perhaps." He gestured out toward Lunestone. "Zander has returned home."

"I'm aware."

"With blightwolves," her father added, as though she hadn't spoken. "He is changed, Celine. Something happened to him out there. He's darker. He's more bloodthirsty." Charles faltered, and he gently shook his head, as though still confused about whatever he had seen. "He is more terrifying now than his father ever was."

Fierce golden light brightened the sky, and a clear blue glow hummed above the clouds as the day officially began. The chatter of guards far below filtered through the clang of metal as the shifts changed, but Celine's mind raced with new possibilities.

It seemed so obvious now. The army she had been looking for—and the power to end an ancient abomination—had been staring at her the whole time, just waiting for her to set aside her pride.

"Zander wants Oakenglen," her father said, more urgently this time. "He wants your crown."

"Then maybe I will give it to him." A wicked little smile tugged on her lips. "Perhaps Zander can be more useful to us than we imagined, Father."

Beside her, Charles Jasper frowned. His brow creased with concern, and his gaze roamed her face as he no doubt fought to understand the sudden change in her demeanor.

Celine needed a way to lure the Wraithblade to her, and the Starlings' feud with this peasant could prove to be the perfect bait. All it would take was a little persuasion and the opportune moment to stoke the fires of Zander's greed.

Perhaps she didn't need to burn the world at all.

Maybe—just maybe—Zander Starling would do it *for* her.

CHAPTER SEVENTY-EIGHT

CONNOR

Connor stood on the cliff's edge, far enough back to remain unseen from anyone below, as the evening wind rolled off the lake.

A kaleidoscope of color sifted through the gentle waves, and a school of fish splashed across the water's surface not far from the shore. Amber clouds swirled on the horizon as the sun clawed back the last of the day's sunlight. Hints of pink along the sunset's edges faded into a dark purple sky spotted with flickering stars, and all was quiet.

For now.

Lunestone dominated most of the landscape. Its blue banners waved from every spire, the Lightseer insignia proudly displayed in silk that fluttered in the breeze. The white stone fortress blocked out the last bit of sun and cast a long shadow over the city at the base of the cliff.

The Lightseers ruled this land.

After five days of preparation, they were finally ready. The new moons would arrive tonight, and that would give them all the darkness they needed to raise hell.

Behind Connor, a boot scuffed over the grass. It only happened once, but he reflexively stiffened all the same. He had spent enough time with Dahlia and her soldiers to learn their basic gaits, but this one eluded him.

It had to be Quinn, then.

"Is everything ready?" he asked her.

Quinn Starling chuckled and, moments later, stepped into his periphery. Together, they watched the approaching stars as dusk settled over the water.

Another gust rolled off the lake, and her fire-red hair snapped around her face in the gale. She ran her fingers through it to tame the loose curls, and a beam of fading sunlight flashed across the purple scales on her wrist.

Part dragon.

It was still so hard to fathom.

Lilac scales dotted her arms, so pale that they nearly blended in with her fair skin. The scales lined her forehead in an odd shape that reminded him vaguely of a tiara. Ribbons of lavender light swam through her otherwise fire-red hair, and she watched the horizon with an intensity that made him wonder if she had noticed something he couldn't even see.

She was captivating.

Her hazel eyes flicked toward him, and she smiled. "You're staring."

"Apologies, Lady Starling," he said with a wry grin.

She shook her head and chuckled. "Don't call me that. It's strange coming from you."

"It is," he admitted.

I have a few ideas for better names, the Wraith King grumbled from somewhere in the in-between. *For the Fates' sake, Magnuson. You can't even choose a human lover?*

"Stop talking," Connor muttered under his breath.

In the back of his mind, Doom chuckled darkly.

With a sigh, Quinn tugged a pendant from her coat pocket and put it around her neck. From the moment the clasp secured it in place, the lavender scales faded from her skin. The light in her hair faded, and she looked the same as the first day he'd seen her.

"Why would you put it back on?" he asked. "Out there, we're going to need all the power we can get."

"This one doesn't limit my magic," she explained as she tapped the Starling crest around her neck. "Mother made me two of them."

Connor frowned. "Then throw the other one away."

At that, Quinn smiled more broadly than before, and she briefly scanned his face. "It's not that simple, outlaw. If Nocturne's right about me having a feral side, I need to keep it close. We might need it."

The very idea seemed utterly insane. Quinn had aways been cool, calm, and collected. It didn't seem possible for a woman like this to have a wild side, but he chose not to respond.

As they stood in silence on the edge of the cliff, Quinn slipped a folded piece of paper from her pocket. Deep lines had creased into the note, and she opened it with practiced ease.

"Is that the note from Gwen?" he asked.

Two days ago, the note had appeared in a safe box the sisters kept for each other. Just a few lines with the best time to attack, unsigned and undated. Even the handwriting, apparently, had been altered so that it couldn't be tied back to her.

This woman was *good*.

Quinn waved the note with a halfhearted flick of her wrist. "I know I shouldn't keep it, but I can't bring myself to destroy it. Right now, it's the only piece of her I have."

"I know," he said gently.

He wordlessly set one arm around her shoulders, and in the billowing dusk, he let the night take the lead. The soft nicker of the Freymoor horses, deep in the forest behind them. The honey-dusted wind through the trees, like the haunting applause of a long-dead orchestra. The warmth of Quinn's body as he held her close.

Sometimes, a man had to step back from the chaos and simply enjoy what he'd been given.

With a reluctant sigh, Quinn bunched the paper and shut her eyes tightly. The Starling warrior bit her lip, as though she were waging some internal war, but a flicker of orange light erupted in her palm. Seconds later, flames engulfed the note, and it burned instantly to ash.

"Can't have evidence," Quinn muttered as she shook the last bit of fire from her palms. "Can't be sentimental."

He shrugged. "You can be a little sentimental."

Quinn took a shaky breath and stood taller as they stood together in the wind. "The potions are done. Tove and Sophia just finished the last batch, and now they're distilling what's left. Won't be too much longer before the vials are ready."

"Down to business, just like that." Connor's grip on her shoulder tightened with a gentle squeeze. "That's how I know you're nervous."

"I'm not nervous."

He grinned. "You can admit it. I'll only judge you a little bit."

Quinn laughed and playfully elbowed him in the side. To his surprise, a brief jolt of pain shot through his chest, and his smile faltered.

Whatever she was, it had made her far stronger than anyone realized.

"I can carry the potions," Quinn said, oblivious to what had just happened. "That leaves you to take the front."

"No, I'll carry them."

She frowned, and her brows knit in momentary confusion as she scanned his face. Something must've clicked in place for her, however, and she quickly looked away. "Alright."

"It's nothing personal," he said.

"I know."

Once again, a serene lull settled between them, filled only with the rush of wind over the cliff's edge. More stars blinked to life in the depths of the tar-black sky, and for a while, there was simply nothing to say.

"What happens next, Connor?" Quinn eventually asked. She lifted her chin, but even as she spoke, she didn't meet his eye. "When we're done with that island. When we all head back into the Decay. What does it mean for you to have two simmering souls?"

It was a good question, and one he couldn't fully answer.

"I guess we will find out," he confessed. "The Fates never keep us waiting for long."

Quinn's lips pursed, and he waited for her to say something else. To probe. To prod, maybe, or pick apart the political implications he didn't understand. But after a second or two of quiet debate, she leaned into him.

"Yeah," she said. "I guess we will."

Back in the forest, the steady murmur of voices grew. Any time now, Dahlia would give the order for her troops to move, and that would tip the first domino of a night they could never take back. Whatever happened, his life would change tonight. For better or worse.

But for now, he stayed put. With Quinn's head on his shoulder and the night's melody buzzing through the air, he simply enjoyed being alive. It took effort, really, to simply exist. To savor what was, instead of what might be.

Moments of peace like this didn't last for long—not in Saldia, at least—and he intended to enjoy it while he could.

CHAPTER SEVENTY-NINE

CONNOR

Wind snapped against Connor's face as Nocturne circled the island fortress far below. His eyes had already adjusted to the serene midnight, and Nocturne had settled on a flight path low enough to give them a lay of the land, but also high enough that the pitch-black dragon blended in with the moonless sky. It tested the full range of his connection to Doom and the Wraith King, but they would have enough leeway to do what needed to be done.

Quinn sat behind him with one hand around his torso to root herself in place, and the glamour she'd taken stained her hair almost black. The thick curls whipped around her face in a frenzy as they both leaned toward the island. Her stolen Lightseer tunic creased as she leaned forward, and he glanced down at his own with a bemused frown.

Of everything that had happened thus far in his time as the Wraithblade, wearing a Lightseer's garb shouldn't have been one of the most surreal things to happen to him—but it was, regardless.

Here he was, a wolf dressed in wool, ready to set fire to the world.

Nocturne banked left to circle the island yet again, in tune with the gentle breezes rolling off the mainland cliffs. The wind drifted over the vast lake, stirring up gentle waves, as silhouettes patrolled the torchlit walls. Ballistas dominated the top of every tower, each already aimed at the sky, and even more giant crossbows dotted the interlocking ramparts of a deceptively massive fortress.

It had to be big, Connor figured, to house dragons.

This high up, their breath froze on the air. Pale plumes dissolved into the gusts around them, though none of them shivered in the cold. Nocturne drifted through a cloudbank and left a hole in his wake, and through the gap, stars shimmered like fireflies darting past black velvet.

The perfect backdrop for a raid from above.

A churning black fog bubbled from the air before them. It rolled over the sky, as thick as a cloud and as dark as depths of the ocean. Nocturne shot through it, unable to swerve in time, and Connor squinted as they dove into its midst.

When the dragon emerged on the other side, two wispy ghouls flanked them. The Wraith King glided through the air to Connor's right, his cloak whipping about in the wind like a grizzly specter of death. To his left, Doom soared through the air just below them, perfectly timing every wingbeat to match Nocturne's. The Dragon King's massive bulk blocked out the world below. Their edges blended and blurred, never still, and bits of black smoke sizzled along the tips of Doom's wings.

Power incarnate, and ready for his command.

I shall enjoy this, Magnuson, the Wraith King said with a wicked cackle.

"Focus," Connor chided. "Remember the plan."

Yes, yes, the ghoul said dismissively. *Scouting first. Chaos and murder second.*

"Glad you've managed to prioritize," Connor muttered dryly.

WE FIND MY PEOPLE FIRST, Doom interjected. ONLY THEN CAN WE ATTACK. THERE IS NO TELLING WHAT THESE HEATHENS WILL DO TO THEM, SHOULD THEY REALIZE WHAT WE WANT.

A fair point. It was yet another unknown to add to the ever-growing list of things that could go wrong.

By now, Dahlia and her army had to be in place. She, Murdoc, and Sophia had led the soldiers along the cliffside just after the last threads of sunlight had burned away. Their ice arrows would buy him much needed time, but he still needed to be quick—and hurrying through an onslaught with impossible odds wasn't usually a great way to stay alive.

"Wraith King, stick to the plan," Connor warned again. "Don't do a damn thing until one of you can stand guard over any dragons in that place.

As soon as you find them, coordinate your attacks." Connor pointed again at the ghoul floating at his side. "Remember. No murdering anyone until you break those chains, got it?"

I heard you, you twittering old hen, the ghoul said with a dismissive flick of his bone-white wrist.

"Right," Connor said, ignoring the jibe. "After that, Doom will give the rest of us a way in."

A dark chuckle rumbled through Connor's head, and Doom's blue eyes darted briefly toward him.

They all knew exactly what that meant.

"Alright, you two," Connor nodded toward the fortress. "Let's see what you can find out."

In his head, Doom's furious growl blended with the Wraith King's devious laughter, and both dissolved once more into a rolling blanket of black smoke.

All he could do now was wait.

In the corner of his eye, Quinn shifted her attention to him. "Having second thoughts?"

"Second and third thoughts," he admitted over the roar of the wind. "But this is the closest thing to a plan we've got."

She set a reassuring palm on the center of his back. "It will work."

It was confidence he didn't quite share. This onslaught of theirs had so many unknowns, despite the vast power at his disposal. The assassins. The numbers. The layout. Back in the Decay, Teagan Starling had brought the sort of heavy siege weaponry no one in Saldia had ever before witnessed, and that meant there had to be an astonishing amount of firepower buried throughout the halls and warehouses in this keep.

Even with Doom and the Wraith King on his side, five against hundreds weren't great odds. As the ghoul had warned him long ago, even he could be outnumbered. Henry Montgomery had died while fused to the Wraith King, and that meant Connor could, too.

Moreover, he was about to unleash the true power of the simmering souls. Just one of these abominations had been enough for Henry to conquer the continent, and yet Connor had *two*. If he lost control of them, they would do more than vanquish whatever lay before them.

They would burn it—and even he might not be strong enough to stop them.

Quinn hadn't yet witnessed the true depths of the Wraith King's devastating power, but she was about to. Once she did, she would understand why Nocturne had urged her to make that pact of theirs, back in the Blood Bogs.

"Listen," he said under his breath, just loud enough for her to hear. "What you're about to see… what they can do…"

As he trailed off, he growled in frustration and fought to find the right words. Through it all, Quinn watched him in a stony silence, as though she knew what he was about to say.

"Remember your pact with Nocturne," he eventually warned her. "If I get caught up in the chaos, too. If I lose my way."

Her lips pressed into a hard line, and she met his gaze with an intense glare of her own. "You won't."

"If I do—"

Quinn grabbed his collar. She pulled him close, until their noses nearly touched, and her eyes narrowed with fury. "You won't, outlaw, or I'll beat some sense back into you."

He raised one curious eyebrow. "Are you threatening me?"

"Damn right."

"Fair," he said with a wry grin. "I'll hold you to that, then."

This is impressive, the Wraith King said begrudgingly. The undead king's gruesome voice snapped through Connor's head. *I've counted one hundred thus far. It's so tempting to snap their necks.*

Connor groaned. The ghoul was too far away to hear him speak, so he didn't even bother telling the specter to focus on their mission.

I have seen as many to the south, Doom reported. *Many in those idiotic white and blue tunics. Many more in black garb, slipping unseen amongst the soldiers.*

Interesting.

Teagan Starling had apparently ordered the Unknown to remain hidden even from the Lightseers guarding the island.

There are spellgust stores to the northeast, the Wraith King added. *Dozens of rooms filled with powder, raw ore, and gems. Surely we can pillage some of this before decimating the fortress? What a waste to let it burn.*

Or a blessing.

A wild idea came to Connor, then, and he grinned with devious mischief at the thought of what that much spellgust could do, if combined with the right ignition.

Doom snarled, furious and loud, and the rumbling roar built to a crescendo. Connor grimaced at the overpowering thunder in his head, and a dull pain pulsed against the base of his neck.

They are chained, the Dragon King growled. *Eleven of them, like lambs for slaughter, buried beneath iron and ore. No human in this fortress survives this night, Magnuson. Not one. They all deserve to burn for what they've done.*

Connor couldn't agree more.

And one— Doom snarled again, more fiercely than ever, and a flash of heat shot deep through Connor's chest. *And one has lost his way.*

A feral dragon.

Connor shut his eyes, and a heavy breath shot through his nose. His hand balled into a tight fist, and deep in his soul, he wondered if they truly were too late. If, had they come sooner, they could have saved this one, too.

It is a king's duty to his fallen, Doom said somberly. Gruffly. Certain. *He is mine. He will feel no pain, and then he will be with his brothers in Death.*

A knot formed in Connor's throat. Though Doom could neither see nor hear him from this far away, he nodded once in solidarity.

"May the fallen be at peace," he said quietly.

What have they found? Nocturne asked through their connection.

Doom found them, Connor answered.

Thank the old gods. The relief in Nocturne's voice punctuated every word. *All of them? Have any gone feral?*

At first, Connor didn't reply.

All those centuries ago, the prince of dragons had flown out to Saldia to find the lost ones—dragons who had gone missing through mysterious means. He had sacrificed so much and lost so many years to find them. He had been burned and nearly broken in his valiant attempt to rescue them all.

But they wouldn't leave with everyone he had come to collect.

Connor wasn't sure how Nocturne would react to hearing that even one of them had gone feral. He needed the regal creature to be sharp. Focused. Brutal. Most of all, he needed Nocturne to attack with a clear head. Blind rage at losing a brother in arms might end in a life-threatening error of judgment.

For a moment, Connor debated lying—but given Nocturne's uncanny ability to sniff out lies, the dragon would instantly know.

Yes, Connor finally admitted. *But there are others who haven't. You and I need to focus on rescuing the ones we can still save.*

At first, Nocturne didn't reply. Their connection went dead, and a furious growl shook the dragon's body. Beneath Connor's seat, the regal creature's scales warmed to an almost painful degree, and Connor set his palm on his scaly friend's neck to soothe the dragon's rage.

It worked, for the most part, and the furious rumble faded to a low growl. Sparks skittered down Nocturne's spine, and he snarled at the fortress far below.

MY PEOPLE HAVE BEEN ENSLAVED FOR TOO LONG, Nocturne's voice snapped through Connor's head as the dragon reopened their connection. *LET US SHOW THEM ALL THE SKY.*

The chains are broken, the Wraith King grumbled. *Now let me work.*

It was time.

"Have at them, boys," Connor said under his breath.

In the wake of so much chatter, the eerie silence that followed felt wrong. Heavier than it should have been, perhaps, or too peaceful. Another gust shot by as Nocturne circled once more. The trees shielding the island fortress from the mainland shivered and shook in the midnight breezes, and a distant owl hooted in the pitch-dark night. Stars shimmered on the horizon, dotting the night with their glittering brilliance, and the rolling clouds tumbled through the sky.

No screams.

No fire.

No bloodshed.

Just a cold, surreal silence that stretched on for far longer than it should have.

After what felt like an eternity, a wild and wicked laugh built in the back of Connor's mind. It simmered like a pot about to boil over, deep and low, and built slowly to a manic cackle. Nothing in the Wraith King's tone sounded familiar. It was as if a demon had possessed him, and he had freely given himself over to its darkness.

It sent a cold shot of dread clear through Connor's blood.

In the gentle ebb and flow of the wind through the trees far beneath them, a dark plume of smoke bubbled forth from the in-between. It rumbled and rolled over the battlements, as dark as the night beyond the fortress, and it slowly ate the warm amber glow across the stone as torch after torch went out. The figures nearest to the billowing shadow stilled, all focused on the plume of smoke, and a few drew their weapons.

Little did they know it wouldn't do them any good.

Before any of the silhouettes on the walls could so much as call for backup, the smoke consumed them. It raced across the fortress like snow down a mountain, fast and fierce, and no one in its path could even scream before it ate them whole.

"Fates be damned." Behind him, Quinn's breathless whisper carried a blend of awe and horror. "I see why you held them back," she confessed. "This—this is—"

"That's just the Wraith King," Connor warned her. "It's about to get worse."

Their eyes briefly met, and her lips parted in her stunned silence. It must've dawned on her, now, just how much devastation he and these two ghouls were capable of inflicting on this continent.

A single, heavy boom rocked the air. It reminded him of what a ship might sound like, if one of the Fates dropped it from the heavens and let it shatter on the earth. Ripples spread across the water from the fortress, ending in a tsunami that slammed against the mainland cliffs.

Even the Wraith King's wicked madness stilled. In a wispy rush, the plume of smoke on the battlements faded to nothing, and the undead king disappeared. The corpses of his victims littered the dark ramparts, their useless weapons strewn about the ground around them.

And all was still.

Connor waited. He gritted his teeth and scanned the fortress, waiting for the hellfire to hit. Tension built in his spine, between his shoulder blades, and his body stiffened as he braced himself for the inevitable fight. Sweat licked his palms, and he took a shallow breath to clear his head.

A blisteringly loud roar shattered the tension, and he grimaced from the sheer weight of the sound.

As if awoken from a spell, the island trembled. The fort's stone walls leaned, buckling under the weight of something he couldn't even see, and the entire structure caved in on itself. Screams followed. Men barked orders, only for the splintering crack of tumbling stones to drown out their voices. A long tail carved through the building from below, and it left a trail of dust that lingered in the air like smoke. The haze gathered at the center of the garrison, thicker with each passing minute, and a flash of red illuminated the fumes.

In the churning cloud of dust and debris, a monstrous figure rose from the depths of the stronghold.

The blood-curdling roar stretched on. Debris shot into the air as Doom's jaws emerged from the smoke. Another flash of red illuminated the depths of the fortress, and the hazy silhouette of Doom's claws dug into the surviving structure. The rock crumbled to dust under his grip, and the plume of smoke around him grew.

Amber eyes glowed brightly against Doom's black scales as his mouth opened to reveal teeth as long as a man. He stretched his powerful wings wide, and they tore effortlessly through what few of the stronghold's walls remained. That simple movement shot a tremor through the island's foundations. Stone bricks and broken corpses alike flew in every direction, propelled by the sheer strength of an undead legend. Debris plunged into the lake, and the water frothed in the wake of everything it dragged to its depths.

Doom the Battleborn had awoken, and there would be no going back now.

Bursts of blue and red spells shot from within the fortress, from the floors below the ramparts that Doom had ripped apart. Ice crackled across his scales. Blasts of light shattered uselessly across his underbelly. Because only the Bloodbane magic could affect a wraith, however, the Lightseers' attempts at defense did absolutely nothing—except irritate an already furious king.

The mighty dragon snarled, his snout creasing with disgust, and flickering gray light burned in the depths of his mouth. He roared again, even louder this time, and unleashed a torrent of blackfire on everything within reach. The flames charred everything they touched, and what few silhouettes Connor could see from this angle burned instantly to ash.

From behind Connor, a small gasp escaped Quinn. Other than that, she said nothing.

With another swipe of his wings, Doom cleared a hole wide enough for Nocturne. The plume of ash swirled over the new access point to the depths of the stronghold, and breaks in the cloud of debris revealed only glimpses of the foundation.

Billowing flames.

Twisted metal, piled in a heap.

A white dragon, wide eyed as she stared up at the stars.

Magnuson, you must come at once. Doom's voice rumbled in Connor's head, and it carried an uncharacteristic undertone of something new. Not panic, exactly, nor dread, and it took a second longer to place it.

Fear.

Doom was afraid.

The kill order has been given, the Dragon King continued. *They will kill the infants first. I cannot fit in the chamber where my people are held captive. I have tried. You must hurry. I will do what I can to shield you all, but you must stop them. Now!*

Those Fates-damned cowards.

It wasn't enough to enslave these powerful creatures. Not for Teagan. If the Starlings couldn't keep their dragons, apparently no one else could have them.

Dive, Connor told Nocturne through their connection. *These bastards are trying to kill the newborns.*

A rageful roar burned in the depths of Nocturne's body, and sparks once again skittered over the dragon prince's scales. Something echoed in Connor's head through his connection with the regal creature, but it didn't sound like words. It was a deep, primal anger, and it bubbled through every inch of him.

Nocturne dove. The fierce and sudden movement kicked the air out of Connor's lungs. It was as if the ground had dropped out from underneath him, and he grabbed the nearest spike along the dragon's spine to keep himself in place. Quinn's grip on his shoulders tightened, and her nails dug deep into his skin as she also did her best to stay on the dragon's back.

"YOU WILL DIE FOR WHAT YOU'VE DONE!" Nocturne roared into the crumbling fortress. "I WILL KILL YOU ALL!"

The now-familiar heat of Doom's blackfire pushed against Connor's palms, and in his own rage, he barely kept the powerful urge at bay. The biting wind zapped his face as they fell, propelled by anger, toward the crumbling haze of a dying fortress.

Tonight, all of them were out for blood—and they would get it.

CHAPTER EIGHTY

DAHLIA

On the island, chaos reigned, and it was beautiful to behold.

Dahlia stood with Duncan at the edge of a sheer slope that led to the lakeshore far below. Out of habit, she once more tapped the quiver of arrows slung over her shoulder, and her grip on the bow in her other hand tightened.

The creak of skin on well-worn wood blended with the blustering chorus of a storm whipping through the branches overhead. A few curls broke loose from her tight braid and fluttered around her face, but she didn't care. Trees buckled and swayed around her as an unnaturally cold gust snapped through the canopy, and the haunting char of roasting flesh wafted past. It was a putrid odor from her childhood, one she could never quite shake, and her jaw clenched as she watched the carnage from afar.

Tonight, Connor's onslaught would keep Death quite busy.

A white tower at the north end of the fortress crumbled in on itself as a dragon's black head rose from the center of the imploding stone. The Lightseer banner fluttered as it fell into a pit of red and black smoke, and its hem caught fire in the seconds before it disappeared into the smog at Doom's feet. The dragon's wings spread wide and all but faded into the darkness behind him, as though he and the night were one. His impenetrable scales glinted in the firelight, as sleek and polished as any sword, and the wispy edges of his form mesmerized Dahlia as she watched in awe.

And through it all, the dragon's fearsome roar thundered through the air.

Dahlia had spent half her life in the in-between, and the goddess had taught her much. Even outside of Freymoor's walls, she saw what others could never dream of seeing: the world as the wraiths saw it, and as Death had made it. Where others saw a grave, she saw the wandering soul waiting for Death to take him. Where most saw the bloody aftermath of a battle, she witnessed the steady march of broken bodies, all stumbling toward the creator.

She had seen Death, and He no longer frightened her.

The world around her experienced only the aftermath of Doom's rage, but the chaotic screech made the pale hairs on her arms stand on end. It carved through her thoughts like teeth into bone. The Dragon King must have been a leviathan, back in his day, and she shuddered to think of what had happened to the fools who tried to take him on.

The tar-black dragon opened its mouth, and blackfire erupted from between his teeth. A blast of hot air hit the trees shielding the island from mainland view, and the ensuing inferno set everything ablaze. Amber light crackled over every surface, casting devilish shadows on the surviving walls, and the inferno burned ever hotter.

The Dragon King, in all his glory.

A deafening groan, like a cannonball wrenching its way through a ship's pierced hull, vibrated over the water. The very ground shook, even at this distance, with every wall of the fortress that gave way. Smoke billowed out of the holes forming in the once indestructible stone. Towers collapsed, and they were nothing but boulders by the time they hit the water with a soul-shattering crash.

Ever at her side, Duncan clasped his hands behind his back as he surveyed the carnage. "You chose well your Majesty."

"Yes," she said as another rampart collapsed in on itself. "We certainly did, Duncan."

Her general cast a sidelong glance at her face, but his gaze quickly shifted to something behind her.

Approaching footsteps on the grass, whisper-quiet and barely there at all.

Dahlia peered over her shoulder as her four Captains arrived. They saluted—rough and quick—before sliding the bows off their shoulders and notching their arrows.

It was time.

At the silent warning, Dahlia notched one of her own arrows and scanned the pitch-black sky between Lunestone and the carnage just offshore. Her small army followed suit, and those she could see through gaps in the trees adjusted their positions to focus on their own part of this mission.

On the ledge below her, Sophia and Murdoc stood side by side. The former Blackguard aimed his bow over the lake, arrow ready to fly, while the necromancer summoned two small blades into her palms.

Not once did Dahlia think she would fight alongside a Nethervale elite, but Connor and his team were full of surprises.

Duncan trained his arrow on something moving in the darkness near Lunestone. His eyes were even better than hers, and he went rigid as he took aim. He whistled, sharp and shrill, in a silent command that any witness would take for a mocking bird.

But the Freymoor soldiers knew what it meant.

Fire at will.

Seven silhouettes emerged from the darkness like ships emerging from a heavy fog. The winged tigers sped toward the island with armored soldiers on their backs, each little more than an outline in the pitch-black midnight, and not one of them looked her way.

They had no idea of the danger lying in wait. If all went to plan, not one of them would even realize they were dead until they crossed over to Death's domain.

Dahlia took a single, slow breath to steady the slight shake in her hand. Her bow went still, and her arrow focused on the nearest soldier's heart. In the low light, she couldn't even see his face—just his broad shoulders, and that infernal Lightseer crest etched into his armor.

Her arrow would pierce even Lightseer metal. She had tested it herself.

She released the enchanted arrow, and it disappeared into the night. The only hint it existed was the thin trail of emerald green light from the glowing spellgust gem embedded in the enchanted weapon's tip.

The man didn't stand a chance.

Her blow hit, and he went instantly rigid. Ice snaked across what little of him she could see, and he tilted toward the water. His vougel roared and looked back at him with hesitation, but the soldier was already dead.

As he fell to the dark water below, eight more silhouettes zipped skyward from Lunestone's main fortress, each headed for the crumbling inferno and entirely unaware of what had happened to their comrade.

Dahlia's forces still had the upper hand, but it wouldn't last long. This would buy Connor time, but even she couldn't keep this going forever.

By dawn, it would be like she and her soldiers were never here—and Connor was wise enough to do the same.

He knew what was at stake if he failed.

CHAPTER EIGHTY-ONE

CONNOR

When Connor and his team landed, they touched down in chaos. Smoke. Flame. Debris. The smoke clogged Connor's lungs with a mixture of rubble and ash. In unison, both he and Quinn lifted cloths over their noses to filter out the worst of it, but the suffocating musk lingered.

Overhead, Doom's broad wings shielded them from the collapsing ramparts. He roared into the sky and unleashed another devastating stream of blackfire into the lingering walls. The blast obliterated a tower on the southeast wall, and more heaps of rock shot into the sky. A blistering orange fireball rose into the air and cast surreal shadows through the fog.

Nocturne's claws dug into the stone floor of the stronghold's dungeon. Wings spread wide, he roared at the silhouettes scampering through the haze. Sparks shot across his scales as something rumbled deep in his chest, and Connor grabbed Quinn's arm as he jumped from the dragon's back.

When the prince of dragons unleashed his fury on the assassins in this place, they would want to be as far away as possible.

He and Quinn hit the ground hard and rolled. Connor skidded the last few feet, and Quinn hit the wall behind him. Before he could even ask if she was alright, she waved away his concern with a quick shake of her head.

She was a Starling. She could handle far worse than this.

Nocturne roared, and a blinding arc of lightning cut through the smog in front of him. It sliced the haze like a blade through a vein, and something on the far wall exploded from his raw might.

"You will burn!" Nocturne screamed between blasts of lightning. *"You will pay! You will drown and die in your shame!"*

The dragon's eyes flashed amber, brighter even than the dizzying light streaming from between his jaws. Connor sat there, momentarily torn between his mission and ensuring that his scaly friend didn't turn feral in the process of saving the others.

Nocturne's amber eyes darted toward Connor, and the regal creature snarled. *"Go!"*

Alright then.

Connor pushed himself to his feet, and Quinn followed. He led the way into the haze, careful to scan for threats with every step. More backlit figures ran through the churning smoke around them, and another red flash lit the chaotic scene.

Towering silhouettes reared their slender necks over a gathered throng. Wings opened. Tails whipped through the smog. Blasts of blinding light snapped through the haze like lightning. New roars, unlike any Connor had ever heard, joined the building screams in the air.

The kill order had gone out, and those dragons didn't stand a chance.

Connor sprinted through the bedlam. A flaming beam fell in his way, and he propelled himself over it with ease. Rubble fell from above. He and Quinn dodged each boulder that fell to the ground around them. Each kicked up a fresh plume of ash as it landed, and Connor coughed violently to clear his lungs.

A gap appeared in the smoke to his left, and a massive red eye stared at him from afar. His heart skipped a beat in surprise, and he slowed.

The feral dragon.

Its scales were as gray as the floating ash around them, which meant it would easily blend in with the smoke. He didn't dare look away, or he would lose it.

He waited for it to attack. To fire. To charge. But it simply watched him, unblinking, from the depths of the fog. A thick gold liquid streamed from a gash between its eyes, but he had no idea what it was. Seconds later, Doom's tail swept overhead, and droplets of that same golden liquid splashed across the floor from the jagged spike on the tip of his tail.

Oh.

That golden stream was dragon blood, and the feral dragon was dead.

With a nod of respect toward Nocturne's fallen brother-in-arms, Connor resumed his charge into the ash-ridden hellscape. They'd already lost one. He didn't want to lose any more.

The bitter char of smoke and flame filled his head. His eyes watered from the intense heat, worse with every step, but he didn't dare slow. Quinn drew her sword, ready to add to the bloodshed, and he summoned his own enchanted blades in a rush of black smoke.

He and Quinn reached the cluster of assassins around the dragons, and the smoke cleared in a rush.

Within seconds, he scanned the half-destroyed chamber and made sense of the anarchy. Ten dragons had been backed against the only surviving wall. Chains dangled from shackles around their necks. Twenty three assassins clad in black garb clustered between them and the exit, unleashing blast after blast of magic into their faces. Fire. Ice. Roots. Rock. Water. Metal. Any and everything hurled through the air, and almost every blow hit a target. Long gouges ran across the dragons' necks. Glimmering golden blood streamed down their hides, and small holes punctured their wings.

One dragon loomed above the others, her pale white scales almost sickly against her famished frame, and she wrapped her giant wings around the others. Two red dragons. Three green. Two black. One violet, and one gold—all of varying ages. All skin and bone.

Enslaved and starved. Hidden from the sky and left to wither away in the darkness.

Their agony ignited something in Connor. Something deep. Something painful. Something that blistered in his core with all the hatred and fury that had been poured on him throughout his life, from everyone who had kicked him in the teeth when he was already down.

It was primal.

Violent.

Connor didn't blink. He didn't pause. He didn't stop to question who these people were, or why they would stoop to such a low. All he knew was they stood between him and doing the right thing.

A mistake.

He swung at the nearest bodies, and their heads left their necks before they could even look his way. He drove his dual swords through the next man's torso and twisted. The assassin gurgled, and the ice in his palms melted away to steam as Connor withdrew his blades.

Nearby, Quinn swung her own blackfire blade. It shimmered in the light, slicing two throats in one blow, and she spun with all the grace of a dancer as she drove her knee into a woman's gut. The female assassin sputtered curses, but they were the last words she spoke. Quinn punched her in the jaw and drove the blackfire blade clean through the woman's eye.

Brutal.

Merciless.

Efficient.

In this chaos, they had to be.

An arrow whistled through the smoke, aimed straight for Connor's heart, and he reflexively twisted out of the way. It whizzed past, but he grabbed it and drove it into the nearest assassin's throat.

The dust billowed around the hole in the smoke left behind by the arrow, and he saw a silhouette pull another arrow from a quiver on its back. Before they could fire, however, an inky darkness appeared behind them, and a bony hand reached for their neck. The silhouette's head snapped at an odd angle, and the body went limp.

In Connor's head, the Wraith King clicked his tongue in mock disapproval. *Now, Magnuson. Surely you wouldn't dare have fun without me?*

"Wouldn't dream of it," Connor muttered. "Handle the rest of these. Quinn and I need to get to the dragons."

Demanding as ever, the Wraith King said.

One by one, the assassins looked over their shoulders at Connor. Several cocked their arms and summoned blinding flashes of light into their palms, ready to fire. The moment slowed, and in that suspended unknown, Connor waited for the ghoul to fail him. The Wraith King had had his taste of bloodshed, and now would come the test.

If Connor couldn't control these simmering souls, Saldia would fall. Everything he had done up until now—from the Ancient Woods to Slaybourne to Kirkwall—culminated in this moment.

To see if he could, in fact, make an alliance with magic that would've corrupted any other man.

A blast of blinding blue light shot toward his face, but the Wraith King was nowhere to be seen. In the second before the magic hit him, Connor dismissed one of his blackfire blades and summoned his shield in a rush of black smoke. The enchanted metal sizzled in his palm, hot and heavy, as he lifted it to shield both him and Quinn.

He growled in disappointment. Fates be damned, sometimes he hated being right.

The fog from his shield, however, didn't fade. If anything, it thickened, and the darkness consumed the surviving assassins. It rolled over them like fog over the ocean, and it swallowed even the piercing glow of the fizzling magic in their palms.

In his head, the Wraith King laughed gleefully. He said nothing even as the screams within his dark shroud grew louder.

Despite the pandemonium in the depths of this crumbling fortress, Connor let out a sigh of relief.

"Come on!" Quinn smacked his bicep and charged around the edge of the churning black mist.

Connor ran after her, his legs pumping faster even than hers, and they easily rounded the ever-expanding cluster of black smog. As they passed, a hand clawed at the clear air beyond the rumbling smoke, only to be yanked violently back inside.

Gruesome.

THEY HAVE LOADED HALF OF THE SURVIVING BALLISTAS, Doom reported. YOU MUST HURRY. THERE ARE TOO MANY EVEN FOR ME TO DESTROY.

As the Wraith King's darkness swallowed the last assassin, the screams died. Fire crackled somewhere nearby. A deep groan shook the ground beneath his feet, and the rumble of something large falling to the earth sent tremors through the stone.

Along the back wall, the prisoners clustered beneath the large white dragon's wings and snarled like beasts in a cage. Golden light burned in most eyes, and flashes of red hit others.

Shit.

If he didn't do something soon, they would all go feral.

"We're here to help!" Connor shouted over the crackling chaos around them. "I need you to—"

The white dragon roared at him, her voice shrill and desperate, and her wings closed tighter around the dragons in her care.

"You made it worse!" Quinn hissed under her breath.

Do not ask! Doom's voice shook his skull, and Connor winced as he was set momentarily off balance. You are a king. You are my voice. Do not ask for what you want, Magnuson. Command them!

So be it.

"Quiet!" Connor shouted.

His voice had carried all the power of a dragon, and it surprised even him.

At his command, everyone went still. Though the bonfires around them crackled, and though the shuddering tremble of a broken fortress shook the ground, every living thing nearby went silent. The flickers of red and amber light in the dragons' eyes faded. Even Quinn went rigid, and her lips parted in shock. She and the dragons alike watched him with wide and wondering eyes.

He finally had their attention.

Connor reached into the pack on his shoulder and pulled out a vial of glittering silver liquid. With their full attention already on him, he relaxed into his regular voice. "This will give you enough energy to fly. Swallow it whole and get into the sky. If you can, carry the little ones on your back. Now!"

With a grunt of effort, he hurled the vial in his hand at the white dragon's face. Her jaws snapped around it, swallowing it in one go, and her eyes sizzled with a rush of amber light. She growled, her throat vibrating with the sound, and Connor tossed another at her for good measure.

A dragon that big would need more than one, even if these were concentrated beyond belief.

Quinn eyed the bag on his shoulder, and her knuckles went white as she gripped the hilt of her sword even tighter. As he threw vial after vial into the air, he kept a careful watch on her through the corner of his eye. The dragons snatched the Dazzledane vials from the air, and the rumbling growls of ten buzzing dragons blended with the tremors rifling through the ground. As they dined on the potent brew, Quinn bit her lip with longing.

This much Dazzledane had to tempt her more than anything else could.

"Keep watch," he ordered, mostly to give her something to distract herself from the craving. "In case the Wraith King missed one."

The gall, the specter grumbled. *What an insult to my—*

A dazzling burst of light engulfed them. It blinded even Connor, and he raised one arm to shield his eyes. Hot air blistered across his skin, and he yelled in pain as he braced himself against whatever the hell had just happened.

WHAT IN THE NAME OF THE OLD GODS WAS THAT?! Doom shouted.

"Aren't you the one keeping watch?!" Connor snapped back.

The light faded in a rush, and it left lingering spots on his vision. He blinked to clear the splotchy daze from his eyes, and he felt the spear before he saw it.

Aimed right at Quinn.

He moved without thought. Without a plan. Without direction, even. He just knew what he had to do.

Connor hit her with his shoulder, and as she fell to the ground, he took her place. He grabbed the spear and pivoted, using the momentum that had come with the weapon, and he hurled it back at whatever fool had thrown it at them.

It landed with a wet thunk in something solid. Seconds later, something heavy collapsed to the floor.

The reinforcements hadn't attacked, and that likely meant they were waiting for a clear shot to understand who they were about to fight. That would buy him a little time, but not much.

In the backlit flurry of ash and debris, a silhouette walked in front of a raging flame. Two followed. Then eight. Then twenty. Then forty.

With each passing second, the approaching threat grew. White light shimmered above them as each figure reached for the ceiling. Their hands glowed with white light that reminded him of Quinn's light shield. Falling debris tumbled harmlessly off the glimmering Shieldspar charms as the soldiers kept conveniently out of range from Doom's claws.

How unfortunate, the Wraith King muttered.

"You're going to have to be more specific," Connor snapped.

It appears there is a narrow tunnel beneath the lake, the ghoul said gravely. *They're wearing Lightseer garb, so it must lead to Lunestone. The passage is only wide enough for one at a time, but they assembled in secret below us. We now have quite the audience, and more funnel through every minute.*

Connor grumbled obscenities, and they came out more as a prolonged growl than anything resembling coherent words.

It was time to use his backup plan—the one he'd devised in those moments before the attack had begun, and one he honestly was certain would work at all.

Desperate times, desperate measures.

Connor's grip tightened on his blackfire blades. He took a settling breath as he lowered his voice so that the newcomers couldn't hear him speak. "You remember those spellgust stores?"

Of course, the ghoul said with a huff. *Have you finally seen reason? It's best to raid it, rather than let it go to waste.*

"On the contrary."

You can't… The Wraith King trailed off, apparently connecting the dots on his own, and a scheming laugh echoed through Connor's head. *You're devious, Magnuson.*

"Flatter me later." A beam tumbled from the raging inferno above them, and Connor barely ducked out of the way in time. It landed hard in the soot and sent a spiral of dust into the air. "You know how to set it off?"

I can do one better.

Connor frowned, not entirely sure he would like the ghoul's plan, but he didn't have the capacity to rein in the undead king's bloodlust right now.

"As soon as we're clear, burn it all," he ordered.

With pleasure. The ghouls wicked chuckle rumbled, deep and dark, before fading into the ravenous crackle of the fires around them all.

This would either go brilliantly, or it would make everything so much worse.

By now, all of the dragons that could fly had gotten Dazzledanes. They shook their heads as the magic took root. The thrumming hum in their throats built to a crescendo. Their noses flared. Their wings snapped at the air. Their claws extended into the rock, and cracks splintered through the floor from the sheer force of their budding strength.

"Hold!" a voice shouted from the depths of the smog.

Quinn went still, and she stared breathlessly at the haze. "I know that voice."

"Fantastic," Connor growled under his breath.

If she knew the voice well enough to place it in this deafening rubble, she must've spent more time with the man than most. That meant their new visitor was a high-ranking officer, and it looked like he'd brought a small army with him.

Quinn pushed herself to her feet and snatched her blackfire sword from the ground. She glanced at him in confusion before raising her blade toward the looming onslaught. Her braided hair hung over one shoulder, still black from her glamour, but now he questioned if that would be enough to mask her identity from these soldiers she had once fought beside.

"Why can't things ever just go to plan?" Connor said under his breath.

It was like the Fates themselves were trying to kill him—but he wasn't the sort of man who knew when to quit.

If this was going to end in hellfire, he would do it on his terms.

CHAPTER EIGHTY-TWO

CONNOR

In the crackling hellscape deep within the crumbling ruins of Teagan Starling's fortress, Connor held his ground. The Lightseers had come in force, and they had only one goal—to kill him and everyone he'd brought into this Fates-forsaken ruin.

The blackfire in his blood raged hotter with his frustration, with his fury, and with the grief that they had already lost one dragon tonight.

He refused to lose even one more.

"Wraith!" he shouted, not caring if the newcomers heard him. "Help the dragons!"

The ghoul scoffed. *You must be joking.*

"Just do it!" Connor demanded. "You can fly—or hover, or whatever the hell you call it—so help them get off the ground. They need whatever assistance they can get."

You're outnumbered, you damn fool, the wraith snapped. *You need me more than they do.*

There was a possessive hint in the ghost's tone. Pride, perhaps, or sorrow.

"We can handle this," Connor promised, though he wasn't sure if it was a lie. "If we don't get those dragons airborne, things will be so much worse. Go!"

I couldn't possibly—

"Please, damn it! For the love of the Fates, just—"

Yes, yes, fine. The ghost let out a strangled growl of frustration, but the protests ended. Moments later, a black plume rolled over one of the dragons closest to the floor, and the ghoul's bony hands lifted it from below.

Thank the Fates. For a second there, Connor thought that wasn't going to work.

Nocturne, he said through his connection. *Wherever you are, I need you over here. Get these dragons airborne. They'll need all the help they can get.*

Something has happened. Nocturne didn't bother to mask the pang of concern in his voice. *Tell me.*

We have visitors. No time for questions. Help them!

Connor didn't wait for the regal creature to respond.

"Get into the sky!" he ordered the dragons behind him. "Coast on the air currents. Now!"

The white dragon finally stretched her wings wide, releasing her grip on the others, and she beat at the air with all the fury of a hurricane on the sea. The gale stirred the thick cloud of smoke blanketing the room, and it only grew with each passing moment. Connor sank into his stance as planks and boulders drifted across the floor.

But her feet finally lifted off the cracked stone ground, and the dragoness was airborne.

The others joined her. The slow snap of her wings on the air became an eruption of wind and fire as the prisoners slowly lifted off the ground. Fueled by magic and sheer will, they lifted higher and higher with each second. Their heads craned toward the vast opening above, where Doom still shielded them from the crumbling fortress.

The stars winked at them all, beckoning them onward—but their tired bodies could only do so much. Even the Dazzledane wasn't enough to hurry their climb toward the heavens.

If Connor didn't act, the approaching Lightseers would kill them all.

A blazing shadow shot toward them from above, and Connor instinctively tensed as he prepared for it to attack. Instead of diving, however, the silhouette shot from the depths of the churning haze, and Nocturne roared as he kicked up dust and ash with each stroke of his broad wings. He doubled back and grabbed one of the red dragons who hadn't yet made it off the ground. The two rose skyward as Nocturne's rough help finally got the wounded creature airborne.

Inelegant, perhaps, but effective.

The dragons' wingbeats thinned the smog, siphoning away what little cover they had from the approaching forces, and there wasn't time for a standoff.

He had to end this.

Now.

Connor stretched out his fingers and took a settling breath. With a sidelong glance at Quinn, he tilted his head toward their new opponents in a silent indication of what he was about to do.

Her lips set into a grim line. Though she swallowed hard, she eventually nodded.

Good. She was on board.

"Now or never," he said under his breath.

As he had felt so many times before, the blackfire pushed hard against his palms. It slammed against his skin, again and again, desperate to break free. As always, his reflex was to contain it. To bury it. To hold it back and rein it in to protect others from seeing what he truly was—and what he could truly do.

This time, however, he let it ignite.

A rush of pain and blissful ecstasy shot through him, starting from his toes and shooting up the full length of his body. The fire consumed him, and though his dragonscale armor didn't burn, the flames rolled off the polished black metal.

Beside him, arcs of lightning coiled over Quinn's arms. Her eyes flashed amber, and as the lightning in her palms built, the brilliant glow in her eyes only brightened. Her hair whipped around her face, and she focused the full intent of her fury on the people who had come to kill them all.

She wasn't just ready to fight her former comrades. This time, she was apparently willing to kill them, too.

In the final rush of dragon wings, the air before them cleared. It finally gave them a glimpse of the hundred or so Lightseers gathered beneath the massive Shieldspar charm on the opposite end of the devastated fortress.

Those weren't great odds, but he'd come a long way from his time in the

Ancient Woods. He wasn't an orphan lost in the forest anymore.

He was a Fates-damned *king*.

With a furious roar of effort, Connor raised his palms and funneled the full brunt of his blackfire through his hands. The torrent blazed in front of him, stronger than any bonfire, and it singed anything it touched. Beams melted in seconds. Metal pooled in silver puddles on the floor.

The formation of Lightseers shifted on a dime, reacting instantly to his attack, and their Shieldspar dome repositioned to concentrate most of its power on the frontline.

It wouldn't be enough.

Deep in his bones, Connor could tell that he had barely scratched the surface. He leaned into the fire, releasing the torrent into the scalding air, and the crumbling fortress sizzled around him. Sweat dripped down his brow from the heat, but he didn't care. He relished in the raw power burning through his blood. It fed his mind and filled the scars deep in his soul.

It was beautiful, and it was his.

To his surprise, the Shieldspar charm mostly held. Cracks snaked along the blinding light, and those in front gritted their teeth as they leaned into their magic. The shield hummed and fizzled, sputtering under his blackfire, and it couldn't possibly hold much longer.

But he had no idea how many waited behind the frontline, nor did he know what sort of firepower they'd brought with them.

Better not to risk it.

Quinn let out a strangled yell, something between a scream and maniacal laughter, and a blistering arc of lightning ripped through the air. It splintered, little tendrils of light snaking off the bolt like roots on a tree, and the hair on Connor's arms stood on end. Her lightning collided with the Shieldspar. The cracks grew, and those on the frontline skidded farther backward. Their boots cut through the thick layers of ash on the floor as the sheer power of the combined attacks overcame them.

As they grew weaker, Connor's blackfire burned hotter.

It was a gleeful thing, this power. It snaked through him. It lit him up from within. Now that he had it, he could never dream of going without.

It flickered and popped within his soul, rife with potential, and only one thing could ever feed it.

Blood.

With a broad grin on his face, he cast a sidelong glance at Quinn. Surely, she must've felt this, too. Her lightning burned brighter than any star, and it hit their enemy with power that matched his.

But as she met his gaze, her eyes flashed red.

That, and that alone, snapped him from his bloodlust.

She is new, Doom had warned him. *She has a feral nature, Magnuson. I can almost taste it on her. It has been repressed for so long that it will become untamable, now that it's free.*

The fire in his hands weakened, and he grimaced as he fought to come up with a plan. He had to stop this. He had to end this before he lost her—and in so doing, unleashed her on the world.

Nocturne, he said through his connection to the dragon.

They are airborne, Nocturne said, misreading the tone in Connor's voice. *They are in the sky.*

I need backup. Connor didn't bother to mask the dread in his voice. *Now! Get us out of here now!*

The dragon didn't respond. Perhaps Nocturne had slipped out of range, and if so, Connor would have to somehow do this on his own. With the Wraith King getting the dragons into the sky and with Doom still protecting them from the ever-crumbling building, he might not be able to find cover fast enough to snap her out of this.

If he managed to do it at all.

Damn it, Magnuson, the ghoul growled in his head. *Aren't you free yet? There's a glorious stockpile of spellgust that I wish to destroy.*

An irritated huff of air shot through Connor's nose. The ghoul already knew the answer and, most likely, wasn't anywhere close enough to hear him.

That infuriating ass.

Mind racing, Connor sifted through his rapidly dwindling options for escape. Through the guards meant certain death. Through the collapsing walkway to his right would also end in certain death, given the unstable fortress walls. No access to the water. No access to any visible exit.

They were trapped.

Then, he heard it—a shrill whistle on the air. It plummeted toward the earth, quietly at first, but it grew louder with each passing second.

If any of the soldiers heard the approaching Armageddon, they didn't show it. No one looked up, and no one eased their stance as the dueling lightning and blackfire slammed against their shields.

Yet again, Quinn's eyes flashed red. The bloody glow lingered this time, and the lightning in her palms grew stronger. Though her mask covered most of her face, her eyes creased with joy. Her fingers stretched wider as lightning funneled down her arms.

Even I cannot hold this crumbling ruin much longer, Doom roared in his head. *You must escape now so that I can finally obliterate this steaming heap of an island!*

Before Connor could answer, a shadow dove toward them from the vast hole in the crumbling stronghold's ceiling. With wings tucked tightly against its back, the figure moved faster than Connor's eye could even track. At the last second, its wings stretched wide, and the movement carried it toward them in a blindingly fast arc.

Nocturne's eyes burned with amber light, and smoke billowed from his nose as he flew with all the hellfire of a storm.

Across the fortress, the Shieldspar broke. The splintered shards of light dissolved into the smog around them, and the frontline took the brunt of both the blackfire and lightning.

Powerful though they were, they never stood a chance.

Their bodies melted on impact. Some had time to scream, but most burned instantly to ash. Blood and bone sizzled in the onslaught, and the putrid stench of roasting flesh coiled through the air.

Magic always came with a cost, and Connor would not let either he nor Quinn pay more than they already had.

With one last glance at Nocturne's rapidly approaching form to gauge his timing, Connor reined in his blackfire. It fought him, all too happy to be finally freed, and a strangled yell escaped him as it took every ounce of his strength to contain the torrent. The blackfire weakened and then, blissfully, ended altogether.

Quinn's lightning, however, raged on.

Connor hooked his arm around Quinn's waist, and he lifted her into the air as Nocturne passed. She hit the dragon's back with a grunt of pain, and the splintering arc of her lightning ended. Connor jumped onto Nocturne's back after her and hooked his arm around her torso once more to keep her planted on the dragon's back. Nocturne climbed to the stars, and the fallen fort's twisted remains blurred as they whizzed past what was left of Teagan Starling's legacy.

The second they left the fortress and sped into the sky, however, Quinn punched him hard in the gut.

He doubled over, the wind momentarily kicked from his lungs. She cocked her left arm, ready to land a hook in his jaw, and her eyes once again flashed red.

Angrier than before, and still very much thirsty for blood.

In the second before her blow could land, Connor grabbed her wrist. She wrestled with him on Nocturne's back, and the prince of dragons glanced over his shoulder as they grappled above the churning waters far below.

A fall like that would mean instant death—possibly even for him.

With his hand still firmly on her wrist, he spun her around and pulled her tightly against him. Her back slammed into his chest, and he pinned both of her arms across her torso to keep any more brutal blows from hitting him. With his spine against one of the spikes on Nocturne's back, he set his legs out wide to balance them and keep them both in place.

"Quinn!" he shouted. "Quinn, snap out of it! This isn't you!"

She writhed in his grip and cast a withering glare over her shoulder. The red light burned again, shorter this time, and something in her expression softened.

"Look at the sky," he told her. "Remember who you are, and don't let it win."

Please, he wanted to add. *For the love of the Fates, don't let it win.*

She stilled, and the red light slowly faded from her eyes. She did not, however, look at the stars.

Instead, her focus remained on him.

The last of her fight left in a rush, and she collapsed into his chest. Her chest heaved, and her vicelike grip on his hand went limp.

"That... that was..." Between her pained breaths, she couldn't even speak.

Though he released his tight grip on her, he kept his arm around her waist to stop her from plummeting into the dark lake. "Don't talk. It's done. You're alright."

"It was so strong." Her voice was barely audible over the rush of the wind. Sweaty and weak, her hair stuck to her face as she looked back up at him once again.

Her feral side. Had to be.

"You're stronger," he reminded her.

"Yeah," she said weakly, as though she didn't quite believe it.

Nocturne banked hard to the right, and he circled the pitch-black water as they once more angled toward the crumbling fortress. Doom rose from the firelit cloud of ash, and he roared into the sky.

Finally, the Wraith King growled.

"Let it burn," Connor said under his breath, knowing full well the ghost couldn't hear him.

One of the few surviving towers trembled. It shook like ripples through a puddle, just once, almost too subtly to notice over the raging hellscape around it.

The Wraith King chuckled, softly at first, but it grew into a diabolical cackle as the tower shook again.

This time, a green flame shot through the windows along the bottom floor. It raced upward to the spire, spewing out each window as it raced skyward, and it hit the rooftop with a deafening boom. Shingles launched in every direction. Stone arched over the water, leaving a black trail in their wake as though they were burnt stars shooting across the sky. The green inferno raged hotter, ever higher, as the flame ripped across everything it touched.

An unstoppable force, and one that scorched everyone in its path.

The ghoul's laughter deafened Connor, louder even than the crackling inferno below. That had probably sated the ghoul's bloodlust for a time.

Maybe.

The Dragon King pushed off the smoldering ruins, and his wings carried him into the sky. His spiked tail swung in a wide arc, and the effortless blow knocked down the last two surviving walls. Soldiers flew in every direction. Most landed in the water, but some fell into the smoking pit at Doom's feet. The scorched air shook around him, quaking with every wingbeat, and starlight shimmered over his scales like a midnight river.

Mankind has forgotten the might of dragons! he screamed. *Let us remind them all!*

Doom's wings spread wide as he circled the fortress, and his throat glowed with the bubbling blackfire in his belly. A roar built in his throat, trembling and fierce, before he unleashed hell on the ruins.

An inferno rained upon the fortress as Doom flew around it, and black smoke billowed into the night sky. The fiery blast hit its target and destroyed it—the fortress reduced to rubble in an instant. Soldiers scattered as debris rained down around them. The heat built, and each gust of wind over the lake water carried another burst of sizzling air in every direction. Even from this far away, the heat singed Connor's eyebrows.

Nothing and no one could survive *that.*

Doom circled above it all, surveying his victory with pride, and his triumphant roar echoed through the in-between.

Whatever undead could hear him would be wise to quiver with fear.

I've collapsed the tunnel leading to Lunestone, the Wraith King grumbled. *It was a painfully obvious oversight, and you're lucky I was here to ensure there were no survivors. You're welcome, Magnuson.*

Connor let out a sigh of relief. He figured the ghoul was too far away to hear him reply, and he was too tired to exchange barbs.

Happy roars filtered through the sky from above him, and he glanced upward as the newly freed dragons coasted by on an air current. Their wings wobbled on the gusts, but every last one of them raised their snouts toward the stars in blissful relief.

Reunited with the sky, after all this time in the darkness.

Once again, Connor watched the smoldering wreckage of the island fortress. Everything was either rubble or on fire—or, in many cases, both. Raging flames scorched the forest canopy around the stronghold, and ash floated on the air. His focus shifted toward the glittering lights of Oakenglen, out there on the far lakeshore, and something deep in his soul clicked into place.

Perhaps Doom was right.

Since fusing with the Wraith King, Connor had been hunted. He was quarry for those in power. Prey to be skinned and eaten.

Not anymore.

It was time Saldia understood what would happen to those who threatened his home.

CHAPTER EIGHTY-THREE

CONNOR

As Connor left the smoldering ash of the island stronghold in his wake, he set his sights on Oakenglen.

Doom's wraithlike form glided beneath him. The city's lights cast a warm glow over the water, and the Dragon King's shadow rippled across the waves as their winged army neared. Shouts echoed across the walls as officers barked panicked orders, and the ballistas along the ramparts rotated their deadly spears toward him.

It wouldn't do them any good. Not against a wraith.

Quinn now sat behind Connor with one arm curled loosely around his waist to keep herself rooted. She peered over the side of the dragon to get a view of what lay ahead of them, but the spark had faded from her eyes. Whatever she had faced back there in those ruins, it had drained her.

Overhead, joyful growls rumbled through the sky like thunder. Far above and out of range of Oakenglen's weaponry, the newly freed dragons wobbled on a headwind. The gusts carried them south, and Nocturne had already warned them of which path to take until he and Connor's team could rejoin them. Though there had been concerns of the dragons branching off to attack on their own, he doubted any of them would be able to take off again once they landed.

Besides, disobedience would end with Doom snarling over them.

I wonder if Celine has crafted any more Bloodbane daggers, the Wraith King mused.

Connor didn't know, and right now, he didn't care. "Stay out of sight. If you go down there, they'll know this is my doing."

I don't need you to repeat yourself, the specter groused. *I have no intention of returning to the place where I was nearly destroyed.*

On the castle walls, lines of soldiers marched across the rampart at a brisk pace. They took their positions along the wall, and each of them wore the same golden armor as those men in the field had the night Connor fused with the Wraith King. The gleam along that golden metal reminded him of how close to death he had come back then.

In unison, the soldiers of the King's Guard raised their palms. Blistering white light erupted in their hands, and each of them stared him down as he neared. The ballistas tightened. Armored men stood at the ready, and all of them waited for the signal to fire.

Connor didn't slow, nor did he bank upward.

Not yet.

This had to be timed perfectly. Before Nocturne could bank upward, they had to ensure the soldiers saw the Lightseer tunics Connor and Quinn wore. Otherwise, the onslaught might be pinned on him after all.

Connor, Nocturne said through their connection. The dragon's voice carried all of the unspoken anxiety and dread pooling in Connor's spine as they bluffed their way closer to the walls.

Not yet, Connor replied.

On the walls, the ballistas rotated on iron wheels. The steel-tipped point on the massive spear followed Nocturne's flight over the lake, ever closer.

Connor! The dragon snapped at him.

"Ready! Aim!" someone shouted from the ramparts. The voice carried over the still midnight air, and the distant groan of a tightening ballista croaked through the air.

They need to see the tunics, Connor reminded Nocturne.

The dragon growled. An irritated rumble vibrated through the regal creature's body and up Connor's arms, but Nocturne indulged him.

On the walls, faces came into view. Helmets, mostly, and a few trembling hands. A few gaped at the dragon in fear, but more than one looked directly at Connor.

Their eyes drifted to his chest, and their bodies froze with terror.

There it is! Climb! Connor patted his scaly friend's hide.

Finally, the dragon growled.

In a blinding rush, Nocturne pivoted. He propelled them upward so quickly that they shot vertically into the sky. A heavy pressure settled squarely on Connor's chest, and Quinn's grip around his waist tightened as they zipped toward the stars.

Spears shot into the sky around them, some missing by mere feet, while the twang of firing ballistas drowned out even the raging scream of the wind. The weapons arched and careened back toward the lake, and each plopped harmlessly into the water.

Doom's massive form pulled upward at a slower pace, and the ballistas aimed at him sailed clean through his body. His wraithlike body sailed over the castle ramparts, up the full length of the stone walls, and clear over the iconic lakeside towers. His tail writhed in his wake, and the massive spikes effortlessly carved their way through the ancient stone. He roared into the city as blasts of blinding white light shot toward him from below, but the soldiers' magic did nothing to his immortal form.

Alright, Nocturne, Connor said through their connection. *Remember, keep to the walls and castle. Leave the townsfolk alone.*

The dragon growled. *If I must.*

You must, Connor replied. *Now, let's give them hell.*

The prince of dragons didn't reply. Instead, sparks skittered over his scales, zapping Connor as they raced along Nocturne's body, and a low hum built in the dragon's neck. His massive jaws opened, and yellow light poured from the depths of his throat.

Lightning ripped from Nocturne's mouth, and it obliterated whatever stood in its way. Stone shot into the air, nothing but dust and rubble. In seconds, the massive stone walls along the city's northern wall crumbled like paper, sending thick plumes of smoke and debris into the night sky. Boulders rolled down the cliffside and into the lake, churning the water below.

Before Connor could survey the aftermath, however, Nocturne banked hard to the left and circled back toward the rows of ballistas. He flew overhead, just out of range, but the soldiers fired regardless. More spears sliced through the air, falling just short of the dragon's feet.

It is a shame that we must leave enough of them alive to fight these Lightseers, Doom's voice echoed in his head as the great dragon circled the castle in a slow arc. *How delightful it would be to burn them all.*

Connor frowned, but they'd already discussed this. Time to see if Doom would stick to the plan—or go rogue.

In the wake of Nocturne's fury, a large section of the outer defenses had been reduced to a pile of rubble and smoldering ash. Red-hot embers glowed in the night air, and Doom scanned the walls for an ideal place to attack.

After all, this had to look like a real onslaught from the Lightseers, and that meant leaving a fair bit of chaos in their wake.

To the northwest, a long stretch of defensive ramparts curved along the cliffside. The stairs built into the stone were wide enough to give a defending army full access to the lakeshore. To destroy it would remove a key access point in Oakenglen's walls and cut it off from a key point of attack.

Clever.

Doom's wings caught the air, and he banked sharply toward it. The massive creature dove, and his claws stretched out in front of him. With a furious snarl, he dug his thick talons into the stone and ripped a devastating hole through it. Entire chunks of stone broke away and rolled downhill. Boulders plunged into the water as smoke rose from the gaping cavity in the wall.

But Doom wasn't done.

The Dragon King's jaws opened wide, and he roared. Blackfire spewed from between his teeth, and the sizzling flames roasted everything along the hillside. The grass singed. Trees burned to ash in an instant. A black haze coated the steep slope, and his blaze of fire ripped through the stone that had survived his first attack. The blast incinerated mortar and stone alike. Flames danced across the fallen stones in an inferno, consuming everything it touched, and the world was ablaze.

All this, and Doom had *restrained* himself.

The sky lit up with reds and oranges as Doom flew away from the raging hellfire below. Doom angled over the water and soared into the stars, where his hulking black form dissolved into the endless void above them.

After so many bloody battles, it struck Connor as odd for this to end almost as quickly as it had begun. The goal wasn't to burn them all, but something in him warned that he should do it anyway.

That, if he didn't, he would one day regret letting someone in that castle live.

It didn't make sense, not really, and he shoved the fervent warning into the darker parts of his soul. This was all they had come to do, and they needed to leave before any real Lightseers made their way to the city.

That's it, he told Nocturne. *Time for a hasty retreat.*

Very well. Nocturne's voice echoed through his head, weary and relieved, as he propelled them into the sky after Doom.

As Connor cast one last look at the castle, a woman with bone-white hair walked out onto the balcony. Despite the flames burning away at the castle foundations, she walked with grace and ease. Her loose hair whipped about her face, but they were too far away for him to see her features.

"Think that's Celine?" he asked anyone who could hear him.

"I couldn't see her face," Quinn admitted. "But judging by that hair, I'd say yes."

It is, the Wraith King confirmed.

Connor's jaw clenched, and he stared down at the receding figure until she was nothing more than a dot in the distance.

"Do you think she called our bluff?" he eventually asked.

Quinn's grip on his waist relaxed, and she rested her forehead against his back. "It's possible. Even if she doesn't, most people will believe this was an overt attack. That's what matters."

Hmm.

Maybe.

Either way, she deserved what she got, the ghoul said with contempt. *Let Lunestone and Oakenglen kill each other.*

That suited Connor just fine.

As they banked to the north—just far enough to stir gossip—the dragon's chest rumbled with well-deserved victory. Once they had passed out of view of Oakenglen, they would fly out of sight and circle back toward the wobbling dragons riding the southern wind toward the Decay.

Let's go home, buddy. Connor patted Nocturne's side and let out a settling breath as they left the smoldering city to deal with the aftermath of dragons' fury.

Happily. Nocturne's head tilted toward the wobbling dragons overhead. They had done what they set out to do, and they had to get the hell out of here before anyone realized who was responsible.

ROWAN FREEROCK

Pillars of smoke spiraled into the clouds in the wake of a bloody sunrise.

Battered and barely breathing, Freerock stumbled onto the lakeshore. His ripped tunic clung to his tired body, and streams of water dripped from the heavy fibers. Soot and blood stained the edges of the once crisp uniform, but he had burned through many Lightseer robes in his days as a soldier. Gear was meant to be destroyed, and the gritty remnants were testaments of a battle well-fought.

This battle, however, had not gone to plan.

He shook out his drenched sleeves as he hauled himself out of the lake, every bit of him dripping from the near-drowning that damned dragon had given him. Water seeped from his boots and dripped off his nose, but he barely felt any of it.

Those two in the fortress, standing among the smoke, had both struck him as familiar. The man was from the wanted posters, no question, but his accomplice was new. Like the Shade, her eyes had struck him as out of place.

They, too, were familiar.

Too familiar.

His knees hit the finely ground rocks that coated the lakeshore in lieu of sand. They bit into his kneecaps, but he barely felt the pain. His lungs ached, and bile rose in his mouth. Without warning, a violent surge of water rushed out of his mouth, and he collapsed into a heap on the shore.

Damn it all.

Though every bit of his body ached, Freerock pushed himself upright, and he tugged off the cumbersome cloak that had nearly pulled him to the lake depths. It splashed into a heap beside him, and his chest heaved for air as he once again stared up at the bloodstained sky.

His mind wouldn't stop racing. Despite the pain, despite the agony and the water still sloshing in his lungs, all he could think about were the woman's eyes.

It couldn't have been her.

Not Quinn.

It just wasn't possible.

On the horizon, at the far edge of the lake, more black smoke spiraled from the besieged Oakenglen Castle. The dragons had ripped it asunder, and he figured what came next would be inevitable. The dragons had come from Lunestone, after all, during an intense shift in power on the Oakenglen throne—a crown Zander Starling had always wanted for himself.

The world didn't know Zander and Teagan were dead. Frankly, Freerock didn't want anyone to know, but these assailants must have been all too aware that the master was away. Only a fool would've attacked without knowing for certain.

So much of last night should have sent him running to find Gwen and Victoria. They needed to know about the bristling black dragon that had destroyed their secondary warehouse and spellgust stores. They needed details on the onslaught, as well as confirmation about the second black dragon that had been circling the island before the attack. A thorough investigation needed to occur so that they could figure out how the blazes twelve dragons had gotten in there to begin with, since that wasn't something one could simply overlook. That white dragon alone had dwarfed anything Freerock had seen in his life, save perhaps the black dragon from the same attack.

And yet, none of it took root. He had no orders to give, nor could he think straight as his mind buzzed with the most impossible part of it all.

Those eyes.

Out there in the Decay, he had feared the worst. He had been certain that he had lost not only his surrogate father, but two warriors he had thought of as siblings for all of his life. It seemed the worst possible fate to lose them all to one enemy.

But now, he found himself wondering about a fate far worse.

He wouldn't tell a soul about his suspicions, not until he was absolutely sure. If there was something left of her to save, he would do it. The youngest of the Starling children was like a sister to him, after all.

It felt insane to even consider, but perhaps Quinn Starling hadn't succumbed to the Shade at all.

Perhaps, in the end, she had *joined* him.

CHAPTER EIGHTY-FOUR

CONNOR

In the peaceful morning, only the roar of the wind kept Connor company.

For the last few hours, he had taken watch over the expansive darkness of the Decay. Quinn lay against his chest, her breasts rising and falling with each of her steady breaths, while Murdoc and Sophia slept behind him. Nocturne growled softly to keep himself awake on their long trek home, and the regal creature's voice rumbled through Connor's body as the prince of dragons carried them through the desert.

As light returned to the world, the sun cast a backlit glow on a cluster of mountains in the distance. Heat baked the air between him and Slaybourne, but this was no mirage.

They'd made it.

Finally.

A sharp gust of wind slammed into Connor's face, and he raised one arm to shield his eyes. The first threads of sunlight filtered through his fingers as dawn finally came, and the steady creep of golden light bled across the sky as the sun chased away the stars.

Silhouettes clustered in the air all around him, and their shadowy wings coasted on the current carrying them through the Decay. Though he'd spent so much time with Nocturne, seeing so many dragons together sparked something deep in Connor's soul. It took him back to when he was a boy—when wonder and awe still came to him so easily—and he was reminded of the same raw delight he'd felt when he had first freed Nocturne from that frozen stone prison.

Unlike Nocturne, however, they all had advanced warnings of the dangers Slaybourne's walls posed. None would fly too close.

These newcomers wobbled on the gusts whipping past, and some growled in frustration as their wings refused to work. He had already warned them all to take it easy on the trip to Slaybourne, but old habits were hard to break. Exhausted as they all were, some of them dropped a hair lower in altitude with every passing moment. Others managed to carry themselves a little higher, though not by much.

Rich rays of pink and orange light glinted across the dragons' scales. Their long, slender bodies stretched across the sky. Half of them had curled horns, woven around their heads like crowns, while others had claws longer than Nocturne's teeth.

If he didn't know better, he might've thought these diverse and varied dragons were part of six different clans—but except for the infants, Nocturne had recognized them all. Once things had settled and the elders had healed, Connor would sit down with them all to learn as much as he could before Nocturne took them back to the dragonlands.

At the thought of losing his scaly friend, Connor set his palm on the dragon's hide. Another rumbling growl thundered through the regal creature's chest, and it seemed wrong for the prince of dragons to leave now.

But their bargain had been fulfilled, and Nocturne had to tend to his own people just as Connor had to tend to his.

As the dragons glided through the open sky, they slowly closed their eyes. One after another, they lifted their jaws toward the sun, and their happy growls became a thunder of voices. Their jubilant cries mixed with the scream of wind rushing by, and the blissful symphony stirred something deep in Connor's soul. It built to a crescendo as they savored the sunlight and their precious sky.

Free.

Nocturne roared. The ear-splitting bellow shattered the air, and the other dragons followed suit. The deafening thunder cracked across the landscape below, stirring up dust into tiny tornados, as their band of outlaws shot toward the ever-nearing fortress on the horizon.

As the dragons' voices echoed across the desert, Quinn stirred. She yawned and leaned into a deep stretch as she raised her palms toward the sky.

"You snore," Connor said with a playful grin.

Instead of defending herself, Quinn smacked him lightly on the arm and once again leaned into his chest. "Liar."

"What—" Murdoc's muffled cursing followed as the baffled soldier slowly woke. "What the hell was that?"

"Dragons," Sophia said over the wind. "Or have you already forgotten?"

In Connor's periphery, Murdoc stretched and leaned his back against one of the spikes along Nocturne's spine. "Oh, good. I was worried all of that was just a nightmare."

"It's not over yet," Sophia muttered. "There's still time for this to go terribly wrong."

Connor laughed and glanced at her over his shoulder, but she just shrugged.

YOU SAW IT. Doom's voice boomed through Connor's head, louder even than Nocturne's roar, and Connor grimaced in surprise at the intrusion.

You will have to be more specific, the Wraith King interjected. *Magnuson sees many things.*

Doom growled, deep and low. THIS DOES NOT CONCERN YOU, GHOUL.

Doesn't it? the wraith prodded.

As the two immortal demigods bickered, Connor merely sighed in irritation.

That flash of red, Doom continued, as though the Wraith King hadn't spoken. *You saw it in her eyes, back there on that island. You saw that glimpse into her feral power.*

Connor's jaw tensed, and it took effort to keep his breath steady. He let the silence be his answer.

Of course he'd seen it.

Of course it concerned him.

But it still didn't change a damn thing.

She is more at risk than the others, Doom continued relentlessly. *Her rage, her power—in all my centuries, I have never seen that before. Whatever lies dormant within her is a threat, and it is getting stronger.*

The Wraith King huffed indignantly. *I suppose that will do, Magnuson. If you won't give me a dragon, then at least tame her if she goes feral.*

Connor bristled, and for a moment, he wished the Wraith King were close enough to punch in the jaw. "Too far, asshole."

The ghoul groaned in annoyance but didn't reply.

"What are they saying?" Quinn asked.

He instinctively set one hand on her stomach. Though he didn't need to root her in place—she had better balance than most sailors he'd met in his life—the gesture carried weight all the same.

She's mine, it cautioned.

And Doom would do well to heed that warning.

"That bad, huh?" Quinn sighed and readjusted in her seat. Her shoulders pressed harder into his chest as she tried to get comfortable, but they didn't have much farther to go.

Any moment now, they would begin the descent. The Wraith King would open the doors, and they would finally return to the patch of dirt he had sworn to protect.

"It's good to be home," Connor said.

"Yeah," Quinn said, and he could hear the smile in her voice. "It is."

CHAPTER EIGHTY-FIVE

QUINN

Quinn lay in the summer sunlight, her head resting on the glowing green grasses of a half-flattened field within Slaybourne. Heat soaked into her skin, and she smiled as a breeze ambled by. The gentle whoosh of air through the forest branches blended with the twittering chirps of the nearby birds. Beside her, Blaze's soft growls blended with her own steady breaths, and they allowed themselves a moment of peace in the sunshine.

They had earned it.

She felt alive in a way she hadn't in a long time. Every whiff of honeysuckle on the wind felt fresh, as though she had never before smelled something so sweet. The meadow grasses beneath her tickled, and each brush sent a shiver over her skin. Summer had never carried this much joy on its sunshine, nor had it ever breathed this much life into her soul.

Maybe this was what joy felt like.

Or, perhaps, this was what it felt like to truly be home.

Out there, on the island where she had nearly gone feral, it had occurred to her that she might not make it out. It had seemed rather foreign, at the time, to think her life would end there.

To think she might've gone that far, only to succumb too soon.

Her eyes opened, and the brilliant blue sky stretched out above her. Despite her grim brush with death, she smiled as she drank it in. The layers of each passing cloud. The gilded edge on each, where the sun cast golden ribbons over each curve. The expanse of brilliant blue light, endless and epic, beckoning her upward into the unknown.

The sky called to her, now, as it had never called to her before.

Blaze stirred in his sleep, and she sat up just as he rolled onto his back. His wings stretched out beneath him, flat against the grass, and he peeked through one eye as he continued his feigned snoring. When he caught her looking, his tail smacked her lightly on the back of her head.

She laughed and rubbed his stomach. "Alright, alright. You're not exactly subtle, you know."

In answer, he growled happily and shut his eyes once more.

Another breeze sent a rippling wave across the meadow around them, and glimmers of green light sang through every blade of grass. Wildflowers dotted the field, their bright yellow petals a stark contrast to the endless ocean of green. Pinpricks of light floated off the grasses like dandelion seeds on the wind, hinting at the vast stores of spellgust ore beneath her feet.

It struck her, then, that Slaybourne had more than one kind of magic.

A figure in her periphery wandered out of the forest nearby, and she leaned backward onto her palms as Connor stepped out into the sunlight. He walked toward her, a thin smile on his face, and sat down beside her with a grunt.

Blaze peered again through one eye after a moment or two without pets, and his tail twitched in irritation at the lack of devotion.

Connor laughed. "Don' worry. You'll get her back."

Blaze snorted and rolled back onto his stomach. His ears pinned against his head, and he made a show of looking away from them both as he fluffed his wings.

He apparently didn't believe it.

"How are you feeling?" Connor leaned one elbow on his knee as he studied the field around them. "You had a close call back there."

"I did," she admitted.

His smile fell, and he turned the full weight of his intense gaze on her. He studied her face for a moment. "I thought I'd lost you."

"You almost did."

He frowned, apparently unsatisfied with that answer.

"I didn't believe it," she said haltingly. She grabbed a piece of trampled meadow grass and absently ripped it to shreds as she spoke. "When Nocturne said I had a feral side, I thought that was ridiculous. I figured I would've felt it." She swallowed hard and tossed the ripped fragments of grass aside. "I was wrong."

"Nocturne will help you learn how to control it."

Quinn shook her head, lost in thought as she relived that night on the island yet again. "It felt so untamed. So… *wild.* I don't know how any dragon can tame something like that."

"Tenacity and grit, I figure," Connor answered. "Stubborn as you are, you'll be a natural."

Quinn laughed and smacked his arm, and he grinned right along with her.

They sat together for a while in silence, enjoying the sunshine and each other's company as the breeze carried fresh waves of summer perfumes across the air. Lavender. Honeysuckle. A hint of rose, and the heady musk of freshly cut wood.

"I have news," Connor eventually said.

Quinn studied his expression. He tensed as he spoke, and he glared off in the direction of the nearest door to the catacombs—the one that led to the dungeons, and to the Lightseers locked away in the dark.

"What have they done?" she asked grimly.

Instead of answering, Connor's head tilted to the side. He adjusted in his seat, and as his arm draped again over his propped knee, he absently tapped his finger against his calf.

"Tell me," she prodded.

He sighed. "Generals Gregori and Yao gave me an update while you went to find Blaze. I figured it was best to let you recover, or I would have made them wait."

She nodded in thanks and waited for him to continue.

"The Lightseers got complacent," Connor explained. "They thought the guards weren't listening, and they've said some treasonous things. About me. About you. About everyone here. They even took Isabella captive."

Quinn bristled. "Who was it?"

"She's alright." Connor raised one hand to soothe Quinn's rage. "Isabella's fine. She chastised them more fiercely than I think even Kiera could've managed. They let her go."

Surprised, Quinn raised one eyebrow and simply looked at him, baffled. "They let her go? On their own?"

Connor nodded.

"Interesting." Quinn bit the inside of her lip and stared at the ground as she sifted through the implications and what that could mean.

A Lightseer never willingly surrendered their leverage in a situation. It went against every ounce of training they received.

"There's more," Connor said. "They know we were gone. They want out of those dungeons, Quinn, and they'll do almost anything to make it happen. They want to challenge you to the Rite, whatever that is. Some want you to prove yourself as a worthy leader, while others want to use it as a trap to overpower you and kill us all."

Quinn scoffed in utter disgust. "And I bet I know whose idea that was."

"Halifax," he confirmed.

Those damn fools, listening to that bloodthirsty officer. Sometimes, Quinn regretted saving that woman's life.

Quinn cursed under her breath and pushed herself to her feet. Blaze craned his head as she stood, and he growled softly with concern as she paced a short stretch of grass.

"Heal," Connor ordered. "Take this time to rest. They're under lock and key, so there's no urgency here. We can deal with them later."

"No," Quinn said. "We may have already let it go for too long, Connor. Every day we wait is another day she has to convince more of them to ignore reason. Halifax might be a lost cause, but the others aren't. There are good people down there who just want to do what's right."

He frowned. "What exactly are you suggesting we do?"

Through the furious torrent of her racing thoughts, an idea sprang to life. It surprised her with its brazen gall. It seemed too outlandish to even consider. Too arrogant.

Too *wild.*

But out there, on that island just beyond Lunestone, Quinn had accessed her true power for the first time. Zander and Teagan had pushed her limits throughout her life, but she had only begun to access the depths of her abilities.

Talented as they were, even the Lightseer elite could never rival the Master General's power. The Rite was a duel to be fought one-on-one. It had laws, and laws had consequences if they were broken. If any contenders cheated—if they tried to overwhelm her—they would learn the hard way that she no longer entered any arena alone.

A wicked little smile spread across her face, and Connor's forehead scrunched with concern.

He stood and brushed the grass off his hands. "Should I be worried about whatever's going through your head right now?"

"Probably," she admitted.

Connor tilted his head and, eyes narrowed, waited for her to elaborate.

"We will need the dragons' help." Quinn raised her chin and set her hands on her hips as she met his eye. "We will also need Tove and Sophia to work together, as we're going to need dozens of very concentrated Hackamores."

"Curse the Fates," Connor said with an incredulous laugh. "What the hell are you planning?"

"Trust me, outlaw. You'll approve."

He chuckled and, with a shrug, gestured for her to follow him toward the ever-growing cluster of newly built homes. "Alright. Show me what you're made of, General Starling."

Huh.

General Starling.

That had quite a nice ring to it.

CHAPTER EIGHTY-SIX

QUINN

Overhead, the sky rumbled.

Quinn closed her eyes as a dew-dusted wind rolled past. The air tasted like rain, blended with the heady char of burning wood. A thin crack of lightning snapped through the churning gray clouds above her, and she felt its power jolt through her veins.

No glamour. No Bluntmar. No pendant.

Just her and the sky.

The rainfall hadn't started, and the blurred sunbeams of an afternoon sky filtered now and then through the cloud cover. The overcast sky cast a surreal gloom over the barren stretch of rocks that she and Connor had chosen.

The Wraithblade stood beside her on a platform high above the makeshift arena. A throne carved from the black mountain rock sat in its center, marking the spot with the perfect view of every crevice of the small, cliff-lined valley.

The monarch's throne, carved for the Wraith King himself all those centuries ago.

Connor paced behind her, one blackfire blade already summoned, and he watched the sole entrance to the cliff-lined alcove at the western edge of Slaybourne. The Wraith King had apparently suggested this long-forgotten arena for their confrontation, as it had the greatest strategic value should things turn south. The entrance led to the catacombs, and positioning the undead soldiers in front of it would prevent any wayward Lightseers from escaping.

Quinn still found it baffling each time the ghoul proved helpful. It seemed wrong, somehow, for the Wraith King to be anything but an obstinate ass.

Sophia paced a long stretch of gravel nearby, and Murdoc leaned on the sheer cliff wall behind them with one foot propped on the stone. Blaze stood beside her with his wings tucked tightly against his body. His lips curled as he snarled in the brewing tension, and Quinn patted him lightly on his neck.

Everyone watched the tunnel exit that led into the arena, and no one spoke.

"Last chance," Connor said under his breath.

She raised one eyebrow. "To change the plan?"

"To throw them back in their cells." Connor cracked his neck and stretched out one arm, fully prepared to slice throats at any second. "You heard the threats they were making down there, Quinn. You heard what Halifax did to Isabella."

Quinn's jaw tensed again at the thought of that damned idiot pinning Isabella to the jail bars, and a flash of rage ripped clear through her soul. She paused, refusing to let her feral side gain even an inch, and she took a settling breath to quell her ire.

A low growl rumbled alongside the thunder, and she glanced upward to find Nocturne resting on a perch that overlooked the arena. His jet-black eyes studied her, clearly picking up on more than the others could see.

She frowned.

Nearly a dozen other figures dotted the walls, each dragon having found their own perch. They stood as still as the stone around them, but each tilted their horned heads to the sky they had so long been denied.

"Are you two sure about this?" Murdoc asked. "It's risky."

Sophia huffed. "No, it's *insane*."

"A little," Quinn admitted, her voice even and calm.

The necromancer paused midstride to stare at her incredulously, but Sophia ultimately scoffed in astonishment and continued her anxious pacing. "Connor, surely *you* see the flaws in this plan."

"There's always danger with this sort of thing." Connor spun the black-fire blade in his palm, and the crackling flames raging on its steel whooshed through the air with each deft movement. "But this time, Sophia, we have the upper hand."

Dark smoke coiled over the ground like a thick fog. In unison, both the

Wraith King and the Dragon King emerged from the haze and flanked the throne's raised platform. The Wraith King drew his sword and pulled off his hood as though preparing for a bloodbath.

Opposite the king, Doom spread his wings wide and bared his teeth in a silent snarl. Wisps of shadow flew off Doom's hide like snow off a mountain's slope, and his piercing blue eyes shifted toward her.

"Get ready, everyone." Connor stood taller, and he squared his broad shoulders. "They're coming."

Sure enough, long shadows stretched across the steep cliff walls that funneled into the arena. The steady thud of hundreds of feet hitting the rock echoed through the arena with a steady cadence until, one by one, figures rounded the corner. Hundreds of Connor's undead soldiers led the surviving Lightseers out of the oppressive darkness and into the overcast daylight.

Even now, she wondered how many of them were Unknown assassins. It had seemed impossible, once upon a time, to consider that her father had assassins stashed away in every corner of the continent, but the ledger had shown otherwise. They had more to glean from those hundreds of pages, and perhaps his notes could pinpoint any among the survivors.

Time would tell.

Quinn rested one hand on the pommel of her new sword, eerily calm given what was about to happen.

She knew, deep down in her bones, that there was at least one person among those Lightseers whom she would have to kill today.

Maybe more.

Quinn watched the approaching soldiers with cold detachment. She scanned each face in her hunt to place the ones Gregori and Yao had pinpointed as the worst of the traitors. The ones who would cheat.

The ones who wanted her dead.

Captain Oliver led the way, and from the moment he first stepped foot into the ring, his focus remained entirely on her. His brow creased with his intense focus, and his gaze snared her in a way only her father's had.

For the first time since she and Connor had hatched this plan, her resolve faltered. It was only for a moment, but it happened nonetheless.

He was a good man, and even during all of the treasonous chatter, he had been a voice of reason. If any of the captives listened to her, it would be him.

One by one, her former allies craned their necks upward to gaze in awe at the dragons perched high along the cliffs. Hushed murmurs filtered through the storm's distant rumble, and as she studied each approaching soldier, she caught snippets of the overlapping conversations.

"—Fates be damned, that can't be—"

"—this is impossible—"

"—but imagine riding one of those into war."

Quinn's ear twitched as that last familiar voice stood out from the others.

Halifax.

The Lightseer Major watched Nocturne, and her eyes narrowed with all the icy bloodlust of a predator singling out its prey. Though it shouldn't have come as a surprise, Quinn still bristled at the woman's audacity.

At that blatant *greed.*

No one could own a dragon—especially not Nocturne. These stunning creatures had already endured enough torture, and if anyone aimed so much as a blast of light their way, Quinn wouldn't hesitate.

Today, she had no reservations about murder.

With her blackfire blade in the sheath at her waist, adorned in the jet-black dragonscale armor from Slaybourne's vaults, Quinn Starling stood at the edge of the throne's platform. Wind danced through her fire-red hair, and she caught snippets of lavender locks in her periphery.

One by one, the gathered Lightseers looked up at her. They went eerily still, and whatever they saw in her—the soft purple scales on her arms, the ribbons of lavender light in her hair, or perhaps the fearless glare—it made them all stiffen.

Good.

"Ready?" Connor asked under his breath.

She nodded.

When the undead guards had herded the Lightseers into the center of the arena, Quinn jumped off the platform without a sound. The movement was quick. Decisive. With the newfound power crackling through her blood, the thirty-foot drop was easy enough to manage. Sure, the winding stairs on the left side of the platform might've been more practical, but this entrance had a theatrical quality to it that she rather enjoyed.

Her Strongman augmentation kicked in as her boots hit the dirt, and her enhanced strength protected her body from the jarring blow. Effortlessly, she stood and made her way toward them at a slow saunter.

Each step brought her closer to the center of the ring—and toward the inevitable conflict.

With every Lightseer glare focused intently on her, she quickly closed the gap between them. No stumbling. No doubt. Nothing but confidence and a slow gait as she staked her claim in this ever-changing world. She borrowed on the performances she had witnessed all her life from Zander and her father as they'd spoken to their troops, and she channeled that energy now.

Zander might've been a manipulative asshole, but he certainly knew how to command an audience.

"It's strange to me," she admitted as she finally reached them. "How freely you all spoke with four guards in each cell. You got complacent. You got lazy. You got *sloppy*."

A few of the Lightseers bristled, including Halifax, and Quinn made a point of catching the woman's eye.

Halifax went still, and she glared at Quinn as though her mere hatred could set Quinn on fire.

Unfazed by the taunt, Captain Oliver took several steps toward her. The undead soldiers surrounding the prisoners aimed their spears at him, ready to kill in the blink of an eye, but she raised one hand to stop them.

They obeyed.

His eyes narrowed, and he only stopped when he was standing a few feet away. "If you heard our discussions, then you know about the Rite."

With a calm glance across the captives, she simply nodded.

"Good." His gruff voice grated through the air, and he raised his chin in defiance. "Then as the last survivor of Unit Zero, I call upon the authority of the Lightseer Regents. I hereby challenge you to the Rite. The laws remain unchanged. Should you accept, you will face us, one by one, until we are satisfied in your superior power. Only upon the mercy of the victor may the loser still live."

Thunder rumbled through the silence that followed, and few of those gathered around her dared to breathe. The soldiers watched her through bloodstains and scars, their wounds still healing after the devastating battle out there in the Decay where so many of them had lost those they loved.

Their brothers.

Their friends.

These soldiers thrummed with anger and ached for revenge. No Rite would ever satiate their bloodlust. No speeches would sway them, nor would calls to their reason. They had lived under Teagan's thumb for too long, and their idealism would not be so easily shattered.

Blood would not sway them, but perhaps mercy could.

"I refuse," she said flatly.

Captain Oliver's head snapped backward, and that broke his composure. He gaped at her, brows furrowed in utter confusion. For a time, only the hollow whistle of the storm winds through the rocks filled the silence.

"You're a coward, then," Halifax snapped.

That broke the Lightseers' dazed spell. Many tightened their hands into fists, while others settled into their stances, as though they would rather die with the odds stacked against them than spend one more day in Slaybourne.

"A coward?" Quinn laughed. She couldn't help it. The sound was light and carefree, and it filtered through the befuddled crowd before her as they once more went silent.

Halifax thought she was stupid enough to take such obvious bait. The woman wanted bloodshed, and that was probably only going to happen if she could rile Quinn into war.

What a fool.

"Quinn," Captain Oliver said firmly. The man's voice dropped an octave, until only she could hear him. "This is the only way for you to sway them. They need to see your power."

She met his eye, cool and unfazed. "They will."

He went eerily still. Whatever he saw in her face had stunned him yet again, and he studied her expression as though he were trying to decipher a puzzle that had eluded him for years.

"The Lightseers are not mine to command." She spoke loud enough for everyone gathered to hear.

Stunned murmurs bubbled through the captives, and she let them debate among themselves for a moment before she continued.

"Keep your Lightseer oath, if you want," she said, her voice drowning out theirs as she regained control. "When this is over, we will free you. In the meantime, we will improve your accommodations. There's no reason for you to waste away in the darkness."

Through the corner of her eye, the Wraith King shook his skeletal head. Apparently, he wasn't fond of this option.

Captain Oliver watched her warily, and his jaw tensed as he no doubt searched for the trap in all of this.

Quinn met his eye, as her next offer was intended for him—and any of those he could sway into listening to reason.

"Or you can defect," she continued. "Like I did. You can ask yourself who you truly serve—the light, or my father?"

"They're the same!" Halifax yelled.

"No," Quinn replied calmly, her intense gaze still fixed on Captain Oliver. "They never were."

The good captain sighed and, for the first time since he entered the arena, his attention shifted toward the ground.

He knew the truth, and he was so close to accepting it.

"You must be joking," Halifax shoved her way through the others. Yet again, the undead soldiers raised their spears.

Quinn lifted one hand, her fingertip already pressed against her thumb, and she braced herself to order the major's death if the infuriating woman took one more step.

"Stop where you are," Quinn ordered.

Halifax gritted her teeth and, with a strangled growl of frustration, paused midstride. "You can't con us into abandoning the oath we made to Lunestone. We're Lightseers, Quinn—real ones. You're nothing but a cheap imitation of your father. We would *never* take commands from you."

The barbed insults slid off Quinn's back, and to her surprise, she simply didn't care. Halifax had no power over her anymore, and she would not rise to this woman's bait.

"This 'cheap imitation' made it off the battlefield," she said calmly. "Your Master General didn't."

An eerie silence filtered through the Lightseers at her sheer audacity. Even Halifax paused, momentarily stunned, before her cold fury finally returned. Halifax stiffened, and the woman stood taller in silent challenge.

If not for the armed soldiers surrounding them, Quinn figured the major would probably have thrown a punch.

"I don't need you." Quinn gestured to the undead guards that outnumbered the Lightseers by a landslide. "In case you hadn't noticed, we aren't hurting for soldiers. I have no claim to Lunestone, nor do I want it. Not after everything I've learned."

She tensed, bracing herself for the next phase of her plan.

"I'm not a Lightseer anymore." Her voice softened, and the icy edge to her tone faded completely. "But not because I've abandoned the light. You aren't needed, no, but you *are* wanted. I don't hate any of you. I don't want you to rot away in a cell."

"This won't work," Halifax interjected with a haughty sneer. "Pretty words aren't enough for us to break rank. We won't fight for you."

"I'm not asking you to," Quinn explained. "In fact, I forbid it."

Another ripple of confused muttering rippled through the gathered Lightseers, and Captain Oliver leaned close to her once again.

"This is insanity," he said in a harsh whisper. "Whatever you're playing at, I suggest you get to it quickly."

"Patience, Captain," she chided.

That, for some reason, seemed to disarm him more than anything she had said thus far. His eyes narrowed with recognition, as if he had detected something in her tone that even she had missed, and he took a cautious step backward.

"Before you choose, there are a few things you must know," Quinn announced to them all. "If you defect, you will be protected here in Slaybourne like any other citizen. You will be forced to take Hackamores until we are satisfied that you will not harm anyone here. You will surrender all weapons and be given a Bluntmar augmentation, blocking access to your magic until your other augmentations naturally fade."

She had expected furious protests at the mere idea—to block a Lightseer's magic was to remove a part of them. The gathered throng, however, watched her in furious silence.

Waiting—no, *daring* her to continue.

"This isn't an offer," Halifax spat. "It's extended imprisonment."

"It's prudent," Quinn corrected, not bothering to mask her irritation at the woman's constant interruptions. "My trust is earned, not given, and this offer is more merciful than my father would have ever granted."

A few Lightseers in the crowd looked at the ground. Others shook their heads. Most, however, watched her in that unyielding, stony silence.

"I will not lie to you," she continued. "Nor will Connor. You've endured enough, and I won't dangle carrots over your heads to make you dance. Do what you will. I don't care. You don't even have to decide today. Sleep on it. Think it over. Decide when you're confident in your choice—because there will be no going back."

Lunestone did not take well to defectors. Her father had forced her to watch more than one execution carried out in the central courtyard.

Captain Oliver shook his head in disappointment, as though all of this had finally gone too far. "Think about what you're saying, Quinn."

"I have." She raised one doubtful eyebrow. "Would you really expect any less from me?"

The captain sighed, and yet again, his gaze swept the ground in unspoken defeat.

"It's your choice to make." Quinn's voice carried over the arena. "If you keep to your oath, just know that you won't be returning to the same Lunestone that you left. The world has moved on, and no one even knows you're alive."

A chilly lull settled on the air, and everyone watched her.

Intently.

"And this?" Captain Oliver gestured to her body, no doubt in reference to the scales along her arms and neck. "What happened to you?"

"Earn my trust, Captain," she said calmly. "And perhaps I'll tell you."

He crossed his arms, his glare as intense as ever, but he didn't reply.

"If you want a duel, I'll grant it." Quinn caught his eye and nodded to the arena at their feet. "Just know that not every battle needs to involve steel."

At that, his resolve finally fractured. He rubbed his eyes, and though he tried to tilt his head away, he couldn't fully hide his proud smile.

"Well said," he admitted quietly.

Halifax scowled and pointed one finger right at Quinn's chest. "Captain Oliver might be broken, but I'm not. If he won't challenge you, I *absolutely* will."

Quinn stifled a disappointed groan. She had seen this coming, of course, but she had secretly hoped the major might surprise her.

How disheartening.

"Stand down." Captain Oliver shifted his furious glare toward Halifax. "There's no Rite. That means there will be no duel."

"It's alright." Quinn stood taller and nodded to the nearest undead warrior. "Fetch the major's sword."

Captain Oliver frowned, and in the silence that followed, everyone waited for the trap to spring. They likely figured this couldn't be real, and that Quinn would inevitably do something stupid. Rash, perhaps, or desperate.

After all, Halifax had a reputation among those involved in Lunestone's dueling organization, and the woman rarely lost. In fact, most of her opponents ended up in the medic tents, bleeding profusely.

Halifax never held back, even in a fake fight.

This would be a duel of masters, and with all that was at stake, Quinn wouldn't hold back either.

The rumbling thunder grew louder as the storm neared, and Quinn cast a quick glance over her shoulder to find Connor standing on the edge of the platform above. He met her eye, and in the tense silence, he took a settling breath.

Good luck, he mouthed.

She offered him a thin smile, but her thoughts raced yet again with possibilities for the ways Halifax could spin this to her advantage. Quinn had already debated the risks in depth, and she walked through her rehearsed counter attacks, one by one.

Each of them ended the same, and she braced herself for what she had to do.

Quinn snapped her fingers, and the undead army before her fell effortlessly into formation. They herded the Lightseers to the edge of the ring and split the prisoners into groups of two to prevent a full-fledged mutiny once she was distracted. Only Halifax remained in the center of the ring as a lone undead soldier returned with her blade.

"Free her." Quinn gestured for the undead soldier to remove the major's Bluntmar collar, modified for any Slaybourne soldier to remove, and the undead warrior obeyed.

The iron circlet clattered to the ground, and Halifax gasped as the enchantment faded. She fell to one knee as the augmentations along her arms glowed brilliantly green. Her eyes fluttered closed in either relief or raw bliss, and a broad smile crossed her face.

"That's more like it," Major Halifax whispered, almost too softly to hear.

The undead warrior tossed the major's blade onto the rock in front of her and retreated to the edge of the arena, like all the others.

And, just like that, the duel had begun.

Quinn could have attacked. With her opponent's guard lowered, she would've had an easy end to the duel. Even a soldier as talented as Halifax wouldn't have stood a chance in this weakened state.

The minutes ticked on, however, and Quinn waited for her opponent to recover.

After a minute or two, Halifax reached for the hilt of her sword. The woman's hand trembled at first, but her strength quickly returned. The augmentations in her arms burned brighter, almost blindingly green, and the major let out one more satisfied sigh as she finally stood.

Only then did Quinn draw her own weapon. Enchanted blackfire raged across the dark steel, almost identical to Connor's own blades, and she pointed the tip of the sword at Halifax in challenge.

"Weak," Halifax said with a wry chuckle. "Pathetic."

"Do elaborate," Quinn said dryly, mostly to indulge the major's attempt at banter.

Slowly, Halifax circled, no doubt looking for a chink in Quinn's armor. "I gave you ample opportunity to take a swing, and you couldn't even manage that."

Mockery.

Insults.

That stupid, cocky grin.

All of them were weapons in a Lightseer's armory, and they sometimes had greater impact than any steel ever could. Rile up the opponent, especially in a duel, and watch their defenses crumble.

So *predictable.*

As the major walked slowly around her, Quinn circled in place, always keeping the Lightseer in her sightline. "Is this really what you want?"

"Of course."

Quinn shrugged, genuinely curious. "Why? What will this prove?"

"That you're worthless." Halifax gestured to the captives surrounding them. "They will finally see you for what you truly are—and your sterling reputation is all you have. Without that, you're *nothing.*"

Quinn almost laughed, but she held the snicker at bay. "I guess we'll find out."

Halifax frowned as her enemy yet again refused to take the bait.

"Tell me, Major," Quinn prodded. "Have you thought through what will happen if you do kill me? I convinced Connor to give you all this offer. If not for me, you'd all be rotting down there with no hope of seeing the sun. What will happen when I'm gone?"

"I don't care." Halifax's voice dropped to a wicked whisper, barely loud enough for even Quinn to hear. "If we're all dead anyway, at least I can avenge the Master General."

Quinn paused, even as Halifax continued to circle her. It almost hurt her, really, to see a soldier this loyal to a man who had used them all as disposable pawns.

What a *waste.*

"To the death, then?" Quinn asked.

"To the death," Halifax agreed.

So be it.

Quinn still had not moved, even as Halifax continued to circle. She watched intently as the Lightseer walked to the edge of her field of vision. Her grip tightened around the hilt of her blackfire sword, ready at a moment's notice to swing even though it was no longer pointed at the major.

Now, to see if the major walked into her trap.

A bolt of lightning snaked through the sky overhead, and sparks skittered across the scales on Quinn's arms. It was a quiet warning, for one smart enough to heed it, that Quinn carried magic within her now that hadn't been there before.

But Halifax didn't falter.

A burst of green light snaked up the woman's arms, and a dazzling fireball appeared in the palm of her free hand only a second before she hurled it at Quinn's head.

The distraction, most likely, to draw attention away from the death strike that would follow.

Quinn barely moved. Her blade sliced through the air, and her steel blocked the ball of fire heading for her chest. The black flames on her sword swallowed the onslaught, and the blackfire erupted across the steel as it fully absorbed the blow.

Another bolt of lightning cracked through the sky, closer than ever.

This time, she called to it.

As the blackfire raged on the blade Connor had given her, Quinn raised one hand to the raging sky. Sparks thrummed over her skin as she summoned the chaotic arc of light splintering through the dark clouds.

And it *obeyed.*

Halifax raised her sword, and a flash of light glinted over the blue Lightseer crest engraved on the base of the bloodstained steel. Instantly, a shuddering boom echoed through the arena, and a flash of blinding white light hit the major's sword. Quinn's fingers spread wide as the lightning's chaotic energy fought her, and that one gesture unleashed the full rage of a storm.

The ground trembled. Quinn's bolt of lightning thickened. Earth-shattering booms shook rocks from the cliffs around them, and the splintering crack of snapping boulders threatened a landslide. The storm's bedlam thrashed in her grip, trying desperately to snake out of her grasp, but she held firm.

But her point had been made, and as the storm fought her yet again, she finally released it.

Before the blinding light even faded, steel clattered onto the cold ground. Imprints of light danced in her vision, and it took her eyes a while to adjust. Quinn's ears rang as she waited for the first signs of movement through the lightning strike's hazy aftermath. Dusty black coils spiraled from patches of cloth strewn across the rock, and thick smoke crawled over the arena like a charred fog.

The storm winds snaked through the cliffs, and in the dead-silent aftermath, the air currents ushered away the smoldering haze. Smoke billowed from the charred rock where the Lightseer soldier had once stood, and nothing remained of Major Halifax but a soot-stained sword lying in a pile of scattered ashes.

Even as the shrill scream in her ear faded, no one spoke.

Quinn studied the blackened rock, waiting to feel remorse. Guilt. Shame. She had prepared herself for them all and steeled herself against living with the weight of having killed one of her own.

It didn't come.

Instead, a flicker of that wild rage scorched through her soul, and she winced at its sheer ferocity. She set one hand on her abdomen, willing it to fade. It refused, for a time, but that feral flicker eventually died out.

For now.

"Anyone else?" she asked the silent arena.

None of the Lightseers moved, and she was met with a surreal and painful silence.

"It's settled, then." Connor's voice echoed across the sheer cliffs. "Those of you smart enough to take our offer can do so in the morning."

All at once, the dragons around her roared. Their voices blended with the rumbling thunder, and the cliffs shook once again. They spread their wings, entranced by the storm winds and her display of raw power, and their massive silhouettes cast shadows on the tumultuous sky.

Quinn didn't look at the Lightseers as the undead guards silently herded them back into the catacombs. She didn't hunt for Captain Oliver's face in the crowd. Though she could feel Doom's heavy gaze on the back of her neck, she instead shifted her attention toward Connor.

He was already watching her, as was everyone else on the platform above.

As their eyes met, Connor let out a quiet breath of relief. His shoulders relaxed, and a small smile tugged at the corner of his mouth.

Hell was already on its way for them both, but she was no longer afraid. The Fates had tried so very hard to break her, but this ragtag group of misfits had pulled her back from the brink.

In Slaybourne—and in Connor—Quinn Starling had finally found a home.

CHAPTER EIGHTY-SEVEN

CONNOR

In the peaceful sunshine of another brilliant morning, Connor watched the sky.

He sat on a grassy knoll beside Ethan, and the two of them stared up at the swirling silhouettes sailing through an ocean of clouds. The dragons' long wings sliced through the white fluff around them, leaving trails in their wake, and their tails angled to guide them through the air currents.

A whistle cut through the air, closer with every second, but Connor had grown accustomed to it by now. He leaned his elbows on his knees just as Nocturne shot overhead with four dragonlings in his wake. Plumes of white smoke shot through their noses as they chittered happily behind him, coasting on his currents, and the prince of beasts glanced over one shoulder as they slowly built the muscle in their wings.

Soon, the babies would be flying alongside their parents far above.

Nocturne's dark form shot over the nearby forest with the dragonlings in tow, and the last one in the line hiccupped. A small puff of fire snorted through its nose, and it violently shook its head to clear the pain.

In unison, Connor and Ethan chuckled.

"Fire-breathing dragons near wooden structures?" Ethan clicked his tongue in disappointment. "That's not going to end well, son."

"I'll make sure he keeps them on the far end of the valley, at least until they control it." Connor adjusted in his seat as a cloud rolled across the sun.

Overhead, a dragon shot through the fluffy blockade, and a single sunbeam cast a lonely spotlight on the nearby field. Wesley stood in the center of a flattened stretch of meadow grasses, swinging the silver swords that had once belonged to Connor. The blades carved away a weathered old stump that had, Ethan assured him, once looked like a torso. While he grunted with effort, Kiera and the girls snuck occasional glances at him as they rifled through a picnic basket for their breakfast.

"Did she save any of those breakfast rolls for me?" Connor asked with a nod toward Kiera.

"Tried to." Ethan shrugged. "Murdoc burst in like the hurricane he is and claimed them all for himself. Made a show of it, too."

Connor laughed, but that wasn't a battle worth fighting. He could probably convince Quinn to swipe a couple for him later on.

Overhead, the white dragon dove toward the sprawling forest. Her wings snapped open as she approached the ground, and she roared happily as she maintained control of the descent. She angled away, her tail angled perfectly to guide her turn, and her broad wings snapped hard against the air.

True to Nocturne's word, the dragons had already begun to remember the sky.

Ethan nudged him gently in the side. "These gorgeous creatures are nice, Connor, but I notice you didn't bring me any new carpenters."

"I'm working on it," Connor promised, grinning. "There isn't exactly a queue of people waiting at the gates."

"Yet," Ethan corrected.

Connor's smile fell, and he didn't reply.

A gentle breeze ruffled the grass at his feet, and he once again listened to the peaceful day's song. Birds twittered somewhere in the nearby trees, and a dragon roared happily in the distance. Chatter filtered up the hill from the newest cobblestone road Ethan had built between the houses on this end of the valley. Fresh cabins, their boards still fragrant with the bite of fresh pine, lined the path. A cluster of children raced across the stones, laughing as they ran, and two of them held long ribbons that fluttered behind them like kites.

Two former Lightseers, both clad in simple black tunics now that they were citizens, passed the children. Six of Connor's undead soldiers walked in a steady pace behind the two men, but the children didn't bat an eye at the walking skeletons on the path.

Instead, their gazes lingered on the former prisoners—newcomers in their midst, and men they didn't yet trust.

"I don't like it." Ethan's voice dropped an octave, and he glared at the men as they entered one of the homes delegated for the prisoners who had chosen to abandon their old lives.

"I know," Connor said.

"It ain't right." The man bristled. The hand resting on his thigh curled into a fist, and the enchanted leg Tove had made for him hummed with the magic in its spellgust stone. "Those are powerful soldiers. Murderers, might I add. You heard what they did to Isabella. They should be in a cell, every one of them."

Isabella.

That poor kid.

"She's capable, Ethan, and she's brave," Connor said gently.

"A little too brave." The carpenter gritted his teeth.

"I don't know about that."

"No, she is," Ethan muttered under his breath. "Maybe it's my fault."

Unsure of what to say, Connor shifted in his seat and set his palms on the grass behind him. He scanned the growing homestead at the base of the hill, still astonished at the new roads and towering roofs, but that was Ethan's gift.

Wherever the man went, he built a home—and there was always room at the dinner table for a tired traveler.

"You're really going to let them live among us?" Ethan's glare rested squarely on Connor, and the man's mouth set into a grim line.

Connor's father had made that expression plenty of times over their years in Kirkwall, any time Connor had done something that tested the man's patience.

"Some of them," Connor admitted. "To step out of that dungeon, those men and women chose to defect from the Lightseers, but that doesn't mean they can wander freely. They'll be guarded, blocked from their magic, monitored constantly. The generals Quinn and I found in the vaults are keeping close watch, and they will administer Hackamores on a regular basis. They have to earn our trust, Ethan. Including yours."

At that, Ethan scowled out over the valley. He grumbled under his breath, but his tense shoulders finally relaxed.

Not an outright win, perhaps, but it was progress.

A dark shadow fell over the hill from behind them. As it passed overhead, an ominous chill chased away the sunlight's lingering warmth. Ethan shivered, and Connor glanced upward as the Dragon King soared overhead. The massive wraithlike beast snapped his wings against the air with a relaxed cadence, but the shadow he cast on the valley siphoned the joyful chatter from everyone he passed.

They merely gaped up at him, frozen in a blend of awe and outright terror.

"I swore I wouldn't ask this." Ethan sighed heavily and rubbed his palm against his forehead. His eyes squeezed shut, and he took a few settling breaths.

A muscle in Connor's jaw twitched, and he braced himself for what he already knew would come.

The question.

The one he'd been dreading all this time.

With one arm draped over his propped knee, he tensed and relaxed his fingers, over and over again. The movement kept his head clear, and he leaned forward as he waited for Ethan to speak.

Thank the Fates the Wraith King had gone to scout the prisoners. Connor didn't want either of his simmering souls anywhere near this conversation.

"That wraith of yours, he—" Ethan stumbled on his words, fumbling with what he wanted to say. "And now this dragon. They both look like… like…"

"Death," Connor finished for him.

"Death." The carpenter let out a slow breath and nodded. "Death, exactly. Like the old magic in the legends, when necromancers had more power than the Lightseers. When the dark magicks had more power."

So be it. Ethan and the Finns deserved to know the truth. All of it. If anything, this conversation was overdue. Part of Connor hated himself for letting it go this long.

Keira knew about the wraith—but not what he was. Connor had learned as much back in the Ancient Woods, after he had saved Kiera and the girls from those slavers. Though she hadn't shared her discovery with Ethan, something she said that night had stuck with him all this time.

I didn't want Ethan to lose faith in you, she had confessed. *He wants nothing to do with magic like that.*

The risk of losing them all had kept him silent. They could never kill him, nor would they try, but they had the power to deliver a far worse punishment. He braced himself for the idea that they would grow distant. Cold, even. That they might regret calling him family.

But it was time, and he would suffer whatever consequences followed.

"You're right," Connor admitted.

Ethan was still. The man didn't speak, and he watched Connor in a transfixed daze. Breathless. Unblinking. Waiting for more, and yet not sure he wanted to hear another word.

Connor knew the feeling all too well.

"The simmering souls were never destroyed," he continued. "The Lightseers lied. That night, out there in the ruins of that cathedral where we met, Kiera saw one of them. She thought it was Death, but it wasn't. It was the Wraith King."

Ethan's eyes pinched shut at the name of a long-dead warlord people still feared. The carpenter clenched his fists so tightly that his knuckles went white, and his pant legs bunched under his painfully tight grip on the fabric.

"That's why we're here." Connor gestured to the valley nestled between the Black Keep Mountains, in a land that had belonged to the Wraith King in the undead king's mortal life.

The Dragon King's looming shadow swept across the far end of the valley as he soared above the mountains, immune to the occasional spike that shot into the air as he passed over the enchanted walls.

Briefly, Connor wondered if it was best to stop here. To quit before he shared the worst part of it all. The bit most would see as a power-hungry madman only out to obtain more and more power, but he steeled himself for what he knew had to come. He was fully committed at this point. Now that he had begun, he wouldn't hold back.

They would find out eventually, and they deserved to hear it from him.

"That's Doom." He pointed to the wraithlike dragon at the far end of the valley. "I didn't intend to fuse with him, but I can't change it now. That leaves me with two of the four."

"By the Fates," Ethan whispered.

The man set his head in his hands, and his fingertips dug into his scalp as he stared at the grass between his legs.

As Ethan sat with the confession, Connor let the silence linger. There was nothing to defend. Nothing he said now would change any of what had happened. Whatever happened next was for Ethan to decide, and Connor had no right to press him for answers.

In the silence, the clouds shifted. Sunlight once more bathed the nearby field in a golden hue. The sunbeams highlighted the lush green meadow and wildflowers that had sprung up among the glowing grasses. Pinpricks of light floated off each blade of grass as the wind stirred the meadow, and the little emerald stars twirled upward on a desert wind.

"I don't—you can't—" Ethan fumbled with his words and fell silent once again. A vein pulsed in the man's temple, and he leaned his jaw against his palm as his gaze finally shifted to Connor. "There was a time I would've put you in chains just for saying that out loud."

"I know," Connor said, his voice never betraying the brewing tension in his shoulder blades.

"It's a death sentence," Ethan continued with a furious shake of his head. "Back when I was a lawman, I would've gathered every man in all of the southern towns if that's what it took to see you in a jail cell. I would've thrown you in with the other vile lot of the Ancient Woods, and I would've done all I could to see you rot."

Connor kept his gaze focused on the grass in front of him. His chest tightened, and he waited for the worst.

"But that—it ain't—" Ethan growled in frustration and once more pressed his fingertips into his scalp. A slow, weary breath escaped him, and his ragged breathing settled. "Is that why Kiera didn't tell me?"

"Yes," Connor admitted.

"Damn it," Ethan whispered.

The man stared off at the forests around them, and another tense lull settled between them. The pit of dread in Connor's stomach tightened with each passing second, and his increasingly shallow breaths weren't helping.

"Some men, you can judge by their past," Ethan eventually said, though he still wouldn't look Connor in the eye. "Others, their actions."

"Where do I fall?" Connor asked.

Ethan thought about it for a second, his eyes glazed over and foggy. "Actions."

With a cautious sidelong glance, Connor studied Ethan through the corner of his eye. "Is that so?"

"It is." Ethan sighed, and the last of the tension in his shoulders melted away. "Let's face it, son. I wouldn't be here if not for you. None of us would. I owe you my family's lives. Evil men do good deeds, don't get me wrong, but I don't count you among them. Whatever legacy you inherited from those two, that's not who you are. I may not know everything, but I know that much."

In a rush, the building pit of dread in Connor's chest faded. He could breathe again, and he let out a slow breath of relief.

"Magic like that has a steep price, son." Ethan finally looked Connor in the eye, and his grim frown deepened as he pointed right at Doom. "Don't sell your soul to pay it."

With that, Ethan stood. He got to his feet with practiced ease despite his prosthetic leg, and ribbons of emerald green magic hummed through the enchanted metal as he took his first steps down the hill.

Over a distant stretch of the forest, the two black dragons dove toward the canopy. They plummeted toward the earth at blinding speeds in a game he had already seen plenty of times since his return to Slaybourne. He watched the two magnificent creatures as they tested each other's strength, and the last to pull up from the dive roared in happy victory. The loser snapped playfully at the winner's face, and they shot up into the clouds to go again.

Through it all, Ethan's warning lingered. Connor had a feeling those words would settle into his bones, right alongside his father's lasting wisdom.

This world had not been kind to him, but he was better for it. Stronger. Capable and resilient to whatever lay ahead of them. In his time as the Wraithblade, however, he had learned something even more powerful.

No leader could achieve this much on his own. Everything before him had been built with the blood and bravery of those he had come to trust.

For that, he owed them more than they could ever realize.

Though she didn't realize it, the Antiquity had given him a way to repay those debts. She had chosen him for something more, even than the tranquility around him now, and he finally understood the truth of what it meant to be her Champion. She wanted him to travel to South Haven to meet the Morrow, and he would leave with enough magic to become a god. It would give him the power to protect these people.

His friends. His family. His home.

Despite all her tests and riddles, the goddess had been right. The continent was vast, and more people depended on him with each passing day. Far more was at stake than his life or even his team's. Not once, in all his years, did he imagine he would carry the burden for so many.

But it was a burden he was finally ready to bear.

CHAPTER EIGHTY-EIGHT

ZANDER

In the distance, men yelled panicked orders.

As Zander rode on Alistair's back, he eyed Lunestone in all its glory. In the darkness, under Saldia's twin moons, the fortress towered above the lake. Moonlight glinted across the gentle waves, nothing but flashes of soft blue light across the tar-black water, and a rich orange glow permeated from the hundreds of windows along the northern side of the castle.

Home.

He had finally made it.

A thousand blightwolves walked behind him, all perfectly quiet. No murmurs. No barks. No growls. They marched with steady precision and absolute obedience.

The perfect soldiers.

His army walked the stone road along the cliffs, and a cold wind blew up from the lake. It snapped against his face, sharp and crisp, before fading into the warm summer air. A heady aroma wafted past with each gust, however, and the smoky char of a smoldering ruin carried with it an ominous warning.

The island.

Something had happened. Something dire.

But he had his wolves and enough newly attained power to face any obstacle. Whatever had transpired, he would have more than enough strength and manpower to contain it.

With the blightwolves at his side, it was time the people of Saldia remembered why they once feared the night.

Though part of him wished he'd kept the wolves a secret until the last moment, simply to see the surprise on his human soldiers' faces, he'd sent messengers ahead of him to ensure there would be enough food to sustain the pack.

He couldn't let his new pets go hungry, after all.

One last time, he scanned the air behind him to ensure the Feral King had remained hidden. For this to work, the ghoul could never reveal himself unless Zander gave the word.

To his relief, the landscape remained empty, save for the trees and hundreds of wolves.

Good. This would work after all.

As he led the wolves around the final bend in the road and up the last hill, the long bridge to Lunestone finally came into view. At the mere sight of the imposing stone bridge, wide enough for ten men to walk side by side, he sat taller. The bridge itself had walls that stretched along its full length, and men gathered to watch him as he neared. Each held a bow with an arrow already strung, ready to defend the only entrance to Lunestone.

Finally.

He had waited nearly eight weeks to see this sight, and he'd be damned if he kept himself from enjoying it.

So many morsels. The Feral King voice echoed like a wheezy cough in Zander's mind. *Might I have just one?*

"Not yet," Zander said, choosing his words carefully to ensure the creature's obedience. "If they cause trouble, I'll consider it."

Hmm.

Zander rested his hand on the hilt of his sword as he scanned the walls. Hundreds of soldiers stood along the ramparts, many of them with bows, and another panicked shout echoed through the night.

In unison, they lowered their weapons. He was finally close enough to see their faces, and one by one, they stared at him in vacant horror. Even as the bowstrings relaxed, the men and women on the walls gaped at him. Their white military garb practically glowed in the dim moonlight, a sharp contrast to the darkness behind them, and not one of them spoke as he finally reached the bridge.

Alistair growled softly as he passed by the soldiers gathered on the bridge's upper ramparts. It was a warning to anyone watching that the wolves—even the one ridden by their Master General—were still to be feared.

A wise move, and Zander allowed it.

As the wolves stepped onto the bridge's cobblestones, Zander counted the distance to the failsafe point, mostly out of habit. Should the need ever arise, the bridge could be destroyed in eleven seconds. A system of enchantments stretched along the underside of the road to ensure total destruction—including the poor fools crossing it when it imploded. It was a rife spot for a trap, and as such, the Starlings rarely walked across it.

But tonight, he needed to indulge the Feral King's love of theatre.

I confess, the creature growled in his head, *you have outdone yourself, Starling. Their fear is decadent. Something about a soldier's terror tastes so much better than a peasant's.*

Curious, Zander sniffed the air. A sickly sweet honey-stench wafted from the walls, unique from anything else he'd ever smelled—except when he had discovered his wife's betrayal.

The reminder of her treason sparked his white-hot rage. His jaw tightened impulsively, and his nose flared with his barely suppressed disgust.

He had to focus, and that whore wasn't worth a second thought.

As for the scent, yes—the Feral King was right. These powerful soldiers, all of whom had trained under his father and alongside him, were afraid.

The cowards didn't trust him to keep the wolves at bay. In their terror, they betrayed how little they believed in him. He grimaced, disappointed, but he ultimately said nothing.

They would learn.

You've done well, the Feral King continued, thankfully still out of sight.

"As have you." Zander scanned the walls around him, careful to keep his voice low enough that the soldiers above wouldn't hear him. "Remember our bargain."

The undead wolf chuckled. *But of course. You are the alpha, after all.*

Even just four weeks ago, Zander would've taken that as a silent challenge. He would've bristled at the possible implication that the creature was biding its time, waiting to strike him at his most vulnerable moment, but now he knew better.

The thing was simply enjoying itself.

A figure stood ahead of them in the center of the bridge, right over the failsafe point. Zander lifted his chin, studying the silhouette until his features finally came into focus.

Colonel Rowan Freerock.

Interesting.

Teagan doted upon Freerock as though the man were a pet, and Freerock would've been with the man on his trip to the Decay. To see him here added an element of curiosity and interest he hadn't felt since he'd faced the Wraithblade.

Perhaps Zander would find out what had happened out there in the Decay, after all.

As Alistair and the wolves approached Freerock, Zander kept a careful watch on the man's face. The colonel had developed something of a reputation for himself as a man without fear, and he wanted to see if the stories were, indeed, true.

To his credit, Freerock didn't move. He stood with his arms behind his back, chin up and eyes locked on Zander even as the hundreds of wolves approached. No reservation. No fidgeting. No creases of worry in his brow, nor sweat along his temple.

The man simply stared dead ahead, without a trace of fear.

I do not like this one, the Feral King grumbled.

Zander grinned. It seemed as though Freerock might be useful, after all.

He whistled, and at the sharp command, the blightwolves immediately halted. Though murmurs filtered through the soldiers gathered on the walls above, not a single blightwolf so much as growled. Alistair watched Freerock like a fox would examine a hen, waiting for the moment to strike. Though the wolf's muscles tensed underneath Zander, the beast didn't attack.

"Easy, Alistair," Zander warned.

The blightwolf let out a slow breath, and his body relaxed.

"Welcome home, sir," Freerock said with a curt nod. "We were beginning to worry."

Zander chuckled. "Were you, now, brother?"

Brother.

Teagan had many flaws, but he had also taught Zander a great deal about how to manipulate the hearts and minds of the soldiers under his command. Freerock, especially, had been treated with the sort of deference few others experienced in even the most distinguished career. The man was not an equal—no one was, after all—but Zander had long ago become accustomed to using the overly familiar terms his father had showered upon the colonel through the years.

Mainly because it worked so damn well.

Freerock's shoulders relaxed, and a small smile tugged at the corner of his mouth. "It's good to have you back, Zander."

"It's good to be back," he admitted.

For the first time, the colonel glanced behind Zander to survey the blightwolves gathered on the bridge. "You seem to have kept yourself occupied."

"I have." Tired of milling about on a road that could burst into flame with a few strategic blows, he nodded toward the fortified island at the end of the bridge. "Shall we?"

"Of course."

Freerock turned his back on the wolves, and though the sickly sweet scent of terror still radiated from above, the colonel carried only the scent of oak resin and whiskey.

Fearless.

"Resume post!" Freerock shouted. His authoritative command carried through the night air, and soldiers snapped to attention on the ramparts. Their eyes finally broke from the procession of wolves below as they continued toward the castle.

"Walk beside me," Zander ordered.

Freerock complied, pausing momentarily until Alistair passed, and then he easily matched the wolf's long stride as he stayed perfectly aligned with Zander's boot.

As obedient as any blightwolf.

"What happened to the island?" Zander asked. "I could smell the smoke from the shore."

With a heavy sigh, Freerock simply shook his head. "It's a long story, sir. One best saved for a secured war room."

Hmm.

Very well.

"I heard about your report," Zander said in a low tone that no soldier above them could hear. "About my father."

Lightseers along the southern road had briefed him on all that had happened in his time away, including things the common folk could never know. He had pieced together the rest for himself.

Freerock sucked in a deep breath, and his eyes remained glued on the path ahead of them. "I'm sorry for your loss, sir."

"And to you for yours." He studied the half of the colonel's face that he could see from this angle, and the man's brows pinched with restrained grief.

"Thank you." Freerock's voice cracked briefly with sorrow. Though the man's gaze never strayed from the path ahead of them, he nodded once in gratitude.

Astonishing.

The fool had truly loved Teagan like a father.

"What about Quinn?" Zander continued. "Was she recovered?"

At that, Freerock stiffened. His eye twitched, and a muscle in his neck stretched taught in an uncharacteristic reaction to an otherwise simple question.

"No, sir." Freerock cleared his throat abruptly to maintain his composure.

Zander narrowed his eyes in suspicion. The colonel had just lied to him, and it struck him as odd—mostly because he'd never seen it happen before.

It seemed as though Rowan Freerock had secrets he was not yet ready to share.

"There's a slim hope that Quinn is alive," Freerock continued. "But it's not something we can depend on. Especially not after the bloodshed I witnessed out in the Decay. Not many could make it out of an aftermath like that, sir."

It seemed as though many of Teagan's elite had died out there. Unfortunate, since Zander had plans for those men and women.

What a waste.

"But you survived," The colonel continued. "We were concerned you were also among the fallen, but I can't tell you how grateful I am that you survived. Maybe she did as well."

Most likely.

It took effort for Zander to keep from sighing in disappointment. Though it would've been a delight to find Quinn's corpse, he doubted the Wraithblade had killed her. It would have made strategic sense to keep a prisoner like that alive.

"Stoic as ever, sir." Freerock studied him through the corner of his eye and nodded appreciatively. "You inspire us to be strong."

Zander almost laughed at the ludicrous idea, but he managed to restrain himself. "Such is the Master General's duty."

"Such it is, and we are grateful."

"How many soldiers have arrived?"

"Almost all of them." Freerock shook his head. "It's been hell trying to find lodging for everyone. Many have been given rooms in Arkcaster, simply for lack of space. Before we left, Teagan ordered everyone to assemble, but few of them know why."

"You do."

Again, Freerock let out a long, slow sigh. "Nothing went to plan, Zander. Not a damn thing."

"Given our opponent, I'm not surprised."

Freerock frowned and, for the first time since they'd begun their march toward the castle, looked Zander dead in the eye. His mouth parted in confusion—or maybe shock—but he kept the colonel's eye and let the unspoken implication weigh between them.

"You've fought him?" the man whispered.

Zander nodded. "And I will not make the same mistakes again. When we face him, Colonel, he will burn for what he has done."

The promise breathed fresh life into Freerock, and he stood a little taller as they neared the end of the bridge. "I'm glad to hear it, sir."

"As for the loss—we will endure. We've recovered from worse."

"That we have," the colonel agreed.

Yet again, a twang of betrayal hit him hard in the chest, and he hated how many things reminded him of his whore of a wife. "Where are my children?"

"With your mother at your family's estate. We've added extra protections to ensure the family is safe. Your sisters are here, however, to help with the void in your absence. Before the edict from Teagan to assemble, your wife left for a goodwill tour through the south. The locals were troubled by our trek through the Ancient Woods, and she has always had a way of soothing them."

It took effort for Zander not to growl with hatred.

"We've sent word for her to return," Freerock continued, oblivious to Zander's rage. "It takes time for messengers to follow the full road south, but I suspect she will arrive soon."

Good. At least no one knew she was dead, yet, and the risks of him or his blightwolves being implicated in her murder were slim.

The bridge to Lunestone stretched ahead of them, but they were nearly to the island. Two figures now stood at the opposite end, waiting for him, and their fire-red hair stood out in the night.

Gwen and Victoria. The Starling siblings, reunited at last—the ones he enjoyed, anyway.

Even with his enhanced vision, it took a moment longer before their features came into view. As his eyesight was superior even to theirs, he studied their expressions in the seconds before they would be able to see his face. Victoria smiled broadly, her eyes roving the blightwolves behind him with a greedy hunger. Her chest rose and fell with almost panicked glee, as though she couldn't get enough air.

Gwen, however, merely watched him, as though the wolves didn't exist. She stood there, hand on the pommel of her sword, her shoulders relaxed and her chin raised. Calm. Quiet. Unfazed by anything.

Unafraid.

"Schedule the coronation immediately," Zander said to the colonel beside him. "Lunestone cannot be without a Master General."

"Of course, sir. With everyone here, it won't take long to coordinate."

Up ahead, Victoria's gaze finally shifted to him, and it seemed as though he was finally close enough for them to see his face. His older sister nodded once to him in a rare display of respect.

Marvelous. He had impressed her, and that meant she would go above and beyond with whatever he asked her to do.

Though Gwen's expression never changed, she and Victoria both stepped aside to let his blightwolf army through. Alistair carried him onto the island fortress that was and always had been his birthright, and the air had never smelled sweeter.

Lunestone was his—and he had quite a few changes to make.

GWEN

Zander was alive.

Bless the Fates—or curse them. Gwen wasn't sure anymore.

Mere hours after Zander's return, she now paced the edges of the same room where she had discovered Quinn, standing in the shadows and very much alive.

Now, their brother's return had threatened that brief moment of joy.

Though she often mumbled to herself while she paced, working through her thoughts, she didn't dare say a word now. With her father and Zander gone, the walls had felt almost quiet—but with Zander's return, she no longer trusted the silence.

With the vast network of secret passages Quinn had shown her, anyone could be listening, and at any time.

Her ear twitched as the barest hint of footsteps scuffed across the hallway carpet. She paused mid-step, her back to the empty fireplace as she watched the door to see who would enter.

A long stride. The brief, hollow thud of a boot heel. A man's gait, but one she couldn't place. That had always been Quinn's forte, not hers.

The knob turned, and seconds later, Cade entered. Their eyes met, and she let out a slow sigh of relief.

For a moment, it had almost sounded like Zander's footsteps.

As he shut the door behind him, the hinges creaked by design to alert anyone inside that they had company. It screeched against her enhanced ears, but she didn't dare oil the tarnished metal—especially not now that her brother was home.

In the tense silence that followed, Cade scowled and watched her face. His eyes narrowed, his lips pressing into a hard line, and she had seen this expression plenty of times in their many years together. He wanted to speak, and this was his silent way to question whether the room was safe.

Gwen shook her head.

He grunted in frustration and paced the far wall by the door with his hands in his hair. Elbows spread wide, his nose briefly flared as his boot heels clacked carelessly across the floorboards. They didn't need to be stealthy in here, after all, and sometimes it helped to let loose even when the world expected constant perfection.

They needed to discuss everything that happened, but with hundreds of blightwolves roaming the grounds, there wouldn't be a way to sneak out undetected—unless they used the Starling Tunnel.

She shuddered at the thought. No, to devise their next move, they would have to find a room where they could guarantee no one overheard.

Blightwolves.

The thought rooted her in place, and her eyes glossed over as she stared in silent horror down at the carpet beneath her feet.

Fates-damned *blightwolves.*

Whatever had happened to Zander out there in the Decay, it had done more than break him. Her beloved brother had fractured, and whatever had been rebuilt from the pieces no longer resembled the man she knew.

Not even the great Teagan Starling had been able to tame the blightwolves, and yet Zander had waltzed up to the main door with nearly a thousand in tow. To achieve such a thing, he must have sacrificed. He must've bled. Whatever he did to win their affection, she doubted it would last—and this close to those teeth and claws, the Lightseers would suffer the consequences.

Worst of all, this changed the plan.

Though she would still be able to pull strings from afar, she would no longer have the authority as acting Master General. Everything she and Quinn had begun to plan was in jeopardy.

"Good luck," she whispered to her baby sister, so softly she could barely hear her own voice. "You're going to need it."

EPILOGUE

NYX

With a strained grunt, Nyx fell onto her back and rolled. There wasn't time to think, and her body moved on impulse.

A split second later, the sharp crack of splitting rock echoed through the hollow mountain. A long, armored tail shot out of the shadows between two boulders, aimed right at her. She rolled again, and a stinger the size of her head slammed hard into the rocky terrain where her face had been moments before.

These damn giant scorpions.

Curse the Fates, how she *hated* these things.

Her momentum carried her across the uneven floor of yet another towering cavern somewhere in the deepest parts of the Mountains of the Unwanted. As she regained her balance, she rolled onto her knees. Her bloodstained boots kicked dust into the air, but she finally had the upper hand again.

With exoskeletons tough enough to protect them from even the enchanted blades sheathed to her wrists, these bastards refused to die. She had only one advantage, and she just needed a clear shot to use it.

Palms flat and brows furrowed, she waited for the damn thing to scuttle out of the darkness before she froze it to death.

Its stinger receded into the shadows between two towering boulders, and in the silence that followed, she waited.

The stillness lasted too long.

Nyx's ears rang. The soft emerald glow of spellgust ore in the walls offered the only light, and to her irritation, the abomination of nature didn't move.

Perhaps her map was faulty after all. Under torture, the Lightseer Regent she had captured all those years ago had drawn the one and only map in existence, and it was possible for little tricks and traps to have been discretely added out of spite. Rough terrain. Steep cliffs. Spikes beneath the one surviving rope bridge. Little beetles that had chewed a hole in her arm. A fanged bat that had nearly carried Reaver into the dark recesses above them.

The Lightseers kept their rejects in here, where they could be stored away and forgotten, and these beasts were *hungry*.

From the darkness came the scurrying clatter of armored claws across the rocks. A soft clicking followed, like the rumble of a dozen claws clacking against each other. Something shifted in the darkness, just beyond what even her enhanced eyes could see, and she tensed as she tracked its movements.

In her younger days, she would've fired randomly into the void, but she had developed restraint after so many years running Nethervale.

Ice crackled across her knuckles, and she couldn't wait to freeze this infuriating creature to death. She would leave its head until last, if possible, just to watch the thing suffer.

Perhaps one of these monstrosities had already eaten Reaver. He was hard to kill, mostly thanks to her training, but she hadn't seen him since the scorpions attacked. If he died in a monster's stomach, she would be just as disgusted with herself as she would be with him.

With as much as she had put him through in her years as his mentor, he could survive worse than a few giant bugs.

In a violent rush, two claws shot out of the darkness. Her blood already stained the serrated edges along each interior curve. Her body tensed, ready for more pain, but she didn't want to get caught in one of those again. Its beady eyes glistened in the green light from the walls. The serrated bone daggers across its mouth quivered, drool oozing as its teeth gnashed against the air.

It lunged at her, faster than anything this big should ever be.

Her blood hummed with all the power of her Crackmane augmentation, and a thick layer of frost coated her outstretched fingers as she summoned ice from the air. Bone-tired as she was, she didn't need to aim at this thing. She unleashed the blast in a wide arc, already knowing she would land the death blow on this monster trying to eat her alive.

Her ice hit it square in its open jaws. It screeched in pain, and its tail curled on itself as it arched its back. Its momentum carried it ever closer toward her as it teetered, and she pushed herself to her feet as she waited for it to fall.

In the meantime, she relished its pain.

Filthy bastard. It deserved this.

Its pincers clacked above her head, but it tilted and shuffled backward as it fought off the ice slowly creeping across its body. The frost coated the inside of its mouth, and its shrill screech finally died. It arched backward, still writhing, until it finally keeled over backward. Lying on its back, its legs curled inward, and its claw twitched one last time as the ice slowly crept over the last untouched patches of its corpse.

Nyx spit on it and wiped her bloody mouth on her ripped sleeve. "Serves you right."

Chest heaving, she stood and watched the final twitches of its legs. She wished it had screamed more, but she couldn't waste any more precious energy on revenge.

With no sunlight, no moonlight, and only the steady green glow from the spellgust in the walls guiding her through the mountains, Nyx had no idea how much time had passed. It could've been days, but the exhaustion in her bones suggested they had spent far too long down here.

Weeks, more likely. Time she couldn't spare.

She and Reaver had encountered something crawling on the walls, ceilings, and floors of every inch of this hellhole. They had been besieged at every turn by overpopulated clusters of the monsters the Lightseers had collected over the centuries.

The black unicorns and swarms of blood-sucking leeches had been easy enough to kill, but these scorpions were everywhere.

From the shadows to her left, something launched at her. She rolled out of the way and raised her palms as she scanned the cave for something else to kill.

Ready.

Willing.

Bloodthirsty.

Instead of a living thing she could murder, however, a giant severed stinger rolled across the ground. It slid toward her, and with a furious growl, she stopped it with her boot. The sharp tip glistened with venom, and she kicked the thing to the side.

A figure appeared at the edge of the shadows, but it made no sound. Not a footstep. Not a breath.

Reaver.

With an impatient sigh, Nyx brushed off her shirt just as her most promising student stalked from the shadows. He held his sword in one hand as he glared down at the severed stinger. Blue goop coated both his blade and his face, and without even a sideways glance at her, he cut the damn thing in half one more time for good measure.

His shoulders heaved as he fought to catch his breath, and his brows furrowed with hatred. Whatever he had endured, it had been enough to make him emote—something she rarely saw.

"Get ahold of yourself," she ordered.

His gaze darted to her, and he gave her an exhausted nod as he withdrew his sword from the insect. He pulled a black cloth from his pocket and wiped his blade as he scanned the cavern.

Nyx, however, was more intrigued by his weapon. Her poisoned darts hadn't been able to pierce these creatures, but he had clearly done something special to his own sword if it could cut through the hardened layers of their armor.

When they returned to Nethervale, she would have to find out what he had done—and steal it for herself.

Nyx picked up one of her loose daggers that had fallen during her duel with the scorpions and lifted her shirt to slide it into the sheath strapped to her chest. "How many more?"

"Twelve," he said, his voice raspy from disuse. "Not a threat until we leave. Too far."

Nyx tugged down the scarf that was still covering her face and used the back of her hand to wipe away the sweat dripping down her temple. She wanted a hot meal and three days of drug-induced sleep, but she would have all that and more just as soon as they found what they had come here for.

Reaver's chest still heaved as he cast one last wary glance around them. Just as Nyx reached for her canteen to take a carefully measured sip, his eyes lingered on something behind her. She paused mid-drink and followed his gaze.

The emerald glow behind the boulder at her back burned brighter than the rest of the cavern.

The tomb.

Nyx hooked her canteen onto her belt and stood, careful to scan the world around her as she swallowed the hope in her chest that they had finally found it.

Around the boulder, hand-hewn stairs cut into the rocky terrain and circled around a giant pillar of rock that disappeared into the shadows above them. Each of her steps cast a glittering ripple of green light through the murky brown stone.

The magic here pulsed. It had more power than anything she had felt in her life. It practically breathed, like a gale off the sea hitting her in the chest, and her body hummed with potential.

For this much magic to be buried this deep into the mountain, the Lightseers must have stored something truly special here.

Nyx led the way up the stairwell, careful to angle her body enough that she could always keep a wary eye on Reaver.

Just in case he—like everyone else on this damned continent—got greedy.

The staircase ended at a massive door. As tall as a church spire, the towering doorframe glowed green with all the magic keeping it sealed shut. No visible seal. No hinges. For all intents and purposes, it seemed more like an ornate carving in the stone than an actual entryway.

Undone by her exhaustion and the sheer awe of finding something she had hunted all her life, Nyx's mask of cool indifference faltered. She grinned, broad and beaming, and her breath quickened as she beheld this place of legend.

A small basin made of solid spellgust protruded from the door at waist height. It was the closest thing this door had to a knob or a lock, and it looked exactly like the sketch the Lightseer Regent had drawn. The woman had warned that the basin served as a place of offering.

As with the Rifts, powerful magic like this demanded sacrifice to function.

Ordinary blood wouldn't suffice. Instead, she reached into her bag and tugged out the smallest vial she carried. Bubbles gathered along the surface of the golden liquid inside, and though she wished she had brought more to be safe, dragon blood wasn't easy to acquire.

Not when Teagan had a monopoly on the supply.

With a flutter of disappointment, she poured the entire vial into the small basin. To think of the spells she could've created with this much ancient blood—but no matter. What lay in this tomb would dwarf anything she could create on her own.

As the blood pooled in the basin, the gemstone bowl glowed with all the fire of a star. She squinted her eyes, refusing to look away, as a heady hum filled the air. She could feel it vibrate clear to her lungs, and she could only imagine how many other creatures in this place could hear it. She reflexively twisted her wrists, ready to summon her blades in case the noise attracted more of those damned scorpions.

These treasures belonged to her, and she would be damned if something killed her before she could unleash them on Saldia.

A bright green light snaked through the runes etched along the edges of the door. It shot up into the cavern's ceiling, higher than even she could see, and circled back seconds later.

The door opened outward on its own, and a gust of stale air rushed past them. The creak of ancient hinges rattled the mountains, and she waited for the telltale screech of something hungry skuttling through the darkness.

As the heavy groan of the opening doors slowed, the cavern was silent, and nothing raced toward them. It was as if the monsters of this place feared what lay beyond just as much as the Lightseers did.

Her moment had finally come.

A green glow emanated from beyond the door, so dull and faded that it offered almost no light at all. Her smile faded as she scanned the dark interior, and she tilted her body enough that she could keep an eye on Reaver even as she cautiously entered. She tapped the floor, ready for a trap to spring at any moment, but nothing happened.

The Lightseers had played all their cards, and she had won.

Beyond the door lay a narrow circular chamber. Walls made of solid spellgust surrounded the narrow space like the toppled dome of a castle ruin.

In its center, a simple leather book rested on a black pedestal. A green gem embedded in its cover glowed faintly green, securing the leather strap that bound it.

The Deathdread—and it was finally *hers*.

Beside the book, however, lay the true prize she had come here to find. A rotted skeleton rested on a stone altar, its brittle bones stained yellow with time. The bony hands of a long-dead man clutched a bottle that glowed with dazzling green light. Black mist floated within the faceted curves, and the smoky edges blurred as it pushed against a cork encased with a red wax seal.

Despite the stories and lore around this place, the Lightseers had chosen to call this Aeron's Tomb for a reason.

"That's him?" Reaver asked as he stepped over the threshold, his eyes glued to the skeleton. "That's Aeron Zacharias?"

At first, Nyx didn't answer. She needed to be certain. Shoulders tense in case a trap sprung, she circled the skeleton and examined the bottle in its clutches. Her information on this place had been limited from the start, but everything she had heard confirmed what she had always hoped would be here.

A spellgust jar with black mist inside. A lone skeleton clutching an unassuming treasure. A red wax seal with the Starling crest stamped over the cork. A chamber powered by timeless enchantments, fueled by the mountain itself to contain their greatest enemy.

"It's him," she said calmly.

The whistle of a blade through the air interrupted her thoughts, and her body moved on instinct alone. She snapped her head back a second before an enchanted Nethervale dart embedded itself in the spellgust wall by her face.

Reaver launched himself over the skeleton, his intense eyes focused entirely on her as his other enchanted blade soared through the air. He drew his sword, ready to strike if his second dagger missed.

Betrayal.

How disappointing.

His first dagger wriggled in its hole in the wall and broke free, but she effortlessly sidestepped it as it sliced through the air by her head. His dagger arced, racing back toward her for another attempt. With a twist of her hands, she summoned her blades from the sheaths on her wrists and hurled them at the enchanted metal headed for her face. He swung his blade, but she leaned backward as it cut the air where her neck had been.

Their enchanted Nethervale darts collided, and sparks lit the small room like bursts of lightning in a storm cloud. All four blades fell toward the ground, their momentum lost, but she tugged on the invisible tether between her and her daggers. They reacted instantly, flying back to her as she prepared another blow.

Reaver swung his sword at her neck yet again, and his darts curved back toward him as he regained control over them.

She ducked and, with her body hiding the movement from his view, drew the dagger strapped to her thigh. His sword sliced off a lock of her blonde hair as it missed her by inches, but she didn't care. In the seconds after he swung, he had given her what she wanted—an opening.

With a grunt of effort, she twisted her hips and drove the secret dagger into his armpit. The blade sank to the hilt, but he didn't grimace. He didn't even flinch. If she hadn't trained him for much of his life, she wouldn't have even known he'd felt it.

She tugged on her enchanted darts and aimed for his eye. Time to deliver her poison and end this.

Though the dagger still burrowed deep into his armpit, he groaned with effort and summoned his enchanted darts to block hers. More sparks shot through the air as the blades collided again and again. Though she felt the gentle tug each time she changed her poisoned darts' direction, their movements had become second nature to her—and to Reaver.

His jaw tensed as he grabbed the hilt of the dagger embedded in his torso. His eyes never left hers, and he tugged the blade out with a swift yank. She had burned the fear out of him long ago, just as her mentor had burned it out of her.

Above their heads, their enchanted daggers clashed with the steady clang of steel on steel. One of the poisoned blades sailed by her face, and she barely ducked out of the way in time.

Even as blood seeped from the wound in his armpit, Reaver closed the distance between them and swung. Nyx summoned her Crackmane augmentation again and shot a blast at his face, but he twisted his sword and blocked the attack with the flat of his blade. The ice dispersed, hissing as it faded away into steam.

"Impressive." A small smile tugged on Nyx's lips. "Tell me how you enchanted your sword."

He didn't answer. He didn't flinch or acknowledge that she had spoken in any way. He merely swung again, his blood spraying the walls with each step.

Fine. If they weren't even going to banter in his final moments, it was time to end this little charade.

Nyx feigned another blast of ice, even going so far as to summon frost into her palms. Reaver raised his sword again to block the blow.

The gullible fool.

Instead of firing, she dropped to a crouch and swept her leg under his ankles. He fell backward and hit the ground with a thud. More of his blood spurted onto the floor. His sword clattered against the stone and slid out of reach.

Before she even had the chance to stand, he pulled another dagger from somewhere in the depths of his shirt.

She clicked her tongue in disappointment. This was the one thing they had always disagreed on—weapons. The fool relied too much on his blades, and that always gave her the openings she needed to use her magic. It was the one lesson he simply refused to learn.

How fitting, then, that this would be how he died.

As a cascade of sparks fell from the dueling enchanted blades above them, she pressed her palm flat and summoned forth her Crackmane magic yet again. Before he could even blink, the ice splintered through the air.

Only too late did he realize his mistake.

The blast of ice hit him hard in the chest, so hard that he slid backward over the stone. The frost crept over the cloth, freezing him more with each passing second, and he dropped his dagger as he clawed at his shirt to get it off before the ice could reach his skin. He tried to stand, only to grimace and throw his head back in pain as more of his blood leaked from the gushing wound under his arm. He groaned in agony, trying not to betray his misery even as it was written on his face.

His enchanted daggers fell to the ground, and she summoned hers to her side with a sharp tug on the unseen tether. The merciful thing would be to kill him now with a bit of fast-acting poison, rather than letting him slowly freeze.

"Give up?" she asked.

He eyed her, knowing his fate even as he waited to see what she would do.

Nyx stretched her fingers wide, and her enchanted daggers obediently slid into their sheaths on her wrists.

There would never be mercy for those who tried to kill her.

His jaw tensed, but he couldn't keep his teeth from chattering as the ice spread. His eyes went wide with bewildered disbelief, and for the first time in over a decade, he betrayed his fear. The frost crept its way up his neck, inching over his body bit by bit, but she figured the cold dread of his failure had to sting more than any magic ever could.

With an exaggerated sigh, she kicked his two enchanted blades to the far end of the room, just to be sure he didn't try anything in his final moments. "It's a shame, really. After a few more years, you might've been ready to take over. You tried to take my seat too soon."

He shivered in the growing chill creeping over him, his lips already turning blue, and yet he never took his eyes off hers. "B-but if you have a simmering soul, I'd n-n-never have had the chance."

"Fair point." She grinned and crouched beside him. "Guess you were just unlucky."

The icy frost finally reached his mouth, and his lips fused shut as a sheet of ice splintered up toward his nose. His shaking eyes watched her until the last moment, until the ice swallowed them too, and only then did he finally stop shivering.

When her magic had worked its way over his entire body, an icy sculpture resembling Reaver Solomon lay on the ground, still staring up at her in shock.

With a grunt of annoyance, Nyx snatched his sword off the ground. She twirled it in her hand, studying the flash of light across its perfectly polished steel as it spun, and she grabbed the simple gray hilt. It nestled in her palm, a little too big for her liking.

A good weapon was light. Thin. Versatile. A proper weapon hit its target before the victim knew what was happening.

This hulking behemoth, on the other hand, was only good for one thing.

With a twist of her body to add momentum to her blow, she drove the blade deep into his chest, right where she had nailed him with the blast of ice. The blue sculpture shattered, and shards of ice skittered across the floor in every direction.

"What a waste," she muttered in disgust.

Nyx tossed his sword aside, and the iron clanged against the ground. Now she could focus on what truly mattered.

The skeleton and its glowing green bottle. More importantly, the writhing black smoke inside, still pushing against the red wax sealing the cork shut.

She cast a sidelong glance at the Deathdread, but not even the legendary book of ancient necromancy could tempt her as much as a simmering soul.

To her surprise, the spellgust bottle warmed her palm as she grabbed it. The skeleton's fingers resisted her tug at first, but as she yanked it free, the curled hands snapped off. The frail bones of Aeron's corpse clattered over the floor like dusty rain as she pried off the wax seal with her fingernails.

The Lightseers had buried their greatest secret in here with the Deathdread, and they had fought for centuries to keep their shame from reaching the public. That fateful night when they had tried to kill the Great Necromancer, they had failed. He had done what he had set out to do from the very start.

None of the other simmering souls mattered. Everyone had assumed he wanted them for himself, but they were merely practice.

Not even the Lightseers could have predicted Aeron Zacharias would bring himself back as one of his own creations.

And now, the Great Necromancer and his book belonged to *her*.

Nyx clawed at the thick wax coating the spellgust bottle. It fell like shards of dried blood. The cork resisted her at first, since whomever had sealed the bottle had shoved it deep into the bottle's neck, but she quickly pried it out. In her blend of excitement and disbelief, Nyx could barely breathe, and her heartbeats practically echoed through her skull.

The cork left the bottle with a soft pop, and her world went eerily still.

Around her, the spellgust walls glowed brighter than ever, and a black mist spiraled out of the small green prison. Her shoulders relaxed as she marveled at the churning smoke, and she didn't feel a thread of fear. Her lips parted in the seconds before the magic hit her, as eager and excited as a maiden waiting for her lover.

Nyx had dreamed of this day since she was a little girl, but she had never thought it was possible—until that Lightseer Regent had so foolishly walked into her domain.

Since then, Nyx had bided her time.

Listening, and waiting for a chance to strike.

Power awaited her, raw and real. Power beyond anything the world could comprehend.

The smoky cloud darted toward her, faster than her blades could ever be, so fast her eyes couldn't even follow its movement. The mist hit her square in the chest with all the force of a war hammer.

It knocked her backward, and she hit the ground *hard*.

She saw stars, and her world went white as every vein and fiber in her body roared with fire. The pain consumed her, eating away at her, almost too much to bear. For the first time in years, her mind went blank.

She couldn't think, and she didn't want to.

She merely lost herself in the ecstasy of such overwhelming *pain*.

Nyx arched her back as she writhed on the floor, and she couldn't contain the moans of pleasure that escaped her as the misery ripped her flesh from her bones. Her voice echoed in her head, and ribbons of pleasure followed each burst of pain, so intensely that she moaned even louder.

Sweat rolled down her cheek, down her neck, between her breasts. Every exposed inch of her shivered in the alternating waves of fire and ice, of pleasure and pain.

Her palms flattened against the cold stone floor, and she tilted her pelvis upward as another ripple of orgasmic agony ripped her apart. She almost wished a man were inside of her to make this even better, to build her to an even more powerful climax as her screams of agony blended with those of her unfiltered hedonism.

She lost track of how long she laid there on the floor, sweating and smiling, with her vision blurring and with strands of hair stuck to her face. Her chest heaved as the pain slowly receded, and she shut her eyes to enjoy the last tremors of utter bliss.

Curse the Fates, she hadn't cum that hard in at least a decade.

Well now, a grim voice said.

It came from within, from deep in her mind, and it echoed through every inch of her. The vibrations rumbled clear to her bones. The words warbled and shook, and for a moment, it made her feel nine-years-old again.

The trill reminded her of how her father had sounded, all those years ago, whenever he held her head below the surface of the lake as punishment.

The memory brought no emotion with it. She had buried her hatred for that man with the hatchet she had used to kill him in his bed.

Aren't you a delightfully wicked little thing? the voice asked.

With a happy sigh, she rested the back of her hand against her sweaty forehead and closed her eyes. Nyx smiled so wide that her cheeks hurt, and she savored the warbling tenor of the voice that would make her immortal.

"Aeron, my love," she said as her devious grin only widened. "You have no idea."

Thank you!

PLEASE READ

Hi, there. Boyce here.

Thank you for reading *Wraithstorm*. I know it's a month late, but I hope you found the delay worth it now that you're done.

As always, I'm beyond grateful for you. I'm thankful you took the time out of your day to go on this adventure with me.

Before you head out, there are a few things I'd need to share…

Thing #1 – Please consider rating and reviewing *Wraithstorm* on Amazon and Goodreads. Doing so will help more amazing people like you find the series. I would be immensely grateful.

Thing #2 – I made you something. Check out my Author Notes, where I share my experience writing *Wraithstorm*. You can find them at smboyce.com.

Thing #3 – The folks on my Boyce Nation email list get updates on Wraithblade 4 & the link to the discord server. Sign up on my website (smboyce.com) if you haven't already.

Regardless of whether or not you choose to review, reach out, or support me elsewhere, thank you again for taking the time to read *Wraithstorm*. There's one more book to go, and I look forward to hearing what you think.

Your biggest fan,

Boyce

Printed in Great Britain
by Amazon

47644533R00453